Adam Thorpe was born in Paris in 1956 and brought up in India, Cameroon and England. He has published two collections of poetry, *Mornings in the Baltic* (which was shortlisted for the 1988 Whitbread Award for Poetry) and *Meeting Montaigne* (1990). He is the author of three novels, *Ulverton* (1992), *Still* (1995) and his latest, *Pieces of Light* (1998). He now lives in France with his wife and three children.

BY ADAM THORPE

Fiction
Ulverton
Still
Pieces of Light

Poetry
Mornings in the Baltic
Meeting Montaigne

Adam Thorpe

STILL

V

VINTAGE

Published by Vintage 1998

2 4 6 8 10 9 7 5 3 1

The author was the grateful recipient of a Wingate Scholarship from the H. H. Wingate Foundation during the writing of this book.

Extracts from *Notes sur le cinématographe* by Robert Bresson appear with the kind permission of the author.
Extracts from *Zen Flesh, Zen Bones* appear with the kind permission of Charles E. Tuttle Publishing Company Inc.

First published in Great Britain by
Martin Secker & Warburg 1995

Vintage
Random House, 20 Vauxhall Bridge Road,London SW1V 2SA

Random House Australia (Pty) Limited
20 Alfred Street, Milsons Point, Sydney
New South Wales 2061, Australia

Random House New Zealand Limited
18 Poland Road, Glenfield,Auckland 10, New Zealand

Random House South Africa (Pty) Limited
Endulini, 5A Jubilee Road, Parktown 2193, South Africa

Random House UK Limited Reg. No. 954009

A CIP catalogue record for this book
is available from the British Library

ISBN 0 7493 9622 9

Printed and bound in Great Britain by
Cox & Wyman, Reading, Berkshire

In memory of
Samuel, Malcolm *and* Nancy

The most beautiful thing of all
is the complete stillness of an audience
so intent that it hardly breathes.
Charles Laughton

handspring over my neighbour and check out the wing fire fairly frequently. Hey, it was hard manœuvring my own face out the way, it looked very old and lonely out there and wanted to tell me things, the pallor was exaggerated I hope by the cabin lights and three inches of perspex. I'm guessing three inches, by the way. Three inches sounds dense enough because any less and I'd start to get worried, I'd start to think twice about placing my face so close to somewhere very high above the Arctic Ocean and there's still a draught that gets your nose iced over. You'd thought the whole thing was sealed up and triple-checked because if it isn't sealed up the eccentric but adorable bobble-hatted old lady or whoever sitting next to you gets sucked out screaming suddenly and you're only staying put because you're clutching your in-flight movie headphones or the stewardess's thigh or whatever. I thought about showing my movie in a 747 actually but I had to pay a pilot, they didn't do a self-fly. Anyway, this wing fire was doing fine despite the ice particles, I could see it clearly beyond my wide and terrified eyes if I barn-doored the night lights, there was a kind of red flame and sparks and the wing looked like it was about to fall off, it was doing hand flexions or whatever, these 747s are getting old, they can't just go on forever, something's gotta give if you're a lump of metal ploughing through alien air at some God-forsaken hour in some totally God-forsaken place just under outer space with only five hundred military personnel in ski suits and maybe a few white seals below you for thousands of miles and this ectoplasm over your shoulder that turns out to be the aurora borealis. I must have been saying oh God oh God or something over the snores of every single other passenger dribbling onto their neighbour's shoulder or groin or even sockettes in some cases if they'd really slumped because this stewardess came up to me and said relax, sir, it's only Arctic thermals, is this your first time up and I unstuck my nose and my twin plunged away screaming and I said, no, if you're talking about aeroplanes, it's my seventy-seventh, actually.

If you're late and you missed the beginning then frankly you won't understand a single thing for the next twelve hours, you might as well go learn some manners someplace else.

OK OK, it was the traffic, London has terrible traffic, you didn't think of leaving an hour early despite the fact that you have lived here all your

1

life or whatever and know for sure that you can only jerk anywhere. So you got very stressed up and kept looking at the invitation and pointing out to your chauffeur or whoever that it started at eight o'clock and you still had to park, Richard would be very upset if you came in late and then your chauffeur told you to shuddup for Christ's sake because living together's like that, instead of chilling each other out in a five-mile tailback with some vertebral massage you work each other up and shout and jerk and then say what you've actually now you've mentioned it been meaning to say for five years ever since and by the time I open the door and say *hi, you people, come on in, you're late* you're already negotiating on the splatterware vase with the chip you paid through the nose for but what the hell on that amazing weekend in Cromer when you couldn't stop looking at each other in the bus shelter.

Call me Ricky. Richard is granted to a select few, mostly dead.

The bit you've missed was vital but I'm not rewinding and this is a unique screening, so shucks. It was something I wrote on the flight over, which if you weren't trying to find your seat or grabbing a highball at the bar or yelling hi to everybody as if everybody wasn't staring up here with their mouths open and their eyes flickering because they're hanging on to EVERY WORD you'll have realised I've just been talking about, so concentrate. It was a pretty scary flight because all the cans were in the hold and all of me was in the cabin and if the thing went down blazing and got the polar bears looking up for a moment there'd be nothing left of me anywhere else and NO COMPLEX MASTERWORK either, you'd just have been drinking highballs and jiving and cramming your mouths on my tick and maybe mentioning me about once, *yeah, what a shame, they've found the wreck with sonars I think but it's too cold to go down, what are you doing these days?*

Because I know this is a very exciting time, I know there are distractions.

I hope you're keeping your head dipped if you're stood up in front of this, because if you have a large head or a ridiculous *coiffure* for the occasion or some fucking stupid fedora that keeps knocking everybody's glasses off then you might be wiping out several days' work on my part, light travels in straight lines, it doesn't curve for anyone, not even you. Unless your brain's a prism or you are a very special visitor from some hitherto unknown galaxy with an important millennial message to impart, biding your time. Bide your time a little longer and duck, will ya? You have another thousand years in front, don't panic.

This is the trailer, by the way. Or maybe the foreword. It's filling in some large holes. It's important, you're not looking up and seeing this giant Coca-Cola can waterfalling while you're treading on everybody's toes nor are you wincing while everybody seems to be shooting everybody else one hundred times too big and missing the gangway step because Next Week is *Mad Bastard 3* now the school vacation is over – we're talking serious informational content here and if it's smeared it's not your contact lenses playing up it's because this reel's a daily and going in practically green, I'm scribbling in my kitchen, I'm between time zones and feeling like the Blob from Sirius after Commander Cody's dealt with it, bear with me, I know this ninety-nine-year-old who's got the keys to the Shepperton processing lab, they fired him or something for hand wobble or head shake, he's worked with Max Sennet and maybe Frank Tuttle and he's a genius, he has nitrates instead of blood, he'll rush my rushes through and it'll be rolling loud and as clear as can reasonably be expected given this fucking biro and my brain and the fact that it's TOMORROW you're gonna be looking at this, cor blimey luvaduck guv, if only I had a little more peace of mind ummmmm.

It's certainly not the camera and it's certainly not the projector if Joe the Gel's on it. The projector is antique, it's reliable, it cost a bucking bronco off a specialist dealer with sprocket holes each side of his brain, it takes 35mm silent like you've given it a free trip to the Seychelles or someplace, oars included. Don't knock it. Don't give Joe the Gel anything that might make his breath inflammable. If you feel a warmth on your head, DUCK. Crawl to your seat. Don't wave your arms in the air. There'll be intervals for your bladder contents to get recycled in, OK?

I was never late, actually. I was always very early. I got there so early I was scowled out by the kiosk lady and sometimes by the big padlock

3

and chain across the double doors made of laminated bronze or something. I'd go round the side and look at the back of the screen like I was looking up a girl's skirt, it was all raw naked brick and there were no windows, the drizzle played on it, there were stains off the gutters at the top and it frightened me because it was so BLANK. I'll talk about this in about two hours, right now I need to cover some lost ground before the main feature. I was talking about the flight. I think I nearly died from heart strain over this wing blaze because I was the only one awake who realised except for the stewardesses who were either very cool or androids, they had built-in gyroscopic stabilisers or something – I'm checking out the conflagration trying to count the red sparks and then the nose-cone hits a very tall iceberg or whatever and Miss Gotta-Be-A-Wig comes running up to tell you to keep your voice down and your language clean because, sir, EVERY SINGLE OTHER PASSENGER is asleep. Hey, they are, it's true, it makes you feel lonely and unwanted under your nose-bleed and if Miss Gotta-Be-A-Wig wasn't actually only about five years younger than you if you were to peel everything off of her face you'd try maybe to start something at 3.21 a.m. But she trips back down the aisle as you're zigzagging on the spot and you haven't even mentioned the wing falling off in a fire-ball, she looks the kind of person who might scoff and make you look a real jerk. On the other hand, you don't want to be the jerk who killed five hundred people because *I didn't want to look a jerk*, he commented afterwards. From fifty feet down in this chance snowdrift.

My table's scratched. OK. Leave it.

Planes are ships on borrowed time, you yell after her. But she's already straddling the navigator behind that creepy closed door at one end the stewardesses always come out of with a sly smile giving you just a teeky-weeky glimpse of balloons and winking lights and highballs and party poppers like right now, like right now in every house worth peeping into all over the world, heading for the unknown on only one good wing, bub. And now your hands are moving because you're trying to remember which is port and which is starboard, you're swaying up the gangway past the galley towards the cockpit because you have to speak with Captain Peck personally but you can't say there's a worrying flame situation in the left wing, he'd just shake his peg-leg at

4

you from under Miss Buck-Teeth '99 and tell you to jump overboard, so instead you just go soak your sockettes in the toilet and pray.

OK, God listened, obviously. Or He lip-read because I cannot imagine for a moment that He could hear anyone stuck in a stainless steel toilet inside this metal prophylactic Somewhere in the Night over the greatest ice sheet known to man however loud the appeal. My granddaughter can lip-read, by the way. She loves silent movies because they use such filthy language. Hi, Hilda. Glad you could make it.

Yeah yeah, and the Lord did respond. The landing was hopeless because of the peg-leg probably or maybe Heathrow Inc have put down some authentic hand-chipped cobbles on Runway Three for the Japs or whoever but the trees slowed down and so did my heart and I fell asleep for fuck's sake, I slept for the five miles it takes to get to passports on that moving belt that turns your stroll into a joy-ride and I slept on the baggage carousel until some amazing Colombian brunette picked me out and also in the train despite all the jerks and all the way up the stairs to here. To my ridiculously dear walk-in England so tiny the broom has to wait outside.

Ho ho. You know what this is called? It's called a warm-up. It's called a dope-massage. It's called firing-the-brain-dead so they actually move their jaws to the right position every now and again. I hope y'all doing that. Ricky Thornby's back in town.

I fell over. Kind of. I slid off the table. Nervous exhaustion. I woke up immediately but my clock says it's been two hours. You can't do that at fifty-nine. You can't adopt a position with your butt up in the air and your wrist torqued and sleep for two hours unless you're twenty-two and flexible. But from my general pain situation I think I did. Hey, I feel mentally MAHCH BETTER, GUV. Which means chilled out and dreadful. I've just shot what I've scribbled and I'm ashamed. But there's no time for a remake. No time. Cor blimey no.

I thought the trailer would be finely wrote, as a matter of fact. I don't mean italic handwriting, dumbos, I mean *content*, *style*, all those things you people don't believe in any more. I thought all you guys and gals at the party'd be drooling over it. Hey, Dick the Prick can write! He took a wrong turn way back! Too bad it's too late! Maybe it's not too late! It wasn't too late for Mary Wesley!

Mary who? You mean *Wesley*? You mean the one who wrote that crap my pal Jerry Freeman lost the film rights to back in '89 and said it was all my fault because I'd kept him too long on the phone and that's when I told him to fuck off out of my life because I'd talked for about ten seconds and I'd been trying to get him for weeks? Give us a break, I might get jealous.

That reminds me. Fanfare. A coupla thousand of Cecil's trumpets and a gong. Now's the time. It's as good as any other.

> The poor soul sat sighing by a sycamore tree,
> Sing all a green willow;
> Her hand on her bosom, her head on her knee,
> Sing willow, willow, willow.

You know something? About this song? (*Othello*, dumbos. The William Shakespeare version. A great scene. I'll have you know, who might not for some incredible reason like being in an iron lung for thirty-three years, that I was on set for the Larry screen version in '66 giving kind of technical advice, I was at my peak, my advice was ACTUALLY BEING SOUGHT AFTER, I fell in love with Maggie as in Smith, I watched her sing it and cried – I really cried, my nose ran, I was sacked because I became totally useless. *I started at the top and worked my way down* etc. Big deal. No one knew why I cried. It had nothing to do with Maggie, it had everything to do with the raising of some titanic memories best left to the barnacles. So stick around.)

You know something?

I want it carved into my tombstone. The willow song.

Seriously. It's in my will ho ho. It's written down. I've written it down because if it wasn't in black and white and blotted carefully my lousy relations wouldn't do it. I mean, Gregory my son might, and Hilda my granddaughter might, but my nearest and weirdest and their terrible spouses'd stop them. They'd say it's too expensive, they'd say it's not done, they'd sip Australian brake fluid at my funeral and say it's not done, he was always barmy, what's good enough for Mum is good enough for Dicky, and I'll end up with just my initials and a couple of dates and my initials are R.A.T. Des'd love it. Des my brother has been waiting for me to cop it for years so as he can put *RAT* on my tombstone. Richard Arthur Thornby. Christ, my parents were thick. Nay – my mother was thick, my father was (is) malign. He did it deliberate, dinne? Good for a chortle, eh? Oof. I'll bet he did. Most of you don't know this little legacy of mine. I've been R. T. for forty-five years. I let the trapdoor open under Arthur when I was fifteen. I heard him scream all the way down, out of my life, and walked forth R.T. for ever and ever amen. But Des remembers. He's a fucking elephant. He calls me Ratty. We have to meet now and again, every funeral, every wedding, every so too bloody often. Hallo, Ratty, he chortles, how's tricks? He likes slapping guys on the back. It's how the English cope. They don't kiss, they don't hug, they just disable you. They? I mean we. I'm one of them. I'm Des's closest relative after our mutual progenitor. We shot out of the same organ. Imagine that. He takes off my accent. Waal, whad'ya know, it's the Yank! Over-sexed, over-paid, and over here! Great joke. He's always joking. Every time he opens his mouth it's like pulling a cracker. Actually, he's very depressed. I know. I can tell. He stayed, I got out. But they're all back there with him, waiting. They've got your old skin in their hands. They're waiting until you're helpless, dying, dead. Then they'll zip the skin right over you, the old sloughed skin, right over you and over your head. Hoi, I didn't want to get on to this. Not yet. I'm scribbling against time. I have to fill in some holes.

Maybe I should write in block capitals but it's slower. I don't know what the fuck the time is. I'm between zones. I'm feeling terrible. I'm thinking – this party tomorrow night, it's too much, I want to bury my head in the futon, ouch, I can't face it, I can't face all those people, I can't face the most important day of my life, how did I get to this point? I don't know, I don't know what I'm doing here, I'm still bucking, the kitchen floor is not stable, I'm nauseous, we'll crash, we'll crash in flames at any minute, into the waves, into the anomynomynymous waves of slumber and I'll wake up and I'll have blown it, I'll have missed the party, I'll have wasted the day, I'll have wasted twelve years of my life, you stupid cunt.

I'll fix myself a coffee in a moment. Right now I'm too stressed. I need the toilet. I'm intercontinent. Hey, that's the first joke! Dick the Prick's on form! Things are going to be OK!

I hope I'm getting the focus right and hey, sorry about my thumb if it's bothering you. I'm working in terrible conditions, the Sellotape's run out, Greg and Mee stayed here over Christmas so all the fucking vital things like Sellotape and string and toilet paper and whisky are missing. I've picked the pink Blu-tac off of the Christmas cards they've stuck up all over my pure white walls which is why you're getting speculars off the glitter. I apologise. I've tried blowing but the stuff catches in the little hairs on my palm. I've NO TIME TO CARE. Holy shit, the camera's making the kind of noise my neighbour with the cockroaches just overhead likes to report, it's very old, the intermittent's a couple of pterodactyl claws, the actors had to shout to make themselves heard, you're lucky there's no soundtrack on this one or your teeth'd be coming loose. Or maybe looser 'cos, hey, we're no longer what we were, huh?

Cor blimey luvaduck. I hope I'm not repeating myself. I'm thinking about y'all. I'm thinking about all those people who're going to be there tomorrow. I'm thinking about you reading this and saying, hey, he's still repeating himself. I can see your faces. I can see you squinting at this. At this. At this.

At this.

Wow, that's weird. Some of these faces I know so well I don't even have to imagine them, they're just kind of more slouched with bad hair around them. Hiya there, Ossy, y'bastard!

Some of the other faces I'm not so sure about. The phantoms'll be in the front row. Hoi, it's their film. Don't sit on their laps. Just don't get in their way.

Christ, this party. I can't stand it. I can't stand the fact that it's tomorrow. As long as it was next week, or next month, or next year, or in nine years' time, I could stand it. But it's tomorrow. My party's tomorrow. Tomorrow is my birthday. Tomorrow is the Big One. Once this tomorrow was in nine years' time. I mean this. It was, once. Hey, seriously. What d'you expect? You've got a suite, a suite with a terrace, a suite with a terrace overlooking the fucking Thames. I booked the last one available. I booked it nine blahdy years ago, mate. I worked out how, leaning out a little, you'd get the official fireworks, the big jobs, the ones that burn out their hundred quid in ten seconds of the Second Coming, then pop some more, then bloom into a thousand crimson blooms, then go quiet and dark, then spray a million peacocks over the city with a Semtex bang and a mass *whoo* from underneath and a *yaroo* from whoever's got it melting their shoe. I thought, there won't be room for everyone to lean out. There'll be shifts, or some people won't like bangs and whizzes and stay inside, or others'll be English and stay pissed off and polite at the back, seeing only the rockets if the arc is tight. The bigger ones were all booked. They were booked *ten* years ago. Hey, I apologise. At least you've got the bleedin' river, mate, the cobbled wharves slapped at an' all that, ghost ships swingin' their crates, the sound of peg-legs tappin' an' inn signs creakin' an' me dad wiv his barrer, yellin' 'orribly. There'll be some minor B-rated fireworks around. People will bring their personal squibs. We can light the blue touch-paper on the terrace and stand back and try to look impressed for Christ's sake. There'll be boats. There'll be pleasure-boats plying up and down gushing with peacocks and their reflections we can all ooh and aah over. If anyone's grumbling I say to you hey, why didn't you git up off your fat arse ten years ago, huh? Because that's when the big suites were booked. I thought ahead. I mean it – this was the last one available, on the blahdy river, anywhere. Now hold up yer mitts and count the fingers if you can count that high 'cos that's what it cost me, guv. A cage o' monkeys at bun-time. Poetic thought, faintly Japanese: no party tonight will be quite right unless it faces flowing water. Hey, way above y'heads, dumbos.

Oh Zelda.

I haven't invited my first wife. My second is dead, of course, some of you know this, so she might or might not be there. If she is and she's not snoring – ignore her, she doesn't mean it. My first wife is currently under the notion that I'm tacky, that I've done a very tacky thing with Hilda, which is simply not true. Hilda wanted to be present. She wants

9

it. She wants to be with her grandad. As her grandad, I can only open my arms and say, honey-bun, come right in. Just don't bring any of your Friends of Woodstock '99 to shame us. It's my party. I did not write to Hilda insisting. There were no bribes. Hilda's had nothing more than a box ticket for *Hotchpotch* (the crap musical, not the great film) from her grandpop for two years. (Lighting box, I mean. My friend Joe the Gel was doing lights.) No bribes, no bribes whatsoever. I'm too damn skint, for starters.

That's me dad speaking. Nasal, Enfield coming on Cheshunt. He never had no pretensions. Too damn skint, for starters.

Hoi, listen. The Earl of Sandwich saved the King. Naval battle. Can't recall the details. Charles, it was. Poncy Restoration types lining the poop, misty, a slight swell, moisture beading in their wigs. You're an earl, says Charles. Cor, says the Earl of – oops! Earl of what, Your Highness? Earl of wherever we touch first, says Charles. The Earl of Wherever We Touch First is quite excited, standing on the poop, his toff gloves feeling the wetness off of the poop-rail. The coast looms. He quite fancies the Earl of Dover (my father winks at me mum, I fake a grin). Cor, says a partially deaf ancient mariner, it's England. Where are we exactly, where is that? lisps the Earl of Whatever-the-ancient-mariner-is-about-to-reply. Sandwich? says the partially deaf ancient mariner, undoing his greaseproof. I've got tomato-and-herring, if you're partial.

Yup, that's how Dicky Thornby learnt history, at his father's elbow, jabbed on the end of it – *oof!* Geddit, son? He had one book. *The Percy Anecdotes.* Anecdotes collected by the Percy family. They'd sell books off the barrows, along with the fruit and veg. Our lot, not the Percys. Old books. Books from bookclubs run by crooks as cover for the white slave trade or whatever. This one they couldn't sell. He claimed he'd filched it off the barrer. Crap, Pop. It slipped into the interstices (now that'll fox you, mate) of the free market. He still has it. It's his Bible, for crying out loud.

Sing willow, willow, willow.

None of the uncles is coming. They weren't invited. Anyway, most of them are dead. The least dead one got out years ago. He's in Melbourne. Eighty-eight and fighting fit. He writes to me. He wants to be in one of my movies. He thinks I'm still in movies. Well, I AM. He's seen *Ridden Out*, *Honky Tonk* and *Honky Tonk Two* (the better half, if you harken to the critics. Derek Malcolm said so. The lesser of two evils. Yah, yah). The others weren't dizzed in Australia, not on the big screen. He has a video but I haven't told him. Anyway, they're rare, they're collectors' pieces, they're hard to track down. I'm talking of *Will There's a Way* and *Homhitch*. These titles. They're like a woman you wake up to in the morning and don't recognise but she's made you tea in the right mug.

I should be so lucky.

The second least dead one most of you know. He's been in all my films. He was Kierkegaard in my first short, print lost, history down the plug-hole. But he can't come. Gerald can't come. He's busy. He's building a wind machine on the beach of Bognor or someplace. He's tied his trilby to his head with elastic. Otherwise it'd bowl along like nobody's business, way off along the sands of Bognor, the shingle of Bognor, the fucking agonising pebbles of Bognor – whatever, I haven't been there. Gerald Ursule Thornby. Ursule? Is that a slip of me blotty biro? Nope. Ursule it is. Like some medical appliance one don't mention, as my pop would say, what didn't like Gerald very much. Gerald'd only have to crack his knuckles to get everyone falling about, that's why, and he was too feeble as a kid to push a barrer the requisite distance. My old man always was a bully, not so deep down. He lacked 'uman sympafy. My films lack 'uman sympafy. Derek says so – has said so on many occasions, I can show you the cuttings if you handle them carefully 'cos they tend to crumble. Toff. Ponce. Wouldn't know what 'uman sympafy was if it smashed him in the teeth.

Yup, I've always had a soft spot for Gerald, if I could find it.

Listen. I'm getting derailed. It's not deliberate, it's not me being smart, it's me with an iced nose still winding the big hand in me small brain forward, OK? I'm no moth, mate. I'm lagged. Yeah yeah, I kipped. I kipped for ten minutes on Norman Mailer's latest and I need to see my chiropractor, bom bom. Have I said we had turbulence? We had

11

turbulence. I hate flying in the winter. I have this thing about snowstorms at night twenty thousand feet up. This film I went to see as a kid, the first film I ever went to totally on my own, I was nine, the old Enfield Ritz, Saturday morning, a drizzle, it always drizzles on Saturday morning, it was called, it was called – heck, I've forgotten – anyway, it had this sequence which had me sucking on my duffle-coat's top toggle so hard it came off and I nearly died. These toggles were the size of enemas. I reckon they were enemas. It got caught in me red lane. They fitted a young boy's red lane (look it up, look it up) exactly. I didn't try the other place. If I'd had a sister I'd have hired it to her. For a shilling, of course, 'cos I wanted to haggle with Donald Benson for his Lotts Bricks Box, Set E. You could build a Municipal Sewage Works with it, Tudor style, with gables, mullioned windows, the works. Blow me down. This sequence, I was talking about this sequence – it was great, it was awful, you were looking at the cockpit, the lens was set on the twin-prop's nose and it made me feel carsick. Screams. Snow. Oh crikey, thick swirls of it, against the cockpit, just about see the pilot's eyes, oh crikey. Wind machine going flat out, buckets of fluff tossed in front, cockpit bouncing like crazy, pilot's knocked out or got the vapours, hero grappling with joystick, joystick comes off, top toggle comes off, sticks in throat, I'm dead. My fear of flying is nothing to do with sex, OK? I explained all this to my analyst when I had one. (A phase, a phase.) She said I was projecting. I said hey, I've always wanted to project. Sweeping the smoke for the screen, finding a film at the other end, hoping it doesn't bomb. Miraculous. Works every time. She nodded carefully. I had to be carried out. Of the Ritz, I mean. They whacked me on the back and out it shot, rolling under the Number 49 to Palmers Green. Me mum'll kill me if I don't get it back, I rasped. True. The Number 49 ran over it, Stevie Smith bumped her head on the top-deck rail, I got my top toggle back, intact. The Princess and the Pea, Enfield version. They knew how to make stuff in those days. Oh yes.

That thing about projecting. Part of another little party popper. Blitz in the Ritz. Hoi, geddit? Me dad's legacy. Jokes that need explaining. Damp squibs. Fireworks and a torch with the jitters. The Catherine wheel that believes in only one revolution a century until you get too close. Whop! The sound of fireworks even cheaper than your neighbours. I mean, even cheaper. At least their rockets *fart*.

Hey, why am I so angry?

This was going to be cool and explicatory, not angry. My classes'd start cool and explicatory, I knew the ropes, I got angry later. My kitchen table's been *scratched*. I don't care. I feel terrible. I'm nervous. I'm about to be sixty. I'm about to be old. Do not go gentle into that good night. My father's still alive. I'm about to be old and my father's still alive. We'll both be old at the same time. It's not fair. How can he do this to me. How can *He* do this to me? I jog now and again, I wear casuals, I don't have a tie, I've never seen *The Sound of Music*, a million-to-one-chance, I know, it's never seeing snow on a mean person in Switzerland or seeing my lips flapping in slomo with the sound not off, it's incredible but possible, I was avant-garde, I had the film rights to *Narziss and Goldmund* before Hermann Hesse was invented, I made love while John Lennon was playing with his lead soldiers, I was hip, I was cool, I was outrageous, I bombed up the Marylebone Road in a Daimler Conquest Open Roadster once, I took drugs, I took Diana Rigg to the movies, it was *my* movie, I had a Cocteau cap and cigarette holder, I chortled in French. Remember?

Hoi, I'm talking to you people. Remember?

Great days, great days.

I think of Roy, Roy Plomley. I knew Roy, Roy Plomley. He promised. He promised I'd be on it (*Desert Island Discs*, deadheads.) One day Dicky, he said, you'll be washed up, I'm sure.

Great joke, huh?

Actually, I never thought that others'd creep up on you so quick. I'm talking about youf. I'm a grandad! You know who I hate? I hate the boomers, the groovy boom-babies, the boom-baby-boomers in their tie-dye bloomers. (Opening song from *Hotchpotch*, you ignorant bastards.)

Seriously, I have relational problems with a generation.

You don't know this?

I wasn't one. You know that, you know what I was. I was a BOOM-boomer, born in an air-raid shelter, the stupid type which killed you. They took away my youth, that peacetime polio washed-in-Daz lot. I'd just got rid of my spots and they made me feel old. Christ, I was on the edge of thirty in '68. Thirty, sixty, what's the difference? I'd made a few movies but suddenly I was old, comfortable, clapped-out, a fucking Morris 1100 Saloon with Grandma in the back feeling very comfortable, thank you dear. I was idiot enough to wear a black polo-neck when bandannas were in. I looked like Colin Outsider and felt it. I made the right noises, oh yeah. I squirmed naked in some mud, once, on stage, for Ken. Ken Campbell. Made no difference. It washed off. Very comfortable, thank you dear.

Phantoms.

I'm not feeling angry. I'm feeling nervous. I'm still feeling nervous. That's why I'm not going to have a coffee. I drank coffee all the way over. My ears are still humming, humming *One of Our Aeroplanes is Missing*. Hey, yeah, I *know* it's safe as houses, million-to-one copper-bottomed safe, the flames were the fucking wing-lights given the nadgers by the ice particles, etc etc. But you know what keeps a big heavy jet high up in the sky? A vacuum above the wings. Think about it.

And thrust.

Thrust and vacuum. That's me. That's my life.

Sing willow, willow, willow or whatever.

Anyway, who said houses were safe? Most accidents are in the home, for God's sake. And mine's been smashed up twice, back in Houston. Nice neighbourhood. Nicely distressed fronts. Nice English statuary, authentically nicked, lifted out of some forgotten corner of a genuine English lawn so big they thought the Sikorsky was the flymo – Echo with hand up crotch, Pitys scratching her moss, Syrinx squeezing into her swell reed outfit, dip the hysterical laughter, I haven't finished. Tudor Mansion Kits (real woodworm, real woodworm, guv). Sprinklers with built-in radar, mastiffs who don't like their analysts, gravel driveways you have to wade up – get the picture? I say to them, what's so great about England? It's a dump. It's mean, peevish and little, as my pal Jonathan Windmiller put it once peevishly 'cos someone had said his Show wasn't the greatest thing since the Siberian shamans. They love it. The Texans, I mean, not the blahdy shamans mate. They've only been to Windsor Castle and they love it. We even have a pub. It's an exact copy of a pub I happen to know, back in the old country. I say, sipping my Pigge Swille, shielding my eyes from the flare off of the horse brasses, this isn't England. This is about as English as the set of *Suspicion*. People drift away like I smell. Maybe I do, but that's not the point. I stand alone. They don't want to know. They don't want to know the genuine cast-iron authentically traditional hand-buffed troof, guv. I try not to get pissed. When I get pissed I get magdalene. I went to Magdalene College, Cambridge, I say. Magdalene with an *e*. If it hasn't got an *e* it's the Other Place. I wasn't a blue, I was a red. OK OK, maybe I start to shout now. Dudley was at the one without an *e*! That's why he's a scug! I made love with my bedder! I bet he didn't! They don't understand what I'm yelling. I feel Union Jacked down to my underpants, my tinnitus is whistling the Selected Beatles, I raise my glass and look around with this Alec Guinness grin playing over my bottom lip. There's a crop-headed barman out of *Terminator 2*. He wears these terrible sort of solarised shirts. I thought, the first time I went in, he's the only orfentically English thing in here. I was right. My act gets nowhere when Jason's about. Tinkerbell's tiddly again, he says, so why doesn't Tinkerbell fuck off out and join Wendy in *Never Never Land*, eh? I don't know why he has this nickname for me. It's worrying. It takes the wind right out of my gaff topsail. The beer's terrible. He waters it down. He mixes the IPA with some American junk that has a big head and a big flavor. Otherwise no one'd come. Who can blame them? Real real ale's so real it tastes like it isn't. That's why I like it.

Sorry about the corner on that last one. I could wind it up, scroll it up on a toilet roll. I'd have problems with the focus. Stay with me and ALERT. Anyway, I'm out. Retired early without honours. The Houston Centre for the Dramatic and Visual Arts (Film Section) is gonna be sunk without me. I'm shaping the future. I've seen it, it aches, it needs a massage. At least I have a walk-in swimming pool. I walk into it every morning and eat an avocado. Seriously, I do, a whole one and they're Texan. The pool's small but it can take my Monroe inflatable and the ripples cluck like my mother used to when I chewed my Wrigley's Spearmint Chewing Gum and I was doing the advert for Christ's sake. Very early days, but still. Have style, right?

So, about this plane trip: I drank coffee through the night when I wasn't tucked up with Norman Mailer and my neighbour's elbow and now I feel terrible. I'M OUT OF CHICORY AND THE LAST TOILET ROLL'S DOWN TO THE SUTURE. I can't cope with having two homes each side of the Atlantic either financially or mentally. Someone's used up all the chicory and not replaced the essential. That'll be Mee and Greg respectively – Greg has always spun the roll until it touches ground before tearing it off seven times over, it's a childhood habit, he practically ruined us, maybe I should have lowered the holder, maybe I should have done a lot of things when I think about it. Have I mentioned Mee? Mee, or Mi, is my son's partner. She's Chinese-American with a pinch of St Helena. St Helena! Hey, she could be related to Napoleon in some sneaky way! She's beautiful but she's a health freak. She uses up all my chicory powder and all my lentils and anything in big chunky blue-glass jars with cork lids because anything in those looks pure, unmilled, all that crap, even if it's not. I'll lay traps for her. I'll empty the best the US can offer into one of those jars – real Agent Orange schmuck the colour of bri-nylon striped underwear and see if it goes. It will, it will. When I'm next over.

Mee's coming, I know this. She wrote me. Hiya, Mee! My son might be out there with you, too. He's not getting on with his mother, so it's touch and go. (Hiya Greg, if you are.) Mee wants to come because she thinks I'm famous. She's a sucker for fame. I've touched her knee. I was pissed, Greg! It was in Ashby-de-la-Zouche. Remember the Green Horn, Ashby-de-la-Zouche? August 1995? (Hey, is that *19* looking antique already? Does it wear a high collar, does it talk kinda funny?) We were jerking up to Edinburgh for some private view (the car was fine, it was the traffic) because my son's an artist, in case any of you deadheads didn't know. He lays carpets. No, he doesn't even lay them. He gets the carpet layers to lay them while he lays Mi, probably. He's into carpet squares, these days. This is a big development. It used to be nothing but fitted stuff with one end left unrolled. They're called deep things like CARPET SQUARES #32 and sell for a

THOUSAND BUCKS A YARD OR SOMETHING. I'm a Morris 1100 with Grandma in the back. Fuck the carpets. I put my hand on Mi's knee in Ashby-de-la-Zouche, Greg. You were out at the toilet. Her knee was bony. There was a stretch of naked thigh above it, like a beach. My hand wanted to move up there. It wanted to leave the bony country and make out for the beach, maybe hit the frilly white surf. It did so. The going was easy, soft, warm. No thunder. Only a giggle. A Chinese-American-St Helena giggle, soft as breakers heard from a far hut.

Then you came back in, Greg. There were some interesting beer-mats. We did the quizzes on them and I said Miami Dolphins to every one and got a point. You said well done, Dad, and bought me a half. Hey, Gregory is a saint. He's a nice bloke, guy, whatever. He's a saintly fool who makes bucks. Somewhere between him and what he creates there is a gulf with a swing-bridge. He shouldn't be creating what he creates. He deserves Mi, or Mee. He really does. But so do I. I've seldom met anyone I thought I deserved more. But the thing is, I think she feels sorry for me. She thinks I'm more famous than I really am (wow) but she still feels sorry for me. I don't know why. It's just a feeling I get. She borrows my flat now and again, when they're down from Stoke-on-Trent (it's hip, it's hip, you're out of sync), and she sits there in the empty kitchen and I think she thinks it's sad. She thinks it's sad to see my posters, my old movie posters, nicely framed and ranged on the kitchen walls. They're terrible posters, most of them. The colours are going. All except the red. Not even Technicolor red. Oh no. Not the ripe incarnadine throb of Technicolor, to quote myself (*A Student's Introduction to Film Techniques*, Nonumque Press, Houston. It bombed at $5. It bombed at $1, remaindered. I shipped some to Manila. It bombed. No student buys a book, period. Not by me, anyway).

Yup, cheap carmine red, on my posters. Which is just as well, because most of it is on the mouths of the posters. There's a lot of mouth on my posters. I was always into mouths. They're leaning up against the miniature dishwasher now because I needed the white walls for this. Otherwise I'd pan them to remind a lot of you of old times. Your hot cheeks would go with the mouths.

17

Sorry, I've interrupted. So she sips my chicory coffee and looks around and says, Greg, don't you think it's sad? And Greg pauses. If he was in one of my old films he'd say whassat or come again or sing a song for about ten minutes. But he doesn't, because he's not. And she doesn't reply oh, it doesn't matter, in close-up, blinking fretfully. Nope. He just pauses and then he nods. He nods and gives a little snorty sigh. Yeah, he says, softly. Yeah.

I was never that blisteringly realist. Till now.

Christ, I'm getting myself worked up. I can't stand people feeling sorry for me. I want people to think I'm so great they hate me deep down under. I'll bet everyone hated Andrei Tarkovsky deep down under. I'll bet Alfred Hitchcock got right up their noses. Ford, too. Bresson and Godard and Carl Theodor Dreyer. Gods. All of them. They tower above me, gloating. No, not even gloating. Great men don't gloat. They don't need to. They don't notice me. That's it. They don't even notice me. They think I'm Second Grip. They think I'm the jerk with the walkie-talkie who keeps the onlookers out of line and kicks them if they cough. They think I'm the one who oils the tracking rails and can't get the coffee machine to work. They think I'm practical with limits. That's it. Christ!

But what Mee doesn't appreciate is that Gregory has crept up on me. He's overtaken me. He has a quietly solid reputation. I'm not Dicky Thornby any more. I'm Gregory's father. I'm Any Relation, question mark. A few fucking carpets and some crap about the *I Ching* (I'd forgotten the *I Ching* crap, it's normally at one end of the room so you have to walk across the carpet, innit brilliant?) – this lousy scam has overtaken all my years of hard graft, all my aeons of blood and sweat and tears and, OK, *semen*. That's why I deserve Mee. He can't have the whole bleedin' can, can he?

Sorry, Greg, if you're out there. I'm emoting. Take no notice.

I'm getting myself so worked up I've left a bit of white wall for you to kind of space out on or go get another drink. In that beat I've drunk some real coffee. I feel better. My apartment's born again. The air is roasted, ground, and boiled. There are some fings in life better than Dick Van Dyke in *Mary Poppins*, I can tell ya.

Also, I've been to the lavatory. I eked out the roll, I managed, I found some face fresheners in my back pocket, it was a new sensation, my butt never gets that kind of privilege normally. Hey, I feel nicely voided, I can begin to picture the curry I've been picturing for six months now, the airline food did something, I don't know what, it always does. Perhaps it's not the food. Perhaps there's something about turbulence that stays. Like my English accent. Gregory's posh pretending to be not. I'm not, pretending to be posh. By posh I don't mean Harrods posh, I mean International Artiste posh. But Pop won't let go. Enfield-coming-on-Cheshunt's got its claws in. It's got its claws in my nose. Just when it's safe for my voice to go out the Thing From Enfield-Coming-On-Cheshunt pops out of my nose and screeches. No, it whines. It slobbers over my wotsits, my my my my diphthongs. It particularly tucks into the word 'field'. If the aliens in *Alien* could speak, they'd speak Enfield-coming-on-Cheshunt. Eighteen years in the States, *all in the state of Texas*, and it's still slobbering. But no one

19

over there thinks it's ugly, no one over there thinks it's anything but quaint. Like Tomato's four parnd fifty. Only the English barman knows. Jason knows I'm not a gentleman. He knows that, because I'm not a gentleman, he can say fuck off and pitch me out on the end of his tie-pin, the rotter. He knows this because he's English, he's from Wokingham of all bloody places. I revile him. I'm going to send him a postcard of the High Street of Wokingham with WANK OFF OVER THIS, YOU BASTARD, under highlighter on the back.

No, no, Dicky. About as subtle as a gas – hey, sorry, *petrol* pump (Derek on *Honky Tonk*). Let us think.

MUCH MISSED, FROM ALL AT THE EARLY LEARNING CENTRE.

Maahch better.

No. He won't get it. You can't have a chortle at someone's expense unless they Geddit. He'll show it to the customers and they'll all shake their big, stubbly, Texan heads and say, sorry, Pat, me neither, as if they're bit-parts in *The Searchers*, the stupid cunts. Nope. How's about: *Thank you for your enquiry. A post is currently available for a traffic bollard on the A327 turn-off.*

Hey, hey, that's good. I could filch some Berkshire County Council notepaper from somewhere. I could make this my first big proj for the new millennium.

OK, I had to look up the road. The A327. I've got a Great AZ Britain Road Atlas with an Index to over 30,000 places and it was in the right place. That's because I hadn't unpacked it yet. I keep it in my suitcase, and I haven't unpacked my suitcase. It fits right at the bottom of my green Globetrotter that's been a constant companion since, ah, 1963. (*1963*. Where's my plume?) So after *traffic bollard on the*, I went over to my bedroom about ten paces across some coconut matting that's hell on bare feet but aw shucks and through a door because right now I'm in the kitchen (have I said that?) and worked hard at this tricky-dicky lock on the Globetrotter until as usual it ended up embedded in my nostril and had to rummage through two pairs of sneakers, ten underpants, five clumps of socks, my inhaler, the Norman Mailer whopper and a dirty magazine. The dirty magazine is called the *Spectator*. Yes, the same. I admit it. It's my sort of magazine and its lousy politics keeps me on my toes. It reminds me of pigeon shit on the church porch of Bloody St Mary's, England. It reminds me of the Golden Age of British Cinema just round the corner, if only the steeple-fund barometer would hit room temperature. Its very own Auberon Waugh once called me the faintest hope of British film ever to have flickered out. Yup – I'm that guy who had thirty years of the *Listener* bound in leather and they blew my cover, the old devils. Or was that in *Private Eye*? Same gang-bang. All ye who enter here, wear a tie and testicles and chortle in Latin, or else. I'll send them a postcard, too. From a Reader in Houston. Hi. I think you're all great. All my friends think you're great. We're coming over next week and we'll be dropping by. We admire your deeply held convictions and want to meet up in person. Mothers of Serial Murderers Friendship & Support Club, Houston.

Kill the roars. That wasn't very funny.

I'm even getting to look like him. My pop, I mean. My old dad. Grey hair out the ears, Goofy's dewlaps, lousy double-act in *They Came from Planet Age*. He tells 'em backwards, now. Tomato-and-herring, if you're partial, he says. That's right, Dougie, says the nurse. She never stays long enough to get the opener. The Earl of Sandwich saved the King makes a great punchline, but she's off hospital-cornering some other poor bastard with no teeth. Poor bastard? Sucks. She can hospital-corner me any time. I like to trampoline. She murmurs to me – well, he does talk but it's all nonsense, I'm afraid. 'Twas always thus, I say, in my RSC croak. Prithee, unpin me. These nurses, they never geddit. They glance at their stop-watches instead. What a carry on. No need to hold their stop-watches up because they're rested horizontally on their chests. It's all rather confused, Mr Thornby. Nonsense, I say, you just have to put him on rewind. Then you'd get the joke.

Hey, I really do find nurses' uniforms attractive. I really do. I want to die in hospital. I want to go out with them perched on my bed like starlings about three minutes after they've given me my daily all-over soap. I want to go out clutching one of them by the ass, and she not minding. Perhaps minding a little bit. A giggle. I hope you don't mind my old geezer's reverie. I couldn't say this kind of thing where I worked. I had to hold myself on a very tight rein. I had to look at my male and female students equally or I'd get hauled up for one of the seven deadly sins, I forget which. It was tiring, I didn't have a stop-watch, I got migraines. I want to go out clutching a nice little nurse's starchy ass. Or arse, if it's over here. They're nicer over here, nurses are. They're starchier. They're young. They've got tiny teeth.

Hey, I'm getting myself really excited. I'm bursting through the mould on my chakras. The coffee's coursing. I was talking about my father. Why am I always talking about my father? Why not my mother? It's because he's a malicious person. Even backwards, he's malicious. You look younger every day, Cyril, he says, tucking into his Smarties. I'm not Cyril, I say, I'm your son, I'm Dick. Spotted! he cries, and rasps. The rasp is him chortling. The bed shakes and squeals. There's a tip-tap over the lino. Everything all right, Mr Thornby? Nurse Luscious is bending so close over me I can tell the time to the millisecond. No, I say. He's just dusted off my school nickname and I feel very upset. He's still a right bastard. When's your shift over? Let's go out. Let's go out and skiffle a bit and then nip back to my flat and discuss your favourite operations over a pillow or two with the lights out and that dicky street lamp giving a great strobe effect on your hip-bone.

Uh-huh.

Actually, I clear my throat and enquire if there's a cup of tea available by any chance. In about an hour, she snaps. It's always in about an hour, whatever, whenever. Not that I've visited more than about once a year. I can't afford the Smarties. They're a shocking price, don't you know. And he never chokes on 'em. Never offers me one, neiver. His Norf Lunnun's got thicker. I can't pretend he's Michael Caine any more, it's kind of brewed over the years, it's got this whine in worse than Steptoe Senior, it makes me jump up and look for the shelter practically. When he begins the ends of his jokes, I wince. When he ends the beginnings I sigh with relief because hey, you get about a minute's break before the beginning of the next end. I try not to look at him. He's unpleasant to look at. It's not the forgotten-satsuma-found-behind-the-fridge face so much as the eyes in it. The eyes weep a kind of pus, a kind of snot-green pus no one does nuffink abaht. Son, he says, these eyes have seen so much in their time they've rotted, they've gangrened: LOOK! I wish he did say that. It'd make a great line. But he doesn't. He whinges on instead about there being no white ones. All the colours of the rainbow, he says, that's the trouble. Like he used to talk about the immigrants. Oh, I remember, I remember the Book According to Enoch glossed by Douglas Thornby. Suck 'em, I say, before he can start shouting. Suck 'em and then look, Dad. He scowls at me and rattles the packet. Or maybe it's his cough. Cyril, he says, you're a ponce. I'm fit as a fiddle! Fit as a fiddle!

Cyril, by the way, was his pal in Forsyte Avenue. Are you all sitting comfortably? Then we'll begin. So shuddup. Once upon a time there was Cyril. Cyril's father was a baker, a rump-cut above the coster-monger lot. Cyril died in the rubble of his shop, three o'clock a.m., baking wartime bread out of road-grit and boiled fag-ends. Direct hit with a V1. Um, I think my father's shrieking off-set, excuse me a moment, something about a V2, sorry, I think it was a V2, that's an important correction, we'll trim this up later, meanwhile let's have a slow pan of CYRIL HATH RISEN wot some berk with a great sense of humour scribbled on the brick wall opposite. You had to laugh, apparently, in those days. You had to laugh, or weep. Same difference. Cor. Poor old Cyril. Maybe I look like him. Hang on, I'm twice his bloody age. Work it out! I'm older than Sid James in *Carry On Camping*. Oh, crokey. (Would you believe it? That was a slip!) Hey ho the wind. I'll be fancying Hattie Jacques, this rate.

Jokes flying like penguins, eh, son?

Thank God Cyril didn't die in the first wave. I'd have been called after him, for certain. No person called Cyril Thornby could ever have made it as a really great movie director so IT WAS JUST AS WELL, HUH? Dick was bad enough. After – wait for it – Dick Whittington. Naff, eh? Then my progenitors rubbed wartime lard into my cheeks and stuffed me full of fake sausages to get me spots just right because they'd heard the bells of Ponders End and the bells of Ponders End had said I would be called Spotted Dick. And lo, I was. I had the worst fucking spots in Jubilee Road, not counting Stephen Arkwright, who'd walked into a blowlamp or something. Jubilation. The Thing from

23

Jubilee Road, The Gong with the Luminous Zits, all that. Wandering the early fifties with his hand-cranked Oxo box, too busy tracking old ladies with hairnets yelling bugger off or zooming the wheezy old weirdo in gumboots waving his medal at the ducks or panning the grey early-morning light on trampled fish-guts in his grim social comment phase to be a great costermonger. The early fuck-all Fifties. Who remembers them? Who remembers him? Who but he has framed his mum's ration cards and hung them in a Houston lavatory (his own)?

Me mum. I must talk on me mum, guv. The sun is now as risen as it'll ever rise, the shops are open, I'll nip out in a tick and smash-grab the fireworks and sundry other items that'll get the party swinging groovily. I'm not organising it, I'll have you know. I've paid good money to get it organised. Actually, it's Hilda's second cousin/my whatever who's got a little catering business and I hope she's got the date right because I couldn't get hold of her from Houston. This is my opening line to her. Her name is (I'm checking up) Zoë Brand. How could I forget? My opening line is: Hi, Zoë, it's Richard, Richard Thornby. Hallo. Great weather (first joke). It's about my birthday party. I hope you've got the date right, Zoë (second joke).

Zoë Brand, *Miss Tiggywinkle Catering*. Hey, that's awful. Miss Tiggywinkle, I ask you. We got organised last year, over a Sarf Bank sandwich. I had to check up on her. I mean, she's English, she might have been into Tanzanian goulashes or supp'n. I had a Brie & Cranberry Sauce Wholemeal and she had a Taramasalata & Prince Albert's Green Chutney Brown and I said hey, I hope that's just his chutney, Zoë. She didn't click, she just flushed so I waved my sandwich around and said, so what's your professional verdict? She said, extenuating circumstances, it's an English sandwich. She smiled. I tried to smile back but the brie had kind of glued itself to the roof of my mouth, my tongue was planing it, I think I frightened her because she showed her profile against St Paul's (it's a montage shot, give me a break, London's always got something in the way, for Pete's sake) and then, over some fairly sinister strings, *I realised I knew her from somewhere.*

Maybe in a past life. Maybe Zelda is a red herring, Ricky.

24

I got excited for about as long as this pigeon took to haul the rest of my sandwich off the ground before I remembered she was related. Yeah yeah. Just my luck. I'd taken her in at all those family occasions through fans of twiglets and the chronic congenital deformities I have to be nice to because you NEVER KNOW, you never know what they've got stashed away and some are very old. Each time I'd thought it was a different person but she'd just grown. She was the only catering outfit not booked for my birthday. I don't mean I'd booked them all, either. I mean that my sixtieth birthday is in competition. If I called it my sixtieth birthday and had a quiet do in here I'd get no one, probably, except my neighbour overhead with the cockroaches and, of course, Ossy. Huh, Ossy? No? Aw, shucks. I mean not even Mee'd make it. So I've had to relent. My birthday's barely mentioned on the invitations –which, I'll have you know in case you've forgotten, y'all, I sent out THREE YEARS ago. So did everyone else. Like panic buying in Russia. Cor blimey. Remember? One fucking paranoid with halitosis sent his invitations out three years ago and, waal, whad'ya know – every dinner table got to hear of it and panicked. I was in Houston. If I hadn't read about it in the *Guardian Weekly* or someplace I'd have been sending my stack off about two years late. They're coming through so fast it's like flash cards, yelled the report. They're smothering the doormat and they are (oof) flashy. Two types. Huge'n apocalyptic with bloody tasteless terrible jokes or small, gilded, classy. Take your pick. Mine were a third type, unique type. Hand-crafted, I'll have yer know. I spent two weeks painting each one. OK, two weeks preparing myself and humming and then a couple of seconds for the artwork. Chinese ink onto silk paper. They were Zen. They were minimal. They were brill. Don't say you haven't bloody well *framed* them. Hey, I look at them now and I feel, well, bashful. But we're talking aeons ago, the last millennium, we're talking *three years* ago, when Zelda was still around. Zelda. I call'd my love false love; but what said he then? Look it up, dumbos.

Ivory Zelda with the yellow front tooth. That was the loveliest thing about her and the rest of her was pretty lovely, too. No dentist should ever touch it. That little bit of canker on the glossy apple's what every painter craves, innit? Tarkovsky would have really liked her. Fellini did. She was one of the Serbian refugees in *E La Nave Va*. She joined the queue of hopefuls outside his office and he picked her. There were

25

thousands and thousands of hopefuls and he picked her. I know, because I was there. He didn't realise I was just holding her hand. He wanted me, too. I said, Mr Fellini, you're talking to Richard Thornby, the film director. I don' care, he cried, you are parrfet. Parrfet for what, Mr Fellini? Ambidextrous Siamese twin? Grizzled cherub with club-foot? The lead role? I can't juggle with my toes, by the way, but I can skip on two legs without a rope. Ha ha, he laughed. You are parrfet for dead man on wharf who is trampled underfoot. Percipient, was our maestro. I'll let you know, I said. I didn't. I've got it on video. There is no dead man on wharf trampled underfoot in *E La Nave Va*. There's not much of Zelda, either. But enough. The greatest moonlight scenes in the history of film making and Zelda's tooth flashes for an instant – pure rotten gold, guv. That's all I'd watch it for, towards the end.

So my sixtieth, the door into senescence, the gateway to the wintry, my farewell to the last loony pulse of youth, is gatecrashing itself. How about that? Intruder at the feast. At its own feast. I hope Zoë's remembered the cake, that's all. And wow, the candles!

Has she remembered the cake?

This is audience participation, dumbos. Dick Whittington on ice. Oh no he isn't. Oh yes he is. Come on, come on. Did I hear a murmur?

Talking of noise, I reckon it wasn't the bomb on poor Mrs Jackson's. I reckon it was my father. I reckon it was one of his little jokes. I reckon it was him got my mother going that starlit night under the rumble of the Heinkels, under the corrugated iron of the Anderson, under this lyrical bit of English prose. Nice number, guv. It'd come up lovely, spotlit.

I reckoned he got her going, frankly. On purpose. He was capable of that. And he was pissed. In sixty years time, lovely me duck, he'll have the birthday of his life, I don't think. Eleven-firty. The bomb dropped at eleven-firty, me mum said. The poor souls were having a quiet get-together for the new decade. Total shash then quiet again except for the water-pipes. Did for the lot. All the family. Not a Jackson left. Just the dog, in his kennel. Horrible dog, too. Mind you, said me mum, in her quiet way, they weren't everybody's cup of tea, the Jacksons. Half an hour later – whaaaa! No wonder I've always been susceptible, like. To noises and cold, oh Zelda my love, to noises and cold. I came out to the All Clear and the comforting wails of ambulance sirens and drunks and the rasp of a lotta Brooke Bond being sipped and was wrapped in a blackout cloth, which I'll have you know prickles dreadful. What an entrance. What an entrance. None of my students understand. They've never heard of the Blitz, out in Houston. They think London's a waxwork you have to queue five hours for. They're right.

The phone has just rung. It was Ken, another Ken. Incredible, the number of people I know called Ken. Ken Loach, it was. The great Ken Loach. *Kes*, *Raining Stones*, *Ladybirds* or whatever it's called – they're all bloody masterworks. What did he want? I'll tell you. He wanted another number. For some inexplicable reason my name was in his address book. It's crammed with the great and the good, Ken Loach's address book. Is that Bertrand? he asked. No, I said. It's Dicky. Dicky? Yup. Alias Richard Thornby. Silence. Oh, Christ, I'm sorry, it's Ken here. Ken Loach. I wanted bloody Tavernier. We're doing a big thing together. Top secret. Well you've got Richard here, Ken. Christ, I'm sorry. Did I wake you? How's tricks, ah, Richard? I can hear him pounding through his memory cells. He must know who I am, for Christ's sake! I'm just over for a few days, er, guess why? Oh, that, says Ken Loach, yeah – we're just having a quiet do at home. Well you can come along to my do, if you want, at the Waterfront Hotel, Ken – we'd be honoured. A bit of a knees-up. Silence. He's probably handing out soup to dossers tonight, or something, and too damn modest to say it. Change the subject. This big proj, sounds great. You know what it is, Richard? He sounds upset. No no, I hastily respond. But working with Bertrand and all that, y'know? I've diminished in size. Literally. I'm crouched over the bloody phone as if I want to get into the mouthpiece. Ken, on the other end, is enormous. He's a granite cliff. He's a masterwork. I nearly call him sir. Sorry, sir – Ken? Not yet, not yet, Richard. There's interference, sounds stellar. He's probably phoning from somewhere bloody interesting, like the multi-storey in Salford. Somewhere with lots of texture.

Yeah, well, says Ken. Great talking to you, Richard. Still out there, then? A spark of interest! But he's bluffing. He doesn't know where out there is. It could be the Riouw-Lingga Archipelago, for all he knows. (The what, son? I did a shoot out there, long ago. Great surf. Great girls. Indonesia, by the way. The shoot for my unfinished masterwork, *After the Bounty*. My *first* unfinished masterwork. Actually – honest now, guv – it was for *Let's Go Places* on ITV. Nicest job I ever had. Just before *Clive's Seasons*. '87, or something. Probably ruined it. The archipelago, I mean. Mind you, it doesn't exactly trip off the package holiday tongue, Riouw-Lingga, does it? Sounds a little like what I got up to one night, under the coconuts, our toes tickled by surf, her skin as warm as sand and the colour of the opening shots in *Stalker*. Blimey, son. 'Nuff said. Over to Ken and me.)

Yup, I'm still out there, Ken. Teaching. Till recently. I haven't done a thing in ages, except yak. Except what? Yak. Oh, *yak!* Giggle, north of England style. I bring the receiver back to my ear. But I've got something up my sleeve, something big. Oh, yeah? Yeah, Ken. Poor sod wants to phone Bertrand Tavernier and he's wasting his priceless time listening to some clapped-out jerk kidding himself he can make a comeback. Must happen all the time. Silence. Well, good luck with it, Richard – sorry to bother you. Hey, Ken, you can phone me whenever you like. Any hour of the day or night. When I'm over. You can phone me in the States, you can phone me when you're out there. I'll put you up. I'll put you up and we can talk far into the night about kestrels, about Manchester, about the revolution, about the cosmos. I'll tell you about my mum and my project. You'll fall off your chair and I'll carry you to bed. I'll tuck you up. I'll lie on the sofa and watch the fire die and listen to the toads and the ambulance sirens and think this is a very important day in the history of British film-making. Merchant-Ivory, get lost. M. Tavernier, *je m'excuse*. Ken and I have shared something infinitely precious. The films we are going to make together are all going to be infinitely precious. They are going to be the early jewels of the lustrous twenty-first-century renaissance. The renaissance that'll spread its brilliant peacock tail through all the arts. Unstoppable. Magnificent. Fanned out, flowering out of the dung-heap of the twentieth century, out of the million upon million of the murdered and abused and forgotten of the twentieth century, out of their hearts and minds and Technicolor mouths. Ken, we can do it.

Click.

Heck, I wish I'd said it. It's down there, curled on the cutting-room lino. The lost rushes of Orson Welles That Ends Well. Unspliceable. Be content, be content with stills. With frightening stills. Frightening, unflickering, slightly tramlined stills.

I think I said, instead – good luck, Ken, thanks for calling. What a jerk. Thanks for calling! But he didn't mean to call! Why do I always fuck it up at the end? I sounded like I felt, that's why. I sounded miniscule. Bet you my last Wrigley's he hated my accent. He's from nowhere and he's going nowhere, I bet he thought. Treading water in mid-Atlantic, riding the big swell to nowhere. It's not my fault, Ken! I'd love to be real, I truly would! No froth, no chemicals, just handpicked and yeasty in my own china mug unhooked from the ocean-hardened truss, spit on the floor, sawdust on my toes, the old geezers singing their incomprehensible songs and me – me joining in because I know the words backwards and no one's sniggering behind their Woodbine-kippered, England-encrusted nails!

Aw, shucks. Cor, blimey. Well, that's the cue for me mum. And behind me mum, the phantoms.

Chill. They're in here. OK. Let's go.

Zoë rang. I gave you a lot of held white wall and was just about to start the countdown when Miss Tiggywinkle rang. Zoë is, if I remember rightly, nothing like Miss Tiggywinkle. She is slim, dark-haired, efficient. Get that. Slim, dark-haired, efficient. Zoë, I really lust over your voice. I lust over what you embody. I would like to have married you, thirty-odd years ago, before you were born. Now it's too late. You are the mistress of the ceremonies that are about to consign me to senescence. (Look it up, Ossy, look it up, I've used it before.) I don't feel my age. I feel very young. I feel, as a matter of fact, as if I've only just been born. Hey, no, don't go back to that bloody terrible night, those bloody awful nights of infancy, the night skies raining terror, bright as day up there and dark as the pit down here, serious testicular abrasions from the war-issue diapers, Des's shell-case rattle with my fontanelle coordinates on it, superficial crush injuries against me mum's Oxo pinny every time the siren went, stuffed onto a train, getting out at somewhere unspellable even by a grown Englishman 'cos there were literally thousands of *l*s in it, guv, bundled past scowling chapels and friendly sheep, mired thigh-deep in sopping grass as we crossed the field's short-cut look you, hugging my teddy, what the hell is happening, where am I going, who are you, what is this country, and where are the whales that are going to save me? Because I have a great and abiding terror of them. They're too large. Call me Ricky. Ricky please, not Dick.

Above all – where's me mum?

Ah, Zoë. How I wish you were running my life perpetually. How I wish you were running the world. One big party. Remembering the candles. Remembering the doilies. Remembering that I liked pink marzipan and – oh joy, FRESH CREAM ECLAIRS which have to come as you bite them or they're inauthentic. Not that you used that term, come. Not that I used it, either. Oh no. You are brisk, slim-haired, darkly

31

efficient. Zoë Moneypenny. I could hear your horn-rims cluck against the earpiece as you noted, noted my desires down in your little electronic pad. Cool, calm, collected second cousin of Hilda and something-not-too-close of me. What opposites! All the women in my life have been wild, wild and brunette and emotionally awry. Dark-tressed Zoë, you are my salvation. I can splice and edit my wet green rushes all day, rise from the table at six, change and scrub myself (maybe not in that order) by seven, saunter by foot with my film cans in the old perambulator through the gaily-apparelled and pissed throng to the Waterfront, ascend in the whispering lift, hush-puppy along the corridor to Suite Y, open the door softly to a forest (OK, a small but intimate English copse) of applause, the last balloon in place, the last doily settled, the sago browning, the screen up and the projector set (thanks, Joe, thanks), the terrace garlanded with winter roses, a well-rendered chorus of Happy Birthday plus serial descant from Ossy and the other event temporarily forgotten.

Thank you, my dearest Zoë, Zoë my lass! (Mind you, guv, I'm paying her enough. Fifty per cent up front, too. Orfenticity, see. Cor.)

Where's me mum?

Me mum is dead.

Rough justice. I bet she wore herself out tending to your horrible dad, you're thinking. I bet she laboured over the iron and the stove and maybe the haberdashery-till on Saturdays ping till, tucking her loose strand of once-lovely locks into her headscarf, she turned and said to your belching pop with his feet up on the meticulously-scrubbed table: I don't feel well, Douglas. Grunt, because Douglas is tackling the *Enfield Times* crossword: six across, begins with C, ob-lit-er-ate at once, lovely me duck. I have to tell you it's cancer, Doug. Thank you, Marge. You're a doll.

Not quite like that, but all but. Steady decline, put put, bits of her going, not enough to excuse herself from duty. Hip joints ground down to powder waiting for the op, a list of ailments ending in orosis, the *coup de grâce* indecipherable on the death certificate but probably something nasty and Victorian from the lousy hospital, crawled out of the peeling woodwork, a sort of Fagin bacterium last heard of in 1848. *Thatcherismus stridulus*, most like. Hospital knocked down a year or so later. Made into a car-park for tax-perks. Amen.

Phantoms. Hey, she never told me much. Let's get this straight: she was not posh. But she had class. You could tell. You could tell she had some right royal blood in her. Cor, I'm sounding just like David Herbert Lawrence in that massive biopic proj Ken (as in Russell) wouldn't bloody touch in '65, holed up in Zennor, getting flat-irons chucked at his head by that horrible Frieda and shouting it was all his dad's fault, or maybe it wasn't, maybe it was his overweening mum had made him go after spit-cotton slick-saddled Boche aristos who didn't wash a dish if they could chuck it some, son. Anyway, I loved me mum and I still do. I've got to visit the cemetery day after tomorrow. OK, I haven't got to, but I will, come hell or hangover or, hey, death by drowning. It's the worst cemetery this side of Calcutta, it's practically on the North bloody Circular, the ground throbs, I bet there isn't a corpse with a tooth still in its head. There've been incidents, naturally. Great-great-grandsons of Burkett and Hare, pillaged plots, hearse thefts, abandoned mourners. Me mum's grave had its begonias pinched, along with the pot. It was her favourite pot. Bastards.

I've thought of moving her but it's too complicated. She wanted to be buried out to sea, would you believe. Well, scattered from a cliff-top, that nice romantic and extremely filmic type of thing. The relations wouldn't hear of it. She'd not got it written down. It had to be Enfield. They're rather cocky about Enfield. They're so darn cocky about it they've never left it, except to go along to Epping Forest to do a bit of flasher-spotting. My cousin Rog (hang your head in shame, Dicky, dim the lights) is on the council. He's Tory. He's Tory to the last bubble of spittle on his niblick. Like Des is something worse. Talking of golf, I've got a return match with John Schlesinger that's been waiting for twenty years. My clubs have congealed, rusted, coagulated, back in Houston. They're all too keen out there. But they're not much cop, I can tell you. I abut a golf course. Weekends and it's like the hammattan, they're that bad. I step out onto my porch and get half a bunker down my throat when the wind's right. I tell yer, it's bleedin' *Paths of Glory* out there, guv: divots the size of shell holes, massive eruptions, fat Texan wives who forgot to let go of their Number Ones whining over your head, overweight trolleys lumbering into trenches, the rattle of machine-guns resolving a quibble up at the eighteenth. I've thought of moving, but I like my wee hame. I do. Maybe my mother likes to be juddered by trucks. Who knows? Who knows why we end up where we do?

Sorry about the golf act. It's my after-dinner number, I don't get to use it much these days. I tend to spray my Scotch when I do. My fifth double, usually. That's what it takes. I've never seen it in black and white before. It looks weird. And trite, over-ambitious, seriously unfunny. (Philip French on *Will There's a Way*. Or Barry, me old ex-chum Barry Norman. Hiya, y'bum, if you're out there. Treachery. Life's all blahdy treachery. Me table's *scratched*, for God's sake.)

Where was I? Ha, me golf party pooper. Hey, and I've been using it for years. Zelda would scream with laughter. So would my mother. That's what I liked about my mother. She laughed at me jokes.

Phantoms.

Sing willow, willow, willow etc.

I wanted this whole thing to be poetic. It started out poetic. Now it's just me, yaketty-yak.

I'll let you into a secret: I spent half a night-flight on the first three paras. I think I might have mentioned this already. I didn't read Norman for more than about ten minutes. Mailer, not blahdy Barry. I spent four and a half hours composing the start. That's why it's so damn good. The bit about the hand flat against the wall was composed in my sleep, in my dreams, because the moment breakfast came and everyone woke up and started yelling *hi* at each other I couldn't keep awake. When I started I had to memorise it because the fucking stewardess didn't respond to my panic-button. I needed a pen. I hadn't got a pen on me, would you believe it. I was in the middle of the middle row. My knees were up to my chest. I couldn't move yet again to check out this wing-inferno thing or go see Miss Buck-Teeth-But-Very-Nice-Everything-Else '99 because I might wake up my enormous neighbour from a little village fifteen und a half kilometre souse of

34

Düsseldorf and he'd start on yet a-bloody-gain about his fucking little village fifteen und a half kilometre souse of Düsseldorf like he was doing a one-man *Heimat*, Parts 1 to 28, no commercial breaks. So I memorised the beginning. It was good for me. I had this crazy notion that the plane would crash flaming into the ocean if I didn't memorise it before my enormous neighbour woke up for breakfast. He stirred once and I hummed him a little lullaby and this sweet smile broke across his face and he snuggled up to me. My heart was hammering. I was sure it would wake him and we'd go crashing into the sea, the night sea, the murky not even moon-glittering sea and down, down, down we'd go with bubbles coming out of our mouths and giant creatures of the deep nosing at the windows until we bumped bottom where the blind fish roam and gobble through their pointless, unobserved existences, to quote me old mucker Henry Peterson the unobserved poet, long dead. But we didn't, quite possibly because he started snoring to my lullaby. The ghosts of my grandfather, great-aunt and great-uncle, I murmured. Yah, he grunted. Then snored again. That didn't count. He had not woken up. There was a jolt. The whole plane jolted. Oh well, I thought, wanting to check out the sick-bag but my knees were in the way. I have so many plans. So does everyone else on this plane. So many plans. But my plan is more important than anybody else's and all the fucking cans are in the hold forgive my language just this once. Please, O Lord, give me a bit more time. He did. My neighbour only woke up for breakfast. He laid his enormous hands on the Continental and it kind of vanished. But I loved him, by then, for not waking up. I manœuvred my marmalade onto the croissant and I loved him. Dawn shone on his nose-hairs. In my villedge, he started. I woke up. Go on, go on, I said. In your village. I fell asleep again. He had a soothing voice. My favourite blonde student was undoing my fly. We were on a boat. You don't have the right, Candidia, I protested. Relax, she said. I was trying to get my shoulder round but it wouldn't come. A flotilla of pleasure-seekers with blue hair were looking on. They were prim. They had guard-rails round their teeth. They were humming with their mouths open. My (sorry about this) dick pressed against her cool hand. I don't want to éclair just here, I protested. The boat rocked. In my villedge, came the announcement over the swimming-pool tannoy. Candidia turned into oh no Zelda surprise surprise and bent her face down and her loosened locks swept across my chest. There are seat belts for every person on the planet, she enunciated, her lips striking the top of my swollen microphone in time to the plosives. We haf much manufacture of small parts, before. My shoulder came off. It was the stewardess. I blinked. Your seat belt, sir, she said. We're about to land. She nods towards my lap. She must be able to see it, it's through my underpants and against my zip, it's about to be lacerated. Christ, I think. I could be chucked off. She leaves me with no further comment. She's probably used to it. Like nurses. Und the immigrants, don't you sink, hm? Eh, what? Oh yes. Und the immigrants, und the immigrants.

Wasn't I talking about my mother? Bear with me, guv. I'm still lagged. It's not the right time. I'm wading against the clock. When I smile to myself I feel like I'm one of those old portraits the charm of which is in the craquelure. Ain't that just a lovely lil' ol' English sentence, son? The grey is getting into me. Ma grits is gone cold. Texas is a faraway siren, a ten-gallon pick-up on the wide horizon, the credits about to roll, a disappearing dust cloud, the silhouette at the end of *Unforgiven*, Clint indistinguishable from a cactus, not wanting to move as the seats clack back all round and the lights drag you back to some lousy multiplex with a built-in depression system and the rumble of *Rocky 5* coming up through your boots from Screen 58 and a November evening in Flatulence-upon-Effluent waiting to hug you. I've been there, I've even opened them. Helped open them in the kinds of places that hadn't caught up with the fact that Richard Thornby is a no-no these days – and I'm talking about the *seventies*, for Christ's sake. I'm one of the guests, the one without a title and a gold harness round his neck, the one who doesn't look as if he's been dry-cleaned in his suit because, hey, he's the artiste, he's allowed to wear casuals, he's hip, he's the one we expect to get legless on the Piat d'Or (thank you, Chairperson of the Council) and hog all the peanuts (thank you, Rapentheft Development Corp) but he doesn't, he drinks orange juice and is on a salt-free diet and can't give a hand carrying Lady Toper out because he's just seen his chiropractor.

Yup, I'm back. I'm in orbit again, I'm circling, I'm bringing a groan to a thousand mouthpieces, a hi and a hey and a *here, what's up next week?* Only this time you're coming to me. I'm paying. I'm providing. I'm promising.

What am I promising?

Phantoms.

The film that never was and never shall be.

The ultimate masterwork.

Stills. A handful of stills.

Thirty-two.

Why the heck thirty-two, Dicky?

Duff-head. Illiterate sponge-brain. Does the name Glenn mean anything to you and not as in Glenn Close, for fuck's sake?

You mean John Glenn, Dicky? The astronaut? The first guy to orbit –

Oh, you film people. Give me your head a minute. Is there intelligent life on it? Yeah, the lice. Now listen. Picture a big black grand on the TV. A Steinway so buffed it must be giving the studio lights a migraine. Picture a guy crouched at it, keeping osteopaths in a living, attempting to squeeze in between the keys. His fingers are moving. He's singing but the sound is coming out of his fingers. The sound coming out of his fingers is doing something to you. It's making love to you like an angel might make love to you if you were incorporeal. You are incorporeal. Even your breakfast isn't repeating. This is because Glenn as in Gould is playing Johann as in Bach on Channel 98. You've hit it by accident, searching for a re-run without either Depardieu or Hopkins or Streep in it. This hasn't got Depardieu or Hopkins or Streep in it. It's terrible quality. It's lit as for open-heart surgery and there's bad lag on the hands and they're not even moving that fast, they're kind of floating. But it's doing something to you. You decide to change your life. You decide to create something as delicate and beautiful and deep as Glenn Gould playing Johann Sebastian Bach's *32 Variations*. Then it's the commercial break. Your breakfast starts repeating. You feel sick. The meaty chunks slide onto the plate. You've been dreaming. The mouths flap and smile and talk. The dogs gambol. Blip. The screen dies. Your life has changed. You don't move. You don't move for an hour.

Got me?

This is personal, by the way. It personally happened to me. In a motel outside Toronto. I was trying to see Zelda. She was cleaning out her mind of material things on some course that was certainly doing that to her wallet. It was mid-winter. I was holed up in a motel where the pipes were still organising themselves into a heating system and the motel manager was called Jeroboam. He bore absolutely no resemblance to Anthony Perkins, unlike in every other motel story you get to hear. He was a lapsed Mormon and drank a Bourbon & Coke an hour and told me not to leave my hairs in the shower or on the pillow or anywhere, because he'd had a lot of problems with hairs, especially the spirally kinda hair, sir. He'd enjoy being a motel manager were it not for the hairs, because you couldn't find a cleaner these days who'd poke 'em out. He had to use a fork, he said. I hope you wash it after use, I said. He gave me my key which had a sort of rubber sex-aid dangling from it. I stayed three days because it was the motel nearest Zelda's hideaway. When I eventually caught up with her building her personal image out of snow she was very surprised and I said if I'd known I'd have bought you a carrot for the nose and she glanced at my jeans and said, honey, I think you have. I pulled out my key. My talent falls within definite limits, I japed. She laughed and laughed without recognising it and we had a nice week together motoring about and eating and laughing. Then she left me for A. N. Other Jnr you'll be hearing about soon, I'm trawling, stick with me, it gets very exciting. But I didn't mind at that point. I'd caught this Glenn Gould thing on the second night in Jeroboam's little kingdom and I was somewhere else. Hey, I was orbiting. I was not touching earth. My nose-hairs tinkled but I didn't feel the cold. I had this Big Idea forming in my head. This Big Idea had to do with me making a comeback. My favourite film is *The Secret Life of Walter Mitty*. I even look a bit like Danny Kaye. Shucks.

Get the picture?

Come on, son, pack it in. Anyone'd think you were a bleedin' Yank, talking like that.

38

I am, Poppa, I am. Except when I say field or round about especially as in the angels of the Lord shone round about them or start getting unemotional, thinking about you.

Cor. You used to talk posh, too.

I still do. In Houston everyone thinks I'm posh. I could talk like a dishwasher and they'd think I was posh. It's because I don't have a drawl so stretched you can pop out and make a nice cuppa while they're getting through 'well'. As in 'Waaaaaaall, whad'ya know some, it's Tricky Dicky'. Naff, eh? Tricky Dicky. I don't even look like the bastard. It's because that's the only nickname they can think of, they're so bloody thick. It's affectionate, of course. Bear-hugs follow, usually. There's lots of affection around, in Houston. Lots of big grizzly bear-hugs. I like it. Bear-hugs or a silent, mean look over a gun or OK maybe a plate of grits. I like going downtown thinking I'm either about to be bear-hugged or blasted. It gives one zip. Enfield could do with some footpads, I'm thinking, Pop. A few big pick-ups to hold the sawn-offs, a few stretched limos the length of our street, a few deadly youf gangs. Or has it arrived already? I hear Cricklewood has problems, from Geoff. It doesn't have problems from Geoff, I don't mean that. Oh, I got bad slick on ma tongue. I mean that it's as safe as houses. They come in through the roof, according to Geoff. Without lifting a tile. They're so skilled, the unskilled, they can remove your video in the middle of *Suspicion* without you noticing. Have style, will steal. End up in Enfield a long long way from the wharves, right, Pop?

Let's not get onto that, not now.

My kitchen clock hath just spoke. I wound it up when I got in and it's just shrilled at me, because I did something to the button when I was winding. The alarm button, I guess. Sorry – I suppose. I suppose. I suppose. I don't want to be taken for a Yank by the Waterfront's doorman. He'll expect a tip. I'm skint. This clock, it cost me an arm and a leg duty-free. I've had it for five years and I've never worked out how to set the alarm. It's all in sign language, it's like the console of a jumbo at the back. Perhaps it was Mee. Perhaps Mee and Greg set it for something. Ten-fifteen. That figures. They're late risers. I like its tick. It breaks the uncanny silence so it's the first thing I do, wind up the kitchen clock. It's got a tick so quiet it must be Japanese. Tlick, tlick, it whispers. I wonder what makes it tlick, sometimes. I think it's admonishing me. Christ, I sound as though I'm writing a novel. Clocks are always admonishing people in novels. I'd like to write a novel. Richard looked up. The clock was admonishing him. He grimaced and set to again, flensing her with such delicacy that she didn't notice her skin had been removed until she saw it on the back of the ottoman. Don't put it there, she said, Ramona is coming to clean. She'll only spill something on it. Richard smiled grimly. Ramona won't be coming, not today. He wiped his flensing tool on the side of his Burton's handkerchief, size L, and flinched. In his frenzied haste he had forgotten

Give up.

Here I am, in England.

England.

England my England.

Something in Old English finishing in wod.

A verray parfit gentil knight

Unsex me here, you murthering ministers

It is a truth universally acknowledged, that a single bloke with his arse on a fortune, must be in want of a wife. Something like that, guv.

Fog. Fog and more fog. Fog fog fog, fog in the guttering and in the funnels and up the costermonger's nose. Fog everywhere. Fog. I could go on. I will. Fog . . .

Grey fog of a winter dawn. I had not thought death had undone so many. Too right.

Yeah, I could go on. I've read a few modern novels in my time, for the film rights. I just missed *The French Lieutenant's Woman*, for starters. I don't have the clout now, and didn't then. Bloody producers. Illiterates. They dream in figures. Edicated, too, most of 'em. I mean, they've got an O level or two. Know what I mean?

Ponce. Spotted Dick. Fancy ideas, eh?

Oh yes, I went up, grammar school genius, cleverclogs of the Sixth, hoity-toity of Enfield, did English with Mr and Mrs Leavis, no less. Old English, Middle English, Golden English, Midden English, Old Heap of Junk English (speaking chronologically) – you name it, I've done the lot, mate. You should have heard my accent then. I mean, when you've got dons what make BBC Home Service announcers sound like my old man the dustman, you can't do nuffink at all, can you? So I gave it a good thrashing, bashed all the muck out, and opened me gob at the fifth seminar. Silence. Mr and Mrs Leavis Enterprises looks askance. The mob hath spoke. The masses have given voice. Actually, they liked me. Frank and I got on. Q. D. was a bit tricky, but she made good buttered buns. I can't deny it. I was a cocky sod. I got a third, just. I was far too busy to get anything else. I was the Jean Cocteau, fuck it, of Magdalene with an *e*. I got my Orphée to wade into the Cam where we had to fish him out because the stupid bastard couldn't swim. Lost his bloody wings, too. Christ, it was hard work, starting out with that bunch of public school nitwits. Casts of thousands all looking suspiciously the same. They were the same. They were mostly Dickin Cartwright and Gerald Hallerby-Baste and me.

Great days, great days.

Have a bit of my nice white wall to go fix another drink and watch a rocket. Get some popcorn. Be my guest.

You know what Kubrick used to do? He'd control his films to The End. I mean The Very End, The Popcorn-Down-The-Edge-Of-The-Bleedin'-Seat End. He'd get the family to check out the movie theatres (sorry, Mr Doorman – the cinematic establishments). He had family in every major capital. He'd get them to go along and check there wasn't light bouncing off the walls or the seats weren't too close or the screen was nice and smooth and didn't have a bulge or a patch or a rip or so much as a fag scorch. Because when you've made *Paths of Glory* or *2001* (*sic*) you're not going to have it fucked up by some lousy flea-pit of a nickelodeon charging a half-bottle of Laphroaig a throw, are you? For Kubrick it had to be OK Corral until the hordes descend blinking into the house lights of Earth and close their parched mouths and check for their wallets and their pardners. So you jes make darn sure that projector blonde ain't a-dazzlin' some and that the ol' sound track ain't out o' sync with the lips a-flappin' real big up there and lie back and don't rustle your popcorn while the action's rollin'. Or I is gonna get riled.

OK.

Hey, you see why I go down a bomb in Texas?

I said I'd write the trailer in England on the first – the last – OK OK, the last-but-one with the last for trimming up and stuff – day. Ah declare, ah declared, it'll be the last act of the twentieth century and of the second millennium following a certain little scuffly spot of pother in Palestine. So be it. I've got to come into this new one on a high, shed skin left on the flanges of the security wall that'll shield us from that bad past and let us roam forward with our backs covered. I said it would be mildly (nay, allusively) poetic, recalling my early scenarios, my early poetry, my early letters, my early unfinished novels, my early angry young plays I had to pay my students to perform because there

43

was some essential nudity involved, my early just about everything before the vision flickered out and the spool spun round, empty, because some mad bastard had run off with the only darn print. I said all this on my Marilyn inflatable one morning, so excited that I'd gotten myself my own wave machine, so high that I could have taken the stopper out of her bum and still floated. Hey, the millennium's just about tailed out. Everybody is miserable because the tenth instalment went real hairy in the fourteenth minute and wasn't just unsuitable for kids and dogs – it should never have been screened at all! I mean, it was more than murders and tongues, Mum. It was massacres and violations. It was even worse than the ninth instalment. And the ones before that weren't so great, either. We'd tried, we'd tried. Am I mad? Am I insane? Am I twelve screws loose thinking we might just be able to start all over at sixty? Hey, this is going to be one hell of a party. I'm high. I'm back on my inflatable getting avocado all over my chin it's all so swell and I'm thinking big, I'm thinking Texan, I'm thinking we don't have a problem, Houston – or if we do we're gonna make it back. Lovell, Halse, and Swigert. Frontier spirit. The third millennium. I'd really like to make a movie but no rich bastard's gonna stump up the spondulicks, guv, so over to you. Settle down. Enjoy the comfy seat with no gum on the base, the perfect air-conditioning, the hush-hush Bach over the system, the guy/gal sitting there in prime position, really nice and sensitive people all around discussing in low voices just about everything from Pete Abelard to Zoroaster, really great hand-tossed popcorn, lots of elbow room, a mathematically-calculated rake so even a middle-aged Mohican bang in front of you would be just fine, and no shiny walls. In fact, it's Stanley himself sitting bang in front of you and he's nodding happily. He likes it. It's his perfect picture-house. Pity about the picture. Let's roll. Duck if your head lights up.

Not quite. Hands off the halogens. You're in the Enfield Ritz in 1951, I'm afraid. Sorry about that. It won't take long. It's a short. Saturday morning drizzle. You're in the lobby, in actual fact. It's your first time. You're early. You're the first mug there. You're so early the ticket woman's putting on her lipstick in the kiosk. You didn't realise she ever wore lipstick. It's crimson. You'd always thought it was her real mouth. She puts it on badly. She looks as if she's just got back from a round of blood-sucking with Boris Karloff. She scowls at you. No one comes this early. Your sixpence is melting in your hand. It's turned to goo. It wasn't your sixpence. Your sixpence is in your secret pocket which is hell to get even your small fist into. The goo was a piece of chocolate your mother gave you at the last minute, as if you were off on an Antarctic expedition. The chocolate will reappear in the last frame, it will be your salvation, you won't have to eat Bingo the husky who earlier on licked you awake out of a deadly nap. She's rearranging the popcorn and the toffee bars and even the chocolate-boxes that are only for the very rich and so have dust all over them. The kiosk woman, not your mother. You wish your mother was the kiosk woman, then you wouldn't have to pay and you could eat up all the chocolate-boxes and you could go to every showing except the late night ones where they peck, apparently, and don't watch. The whole of the back row pecks. It's part of the thing about a late-night showing. You can't go in on your own. You have to have someone to peck. If there's no room in the back row you can't peck, you just have to hold hands. Some in the back row use their tongues. You can't quite put a picture on this one, but as the kiosk lady rearranges her blouse you try to. Perhaps they show their tongues to each other and place expensive chocolates on them. You can't think of anything else more pleasurable for the moment. It's 1951, for God's sake. You look at the stills. You have the stills for this week's film and the stills for next week's film. They're outside and they're inside. Inside they're easier to see because outside the rain has spotted the glass and seems to have got inside because half of the stills are curled and one of them has dropped to the bottom where it just looks like any other snap. In here it's like looking into an aquarium full of exotic fish. You don't think that, of course. You're not old enough to be that pretentious. There's enough poetry in the stills for you to think of them as just that. You're staring up at this week's stills in little brass frames because next week's stills are next week and next week is unimaginable while the Hoover purrs beyond the magic door and the kiosk lady is phoning someone and giggling. You're happy she's not scowling at you. You're happy that she's otherwise occupied because you have the feeling she might snap and toss you out into the street at any moment and the street is somewhere else, the street is not in here, the street is far far away and in some other universe you can vaguely remember because your duffle-coat is still smelling of it and its dampness. The stills. You gaze at them. The colour isn't very good. They look as if they've been up a very long time. They look as if the sun has been on them too much, which is unlikely, because you haven't seen the sun over Enfield for three weeks. But it doesn't matter. This is the film you are about to see. You don't know what the film's about. You don't care what the film's about. You look at the photos and you think you're going to like the film. You have a terror that this is all you're going to see of the film because it's floor-wax early and probably the cinema's about to burn down and some nutter's run off with the print. I threw my toilet roll away by the way so I'm gonna do a slow tilt on this long one starting high up because I don't want to interrupt, it's all one take, it'll be fine so long as the print doesn't smear. You don't know the word print, of course. You know only screen, projector, film. That's enough. And Action. You know Action. When you play at making films with the dog and your hand-cranked Oxo box you say Action. The dog takes no notice. The other kids on the street think this game is bloody boring. They prefer to kill each other because that's what their fathers have been doing recently, according to their mothers and their grandmothers and the Prime Minister. You shout Action at Rufus and Rufus begs, which is something. Back to the stills. You've licked your hand clean of chocolate but your mouth is now soiled and you've forgotten your handkerchief like your mother said you would forget it if you didn't put it in your pocket right now. Your tongue comes out and you wipe all around your mouth with your tongue which is probably what they do in the back row in late night shows so you make sure you've got your back turned on the kiosk lady who's now rearranging her hair. You can't actually see she's rearranging her hair because your back is turned but take it from me that's what she's doing. I'm the guy waiting for his girlfriend at the door, looking in, cheek on the glass. I'm watching you gazing up at the stills. I know what you're thinking. You're thinking about what happens either side of each still. You're thinking whether that tall handsome bloke with the quiff has just raised his hand or is in the middle of lowering it. You're thinking whether the blonde lady with the big bosoms lying on the sofa is asleep or whether she's just been murdered. You don't think she's been murdered because the film is suitable for kids and your mother checked there wasn't anything scary by phoning someone. Perhaps she phoned the kiosk lady. Perhaps the kiosk lady tricked her with a cruel crimson smile and the film will be full of murders and tongues doing things. You're thinking about going home and just checking again with your mother. Then you're thinking how it might be quite fun telling the other kids about the murders and tongues. There aren't any tongues on the stills. You're glad to see a dog in one. It's a big, hairy sort of dog and there's someone, a boy, good, kneeling by it and pointing. You wonder what's going on. Your favourite still is of a man on a horse with big mountains behind him but it's not like in the cowboy films. He doesn't have a big hat. He has a sort of tartan thing with ear-flaps and a thick coat with, hey, toggles. There's snow on the mountains. There are forests with snow on them. The horse is rearing up. It's white. You wonder what happens just before and just after. You want to see more of the mountains. You think that when you get into the film you'll see more of the mountains because the horse will move along and probably gallop. For some reason you can smell the mountains, you can smell the forests on them. They're high and cold and full of snow but it's not the slushy brown muck you get in Enfield. It's white and cold and high and you can breathe it in and the horse is panting and you can practically sit on the horse and move along very fast but actually it's me giving up on Barbara and opening the door and entering, panting the chill away, giving you a wink because you've turned round and I know just what you're thinking, kid, I know just what you're thinking.

OK? Get the picture?

I did think this was going to be a trifle more poetic, as Dr Foliole (Leavis) would say. He'd have hated my films, but let's not go into that. The point is, the point to remember, is that the film was never as good as the stills, was it? I don't mean to say that a bunch of lousy photographs gently curling in the Enfield Ritz was better than, say, *Passport to Pimlico*. But that feeling, that feeling. The horse did move along and you moved with it and there were the mountains and it was great, but –

Right – it wasn't the same feeling, was it? Is there life out there? Are you all yelling NO! No? OK, let me tell you something: Signor Fellini never looked at his rushes at the end of the day. He drove technicians crazy. He preferred the rushes in his head. Once he made a whole film without rushes. Then he got them done and watched. They were good. I forget the film. There was some kind of strike on down at the labs. A friend of his, one of his unit, told me this at a party. The opening night of *E La Nave Va*. The launch, in Paris. Great days, great

47

days. Think about it. About Signor Fellini never looking at his dailies because he liked to keep things pure.

That haunted me. No, it didn't. I forgot about it because I was pissed at the time and then it popped up again in some interview on TV. I was in a motel in Arizona, years later. Serendipity. For the whole of the next day, up with the Hopis, watching them pop in and out of their buried temple for the Butterfly Dance I think it was – hey, I couldn't muse on anything else. I stood on the lip of the mesa and stared out at the wowee desert and I thought: that's what's wrong with everything. That's what's wrong with my life. That's what Zelda might have meant if she'd said it right but she didn't, she just said something halfway between Sufi and Zen and it sounded like she was telling me I had a low grade in math. (Sorry – poor marks in maths. Mr Doorman'll be pawing me at this rate.) He never watches his rushes. I repeated this so many times to myself it sounded like another language, it sounded like Latvian or something. He never watches his rushes. He never watches his rushes. He never washes his undies. That's my mother. She's always interjecting. I bear no resemblance to Anthony Perkins. They say I do remind them of Danny Kaye, however. My mother was a very nice and kind person, salt of the earth and a bit of a toff to boot. Which reminds me.

Sorry – that was Zoë on the phone again. Have I got a guest list? She needs a guest list. Why does she need a guest list? The hotel needs a guest list. Why does the hotel need a guest list, Zoë my ducks? The hotel needs a guest list for security reasons. Apparently the Queen of Sheba or somewhere is having a ball in the room below. At least she's in the room below. At least if someone's planted TNT under her throne the ceiling won't fall on top of us. Semtex, these days, Richard. This is ridiculous, Zoë. None of my guests would want to kill the Queen of Sheba. None of my guests would want to kill anyone. Except possibly me after inviting them to my party on The Big Night and then getting them stopped at the door by the Queen of Sheba's personal security service who've probably only just taken early retirement from Broadmoor, Zoë one of the lasses O. But you must have a guest list. I don't. I don't know how many people are going to turn up. But you gave me a number to cater for. I gave you a number, Zoë, which was

48

the number of invites I sent out and then some more. Oh, Jeeesus! Zoë, I didn't know you were a blasphemer. What's wrong? You think we're going to run out of Miss Tiddleywink's carrot cake? Miss Tiggywinkle, actually. Oh, crumbs. Hey, Zoë, I thought you were slim, dark-haired, and cool as a cucumber. Put your horn-rims back on, Zoë. What am I going to tell them, Richard? Zoë, you tell them from Rick-No-Tricks Thornby here that my guests are going to glitter so brightly the doorman'll have to wear shades or he'll feel like Scott of the Antarctic who ate all his huskies up. All except my relatives. Sorry, Richard? And my relatives are nothing to worry about. Save my daddyo. And he's not coming. He's going to be wrapped around Nurse Luscious in Chestnut Grove Home for the Intolerable, Havant. He's what? Zoë, you tell them that. You might also tell them that I'm paying for the privilege of abusing their Suite F. A., and they can go stuff their Queen of Sheba because we're just as vital. I mean, someone might want to blow *me* up. Have they thought of that? Zoë?

She put the phone down on me. I guess – sorry, I suppose – I overran some, somewhat. Thornby In The Flesh. Dick the Prick. Rick Thornby: Houston's answa to the ansaphone. I've seen all these scrawled up in the student's lavatory when I've been caught short. Heck. Aren't they original? The first was doing the rounds when a gas mask turned out to be Winston Churchill, for God's sake. My late-lamented students wrote with their tongues stuck out. Or they would lean back and rest their feet on the desks and nod and I thought for years I'd hooked them with my exposition of doubles in *Strangers on a Train* or whatever but the nod'd get frantic and continue even when I was saying how the blobs from Sirius had just landed on the HCDVA lawn at my command at last and I realised they were tagged into a personal stereo so discreet it barely existed. And hey, I'd thought it was the air-conditioning system all those years. I went on yakking because I reckoned it was their bloody funeral. I never once used videos, incidentally. I used stills. That thing about stills in the Enfield Ritz was my little introductory piece for stale freshpeople. It helped clear out the chaff. About half of them didn't come back to my module and it meant I could get between the desks to strap knuckles. Seriously –I NEVER USED MOVING IMAGES. Their eyes'd be less glazed, they'd maybe start to listen, maybe now and again I'd start to see something other than the drawing-pins and gum blatches on the soles

49

of their giant trainers because they liked to rest their legs after sex or advanced trampoline or whatever. My colleagues thought I was crazy. They have big video screens in the College – the kind that disappear if you look at them from the side, they're so Japanese. The HCDVA has a lot of dough, a lot of the readies, guv. But the pay was lousy. I got paid basic and I got paid boost. Boost was dependent on the number of students attending my module. Basic was so basic the bank'd charge you for wasting their time. It was embarrassing unrolling your hand-kerchief on the counter each month and counting out the cents. It'd get the queue of furred old ladies and the guys in Mickey Mouse masks really impatient. I'd shrug my shoulders and say, hey, schmuck, where d'you want this? Under my Bultex? Remember the Princess and the Pea! Besides, I'm British. I'm mean, peevish, and little. Give me a break! Boost was hopeless, by the way. I had an attendance number which would've made a great golf handicap. There were others whose boost was so big they had to carry it out in a sack. This was because their lectures had titles like *The Valorization of the Vagina in Twentieth-Century Cinema* or *Copulation and Closure: A Critique of the Hard Core* (I read between the lines, I read between the lines) with plenty of illustrative material and all that and there were fights at the door, it was like the Japs trying to get on a subway, it was deeply depressing to watch – especially from the other end of the corridor with a lecture in your hands that'd get Susan Sontag to shut up and listen and there's this one student approaching, the mature student, the one with the whining hearing-aid and the dayglo satchel who's got a crush on you because you bear oh boy just such a weird resemblance to her dead brother before they cremated him back in '48.

OK, OK, I dramatise. It's the coffee. I'm getting nervous. I'm getting wound up, for Christ's sake. Wound up. When I say wound up out loud it smacks its vowels against my adenoids, against the quiff-greased walls and choking chimney-pots of Jubilee Road, against the grey drizzle of a Saturday morning when the Ritz is closed for refurbishment. It was. When it reopened, refurbished, the lipstick lady had gone and there was a new name. *Bingo*. I liked it. It reminded me of Fred Astaire and Ginger Rogers and some husky or other in a Disney. There were no stills. There were two doormen in green pullovers. I held up my sixpence and they laughed. They wouldn't let me in. Gambling, they said, not for toddlers. I asked my mother to phone up and check. Gambling must be full of murders and tongues, I thought. She said it's a Bingo Hall, dear, I've told you before. I know you've told me before, Mum, but I was pretending to play with Meccano and I wasn't listening. Don't go on about Donald's Meccano again, dear. You know we can't stretch to it, not with the heating bills and the protection money and the price of Wall's this and that and your father's cigarettes and your father's drop of an evening. He does like his drop of an evening. Listen – there goes the gas again. Pop another guinea in, would you, love? We need it for luncheon. I can't see a thing, otherwise.

Great days, great days.

Happy days.

I saw Peggy in it of course. *Happy Days*. Sam Beckett. Remember him? Before your time, perhaps, before your time. Hog bristles. Male castrated pig. Peggy was – Peggy Ashcroft, this is – she was a dream. She was wild. I did a whole season with her. The Rose Theatre. Remember the Rose? Course you don't. She was in a wheelchair in the mud, I held the mike and she made us all cry, the builders climbed up into their saddles and yelled good luck and rumbled away, they were on our side, she'd moved the earth-movers, she'd made history, I should have stayed with just holding the mike in a non-speaking role but I fucked it up, I got all overwhelmed and kissed her on the forehead and leapt down and embraced this broken white column and said into the mike *you've saved our Acropolis, Peggy* in my patent Larry-as-King-Harry and then some fucking archaeologist said that's the concrete footing of the old office block actually and please get your big feet off the original nutshells and good old Peggy giggled along with the crowd's roar of derision or whatever it was, maybe it was just general cheering, maybe no one had heard in the general mêlée. Still, it was great to be in England for about ten minutes. HCDVA gave me a sabbatical, hoped I wouldn't come back. A sabbatical on basic, just so lucky. Hey, how am I gonna eat? I pleaded with them. Give it to someone else! Nothing doing. Their stony hearts didn't chip. I took a bucket-shop to London. I have three more friends in London than New York and two more friends in New York than St Lucia where I have none but where I'd really liked to have gone and been a beach vendor but you have to be beautiful, young, and black. It was raining in London. I'd got worried for a moment because sun had been pouring into the Terminal, Mike would've loved it. I put flowers on my mother's grave and ticked off a dog-handler for letting his dog crap on her and he beat me up. After a few days trying to sort out my social security situation on the end of a drip I gave up and released myself and went to see Jerry. It was either seeing Jerry or doing my Marcel Marceau act on the subway. Sorry, Tube. Jerry Freeman, Viper's Bugloss Productions, hotline to the happy hunting ground of Channel 4 because he's married to one of them and plays Oxbridge Snap in the Groucho or something with the rest. He gave me a job. Well, OK, it was my thrust and his vacuum – I crawled into his office about the size of a hogshead in some refurbished fish warehouse in Shadwell not too far from where you're swilling your snouts on my tick right at this present moment. In Shadwell, son? Hoi, that's where the Thornbys rose. That's where we plied our trade in the grease of our mits, my lad. Joshua Thornby, Jericho Thornby, Jonas Thornby. Father, son, and holy post. Slept on the barrer, slept on it. Never abandon your post. Slippery, slippery. Apple pulp, fish guts, beer swill. It's where we all rose from, my son. Out the sea, out the Shad, out the Ratcliff Highway. Fog, fog, fog in the cranes and up the costermonger's nose, fog in the bunting and the beer shop. Fog. Great fog, in those days. Proper fog. Not your modern sort. Not your modern filth. Mist, that's all it is. Mist.

Hi, Jerry!

Jeremy's welded to his portable. He waves a little finger at me. A little finger's something. He's got Nikes with dayglo tabs. He's training for the Marathon. He's jumping up and down and talking into his portable. I approach and the aerial gets up my nose. I dangle for a bit. He finishes. He vanishes into his press-ups. This is not the Jerry gentle-ski-run-shoulders, five-joints-a-morning Freeman I remember. Jerry, talk to me. I'm skint. I need a job. Tied me through. They made me take a sabbatical on basic. You owe me since that advert for Cyril Lord carpets. What advert for Cyril Lord carpets, Dicky? I'm not Dicky any more, Jeremy. I'm Richard. Or Ricky. Or Rick. Or even Rico, me old cock. Take your pick. That advert for Cyril Lord carpets. You made the coffee. I slipped you in. I wasn't born when the adverts for Cyril Lord carpets were being screened, Richard. Weren't you? Cor. Anyway, I'm certain you owe me. I'll get you a visiting lecturer's stint at HCDVA. Houston's a great place. They love people like you. People with drive, ambition, an independent spirit of mind, fifty-five push-ups an hour, all that. Houston, eh? Fifty, fifty-one. Yes, Jeremy, Houston. Lots of space. Big Texan girls with desirable T-shirts and no engineering problems. No refurbished dock-pulleys to bang your nut on. Nothing old to refurbish and bang your nut on at all. It's swell, Jerry. Fifty-four, fifty-five! Hey, Jerry, that's great. I didn't know you had it in you. I can just manage three with my knees down. Richard, said Jeremy, sinking into his tobacco bale and staring out over the landing-stage at the teeming emptiness below – Richard, I do have a little proj which might just interest you. Yes? Yes. Pause. He leans on his fish-gutter's slab and catches a little drop of sweat before it spoils the lacquer. What do you know about Nimbies, Richard? Nimbies, Jeremy? Nimbies, Richard.

I knew my Marcel Marceau act hung in the balance. I said, Nimbies is what my dear old dad used to call my mum when he was feeling like it. Jeremy exploded. I didn't mean it to be funny. I stepped back and fell over a gantry. Jeremy wiped his eyes and didn't apologise. Public school sod. Anyway, I got the job. Some of you know this. I got *Clive's Seasons*. Incredible, huh? It's really because the other creep in Viper's Bugloss wanted his girlfriend to direct the shoot and his girlfriend didn't know a barn door from a gobo and I stepped in cheap to save the day. I did it for halves, I did it for halves – but still. I couldn't believe it. Better rub than rust, as my old grandad used to say, dying in the best chair. Thank you, Jeremy, you mean hard bastard. Thank you for everything.

Everything?

Let me grab a crust. I have a mini-freezer. I ask Ramona my favourite Filipina to switch it on and throw in a bagel or two and a Homepride white and some pizzas and a *Jaws*-size packet of Findus fish fingers and a Waitrose curried toad-in-the-hole or whatever so I can arrive at some unprincipled hour and feast on England. Wowee. It still tastes of the packet it came in, does England. Cor blimey luvaduck.

Sorry about the nadgers. This fucking camera's tilt's sticking and Mee's used up all my walnut oil. Bear with me, the main feature's about to be spliced and technically the main feature makes *Moby Dick* look lame. Let me put the toast on. I've checked out the lime marmalade situation and it appears Mee doesn't like lime marmalade, which is the best news I've had yet because my first wife did and I never liked her. Seriously, I never ever liked her. I only got hooked up on account of her being exceptionally beautiful, extremely intelligent, and rich. Men get hooked up for less. But there was a primary flaw in her personality: she really hated me. She thought if she married Ricky Thornby she'd skip a few rungs on the way up to being a great film actress. The truth hurt. It was on the honeymoon. I've put the toast in, by the by. I got the loaf out of the freezer and chipped it out of the berg because Ramona always turns everything right up and popped five slices in because I'm famished, guv – and the toaster appears to be functioning, which is amazing. I did all that between *intelligent, and* and *rich*. And you didn't even notice. Waal, whad'ya know. It's just occurred to me that I could show you my face for a minute and wave but I don't want you all to rush out screaming and fuck up the traffic or hurl yourselves off the balcony, the water's really cold at this time of year.

Actually, I'm clad only in my Kyoto underpants. The heating's been up too high. I hope you don't mind. Zelda bought them for me when she was over there. They have these beautiful Japanese letters on the front which say *wu-shih* which means 'nothing special'. Zelda told me that this was the core of Zen but I wonder. Maybe she was telling me something early on and I didn't hear it.

Hey, I was onto my first honeymoon and now I'm onto Zelda and I'm thinking maybe there's a lovely unbroken curve between the two. Holy shit. This wasn't supposed to happen, honest. I mean, who's paying for this? I mean, what do you think this is? A licensed black cab? We're on the roundabout route with a tricky-dicky meter, mate, and I haven't handled your luggage yet. So sit tight and enjoy the lovely unbroken curves of the scenery.

She thought we'd got fixed up at some mystery destination like Polynesia or the Riouw-Lingga Archipelago or wherever with palms and an above blood-temperature ocean. Deirdre I'm talking about, not Zelda. But I was a busy man. I was also slightly short of the readies. That is, I'd invested unwisely. To be blunt, I'd put it all in me own hole. I'd stumped up when the producer's feet got frost-bite just thinking about it. It was a terrible film. You won't have seen it, not ever. It's due to be rediscovered by some outfit specialising in Great Gaffs so I'm tracking down every last copy. For the personal safety match. My first wife is in it. She plays King Alfred's Queen. It was filmed on location at Wormhill Bottom, Berks, England. I should've known. Michael Caine played A Danish Youth with a great accent. I played King Alfred because I couldn't get Richard Harris to do it for a fiver. And he was a mate. It rained every day for a fortnight. It was a deeply dampening experience. Our extras for the Battle of Ashdown were locals, local youfs let out on remand from their remote downland village pumps. They had this game. It was to see how many watches they could get the camera and no one else to spot. There was a strike or something at the labs. We didn't watch the rushes till the end of the shoot. My middle name's Federico. We offered the Battle of Ashdown sequence to Timex. Well, they didn't want to know. Too historical, they said.

No bloody imagination, these people.

My wife and I, we turned up at Cromer. Her name, as you probably know, was Deirdre Townsend. Not Townsil. Townsend. Her nickname was Dreary. I thought it up on our first night, but didn't tell her. She was displeased with our mystery destination. I said I was killing two birds with one stone, which she took ill. She wouldn't get out of the Morris 1100. The hotel manageress stood on the crumbling doorstep and sipped her tea right through it all. Deirdre asked, why Cromer? I said I've told you but you were too busy shredding the leather off my dashboard. She said, I should never have married you, you bastard. I said, don't jump to conclusions. Look, this is the film business, Deirdre. We're gonna make a great film out here. It's about these newly-weds stuck in Cromer off-season when a catastrophe has smitten the rest of the country. What catastrophe, for God's sake? Deirdre, I'm working on it. It could be the Bomb. It could be the Plague. It could be a Comet. It doesn't matter except it's not the Blobs from Sirius, that stuff is out. The film's going to be poetic, allusive, and in muted tones of grey. You mean mostly out of focus, she snapped. Not necessarily, I chuckled indulgently. But it is definitely going to rain a lot and when it's not raining there'll be sea-fogs. Yet through all this love survives. There's gonna be an amazing amount of sex, by the way. And a murder. There's gonna be a murder. Not the wife, I might add. And a white horse moving very fast along the beach. Why? she asked. I don't know. It's just an image. It's poetic. We're going to keep cutting to this white horse moving very fast along the beach and the beach seems to go on forever. They do out here, she said. I know they do, I said. Could you at least leave the knob on the gear-stick legible? I can never remember where Reverse goes. She was stubbing out her fifteenth Pall Mall on it. She'd locked me out of the car. I forgot to say that I was shouting all this through the window at this grey fog in which I could just about see Deirdre's fabulous face. The hotel manageress had finished her cup of tea and was shaking her head. I could see her in the wing mirror, shaking her head and looking melancholy. Sorry, somebody's shouting again off-set, apparently the Morris 1100 of this period had no fucking wing mirrors, I'm about to be arrested for inaccuracy, well done Hercule *alias* some jerk called G. W. R. Ashby (Mr) who never left me alone, every movie I made he wrote me with a list as if I could rewind and correct it all, hey, never work with any form of motorised transport or uniforms, stick to symbolic nakedness on a beach. I had to admit Cromer in November made this pretty difficult. Eventually Deirdre relented when I told her how Jean Cocteau would be visiting the set. I'd thought this up on the spot. I didn't know Jean Cocteau personally. I knew his films backwards but not him. I learnt French via the subtitles. That's why my French is so admired but I can't ask for a room without sounding brilliant. Our first marital night was first of all marred by having the hotel manageress's wireless right below and she had a hearing problem. Believe it or not, Deirdre was a virgin. I'd never seen her with her clothes off. I was very worked up by the time we'd had our quick stroll along the sea front. She wasn't. She was thinking of Polynesia, shaking out the scurf and the greased scraps of *Daily Heralds* from her fedora and thinking of Polynesia. She was thinking how she could have got her rich dad to help out. But Dad didn't like son-in-law, that was the problem. We got upstairs. I sat on the bed and I have to tell you this: every time you so much as winked the bed sounded like the Titanic hitting the iceberg. You know what the Titanic hitting the iceberg sounded like? Like someone tearing

56

tissue-paper, they said. *Heugh*. Yeah, yeah. Who're they kidding? It sounded like our honeymoon bed. Not even the wireless popping its valves out in the room below would have drowned it, because I'm talking about each spring. Each spring sounded like the Titanic hitting the iceberg, not fucking tissue-paper. So in actual fact when we both lay down on it in our respective night attire it sounded like fifty Titanics hitting fifty icebergs. In order to speak to each other we had to stop blinking and open our mouths slowly. But you have to breathe, even you really intent people out there are breathing. The sexual act was out of the question. To have had sex would have shashed Cromer in white noise. People would have come out of their houses screaming with their hands over their ears. I suggested we have sex on the rug in front of the electric two-bar like at Cambridge or in *Women in Love* but Deirdre had not been to Cambridge and Ken Russell was still in his non-pansexual phase so she just lay there under a pall of smoke, not saying anything. Dreary, I thought. Underneath it all she's dreary. When she went to sleep she snored. I couldn't even work myself off because of the bed. Every down-stroke deafened me. I went to sleep. I dreamed. I dreamed I was in Polynesia under the coconuts taking Deirdre's clothes off one by one. I éclaired and woke up. I'm sorry about this sensual detail but it had got onto the front of her nightie. I tried to scrape it off with my comb but she woke. She stared at me. You're disgusting, she said. I didn't mean to, I replied. Even monks don't mean to. We were yelling over the springs. She started thumping me, rhythmically, with her feet. I got out of the bed and went straight to the door because I couldn't stand the noise and needed to relieve myself. I opened the door and the hotel manageress keeled over on top of my slippers. Her left ear was red and had an attractive drypoint of our keyhole on it. She picked herself up. A cup of tea? she said. That would be very nice, I replied. You could tell we were both embarrassed by the situation, mainly becauses the front of my pyjama bottoms was still sticky. A stiletto shoe flew over my head but not the head of the hotel manageress. It stuck in her beehive and she didn't notice. I didn't like to say anything. She went round with it for days and no one said anything. They don't, in Cromer. She had a room full of caged birds and a dicky television striated with guano. Deirdre spent most of the rest of our honeymoon blowing smoke at crazed budgie eyes and watching the test card, dreaming of surf. Somehow, we managed to make Gregory. I don't remember how. Christ, I hope he doesn't read this. Ach, we were so young.

The toaster's popped. Toasters popping always make me chortle. They remind me of Danny Kaye as Mitty. You know it's going to pop and make him even scareder than he already is and you wait for it and you wonder how he's going to do it every time but he does he yowls like it's the first time he's ever done it and you weep like it's the first time you've ever seen it and you both join hands and are glad. That's genius, mate. That's why I chortle. No one's got it these days. No one can hang from a window-ledge like Danny Kaye could. No one.

I've just been chipping away at the butter without my safety visor, I'm irresponsible in my twilight. I'm waiting for it to soften on the toast, because I can't stand English toast without butter. It's not even cold in here. Romana had put the heating on. I've just remembered it's Romana not Ramona, it's because she complains the whole time, G. W. R. Ashby (Mr) will be having a field-day if he's out there amongst you all, he'll be the one with binoculars and a little pad and a V-neck smelling of sheep-dip. I invited him. I invited all the people I have strong feelings about, except Jerry. Romana turns everything right up. I've told her, I've told her. That's why the windows are open and I'm in my wooshy underpants. It's like the Kalahari without the breeze. But I trust Romana. Everyone has their little blind spots, their little foibles.

So I got to make *Clive's Seasons*. What a doddle. Four weeks shoot, two weeks in the can, a day for Jeremy to unravel all my good work but I can't complain, he knows he's hopeless, underneath. I couldn't have cared two roubles either way. Journeyman stuff – just point the lens at human kind and nod, it makes it feel important, it falls right into it, it yaks. It's all in the editing, mate, it's all in the editing. The only trouble was, it had to be spread throughout the year as thin as marge. No wonder no one wanted to touch it. Seasons, geddit? You can't just put cotton wool on the hawthorn, now can you? Oh no. You can't fool Mother Nature, dear old soul, hey ho the wind and the rain and the rain it raineth every day on location, that's the rule. Otherwise it was cast iron, guv – villains and goodies over the hedgerows, defence of the elm and the natterjack and the cleg horse-fly what jabs in complete silence and did, on my shin, chatty Clive the underdeveloped developer versus the trees and the meadows and the folk what like their back yards nice and leafy. Does it have to be all year, Jerry old soak? Yes, Rick. That's the notion, the core, the nub, the fulcrum, the cleg, the main thrust. He chose the weeks, too. One for each season, in case you haven't got the main thrust yet. And you know what I did? I quit the city, the main thrust, the fulcrum, the pussy, the nub – and hit the hedgerows. I rented a wee cottage, fourteenth-century, thatched. Honeysuckle Cottage. OK, it would have been smothered in honeysuckle if there'd been more than a duck's arse between it and the main road. Hey ho. I crouched behind the front door waiting for a gap. I threaded a volley of wing mirrors to go get my sliced white from the Co-op. I ducked the trucks and jumped the coupés. There wasn't a lot of choice. All the wee cottages smothered in honeysuckle had been appropriated by retired high-rise architects and Blue Circle Cement executives. Still, it was my fault. I'd picked an emsav (much-sought-after-village, noodles) with a church that gets a whole half page in mingy old Pevsner on account of the Victorian corbels and a great pub known for miles around with room for coaches where the hay-barn used to be and a firm promise of a bypass through the water meadows if the Stinging Fawholt Cleg's rehoused or something and roots. Roots? Yup, Jerry, roots. How's the push-ups? Sixty. Congratulations, Jerry. What roots, Dicky? Ricky to you, Jerry. My roots. My maternal roots. What, you mean Ulverton? No no, not that dump. Next one on. Fawholt. Tiny. One church, one spittoon, one retired banker, ten yobs. Would have been eleven but young Spearhafoc was slain at the Battle of Ashdown. Or Arsedown. What are you on about, Ricky? Your family village or something? Ah, there a tale I shalt woof, some day, Jerry: make it a hundred and I might tell you. A hundred? I'll have a coronary, Ricky. I'm not talking push-ups, Jerry my chinless nitwit, I'm not talking push-ups.

He put the phone down. Mean hard bastard. A hundred for expenses, that's all I was asking. I had to hitch up the M4, practically, carrying the boom in me backpack and Second Grip on me shoulders.

Seriously: it wasn't a chief dover, but it was run-of-the-million good. Eh? I tried to keep it balanced and all that, son, but you knew which side me apples rolled off, you knew which side. No voice-overs, nothing overt, Rick, more fly-on-the-wall than spider-in-the-pantry, tender shots of misty cows, sunsets over the dolmens, easier to sell to the Yanks, OK? OK, Jerry my bean. I gave Clive the Cleg plenty of rope to have his swing. He was a right thick dickhead. Full one minute, bust the next. I thought I'd given him enough but no, Nancy Banks-Smith felt sorry for him. She would. I was back in Houston by then. Pat Batskin sent me the clipping. So I got the whole review off Pat. Let's have uncontrollable hysteria on that one, full up. I have, actually. I've copied it so many times I've got ultra-violet burn on my corneal epithelium. Look it up. There's a lot about eyes in this film, it'll come in useful, I spent my life making movies without knowing how an eyeball makes movies. Hey, I copied it for my students, who'd otherwise reckon I'm as faky-flaky as all my colleagues with their PVC CVs and 50,000 word faeces on Streep's left nipple in *Kramer vs Kramer*. Wowee. You mean you did make films, Mr Thornby? Then we'd spend two hours deconstructing the review and get nowhere. They'd love it. HCDVA is behind the times. They're faithful P of C and they're into Lacan and Derrida instead of Dorothy Parker. I'd say, listen, the only thing I like about Doc Diarrhoea is that he's a Sephardic Jew. He's a what? they'd expostulate. A Sephardic Jew, I'd say. He keeps it hush. But that subverts everything we know about Derrida! went the cry (I'm talking here about my graduate students, OK? The ones who had some brain left after high school crack and video sex and swimming in their pools without ear plugs. Not a lot, but some. Enough to say the right things about the right things). *Touché*, I'd quip. Isn't he swell?

I don't know why I'm behaving so like a recently-retired person. Anyone'd think I miss the place. Over to you, Nancy. I rather liked Clive, wrote Batty-Fangs. He was a shepherd really. Then he discovered bricks. Bricks with Olde English written on them. My sheepdog eats Weetabix but doesn't speak. Clive does. He's not a bit like a sheepdog.

Oh, I've forgotten the rest. But you get the drift, mate. You get the drift. (This is me now, by the by.) Oi, stop fiddling with that meter! What's wrong with the scenery? It's coming, it's coming!

No one else reviewed it, not properly. Some old wanker in *The Times* used it as a handle for an article about the abuse of Great Composers (Vivaldi, in case you didn't see it and you're too blubber-headed to work it out) on film'n TV as if I'd made a bloody commercial, and the *South-West of North Swindon Journal*, or something, called it a fairly interesting programme on a burning local issue and spelt my name wrong twice (Throneby and Tornby, *sic*). Jeremy was smiling. He sold it to various nations including the Russians. I've not received so much as a blackmarket dwarf tomato from these. He won't answer my calls. I think he might have knocked himself out on a winch. Good bloody riddance.

I'm starving. Toast: cold. Butter: slush. The lime marmalade awaits my attentions. Wait a little longer, my love. (Opening song from *Honky Tonk*, in case you etc.) I bought a Mars Bar at Heathrow, for old times' sake. You can't eat Mars Bars for breakfast, not in England. Slippery slope. You gotta start as you mean to go on. Go on.

Didn't you just now say that this guy Jeremy was your benefactor in some way, sir? I did indeed, my man. And didn't you just hope he had somehow hurt himself badly, perhaps even fatally, Mr Thornby sir? I did indeed, Marcus Aurelius Samsonite the First Jr. But that doesn't quite figure as logical to my personal way of thinking, Mr Thornby our teacher at HCDVA sir. Of course not, because you are thick. Sorry, sir? No need to apologise, Yank dickhead, it's not your fault. Is that an insult towards me, sir? No, no, only joking. Put away your AK-47 and listen to me.

This is the nub, at last.

Loaded Magnum pause.

Where did my mother come from?

From the union of my grandmother with my grandfather. Unless I am Jesus.

Sir?

Skip it. Who was my grandmother?

No, leave that too. Advance the portaprompt. Watch my lips.

Who was my grandfather?

61

My grandfather was a toff. That was my father's term, by the way, for anyone who was not born within snotshot of Shadwell. But my grandfather was more than a toff. He was a proper toff. That was my father's term for anyone who owned a reasonably large motor car and didn't swear. There were gradations of proper toffs, of course, and my grandfather came reasonably high. Somewhere between a right proper bleedin' toff and a bloomin' right proper bleedin' toff. The Queen was the Queen. Immediately below the Queen were the fuckin' parasites. Immediately below the fuckin' parasites were the bloomin' right proper bleedin' toffs. Geddit?

I say, my man, have you got it? I hope I am not addressing an empty classroom.

I thought we were at the movies, sir. I've ate all of my popcorn.

My man, the fact that you have consumed all your provender is neither here nor there. The house lights are up. They will remain up until this discourse is finished. Bach plays his cantatas. Nurse Luscious ticks beside you. Zelda hums at the side showing an absence of panties in the lotus position. Tongues pass melting Maltesers to each other in the last row. What more can you want?

I want to see the movie, sir. We haven't even had the commercials.

There are no commercials. This is an art house.

Wow.

Nurse Luscious is showing you the time to the millisecond. Be content.

Yes, sir. Wow.

You've heard of trails? This is the trail. Or trailer. Take your pick. You know my fondness for lecturing without the moving image. Be content. The feature will shortly follow. Drinks will be served in the bar. My books will be on sale at reasonable rates. The rain in Spain falls mainly on the plain. Autographed stills of Julie Andrews in *Clockwork Orange* will be subject to all the usual availabilities. OK?

Yes, siree.

And, as this is a picture-house of more than equal opportunities – how're y'all, gals?

Jes fine, sir. Jes fine.

You think I was merely wagging just now, about my books? You mean you haven't perused my monograph on Douglas Sirk in which I claim him to be the greatest thing since unspliced Carl Theodor Dreyer? My frame-by-frame analysis of *Written on the Wind* published in the highly prestigious Buff series from Auteur Books? Don't you know anything?

Evidently not, my dears.

Tlic tlic. Time passes, Mizoguchi style. I am eating my toast. Ghosts swarm. I had not thought death had undone so many flies. I am being niggled at by my conscience. I told a lie, earlier. A lie is too strong. A fib, then. I fibbed about Cambridge. I did not do English. I did Danish. I did Danish because otherwise I would not have gone up as the bishop said to the Copenhagen porn queen bom bom. Nobody had gone up from the school in centuries, my English master assured me. You are bright, but not brilliant, Thornby. (How true, how woundingly true!) Nobody else in the country wants to do Danish. The Danish don feels lonely, undesired. It is the secret door covered in ivy, Thornby my boy. Every year, it works. It worked. The Danish don was so lonely he put his hand on my crotch in the second supers. I rapped him over the helmet with my *Basic Old Danish. Til døden!* I cried. I sidled into English seminars and no one cared, no one noticed. Eventually, at some indistinct but deep point mid-stream, I changed horses. The Danish don was lonely again. I can hardly be blamed for his suicide. No one blames Miller for Monroe. No one blames Thornby for Thierkegaard swinging from his napkin off High Table. I learnt sufficient Danish to swagger about pretending I was Carl Theodor Dreyer. Thus my quirky interest in Sirk. I am eating Pure Danish Butter, apparently. Ah, these *smuler*! These *smuler til døden!*

Weren't you talkin' about your grandfather or supp'n, sir?

I was, I was. The great, grand old days were leading me astray once more. Turn left here. That's it. Here's the scenery. Now for my grandmother. The grandmother at the top of the stairs by the stuffed lemur, wild and angry. My grandmother, not the lemur. Very angry. Take no notisss. Sneak preview. Trail. Follow it, they who dare, etc.

It was like this: my grandmother had a certain connection with Fawholt. So did my grandfather. Going west out of Fawholt there is a little lane to the left. A small bungalow has been erected on the corner. It surpasses in hideousness almost all the small bungalows I have ever seen—

Sir?

You interrupted me, Marcus Aurelius—

Pardon me sir but I just wanted to know why you were talkin' so funny.

Was I?

Yessir.

How was I talking, exactly?

Like you're talkin' now, sir. Like John Gielgud in *Arthur*, sir.

General giggle, of course, presents arms. Marcus Aurelius Samsonite the First Jr is the college wag. His waggishness is legendary. When he is not being waggish he is a born-again Christian. He appears to wear hair oil, though his hair is very short. His shirts have collars and are white. His skin is pink. I look at him and I feel, sometimes, I am looking at the image of God. Only then do I fear death. Harrumph.

So what do I normally sound like, funnyman?

Like Cary Grant on speed, sir.

Ha ha. Very droll. I know exactly what he means. Neither here nor there nor there nor here. Jack of a thousand voices, master of none. Dangling off Rockall, screaming into the spume. Now I'll show 'em.

Don't you mean Dick Van Dyke in *Mary Poppins*, arse-hole?

General consternation marches past. Our scrubbed wag assigns me with his clear blue eyes to the seventh circle. I go there. I sit on my big throne, spitting fire. Right. No murders, no tongues, no interruptions. Not yet.

You take this lane past the bungaloid and keep going for about a quarter mile, right? You hit some trees, big trees. You go under them and look to your left. There are two houses. One is a receptacle, the other is a residence. The receptacle is of a lipstick-carmine brick and the residence is of a peeling paintwork that might once have been cream. The receptacle has a 1988 Vauxhall Cavalier on its gravel and this is 1988. The residence has a bicycle on its lawn with a wicker basket at the front of it and it might be 1888 but it isn't. You get the feeling that the size of the houses has nothing to do with the owners' incomes, because remember this is England and we're into class. We're into accents. We're into the real thing and it's not Coca-Cola. The receptacle, a little voice tells you, was built in 1984 on the former old walled vegetable garden of the residence because the residents were skint and needed to mend a leak or twenty. You look at the receptacle and because you've been filming around here a touch you recognise the hand of Mr Clive Walters in the cottage-style porch made out of dowelling rods and the lovingly individualised crooked chimney. You know by now that if you switch on the fan in the Victorian-style conservatory the thing'll take off and do a Bleriot in the Jemima Puddleduck-style pond with the Yorkshire priory-look paving stones ready to be grouted by the owner of the receptacle if he ever finds the bloody time, Josephine. You think, given the choice, and because you're temporarily English, you'd really rather go to tea with the owner of the bicycle. There'll be better biscuits, for a start. Out of an old tin. Just for a start. In fact, you don't give the receptacle owners a chance. You go up to the front door of the residence and take hold of the dog's paw and knock, thrice. Geraniums spurt out of broken pots. Ivy sports through the sides of the porch. Spiders spin and bees slumber. An ash-bin squats to the side of the door, full of ash the colour of rain. You could stand here forever and not grow cold. You seem to. Because no one answers. Only then do you notice the convolvulus woven through the bicycle's spokes, the bird's nest in its wicker basket, the capless bell, the grass waving in the drive and on the lintel of the cracked window. Ha, you think. Abandoned, abandoned and echoing, dust's footfall, the scatter of phantoms and mice, perfect location for that Vauxhall Cavalier commercial, must tell Jerry—

When the door opens.

Hallo?

Hallo, sorry to bother you. You made me jump. I thought there was no one here.

Well, there is. It's sold. We bought it. We've exchanged. Sorry.

No, no. I don't want to buy it. I just wanted a look.

Really, these agents. You're the third person today. It's this multi-agent thing, you see. We're in so many windows. Word'll get round, I suppose.

I suppose it will.

Sir?

Ye-es, Marcus Aurelius—

Who's this other guy, sir?

How do you know it's a guy? And stop interrupting.

I didn't. You paused. You looked up at the ceiling.

It was a dramatic pause. A Pinter pause. What we call a beat. Do you turn to your partner and natter in the middle of a film? A film by, say,

Andrei Tarkovsky? Or Carl Theodor Dreyer? Or Robert Bresson for Christ's sake? Just because no one's talking?

Who are they, sir?

Never mind. Module Two. *In the Mirror: Illusion and Reality in World Cinema.* Or: *My Favourites So Shuddup and Listen.*

But that's when you have pictures to look at, sir.

And don't you have pictures now, dope?

Aw, no sir. Nope, I don't.

You mean my laborious efforts to paint the scenery for you have come to naught?

Pardon me, sir?

Never mind. He never watched his rushes.

Whassat, sir?

Enough, Marcus Aurelius etc Jr. You have dived into your kidney-shaped pool one too many times. You are beyond redemption—

Sir, I regard that as a deeply insulting personal remark against—

I'm sorry, I'm sorry. I forgot. You've flicked hair oil in your neighbour's eye. You are a true believer. You will be ejected without pause into a heaven of moving images and choo-choo trains and final causes where the films of Robert Bresson are banned. Well done. Now shuddup and listen.

OK. But be careful. Sir.

I will, I will.

Christ! – the phone again. The bloody phone.

That was Gregory. He says hi, Dad. I say hi, son. How's tricks, Greg? Are you coming? He says I'm working. You're what, Greg? Working? Tomorrow of all days, tomorrow night, tomorrow night of all nights? Sort of, Dad. We're having a párty at the gallery. My new work's the centre spread. That's nice, Greg. What's your new work? Can I come and see it some time? Can I come and see you sometime? Don't get like that, Dad. How long are you over? The usual, Greg. High days and holy days. Cut-price ticket. Have to head back within five days, five hours, five minutes and fifty-five seconds of my arrival time or they'll charge me the cost of the engine fuel plus VAT. Same old dad, Dad. Same old dad, Greg. No, that's not true. I have a film out. A *what*? Did I say something, Greg? You said you had a film out, Dad. And what's so deeply shocking about that, son? Don't call me son, Dad, it sounds so American. You haven't made a film in years. What film is it? I'm showing it at the party tonight, Greg. I'd hoped you'd be there. It's about us. Oh no, Dad. No, Greg, I mean us as in our roots, our genes, our blood, our memory banks and all that. It's great stuff. It's kinda revolutionary. In fact, it's definitely revolutionary. It's a film without pictures. Are you still there, Greg? I'm here, Dad. A film without pictures, eh? A film without pictures, Greg. Fellini never washed his undies. Dad? Yes, Greg? Have you been drinking again, Dad? What, me? I'm a reformed character, son. Renewed. Reborn. You must come along and see. Hey, Greg, how does it feel? How does what feel, Dad? How does *today* feel? Today feels OK, Dad. Just OK? The day before the Big One and just OK? Is that all you can say? You sound like your mother. Mum's not very well, Dad. Oh? She's got a thing with itis on the end. It makes her limp. I'm sorry to hear that, Greg. No you're not. Is it life-threatening, Greg? She won't say, but I think it can be, according to Sally it can be. Hey, what's this new piece about, Greg? Still carpet squares and the *I Ching* and the fifty thousand bucks price tag attached? You're behind, Dad. I'm not into carpets any more. You'll have to come and see. I think you might like it. What you said about a film with no pictures, that's amazing. You mean you like the idea, Greg? I do, Dad, I do. Is that because you hate my other films so much, Greg? I do but that's not why I think it's amazing. I didn't have the money, Greg. I didn't have any choice. Dad? Yes, Greg? Don't put it like that. Don't be cynical about it. A film without pictures is

68

beautiful, Dad. Thank you, Greg. Is there just the screen and a blue light on it or something like Jarman's a few years back, Dad? No, it is nothing like Jarman's a few years back, Greg. It's a silent. A silent with no pictures? There are words, Greg, calm yourself, there are lots of words. How are you showing it, Dad? How am I showing it? Yeah. On a screen, Greg. I've bought my big screen over – a whole superwidth double, Texan cotton, no stains, start with a clean sheet. Hey, this is great, Dad, but stains would've been better. Greg, you'll just have to come and see mine and I'll have to come and see yours. There's nothing to see, Dad. There's nothing to see? No. It's the main gallery painted beige. That's all. It's called The New Millennium Giggle. At midnight everyone's going to be in the main gallery and I'm going to take my clothes off and walk out of the door and into the street. I think there'll be giggling. If there isn't, I'm up shit creek. Oh, Greg, you'll catch your death. That's my new work, Dad. Why beige, Greg? Because beige is beige is beige, Dad. I'm sorry you can't make it to the film, Greg. So am I, Dad, so am I. You'll have to do a second screening, just for me. I can't do that, Greg. Why not, Dad? Because I'm going to chuck the unique and only print into the river, if they let me. Except for the last reel. If I tried to take the last reel as well they'd stop me. But I'm gonna wait till the end, Greg. I'm gonna give them a chance to scream and grab me so it's exciting, it'll be a real cliff-hanger, it'll be like those 4d serial matinées at the Bioscope your grandad used to talk about, Greg, it'll be like James Stewart at the top of that tower— He's still alive, Dad. Who, James Stewart? Grandad, Dad. Yeah, but he's unscramblable these days unless you put in a lot of concentration. Well, that really sounds amazing, Dad. Thank you, Greg, I think it is, too. See you, Dad, and good luck. See you, Greg. Good luck to you, too. I'm sure there'll be lots of giggles.

I have to apologise. I'm just feeling the full force of fatherhood all over again. I just need to blow my nose.

That's better. Where were we?

You're standing on this, aw, porch, sir. Talking to this – this person.

Thank you, M. A. You're a pal.

My pleasure, sir.

Right.

Sir?

Ye-es?

You got a drip on the end of your nose.

Oh, Christ. It's a tear, M. A. It's not mucus. It's a tear because I'm feeling very close and very far away from Gregory my son and do you know what?

What?

That's the first phone call in months he hasn't called me a pig.

You mean your son calls you a pig, sir?

He does, M. A., he does. In his own Gregorian way. Softly, like a chant. You're a bit of a pig sometimes, Dad.

Sir?

Ye-es?

I just want to get one thing clear. First, would you please not take the Lord's name in vain? Second, where are we exactly, sir?

That's two things, M. A. First, I'll try not to. Second, where the hell do you think we are?

I'm not sure, sir. It's kinda dark sometimes and sometimes I think I'm in a kitchen and sometimes I think I'm in a taxi and most of the time I think I'm at the movies with this really nice nurse bending over me, sir.

Try all three, old son, try all three. Stick with it. Be content. Don't interrupt. I've eaten my toast. The meter's getting into calculus. Nurse

Luscious is getting into you and drinks will be served on the house and there'll be time to hose down the porcelain before the feature. OK?

OK, sir.

Fawholt. I'm standing on the porch. I say to this guy – it is a guy, forty-nineish, beige-skinned, plump, little veins in the ear lobes, nicely controlled nose hairs, a tarmac executive hoping to go it on his own with a loan from his banker pal, hoping to get into managerial consultancy and earn five thou every time he farts – I say to this guy, hey, I'm a movie director. I mean to say, a film director. I'm making a film next door. I mean, in the next town. That is to say, the next village. So you're the bastard that held me up, he says. Probably. It was probably us. I'm sorry. Film crews are very demanding people. I can hear my Enfield breaking through like the alien in *Alien*. I think: how did Andrei Tarkovsky avoid these people? Why does every beautiful house have one? Why can't they be full of dust's footfalls and phantoms and angels and sweet little mice and those echoes that come before the sound? Why the fuck do I have to endure these fuckers?

Sir—

Shuddup!

The girls are saying—

OK, OK, I'll try to temper my language. I'll try. I'll try. Christ – sorry. Just don't act the mufti and lay a fatwa on me, OK?

A what, sir?

Have you ever been abducted by aliens, M. A.?

Yes, sir, as a matter of fact.

No no, just a joke—

Sir, it wasn't a joke, I can tell you. They took–

OK, OK.

It happened, sir. They left a burn on the grass. They took off all of my clothes except my sneakers. There were lots of rubber knobs. Christ rescued me. He bungee-jumped me out. I was very, very lucky.

Right. Marcus Aurelius etc Jr has hit me way out of play with a juicy B film for the real buff, the real smelly type of buff, the buff smelling of damp mops and engaged to his duffle coat, the one with 3-D contact lenses smirking at everyone through *The Creature from the Black Lagoon*. Brilliant tactic. Chromium bumpers on the spacecraft, Cary Grant haircuts, aliens with wireless antennae on their skull-caps and Cyrillic name-tabs on their bin-lid chests, the whole damn works. The girls are crowding round him. Nurse Luscious and Zelda and the desirable T-shirts. Commander Marcus Cody Jnr's gesticulating and they're nodding and rubbing their hands on his stomach. It's what the aliens did, apparently. M. A. was abducted by aliens. R. T. was abducted by phantoms.

Phantoms. They rose up and they said—

What's that? snaps the Tarmac executive.

I was just reflecting, I reply, on the curious fact that we are what we believe. Don't you agree?

Are you one of these people they've let out into the community?

Yes, actually. I'm on a year's sabbatical.

Ah, I see. Well, if you'll just be running along now. My neighbour – our neighbour might need some work done on his hedge. Run along there and see, would you?

I put my foot in the door like they do in the crime reality junk on TV, so it must be real. Youch.

The Tarmac executive groans, because his wife is out and he's alone and this is how people are murdered deep in the country. He wonders

72

which photo they will use in the papers, he wonders if he'll be important enough to be in colour, he wonders whether that depends on how grisly it is, he wonders whether the lousy tabloid print will catch the tan and he feels sick. He's frightened. I've frightened someone. I've got their attention again. The girls in desirable T-shirts are leaving M. A. alone, they're turning to look at me again, even Zelda with her hair grown back, even Nurse Luscious. They're getting hooked by reality, by words like frightened, the frightened face of the Tarmac executive, the sweat on the faint white tidemark over his cheeks where his ski-goggles lay, the damp collar, the ruffled nose growth, the pudgy hand clasping the door, my *I Am a Fugitive from a Chain-Saw Gang* stare, my foot in the door, the ivy and the ash-can, the slightly-out-of-focus poetic symbol of the abandoned bicycle still upright with the help of some convolvulus, the capless bell, the delicate eggs in the nest in the carrier, a pigeon bursting out of the woods, a white horse pounding an endless beach –

Shit, I've lost 'em again to *It Came from Outer Space 2*, they're gawping, they're all in their 3-D cardboard shades practically. What hope is there for art? What hope is there for poetry? Gee, the Tarmac executive is talking about the police. He's standing there and shivering and talking about the police. Get off my property, he says. I reply, hey, this is not your property. We've exchanged! he cries, with a gleam of triumph between his youthful crowfeet. He's a child, underneath. He had the biggest Meccano set in the avenue. He built the biggest Working Derrick and everyone knew it. I tell him this and how he never let anyone else work it. How the hell do you know? he stammers, terrified suddenly by something deeper than murder. I smile my Ingmar Bergman smile, a flicker of a suggestion on the breeze of a summery day of raspberries smile. It reassures him, because it's wickedly meant. I know your sort, he says, I know your sort. We're moving into a very special genre, gals. Leave M. A. alone. Zelda, stop humming. Nurse Luscious, you're being beeped. We're moving out of reality junk, we're moving out of horror, we're moving out of psychological thriller, we're moving out of anything with *noir* on the end of it, or itis, or ist, we're moving out of rock 'n roll because no Tarmac executive's ever gonna do his Elvis turn in public, we're moving out of light light and heavy heavy, we're moving out of classic adaptation with English nobs on and out of urban grittiness with no

73

English nobs on, and I could go on but I won't because the Tarmac executive is really sweating. He wants to know what genre he's about to inhabit. He wants to know, if it's an action picture, where the helicopters are gonna land because he's just laid some new turf and it's delicate. This is his other side. He loves his lawn and delicate blue flowers. If he's gonna be in an action movie he wants a slice of it without getting hurt. He wants compensation if I so much as lay a finger on his lawn or his house or his wife. He's forgotten about himself. He's too frightened to think about himself. He very much wishes it will be a frankly erotic movie with no discernible plot and lots of swinging basket chairs and then he remembers himself. He's more and more convinced that this is the beginning of the movie and he's the schmuck that says five lines and then gets brutally dumped and it's not even the fulcrum, the crux, the McGuffin, the thrust – just a way of getting the audience hooked and he's the dope at the end of the casting credits, the unnamed one, the Man At The Door, the guy no one even remembers because there were so many others hit and it was 135 minutes ago. Christ, he thinks, I should never have bought this bloody place. It was Suzie's fault. Country living. Knock-down price ha-ha. Dry rot, I'll bet. Please don't kill me, he says, weakly. I smirk. I can offer you monthly at reduced rates, I mumble, not quite bold enough to go for it. He swallows and tries to look pompous. Look here, he begins –

Sir?

Do you mind?

Not at all, sir. I was just wondering, I mean the girls are just wondering, when you're gonna get to let us know.

Let you know what, smidgeon?

About the genre, sir. What real special genre this is. Because I'd got to the scene where the aliens are pulling back my foreskin and the girls are getting kind of impatient.

This cinema is only big enough for one film, junior. It's an art house. It's not a multiplex crap house. Scat.

74

Oh, sir.

OK, OK. But I'm not letting you. Girls, spread out. I mean, find a seat. Leave him alone. Apart from anything else, it looks bad. Dated. Like a lousy forties musical. We'll be arrested for vulgar behaviour in a public place. This is the century of women's liberation, for God's sake. Take off those desirable T-shirts. Thank you. Where was I?

You're about to murder this creep, sir.

Thank you, Hilda. Hilda! What the hell are you doing here?

Taking off my T-shirt, grandad.

No, no don't. Not my daughter's daughter. Oh, cripes. Put them back on, all of you. Hilda, honey-bun, you're practically under-age. Scat.

No way, grandad.

There's murders and tongues. There's massacres and violations. There's—

You've said that before, grandad.

That was pig chitterlings, buckets of them. You laughed. You laughed because your mother told you they were the small intestines of porkers.

I laughed because the acting was real naff, grandad.

OK, OK. But this is different. This makes *Psycho* look like a commercial for Badedas, *The Texas Chain-Saw Massacre* look like a DIY promo, your Jap cyber-snuff movie look like a Zen garden on long hold. I'm telling you, Hild, those guys in three-piece tweed and pipes and spectacles who flicker across our silver screens and grin and can't talk because the coming of sound has not yet come – those cuddly little guys who laugh and stand like they've got something wrong with their underpants and move only in black and white under toff hats or with big ostrich-plumes on their helmets – don't be fooled. Behind them lurks the nastiest movie you'll ever not see. And it got worse.

75

Sounds great, grandad.

Maybe your mum'll turn up. You can hold her hand. Give her a purpose in life.

Tlic, tlic.

OK. Nearly home. I say to the Tarmac executive, sorry, chum, I don't need you. I'm on a recce. What I need is the house. Location shoot. My grandmother's house. I need the rooms, the garden, the trees, the moon. The moon through the window. This is my grandmother's house. Ah, there's my wife, the Tarmac executive cries. He's weeping with relief. The Range Rover growls over the weedy gravel. She alights and smiles. He pushes past me and takes her to one side, murmuring urgently. I'm trying to smile back, because she's wildly attractive. She's tall and fit and seasoned and scarfed. She's fantastically English. Her smile is the sweetness of English apples, the wrinkled kind, the windfall beauties, the profound and the sublime and sometimes the tart. I miss her sort. They were never around when I was sniffing skirt. They'd bound over far-away hedges, just out of sight, sleek and trained and stupid. They'd cook apple charlotte and shoot. They'd screw dukedoms and—

Sir?

Oh, Chri – *what*?

Your nails are dirty, sir.

So they are, so they are, Squeaky Clean the Second.

That's possibly why you never made out with that kinda classy dame, sir.

Marcus Aurelius etc Jr, you sound like James Cagney. Congratulations. I was indulging. You fucked up my punch-line. Listen: she comes up to me and I open my mouth and she opens hers and out comes this whine, this Toujours del Sol, Costa del Provence, spumante-air-freshener-mushrooming-over-the-toilet-seat's-mohair-

cardigan kind of whine and I think it's the Range Rover. I think it's
the Range Rover's security alarm. I say so. Well, it is. It's both. The
Range Rover is being dubbed over, into plain English. It's saying:
would you mind pissing off out of here, at once, this is our property,
you are actually trespassing, Brian please fix that bloody thing. Brian is
struggling with the Range Rover's dashboard. I could slaughter his
wife and burn down my grandmother's house while he's struggling.
Instead I draw myself up to my chiropractor's height and say: whose
bicycle is that? The whine replies, it came with the property. It was
thrown in. Do you want us to call the police? I stare at the bicycle, then
at the house. No, I reply, I don't think that's necessary. I'm sure it
wasn't stolen. *Brian*, I shriek. They both look aghast. They both, for an
instant, look like two little kids caught torturing a bird.

That's nice. You're all so intent.

I smile like I've just come outa the Staked Plains and seen a lot. This
cat's sniffing my trouser-leg. I ignore it. Yeah, we're birds of passage
all, I say – loud enough for Brian to pick it up. Birds of passage all. I
hope the phantoms bother you. Goodbye, goodbye.

I scrunch up the English lane doing a Godard with the trees, the leaves
above my head, the leaves flashing the sun as I take these big strides.
Hell, I feel good. I feel ready. Birds of passage all. The alarm's shut off
and it leaves my tinnitus in good shape as I reach the village, the coach
pub, the very bright and blaring *Half Moon* with an inkie-dinkie snug
on the dark side where I sup alone on undiluted ale and non-terrestrial
chilli con carne and talk to the labrador over his snores. I know what I
have to do. I know it. I stare at this big blow-up of an old wagon and the
wheel starts going round and I have to shake my head. It's a sign. I've
loaded my spool. It's all in there, in the Enfield Ritz or maybe (careful,
little Ricky) the Biograph matinée of my skull. It'll take nine years, ten,
maybe twelve. I know it. It'll ripen and sigh in the hogshead of my
head, it'll strengthen, it'll grow rich and dark and old and ready. It'll be
ready. I'll be ready. I never want to see the house again.

Let's splice.

Let's splice it open.

Let's splice it open and swallow.

5

3

2

I

House lights – someone's hit the fucking house lights.

Thank you.

Phantoms, phantoms.

Mist. More mist. Mist curling over a river, perhaps. Maybe a marsh. I don't want to lay an image on you. You'll have your own. But let's have some studio fog, for the hell of it. I just want to git on thar. The millennium's already five seconds in. Nothing achieved. The bells are still ringing and nothing achieved. We've got the biggest clean-up operation ever and we're going into it pissed. I ask you.

Fog. Swirling about. You're moving into it, it's parting, you know the kind of thing: grainy black and white, creepy billows, hair-tingling but you know it's inside, it's a studio thing, Ealing or Pinewood, the jets hissing as they pour out the fog. Let's have it. Jesus, our budget's limitless. (As my old producer Elijah Wannamakit used to shrug: did He claim expenses or did He not?)

Fog parts, you're going quite fast, it parts to itself, to more fog, my old dad's proper kind of Shadwell greasy wharf mother-fucker Thames pea-souper lamps out consumptive bastard sort of fog, thick and yellow and a killer. We're talking swirls and lumps and flops of fog, we're talking fog that costs a fortune and gets Second Grip hacking, we're talking about the fog of memory out of which anything can lumber, and it's just about to, it's swirling to trees, big trees, dark boles and branches. Trees in a line. The big flat heart-shaped leaves of lindens. Falling, falling yellow. Crushed little fruits underfoot. You know the trees, they're all over London, dog shit piled under the uncropped suckers, never park your car under a lime, honeydew eating the metallic finish, hell to get off, but we're not in London.

A linden tree avenue. Or lime, if you prefer.

Fog fades and swirls away. You're in the avenue. Your feet munch the

fruit and the leaves, the dead leaves of the linden trees every issue of
the school magazine has a poem to. Christ, you're in a bloody school.
The school squats at one end and the laundry chimneys behind and
the air is autumnal, fine, smoky with groundsmen, near the beginning
of things. You're not quite sure whether you're coming or going,
arriving or leaving. The linden trees rear up and shake the sun but the
leaves, the big leaves, drop. You could run. You could run but there
is an awful quiet and it is probably the quiet of lessons. If you ran
you would shake the quiet and bring faces to the distant windows,
hundreds of faces pressed against the distant windows, gargoyle faces
all yelling behind the glass SCUG because that's the way their mouths
are moving. It's that sort of school, mate. It's that sort of date. It's
before the introduction of girls, business studies, the cosy corner of
pottery classes. It's way before the Sony in the study, it's before
electricity practically, it's before your life. You scan about for a handle,
for a main thrust, for a fulcrum, for a core, for a little red cross on a
calendar or maybe a date reading backwards in front of your ankles.
There ain't none.

But hey, the fog's gone, or thinned into the light mist clinging about
the lime trunks and thicker in the meadows where the poplars blow,
thicker in the damp meadows where the grass looks churned by some
rough game and there are horrible horse-flies. You get the feeling that
the school likes its games rough. You get the feeling that you're togged
out for some rough game, because you're cold and breathless and your
breeches end where your shins begin. You must have been running.
You've done something wrong and you're on a run, you're on a three-
mile run, the sun's still low and there's a scent of sausages, sour tea,
and early morning.

With a terrible shock you know that you know the building.

You know that you know its grand if a little crumbling front ranged by
long windows some earl'd gaze through before the invention of the
train, before the great days of the Empire, before the stove-pipe hat.
You know that you know the grand if a little crumbling sweep of steps,
the Corinthian columns supporting the porch, that big mouth with its
big teeth waiting to gnaw you. And the fact that you know this, know it
like it's a feared hard-faced mother, know it like it's occupied one of

87

the small forts in your head – makes you smaller. You're smaller than you should be. Your knees are a boy's. You are a boy. You're a boy at this school, for certain. The camera on its rails ready to track your hesitations down the linden tree avenue has gone. All the people with their walkie-talkies and clipboards have gone. The girl with the pony-tail you really fancy has gone, along with the leather jacket you were hoping to compliment her on. There is no director with his soft jokes and greying sideburns puffed at the ears. There is no other actor to jape with in the interminable delays. There were never any fog machines. There is only the light early clinging mist that you know won't lift all day because the school's damp, a damp pile in a damp low place, and it killed the earl's heirs one by one and their funeral carriages haunt the avenue, the wail of their mother haunts the Upper Dorm, the sobs of the earl can be heard through the drainpipes on certain nights depending on the moon, though you don't really believe that rot.

What did you just say?

Rot?

Ha!

You're in.

The bright red tongue behind the teeth blackens. Someone's opened the main door, obviously. You're way up one end of the linden trees and you're looking all the way down and it's so deep with perspective you want to tap the air just to check it out, just to check it's not trumping your eye with paint or celluloid, a nifty exercise in depth of field across which the leaves float down. But the word rot rings through your head and you daren't lift your fist because someone's appeared, the throat's coughed up someone who stands at the top of the sweep of steps and, anyway, the air is fine and cold and smoky with groundsmen. Shit, if you can see him he can see you, it's a rule of optics, it's the law according to everything. You slip to the side, behind a big bossed bole, and the fumes of wet leaves are already clinging to your shirt. The sweat chills on your shoulders and down your back. You think you might get a chill, the chill might occupy the small fort of your chest, might overrun your lungs and the whole of you might fall to the Gauls.

The who?

The Gauls. The barbarians. The heathen hordes. The white areas on the map that are full of blackness. The ghosts of dead boys. The ghost of the boy who fell. Who was made to. The ghost of the new boy who fell while the others stopped jeering and gazed. The sound of a sheet tearing. The scream of the new boy who plunged. Crikey – you know this place so well you know its phantoms, you know its white areas that are full of blackness, you know its names and the names of its enemies. The swollen bark of the linden tree your fingers are picking comes into focus. You like the name linden, there's a boy called Linden, you like his nose and his mouth but his eyes are murky. You peep out from behind the trunk and it's Streadnam.

Christ. Streadnam. How did you know his name? How come your heart's turned your tonsils into a punch-bag all of a sudden? Why do you fear him? Why do you hate him? Who the heck is he? What's he got that ridiculously tall hat on for and why are his whiskers so enormous? Why, just below his lower lip, is their pepper-and-salt stained orange? How do you know his beard's stained orange just below his lower lip without a pair of telescopic sights on your nose? How do you know so much when all you can see is a dark blob with something puffy and a flue on top in front of the door? For you know the foul redness of his nose and the orange stain on his whiskers as if they were monuments and they stand over you, these things, they stand over your small life as if they have and always will be here.

Not bad, huh? You want out? You want to go out and watch the fireworks? There are still some crazies swimming in the river? There always are and there always will be. Some of them will drown. There's bound to be a drowning tonight or this morning. In the Eros fountain, say, or the big brown superwide himself muscling along, clucking under the barges and the wharfs and the phantoms of the barges and the wharfs, clucking and clopping and rolling the corpses over until the early morning walker with his dog spots them and underacts beautifully because there's no one watching him, just the dog wagging its bloody stupid tail. Hey ho.

But listen – you can't up and out of this one.

If you so much as move Streadnam'll spot you. He'll give you a yell. You'll have to walk the whole length of the lime tree avenue and it's half a Roman mile. By the time you get to Streadnam your knees'll be clutching each other. He'll clip your ear 'ole. Your ears are cold. You don't want them clipped. Even when they're snug and warm it hurts to have them clipped. You have this idea that Streadnam might not realise how much it hurts because he chortles when he clips. You have a fear, generally, of getting hurt. Perhaps this is why you're on a sweat. Scug. Scugs skip games. Or they don't play up.

Play up, or pay up?

Play up.

Perhaps both, in certain circumstances.

Play up is not a misprision.

I don't think the blob has spotted you, you're lucky. It pauses on the top of the steps and then it descends. It's limping. It limps down and the flaps of its black coat are like a crow's wings when a crow hops. Your heart's now practising its upper-cuts and your tonsils are taking it in the way punch-bags do. Streadnam is bad. He locked a boy in a cellar. He locks boys in the cellar where the rats run. He forgets them. The masters forget them. No one remembers them till the end of term because their parents are far away and don't expect letters. By then they're bones stirred by a rat's foot only.

Wassat? Eh? Sounds familiar, does it, that last growl?

Well done, Hilda. Exam text, huh? No? Ha, 'course not – it's all *Superman* comics now, innit? Even better done, honey-bun. Even better done 'cos you were only an egg when me and Ken as in Russell were hustling *The Wasteland* proj down Sunset Boulevard OK up at

Shepperton and everywhere else, same difference, same bloody no-no to the most exciting idea since *The Ten Commandments* remake. Imagine it. Gielgud narrating, Larry doing Tiresias if he didn't mind the dug-girdle, Michael 'Carbuncular' Caine no marks for guessing opposite Maggie 'Fiery Hair' Smith in not even a camisole, *My nerves are bad tonight, Alfie*, cor, that's a shame, Hattie Jacques as Interfering Old Bag in Pub wot likes hot gammon, Sid James as the Barman yelling last orders in slomo between a couple of glass-polishing gags, something for everyone, lots of montage and fade-outs and way-out angles, homages to everybody worth homaging, outside shoots at Margate and the Kew Gardens Palm House and just over the water there, the rest all studio, *magic* but no one believed, all they believed in was bedsit dance-routines and the bloody Beatles. They'd only do it with Julie Andrews and songs and without the wrinkled dugs but I said yes and Ken said no and they wouldn't do it without Ken, they didn't trust me, I said yeah yeah, I'll give you a lot of Julie on the sled and great numbers like *Marie, Marie* and *Hold On Tight* but they lost their initial enthusiasm after about ten minutes in this great lung-cancer habitat, I didn't even try Jack Warner with it. I'd have grabbed the money and run, by the way – fired Andrews, quit Austria, shot *The Wasteland* in secret over at Cromer probably like Kubrick shot *2001* in secret, we'd have had an immortal classic to chalk up on our National Achievements Board. Instead they gave you *Camelot*.

But, hey, you're brighter than your Dad, Hilda. You're brighter than anyone here, I reckon, 'scuse my imbalance. But your great-great-great-uncle was brighter still. He was very bright. He was a beacon on a moor, a lighthouse, a lamp shining in the shepherd's fist, a wise guy. Everyone said so. A brilliant brightness for the fresh century. Hey, you OK there, behind the linden tree? Hilda's my granddaughter. Her great-great-great uncle is about to appear. Don't fuck things up for her – or for him, come to that. Though things are pretty fucked up for him already. And they didn't get better. They didn't.

OK.

Streadnam's surveying from the gravel drive. He doesn't see you. He sees the avenue dwindling to the gates and maybe a flash of cream but he thinks it's the sunlight, or a pigeon. He's in need of a change of spectacles. His spectacles are furred with use, with dirt. When he wipes them on his sleeve they're worse, because his sleeve is greased. But he's settled into his dirt, his use, his grease, and doesn't want out. To take him out would kill him unless it was done like the cleaning of a Goya. The mark of the dribbled cud on his beard deepens each year, but that is all that changes. Streadnam is Streadnam, and always will be. Your mother calls him frightful, but not to his face. Sometimes you have pictured your mother calling Streadnam frightful to his face, but the picture is about as lifelike as your own paintings of cats and dogs Nurse stuck up that time in your room.

PAINTINGS.

That word looms enormous at the back of your mind, it fills this day and is terrible.

PAINTINGS!!!

You press your chilled back against the linden tree and listen to the crows rising above Inkblot Copse.

PAAAAAAAAAAAAINTINGS, PAAAAAAAAAAAAAAAAAAINT-INGS, and so on.

There is something so terrible about this word you want to really bawl it out and see what happens.

Paintings.

An even feebler echo returns. Basically you're a craven scug. You didn't dare to more than kind of yip it because Streadnam might hear above the cawing of the crows and give you a yell. As you wait for what happens something does, but you don't connect it with your pathetic yip.

The gates fill up with a shape and a noise.

The noise is of a clopping and a whoa. The shape is of a horse and a carriage. It is black, all black, an ex-hearse they got on the cheap

92

because it's that kind of mean, peevish school. The out-of-date carriage is so polished you can see the gates and the trees and the dwindling of the trees to the school in the side of the carriage where the door's shut. That also means you're close, three trees away, and Jefferies'll spot you. Jefferies. The name is something dark and rat-like. The coachman. Oh Christ, there aren't any cars, this carriage thing isn't to get the Japs enrolled, it's functional, we're that far back. Or are we? Jefferies drives motor cars fast when he gets the chance. Mr Boulter has a motor car. There *are* motor cars, but not that many. Your image of motor cars is obscured by dust, by white dust billowing behind and gleeful shouts and this faint feeling of fear and sickness. You've seen one in a ditch with its top ripped and its brass horn turned into a flugel. It probably had trouble changing gear when it was going up the hill, it didn't have the sprag down to stop it running back down the hill, you're surprisingly technical about an area you thought you were totally ignorant of apart from nine viewings of *Chitty Chitty Bang Bang* until a few minutes ago – uphill and downhill are dangerous without functioning brakes and a sprag to dig into the grit, you know that, you also know that once you're running backwards down the hill and you let down the sprag you'll leapfrog over it and die. You know hills are tricky from your bicycle, too. You know that even from horses because a horse can refuse to brake. You feel the world tipping up into a hill and you close your eyes to stop yourself sliding and rolling down it. You dig your heels in. You open your eyes and there is Jefferies, standing by the gate, his nose touching the wrought iron of the great gate. Actually, gates. They have a bolt connecting them on a huge latch that sends a shudder through the spikes and the whorls and the plumes of the black iron. Jefferies is looking at you. He's got his mouth open just enough to show off his teeth glint. You're not quite sure why his teeth glint, but they always do, it's connected with the way he rubs them against the ball of his thumb when he's thinking, maybe. Right now his thumbs are on the iron and they're in grey gloves and you know without seeing that the wrists of the gloves have tortoiseshell buttons that Jefferies likes to finger in turn as if they're never quite done up.

You may or may not know that I live next to a golf course out in Houston, Texas.

Forget it. Because if I said it's like you're tied to this dented tree on the

93

practice fairway on the day before the All Comers Championship it would only confuse you. It is, but it would only confuse you. Instead, I'll say this: you're in a pretty negative situation, kid.

But you're not thinking this. You're thinking: this is black-rotten awful, I'll say. This is very fairly hideous. This is a qualified quagmire and I've got the wind up. These words roll through your head like there's someone who knows what they're doing but a bit bored winding the roller. You're surprised at these words. They fit inside you like polished pebbles fit into the pocket of your breeches, like marbles once fitted into your little felt belt-bag in those far-off hols with naughty old Uncle J-J. But they don't get rid of Jefferies. Jefferies continues to show off his dental glint through the gate. But, hey, instead of trying to shrink into an ancient pruning scar on the linden something fairly weird happens: you stand erect and look away, over towards the bladderdash pitch and Fenny Bottom. You casually dismiss the fellow with a casually assumed air of indifference. This is amazing. This is not something you thought you had in you. Your heart's going into the twenty-first round with your tonsils but your bones and tendons know better. Streadnam is a servant. Jefferies is a servant. Jefferies is a servile little rat, actually, a nasty little fellow who some prefects once chucked in the marsh because he crawled from its slime before history started and the smell of his breath proves it and he had to wade back in for his hat, snivelling. He can't do anything to you. He is only the coachman. He can't lay a finger on you, not one jot.

Nevertheless your blood's pummelling and you want to run.

I'm tracking out, up the linden tree avenue. I'm leaving you there, OK? Don't fuck things up by bolting. Stay put. Jefferies is ogling you through the gate, that's all. I'm tracking up the linden tree avenue, towards Streadnam, and it's pretty scary. It's pretty scary approaching Streadnam with the lindens floating past each side and him just watching, staring out through me at Jefferies because I'm invisible. I am, you're not. Bad luck. This is my privilege: the perk of Mr Important, the Number One, the guy in the canvas chair with the giant name-tag on the back and tea on tap and a girl to hold his megaphone. Tea? Whisky, in the old days. The grand old days. I had an antique bronze OK brass speaking-trumpet, in the old days. It shone. Seraphs would polish it. It flashed on set, under the lights. Great days, great days. When I think of them I get a tang on my lips, of Grant's and Brasso. I'm gliding over the morning's leaves, over the red grit of the avenue swept by groundsmen with long rakes each damp twilight. So many have fallen, since. Groundsmen, I mean. There's a plaque of wood in the scullery. *1914–18*, and names. Professionally done, raised by subscription, basically the prizefighter cook's fairly large hat. Not now, of course, not now as I'm gliding towards Streadnam, leaving you in a fix by the fourteenth linden. None of that has happened yet. This is not yet then. This is Before.

Are we that far back?

Yup, we are.

We're following the ground, close. There are no tyre-tracks on the red grit of the avenue because visitors are rare but there could have been, there could have been. There are light combings of groundsmen and the deep thrustings of a carriage and not many heels. There are leaves and the linden trunks' angled autumn shadows, in out, in out, in out, reminding y'all of that creepy ascent in *The Spiral Staircase*, naturally. Now there is gravel beginning, spilt out from the drive. Then there is gravel with the ruts of wheels but only gravel, only gravel passing under with the odd dead leaf. Andrei Tarkovsky would now be adding things, of course. An inch of water all over, dolls with missing eyes, a champagne cork, a revolver, a yellowing journal, you name it, passing slowly beneath us but very close. Thornby tells it as it is. Then suddenly we have boots, scuffed at the caps, prehistory's Doc Martens ending at the knees. Stop. This is Streadnam. I look up and his nostrils are caves through the foliage. I climb into them and inhabit his head. It is not always a privilege, guv, being Number One.

OK. I'm settled in. He has a really disgusting leather chair up here with bad warble-fly holes but it's surprisingly comfortable. He sees you as a dab of sunlight, but he sees Jefferies, he sees the carriage. It is all spick, he thinks. All spick. His head is fumy with porter, because he drinks it and that's what he is, the head one. He found this amusing, once. He nibbles the cud stain on his lower whiskers, as is his wont, baring his teeth like a rabbit as he chews and nibbles. His beard crackles through his head like the fire in his lodge he crouches to most of the day in his disgusting warble-fly homage, keeping one eye out for the truant, the scug, the unwanted bloody visitor rapping on his window. I'm very crammed in up here by curses – big old trunks and valises and strapped-down crates of curses, ten-ton curses he drops now and again, as he drops now and again the little bastards' luggage, just in case they've forgot him. Tuppenny-ha'penny little bastards. Jefferies is waving, the rat-cunt's waving, like it's a fucking fair. It's not. It's a fucking funeral. It's somebody's fucking funeral. Not mine, not his, but one of the tuppenny-ha'penny bastards with golden hair.

Streadnam is talking about my great-uncle. I'd like to hit him, I'd like to clip his lug-'ole from the inside because the inside of one's lug-'ole equals the nipple in pain count. But I'm not there to hit him. You are. You could hit him. You can hurt and you can suffer in your boy's body. From Streadnam's blur you're getting to be a suspiciously bright dab of sunlight, actually – I think it's your elbow or your shoulder, I'm glad his head doesn't have a built-in visual information enhancer to make up for his glasses. But keep in. I don't want Streadnam to see you. I don't want you to hit him, were that in any crazy way possible. That would really foul things up, OK?

How are the fireworks? Hey, how about a little toast, a toast to the not-yet-slaughtered groundsmen with their rakes and struggling bonfires? Huh?

Thank you. Keep the Brut flowing and the buck's fizz out of it. Pass those fabulous canapés around. Be comfortable. Remember one thing, though, and murmur this to the guys 'n dolls out on the balcony or in the lavatory or the cunts among you talking loudly in the corners: I'm going to chuck this print in the river, after. Hey, seriously. There won't be a second screening. That's life. It's up to you to remember.

Don't believe me, huh? We'll see.

Right.

Streadnam.

He died in 1923. Fact. Another decade to breathe and torment and swill and curse by. He retired in 1920 against his will then skulked about the porter's lodge, a cud-dribbling white-bearded dinosaur getting under the heels of Travis, the new sleek kind of mammalian one with what turned out to be Hitler's forelock and nose-bush. Right. I've told you the date, you behind the linden. On the ball, mate? 1913. No-man's-land year, the year Before, the year no one talks about, the non-entity, the non-year, unlucky for some, but for most, in recollection, blahdy wonderful, son. The year my old dad was born so actually he couldn't have remembered it, he wasn't that precocious. Blahdy wonderful. Under a barrer or something, covered in fish guts and apple pulp on the Radcliff Highway with blinkered nags snorting past and right past this 'ere bleedin' wharehouse you've parked your butts in for the night. Amazing, innit?

Streadnam. He's on one of the stills, the stills in the lobby. Our suite's lobby, dumbos, not the main one. Notice them? Thirty-two variations between the fake bale-hook and the coat rack, framed in genuine brass, cost me an arm and all three legs. You'd have to be blind. Maybe some bastard's covered them with his wolf pelt. You can check, after. I'd always check, Enfield Ritz, steal a glance at the stills and try to remember.

Number One, top left. That little blurry fat thing with billows of smoke coming out of his collar, in front of the lodge. Day of his retirement. Dug it out of the school archives. Inkblot genuine. Looks a character, doesn't he? Oh yes, old Streadnam was quite a bloody character.

WHERE'S THE ACTION, RICKY?

There's always one, there's always one.

Friends, relations, the rest, I tell you again if I have already and your hearing-aids are maladjusted: this is not an action movie. It's an epic movie but it's not an action movie. It's hard and big in the saddle but it's not John Wayne or Brian de Palma or Francis Ford Coppola or even John Ford being thoughtful. It's Richard Thornby. It's his deep masterwork. It's his last stand. Don't expect Gordon of Khartoum, Apaches turning cavalry into hedgehogs, flash-forwards to stuttering

97

machine-guns for the backward or the inadequate, fucking heli-copters. This is 1913. We're parked outside a peevish little public school in England on the third of November 1913 and the time is nine of the clock and the leaves are falling slowly out of another year to be raked by the last of their kind. I'm inside this creep and he's waiting. I can't hurry him. You know why I leave a space between the paragraphs?

So you don't choke on your canapés, reading too fast.

I hope the projector's not overheating. It's old, '56, dug out of the rubble of some Cinema Paradiso in West Norwood. I liked the rattle, the burr, the hefty armour-plated kind of look to it and the built-in ashtray WHICH YOU MUST NOT USE, OSSY. No Jap in sight. But it tends to overheat and smoke the dust on top. Perhaps someone can dust it. I'm too pissed to move, probably. Anyway, the director never cleans the projector. Not even Stanley. Don't panic if there's a singed smell. It's the dust.

Thank you.

Ha! Streadnam has lifted a hand for Jefferies.

It's a salute. Streadnam has black fingerless mittens on his hands and the left one salutes. There is a military pedigree to Streadnam and it lingers. He was out in India before the beard arrived, surrounded by blinding whites wot clicked and nodded and got him to scrub their saddles. He took it out on the untouchables. He wasn't kitted out to be a batman. His fart-sucking wasn't the right sort, as a better batman (retired) put it. The young Streadnam beat up an untouchable, basically. The untouchable had left his broom out on the giant verandah and Corporal Streadnam took a tumble, fresh from his umpteenth fucking saddle, flush with porter. He stuffed his fist into this extremely genial sweeper's face five times and dusted his hands and saw the blood all over his boots. He bolted. He tumbled again, this time down the blinding white drop of five steps and crooked his leg in five places. He was invalided out on a tramp steamer. His bone is

98

perpetually infected. The salt got into it, the dust, the untouchable's touch.

Cannon shot on the Khyber, sir. Near took me leg away. I endure it.

Streadnam's hand drops. All spick and in the saddle. It's times like this that brings out the bloody spine in us all. Order. Show 'em a thing or two. The welting could have been public, could have been now, but the others decided contrary, as is their wont. Soft buggers. Soft as babies. He tastes his breakfast on his beard. He belches into the fine air. He can smell his own unwashed smell and it reassures him. His leg has got the fucking damp in, today. He feels the touch of the genial sweeper's five fingers and spits. They ought to've taken it orf. The hand that touched it. It. A light gust blows down between the lindens, there's dust raised, it's India all over again. The avenue blurs further and he blinks it back to the usual. Jefferies is still gawping, it looks like. That's not right. Should be parked by the fucking carriage, not gawping through. He can't be bothered to tell him, to yell, to make a pother out of it. It'll ride. This chair is actually extremely comfortable, I'm sinking into it, it's worrying. I think I need to read some poetry or something.

You over there, behind the linden, pressed against its bosses, shins grazed by its uncropped suckers, gazing at Fenny Bottom, DON'T MOVE. It's good, you're ignoring the hiss which is Jefferies chuckling for the sound that isn't the crows, but, hey, it's like them. You turn to look down the outside of the avenue where the big branches hang over the pasture like they're relieved to be out of things, but can't see a jot. You can't see a jot because the pasture just continues on beyond the avenue, running misty and green down the side of the Pod until the Science Block's erection in 1963 and the all-weather hockey pitch for the flensing of knees about a decade later. Right now the pasture bumps untramelled by anything but the usual scrubby kind of thorny moments you've been thrown into a few times and, beyond the cute wooden fence, brindled cows and some dappled horses. The school is completely masked this side by the giant trunks on parade and then a laurel hedge with ancient dens defended lustily by valiant knights but I think you're a serf, you're never quite sure which den you're supposed to be defending to the death which is why you get hurt a lot. But now

99

something's happening that isn't crows. There is definitely something happening in that general direction.

Shall I tell you? Stay put. If you stick your nose out the other way, someone'll spot you and there's always Jefferies. I sympathise. I have to tell you now that you're in the wrong togs. You should have gone back and changed. You know this. You had time to run to Five Mile Hump and back and change between brekkers and this. You didn't. Now you're gonna have to stand like the naked Emperor in a line of perfectly attired schoolboys, boaters nodding, ties flapping, breeches tucked into ruthlessly steam-pressed shirts, dark blue felty jackets tempting hands with their warm pockets. Because they're pouring out of Cavvie right now and it's too late. The ears are disgorging them, the two ears of the house with the mouth, Miss Cavendish House, the toothy face at the end of the avenue, the terrifying governess's face you've turned it into and that some fading echo from the future tells you resembles a certain prime minister, ranting. Out they come, from either side, as if from a secret door and you can only hear them, I'm afraid, hear them gathering like starlings and crows who've suddenly taken against human beings, what a stupid thought, not the whole of human kind, just certain people, just you as a matter of fact. It's swelling, it's getting louder, it's the voices broken and unbroken, the bullies and the bullied, the brilliant and the stupid, the scugs and the bloods, the keen and the indifferent, the casual and the one who's about to die of some creeping pulmonary problem and is hectic with life, they're getting their beaks nice and sharp from the sound of it, they're ready to swoop. Do you want to make a dash for that hawthorn sprig? Those way-off poplars? That lone ash with its trunk you'd stick out either side of like Badstock's ears? They'll see you, they'll all see you, even without Jefferies waving and hissing. There's nowhere to go, basically. Chum, you'll have to stick it out, trying not to shiver too much in the damp, getting pinched by Briggs or Cowdrey on your plump bottom. Bad luck. I'm a bastard. I'm Dick the Prick. Streadnam's got to me, his chair's cosy. Lucky you're not an untouchable. I'm feeling mean. Make my day. Meanness is what this day's all about. Out of it flowered our century.

Whassat? Out of it flowered our century?

100

I hear murmurings of blimey, it's getting pretentious. He's been too long in the US of Ass-Holes. He always was a Russell in the making. Ken, not Bertrand. Nice rib-tickler that, Ossy. Remember it? Ossy 'Two Shot' Cohen's parting jape, summer of '81. OK OK, I'm not gonna get personal. Just yet. Be my guests. Drink, eat, watch the fireworks and miss a frame or two. Talk, if you want. This is a silent film. But if you don't watch you won't remember. You were actually there, huh? Oh yes, but I didn't see all of it. Went on for hours. Scrolling up the big screen like a bloody computer. No, like the beginning of, say, *Unforgiven*, or *The Grapes of Wrath*, that written bit that tells you you're in Kansas City in 1879 or something, but it went on and on. It went on and on and on, a fucking portaprompt. And I've never been a reading type. Funny thing is, we all watched it, most of it, on and off, and a few just sat there stuck to the bloody screen like it was *Emmanuelle 3* with Princess Di or something. Well, it was a story, wasn't it? I mean, it had that. But he always was a pretentious bastard, was Dicky, was old Dicky the Crown of Thornbies.

Heh? A few red faces, heh? Where am I, anyway? Skulking in the back row? Testing my tongue out on a walnut ripple? Waiting for the white horse to move the snowy mountains and forests? A little scrubbed Enfield boy on the up and up, peering through the curling smoke and wanting his mum because the woolly dog's just been shot by hunters and he can't swallow any more without turning heads?

Aaaaaah. In't that sad, eh? True, though. Bloody true, guv.

I know at this point you'll all steal a glance at me, so I'll give a wave from the screen instead.

Hiee!

This doesn't help you wot's pressed against the linden in the wrong togs though, does it?

Put up with it. Worse things have happened to kids. Are about to happen. You'll have a taste, a feel. Take it. When my great-uncle appears they'll soon lose interest in you, kid. Don't crack. Stay put in the saddle and don't let it buck ya. Be a Texan.

101

I'm back in Streadnam. I just nipped out for a bit of fresh air. He's folded his arms against the boys spilling out, he's folded his arms against the tuppenny-ha'penny little bastards and the Nancy-homeys what are waving them into position like they're practising for the bloody crucifixion. All the young lot are Nancy-homeys, the young lot fresh out of bloody Oxford where they're all bloody bum-boys, anyway. Not like the old lot. All except Holloway-Purse, the army chap. Captain Holloway-Purse of the Hants Fusiliers, late of. He's more bloody like it. Even yours truly's chilled to the bone-juice by Holloway-Purse. The eyes, the eyes. Saw them out in Inja, tucked beneath the piths, out of the sun. Little glints in the shadow of the pith. Killing eyes. Show no mercy. Nigger-rats.

Oh yes, yes. WHP has spine, all bloody right.

The boys are spreading up the avenue, either side of it. Quit Streadnam, track up, track up with the boys spreading up the avenue under the trees, excited, quick, like little pigs with their flushed look from the early morning coldwater scrub, some of them men before they should be, gawky, not knowing what to do with their limbs, high collars lesioning their chicken necks, follow them, follow them up, eyes everywhere, knocking and jolting, knocked and jolted, nervous shrill laughter hushed by hectic young men called beaks funnily enough with old men's gowns whirling about and waving helplessly under the lindens, terrified secretly of Streadnam, of the Head Porter's eye, so they try not to shriek, they try to act the beak, the natural commander, they don imaginary helmets with huge plumes and shout in Thucydidean Greek, they flail at heads in the smoky air, they even kick as if at a rugby ball or clutch at arms as in the wrestles of bladderdash, they sort and cajole and somehow out it spreads, the long line of jacketed boys either side of the avenue and now we've hit you, you're there, skulking in your games togs, looking petrified between howling faces, caps, hands and jackets and the flashes of Edwardian collars but for God's sake stick your bottom in at least, have some dignity.

Track back, I'm not really interested in your humiliation, you can cope, Briggs and Cowdrey are pummelling another little nanny's boy, secretly, the other side of the avenue, doing something clever with the wct dead leaves and his Edwardian collar, track on, track up, glide up the pretty-orderly rows of excitable faces under the lindens, the odd one lovely as an angel, most beginning on the long downward slide to looking remarkably like the worst combination of their parents, moving past too quick to identify or of course to love, whipped away by me while you stay put, getting to know everybody again after an hour or two off and trying to be liked. Up past the last ones joining up and up past Streadnam's scowl and elbows and up the broad stone steps between the pillars into the very throat of Cavendish House, the double doors, the red iron-bossed double doors that open as I approach but it's not for me, it's for the guy on the other side, a short guy with great red whiskers that clash with both the door and his purple gown, it's for Mr Boulter the Master, the Headman, the Chief, the Caesar, disgorged by his school, Big Cunt Caesar hailed by his consuls, by the mob, by the triumphant order splayed before him to the far-flung gates of his conquest.

OK, Cecil Be To God. Let's take a breather. Nero needs a small widdle. Move those five thousand horses slightly to the left.

Dip the chuckles. I have plenty more where they came from, pardner.

Let's just hover.

Let's stand beside Big Man and view his order. It's pretty. Under the lindens there are two thin lines the colour of prunes and the one hundred per cent pink faces on top are swivelled this way. There are beaks in gowns, correctly positioned at intervals. There is Streadnam immediately before us of course. He's turning his beard up this way and giving Mr Boulter a nod, a servile, fart-sucker's nod in which the military pedigree is snappily recalled. It can hardly be other than servile, actually, because Mr Boulter is towering over them all, his squatness psychologically neutralised. Beyond the far-flung gates there is the black polish of the carriage, and a puff of smoke which is no doubt the coachman. Mr Boulter occupies the position, the only position, from which the perspective is perfectly aligned. He is the King on his throne at the masque. If Ossy's out there, explain it. And he could wave it all away, or call *vale* and leave, leave them all gawping, unable to know how to move. *Vale*, Ossy. Varlay. Oh forget it.

103

Mr Boulter's basically weight-challenged and also height-challenged body tucks into this view like a fat little kid into jam and pastries. His stomach swells against the hidden braces, his shoulders pump up against the weight of the gown, his diddle retracts and expands minutely under the starch of his longjohns. I'm focusing right in on his lower eyelid, left side, and its pouches quiver with pleasure. I could cover every inch of his body like this, if needs be, but needs don't, and I'd rather not. Hey, don't push me over my threshold. Do you know what it's like, getting this close to Big Cunt Boulter? It's like sticking your head in a fridge because there's this nauseating whiff and not finding it. Big Chief's gamey, he's hung too long, he's a tangle of trapped snuff, poorly-digested cabbage, badly-ventilated classrooms, something welded into his brain about soap only being good for washing out dirty little mouths, and the kippery beginnings of cancer. He doesn't even use dentifrice, for God's sake: a glass of Martell's swilling between his teeth is all that stands between him and a mouth full of carrion. Hey, don't push me over. This is a nauseating position to occupy. He's the guy in the middle in the second still. Don't rush to look. It's the school photo and the faces are tiny. His is tiny. If I'd found my great-uncle's face I'd have circled it, but there were a few blurs, a few whose heads turned out of life and embraced the fog as an old friend of mine put it. Maybe they saw a bird alighting on the last linden, maybe they saw a kitchen maid ogling from the cabbage patch, maybe they'd just been pinched and were telling Cowdrey to fuck off, *sotto voce*, you beastly rotter. Cavendish House, mainly the steps of, sweeps up behind the terraces of boys and beaks and masters to a pair of feet which are probably Alfred Hitchcock's, I dunno, you expect me to know everything, just put it down to a crap photographer choking on his flash.

Wooomph.

Randle College, Michaelmas Term, 1913.

So what're we gonna do about it? Huh? Yell and wave at them to stop, to whatever they do AVOID 1914 to 1918, go take a trip out to the Riouw-Lingga Archipelago and grow Bibles or develop your family's tendency to club-feet or stress how important the voices in your head are because you always instantly obey them? You think anywhere or any condition short of the terminal in the next four years is gonna be safe or something? You think their job is as easy as mine was in 1957, when all I had to do was show the Board my painted fingernails not too obviously? Huh?

Go take a look. Not too obviously. In a minute. When I say.

Don't disturb the innocence. Don't get in the way of the sunlight, the air, the breeze, don't unblur the leaves against the brick on the left, or kick the fat bearded guy holding the cup with big ears in the front just because it's Boulter because it isn't Boulter, Boulter's the even fatter and smaller one next to the heroically tall chaplain, you'll go kick Hibble who's nice and just happens to be in charge of the Terence Cup for Outstanding Performance in Elegiacs which no one won this year, it was nothing to do with his teaching, there are strict standards at this school, you can fail people. OK, what bastards some of them were, and would have become, if the bad dates hadn't got them young. What nice chaps and brilliant too, didn't make it past the barbed-wire of the bad dates!

Yeah, yeah, this is the mythology of the faces burdened with their own futures, the bastards and the brilliants, the dolts and the nice ones – their grins are all burdened with their futures, their ankles are already in the gin-traps set out neatly for them, their felty jackets are catching already on the tangs of the approaching dates if you believe my late friend Henry Peterson's neglected verse. Yet the fact remains that my great-uncle condemns them all from the grave.

For they did nothing. They are about to do nothing.

Big deal. Isn't that the lesson of history? Hey – you know what I'm doing? I'm shuffling away from Boulter, I'm avoiding occupying his position, because I can't stand it. I'm sorry. I'd like to be neutral, objective, I'd like to give him his own rope and let him tuck himself for you. But that'd be dishonest, guv. I hate the guy. I can barely look at him. I'm too old to be mature and objective and slippery. I'm crabby and mean and honest. The guy wrecked my great-uncle's life. Hey, he wrecked mine, too. We'll come on to that. Look at the still now, if you want. Visit the toilet. Fix yourself a drink. (Not you out there under the

linden, not you. Stay put. You've got a leading role. I'm talking to my
friends in this room. They're free to choose. You're not, bub.) Hey, I'll
give y'all some blank screen, a white-out, a few hundred frames' worth
of pause to do that, to go take a peek in an orderly fashion because I'll
bet you were too busy taking your wolf pelts off and hugging each other
to even notice the stills. I never had that problem back in '51. I went
alone.

You, you out there under the linden, the white grape in a line of prunes
– you stay put. And stop shivering. It looks kinda dumb.

OK?

Stocked up, bladder vacated, sitting comfortably?

Ye-es si-ir.

House lights still off? 'Cos some dumb nutwhacker was bound to have shouldered the button again, lurching off, or some creepy do-gooding practical type will have shattered the ambience by hitting the halogen to make things easier for everybody.

OK, OK, silence and clapperboard and action.

While we've been out things have happened. The masters and prefects and servants have appeared and in that order. It wasn't supposed to be in that order. It was supposed to be exactly the reverse, but some bottlehead's gone and bungled. Streadnam is lead, Boulter is smoulder, Holloway-Purse (right at this moment he's obscured by the balustrade, sorry) is Holloway-Purse or worse. *Worse?* Hey, the beaks either side of him have pins and needles in their buttocks. They know the score. I don't wish to approach HP just now. He's pricklier than usual, which means he's stiff, he's school-ham cold and stiff. What's going on inside his head is busy, it's complicated, it's X-rated unpleasant. He has two sides of him that are sick. It's to do with the loss of his mother as a kid and various concatenations of genes it'd take a ream of Nobel prize-winners the rest of the millennium to decode. It's really not worth it. Take me on trust. He likes to hurt people. He teaches arithmetic. He reads the lesson in chapel every Friday. He's not a virgin. He has hair the colour of beeswax. He has eyes invented by casting directors of concentration camp movies. These eyes of his are before their time. You'll see them in a tick, kid. I mean you behind the linden. What are you doing behind it? Get in line. Sandicot won't touch you. He's a nice boy. Anyway, you're all spaced too far apart now to rub up against each other. You might spread your arms and touch fingers. A genial untouchable sweeper's touch. The beaks have got it really aesthetic, now. You've all been practising. No clumps, no taggles, all spaced out nice and even for half a Roman mile to the big black gates and Jefferies puffing on his Woodbine by the carriage. Wow, out of this order came conflagration.

Obedience. Who needs it?

You do. Because your first period's . . . hey, it's arithmetic! With HP!

You've done half the prep. ½ the fractions set.

Am I mean?

I'm sneaky. It's good for you. It improves your swing. And you gotta change togs. You can't go into your arithmetic class in those. It wouldn't be fair on your fundament. It'd have no idea what might be coming to it – it's made it right through so far with only a nanny spank, the odd half-cock welt. No rod has ever descended on it as Holloway-Purse's might. He doesn't welt, he flays. His right arm no more than flicks but it does something drastic, it tightens your cheeks, it turns them into silk so taut the next stroke nicks it apart and there are four more. You know it's bad when your inside knees get warm and wet. You can't go to anyone because they might tell HP, and he'd do it all over again, and he has terrific aim. He can open up a calloused welt without looking. He's done it before. Thrashing is the thing he does best. When he does it he hears God saying more, more. The Devil comes out when they scream, and when they're silent he's failed, though he admires their tenacity. Or the Devil's. Jolly well done, he says. Hey, he's a fair man. He recognises spunk.

And you've got arithmetic with this guy in about fifteen minutes. And you haven't done your fractions. You're up a gum tree, guv.

I'm playing for time. The fact is, my great-uncle's late, he's missed his cue, time's expensive, what the fuck's he up to? The servants are in a sort of scrum by the laurel hedge. They're listless, surly, y'know – *servanty*. You do know? Hey, I didn't realise my friends were that rich. The servants've come straight from their rakes and colanders and bedpans and giant steam-irons. They think they know what this is all about and the general view is that it's a poor business. They don't like it. That is, they don't like Boulter or Streadnam or that cocky bastard

108

Holloway-Purse and they feel sorry for my great-uncle. That's why they deliberately waited in the kitchens, all of them, until the last possible minute. Mutinous. They're murmuring and maundering and Streadnam's giving them the evil eye. The light's difficult because it's shafting across them and the laurel hedge behind is deep and dark. We'll put a filter on and gild them. Why not? I don't want the group bleached out. This is a high quality work. This is a crucial document. I'm not interested in the laurel hedge. Their jackets are generally dark, their aprons starch white, they're a problem visually. But their faces are gilded, for the moment. Even the maids look pretty heroic. That's how I want it, OK? They're the chorus. The rake looks good. The guy at the front, the young one with the broad hat and slop jacket and corded breeches, he's hung on to his rake and he leans on it. It looks good, the tangs are catching the sun, there's a touch of flare.

Right, Hibble's moment. You remember Hibble. You tried to kick him. He's opposite the rake and next to HP, he thinks the rake reminds him of a painting, a great painting. He was in Florence two months ago. He fell in love with Frenella. The paintings blurred. Frenella sharpened. Hibble is chill in the slight northerly gusts blowing now up the linden tree avenue. There's some sort of beastly delay. The prefects are out, though. They're stood to the left of the servants and facing the avenue. Hibble doesn't like to see them all at once, like this. They look like fellows about to embark on a plundering expedition. His gown lifts and he clutches at it a bit pathetically in case it might brush Holloway-Purse, who is very still. The prefects ambled out in a most desultory manner, after the masters. Something has gone awry. His breakfast is not digesting as it should. He's thinking how Frenella would hate this, would hate seeing him here, dwarfed by Holloway-Purse, dwarfed by the whole caboodle. He was so grand in Italy. He expanded. He kissed a girl. They lay in a meadow full of cowslips. I'm focusing in on a spot just above his right eyebrow. He has careful dark Renaissance-style eyebrows. In three years' time they will be dislodged by a Bavarian sniper with pretty well invisible eyebrows. Holloway-Purse's eyes flicker. Boulter – just at the head of the group now because he's descended the stairs, he's done with his Nero bit, he's now Napoleon leading from the front – is beginning to nod at Streadnam. Sorry, it was a single nod, that was it. It's crazy, keeping track, I thought I had every angle covered but the dope sheet is ancient history now, trust my hand signals.

Streadnam's turned on his heel or whatever and is limping up the steps. He'll sort it out, thinks Hibble. Hibble's worried about finding the passage in Herodotus for the morning class, he's thinking the ticket-stub might have fallen out and he'll be fumbling in front of the Lower Sixth and they'll chortle. This worry is superimposed over Frenella's open mouth and the image falling on his retinas of Boulter's beard and the servants vaguely beyond, sunlit. He wishes he wasn't in alphabetical order, because Holloway-Purse makes him feel dwarfed and awkward and soft. He scratches his eyebrows in turn, then smooths them down with the side of his thumb, but he's not vain, oh no, he's just fidgety.

I don't know why my great-uncle was late.

Was late?

I know the facts, a few facts. A few stills, glimpses, a few moments cast out of the molten whatever. One of the big bronzes is that things were held up because my great-uncle was late. You know who I know this from? I know this from the young guy with the rake. He was still alive in 1988. He was ninety-three. He dug his own salad patch. He kept rabbits. Now he's dead. He told me on a fine smoky autumn morning how it happened. He gave me a ringside seat. And I'll tell you this: he felt bad about what had happened. He felt sad for my great-uncle, this old guy did. And you know what else this guy had seen? He'd seen his uncle at the top of a ladder falling back into the arms of his father – I mean the uncle's brother, or this old guy's father, it's not complicated – and in the middle of his uncle's forehead was this rose petal his father was trying to blow off the whole time. OK, let's start again. The uncle was climbing this ladder and grinning and the father was right behind and this old guy I'm talking about, who was really young then, was waiting to follow because – I think I forgot to say – they were going over the top at dawn or something, out of this trench, with whistles whistling and shells crumping and all that, when the uncle just leaned back into the arms of either this guy's father or the uncle's brother, depending on how you want to think of it, with a crimson thing that

110

looked a bit like a rose petal in the middle of his forehead, and he was extremely dead – dead as a nit, this old guy called it – and there they were in this trench, just the three of them, like a great painting, only it was real, it happened, and I can't find a way of telling it because this old guy told it in the only way possible and I'm not him. He spoke with a huskiness and a cough because the poison was still inside him. He'd worked his back to a dent raking and tying and digging and pruning in the grounds of Randle College for fifty-five years and all the time he felt bad about my great-uncle. I love this man. This man is the only really heroic guy I've ever known. So sucks to you people. Sucks to you all. Toast him, drink to his memory. He's what my father might have been if the apple pulp hadn't got into him, or the fish guts, or something.

You can imagine the situation. I mean the one down there, on the avenue. The beaks are trying to keep cool. The light gusts are getting less light, they're wrapping the gowns about thighs and all that: basically there's a mild wind-tunnel effect, it's well known – it's why the windows of Cavendish are always filmed with grit, it's why ladies have problems mounting the steps and gentlemen lose their hats over the balustrade and the upper dormitory windows rattle like the arrival of funeral carriages for the little earls. A boater goes bowling along and a beak catches it with his foot, which wrecks the crown. Dead leaves stir on the piles at the side as if the mouldering corpses obviously inside them are getting ready. Dead leaves jaunt about and crackle and float through the air and the hint of nicco from Jefferies' Woodbine gets some of the lads salivating. There's some whistling, cat-calling, nice owl effects. Restlessness, basically. Trouble in the ranks. Well it's cold, for a start, it's beastly rotten damp. Hands are in pockets, their fingers are closing round a spare bread roll or a sherbert or a conker or, in some cases, a filched fag. A surprising number are feeling a little pooped from masturbatory action in the night. One kid can't stop thinking about it because it was the first time he'd worked it out and he's relieved and proud and awfully sinful and checking out his eyesight against the entwined RC on the tie opposite. I won't zoom in on him or anything. This is not *If*. I'm just giving you a few scene-setting takes on the general situation. The general situation is looking to be fucked up by my great-uncle, which is just great. HP – I wish he had a nickname, but he hasn't, he transcends them all, they don't stick,

111

they're feeble, they become instantly pathetic – HP's eyes are boring a hole through the back of Boulter's head and Boulter knows it: he knows he's not good enough for HP, he knows he's not good enough for the job, he's not tall enough, he has digestion problems, he discovered nits in his beard last night, he's deeply unattractive to women, his book on Pisistratus is still in the inkwell and he's chronically unable to find small boys unattractive especially when they're surpliced in white each morn and eve, singing to the God he has several niggles against – the chief one being His reluctance to manifest Himself in Randle's cricket scores, which are a personal slight.

Turn around, leave that creep.

There's a leaf mounting the steps. Follow it. It's bouncing on the flat slabs of the Corinthian porch. It gets to the doors. The doors open. The Head Porter has my great-uncle by the ear in the shadow of the doors. What a weird duo they make, like a lousy adaptation of *Nicholas Nickleby* or something. I mean, Streadnam is just so *obvious*, he's just so 'orrible and Victorian and smelly he ought to be preserved as a shining example of an era which has left only phantoms and Margaret Roberts. He has really dry fingers, callouses, scabs of pads which scratch my great-uncle's ear and seem not to know how easy it is to pull an ear off. Or maybe they do. The corridor behind them smells of cabbage, moist loofahs, let-offs, kippers, Latin verbs, a hint of the scent the beautiful pony-tailed sound assistant uses, patchouli or something, as if she has just fled, quick, quick, there! – and a background swell of Izal disinfectant the earl would not have recognised. Neither would he have recognised the corridor. He would have mourned the grand entrance hall with its swell of dark floorboards, its marmoreal busts and bosoms, its ancestral glowerings, its salacious tapestries, its National Trust attendant. Trust the Victorians to carve it up with a corridor, two classrooms, two Upper Sixth studies and a broom cupboard. The leaf whips in and settles temporarily against a wet strand of mop and thrums minutely in the draught funnelled by the avenue and greeted by the corridor and expanded to get the detention lists on the board making a noise like far-off Spartan cohorts drumming joyously on their pectorals. And this is only an autumnal gust. Thank you. Dip the applause, Henry Peterson's dead, he can't hear you, pull up the breathless silence.

Streadnam and my great-uncle are silhouetted against the morning light. I'm turned round, I'm moving up, I'm tagging just behind, I can't stand this corridor a yard longer but Streadnam's kind of paused for acclaim in the doorway, blocking everything but the draught, forgetting about the grip on the ear-lobe, then remembering and sliding it down to the shoulder where even Streadnam knows it's more suited to the bloody grandeur of the occasion. I'm waiting in the corridor. This corridor's not meant for human consumption. Its echoes and its smell are to do with death, detention lists, deadly diseases. Its lino's coming up like sloughed skin. Its walls are a sweaty sort of distemper, something from the bottom of the TB Sputum range, something that later generations' brushes slide over without success. It shouldn't really open, this corridor, onto the linden tree avenue and the woods beyond. It should open onto coils of barbed wire, glistening mud, sleet, ominous booms. Perhaps it will, later, in a two-tone dream sequence I'll be acclaimed for lifted straight out of *What Price Glory?* and Bergmanised. Perhaps it will. Stick around. It must have done, in my great-uncle's actual dreams. I mean, it would be amazing if it hadn't. Really amazing.

He's stepping out. No, Streadnam has given him a little shove, a secret one, just between him and my great-uncle's shoulder-blades, but it still manages to wind. Hey, there's a lot of hatred in that little shove. Streadnam's biggest regrets, in a year or two's time, will be his age and his limp. His little shoves and pinches could've been indispensible along the slimy duck-boards. But he'll make clear his views on shirkers, conchies, scugs all right when the time comes. He'll emphasise his limp till it looks ridiculous, salute visitors, waddle about ramrod-straight and hang Kitch above the fireplace instead of the Faithful Collie. The orange cud-stain on his beard will deepen. He will smell riper. He will tell each school leaver how blasted bloody green he is of their lucky chance, and how it reminds him of his youth, slapping them on the back and winding them slightly as they step into the carriage or the motor car, with their OTC kit folded neatly on the top in the strapped trunk, whirled off to their various deaths.

113

Oh, he's the hell-hound, all right. The porter at the Janus gates. All that. But he is also real. My great-uncle has just felt a real hand between his shoulder-blades, secretly shoving him. That sharp shove is worse than the late thrashing. The Master's thrashings are clumsy, soft-edged, full of grunts and whistlings through the nose. His strokes never cut. They are sort of loving, as if he really wanted to palp the cheeks with his other hand, not catch them with his cane. My great-uncle's bottom tingles, he hasn't sat down for the hour between then and now, but hey, it's only now he feels like he's about to crack. It's only as he stumbles forward with that sharp Streadnam shove that he feels like blubbering, he feels like falling to the slabs and howling.

He doesn't. He blinks away the salt blur and he sees the general situation. He pans over it, over the faces beyond the lip of the stone steps and through the fat balusters of the balustrade and mainly keeps coming back to Mr Boulter's face, separate from the others, right in the middle of the gravel, the gown billowing around it and the purple making his heart leap because it's the royal purple, it's Mr Boulter, it's the Master, it's The Master who he doesn't connect with the thrashing just yet, with the whistling nose and the grunts and the nice lead steam engine in the study with its stopper off, smelling generally of spirits or maybe floor-wax. The wind is making noises in my great-uncle's open mouth, drying it out, making his throat obvious. He closes his mouth. He tries to swallow and steps forward because Streadnam has murmured git going, Nancy homey boy, but his knees have got the wind up. Trust his bally knees to have got the wind up. What rotters they are, letting him down like this!

Now I'll let you in on a terrible fact, y'all out there. You still awake? How are the fireworks? Sizzled out in the sweet dark mother-fucker muscling softly past deaf to ma song? This fact is as follows: my great-uncle looks under the second linden where he sees his brother. His brother, OK, is also my grandfather, it's not complicated, it's logical and straightforward but the slightly older brother under the second linden tree is looking down at the ground. He's avoiding things. He's hanging his head in shame. He's blushing so badly they're giggling opposite because he can't hide his ears, it's not the 1870s or the 1970s – his ears stick out from a kind of Oswald Mosley prototype cut and he's holding his boater by his thigh because of the wind, you're allowed to do that if there's a wind up the avenue. He's feeling utterly beastly. He's wishing his little bro had gone to another school. He's being a selfish prick, is my grandfather, but you can't really blame him. Siblings don't always love each other and even if they love each other they don't always keep it up through thick and thin, and right now it's pretty thick, it's the thickest it'll ever get, and these two brothers didn't particularly love each other, not particularly, but they didn't hate each other either. There's no hate, really, in what my grandfather's feeling.

He's called Giles. His younger brother standing in Sunday-black at the top of the steps is called William. You clutching yourself in the gusts up near the gates, I don't know what your name is but you know William well, you're a mate, a pal, a buddy, a chum; you're implicated and you wish you were somewhere else, you wish this wasn't happening, you wish your mother had loved you enough to hug you each night instead of what she did do, which was peck you on the forehead and pack you off over here for most of the year. Now she's dead. You think she's dead. They sent you this letter from Calcutta. If she's not actually dead then she's pretty much the same thing as dead and it's sorrowfully regretted. Sometimes you see her at the top of the stairs to the Upper Dorms where you're not allowed to go yet. Perhaps when you're in the Lower Sixth and you're allowed to go up there you'll get to meet her at the top of the stairs and she'll peck you on the forehead but it'll be cold, it'll be frost, it'll be sorrowfully regretted and maybe she'll tuck you up in bed before the gas farts and Bates comes to get you out of the dark. Perhaps. You imagine her cold bony hands tucking you up and you'd rather not. The thing at the top of the stairs in the early hours when you've slipped out for a pluve is probably not your mother, it's probably the new boy who fell screaming dressed up as the earl's wife or perhaps it's the earl's wife or perhaps it's just the moonlight through the oval window doing something with the balusters and the cricket-bat stand. Perhaps. One day you'll slip up there keeping to the edge of the stairs where it might not creak and test it by sweeping your hand. Only, if someone collars you on the Upper Dorm landing you'll be properly for it. I mean, you can't go telling Lightfoot or someone you were testing your mother. You just can't. They'd dandle you like they did the new boy and the sheet might break, again.

My great-uncle at the top of the steps, called William, William Lionel Gainsborough Trevelyan – he's not looking at my grandfather any more. He's looking at the lip of the step in front of him. It's worn, chipped, and in all the usual places. The chips and rounded worn bits, the bits where it shines like water going over rock smoothly, these are in all the usual places, the places he hates, the places which say that this step is the top step of the main entrance to Randle College for Gentlemen and it always shall be for ever and ever amen. And it always was. The earl never existed. If he did exist it was just for a flash before the school came along, bustling up the avenue with its purple gowns and its black gowns and its blue jackets and its screams and canes and slates and bladderdash balls and wagon-loads of iron beds and horse-hair mattresses and puffing matrons and a great tureen of pig-slops, making the earl and his little golden-haired children and his white-faced wife flee for their lives across the marsh where they drowned and turned into mist. William knows this. He thought about it once on a butterfly expedition his first summer home at his summer home, at Hamilton Lodge, and he pictured it all and now he knows it was true, he knows it particularly when looking at the lip of the top step he must now go over into all those faces and the thought of going over makes his John Thomas widdle. He didn't mean it to. It widdled and it's still widdling, by itself. It's warming his breeches. He's pluving in front of the faces, in front of the school, in front of this big horrible assembly with Jefferies at the end of it who drives too fast and says obscene things under his breath and sometimes flicks your neck. It's widdling on and on and on, as if he's emptying himself completely of everything inside him but the odd thing is, and this is awfully frightfully odd – he ignores it, he pretends it's not happening, he pretends that there's nothing at all pouring silently out of his John Thomas and now anyway it's stopped. He contracts OK his dick slightly and it starts again, but only for a second. He doesn't even look down at his breeches. Streadnam's saying things to him, right up close, hissing in the ear which is still sore and he doesn't think he can go through with it, he doesn't think he can be expelled like this with Madre at the other end, probably drunk, and maybe the servants, and maybe Father. He doesn't know in what manner Father will receive the news. Father might laugh and clap his hands and say lousy bloody lot, anyway, just to spite Mother, whose cousin went to Randle and liked it and was an awful pile of Blues at Oxford. Perhaps Father will never speak to him

116

again. Perhaps Mr Boulter hasn't told Father and Mother everything. Perhaps by not telling them everything he's made it sound worse. So William my great-uncle finds himself sliding down the side of a baluster the shape of Mr Boulter right on the edge of the steps, which are like a drop of rock to the sea – once upon a time I'd have had some stockshot of Cornish cliffs here with the sea swirling around at the bottom but I'm passed all that, I've accepted my limits, you're just getting the steps with the gravel at the bottom and some upturned faces and now anyway Streadnam's swearing and grabbing the Nancy bloody homey's elbow and someone right up at the other end of the avenue cheers, which is horrible, and there are whistles and a sort of stirring and my great-uncle catches his coccyx on the sharpish base of the baluster and it hurts and a sigh comes out of him and his lower lip is off on its own, talking to itself, in and out and in and out, but there's only a groan from way down in his tummy and he really thinks he's going to be frightfully sick but most of him isn't thinking it all, it's drowning in a sludge of misery and fear and Streadnam's breath and Streadnam's grip on his elbow and a great sound echoes off the brick front of Cavendish House and it's him, it's his cry, it's the cry that came out instead of a retch and it won't stop.

I can't stand it any more. I can't stand being right there and doing nothing about it. And it's only 1913. What'll most people not be saying right now after the fireworks and the duckings in the fountain and the Auld Lang Syne crap? I couldn't stand being right there and doing nothing about it. I couldn't stand being right there amongst the Polish silver birches and doing nothing about it. I couldn't stand being right there in the tidy boulevard with the nice old-fashioned cars and doing nothing about it. I couldn't stand being right there in front of the TV news and doing nothing about it. That's what most people won't be saying, and the rest'll be saying that was a good century, we tidied things up, but we didn't go far enough. We didn't get rid of the last gypsy and the last Jew. The last queer and the last Commie. The last revisionist and the last lousy film director who can't make films any more but still does, somehow. The last Arab. The last person without a bank balance. The last everyone.

Hey, I'm sorry. My dad had a black shirt that wasn't for funerals folded neatly in his bottom drawer and once socked a Mr Weinstein. Mr

117

Oswald Mosley wrote him a letter of thanks. Mr Oswald Mosley had his heart on his sleeve and a nice grip. I've been having a dialogue with my daddy-o for fifty-plus years. He meant well but he would have operated the oven doors and he was a lousy cook. He would have operated the oven doors *perhaps*. Maybe he wouldn't have operated the oven doors but he would have done if Mr Mosley had asked him to nicely. Or not even nicely. My dad's old man was jiggered by a loan shark and the loan shark was a greengage Jew. The loan shark was a rotten apple. Rotten apple's make the healthy apples rotten, it's well known, it's not complicated, it's a fact, son. All manky, son. If he could've cleared out the rotten apples he could've cleared out the slippery sweet mush of his origins. He'd have operated the oven doors on that – making apple stew, polishing society, strengthening the core, the pips, the nice big supermarket Granny Smiths you can see y'scowling mug in, the giant Houston reds you can play tenpins with and then crunch. Perfection. If Hitler had gotten in and still lost I'd have had a very embarrassing time with my dad. The Son of the Oven-Door Operator, at your local saloon bar now. Hey, he might have shopped me, not me him, if Adolf had hung around long enough. He might have done. Blood is thicker than water but I was a freak. I was a rotten apple. I was from my mother's side. The sludge we never talked about over the Kellogg's. My great-uncle's blood flowed in my veins. I was a scug. He'd have shovelled me in, if asked nicely, my dad would've. Clang. The ultimate bloody sacrifice. Bloody fucking Abraham. Arse-hole. Oswald in the skies. Well, if I'd ever been old enough. If Hitler had gotten in for a bit and I'd grown up my true variant self. Why do I bother to go visit him? They should build an effigy of my dad and burn it. The Old Year. The Old Century. The Old Millennium.

I've gotten all worked up, look. All sweaty, all manky.

Sorry, Greg. I know you're quite fond of him. That's 'cos he's old and blameless. The toothless have no bite. Corker of a character, what? Gave sinew to your workin'-class origins, pride of place among all those public schoolers and posh compers palming themselves off as one of ve peep-hole, the wankers. They jeered at y'dad though, didn't they, them art school/film school/poly-put-the-kettle-on poseurs? You only had to say my name and they'd say who? Then you'd explain.

Then they'd look me up in the *Biographica Cinematica* and decide I was OK, I was perfect for tossing casually over the canteen table with a knowing snort, just to impress the others who hadn't a clue, but who knowingly snorted anyway because it was that sort of crew, swinging me and Ken Russell round by the ankles while they slobbered over Jarman or some other fake.

Hey, is this diverting? Am I talking to anyone out there? Can you believe I'm this wound up thinking about my great-uncle who—

Later, later.

Long before I was squeaked aht me mam's mangle, anyway.

Meanwhile: I'm going for a long shot up at the gates. I'm the other side of the gates. I'm peeping through the wrought iron but first I'm focused on the iron. It's got rust spots. There's a spiral and I'm right up close, so close I can break a blister of black paint on the tip of the flange but I won't because Jefferies is right next to me and anyway I'm a phantom. I'm the unseen guest, the unborn blob, the guy who popped out screaming in something not yet thought of on this fine smoky chilly morning back now: an air raid. Air raids hadn't been thought of. If I were to turn round and say to Jefferies the coachman, hey, schmuck, I was born in an air raid, he'd blow smoke in my face and think I was talking dirty. Yehes, so were I, he'd say. And I bin tryin' to get back in ever since. Heh heh heh.

Heh. Yeah, Jefferies is filthy-minded. He was a steam-plate operator in the GWR works at Swindon until he got some of his hand in the way. He usually holds the reins between his right claw, when he bothers. I'm not saying plenty of people don't get their hands in the way of things in 1913, because they do, it's a time full of tackles and weights and chains and grinding tools, of stamps and presses and punches, of an absence of safety helmets and asbestos gloves and shop-floor regulations beyond not spitting 'cos spit dries out and sends off plumes of tubercle germs and not swearing 'cos swearing upsets the ladies and God. I'm sounding like John Fowles in that book I nearly got the film rights to. I'm sounding like Graham Swift in that book I never even tried to get the film rights to because I was already out of decline and

119

into fall by then. Who cares? I can sound like who I like, I'm fifty-three. I'm looking through the gate. I'm changing the focus so the black blister blurs and fades – hey, iron is that insubstantial? – and the avenue turns from a golden fuzz to an avenue with dead leaves and boots on the edge and a big house at the end with steps on which, take my word for it because they're pretty small, two figures descend and a third doesn't.

The boots are boys. They lean in and watch, their hands flutter, their boaters are held, they turn towards me but mostly they don't. The weird pair of boots are yours, because you're in the wrong togs. I won't embarrass you further. But you're leaning in, you're watching, it's getting interesting, you didn't do anything –you're thinking about the arithmetic class and Mr Holloway-Purse more than you're thinking about your chum, Trevelyan. He's a chum but you call him Trevelyan. Actually, you call him Trevels. Bates calls him Margery, for some reason. Cowdrey and most of the boys in the Sixth call him The Purulent Pleb, which is rather tricky to say smoothly but they do, they've practised, they practise it in chorus after lights out to the tune of 'The Eton Boating Song', it's a frightful wheeze, it's bloody. You think this is because Trevelyan's pop is Business rather than Law or Church or Court or Land. They've got a name for you, too.

You know who's coming down the steps? It's my great-uncle and Mr Philips.

Mr Philips and Mr Holloway-Purse have a relational problem. First, Mr Holloway-Purse makes a point of spelling Mr Philips' name with two *l*s. There is a lot of opportunity to do this, because Mr Holloway-Purse is always writing notes to Mr Philips about infractions mainly and leaving them in his pigeon-hole. Mr Philips is a housemaster, his house is the smaller junior house, the tiny one tucked away behind the kitchens in what used to be the earl's mistress's cottage. OK. Ahem. Take a dive into your highball. Relax. The infractions are to do with not doing the right thing at the right time, or doing the wrong thing at the wrong time. Walking on Pod's grass is only permitted if you are not in Lower School with the exception of Sunday till midday. No one knows who made this rule, but it was in the founding fathers' rules, and Mr Holloway-Purse knows the founding fathers' rules by heart. Long before Mr Holloway-Purse came along Sunday until midday had become all weekend. Mr Holloway-Purse rapped on the Master's door one day. The Master had never once looked at the founding fathers' rules. He'd absorbed them like a loofah. There was nothing written down that said Lower School boys could walk all over the Pod's lawn all weekend, although Mr Boulter pretended to try to find it in his drawers, trying not to roll the rum bottles, because it had been like that ever since he had arrived with his downy little beard thirty years ago. Mr Philips had been seen in the company of two new boys walking across the Pod's lawn at one thirty-five on Sunday afternoon. Mr Boulter agreed with Mr Holloway-Purse that this was not what a tight ship was all about, that the Great Randle Rebellion of 1832 grew from just such small beginnings, that the greatest army in the world was not born from slipshod drill and murky buttons, that Mr Holloway-Purse, while having the highest respect for Mr Boulter's Arnoldian reputation, could not expect the Master to have his nose in every nook. Christ, I'm sounding like Dickens. What I'm trying to get over to you all is the hidden import of this action of Philips, this succouring of the boy who was lately in his little Junior House where Mr Philips was kindly but firm. Honeydew Philips, he's called – I'll come onto that, I'll come on to that.

Still Three: go see it. Honeydew Philips, posh portrait of, circa 1910. Note the wing collar, the bow-tie, the lounge suit, the waistcoat, the little snowy range of the handkerchief in the top pocket, the silk topper in his lap. Neat, huh? But irrelevant. It'll make you think he's not around any more, he's a fossil, he's a fly in amber, he's dodo dead and gone because he'd rather die than have to wear jeans. He'll have one of those ridiculous voices that clip and drawl with built-in scratches and static effects. He's a millennium old, he's pre it all except history, he's stiff and respectable, he's the drawer that sticks, he's the one the other side of the fog. He's too real for TV, too *echt* for Merchant-Ivory, he wouldn't know how to move, he'd move funny, he'd move jerky, we'd have to look away and hide our snorts as he flickered and jerked and tried to talk.

But even the eyes are funny. People in those days had funny eyes. Everyone except Mr Holloway-Purse had eyes that you don't find these days, even on centenarians. Everyone's eyes changed, on a certain day, and no one noticed.

Go look at his eyes. Fix yourself a snort of mother's ruin, on ice. Go look at his eyes and then go look in the mirror.

Sorry about the shoving, that was a complicated manœuvre with so many of you out there and lubricated in all the wrong places, especially with that jerk in the dress shaving. Anyway, see what I mean? His eyeballs are kind of rubbed up, like they've been spat on and polished. Those are pearls that were his eyes, as Gielgud might have put it if only. Maybe they cried more. Maybe for them the storms always cleared. There was a lustre to the grey light, the sun was out, their eyes were awash with rain but it was going to be a fine day. I've stared into those eyes and tried to find in them my great-uncle's face twinned and smiling gratefully up – tried to find the kindness and civility that went. I mean, that went generally from the world. I can't. I can only find the kindness and civility that didn't go. That's still around the place. It's like the amount of carbon I think it is in the atmosphere. It doesn't change. Surely it doesn't change. The cornea doesn't change, bar accident or disease. The cornea doesn't change like skin, like the rest of the body, it sticks it out right through until whatever. Bet you didn't know that, fur-eyes. Did you see it in the mirror? The kindness and civility? No? Say, what a shame. It must have got lost somewhere. Mr Holloway-Purse has been up to his old tricks. He's stolen your marbles. He's playing dead-man's tap with your pearls.

There's something else about those eyes that's different – and none of you noticed, huh?

They're different from each other, even in silver-tinted monochrome. The guy has eyes of different shades, of a different hue. I've done my research. His nephew gave it to me down the Transatlantic Cable or however it works now. His nephew is ancient, he has throat cancer, he was kinda hoarse and the computer had problems unscribbling his digitals or something. But I got the gist. Right eye blue, left eye green. Between Mr Philips and us there's someone signalling he's really interested in this fact about the eyes. It's Dr Mengele. He's got a scalpel and a little knife. I tell him Mr Philips is not a gypsy and he's only half-Jewish. That's sufficient, says Dr Mengele. In the interests of medical science. How do I explain this guy to Mr Philips? How do I explain anything to Mr Philips? No wonder our eyes have changed. Kinda shrivelled up and dusty. They've looked at Dr Mengele. And they've turned away. I've thought about this. I think about this a great deal, out in Houston, hearing the cries of despair on the fairway, hearing the whine of the trolleys, hearing the cheers. I think mainly about the Romany girl, the Romany girl with eyes of a different hue in Birkenau. There should be a ballad about her. Eyes of grey and blue, like a sun bar crossing the sea and so forth, Arlo Guthrie or someone. But there isn't a ballad about her. The door slid shut. It slid shut on her and they held her down and Dr Mengele padded up to the Romany girl with eyes of a different hue in Birkenau. That's our century, for Christ's sake. It's not prehistory, it's not the time of the dinosaurs or the Crusades or the invention of the steam-press. I was alive, I was up and walking, I was arsing about with my mother's pinny as Dr Mengele padded up to her. The Romany girl, I mean. Whoever she was.

Hey, wake up. How do I talk to Mr Philips, Samaritan Man, about kindness and civility and oyster-coloured light after storms with that guy stood between us, waving his little cut-throat?

How do we talk to anyone after that?

Really, I'm serious.

You know what happened to Mr Philips? He was spinally damaged by
bloody Streadnam and whirled away by that creep Jefferies. His green
and blue eyes looked out on Passchendaele. And I'm worrying about
talking to him? Yes. I'm worrying about talking to him as he used to be,
before his eyes changed. Because looking at him, in his photos,
afterwards, when he came back, you could see they were really
changed. He lived until 1955. He knew it all. The guy with the scalpel,
the lot. I'm not interested in Acting-Major Philips with the glass eye.
(The green one, if you want to know. He lost the green one. OK, so
they were *really* really changed, but give me a poetic break.) I'm
interested in the guy in the wing collar, in the fossil who ain't, in the
one talking through all the scratches and dust and jerking about.
Because he's the guy who held my great-uncle's arm and helped him
down the steps and spat in Holloway-Purse's eye, an eye worth spitting
into, metaphorically speaking.

Yeah, yeah, the glass eye was blue. He wasn't fussy. Maybe he thought
it was an improvement. Why d'you have to be so blahdy lichrel, guv?

Look: Mr Philips and my great-uncle William are two black dabs on
the grey steps, descending. The dab at the top is Streadnam. The swirl
of purple and orange is Boulter. The black smudge to the left is beaks,
three rows of them. I've got fog on my lens, or maybe it's Jefferies'
thumbprint. Jefferies'd be that sort, the sort you see in war zones
advancing on the picture, waving his thumbs, blocking it out.
Remember Europe in, say, '92? That little shemozzle in Bosnia-
Hurtstocoughinher? No? Well, take it from me, there were lotsa
Jefferies in Bosnia-Hurtstocoughinher, pissed on grandma's plum
brandy. If Jefferies could see me now, he'd thumb my eye and bottle it.

Hey, it's the smoke from his fag, drifting across the gates, blown from
the side of his mouth.

That's disrespect.

Y'know, if there's one thing I can't stand, it's the fucking disrespect. If
there's one thing worse than kicking an old lady you've just shot dead,

it's kicking an old lady you've just shot dead with a fag hanging aht the side of y'mahf. We've all seen it, in those glossy albums of twentieth-century delights. You know what I mean. The barbarians are coming to town with Marlboros hanging aht the side of veir mahves. And some of them talk public-school posh, don't get me wrong, don't get me hung up, Greg. Marlboro, Marlborough, Judge Goddard went to Marlborough. Forgotten goodly Goddard, Greg? The year you were yanked out of Deirdre's nether regions by that pissed midwife because you couldn't wait, 1962, your old dad outside the Old Bailey, yelling *Judge Goddard's a public school sadist*, 'cos he'd just condemned poor simple muddled David Bentley (*Give it to him, Chris*) to the twist. Don't think I didn't do my bit. Don't think Mr Holloway-Purse (Eton, Life Guards) died out on the Hun wire or under *Cunty Lives* in the Carlton. Oh no. Give me a break, son.

And he calls me a pig!

Yarroo!

Jefferies is stamping out his fag in the chalk dust of the road. He's got gloves on, if Sylvia wasn't on continuity it might have been a thumbprint, well done Sylvia. Tarmacadam'll be laid up here in '62, coincidentally. Tyres'll thrum smoothly round their oiled hubs, Jags and Jensens thrumming smoothly through the open gates, barely feeling the bump as the tarmacadam gives out to the same old reddish grit of the school drive. Not avenue, chum – drive. What we're seeing here, this Edwardian perspective under the lindens, the two figures dabbed in front of Boulter, some intercourse we're missing out on – well, it'll all be gone by then, rubbed out, lindens succumbing to honeydew or something, felled in a week, Still Four, look, the woodsmen standing on the fallen trunks, 1953, year of splendours, the New Elizabethan Age, the fly of the avenue zipped open, the light flooding in on the woodsmen's caps, the thresh of leaves, the thud of boles, the howl and whine of progress. How splendid now the broad expanse of pasture, the house seemingly smaller in its tundra of tussocks and cows, the approach airy and petrifying, clean and new, unshadowed by sticky secretions, hints and whispers, or the cell bars of shadow and light climbing up the filmed windscreen!

I'm lifting, I'm virtually realising, I'm malquoting again from one of Henry Peterson's, the most famous poet ever to have never left Randle. It's called *The Lindens*. It's in his *Five Borrowings from the Chinese* (Amoeba Press, 1967). He was into Mao. He was a duffled duffer, a boorish bore. He once lent me a fiver. He nearly drowned in the Yangtze River, if you remember. One of the lesser losses of the Cultural Revolution, almost. He hated the lindens. He was doing a kind of lob return to *Binsey Poplars*. He reckoned the limes'd eaten into his soul. Their sticky secretions had burned his finish. I couldn't have cared one way or t'other, in those days, because Randle meant nothing to me, I was forging a future in film, I was up to my ankles in celluloid, I was burning up the Marylebone road in my Bond Equipe GT 4S Saloon and my great-uncle was a mere rumour on the sidewalk, a murmur from my mother, something about never putting his name up in the Memorial Hall, she would write to them about it, she did, she got a brush-off with a posh header on the Basildon, an embossed RC on the envelope, which I thought was the other Church, I thought she'd broken her covenant or whatever, when really she'd broken the seal on her past and let me have it. I waited. Now the trumpets soundeth and the horse doth pound up the eternal beach.

Oh yeth.

Jefferies is thinking, in his dapper little way, how he could scupper the lot with his Martini Henry, one by one, in the back, grinding his fag into the chalk with his coachman's heel. His claw comes up and scratches at his forehead just beneath the brim of his topper. He has hair on his cheeks, curved towards his big nose. The two horses chomp at the tussocks on the greensward. He leers at Mr Carlins. Mr Carlins is the man who will open the gate. Mr Carlins, thinks Jefferies, is a tuppenny prick who should've been a vicar. Mr Carlin's spectacles flash the sun as he turns his head towards the school coachman, whom he is rather afraid of. Jefferies gives a nasty little nod, which sets Mr Carlin's mouth twitching towards a smile without quite getting there. Mr Carlin is a pale man, he's anxious, he'll end up in a flooded culvert near Boisleux-au-Mont on the Vimy Ridge with the rats all over him turning to ivory under the flares while Jefferies wangles himself some poncy little job as a driver so far behind the lines the booms are like tummy-rumbles.

127

But Mr Carlin doesn't like his position at the end of it all. The boys bob in and out as they peer, golly, it's rather like the keys of a pianola, thumping a mad hatter's tune either side of the avenue, automatically, a thing he's never liked. He blushes because Jefferies is saying *whoa hoot y'fucker* to one of the horses – oh, he hopes it's to one of the horses! Mr Carlin's job is to lift the latch on the gate and push it open and hold it thus as the boy comes through. It's straightforward, it's not complicated, but goodness me he's nervous about it. Mr Carlin has been at Randle one whole year but he still feels squeaky new. He doesn't fit the boot, quite. He's in love with Hibble but that's about it. Everything else he doesn't love, doesn't love at all. He's a man who feels pain with the merest gust of a north-easter on his cheeks, with the merest scrape of his knee on the edge of his high desk, and yet it is demanded of him that he must thrash and rap and cuff and pinch. Which he doesn't do a great deal, but when he does he puts a lot into it because he must not fail, and he generally wricks his wrist. When the shrapnel finally gets him he'll enter into a night of dreams, dreams and discomfort, his spectacles flashing the flares and the shell-bursts, his right hand bobbing in the fouled water on its thread of flesh and so on and so forth – a night through which the wide lipsticked lips of each remarkable laceration will be striving to say how perfectly penitent they are, when he'd rather they wouldn't. This Mr Carlin knows nothing about, waiting under the last linden. He can't even begin to imagine a shell bursting – or a shell not bursting, for that matter. Why the hell should he? He's never even considered it. A shell is something you put your ear up to, trumpet the death of Pan on, try not to walk over at the beach when you're bare of foot and hitching up your cream flannels, goodness gracious. The loudest sound he's ever heard is a station-master's whistle once, right in his ear. *I say, my man, do you mind?* His life is leaning on the little foot-bridge and watching the boys float under, past him, on to their wide and noisy oceans of life. He likes it on the little foot-bridge. He'll get down once a year to go to Greece and Italy, pining for Hibble, having his hole filled now and again by Billy Budds and smelling fish on his fingers for days afterwards, padding back to his post on the foot-bridge until the quiet white-haired furling of his personal flag in a small cottage near Oxford, near the music and the young, punting fellows among the reeds and the nut-brown little Alices trailing their pale hands. But some fucking Serb had to blow the Archduke's brains out, and Mr Carlin got eaten by rats at twenty-five. I like this guy Carlin. Let's not beat about the bush. His depths are hidden. He said something kind to my great-uncle and fucked up the exit by getting the latch stuck, which is just great, it's just blahdy great, mate. Hey, we need these guys, these guys on the foot-bridge, chucking us crusts of Ovid, Petrarch, Theocritus – or whatever they throw down now, whatever wholemeal crumbs of something literate. There aren't many of them left. There aren't many foot-bridges. We're all in the swirl, baby, gasping for air.

Did I say 'blow his brains out'? Waal, I've always seen it like Kennedy in ma home state, that stupid student jerk the Lee Harvey Oswald of Sarajevo, blowing the Archduke's fancy brains out, getting the plumes on the cocked hat nice and sticky for the museum case, the Archduke nuzzling what remains into the Archduchess's taffeta blouse, raising a last hand up and blowing his whistle, blowing his last whistle for the crowds crouched in the trenches, waiting to pour over and get blown away with the rest, the rest of the century a tattered sleeve on a stump, the bloody consequence, the flag of conflagration, a sticky plume. Thank you, thank you.

Wipe that lady's speech of appreciation. He's coming up.

The two dabs in front of Boulter have separated. One's coming up. He's the small one. He's my great-uncle. He has half a Roman mile to walk. He's the guy at the end of Stanley's *Paths of Glory*, one of those three ordinary trench characters about to be shot for nothing. No, he isn't. He's my great-uncle. He's real. He's no one else. Forget the allusions. Forget the name-pellets. He's a dab and Jefferies isn't smoking any more. My lens is fogged. I'm choked. I can't stand it. Mr Carlin's lips are looking penitent. The boys are turned away, I can't see them – yes, one turns to see what his chum thinks of it, turns so I can see his face, and Christ I wipe my eyes and I see him grinning from ear to ear, my heart jumps, I think I could hate this kid for ever and ever, there's a squeak, Jefferies the fucker is mounting his fucking break, high up, taking the reins in his claw, looking poncy, like a fucking undertaker, like the Death in a top hat, Coachman Death, while the horses chomp and the carriage rocks and squeaks and I want to scream out, I want to open the fucking gates and run down the avenue raising the dust at my heels screaming this is what went wrong you stupid bastards or something like that and taking my great-uncle in my arms and hugging him tight and daring them, daring them to come get us.

Then walking with him slowly, held in my arms, up the linden tree avenue, in the great and awful hush, walking slowly and steadily past the faces, past Mr Carlin's amazed lips and through the gates, past Coachman Death who en't doin' nothin' about it, mate, past all hatreds and all wrongs, past all peevishness and all cowardliness, past all absence of love and life out onto the high chalk road where the sun thrills through the elms and the wind is good and we can both walk slowly and steadily towards reparation, forgiveness, humility, an uneventful year and then another, and another, and another.

But I wasn't there.

And I probably wouldn't have done.

I mean, I can hear you chuckling and snorting, you bastard bums. Dick 'Clint' Thornby, taking 'em on single-handed, shooting from the hip, ridin' outa town over the tumbleweeds into the credits, what crap. Huh? Is that what you're saying?

Friends, I wave my hands apologetically. I know myself. I would, sure – I'd have just bloody stood there, son. That's why I'm fogging up the lens. OK, OK. Dickhead Thornby confesses. I'd have been like you, you in the wrong togs, you Chum of Trevels. Flushed and shivering. Grinning back when grinned at. Saving yourself a spot of bother in the dorm. Looking to your back.

Heh?

He's coming down.

He's past the second linden.

He's past his brother.

Change reels, for Christ's sake.

130

I forgot. I forgot something vital. There's so much, I keep forgetting things. And this is really important. This reel is starting with an apology.

I apologise. But I'm not stupid.

I mean, you know how many years I'm working on this baby? Hoi? Yer fink I'm stupid or somefink? Yer fink I'd forget de cello case wiv de money in it?

I did forget. I got carried away and my great-uncle got past the second linden'n his brother with the eyes screwed shut before I could stop him. But I could have corrected myself. I didn't. Instead of splicing in what I forgot I'm telling you I forgot. This thing is revolutionary. Even Godard never apologised. I'm showing you my workings. I'm showing you that there's this key scene and I forgot it. But I'm not stupid. This is what happens. But no film I've ever seen shows you what happens. Not in this way. The mind has holes and you fall into them screaming. You know what my second wife wrote in her suicide note? She wrote that thing from Hopkins, I know it by heart and wish I didn't, I'm clearing my throat, here it is:

> O the mind, mind has mountains; cliffs of fall
> Frightful, sheer, no-man-fathomed. Hold them cheap
> May who ne'er hung there.

Except she didn't quite write that. It bothered me. There was something wrong. I checked it up in my *Norton* an hour before the funeral. Louisa'd got it wrong. She wrote 'O the mind has mountains' instead of 'O the mind, mind has mountains'. There's no comparison. She screwed it up. The most vital note of her life and she muffed it. You can't meddle with Gerard Manley Hopkins. Louisa was like that. She didn't choose a high enough window, either. I don't want to be

132

talking about this but I am. 'O the mind has mountains' goes round my head every day to the tune of *As Time Goes By*. Can you imagine what that's like? Perhaps she knew what she was doing. Perhaps she did it deliberately. Perhaps she wanted to torture me. Perhaps she wanted to torture herself by jumping from a window that didn't break her neck soon enough, and perhaps she wanted to torture me by getting my favourite licherary quotation wrong. One of my favourite licherary quotations. My other one is 'Take a little time – count five-and-twenty, Tattycoram'. (Dickens, dumbos.) I say this to myself every day, every time I want to rip the hide off of some jerk who's getting up my nose. You don't know what Houston students are like. They come from all over but they're made in Taiwan. They come from anyplace that breeds dildos who want to study *Cocoon, The Return* until they burst. They come from anyplace that breeds deadheads who think Andrei Tarkovsky's about as interesting as moving grass. Moving grass is interesting, I say to them. I say Andrei Tarkovsky had a thing about moving grass and leaves in a wind and water rippling with stuff under it. I say to them he's the only guy in the world who ever made moving grass interesting and why is that? They don't know. They don't care. They nod because Bruce Springsteen's on their Walkmans and if they don't nod it's because they've just scored in the toilet and they're numb or if they haven't just scored they've seen Jesus behind me and He's kinda sore about my swearing.

I've swerved. Excuse me. I want to do this scene with Big Cunt and my great-uncle before my great-uncle starts his little trip down the boulevard. Hoi hoi, git yer act togever, guv. Move up close, gerronwivyer, number one cameraaaa.

Play it, Sam.

Ahem. When my great-uncle was stood in front of Big Cunt, something weird occurred. That big burning bush of beard wiggled and the little hole in it opened. It spoke. It said, I have said what I have to say, Trevelyan. But there is one more thing to be said. Or rather, done.

Hands, just hands. Boulter's hands. They have hair on them. Boulter is a hairy man. He has orange hair in places you etc. There are tufts

133

between every joint of each of his fingers. He is like an orang-utan. It's amazing that I can find no record of his ever having been likened to an orang-utan. Perhaps it's because his arms were stubby. These hairy hands poking out of these studded cuffs have a piece of paper between them. This piece of paper has a watercolour painted on it. It might be a person, maybe two, it's not clear. There are limbs, peachy limbs, a huge shock of blue, a really nice deep cerulean blue the colour of the Mediterranean or the Aegean or someplace. It might be a peacock! (I checked up cerulean with my son Greg, long-distance. He does beautiful gouache still lives of jugs and curtains. [I've left that. I wrote this before he got into carpets recently. I've left that because it's poignant and he might be watching this. Greg, they were really beautiful. Really, they were. Grandma in the back says so, too.] Cerulean or midnight or peacock or azure, Dad, he said. In films, I said, we call it Bardot's Bust. Why? It's complicated, Greg. It's folded up in the unwashed seams of film history. It's something to do with her getting chilled one time in a skin shot. My lighting guy called it Siberian Dick. He worked down at Ealing Studios for years. They loved blues. Talking of *The Ladykillers* [hey, I did, a few moments ago, it's scrolled up and gone forever, it was a discreet reference for the buffs, for Ossy, for the guy in the bobble-hat talking to himself at the back, for all you dumbos who haven't even heard of Miss Wilberforce and the trapped cello case] – you watch it sometime, Greg. King's Cross at night. That's cerulean, all right. Righty-ho, Dad. He sighs and the transatlantic cable brings his sigh to me like surf. I will, Dad, I will. The fact is, he hates anything not by Japes Jarman or Fake Greenaway, for God's sake. He's a purist. He thinks painters can make films better than anyone. I say painters cannot. I say painters make terrible film makers. I'm not going into this here.)

Now, if I was a half-naff director I would include a half-naff shot of this watercolour between a pair of thumbs belonging to the hairy guy playing Second Groundsman because the guy playing Boulter's gone off filming the next Bond in Madagascar and hold it for five seconds or something, but I'm not half-naff or e'en a quarter-naff, am I? Am I, yer bastards? Do I hear a cheer? Hey, thanks. Drink more of my drinks, eat my nosh, watch my lips. I'm not naff. I have never been naff. OK, once. Once I was so naff it got it out of my system. Ossy knows about it. He was A Danish Berk. Everyone makes mistakes. Listen, I'm not even pastiche naff. I'm a brutalist. So you hip-hoppers're just getting a tweekiest glimpse of it as it's held up in front of my great-uncle. From the other end of the avenue all *you* can see, Chum of Trevels, is a flash of white. Hey, Mr Boulter might be holding a dove for all you know. Then the hands part from each other, one up, one down, and there are two doves, or the dove has been ripped apart, and you guess what the dove is. The dove is a painting. Your face above the rugby shirt spasms, because it might be your face that's getting ripped apart, and the spasm goes all the way down through your chest and right between your testicles where it stings and you let out a grunt which Cowdrey somehow catches opposite and his grin is infectious, everyone's glancing at you with terrible grins that are leers really, it's really beastly, you don't know where to look through the heat of your face so you study 'the infinite precision of the lime tree's bark' (Henry Peterson, *The Avenue*, 1965) and you let your face burn up and float away in little embers but it doesn't, it's asbestos. Asbestos? It's me who's thinking that, you're not, you're not because asbestos belongs with the new science laboratories and the new pottery classes and the new Panasonics in the studies and we've half a century to go yet. But I'm thinking it's like asbestos. It's like a fire made of fake coals. It keeps on burning but it doesn't burn up. And you know what you're thinking it's like? You're thinking it's like the eternal lingering fires of Hell. Because I'm afraid you believe in Hell, deep down. You believe in Heaven and Purgatory and Hell and phantoms and elves and that your mama isn't really dead and that if you fiddle with yourself you will lose your sight. You also believe that somehow this painting that's being torn up way over there by Boulter is your own graven image and that it's tearing your hope for salvation up. You see the doves becoming feathers, the feathers are scattering about but you're not, you're tearing and burning but you're staying whole, you're a great lump under the linden tree that Cowdrey and the other beasts are leering at and snorting at. You're a great naked lump of boyhood in the wrong togs and you want your mother to take you away but she's sorrowfully regretted. You're burning but the wind is getting up into your testicles, they're shrivelling into themselves, you know that tonight something awful will be done to you after the gas pops out because it has to be done to you after all this tearing and burning and shame. The horrible beasts will probably strip you so that you look exactly as you looked like in the painting except without the wings. They will probably throw shoes at you and flick you with ties. They will probably do the really terrible things they used to do in the old days and which Cowdrey wants to do again and which resulted in death or maiming, sometimes. One thing you really don't want to be is a ghost stuck haunting Randle with his screams and whimpers and maybe a soft whistle. You think of this time tonight coming towards you like a great black ship and you want to yelp but of course you don't, you stare at the infinite precision of the lime tree's bark over which some kind of little winged insect's crawling and you wish you really were that insect, you really do. No, you wish suddenly you were a deer loping deeply out of sight in the deep forest that must be somewhere near, though actually it isn't. You haven't realised yet that England is denuded. You haven't realised yet that England is not medieval England. You haven't realised yet that the great secret about England is that THERE ARE NO DEEP FORESTS WITH KNIGHTS AND DAMSELS TRIPPING THROUGH THEM. There are no deep forests *without* knights and damsels tripping through them, for that matter. Not to speak of, anyway. Not the kind you're thinking of that a knight can get lost in for a week – not the perilous, wolvish, witchy kind with green men and goblins and stuff. Why you love Trevels is that between the water-pipes of the bathroom after lights out, after the pummellings, after Bates has done with you, after the little secret squeaks of bed-springs, after even the prefects have retired from their cigarettes and porter and their unimaginable chat around the smoking coals, Trevels's whispers scroll up an England chock-full of deep forests and tripping knights, of lily-white ladies and murky towers rising out of murkier mere and mist, of all that Tennysonian crap you're really into and that you're really inside between the gurgles and growls of the cistern's pipes cooling after another day's bash. This is why you love Trevels. Trevels leaving like this is a psychological catastrophe for you – though you don't put it like this, you just feel it in your head and your chest and your testicles. You'll sit alone between the water-pipes and try not to think of your mother. You'll think of ladies in medieval gear and you'll realise your cock's going up. You'll think of ladies taking off their medieval gear and your cock'll go up some more. You'll crouch alone in the dark corner of the enormous bathroom and imagine this medieval lady looking like those nymphs in that painting in that book in the school library and you'll screw your eyes up tight and start fumbling down under and you'll try not to think of your mother and try

136

not to think of Hell and try not to think of losing your sight and try not to think of Hylas getting dragged down under the lily-pads by those lily-white naked nymphs prettier than any lady you have ever seen and you'll feel your mouth fill up with saliva and realise that it is going to happen – little golden stars of pleasure are bursting all around you and you don't care if you get dragged under by the medieval lady prettier than any lady you've ever seen and you don't care if the nymphs in the background tear you up into little burst stars of pleasure because this is so frightfully pleasant and her flesh is of the purest white and upon her breasts are two little roses you are pressing with your hands as the water enters your mouth and you lose your sight in the utterly stupendous unleashing of all the slippery pleasures you could ever have imagined but never did over your fingers and even up onto one of the hot water pipes, oh golly gosh.

And afterwards, you'll feel terrible. But that's not my problem. You're not my problem. I've got the Great War coming up. We're talking epic here, son. The Great War'll burst out and you'll still be crouched there in the midnight blue corner summoning yourself from the nymph-pond, smelling of the deeps, water-weed in your hair, until you're caught at it one night by Cowdrey in 1915, Cowdrey the prefect, Cowdrey who'll exact a most beastly retribution the details of which you'll just have to wait for because you're not my problem, I've got the Great War coming up, I've got my relations to think about, this is all taking so much longer than I imagined. I mean, he hasn't even got to the first bloody linden yet.

Move up close. Look at the little shreds of paper fluttering down at my great-uncle's feet or blown about around Boulter's head. One gets stuck in his beard. It's flesh-coloured, peachy-pink, it might be a bit of a buttock. Anyway, it gets stuck in his beard and my great-uncle, through his dizziness, thinks of Mr Lear's limerick about the fellow with the big beard and the bird's nest in it and he wants to giggle. Isn't that incredible? INCREDIBLE BUT TRUE! AMAZING TALES #39!

Hey, that's the scene. That's the scene wrapped up, just about. There's Mr Philips standing to the left of my great-uncle and there's the shreds of paper on the gravel and there's one in Big Cunt's

137

whiskers and there's another thinner one on my great-uncle's
shoulder, as if the black cloth's been torn (did I mention my great-
uncle is in Sunday black, with a dinky black Sunday cap on his head?)
and there we go. That's it. That's what I forgot. Amazing, innit?

I hope you had time to powder your noses before the second reel. I
wouldn't want you to have missed that scene.

I hope your glasses are full and tinkling and the nuts are roasted. I hope
you're not feeling short-changed. England always short-changes me,
as a matter of fact. I say this to our local barman out of *Terminator 2*
back in Houston and because he's English he beats me up. He never
short-changes me. He always gives me a double, as in nelson, bom
bom. I might tell you about him sometime. He's probably Holloway-
Purse's illegitimate son's grandson or something. He has the same
eyes. They're quite common, these days.

He's moving up. My great-uncle. He's, ahem, *running the gauntlet*.
Prissy phrase, huh? Someone got gantlope and gauntlet mixed up
around the time Shakespeare was making a buck and putting it into
property and it stuck. Gantlope means 'course', of course. Running
the course. I like to check things up. I went to Magdalene with an e, I
did Danish and then English and made films with rivers and nitwits in
them and there was always a fucking punt coming in at the back with a
deadhead in a boater screwing the scene up and they didn't have punts
like that in Arthurian Britain. In Randle they call it (I mean, they did
then) passing the pricks. That's because they poke you when it's done
in the dorms because there they do it like it should be done. They
throw boots, too. They hiss as they throw the boots or prick you. It's a
long dormitory, it's always a long dormitory. The posh version is called
walking the *cestus*. Roman boxing-gloves or something. Oxhide and
nice metal strips over the knuckles. I mean, they're *Roman*, baby. They
don't say it's time for a box at Randle they say it's time for a *caedere*. Or
they say today, chaps, it's *cesti* off, it's up with the knuckles as our
fathers did it, and our grandfathers. The place runs with Latin blood.
Sanguinary faces of boys (Henry Peterson, *Remembering Them*, 1967).
Our boys. Lads. Our lovely lads. I'm talking about then. Now – I mean
these days – it's soft as Dunlopillo. There's no boxing, no *caedere*,

there's only one guy doing Latin and he's effeminate. But out on the rugby field they're still breaking their backs and getting their mouths extended several inches. There's still the playing fields. All is not lost. I tell this to our barman back in Houston but he thinks I'm being snotty. That's his word. Snotty. Or rather, sno'y. Sno'y, don't be sno'y, Tricky Dick. I say to him, there's a t in it, Jason. Two ts, as a matter of fact. Queen's English. He socks me one. Queensberry Rules, Jason, I say, spitting out my priceless plate, insured against fire and theft but not socks. *Lapsus caedere*, no doubt, Jason. *Cedant arma togae*. Good old Jason.

How did I get onto *him*, for Christ's sake?

Trevelyan is walking the *cestus*, Trevelyan is passing the pricks, Trevelyan is going out the way he came in, feeling his legs turn to suet, or maybe it's the air, feeling a sense of heightened reality, feeling horrible and sick, feeling this isn't reality at all, feeling that maybe he's in the wrong century and underneath he's wearing chain-mail, thigh-pieces, gauntlets, holding his helm, embarking to fight alongside the Lionheart, and then he sees his brother. Under the second linden. His brother with the head down and eyes screwed tight shut. Oh, Giles, this is horrible, horrible! Perhaps that's what he thought.

I didn't do a close-up of him watching Mr Boulter tear up *The Lament for Icarus*. I only did the hands and the feet with the bits of paper floating down. It doesn't matter. He wasn't watching. He was fogged up with tears. It was like opening your eyes in the pool. I'm talking about the pool in the wood near Hamilton Lodge. We'll come on to that. It's a very important pool. I'm certainly not talking about a fucking swimming-pool. I'll come on to Hamilton Lodge, too. My grandfather lived there. Along with my great-uncle and great-aunt. And grandmother. They lived there in the summer. They were a two-home, two-carriage, two-car family. If Robert Bresson was directing this he'd tell the guy playing William my great-uncle to think about what he'd had for breakfast. Bresson hates acting. He's about 105 or something but he's the greatest. I hate acting, too. I love actors but I hate acting. Maybe Bresson would've done the squeezed onion treatment, but that's about it. So here's a close-up of my great-uncle with wet eyes and looking like he's considering what he had for breakfast just after the shot of his best watercolour getting ripped to pieces.

OK?

Hey, I thought I'd finished with this scene. I don't want to go back to that. He was my great-uncle. His blood flows in my veins. It's complicated. Blow, bugles, blow, set the wild echoes flying! That was Louisa's favourite poem. Or rather, song. She knew it as a song, the Britten thing, we had a Decca recording *circa* 1956 with a scratch and she'd play it over and over, despite the scratch, she'd kick the gramophone to get it over the scratch, she didn't seem to mind, she was crazy right from the start, she was a great actress, she was wasted.

> Blow, bugles, blow, set the wild ech-ech-ech ing,
> And answer, echoes, answer, dying, dying, dying.

I brought her a new one, a glistening pitch-black new one without so much as a thumb-print. It took a lot of research to track it down. She dumped it. Actually, she lifted it up in both hands and broke it against the banister. She was always a nutter, OK?

O-o-o the mind has mou-ountains. All that. Scratches, too.

Back on the gravel in 1913 the bits of paper are getting blown over and up, twirling and fluttering, cerulean blue and peachy pink and snowy white and even olivey green – just a swatch of green here and there. The cerulean ones seem to be particularly active. They're going higher than the others, they're getting caught in eddies of wind, they're going up and up and like little blue butterflies against the boring sky. Can a sky be boring? This one is. It was interesting when this thing started but the wind's brought a thick blank of stratocumulus opacus, blotting-paper stuff, really boring English stuff – it sucks up all the coloured inks out of the scene except these cerulean butterflies and it reminds Hibble standing there beneath them of the field in Tuscany and of his lady's mouth and the jolly queer warmth of it and of her spittle and him having not the faintest what to do with so much spittle and it was just possible he was kissing her in the wrong manner because when he lifted his face it was all over Frenella's cheeks, it was frightful, it was glistening all over her cheeks as if they'd been eating

140

large juicy apples and this thought, as he looks up at the little blue butterflies, makes him blush and he blinks and his Renaissance-style eyebrows quiver and he looks down at his shoes. And if we can just for a moment sidle onto the echoing parade-grounds of Holloway-Purse's mind we'll find it even more interesting, my my we will, because somewhere in there is the flicker of a memory of a picnic, and this memory has to do with deep blue ribbons against a creamy silk dress, and his pater swiping at wasps, and his sister sobbing frightfully, and the governess with the blue ribbons holding Pater's hand at one rather queer point. I look at that flicker and I don't really want to because it makes me feel sorry for Holloway-Purse. I'm feeling sorry for the bastard because that was the first picnic without dear Mater and little HP's world was swirling about with dark mists instead of sunshine but he wouldn't show it, he wouldn't, not like sissy Sis. I could make a movie about HP. I could get really caught up in the guy. He thought of this gauntlet idea so I suppose I ought to get caught up in him but I haven't the time. What I find really interesting about him is that when the war comes along he's not a cad or a coward but a fearless fellow, a fine officer, an exceptionally devoted leader of men. I'm quoting from the citation that was typed out to try to get him off the hook. Because he cracked. He was fine and fearless and devoted and then he cracked. He strangled this old lady. I'm serious. In church. Hey, in a ruined church. This old lady was bringing flowers into this shelled-out church and this English officer just started screaming at her and she spat in his face or something and he strangled her until she was dead. And that was it. That's how this creep ended up. My analyst would say it was to do with his mater, it was to do with things like that picnic and not breaking into sobs for years and years but I dunno, guv. I dunno. And you know what? HP got off the hook. He went back home and it was hush-hush for the rest of his long life at Randle. Yup, at Randle. Because he got Boulter's job. Big Cunt became Bigger Cunt. I want to advertise this thing I know about HP but no one would be interested in the way I want them to be interested. I'd be waving this fact around and people'd be talking about how interesting history is as if it was some kind of college course when I'm waving this thing about and screaming my head off like I think there's justice in the world. I mean, I wrote about this to Randle College in '94 and didn't even get an embossed Basildon Bond *aka* The Master's Secretary reply. One of your headmasters was a murderer, I wrote. I didn't even mention the word sadist. I just gave them the facts about this little old French lady choking between the broken pews with HP's hands around her neck back in 1917 with some photocopies of my research on the subject and they didn't even reply. They probably thought I was a hate-mail freak. They probably didn't even know his name, they probably had to look it up, because they're into coeducational opportunities and business studies and close links with Saudi Arabia and classes in fucking Chinese or something and those old guys are prehistoric. (Hey, I've read the brochure. They sent me the brochure. There was a fucking swimming-pool on the cover, a heated fucking swimming-pool. They do summer courses in everything but sex, which is up to you. I could go there any summer I fancy and do Film Making for Beginners and Judo for Beginners and Tai-Chi-Chow-Chin for Beginners and get my rocks off with some lonely lovely widow gasping for comfort and understanding between the five-course meals in the lovely gentle surroundings of the Hampshire countryside, ideal for excursions on foot and laying skirt. I could. I could'n all. If they'd let me. I'd say my great-uncle and my grandfather were here. The lonely widow would rise up on one elbow and some of the exceptionally attractive Hampshire countryside would be imprinted on her breasts so deeply Pottery for Intermediates might take moulds off them. Were they really, Richard? They were, my lovely. And were you? Was I what? I mean, Richard, are you an Old Boy? I am an old boy. I'm slowly approaching fifty-five. I only look like I do because I have beautycare treatment. It's one of my perks. It comes with the job. Oh darling, she says, twisting round idly to brush some of the remarkable flora of Hampshire off her naked buttocks and loosening her hardly-greying hair with its highlights of gouache and charcoal from Landscape Sketching for the Advanced, you're so terribly droll. Over the summery air comes the fitful clapping from the cricket pitch where the Under-Fifty-fives are getting trashed. Droll, but not too droll, I say, with a knowing flicker of a leer. She sighs an eloquent, under forty-fiveish sigh and a bee sips at the nectar of the buttercup I've just placed on the downy knuckle of her coccyx. The bee's coaxed off and my mouth takes its place. She giggles. I mumble something about liking butter more than marge. She sighs again. We have a quarter of an hour, she murmurs, before my Indian Dance for All Levels. I'm getting behind with my kissing, I joke. And swallow the buttercup. She has to slap my back. Buttercups are poisonous, she says. Cows avoid them. My mouth fills with acrid bile. She cradles me. I'm dying of England, I say. She laughs and I notice her gold tooth. That does it. A deer nuzzles us. Out of the deep deep forest. We hump away as a mounted posse passes so close we can hear the clink of their bugles against their cuisses. A toad apologises but could we help him, he needs to be kissed, he was a prince once in a John Boorman extravaganza, he'd rehearsed for days, they said he wasn't needed, he's weeping, I tell him that's movies for ya, go find Fergie, get stuffed. We grind away through all this, somehow, even through the flitter-flatter over our heads, the thunks and screams of collateral damage from Archery for the Under-Fives. No peace, I gasp, no peace anywhere. I don't care. We set the echoes flying. She's incredible. She was a ballerina, a mime, a black belt in yoga. She's left the Kama Sutra way behind, she's challenging Venus, she does things only water ought to do. Hey, she is water, she turns to water under my rocks, she fills my mouth, there's a stink of the underside of lily-pads, I'm drowning, my feet touch bottom, it's slippery, they cloud things up, I blink it clearer, there's a guy down here, he's draped with the loveliest nymphs I've ever encountered, with Alma-Tadema breasts and Burne-Jones tummy-buttons and Herbert J. Draper bums the minnows seem to like. Hi, he says. I'm Hylas. Join the party.)

Don't y'all rush out at once, d'ya hear? You've got plenty of time, plenty. Randle Summer School, Randle College, nr. Basingstoke, Hants.

Seriously, I have the dirt. On file.

Pssst! I have the dirt on Mr Winthrop Holloway-Purse. I can break him. I can knock on his door and I can enter and I can say what I know and watch his cropped skull flicker as the skin tightens and he covers his face in his hands. I can watch him lift his head with an evil smirk and cry, Do your worst! I was a fine fearless fellow, a devoted leader of men! At any rate, I was provoked. It was wartime. I had just led my men against a redoubt bristling with Hun and won it for several minutes at the cost of only a hundred and one of our boys. She was probably a plant. What species? I reply, certain that these are the last whimperings of a broken man. Get out, scug, he snarls. Certainly, Master, I say. He settles back in his leathery seat and plays with the detention lists

143

fanned before him, only his twitching cheek betraying the smug calm that lies upon him like a miasma. At the inner door like an upended snooker table I turn. Oh, by the way, Master. What is it? he spits, barely bothering to look up. The telephone number of the *Sun* newspaper – do you happen to know it, by any chance? I absently pick at the door's baize. His face breaks through the miasma like a Raymond Chandler novel. There is no doubting his emotion. You wouldn't, he murmurs, you wouldn't. He's stricken and fearful and the hated governess's hand is slipping into his pater's. What do you think, Master? I reply, remembering my mother's dictum that it never does to be impolite, even to a tradesman, even to my dad, even at this juncture. There is a pause. You would, he murmurs, you would. I remain blank-faced, thinking about what I had for breakfast. He sinks back into his chair, as old as he feels. Detention lists waft down to the parquet marked by the nails of those he has thrashed. He would, he murmurs, he would. His face sags and then crumples into age, and more age, until time has swallowed him up in a slurp of wrinkles and rheuminess and falling hair, and it's an Edgar Allan Poe short, for there's nothing except this little pile of dust on the seat that needs to be hoovered up in the morning by Stella, who'll tut about it.

I close the door on him, softly, because it never does to disturb the dead. The little pile of dust might blow all over the carpet. Stella'd be furious. She knew Roy Orbison. She told me this. *Hey pretty woman, walking down the street.* That's right, she laughed, gaily, holding the extension for the hoover. This means I did go to Randle. I did, I did. Early in the morning. Mist, summery morning mist, mist curling around the rugby posts and caressing the all-weather hockey pitch and nudging a linden tree stump in the right place. It was the only one. They must have pulled the others out, like teeth. This one must have beaten them. I sat on it. It had *Fuck Off, Riley*, cut into the top. Note the comma. Public school edication, that. On the side some lonely kid years ago had carved his initials carefully, it was a work of calligraphy, it was real carving. Someone else had sliced *R.I.P.* above it. I took out my Swiss penknife and scraped the *R.I.P.* away. I felt like crying. Seriously, I did. The place was so huge and flat and lonely and lovely, I wanted to cry. I imagined this lonely kid coming back with his kids and showing them his initials and chuckling manfully at the *R.I.P.* though really it was like a stab in the stomach, it practically killed him, it brought it all back, it opened the welts up, the smells, the hatreds. I got more obsessed with this kid than with my great-uncle. I couldn't imagine my great-uncle walking down this long open drive with its smooth tarmac and clipped edges and a sign halfway up that said *Welcome to Randle College* like it was a business park or something. Without the lindens, it was hopeless. I wished I hadn't come, of course. It spoilt things. It snarled my projector. I got up and walked up the drive towards the big red house, Cavendish House, with cars nuzzling its hard bosom like they were feeding off it, pigs or rats suckling the mother pig or rat, and wishing I wasn't walking towards it. I felt like a new boy. I was really frightened to meet a prefect or something, or a beak, or Mr Boulter who was dead and buried and buried and dead and then I met Stella on the steps, in light blue overalls. She was doing the cobwebs, she said. So am I, I replied. She giggled. We liked each other. You know how it is. Her little girl was with her. I made her little girl laugh on the steps. I can't remember how Roy Orbison came up. I was making faces. It must have been the tension. Behind Stella and her little laughing kid was the whole school waiting like Grendel's mother or something to get going. I said there are magic mushrooms in the grounds. I swept my hand. She giggled and then tutted. Are you an Old Boy? she said. Do I look like an Old Boy? I replied. You never can tell, these days, she said. Stella, your eyes were stars and your skin honey. Hoover Holloway-Purse up. Tut tut tut.

Phantoms, phantoms.

The linden trees shoot upright. There's dark and light. There's blown leaves, leaves falling down, there's an avenue and instead of the science block there's tussocks and cows and instead of Stella there's Streadnam because he's still up there, the ponce. Instead of me there's my great-uncle. My great-uncle's turning round. He's just a kid. He can't make it. He's in shock, suddenly. Gauntlet, gantlope, gantlope, gauntlet. Gantlope's the ugliest word in the English language. Running the gantlope is right. He looks back from the third linden and he sees this guy sticking his head out from the gaggle of servants, looking at him down the avenue. He's got a rake. All these faces either side of him and all he sees is this servant's face with the rake stuck up next to it. He's too far to see the eyes. He wants the rake. He wants to hold on to the rake. He's got nothing to hold on to and his legs are

145

going. The face of the groundsman is familiar, he knows it, he's seen it behind webs of twine and through white smoke and above flowers. Let's not get sentimental about this: he wouldn't invite this groundsman to tea, not in a month of Sundays. This groundsman has perpetually dirty boots, like Alf. Alf is my great-uncle's parents' gardener. They've got another one at Hamilton Lodge. He's called Jeremiah and is a little queer, but frightfully good with shrubbery. My great-uncle wants the rake. It's the only thing he can see that resembles a staff. God is my staff. Thou art my staff and my salvation. The rake's far away, like God. My great-uncle holds the air like a pair of banisters. The banisters split apart and the staircase falls, plunges, he hits the ground, his knees roll away, he's got a leaf stuck to his forehead, he wonders where he is for a moment. There's a kind of little gaspy silence a jet might have fucked up if this was now, but it isn't, it's then, very much then. Nothing fucks it up except the crows crowing over Inkblot Copse and a thick-headed sparrow pratting about with a worm on the avenue in front of Tennison (no relation, even a misspelt one) who'd like to catch it with a pebble but he doesn't dare, not with Mr Sitfield so close Tennison can smell the dentifrice. OK, OK: Tennison will lose a knee-cap at Le Cateau and Mr Sitfield will sit it out cooking porridge in Poperinghe on account of his dicky heart and hating the taste in his mouth of gassed air and general putrefaction and all that stuff you know about. I can't tell you about every damn person that pops up. It'll get like *The Omen*, with a little dark mark above certain heads. Hey, while Mr Philips is running down the avenue towards the little black crumple of Sunday best in the middle I'll show you, I'll give you the general picture: wide-angle take, wide-angle take of the whole avenue from the big gates end, perfect perspective, roughly what Jefferies sees from up on his perch, all those heads and hands, grins and a few not grinning, quite a few actually, quite a few actually allowing something like sympathy or even grief to enter their hearts – *wham!* – loop the heads, loop in black the faces of those who aren't going to make it, about a third, about a third are going to be culled, cropped, lopped in their prime, or before their prime, their faces darting about in and out of the black loops, him, and him, and him, and that one with the big flat nose, and this one scratching his knee, and that one standing astraddle who's ace at Eton fives, and this one who's Lightfoot's fag (I'll get on to Lightfoot soon, just wait a minute) and – oh Christ, I've given it away: there's one black circle

146

hovering over the Sunday best crumpled in the middle of the avenue, but the face is down again, folded somewhere in that black cloth, the black cap two yards away, no one picking it up for him. I've let the cat out of the sack. Like my dad used to do. He'd read the last page of every Agatha Christie I brought home and tell me, the bastard. Like father, like son, hoi? This thing won't be the last page, I promise. The black loop's settled like a halo above the black crumple, Mr Philips is there, his arms are going through the loop, blurring it but not erasing it, no one can erase it, no one can scrub the fucker out and say, start again, don't die, just hide your head on that last day – I mean, the last day of the war, the last full day, the day before the Armistice, the day the black loop looped my great-uncle's throat and tightened, tightened, hard cheese, guv, someone has to cop it on the last day of any war and go on copping it after, ploughing up shells, skipping on to mines, fading away in a froth of spoiled lungs, spoiled limbs, spoiled eyes, it's only natural, son, it's only bleedin' natural.

The voice of common sense. Against which all eternity surges. I woke up with that line, a couple of years ago. Not bad, huh? I shook Zelda awake and repeated it. I plunged back instantly into sleep, as is my wont. In the morning I'd forgotten it. Zelda had remembered. I loved her. I still love her. I sit in the Rothko Chapel back in Houston and think of her at least once a month. The Rothko Chapel was her favourite place. I mean, in Houston. It's the only favourite place for anyone who's not a deadhead, in Houston. We'd sit there and try not to think too much of Rothko slitting his arms in the bath, after. Instead we'd think of eternity and color and deep, cerulean things. We'd leave a scent of sweetness in the air from Zelda's patchouli oil. It seemed appropriate. We'd always make love after in a kind of smooth and soft way, as if we'd go on having afternoons to make soft love in until God wrapped things up for the planet or the sun got too big. I'd like to make a movie like Rothko made paintings. Something eternal for the eyes, restful and glimmery and deep, something between Rothko and moving grass, grass in a steppe wind, a soft Mongolian wind, all that totally non-commercial stuff I used to despise in my lousy days. Then I'd probably slit my arms, after. I'd have no place else to go. I'd have said my bit. They'd be fighting over the print and making millions of bucks and I'd be slitting my arms just below the elbow, just above the gauntlet, like Rothko did, going out in color.

147

Sorry: colour. Reading *colour* gives me a hiccup. I've loosed the Old World, sure, off of my oxen. Fix yourselves some more drinks. Drink to Ricky Thornby, Yankee wanker, who can't spell right. Who can't talk right. Who's clinging to a little rock in mid-Atlantic, the fucking limpet. I'm drenched. Get back to Philips, nice decent Mr Philips with the different coloured eyes, one green, one blue. They're looking into my great-uncle's umber eyes and they're encouraging and earnest and kind. The mouth beneath the different coloured eyes is opening and closing. It's saying let's go, old chap, come on, old fellow, you're nearly through, you're nearly home.

Home.

There's a smell of mothballs and old cupboards and pipe tobacco and sherry and stuff from Mr Philips's sleeves. It smells of home, it smells of London, it smells of Dorothy and the big flat-iron and the kitchen and the nursery trunk. William my great-uncle is trying to be a man in front of 351 boys and about fifty men if you don't count the prefects with their rattly voices and the Captain of School who's always been a man from the moment he sprung out of his mother's womb and late tackled the doctor and Ormsby the beak with no pubic hair and a voice so high they have to grip the decanter at Common Room Dinner and all he – my great-uncle – can feel is this hunger for home, for the nursery trunk and Dorothy and the chipped kitchen range and Sparkler the dog who's actually dead. William doesn't know this but he is. Mrs Trevelyan meant to tell him but she hasn't got round to it. She put it off until she forgot. She was going to write to Giles to tell William but she didn't get round to that, either. She knows Sparkler was one of the three most important things in her younger son's life and pretty important in her elder son's, too, but Mrs Trevelyan is not a great mother. In fact, she's a really lousy mother, the kind that cripples you forever. I didn't want to get on to this just now. The fact remains that William is thinking of home as Mr Philips props him up and the gaspy silence descends into a miasma of fart-noises and giggles and jeers from higher up and the local version of a slow hand clap from the creeps in the Lower Sixth which is a clicking of fingers, slow slow, because you can do it behind your back – and home means Sparkler running up to meet him and a smell of wet leaves and Agatha vaguely in the background. Agatha's my great-aunt. She's a year older than Giles.

She has grey eyes. She's been dead an awful long time but I know she has grey eyes. She has eyes the color of driftwood baked by the sun, washed over by countless tides, baked by the sun again, scoured by winds and sand – clear clean grey grey lovely grey driftwood grey eyes that men find unnerving and secretly paint or write verses to or place carefully in novels and if they're not that sort just whimper until they nerve themselves to face her eyes again, holding out their cards like Theseus held his shield against Medusa.

Agatha is not Medusa. These classical allusions are fog. They just hold out their gentlemen's cards and cough politely, OK? I mean that's how they did things then. And it's coming back. Everyone has their card out in Houston. Everyone's hustling each other with these damn little cards and they build up above the freezer because you never know. Agatha or maybe the maid takes the card and they lift their hats and maybe they come to tea. She doesn't go on a date with them. When do you think this is? This doesn't mean that no one's getting their leg over behind the thick curtains, because they are, the human race continues, there's a lot of sex, dirty postcards, wild orgies. D. H. Lawrence is in town. The clitorises are beating away happily under the petticoats and corsets and things. I'm not obsessed. Dicky Thornby's appetite is normal. I'm just making things clear to you guys 'n gals who think no one said penis before 1963. Just because they used breadcrumbs to clean their white silk knickers doesn't mean nothing went on inside them. It did. They got hot. Sodomy and gonorrhoea. Panting under the parasols. It took half an hour to unribbon a dame and unbutton a gent. Imagine it. Now we have T-shirts. It ain't the same. I look at my students (furtively, furtively) and there are the nipples. I mean, there they are, under KEEP KINDA KOOL or GRAMSCI VOTES WOMBAT or a nice picture of a beluga surfacing in the swell. It's instant mash desire, it has no depth, no taste, no nothing. I'm old. They don't fall in love with me any more. I just kinda leer furtively, furtively. Yesterday I was young. They were queuing up. I sweated for three years before I got myself a test. I couldn't open the envelope. I couldn't believe I had not got It. I was getting through two a week. Students, I mean. I was pooped. Now I'm old. Now I'm washed up. I was talking about my great-aunt Agatha. She never got to be old. Neither did my great-uncle William. They stare at me out of their youth, off the hall wall of their home, through this ripply glass with this kind of frozen gilt ribbon between them and it needs a dust, it needs some Windolene, it needs to be buffed up. They just stare at me. They're thinking about what they had for breakfast. They don't know me. I'm holding me mum's hand. There's no recognition in their grey and umber eyes. That's spooky. That really is spooky, mate. I don't want to get onto this now. But Stella with her hoover got closer to me than they ever will. Five minutes of Stella with her hoover on the steps of Cavendish with the same worn bits and nicks my great-uncle saw, plus a few more, I suppose. Plus a few more.

OK, I'll tell you why it's spooky. It's spooky because I'm in love with my great-aunt Agatha, and kind of the same with my great-uncle William. I love them more than love can say. Am I crazy? I want to hug them. I hug them and they vanish. I love them as little kids running across the lawn and as big kids looking serious over books in the drawing-room and as woman and man teetering on the edge of death and not knowing it, not really, because the sun is in their eyes and the grass moves in the wind and they're talking gaily but deeply about life.

It breaks my heart. Nothing else in life has broken my heart like this. My analyst says I have a problem. Not in so many words, but I know what she's thinking. I don't think I have a problem. If I have, I want to keep it. I want to hug it. I want to sit in the Rothko Chapel in Houston tomorrow (I mean, the morrow of the day I'm writing this, OK? Not THE day) and hug my problem to me. I have fallen in love and grieved several times in my life. I say this to my analyst. I have plumbed the depths and soared to the heights and all that. But this is something else. This is looking for the snow leopard so far up above the snow-line there's no one else, not even a monk, not even an Australian in sneakers. This is finding the tracks of what might be a snow leopard and seeing snow puff out and slip from a high ridge as something that might have been a snow leopard skids away out of sight. This is never actually seeing the snow leopard, like in that great book. You mean Matthiessen? my analyst grunts, noting it. Probably, I say. Does it matter? It might, she murmurs, it might. Sucks.

Mr Philips is doing a great job. I'm yakking away and he's doing a great job. He's a doer. He's a great man. He has the boy's elbow cupped in his palm and his other hand is on the shoulder. They're moving slowly up, between the ranks, between the faces, between the linden trees. I'm going for a long shot, from right the other side of the meadow with its jewelled tussocks and morning wisps of smoke or maybe mist or maybe the phantoms are crouched down to watch. Mr Philips and my great-uncle appear and then disappear between the boys and between the trees. It's like a peep-show. It's like the first movies. It's like the thick cards flapping past the slit and hey, it makes that idiot move, it makes the dame lift her leg, it makes them hug each other and kiss and you giggle on the pier in your petticoats, your turn-up flannels – and you all have a red mark on your nose, you've been looking so long.

The mist's thickening. Either that or the phantoms are crowding. It's studio fog, there's a hiss, there's a shout, the beautiful sound assistant with the delicate ears taps me on the hand, the mist is getting into my lungs, I'm getting a cold, my feet are wet, her scent is the same as Zelda's, there's so much love in the world and I've avoided it, ducked it, muffed it, out they come again from behind the tree, Mr Philips and the boy, shadows in the mist, other shadows like paper cut-outs, stretched-out paper-chains, she's shaking my shoulder, I'm sleeping again, I'm drowning, I'm Hylas, I'm nothing, nothing, nothing but fog, fog, fog.

Too right! Ossy shouts, no doubt.

My father was a costermonger, of sorts. He ruined my reading. He told me who dunnit, and chortled. My mother tutted but to no avail. I've always known how things would end. The first day I met Louisa on the set of *Rough Justice* I knew how it'd end. Louisa and me, not the lousy film. Not exactly how, but roughly. Deirdre was there. She could see I'd taken a shine. I was drooling out the corners of my mouth, I was ruining the paintwork on the rhododendrons. It'll kill you, Miss Sway, she said. Then walked out the door and broke her ankle. It was the wrong door. It was fake. The other side of it was blackness, a two foot drop. Pinewood was like that, Elstree, Ealing. You never knew which steps to take. Some of them ended in a mirror, which hurt. Louisa didn't know what Deirdre was talking about, because Louisa didn't know she had fallen for me – she thought it was just the actress/ assistant director thing, it would pass, Deirdre had five more lines than her and didn't get to die. Louisa had the most perfect lips. It was her

151

Jewish blood blooming and she never once used lipstick. She didn't have to. In any other country but Great AZ Britain her lips'd have made her. But they were too big for Great AZ Britain. Great AZ Britain likes its lips thin, tight, Anglo-Saxon. They ended up sucking Corona muck, fizzy garbage, out of a straw, in close-up, between *Magpie* and the *Six O'Clock News*. The last straw, as it happened. She was a nutter, everyone knew it, even my mum, even Grandma in the back sucking her Altoids. But she was driven to it, and not by Dick the Prick, OK?

What I'm trying to say through all this fog and over the patchouli scent of the pony-tailed sound assistant who's wrecking my shoulder is that we know how this is going to end. Mr Carlin will lift the latch and Jefferies will lean down and show his missing tooth from under his black topper and my great-uncle will out and up and off. Out and up and off. Behind him the school will squirm back into its usual bottle and only Mr Philips will be left on the avenue, shaken but not stirred, requested to see the Master before dinner who was stirred but not shaken, though certainly rather cross with Mr Philips for the indignity, the sheer indignity, the sheer crass indignity that had Holloway-Purse thumping the desk so hard one could hear the rum bottles roll, clink, roll.

Only Mr Philips? Not quite. There's the young groundsman with the rake, raking way off up the other end, gilded in the sudden light, the golden light through the leaves and the dust of his raking, thoughtfully and methodically way beyond shaken Mr Philips with the head down and gown wrapped round tight raking through the golden light before the shut gates, held like that with a minimum of sound for three minutes, four minutes, five minutes – because a moving rake is interesting, a man raking is interesting, far off down a golden misted avenue of linden trees in the amazing hush, with no jets to fuck it up.

Fog.

Loads of it. No expense. Canister after canister after canister of the highest quality fog. Blot it all out. We'll come back to the end that we

152

already know, at the end. It's called *structure*. My films were not supposed to have it. What's up, pussycat? Can't take the wild side? Can't take the groovy commotion? Well, this one's got *structure*, right? Ossy won't recognise me in it. He'll feel betrayed. Sorry, Ossy. Sorry, Sylvia. Sorry, gang. The guy who's playing Jefferies, I'm paying him a retainer. We'll come back next year, when the leaves are dropping again. Madness, huh? But it'll all be the same, exactly the same. There won't be so much as a growth-ring under the infinite precision of the lindens' bark. I tell you, nothing will have changed. Jefferies won't have aged a carbuncle. I won't have aged. My great-uncle won't have aged. Jefferies the coachman doesn't age, I tell the guy playing him. I look up. Jefferies is grinning at me. It's really unpleasant. He does smell of bogs, he does. The guy playing him is him. I forgot to say that. This is a quality movie. It's art house. I could've got, I dunno, Roger Rees or someone – no, Ken, Ken as in Branagh, King Ken perched up on the carriage in natty grey gloves and the world falling over itself to see it, even out on the Amazon, even up in Alaska, the film a sell-out forever and ever 'cos our Ken is in it, Ken the Bran-tub with infinite gifts, infinite draw.

But no. 'Cos Jefferies is playing Jefferies. It takes a *real* cunt to play a real cunt. I press a guinea in his grey glove. It's not a glove. It's his skin. Fank ye, sir, he says. Cut the antique accent, I say. The fog's getting on my chest. The canisters are *finito*, says Pierre the mechanical genius from Jersey, it'll have to be ordinary mist, Chef. (Hoi Ossy, hoi gang, remember Pierre?) The black lorry's backing up the avenue. It's enormous. It goes right through Mr Philips. The young groundsman's ninety-three, standing wry and erect next to patchouli girl, who's got him on her arm. My shoulder still aches. What did she want? I'll need a bleedin' massage, mate. The tracking rails go in, the scaffolding, the blind screens, Joe with his yellow gels (thanks, Joe, thanks). Why do they have to shout so much, these guys, these Steves, these bobble-hatted hunks? What the fuck is Mr Philips hanging around for? It's his first class. It's Theocritus. The boys'll be running riot. He can't be that shaken. Maybe he is. It's embarrassing. Nobody knows what to do with him. The Steves in their Doors T-shirts walk through him, no respect. The clash of the scaffolding's a desecration. I want to be left alone. I want peace of mind. My brass speaking-trumpet's nose down in the tussocks. My chair's sinking into the exceptional countryside. I should be on a duck-board. I don't even know her name. I'll call her Julie Patchouli. She has no right to dislocate my shoulder. She has every right to make it better. I wish Mr Philips would go. He's a great man, but he's gotten embarrassing. The Steves are rolling the canisters. Where the fuck are we going to get refills? I should have a duck-board. Stella's talking to the ex-groundsman. Are you an Old Boy? I bet she's saying. There's more boring sky all of a sudden. Christ, careful with them lindens. Polystyrene chips like crazy. Beggars can't be choosers. We'll put the real ones back, I promise, I promise.

Great days, great days.

Bleedin' phantoms.

Check out those whizzes and the boiled whiting while there's still some. Gimme a break.

The thick cards are flapping. Flap, flap, flap. I remember I remember the house where I was born and me mum and Des and I at the buttons in the Science Museum, things flapping and bouncing and grinding and dead, Out of Order, conked. I could make a horse gallop. Round and round and round, cedunk cedunk cedunk. A black horse as ah remember, galloping, mah first motion picture thru' the slit. I went back in '92, research reasons, couldn't find the horse, hey, it was all different, last time was with Maura and Greg somewhere in the psychedelic era when it was the same but smaller. They made the horse gallop and they cooed and I wanted to weep. In '92 I couldn't find the horse. It was all different. It was all explained. You could get a doctorate in physics just walking round for an hour. Hell, it wasn't a playground any more. They have glass lifts which gave me vertigo. I have bad vertigo. The old lifts used to give me claustrophobia. I have bad claustrophobia. It's either vertigo or claustrophobia, take your pick. I'll use the stairs, two at a time, have a little flutter with Old Man Death. I win every time. I'll go on winning. It's all in the attitude.

Science. The, ha, science of hoptics. Ha yes. I made films and I didn't know how. The light fell and I caught it. I left the science to Joe and Pierre and Michael. Remember Michael? Mike Avens? The greatest, the greatest. Shame he had to work with a dope like me, instead of Fellini or Truffles or whoever. I mean, I'd say I want a sad kind of light and he'd say, mournful blue or melancholy blue? I'd say hey, just sort of sad, mate. He'd drench it with a triple bank of cerulean floods and stand there like he was underwater and say howzat? – 'cos he was disgusted. He was disgusted I could be so *crass*. He was into Monet. He was into Claude Lorrain. He was into John Constable. I mean, Michael was not your ordinary camera guy. He's lighting this one, by the way. He's come back from the grave with his palette of Myrals and his light meters and his little funny cardboard thing and he's in seventh bloody heaven. 'Cos this is quality. This is the first quality thing he's ever done. This is the first movie up to his bloody standards. There are Monet mornings and Constable afternoons and Claude Lorrain evenings, OK? There's gaslight, there's fog, there's the big wide chalk country and there's the trenches. The trenches, Ricky? The trenches, Mike. Poppies? A few poppies, Mike. Blood. Mud. White bandages. Dirty bandages. No bandages. Lots of smoke. Big white puffs of smoke. Gas. Yellow, white, hazy gas, ground-hugging gas, invisible gas. Murk. Sunlight through murk. Cross-lighting, lots of specials, the works. Night scenes, Ricky? Night scenes, Mike. Moonlight on barbed wire, maybe. No, bound to be. Moonlight on blood. Moonlight on water, craters full of water, you know the scene. Rats plopping about. Sweaty skin, Ricky? Definitely sweaty skin, Mike. Lots of sweat, lots of gleam, but not Hollywood gleam, Mike. Who d'you think I am, Ricky? I'm going to do it in browns, in umbers and greys, I'm going to drain it, I'm going to use bloody soot for highlights. You'll see. Sounds great, Mike. Sounds exactly what I want. And will there be eyeballs, Ricky? Close-ups? There will be close-ups, say I, hesitantly. Mike comes so near I can smell the weed-killer they put on his plot up at Highgate (Remember the funeral? Dirk Bogarde all choked?) and he murmurs at my eyelashes *a big sooted muck of a face, Ricky. The darkest filter. Burnt sienna of a face. Touch of moonlight on the bridge of the nose. Then it opens its eyes. Eyeballs. White. Pure bloody slaps of white, impasto white, a great gleam, kind of uncomfortable gleam 'cos it's body-fluid, it's not bloody varnish, it's not gloss, y'know? It's eyes, it's eyes.*

I know, Mike, I know. It's not gloss. Sod the gloss. This is art house. This is quality.

We shake hands. His are cold. I forgot to say that his eyes – his eyes aren't there. Mike has sockets. What d'you expect? He's still a fucking genius.

Wasted, wasted. So many wasted.

I want a rustling fern. I want a Steve with a ginormous rustling fern. I want china above the door. Above it? Yeah. In dose days, guys, dey put crockery on de liddle lintel above de door an' a big plush curtain in front of de door yerked back wid a big fat dressing-gown cord an' crockery in every nook an' crannery you can tink of so no kid, absolutely no kid, could move a fucking muscle widout dere being a catastrophe. They put antimacassars on dey fine chairbacks an' dey put Macassar oil in dey hair an' de antimacassar fought it out wid de macassar an' lo, de laundry maid lost every darn time. Dey put photos in all de spaces dat were left by de china an' under everyting dey put liddle lace doilies an' under de lace doilies dey put wobbly tables wid whippet legs an' funny liddle rat's claws for feet an' where dey didn't have de fucking grand piano an' de liddle wobbly tables an' de Empire cabinets an' de huge open dresser wid de Ming vases an' stuff dey put fucking great ferns an' under de ferns dey put slippy liddle rugs in case you were tinking you were sure on your feet wid your wobbly liddle cup of tea but stick to de rugs, stick to de rugs, 'cos between dem dey waxed dem darn floorboards every day in case it wasn't slippy enough, OK?

You get de picture, Steves?

Set it up.

Holy shit, that's twelve crates of crockery.

Sylviaaaa? We forgot to swag the chandelier.

I mean, how could they've hoovered this stuff even if they'd had one? Ramona moans about my coconut matting. I have one coconut mat in all my apartment. It's by the futon, it's for my morning handsprings, it barely prickles. Otherwise the place is stripped to the boards, it's varnished, it's clean, it's Filipina-friendly. Carpets give me the heeby-jeebies, especially fitted. I mean, all that *dirt*! I mean, where does it *go* to? Des my brother has carpets so thick you'd *lose* a bloody hoover in it. But they don't hoover, they don't. Des and Muriel, I'm talking about. I reckon they use herbicide. Every time I visit Des has risen and so has the pile. I wouldn't mind, mate, if it was naaaatural fibres – but it bloody sparks the minute I touch it with me knee-caps (OK, we wear shorts in Houston – so?). I stand there in the living-room propping up the hopelessly-irresponsibly-harvested-mahogany bar and shout, your lawn needs cutting again, I see, Desmond! I always do this when he's in the toilet. He has this thing about being

159

addressed in the toilet. He has a bashful side. Muriel doesn't like me. She doesn't understand me. She takes me licheral, like. I pour out me Grant's. She looks out at the bloody lawn. The lawn's about as unkempt as her hairdo. Not a blade out of place. Des breaks his back doing it, she says. Does he? I say. Well, poor old Des. He ought to give it up at his age, Muriel. Every Saturday afternoon, she says. Well, it's all right for some, I say, giving the soda syphon a good spurt. I pick up the Grant's bottle. There's always this little biro mark on the label. I scuff it out with my nail and fish out my Nixon rotary (collector's item, guv) and correct it. I'm a stickler, Muriel, I'm a stickler: it was at least three inches out. I do believe you don't have lawns where you are, she says, woundingly. Where we are, I say, we have golf courses for lawns, Muriel. Something in the carpet nips my toes. That's another thing Des and Muriel can't abide: I like to take off my shoes and socks. I like to pad about with nude feet. They think I'm looking for the swimming-pool. I am. One day, Ratty, one day. It's the heat, Des, it's the heat. And it's December. Every time I visit Des has risen and so has the thermostat. When I imagine Hell, I imagine my brother's living-room. I imagine Des and Muriel in it. There's no door. There's Muriel's curried-eggs special every day, for ever and ever and some more. There's their conversation and their fave TV programmes and there's nothing else. Des has not mentioned my film work since 1973. Not once. Not to me or anyone else. You in the same line as Des, then? his chums say to me when they come over for some Chilean clutch top-up. You'd think he'd be fucking proud. I've got this brother in films, you'd think he'd say. From time to time. Over the sudded Volvo, the gin and limes, the leatherette attaché case he likes to remote lock whenever I get near it. He was always beastly to me, was my brother. He was always a rotter.

I hope he's not bloody out there instead of at his do – a hundred rare species of quiche, stripper popping out the iced phallus, nice sensitive types eyeing up your measurements for the next piling 'cos the millennium's in the zip bag, there's gonna be a lot of zeros after it, we're not talking chicken soup in a basket, chum. It'd be like him to gatecrash. Bull in a china shop. Arty friends, eh? Let me tell you, little Ricky Dicky here used to play with his little soldiers in the bath until he was sixteen, har har.

160

And *then* what did he play with? you're supposed to chortle, if you're one of his sort.

Cunts. The lot of 'em. I don't mind saying it. How are the ferns? Christ, it's taking an age. Hey, watch that bloody porcelain, Steve! It's real! It's antique! Even in 1913, mate!

I used to talk like that. English, British, a bit like Mick Jagger or someone. I used to kid myself. From Enfield to posh to swinging to sub-Clark Gable. No, as one of Muriel's chums once squealed – ooh, you sound just like Dave Lee Travis! Dave Dee who? I said. She couldn't speak for ten minutes. She'd choked on her scampi-flavoured twirly thing that was supposed to be a crisp. I guess I've been out of circulation, I shouted, rubbing her back so hard she was frightened for her pimples. A pity I didn't fancy her, guv. I didn't. I can't take women who weatherproof their eyelashes. Then Des put on some bloody awful music and knocked the halogens and it was all these breasts bungee-jumping all over the place until the slow track when it was, well, quite frankly it wasn't exactly *Saturday Night at the Palladium*, was it? I got out, quick, before the cops arrived or something. The local had the same music, it must have been wired up or something, but at least I wasn't being pawed. Not much, anyway. This British National Party or something guy dribbled on me, but that was it. At least he bought me a pint. Here's to your dad, he said. I'd told the creep about my dad, about Mosley, about what horrible bastards they all were. That's it, he said, that's it. Real quality, in those days. He wasn't a skinhead, he had hair, he looked like a ferret with specs. Yuk. I got back really late. I really crept in. I waded to the bar for a settler but I was tripped up by something. I fished it out. It was a pair of lacy black knickers with a hole sewn in. I guess they might have been special to someone, they were personalised, so I hung them on the soda syphon. Hey, I was amazed.

Pssst! There's more. I've started so I won't stop. Hold on tight, we're on a sharp curve. I'm the sneaky little brother, OK? Des and Muriel are into serious things. I mean, with their chums. I don't mean the sort of Bacchanalia thing but the sort of Deadly Organised thing. They have some New Zealand lead-free and then they squeeze their tails on to the leatherette three-piece and the wives chuck their car keys into the middle of the room and the men kind of lucky-dip. If a man gets his usual car keys they start all over. The wives are practically wetting themselves 'cos anything's better than the usual. Then they all go off but at five-minute intervals in case the neighbours limpeting their kitchen windows think it really is like *Brooksides* or whatever that thing was called and half of them (not the limpets) get into a strange bed and half of them get into their usual bed but both of them are strange to each other's skin and smell. I'm getting excited. That's really terrible, getting excited over Des and Muriel and chums. You know how I know this? Because my naked foot found a pair of car keys and I yelped and hopped and they were dangling off my big toe and Muriel flushed trout-farm pink and said oh and Des chortled dirtily. So that's where Ted's lot got to, he said. Don't tell him, Desmond, said Muriel. Do, do, I cried. What's it worth, Dicky? said Desmond. Three gin and limes down at the Cock and Bollocks, I replied. Done, said Des, always one for a cut-price bargain. Muriel said, he might put it into one of his films, Desmond. He doesn't make films, pet, said Des. He just teaches.

Hey, that was a great evening. Des and I got plastered, certificate X. We rollicked home arm in arm, almost. We would have done in a crap movie, anyway. Our elbows touched under the coach-lamp as he was fumbling at the lock and we didn't flinch. We were singing softly. I forget what. Lights sprang up all around Glen Close. It was like being in a spaceship or something. Heads appeared in silhouette. They bobbed about. The windows were eyes. Have you seen *Mon Oncle*? I enquired. That was a mistake. He tensed. Don't start talking posh and ruining it, Ratty, he murmured. Actually, he yelled it. He fucking bawled it. Don't start talking bloody French to me! Don't start that! I think it was for Muriel's sake. I don't think it was really him, that one time. Not that time.

I'm serious about that name. Glen Close. It gave rise to my most serious humiliation.

Hoi, Steve!

Yeah, Chief?

What the fuck's that antimacassar doing on the arm-rest?

162

I put it there, Chief.

What's it for – a fucking crippled midget?

I thought it looked nice, Chief.

You thought it looked nice?

Yeah. Kind of dainty. Nice crochet. My grandma—

Listen, Steve. This is my great-grandfather's house. This is 1913.
This is the living-room of my great-grandfather's house. There's a
clock ticking. It's ticking 1913 away, tic by toc. There's a smell. It's a
1913 smell of coal and beeswax and Pears soap and the maid with the
underarms and so on. You can't come in here and just put something
somewhere because you think it looks nice. You put something
somewhere because it's the only place it can go given the socio-
historical forces at work, given the taste, class, standing and financial
position of my great-grandparents, given the fact that it's 1913 and not
1933 or 1983 or 2003, geddit? It goes on the back of the chair, Steve.
Where the head goes. Where the head with half a gallon of Macassar
oil goes. I like the pony-tail, Steve. But get some brain under it, OK?

You're a gas, Chief. Right on, Chief. Y'know, I've worked with Procul
Harum, Chief. I lit them at Hemel, once.

Gerronwivit, berk, or you'll get caught by my great-aunt. She's due to
enter. The cosmos has fixed it implacable, like. You've got four
minutes and twenty-three seconds. Straighten that doily. There's still
no fucking swag on the chandelier. Straighten that Alma-Tadema. I
said Alma-Tadema, stoopid, not the curtains. That one, the one with
the lyres and the rose-bud tits in sunny Umbria or someplace. Thank
you. My great-grandfather liked his paintings straight and he liked
mirrors. He liked to straighten his collar and stuff in great big curly-
wurly gilt mirrors like that one so don't hang it like we're on the
Titanic. Get those bloody cartons out. The place stinks of Steves.
Christ, why do I bovver?

Julie Patchouli, fix me a Coke. Crush the ice so I can pretend I'm at the

163

Big Game. (I've never been to any Big Game or Medium Game or Little Game but Julie's impressionable. She's pretty putty in my palms. She polishes my brass speaking-trumpet so I can see myself in it. Am I a creep?)

I was talking about Glen Close, thoroughly desirable, ooh yeah – about twenty poncy villas in Lotts Bricks style with fluffy bamboo things on the nail-clippered lawns and a big Private Road sign in case you thought it just the verge to let your pet lobster crap on. Des points to the sign, the Glen Close sign. Great, eh, Ratty? he says, not helping with me suitcases (I had to stay the night with him, it's complicated) – great joke, eh? Fatally attractive place to live, eh? Ho ho. I put my suitcase down and prise my hand out the handle and try to straighten the fingers and there's a terrible red welt with stitching where my joints ought to be. Someone had added an *n*. Glenn Close. That was the joke, I guess. Now comes my most humiliating moment ever wiv Desmond me bruvver. He knows I don't make films no more. He knows I teach it instead. That's bad enough, OK? 'Cos he doesn't think very much of teachers, doesn't our Des. It was the teachers' fault kids were taken out of the mines and out of the chimbleys of the greatest industrial power known to man, *ever* (Des after a coupla gin and limes, Muriel nodding over her sputumante) and then got stuffed with useless bloody facts and ended up swelling the unemployment figures and doing sweet Fanny Adams (Muriel chokes a little at that, being upright), Dick. He always calls me Dick when he's being political. It's a concession. Or maybe it isn't. Sweet Fanny Adams or beating up innocent old ladies, Dick. I'm serious. At least the buggers had a job up the chimbleys and down the mines, Dick. At least they were kept out of bloody mischief. At least it sorted out the rotten apples from the decent apples and stopped the whole lot going manky, Dick. Des, I murmur, Dad would be proud of you. He is proud of me, Ratty, says Des. He's not dead yet. Can't wait, can't wait, I say. Muriel arranges her face into Appalled of Friern Barnet. That's not funny, says Des. (But hey, I know it's what he thinks every morning before he gets his dick to go down – *hmmm, I wonder if the old bastard's copped it in the night and we can get our fists on the capital that's bleeding away each day into the coffers of that bloody stiff private nursing-home in Havant?* He knows I know it's what he and especially Muriel think every morning and probably every evening after their hump. But the bastard's still

164

alive, Des. He'll outlive us all.) I was talking about this bloody sign. Yeah, great joke, Des, I say – I thought he was great in *Les Liaisons Dangereuses*. Yer what? says Des, twitching. He can't stand me talking French, especially with a French accent. I thought he was great, Glenn Close was great, in – I thought that's what you said, Ratty, says Des. I also thought you taught Yanks about movies, Ratty. I do, Des, I do: my special subject's Danish post-war cinema, but I do spots on Tarkovsky, Bresson, God—Glenn Close, dickhead, says Des, is a woman. No he isn't, I say, he was very good in *Les*— Have you seen *Fatal Attraction*, Ratty? Er, no, no, Des, I've missed that one. She's in that, too, Dicky my boy. She's definitely got tits and a beaver in that one. I gulp, I sweat, I try to smile, I try to think of what I had for breakfast, I try to recall my own name, I want to play it again and get it right but I can't, Ricky Thornby's feeling sick, and it's not just the jet lag and my extended elbow joint. It's the sickness that comes when you think of all those times you've talked at the Houston Centre of Dramatic & Visual Arts about how great Glenn Close was in *Les Liaisons Dangereuses*, especially when he gets shot at the end. There've been a lot of these times because *Les Liaisons Dangereuses* is the only release you've watched from end to end in about ten years apart from Tarkovsky's definitely-last and Bresson's probably-last but at HCDVA that doesn't count and that was because Zelda craved it for her birthday, you couldn't say how you hate films, may you wait in the lobby and look at the stills and munch popcorn and get off on the quadrophonic effect vibrating your feet? You couldn't say it because you were in love. So I watched it and, hell, I used it. Every time the keenies got talking in the common room I'd butt in with yup, and I thought Glenn Close was pretty good in *Les Liaisons Dangereuses* (in what? they'd say. Ah, sorry, in *Dangerous Liaisons*) – especially when he got shot at the end. I thought they were snuckling at my French. I really thought this. What a stupid fucking name. Des has used it ever since. The whole of Friern Barnet knows I thought Glenn Close was a bloke. Des has absolutely no respect for me any more, and he only had a Cock and Bollocks' whisky measure before. He knows I know he's rumbled me. I know he knows I know he's rumbled me. It makes for a great filial feeling between us. Hey, all our siblings the world over know that we are frauds because once upon a time we picked our noses and played with our little soldiers in the bath and stayed in our diapers and wore sideburns and hugged our teddies till we were seventeen or something. Come to think of it, the whole of HCDVA knows I'm a fraud, but that doesn't bother me one jimp. Why does it bother me that Des knows? I really don't like Des. I have no respect whatsoever for the creep. He embarrasses me. The only reason I've stayed with him two or maybe three times when I've been over was because I wanted this little locket with a tiny blue butterfly in it belonging to my late mother and I knew he had it somewhere and that he wouldn't hand it over unless I crawled and whimpered – which I did, kind of. I had to be humiliated and I was and he handed it over to me like it was a medal. For Grovelling and Whimpering and Letting Muriel Beat You at Strip Poker. It was just worth it. I have it now. It's here, it's on my desk next to the flint from the wind-blowing mind-blowing top of Wot Hill and my Hopi bowl and my little photos of William and Giles and Agatha. Shit, she's coming in. My great-aunt, she's coming in. It's OK, the swag's on the chandelier and stuff, the room's genuine, there's a smoky light, it's kind of morning in London and there's been yer dawn fog that's left its dribble on the window panes and my great-aunt's coming in right now because now is her now and there's nothing in front of it, yet.

Hush.

Sssssh.

She's reading. This is how it was. Her now is is and not was, hers and not ours, our now is not yet and never will be because she'll be dead. Bom bom. You know what she was reading in her right now? Swinburne. Really sexy stuff, swoony, all over the place. She's reading in her favourite place, it's weird, it's behind the biggest fern next to the really enormous piano and at least she has a cushion for her bum. She's dressed in – you know what she's dressed in, you've seen hundreds of these lousy adaptations and you've read hundreds of these lousy contempowawy novels where they tell you what someone's dressed in before she's had a chance to open her mouth, it's like a fucking fashion parade, it's called great art and it stinks of libraries. I've been in the libraries. I've been in the British Library and I've been

166

in the Imperial War Museum Library and I've been in the Public Record Office Library and I've been in the Houston Centre of Dramatic & Visual Arts Library. What's so funny? HCDVA is rich. It's so rich it has at least two of Shakespeare's First Folios or something. Maybe not the First, but certainly the Second. It has Harold Pinter's Laundromat tickets for five years and Sam Beckett's toothbrush. I'm not joking. *The* toothbrush, hog bristles, and worn flat. It also has the finest air-conditioning system *in Texas* (the library, the library) and it's really quiet. There are no golf-balls striking the tinted windows. There are no students, apart from the weirdo in spectacles hung up on Granville-Barker of all people (HCDVA has most of his correspondence, as it happens. I'm serious). It's where I work. On this. On this. Mostly. The librarian is astoundingly attractive, even under neon. Her name is Zelda.

Geddit?

Swinburne.

We have this huge fern and my great-aunt Agatha kind of behind it head down in this white book. It's white and cream, you can sink your teeth into it, she is sinking her teeth into it, metaphorically. It goes with her dress. Her dress is kind of all creamy and fluttery – Edwardian, for Christ's sake. She has a corset on. She has this corset underneath this fluttery summery silk dress and you wouldn't know it except that when she stands her bust and bum stick out unnaturally. Some people find this sexy. I find it a shame. So does she. Well, I probably do find it sexy but I can't stop thinking of whores welting some fat pillar of the community when I think of corsets. Mr Swinburne is unribboning her corset. He actually makes her feel a little breathless. Cor blimey, guv. Doesn't he swing, just?

She looks up. See those grey eyes? I'm filling the whole screen with her face, her grey eyes are as big as the Statue of Taking Liberties, they're beautiful in this lousy light (Mike, I'm talking about a miserable day, it's difficult to get this light as lousy as I want it, she isn't used to switching a lamp on just like that, she hasn't adapted to this electricity thing, she's one of the under ten per cent in this country who've gone

167

over from gas, it's like me an' ma microwave, she doesn't believe it won't kill you, and she's right) – hey, even in this deadhead inkie-dinkie light and what the fog clears to outside, which is a really coaly atmosphere, her eyes are beautiful.

The rest of her is pretty beautiful, too.

If she hadn't been beautiful, I would not have said this. I mean it. I wouldn't have got some prettyface to play her, just for the sake of it, just because no one believes a star can't be plain Mary Jane. I'm not like that. I used to be, I used to be as knee-jerk as all the other movie guys. But I can't help the fact that my great-aunt was beautiful. It was a fact. It was a well-known fact. She had fine features, thick brown locks, a good shape.

A chill. I feel a chill. I shouldn't be talking about her like this.

Listen, you see her how you want. You will, anyway and whatever, even if she reared up in gloves right at this moment and walked across the party suite knocking over your glasses with her trail of silk net and had you all running for the door because deep down you're kids and you're terrified of ghosts, especially ghosts with white gloves up to their elbows.

Because deep down everyone sees what they want to see.

Hrrrrrm. I keep screwing the action. My analyst says I have a projective personality, that I'm in love wid my mother, that I'm one of those really overbearing and deeply insecure jaw-crackers she can go to sleep through but she can't wait to see my backside in her door-frame so she can hoover the couch. She doesn't say this to me, of course. She says this to her sister, who is Zelda's godmother. Zelda is very close to her godmother. Zelda found out about me before she went out with me briefly a few years ago and then got into chastity and Kyoto and then thank God into weatherbeaten time-challenged wise men who made her chuckle and I'm the only one around here right out to the Staked Plains or someplace who fits the bill, so she's back. I like the power I have over my analyst. I mean, I could shop her at any time for professional indiscretion, hm hm. I like to lie there and eat my crackers and talk into her silence knowing she's about as authentic and true as a disgorged peanut. I mean, Zelda's godmother just sits there on the other end of the phone and shrieks, hiya, what whackie-crackies did'ya have today, honey? And honey, alias Moira Kahn, the most respected analyst in all of the Deep South, spills the jelly beans all down her front till she gets real sticky, the prize bitch. Use it, Ossy. Use it.

The *Washington Post*, not the bloody *Sun*.

I call her Ghengis, to her face. It's not funny, but it helps.

How's the Mongol? I say. How's Ghengis?

I get the feeling you're all sick of me. It's me or the dancing girls. You prefer the dancing girls. Bring on the dancing girls.

Not yet. We have a lot of complicated action. We have some history to get through. We have sex and violence and some deep things. She's still reading Mr Swinburne. I can't push her. I can't make her do what she didn't do, can I? The clock ticks, I'm a fraud, I was in love with my mother or maybe my great-aunt and I used to dream about my father getting run over by the 49, I used to dream I was pushing him under but he was laughing too much and Stevie Smith was driving, she's a terrible driver, she swerved every time and missed him and ran over the pea instead. What a mess. Cor. Thank you, Richard. That'll be 150 bucks. Hey, Moira, it's gone up. I must desire you under my loathing. It's normal, Richard, excuse me, I'm being paged.

Holy shit.

You know what Zelda says? She says I ought to shut up and receive. She says I ought to open up my channels and receive instead of emitting all the time. Actually, I'm nervous. I'm nervous because this is the really big action beginning and I've been putting it off for years. All the avenue stuff was just glorified crowd scenes, really. I mean, no one actually had to say anything. They just had to move or gawp or think about breakfast. But this is nitty-gritty close-up jaw-jaw time. This is sensitive performance time. This is the real thing, not on ice. I'm whispering. Why am I whispering? I'm whispering because I'm sitting next to my great-aunt and she's concentrating and the floor's cold and waxy. It'll mark my Levis. I still wear Levis? I still wear Levis. I've got to think what it's like to wear spats. I've got to think what it's like to wear the equivalent of my wardrobe all at the same time and even in summer and not have spray-on deodorant. And I've also got to handle the deep stuff. I mean, I can't be thinking how they wore spats and how they went to the lavatory with a corset on and stuff all the time. I won't git nowhere fast, at that rate. I don't know why I took this damn thing on. It's too big for me to handle. I'm a fraud. You're rumbling me. Hey, she's mouthing it. She's whispering the words, kind of. She has the most delicate ear I've ever seen in my life. She smells of lavender and – I think it's petrol. Why the hell does she smell of petrol? It's sort of petrol. Maybe the maid's crap. Maybe the maid used too much petrol on the wine stain. For always thee the fervid languid glories allured of heavier suns in something skies, thine ears knew all the wandering watery sighs or maybe skies where the sea throbs round lesbian promontories, the barren kiss

Holy shit.

She's paused on kiss. She's looking up at nothing. The fern's just a green blur, a cat's-cradle of greens and shadows, there's a glisten of spittle on her lower lip, the tongue comes out to catch it in, she blinks, she doesn't sigh, I really thought she was going to sigh, she's not thinking what I thought she was thinking, she's thinking the lines through, she's fucking *learning* them, she's not even thinking of a guy, or lesbians, or creamy surf bashing a cliff, or anything deep I could use as a handle for the whole scene – she's just learning the fucking lines!

Shut up, Ricky. Just shut up. Just let the whole thing roll on its own. Trust it. Dare. Just be a little bit daring for once. Just imagine that you can stop hugging the rock for a minute and stand like a grown-up.

I have bad vertigo, Zelda.

Shut up, OK? Or I'll whack you with my *keisaku* stick, twice on each shoulder, like they did to me at dawn in Kyoto.

170

At dawn in Kyoto? That'd make a great title, Zelda—

Youch. OK, OK, I'll shuddup. Shurrup, as my dad—

YOUROOCH!!

Pssst. I'll be quiet as my analyst.

Yow.

Uncle Kenneth thrusts his face into the fern. The greens and the shadows become Uncle Kenneth's face. It's a shock, she didn't even hear him come in. The barren kiss.

Hallo, Uncle Kenneth. Hallo, Aggie-Mags. (Yukoos. Ssssh!) He purses his lips and flickers his tongue. It makes a noise like a helicopter, only he doesn't mean that because helicopters have only appeared so far in Leonardo da Vinci's notebooks. Agatha puts the feather back to mark the page and shuts the book. (She had this feather, I forgot to mention it. It doesn't matter, Ricky, just shut your mouth, I'm trying to listen for Chrissake. Zelda, you're the best thing that could ever happen to a man. It was a dove's feather, by the way. Youch.) Have you had tea, Uncle Kenneth? Uncle Kenneth does a bit more of this rotor-blades-before-their-time thing. Agatha blinks. She doesn't sigh. She ought to sigh, it would relax her. What have I got? says Uncle Kenneth. He's actually finding this head position un-comfortable, because the fern's got sharp blades and he's bent awkwardly, but he's got to keep it up because he's that sort of person. He has these little acts and this little act isn't over yet. He spends most of his time trying to jolly Agatha up. It's heavy. She's heavy. He feels it's his duty in some way. He feels sorry for her. He feels sorry for her because his brother is a selfish cad and his sister-in-law is just frightful. He's wearing spats, by the way, but they're odd, as in not a pair. He's odd and he's a pear. He smells of vinegar. His jacket has a broken belt thingy at the back and food stains. His big rump's sat on something white. We're looking at him from the back. His elbows pump in and out because he's rubbing his hands and the whole fern

171

shakes. The mirror on the left wall repeats it. We could watch the whole thing in the mirror. Same difference.

(Hey, William is on his way back. He's on the train. They don't know this. Mr Boulter hasn't telephoned yet. He's still trying to get HP off his back about Philips. There's lots of time to telephone. The clock in the London room strikes ten-thirty. Sorry, I just needed to say that.)

Or maybe I didn't. Maybe I jumped the gun. Maybe—

OK, OK. *Zazen*. Zzzzz.

Agatha stands up. She smooths her dress. She's chill, she needs her shawl, her dress is too light, she's trying to keep the summer going long after it's gone. Three guesses, says Uncle Kenneth. Oh, I can't, I can't, says Agatha. Her head is full of lesbian promontories and barren kisses and she has her period. I can't, she says again, tucking her hair back behind her left ear – just a stray curl, because generally her hair stays where it should, there are a lot of pins and stuff, it's Edwardian or OK *Georgian* hair and because this is now meaning then there are no concessions, it's pure, it's – I mean, think of how everyone in *The Forsyte Saga* looks like Engelbert Humperdink and you know what I'm saying. Uncle Kenneth gives up and his head comes out of the fern. Agatha steps out from behind the fern, out of her little cosy corner, the fern brushes her shoulder and she gives Uncle Kenneth a peck on the cheek. I've looked at this room, I've rung the bell with the photos of this room in my hand and the drunk who now rents that bit of the house didn't mind, didn't mind at all, olt chup. There was no cornicing and stuff, no fancy plasterwork, no crockery, no piano, no antimacassars. There was some terrible furniture families kill each other not to inherit and some kit pine stuff and a big swanky speaker with an ashtray on top where Agatha read Mr Swinburne. It was a junky feeling, standing in there. You wouldn't have known. The drunk had slippers on with pom-poms. He was Polish, Hungarian, I forget which. An ex-violinist. Probably brilliant until Auschwitz. He thought I was trying to sell him something but he liked it. His carpet had so many ripples in it I felt seasick. It was brown, once.

I'm getting thwacked. By Zelda, it's nice.

172

(We've just ended up laughing so much we had to make love behind the photocopier. Zelda wanted to do it on top and photocopy us like in that book but the weird student was around. He came over to photocopy this huge book and we had to time our grunts. A pity, I'd have really liked a color photocopy of Zelda's flattened cheeks. She says it's sensational, it's warm, you get pressed against this warm glass plate and everything's shunting and flashing away under you but I don't fancy a copy of *my* behind, I'm really anal about this, I'm sorry.)

Hey, we haven't missed much. You gotta live. You gotta live in the now. The now meaning now. Cor, blimey, blow me down. The much we haven't missed wasn't Uncle Kenneth and Agatha having some phatic Edwardian communication with each other – hey, it was just Pinter with spats on. While I was fumbling at Zelda's Levi buttons she made me swear I wouldn't say anything more out of order until the end of the scene. I swore. I wanted to say what's out of order and what isn't out of order or define your terms if you want to be hinterlekshul about it but I just swore, I swore blind – I was fumbling with Zelda's Levi buttons and she doesn't wear panties when it's hot and it's mainly hot in Houston. I'm a weak man. I'm Plywood John. As she sank on to me I nearly swore I wouldn't ever do anything she didn't want me to do ever again but thank the Lord Hallelujah the weirdo student came over humping his book right then and it came out as a kind of ultra-violet grunt. OK. Sssh.

This, my dear, is the Wheel of Life. I know, says Agatha. Uncle Kenneth's crest falls momentarily but he's a great recoverer. A zoetrope, to be strictly accurate, my dear, and accuracy is the handmaiden of intelligence, is it not? Probably. Certainly, my dear.

He gives the zoetrope a little flick and it revolves slowly on its brass-cornered base. A what? A Zoë who? A zoetrope. There's an open drum with slits on top of a brass-cornered base. It cedunks around and comes to a stop. It's really black, except for the brass bits. All in the eye of the beholder, says Uncle Kenneth. The zoetrope is on one of those wobbly little tables with rat's feet in front of the bay window but for some reason it's not wobbling. Maybe they didn't wobble in those days. Maybe a wobble comes with age. Ssh.

173

The Wheel of Life, says Uncle Kenneth. What a fine name, heh? What a perfectly fine and charming name. And look. He taps a little brass plate on the side. Agatha bends and reads it out loud. Hapworth and Sons, Bristol, 1859. Uncle Kenneth is excited. Agatha can't understand why he's so excited, she actually had about ten toy versions of these but they all got walked on in the nursery and wouldn't spin. The significance, my dear! The significance, repeats Agatha. The Wheel of Life, *my* wheel of life, my dear! My great-aunt is not slow but she's still standing on her lesbian promontory. Uncle Kenneth holds her shoulder. He can feel the thinness of it under the silk. It is no longer a girl's shoulder, one outflung region of him thinks to itself while the metropolis speaks. My birth day, dash it! he cries. It's as old as you, says Agatha. The door opens. It's the maid, the new one. Oh, the new maid says. She has a duster in her hand. She sees the funny gentleman who smells with his hand on the young lady of the house's shoulder. Her sister warned her that things would be going on. Her sister told her not to show you'd seen, never to look surprised, never to look surprised were it to be ever so queer, our Mill. The maid has been here one day. Everything has surprised her after her previous five thousand and something days passed in Worksop. Her face has done nothing but strive to look not-surprised since she arrived at the station more thickly greased with smuts than when she puts the washing out, and that's saying something. Oh, she says again. The duster is wrapped tightly round her hand. She can't remember whether you must never ever dust a room with someone in it. There are so many never evers she gets them tangled up. Uncle Kenneth is stretching his arms wide. There's a pack of cards in one hand and a black cloth in another. I'll bet you've been wondering why Agatha hasn't wanted to look into the zoetrope. I mean, it's the first thing you or I would want to do. Simple: there's nothing in it, she can see that, she can see inside because the drum's got no top and you know why it's got no top? Because to see something you need light, and the light has to be natural for this antique. I don't want to get technical.

Ah-ha! says Uncle Kenneth, his arms stretched out. The maid takes a step forwards instead of backwards, it was her mistake, her legs are unpredictable at times like these. Ah-ha, repeats Uncle Kenneth. A big dray goes by loaded with beer-barrels. It darkens the room. I had to mention it because these vintage-hire people charge a fortune and a big dray did go by just then and also now. Let me tell you there's quite a lot of authentically-costumed people out there on the street and there's even a horse and dust-cart coming up soon and you haven't noticed the clop-clops, the gigs and landaus and stuff, the two vintage motor cars that have already rattled past, have you? And beyond that there's more, there's the whole of London, there's countryside with rakes and no motorways, there's sea with 1913 ships and boats on and there's China and India and America and stuff, every one of them looking as they are supposed to look at this now, then. There are no helicopters, there are no sneaky jump-jets, there's not even a vapour trail way up. There's not a hair out of place. If you can't imagine what, I dunno, say, Bolivia looks like in 1913 that's not my darn fault, is it? Because it's out there and a lot of care and Steves went into setting it up. Zelda's advancing towards me. She means business. Uncle Kenneth is gesturing to the maid to advance, which means she takes two steps back. She hits the wall. Oh, she says again. This ah-haing and ohing is ridiculous, but life's like that. Agatha is thinking about her mother getting back soon. She's staring out the window and thinking that. You first, my dear, says Uncle Kenneth to the maid. I don't know what your name is, I'm afraid. Milly, shouts the maid. She didn't mean to shout it. It's like a penny dropped in her slot and she worked. She looks around as if someone else had shouted it. Milly, says Uncle Kenneth, come and have your peep first. Uncle Kenneth is slightly peeved at Agatha's total indifference. She's so difficult to jolly up. Uncle Kenneth gets on with the lower orders, the commoners, the ones who serve the ones who don't as much. This doesn't mean he pays well. He doesn't. But he has no airs. He treats them like they have as much right to exist as he does. This causes a lot of trouble. The maid advances because she wants to do the opposite, she's trying not to look surprised because this is probably the ever-so-queer thing her Sis went on about. She's gawping at the uncle, her mouth is open, she shuts it, she advances until she's at a respectable distance. There's a never ever about a respectable distance, but she can't remember whether it's five inches or five feet. One's too close by half and the other's too far by half. Maybe it's not five anything. She should have writ it all down. So she just stops when she can smell him, which is not very close. Up in Worksop they get so close to each other they have arms around shoulders and kissing and that. She didn't know how close to stand to the memsahib when she was being welcomed, yesterday. It wasn't really being welcomed, more examined, but it was called being welcomed. She nearly said memsahib instead of ma'am which is her brother's fault. He's in the army and he's been out in Inja. He would keep on about it. His back's a broom-handle. Yes ma'am, ma'am, ma'am.

Yes ma'am, she says. Uncle Kenneth's eyebrows go up. His hair is long. It's just conceivable he is a bearded lady. The maid flushes. Oh, she says. Ma'am would like you to give you the honour of a peep, jokes Uncle Kenneth in a dead serious voice. But first, close your eyes, both of you. The maid is really confused. This is definitely an ever so queer. She glances at the zoetrope. The duster is like a knuckle-duster now. She scratches her nose with it and practically suffocates. The house towers above her and all around her. She's tiny in it, she's like a speck of dust and the duster's wiping her away. She's new, says the young lady of the house, she's new. The maid looks across at my great-aunt. The maid feels all shiny all of a sudden, all new and shiny, like she's just been manufactured, like the pans and cutlery and brooms and soap and stuff that issue forth from the factories in Worksop and get crated up to be dirtied and ruined and chucked, eventually. She even feels her spots go away as that word she can never remember, like granted but it isn't, granteeed. Even the blackhead above the left nostril which she knows intimately seems to vanish. Dr Colthrop's Unique Remedy. It comes of scrubbing too much. Nay, it comes of scrubbing not enough. Coal and tar. Coal tar soap. Grease and smuts and smoke. Not enough o' what they fancies, Sis says. Tha cheeks have a shine after it. A bit o' drippin'. Nowt at all till you cotton on. Like pokin' your head out in th'train to view. Lose it. Zelda says this is getting to sound like *Ulysses*. You bet, I say. Any more compliments? Lousy film. Sssh, Zelda. Thank you. You know why my great-aunt said that the maid was new, by the way? First, because she was being nice. Second, because she didn't care too much for herself and the maid being lumped together as Both Of You so she was kind of establishing the maidness of the maid. That's not so nice but, cor blimey guv, who's one hundred per cent nice?

The both of yous close their eyes. The maid squeezes hers really tight because she musn't look surprised never ever and do what you're told be it ever so queer. Agatha kind of tries to keep her dignity so she turns her head and just sort of lets the eyelids take a rest. She hears some fiddling around with the pack of cards which aren't really, they're the set of pictures like a trick pack all joined up, like those fancy postcard sets you can buy in places like Florence and stuff, only these have slots in so they can slot in around the inside of the drum. Hey, this is getting really technical again. The maid's respectable distance is disrespected by the uncle's hand on her shoulder. Her eyelids let some light in but only a flash because she hasn't been told to yet. She's propelled forward step by step. He presses harder, so her back gives up and bends. Have the honour, the uncle is saying. She reckons that's the order to open. She opens her eyes. There's black in front of her. She's been blinded with an ever so queer. It's a black cloth. The thingy in front of her has a black cloth over it. The uncle is a conjurer, oh.

The black cloth, you're thinking, wasn't on there before. Too right, you're on the ball, have another Bourbon & Coke but make sure it's Bourbon. And keep alert. You don't want to miss this. The bar is over there just so you don't, OK?

The maid's shiny-new feeling has already been spoilt. She feels a stain on her shoulder. She's no longer spotless. She bends so her face is at the cloth. Her apron strings are biting into her trapezius muscles. No, that's an exaggeration: they feel a bit tight as she bends. She has some wind. She keeps it in. Never ever *ever*. In front of. Eating. Especially at dinner unless soundless and with strong gravy to hide it. The black cloth smells of mothballs. It's whipped away. There isn't a rabbit, a drum-roll, her sister gasping probably because Dan has put his thumb into her thigh in the darkness (we're talking music hall here, not TV in the lounge, OK?) – there's a slit, moving away slightly. Another slit. Maybe it's the same slit come round fast. Nay, it can't be, 'cos there's another. And another, faster, passing now and another and another and something beyond, something flickering, something alive, and not a rabbit, not a rabbit, but a gent, a gent flickering and walking, how can he be walking in a box, he's naked, he en't got nowt on, there en't a leaf on his privates, the legs pass and he's gone and there's another gent, it's the same one, walking past wi'out a stitch to his name, ever so queer, walking and gone flick and then there's another, the same, Zelda says we've got the idea but I'm enjoying myself, it's a riff, it's cedunking time and she's never ever seed a pair o' privates afore and

177

he's really walking quickly now and back and past and out and back and past and out it must be knackering nipping back like that and striding past quicker and quicker with his hands swinging and his legs and his feet and his privates that she never thought'd look so big oh I've forgot ter breathe and she breathes and comes up as if for air and the room whirls and it's ever so queer and she maun't look surprised at a thing so she looks blank.

Well? cries Uncle Kenneth. He lets go of the handle and wipes his palm on his jacket. He's a little peeved because he was hoping for a giggle or a snort but instead she's come up looking blank.

Still Five: maid looking blank in front of big house. She's the one on the right, the small one, dark hair, even blanker-looking than the other one, on the left. They were shuffled into place between beating the rugs and doing the fiddly bits of silver. The light popping made Milly want to look surprised but she managed not to. She blinked, though. And the funny man with the hair on his cheeks had told them not to. They weren't to move a muscle, he said. They didn't, basically, except for Lily's left hand, which gave a big twitch off its own bat. It was the popping. It was cold. There's the back door behind, with the ivy leaves over it. There are the blades of grass with dead leaves caught in them. There's the shoe-scraper that's still there now meaning now but rusty and no one scrapes their shoes these days, there's no mud, no horse droppings, there's no need – there's only bubble gum and dog shit and gobs. Go take a look. At the still, I mean. Not your fucking shoes.

The phone rings. I mean, the wall telephone on the central battery system mounted next to the hall mirror, the thing which you thought was a brass candlestick stuck out of a kind of fancy walnut shelf, rings. The two little brass bells like tits just under the shelf are getting it. It sounds like a herd of Alpine cows speeded up. It bounces off the lozenge tiles in the hall, it echoes, it's awful. It drowns the click of the door opening. My great-aunt's hand unhooks the receiver on the side and there are just echoes and her mouth gets close to the candle-holder. The receiver's at her ear, horizontal, you've seen it in a hundred lousy adaptations, it's rent-a-vintage-telephone time, there's some guy or lady cranking something somewhere and way off down the other end of the line there's Boulter's mouth. His transmitter stinks, the receiver has dandruff. It's white, he draws it even nearer, it looks like a lamp, he hates using it. Is that, er, good morning, he says. He's nervous. His rum bottles are still rolling. He pities for once the fellows who have arithmetic with Holloway-Purse first thing. Good morning, he says again. There's a soft buzz as usual then there's a woman's voice. It might be the maid's, but it's too posh, it might be the little bugger's mother. A great nervousness grips him, he wants to go to the lavatory, underneath he's a little man who should never have got to be in this position of awesome responsibility. He clears his throat. A great sound of surf washes down the line and Agatha takes the receiver away an inch from her ear. Hallo? she says. Who is it? She's thinking of the maid looking blank in the living-room, not knowing where to put herself. Someone's eating crisps close up. That's not what she thinks, because I don't reckon crisps were invented then, what she thinks is oh blast, this awful line. Something about am I talking to? Miss Trevelyan, she says. Uncle Kenneth's rumble rumbles in the living-room. What on earth is he saying? Boulter swallows and says it. Your son has been expelled, Mrs Trevelyan. Agatha thinks this is queer, there's a madman using the line, it's happened once before, an invader from Mars, it might have been Giles playing the silly fool or something. Not William. William is the responsible type. My son? she repeats. An instant after she has said this, you know how it is, she burns up, her face catches fire, her mouth goes dry, because an outlying region has been attacked by the truth first while the centre takes baths and paints watercolours and embroiders. Boulter remembers there are two just at the same time as he remembers he hasn't introduced himself. He's never been so deucedly nervous in years. Expelled, the younger one (he can't say his name, it won't come out, it has to stay Trevelyan), for what one can only call, Mrs Trevelyan, I'm sorry to say – before the most difficult moment of all can be thrashed the voice at his ear says, who are you, please? It says it in a pressing and frankly off-putting way. Boulter blinks and grips the stem. An obscene thought bubbles up into his mind. His ear itches, it always itches when he uses the telephone. Everyone's shouting at him this morning. This is the Master of Randle College, he announces. Mr Algernon Boulter. I regret to announce – he pauses, expecting to be shrieked at, but no, nothing but a soft buzz, and crackles, and clicks. He takes a breath. He might be talking into the sea. He might drown. The salty sea swirling through his teeth. He lets go of the stem of the telephone because, oh God, it's the same grip. He pushes Jesus on to the stage of his mind, the obscenity withers, he opens his mouth, Jesus is raising his arms, He has a broom and bucket, He's a billposter pasting up BUGGERY all over Boulter's mind, Boulter flounders on regardless. I regret to announce, Mrs Trevelyan, that your younger boy (better, Boulter, better) has been cast from our midst, and has been put on the five past ten Great Western from Basingstoke, Mrs Trevelyan. A picture of the linden avenue stretches out in his head, the boy stumbling, damn Philips, the whole business, nasty business, but must set an example, never again, never again, Mr Wilde's in town, Mr Wilde and Mr Swinburne, all that troop, like ghosts, rearing again and at Randle. The five past ten from Basingstoke sounds common. He blinks, he wants to say something more. A post-chaise would have been better. Galloped out of our midst. Change of horses at Staines. Somewhere. Foaming at the mouth. *Vires acquirit eundo.* Zelda is sighing. She likes Bashō better than she likes Virgil. Boulter has Virgil like he has dandruff, greasy skin, nits in his pubic tuft. It's part of his make-up. The lady is saying something. James Joyce, she's saying. You're getting like James Joyce. James Joyce, I say, is about to start the greatest work of the twentieth century. Next year. Hit that significance, baby. 1914. Now shush, honeybunch. I'm in the telephone exchange, I'm keeping the connection going, I'm in between the two, there's a cat's-cradle of wires on my roof, there's ten tons of scaffolding and wires, it was complicated in those days, my earphones are heavy, the air is full of wires and starlings and the world is growing uglier by the minute. Boulter says, hallo, hallo? He taps his receiver. My great-aunt is steadying herself. Uncle Kenneth is laughing and rumbling the other side of the door. Ha ha haa. The peacock feathers in the big brass jar are staring at her. The nice framed photograph of her as a little girl with Willo's next to it would be staring at her also if the light from the hall window wasn't flaring on it badly. She looks at Willo's flare and the gilded ribbon uniting them perpetually without really noticing, her eyeballs kind of follow the bow of the ribbon like one of Zelda's inner-eye exercises, don't you think, honey?

No?

OK, she's turning her head towards the stairs now. The stairs with the stuffed lemur on the half-landing are waiting for her, she ought to be running up them holding her dress just free of the William Morris runner like Deirdre used to do so well when sober. Mother will be back any minute. She swallows. She's so close in she's practically eating the transmitter, she can taste the Silvo on the nickel plate, it's unhygienic, Father would say so, but she has to keep her voice down.

Please, she hisses, would you tell me why?

The voice in her ear has no shape. It's a kind of mist. She's staring at the twiddly bit of carving on the top of the wall set. Depravity, it says. Depravity, she echoes inside her. The mist fills her head with depravities: vaguely Roman, togas and things, Nero fiddling, rough faces scowling out of the darkness of back alley-ways, whores relieving themselves in Piccadilly, right in front of her, next to the boot-black boy who swears, and further things that are hidden behind red plush, that she might never know of. Not quite the usual depravities, Mrs Trevelyan. I hope he has the spunk to tell you. A letter shall be following forthwith. I do not wish, Mrs Trevelyan, to sully your ears at this difficult, indeed perhaps exceedingly distressful, moment. Boulter nods to himself, in the swing, really in the swing now. He has been, I might add, punished in a way quite fitting, quite fitting, and probably sufficient, though you might yourself decide otherwise. The five past ten from Basingstoke. He may need meeting. He has his trunk and other articles with him. Clearing of throat.

My head-set really hurts. They must have had strong neck muscles or something. My great-aunt is just eighteen. This is the most incredible thing that's ever happened to her in her life, even worse and much more incredible than Evelyn's death because Evelyn was sick for ages before. Her eyes are opened very wide indeed. Her mouth is tight shut. She's blanked out. She wants to say I am not my mother, my mother is out, you wish to speak to my mother, don't you? – but she's blanked out, she can't, she just thinks of the king in her chess-set and how Willo always beats her hollow. I hear a rustle. It's Boulter sitting back. I'm so tense my back hurts, the phone exchange has lousy chairs, they swivel, even in 1913 they swivel, there's all this chattering around me, it's starlings, it's wires, it's work. Done, thinks Boulter. It just remains for me to say, Mrs Trevelyan, how deeply sorry I am at this unfortunate, er, outcome. He was a promising boy. Thank you, comes a faint voice, so faintly into his ear he cocks his head to the right as if he might tip out some more. A most promising boy, and not, I am quite sure, beyond redemption. The receiver tuts. The buzz becomes a hum. He has a momentary fear that he has done something terrible, that she's going to scream and run out and throw herself under an omnibus or something. He crouches over the telephone, as if to coax the voice back. But it's run out, away, and I'm not in the exchange any more. I'm watching my great-aunt and she's not in a good way but she's not about to run out and get flattened by an omnibus. Agatha isn't like that. The living-room door opens. It's Uncle Kenneth. He's dabbing his lips with a handerchief that's well past its allotted span of twelve nose-blows. He's dabbing his lips because he always spittles at the corners when he laughs. Wouldn't you like to know why he'd been laughing? Has blank-face Milly got a comic turn or something? Does she juggle, does she do a great Sarah Bernhardt limp? Hey, I can't tell you everything. Uncle Kenneth laughs a lot. He laughs after he's said something that's not even particularly funny. It's a kind of nerves thing. Here's the maid. Watch her face. It'll have clues in it. It's blank. The more the ever so queer the blanker it goes 'cos never ever. She bobs at Agatha and crosses the hallway. Click clickety-click go her heels. She's wearing boots. The tiles are chess-board black and white. The dining-room swallows her up. Cold air and yesterday's soup waft out as usual. Uncle Kenneth frowns, thrusts his handkerchief back into his top pocket, thrusts it deeper, it looks really terrible and the mucus stains are showing their true colours but I can't change it, live with it.

Bad news, my dear?

Agatha is sitting. I forgot to say that. She's sitting in the big carved oak chair that takes up too much room. She's trembling. It's not really visible, but she is, all over. She thinks it must look frightful. Something's seizing her and shaking her. Willo has committed a depravity. He is on the 10.5 GWR from Basingstoke. Pleasant little country town. She opens her mouth. You'd think she'd say something like, it's Willo, he's done something awful. You'd think that only because you've watched too many lousy adaptations and your mind's a photocopier. She doesn't say that. She doesn't even want to say that. Instead she says, what's the time?

Because my great-aunt Agatha was amazingly practical.

I need a break. Circulate for a minute without me. Dive after those roast fore-quarters of lambs unless you're vegetarian in which case stick with the mashed turnips, it's worth it, heaven's probably a nice place when you get there.

You know why I think I have wasted my life?

You do? You agree that I have wasted my life?

Thanks a lot.

These fragments, says Zelda, I have shored against my ruin. She's reading my notes again. Scat, I say. You're overdue on the overdue books. I want to know what happens, she says. Agatha's in a fix, I say. I want to know how you unfix her, she says. I don't unfix her, I say. I don't do anything but let it roll. Then let it roll, cutesy, murmurs Zelda, or I'll bar you. Half past the hour, says Uncle Kenneth, consulting his fob. Eleven-thirty? Eleven thirty indeed, says Uncle Kenneth. He puts away his fob and sniffs and tucks his hands behind his back. The various clocks ding or ting or bong right on cue. Just one ting or ding or bong each. Agatha feels a great lethargy, sitting in her chair. You know how it is, before an exam or something? You want to sit there forever, you don't want to get up and gather your pencils and mascots and things and go into the exam room. You don't even want to think about doing this, you're so tired. Then you wake up. You took this exam twenty-two years ago and you passed. That's nice. You roll over and sleep some more, snucking into the pillow. That's nice.

My great-aunt Agatha doesn't have that option. She's not asleep. She's awake and its 1913 and really amazing things are going on in the cultural milieu, everyone's really modern, they're all being modern like crazy and Joseph Conrad is bicycling over to Henry James's place and Virginia Woolf is asking D. H. Lawrence to pass the sugar and these incredible magazines are coming out with way-out typography and FUCK OFF THE EMPIRE practically all over them and the Post-Impressionists are blowing the socks off Ezra and the suffragettes are screaming the place down and basically if all we think about when we think of now meaning then is a big hat and *The Country Diary of an Edwardian Lady* and maybe Walter de la Mare having a picnic we've got our arse up a gum-tree in a very bad place because (a) this is not the Edwardian period and (b) these really amazing avant-garde things were going on that make us a lifetime later look like a coach-party of Rotarians broken down on the North Circular Road or something. But the reason I brought all this up is that my great-aunt is stuck in this chair in the hallway in 1913 with a really big problem on her hands and the problem is that none of this amazing modern stuff is inside this house. This house is ticking away really quietly and its chairs are stuffed and it smells of beeswax and it's got twenty-eight crates of valuable china disposed around every place your elbow might be if you were to start getting really modern and jig around to Stravinsky or something and basically sex is not mentioned and nobody jigs around and there are these faces staring at you off every wall which are the faces of your forefathers and foremothers to whom the word bum would've blown their beards off and here's my great-aunt faced with the fact that her sweet little brother is depraved and has been kicked out of his school because he's depraved and the 10.5 non-stop Great Western from Basingstoke is bringing this depraved kid home and no one else knows it.

And Uncle Kenneth thinks he ought to say something because he's only just clicked that his niece is clearly a little ruffled and that it might have something to do with this telephone call. He's opening his mouth at the same time as the front door does and Mrs Trevelyan comes in. He shuts his mouth and turns round. Ah, good morning, dear, he says, instead of what he was going to say, which is drowning in the vast bog of the great unsaid. Mrs Trevelyan blinks at him as if he shouldn't be there. Good morning, Kenneth, she says. She's peeling off her gloves. There are boxes in the carriage, she says. Uncle Kenneth jerks a bit. Ah, he expostulates. He's a gent, a real gent. He goes over to the bell and presses it. It's an electric bell. It's the latest thing. It's very shrill, there's this far-off shrill sound and a pause and then the sound of boots on far-off steps, a stirring, a summoning of the elves deep down in the ground. Thank you, says Mrs Trevelyan. I have a headache. It's all roses, dear. She's saying it's all roses dear to her daughter. Agatha is standing up because she's polite, even to her mother. Roses, Mother?

Roses, dear. Back again, back again. One cannot move for roses. She's touching her hat which hasn't a rose on it, it's got a kind of sprig of heather with a lily on top. It's been roses in the spring, roses in the summer, roses in the autumn, she sighs. You'd think they'd have a new idea, these French, now and again. The hallway is big but it's already filled up with Mrs Trevelyan. Basically, it's something to do with her projective personality. She doesn't like to be ignored. She sets people on edge. She sets inanimate objects on edge. You're an animate object. But even the inanimate parts of you, like your fillings, react to Mrs Trevelyan. They react even more to Mrs Trevelyan than your animate parts. In fact, the inanimate parts of you seem to take over your animate parts when Mrs Trevelyan is around. It's a very curious thing. You feel like slush. You feel like slush to her windscreen-wiper. She wipes you out. I think you must have got the nub by now. Imagine being her daughter. Swish, swish.

Up comes the servant, on cue. It's Milly. She'd gone through the dining-room down to the kitchen, keeping incredibly blank. Then when the kitchen door was shut behind her and Dorothy looked up from out the steam on the range this blank face had kind of crumpled up and tears had plopped on to the original earthenware tiles that (I checked) some bastard's gone and lifted since and replaced with cork. What's up, duck? said Dorothy. Let me tell you here, in case you shrivelled-up cynics think that Dicky Thornby has lost all faith in 'uman koind – Dorothy is nice. She's large, she's ample, she smells of bread if her BO isn't on form, she wheezes a bit, she's straight down the line nice. Nice as in kind, generous, thoughtful, cuddly. She hails from Wiltshire. London gets up her nose and literally. Her cooking's so English but her Irish stew is succulent. She can't handle beans, for some reason. She likes gravy. She likes dishes to look brown and sensible and a lot. She's never heard of quiche lorraine. She doesn't wash her hands after visiting the toilet but who cares? She's wholesome, she's clean, she's a miracle, she tucked up Evelyn and Agatha and Giles and William, in that order, when she was so young she didn't have hair on her chin. Drink to Dorothy, you ornery haute cuisine bastards.

Milly wouldn't tell what was the matter. Dorothy hugged her some and put it down to nerves. She's got just the thing for nerves. Dr Quacker's

Miracle Pills. Guaranteed Relief. Money Back If Not. No Nerve Strain Since, Says Busy Nurse. Bell shrieks, vibrating the pan and Dorothy's brain. Wipe your eyes and nose-parts, dearie, advises Dorothy. Milly goes up. It's the memsahib.

Yes ma'am ma'am ma'am? I mean, one ma'am.

She curtsies. The hall is big. The chequered tiles fan out on every side. She's a pawn, basically. Mrs Trevelyan tuts and moves (Queen to Hall Table with the Carefully Ironed *Times* on 3). Uncle Kenneth doesn't, he hovers and makes his usual little noises in his throat and wonders why Agatha is staring at the telephone and holding her hands very tight and how his little surprises never go quite right. Milly helps Mrs Trevelyan off with her coat. The boxes are in the carriage, says Mrs Trevelyan. Milly has taken off memsahib's coat without too much effort, it's a great milestone, she's sweating but pleased. Ma'am, one ma'am. She's forgotten which hook it's supposed to hang from. Lily said there is only one hook for Mrs Trevelyan's coat and she was showed it. There are twelve hooks in the coat cupboard. Three are unoccupied. She tries the one on the left, the first one. The coat won't hang. It won't hang. She's using the wrong hook, or maybe the wrong tab on the coat, she mustn't look surprised, be it ever so, be it never ever, be it never ever so queer and if you drop it dust it down and don't look surprised. They're talking, amongst themselves, about hats. That's all right then. She finds the tab, it's tiny, the hook's too big, they're all the same size of bloody hook forgive me Lord, it's stupid, fancy that, she hooks the coat by the big furry collar, never ever ever, but it might've been Lily done it, they won't see, dunna fret, it hangs there like it's unhappy, squirrels' fur, a hundred squirrels at least, a hundred hanging squirrels looking unhappy but shrugging it off, look sharp, keep blank, close cupboard, get boxes out th'carriage, don't drop, don't fret, don't expect or 'ate.

Good advice, huh? Don't expect, don't hate. That just about covers the ground. What memsahib had meant yesterday, if you're too pissed or something to have got it, is don't spit, posh version. Milly'd looked blank, but she'd nodded. Don't expect, don't hate. Don't spit in the wind or at anybody else. Not a bad credo for the new millennium. The Anti-Expectoration Movement. The last one, hey, we spat all over. It was an orgy of expecting and hating. There was spittle coursing down the windows. This one, we should keep silent, receive, try to like a bit more, even love. Zelda is getting deep inside me. It sounds better when she says it. It sounds better when it's said from the pillow next to me. Like dawn in Kyoto, nightfall over Lhasa, moonlight through the Sierra Nevada, a grey mizzle over the Thames and Milly humping these bloody hatboxes up the steps under the wrought-iron and fancy glass portico with nicely unpeeling pillars if you can imagine that. Try to. OK, OK, here it is on a plate, here's the shot – rear view, mid, angled up the steps, her black skirt and white apron-ties at the back and black boots and firm black hair that'll have its little fancy white cap at tea-time, humping these big lightweight drums of hatboxes, about the same size and shape as the zoetrope drum – light motifs, geddit? – the front door swinging open to her foot and never ever leave it open for the draughts and drunks. Interior view door swinging open note that nice light shift across the waxed tiles, Mike. Luverly. Milly is in monochrome. Her face is white. She is not robust, but she's not dying either. Until yesterday she lived every one of her thirteen years next to the Worksop soap works. The world's worst soap works were the soap works in Worksop. You got filthy, living next to the soap works in Worksop. All her almost fourteen years Milly has breathed in the equivalent of two packets of unfiltered Woodies a day. Here she's breathing in a little less, but her room is smoky. The chimney is badly aligned, it's under the roof, it's got no draw. I've seen this room. It had an art student in it. The fireplace was blocked. Milly's room, I said. No, Philidea, actually, she replied. Something like Philidea or maybe Philadelphia, even. There was a lot of paint around and most of it on her face. She was a posh punk, I guess. She was maybe how my great-aunt would've ended up if she'd been born in the 1960s. Only maybe, because my great-aunt was quite sensible and practical and serious. Actually, Philadelphia was probably all these, too, but I didn't hang around long enough to check her out. It was the three guys in the room: they looked like they were on stand-by for a lousy Channel 4 drama about this jerk visiting his grandfather's old house and finding it full of art students on a hand-held camera. You know what I mean. I can't help it if they were lounging clichés. That's how they were. It was a few years back. Ripped jeans and Hallowe'en faces were in. Milly would've screamed and screamed. She'd have liked the two-bar electric heater, though. She'd have appreciated that, even without the spit and the fizz.

Zelda's come back from the overdue books. The absent overdue books. The absent centre, as this pseud creep with about three Ph.D.s on Milos Forman calls it. He teaches here. He likes the idea, he tells me, of a library full of books that are overdue. Yeah, shelf after shelf after empty shelf, Rick, an absent presence of books that are semenotically there, y'know? Yup, I say, especially when he gets shot at the end. He gets really flustered when I say that, because I say it a lot these days.

Phantom books, I think he means. Like phantom films. Yeah, yeah. I'll buy him a drink some day, step on his glasses, steal one of his doctorates, lend him *Honky Tonk 2*. He impresses Zelda.

They're all back in the living-room, they've moved out of the hall draughts. The hall draughts are worse than the living-room draughts which, if you position yourself right, can be avoided. The hall draughts can't be avoided, they've irradiated the whole area, they've got every corner covered. Everyone has a kind of draught Geiger counter built into them at this time. It's not surprising: a draught can snuck up under your five layers and settle in there inside your drawers and before you can say lozenge it's manufacturing fluid in your lungs and you're on a downhill slope, guv.

The hats are out. It's admiring time. It's always like this when Mrs Trevelyan goes shopping. It's what mothers and daughters are supposed to do. Uncle Kenneth is hanging around because he knows the tea's coming up in a minute and he wants Agatha to look at the fellow taking a walk through the zoetrope. He's not too sure about his sister-in-law looking at it, but she wouldn't anyway, she's sick to her carious back teeth of his machines and moving pictures and mismatching spats. Milly is sort of waiting to be dismissed because she can't remember whether you never ever or you do. Lily is on tea-duty. Morning tea with a fan of biscuits and the morning sugar-bowl with the fancy coat of arms. Lily comes in while Mrs Trevelyan is lifting up a trousseau with a big bronzed bloom on it that reminds Agatha of a malignant tumour in one of Father's medical books though she doesn't say it she just says very elegant, Mother, it'll suit you I'm sure, while behind this gauzy sentence there are all these Roman depravities in togas and a steam train whistling and smutting and William flying through the air with his articles because he's been booted out of Randle. Where's Giles in all this? She's nodding and wondering if Giles will telephone with an explanation. He's not sure he can telephone. Maybe he'll sneak out and get to a public telephone You May Telephone From Here, if he has some pennies. He must, it's simply essential. She'll shoot to the telephone if it rings. She nods and smiles while the ridiculous number of hats piles up and there's tissue paper all over the place and Milly's thinking she should be tidying up and Lily gives a cool little bob and exits not helping our Mill and there's the japanned tea-tray winking its silver on the tea table behind the chaise longue and on the japanned tea-tray there's a really modern whacky teapot Uncle Kenneth bought for Christmas, which Madre doesn't like too much, it's kind of ceramic bamboo but Lily hasn't got the message yet. Agatha's decided not to tell Madre. When she imagines telling Madre there's this awful blackness and dizziness, there's Madre with her mouth open and her eyes popping out, there's this frightful beastly screaming and the Romans are laughing in their depraved togas, laughing and laughing and waving chicken-bones. She nods and says how charming at a light brown straw with a soot-grey wing on the front. There are enough hats here for a costume museum. *I'm* thinking that, she's not. She's thinking there are enough hats here for a millinery. Uncle Kenneth is helping himself to sugar. He's pouring his tea out. He's drinking it. He makes a noise when he drinks. Milly's staring at him because it's that loud and he sticks his lower lip right out and it's not how Sis said they drink he hasn't even got his little finger stuck up. Mrs Trevelyan's running out of steam, her natter is slowing down, you can tell she's getting irritable and she'll stay irritable until her afternoon nap. Put these back, take them away, into my room, she says. Put these back take them away into my room hits Milly's brain and she jumps. She was gawping, never ever gawp, her mouth shuts, she turns blank. Yes, ma'am. It's a squeak. She clears her throat. Ma'am is looking at her pretty nastily. Make allowances, Mrs T, c'mon. The girl's new to all this shit. But Mrs T isn't like that. The one thing that saves Milly from getting yelled at is that now meaning then was a hell of a time for finding domestics, decent or indecent. There was a supply and demand imbalance. Domestics could be cheeky and survive because it was a hell of a thing to find a replacement. There are articles in all the papers about this, I've read them, on microfilm I've read them, I've taken rolls of microfilm out of their capsules and put them in the wrong way up and got a ricked neck because I'm lazy and I hate machines, it's been like this for years, even the really modern crazy people are moaning about it between jigging around and humping each other and throwing flat-irons at their partners if they're Frieda Lawrence and don't like doing the dishes because she didn't, David did them. He did a lot of things. He did a lot of DIY, painting and decorating and stuff. He washed his clothes and cooked and sewed. He dug the garden. He didn't moan about the servant shortage because he liked to do these things, he liked to wrestle and heave with the great mistress of life, with the elements of earth, air, fire and water, with his vital being, with all that Lawrentian stuff. Peeling potatoes and getting his knuckles chapped kept him in touch with the living man. Zelda's nodding. It's Zen, she's saying. You sit all night in the temple yard and then go off and sweep leaves into perfect circles. Mrs T has never swept a leaf in her life. She can drop a tub of talc and someone else gets to sneeze over it. No wonder she hasn't got this vital thing. No wonder, I'm thinking, America isn't very Lawrentian. I'm thinking maybe I should rent a cottage with no running water and get my hands chapped drawing up the bucket each morning. In England I mean, mate. Roots and that. Foind my voital English bing. Maybe there isn't that sort of cottage left in England. Maybe I'd have to go to Newfound-land or somewhere to find a cottage with no running water and a bucket in a well. That's a terrible thought. But then, maybe it'd drive me mad. Maybe this Third World Thoreau Iron John thing would not suit me after all. Maybe I'd just pine for my Magimix and my electric toothpick. Zelda's saying I should get back to the action. But they're just sitting around sipping tea, Zelda. She says I should try to be Henry James about them sipping tea. Zelda did Henry James for her master's. She's smart. But I'm not Henry James, Zelda. I just see them sipping tea with their little fingers stuck out in this room stuffed full of *objets d'art* and I feel very claustrophobic. What's Agatha thinking, Ricky? I've told you what Agatha's thinking: she's in a mess. She just wants Madre to get out of the way so she can perhaps tell Uncle Kenneth about William but right now she's kind of treading water, she's confused, she's developing a headache, headaches and dyspepsia are really in at this time, practically everyone was trying not to fart the whole time, it must have been the diet or something, they didn't have great stomachs and there was a lot of mental fatigue, probably from straining their eyes in lousy light and breathing in coal smoke and stuff. I think I ought to change the paragraph.

Phew, as me dad would say in World's End Park, nice to git out, eh son? Nice to have a bit o' fresh *oof*. (Chuckle chuckle.)

Too right, Pop, I reply, nursing me ribs. Cor though, that was a short one, eh? That was sort of late-Beckett length, I'd say.

Mrs T's talking. I was going to snip some but what she's saying is quite interesting. Agatha has discovered a bit of sunlight on the window-sill. She's actually sitting on the window-sill. It's a nice shot: sunlight rippling over the creamy dress, her grey eyes, her hair kind of glowing as hair does in sunlight, youthful and fresh, even the soft down on her forearm's glowing, David Hamilton crossed with T. S. Eliot, her Geiger counter clicking but she can take it, the sunlight's keeping her warm mentally, the morning sun, the plunge, that's Virginia Woolf says Zelda, I know the plunge is Virginia Woolf, Zelda, but a film without cultural references is not art house, OK?

bother yourself about me, dear. Isn't it a little late for a frock? They say it will be frightful tomorrow. But I expect you want to keep ahead. When you get to our age, dear, one wishes to conserve. Don't catch chill. We cannot have two invalids in the house. If I may count myself an invalid, if I may have that privilege. Father's habit of encouraging pot-luck is awfully trying. One has to play the hostess when one can hardly see the guests for one's thumping. Though guests, I think, in most cases anyway, is hardly the correct term, since guests are usually invited.

Piercing side-glance at Uncle Kenneth. A twitch of the mouth. Sip tea. It's a great part. Martita Hunt's doing it, of course, someone good at half-crazy ladies stirring behind their cobwebs. Mrs Trevelyan is half-crazy and she's intelligent. She doesn't come at you screaming with a cudgel but kind of pads around and just when you think it's OK, you're safe, she's only talking about herself *out* comes the gimlet and you're perforated, oof, under the second rib. That's why Agatha's sitting on the window-sill. It's safer. And the sun's great. The sun's burning on her eyelids, it's aflame, it's pathetic November stuff but it's turning everything under her closed eyelids into a golden beyond, really incredibly golden and beyond and oceans of it and it's even warm, she's drinking it up, she's got her small chin lifted and it's on her throat above the lace collar, she's showing her throat to the sun, she's letting the sun kiss her on the throat and on the eyelids and it's quite sexual though she doesn't think hey, this is quite sexual, she thinks if only I could stay like this forever and ever and there wasn't this awful thing that is like a frightful dream you cannot wake up from, this beastly horrid thing with William and what am I to do if only Mother would go away Uncle Kenneth would help me oh this sun, this sun, it's so vital, it's probably full of vitamins, I'm sure it is, it does feel as if it is and medically.

Uncle Kenneth is staring up at the ceiling. I'm glad we swagged the chandelier, because his eye is following its folds. There's a lot to look up at on this ceiling. I'm sure, he says, Arthur doesn't mean to be trying. Mrs Trevelyan leans forward slightly. Milly's packing away the hats and trying not to make the tissue-paper rustle, which is incredibly challenging. There's this really big rustle just as Mrs T replies. It kind of dims the effect. It's heard as ssshhArthssshhalwayssshhhto bessshhloved, of courssssshhh. Her irritability count moves up a notch. No, two notches. She's always wanted to say to her brother-in-law this thing about Arthur needing to be loved, because she knows that Kenneth has the same defect and he knows she knows it. This sounds like R.D. Laing, says Zelda. Hey, honey-bun, Sigmund the Fraud is probably giving Herr Adler an inferiority complex and a cigar right now meaning then in Vienna probably. Let me finish. The tissue-paper problem's ruined a major perforation. Uncle Kenneth is still staring at the swag. He's got to the bit that tucks under the central stem. Mrs T leans back and uses the antimacassar, so thank God Steve put it there and not on the arm-rest. I mean, she's narked enough as it is. Milly's doing her hat-putting-away in slow motion, even the blankness is cracking under the strain, because despite doing it in slow motion the tissue-paper is having a ball rustling and going ssssshhh and it's the loudest thing in the room. Would you hurry up, please, bursts through the tissue-paper. This is to her. She's been ticked off, kind of. She flushes but keeps blank apart from her lower lip and starts working really fast, it's noisy, it's like a waterfall, it's like trying to pack a waterfall into boxes and oh Christ forgive me Lord they're different sizes some of the hats don't fit she just has to squeeze and squash 'em in and Mrs T said to be ever so careful because the roses are never stitched on these days they're glued and they can drop off it's like packing birds with big wings you just have to thrust.

There's a silence. Let me tell you, between you and me, Milly's made a mess of the hats. She'll sort it out upstairs, in the privacy of ma'am's dressing room, her blankness ripped away, her lower lip having a very fierce time under her front teeth. Do we have to have so much of the hats business, says Zelda. Yes, actually. Living in this house is a very complicated business. Living in any house is a very complicated business, says Zelda. Yes, honey, but the very complicated business of living in a house is torture when you're not allowed to swear and jig around and you've got a lot of tissue-paper and a whole stack of never evers. In fact, there are more never evers and for every single person in this house than there are alwayses and there are very few what the fucks, if any. And the tissue-paper is just an extra. You should know how to handle tissue-paper like origami or whatever. If you were the real thing you'd know how to handle tissue-paper so it didn't so much as whisper and you could hear a hat-pin drop let alone Mrs Trevelyan saying something she's waited to say for a very long time. Actually, she's already said it before. She said it a week ago and two weeks before that and one of these to her brother-in-law but she has a lot of holes in her memory, it's the drinking probably. She drinks a lot. Hoi, she's a soak then? Yeh, guv, she's a bleedin' soak.

Milly's gone out. She had a tough time with the door because she should have thought to open it before. Before picking up a tower of ten hatboxes, I mean. She's not a great pre-planner. If she had a Filofax the planner section would be empty, like mine. So you know what happened? A never ever. She had the door opened for her by a posh. She was stuck in front of the door trying to balance ten hatboxes about double her height and get her hand to the door-handle when it was opened by a snuffle and a grunt and a hand on her shoulder. Uncle Kenneth would open a door for anyone, maidservant or king. She kept blank and didn't say thank you because it wouldn't come out, she was so upset at a posh opening a door for her. He shouldn't have done it. It demeaned her. She would've got it open. No one should have took any notice. Anyway, she's upstairs in the mistress's dressing room trying to get the hats looking like they haven't just come off a Bring and Buy Sale for Abyssinia stall (how do I know if they had bring and buy sales in 1913? – don't be picky, relax, at least I didn't say Ethiopia) while downstairs Mrs T is easing her lace collar off the weeping sores on her chin by imperceptible movements of her head (hey, it's the lace collar chafing that causes the weeping sores but without the lace collar the weeping sores would be visible and anyway if she didn't wear a lace or something collar she'd one look pretty weird and two her Geiger counter would be going crazy so she's pretty well stuck with a chronic sores problem that even Dr Cheat's Miracle Spot Cream can't clear up in three hours or three months or three lifetimes)

Where was I?

Oh yes. Cor blimey. She's imperceptibly moving her head and Uncle Kenneth is twiddling his thumbs round and round and round and even he sees that his thumb-nails are black so he imperceptibly starts to clean them with one of his clean nails but a surreptitious glance down reveals that this operation makes his clean nail black too so he gives up and tucks his hands into his two waistcoat pockets where they discover bits he can't identify but they're sticky. He closes his eyes. He opens them because a horse clip-clopped past in the street and it's a habit, he always opens his eyes when a horse clip-clops past as if it's someone he knows. Maybe he's taking advantage of the halcyon days of the clip-clop sound effect for real because in 1913 it's the internal combustion engine what disturbs half the time and every day the internal combustion engine is gaining ground over the clip-clop but imperceptibly, imperceptibly. Agatha in the sunny window spot sees the horse and on top of it is Mr Brown or Bran, she can never remember which but both well bread, as the joke used to go when this family made jokes. The dust-cart appears on the corner. And I mean dust-cart, not a garbage truck with electric pistons like something out of *Return of the Empire*. It's a cart pulled by a big old knackered horse with one ball bigger than the other if you wished to crouch down and examine them and a cart behind it full of dust. At least, every time something's thrown into it it's like someone's beating a mattress in there. Up and down the street go people in twills and spats and straw bonnets and shawls and hobble skirts and top hats and ribbons and morning coats and detachable cuffs and puffed sleeves and none of

197

this looks weird to Agatha, she doesn't even notice it except to think how frightfully loud that skirt is or something, even though some of these dresses are really huge and long and the hats are like a joke and half the men look like they're going to a posh wedding because this is a posh street and half the women have enormous bottoms that kind of deign to follow them. I want to know what's happened to all these clothes and these bottoms. Zelda doesn't, Zelda wants the action. I say there is action, there's a street being cleaned, streets being cleaned is important action and especially in 1913. I would like to make a film which starts with a tense family situation in 1913 and you do a profile shot of the heroine at the window and then you see this dust-cart from her point-of-view and then the rest of the film you just follow this dust-cart around and all the guys with brooms and shovels. It would be colossally expensive and very avant-garde and it would make my reputation. The only trouble is, no one gets shot at the end. Zelda says, please don't do that, not now. I want to know what happens when William comes back. I am not interested in a dust-cart, even in 1913. I say – for you, Zelda, anything. Action, she says. I say, action is ninety per cent inaction. Don't believe everything you see on TV. We lie in bed and snore half of our lives. We sit at tables and stuff our mouths or sit at tables and stuff our heads most of the rest. Life is basically extremely routine. You're talking about a very narrow band of people, Zelda says. Did you know that most of the world do not live in proper houses? Zelda comes out with these amazing facts. They turn out to be true. Zelda is my conscience. I like it that way.

We're in a very proper house. It's stuffed with properness, crates and crates of it. It's even got a thick red swag on the chandelier.

How can I help it if they're not talking? This is a family of silences. They're Pinteresque and some more. They're into nattering in short bursts and then long pauses. It's the rhythm, here. It's the Gatling gun rhythm, here.

They don't have radio or TV. Sometimes you hear pretty well nothing but the turning of pages for a whole evening, leaves of leathery books turning like wings of birds, a stream, a breaking wave. The tutting of a fire if it's spring, autumn or winter. The clock agreeing. Clip-clops. Vintage cars on flint-chips passing in rain, in dry, in snow.

Costermongers' shouts distant, costermongers' shouts close. Violet-seller passing on her way home, if she 'as one, a room somewhere, the cold night air, not at the mo shouting vilets vilets, lovely vilets, bit part in the latest Woolf, pays for the urchin's crutch, crunching past the poshie's golden winders, swags on the chandeliers, the turning of pages and maybe the pianer, the usual class gulf, the frayed rope-bridge across, some of us make it, some of us don't, some of us are yelping from halfway down, dangling on the frayed end, nobody takes any notice, we drop, yaaaaaaa, giving it all away, guv, wiv our last yell.

Am I bitter? Am I real ale? Am I Jason's watered-down piss-coloured version? Am I, Gawd 'elp us, a can of Kraut?

Which one was my grandmother? Guessed yet? Gerron, 'ave a go, lay yer bets – five to one on at this stage of the game 'cos we've only got a clutch to choose from, so far. You can pass if you fink she's not appeared yet, mate.

I mean, she might not have done. Delayed entrance. 'edda Gabler stuff, right in the corner of the net bom bom.

Thank God, someone's speaking. My patter has limits. Uncle Kenneth, it is.

I think, Beatrice, I shall dine out tonight.

That's it? Shit.

OK, sub-text, the Woody Allen thing, titles under a shot of the two of them sitting there with their eyes closed like they've got a headache: I think, Beatrice, you are an unholy lump of rancid lard and I'm going to bin you.

Or words to that effect. I've modernised for the historically-challenged amongst you. I'll bet the fireworks have run out. You know what the first news item of the new millennium will be? How many people died celebrating it. It'll be really depressing, you'll have a hangover, don't watch it. Somewhere like Brazil or Mexico will be the worst. It'll be like the Aztecs all over again. That sun's a greedy old sod,

199

eh, Putxekzettleon? Yeah, Zipxundunagin, but there's bugger all we can do about it. Plunge, plunge, pluck pluck. The Abos get Rolf Harris to sing, apparently. Really? Yeah, works every time. More than my job's worth, Putxekzettleon, more than my job's worth. Plunge, pluck. Hup! There's a beauty, nice wriggle, good beat. 24,821. That enough for dawn tomorrow, d'you reckon, Zipxundunagin my blood-boltered old fruit? One never really knows for sure until He appears, Putxekzettleon, does one? But put the kettle on anyway, there's a gore-smeared nice chap, and make sure it boils proper. Nothing I can't stand more than French tea – oops, me zip's undone. That's what I've been surreptitiously (cor!) trying to tell you all this time, Pete – and in front of the sacrifices, too. Tut tut. Shocking.

Yippee, folks – Mrs T is rising. Knuckles to forehead, or *The Bad News* by A. J. Scott-Witherwilly RA, the postboy stamping his feet outside, waiting for a tip, letter skilfully dropped on the slabs so it chimes with her creamy apron and the jug on the mantelpiece. Hey, there'll be plenty of these soon, just be patient, only the tunics won't be red. Anyway, you can tell from the way Mrs T's rising that she's going to continue rising until she gets to her room. This RA way of doing it makes everyone left in the room feel that they have just said something really lousy, and they feel lousy for the rest of the day while Mrs T is raving it above, feeling just great. Sounds like the history of Christianity, says Zelda. Ssssh, no time for jokes. Mrs T hasn't replied to Uncle Kenneth, which makes Uncle Kenneth's remark sort of hang around like a bad smell, he doesn't know whether she heard it or not, maybe she'd nodded off for a split-second, maybe he ought to try saying it again, maybe he ought just to come to dinner anyway and ignore that rude pointed stuff about Arthur's friends (and relations, of course) always coming round unannounced. But she's already at the door with the back of her hand Uhu'd against her forehead, and she pauses because Uncle Kenneth and Agatha know that they're supposed to say something like, is your head very bad today, Beatrice/ Mother? It takes quite a lot of effort to keep your lips buttoned in this situation, because instead of is your head very bad today Beatrice/ Mother? you might come out with, one day, Beatrice/Mother, you really will have a headache and no one will believe you, or, pull the other one, Beatrice/Mother, it's got knobs on, or, for Pete's sake don't be so fucking childish, Beatrice/Mother. Just keeping quiet is a strain against that pause, that expectation. Just keeping quiet will make you feel you're a lousy mean shit for the rest of the day, and just when this feeling's wearing off she'll detect it's wearing off and pump it back up again. She sighs because no one's said anything – a real big sigh, like Sarah Bernhardt in *Hamlet*, clomping around the stage and practically sighing her peg-leg off. Is it very bad today, Mother? Christ, that was Agatha, she said it, she said it with her eyes closed and the sunlight on her face and that's a new variation, it's ironic, it's sardonic, it was sad with an edge of impatience but that might be because Agatha is wound up extremely tight inside, thinking of the train and William and all these togas flying around, and not because she's trying a new tack.

Don't bother yours with it, my dear, says Mrs T. I'm sure you have many more important things to think about.

Brilliant. What artistry, huh? Door shuts. Atmosphere in living-room not good. Atmosphere in living-room temporally disrupted, as pseud creep'd put it. Sunlight on Agatha's eyelids has started to give her a headache, in fact. Suspicion that Madre can read one's mind yet again substantiated. Clock growls, tuts, pings the quarter. Time marches on, thinks Uncle Kenneth. (Hey, you can't think original thoughts all the time. You need the old hands, they're mates, they're pals, they make you feel comfy. Uncle Kenneth needs to feel comfy right at this moment.) Time marches on, he says, it does indeed. The house makes little satisfied sounds above and below, the clocks agreeing and Madre negotiating the stairs and a servant in the room above, making the ceiling creak. And pipes. Agatha nods and watches the dustmen sweeping along the gutters. Zelda's getting worried. The dustmen have high boots and coats too big for them and cocky white hats. There's a sign on the cart: *City of Westminster*. They're shovelling the night's rain, it glitters under their brooms, Agatha marvels at the beauty of it, she's quite Woolfian really, she thinks how the world goes on despite everything and wants just the ordinariness of that water shovelled along past the droppings and oil puddles and down through the drain's grille one of them, the young one, yanked up like he was yanking up the whole street so all the houses toppled over and the swags unravelled and the carriages and motor cars ended up in a heap at the junction.

201

Uncle Ken. Yes, m'dear? He's standing up. He looks dispirited. The zoetrope and its nude fellow has become an embarrassment. He wants to go home and fiddle with his conked-out projector. He has three moving-picture projectors. Uncle Ken and I would have had some great conversations. What's happened to all his stuff? I ask myself every day. Where does everything go to? Where have the stuffed houses of now meaning then unstuffed themselves? Why are we able to move without crawling over hills of antiques and bric-a-brac and junk? I mean, what happened to all their bath-tubs? Who broke up the iron ranges? How come entropy works so bleedin' efficiently? Why am I the only one who lies awake at night thinking these things?

Yes, m'dear?

Agatha slips elegantly off the window-sill and stands. Can I just slip in here very quickly how that slipping-off the window-sill brought a lump to Uncle Kenneth's throat, because he remembers suddenly the days when Agatha'd have to jump it? Or have to arch back with her beribboned tummy sticking out and kind of slither off slowly, awkwardly, humming something sweet? He didn't notice her grow. (Thank you.)

She fixes him with two grey eyes. This is serious, thinks Uncle Kenneth. He clears his throat to hear better. He blinks and his nostrils flare minutely. The sun goes in. Catch it, Mike. Catch the way the net curtains smelling not of coal smoke but of lavender because they've just been washed billow slightly as the sun goes in. Maybe it's connected. Maybe it's because Agatha's just let them drop with her hand and slipped off. Anyway, Uncle Kenneth counts the Coming of the Shadow from that moment. I mean, he will do. In about ten years' time everybody will be saying how human nature changed and the old world was lost and all that guff at, say, six o'clock on 11 May 1915 or tea-time on 8 September 1909 or (bo-oring) zero hour on 1 July 1916 (didn't you learn *anything* with Mr Wilberforce, Ossy? It'll come up again, don't sweat, it'll be my piece de raisin cake, *quiet* in the back row!) and so forth. What I mean, is, they won't be *saying* it at those times they'll be saying it (the world, human nature etc.) was *lost* at those times – oh, you know what I *meeeean*, dumbos. Pretty crazy, huh? But Uncle Kenneth will agree. He'll agree, that is, that the old world was lost and

202

the Shadow fell and so forth at a certain time and his certain time will be when the sun went in just as Agatha fixed him with her two grey eyes before opening her mouth and telling him about William and that was, by the living-room clock, which is always a minute ahead of mean time, 11.47 on 3 November 1913.

Because, I have to remind you I'm afraid, she will already be a phantom when he thinks of her in ten years' time. A phantom with grey eyes who didn't know she was going to be a phantom in ten years' time. Actually, I'm very afraid to say, in almost exactly *five* years' time. Zelda's saying that's ruined it, it's like you said about your father reading the last page of your books out loud, there's no suspense, it's stupid. I say, hey, I didn't say *how* she was going to die. Zelda's upset, she thinks I'm morbid. Listen, O golden-toothed one, I cannot think of my great-aunt who I am also in love with as anything other than a phantom. It's weird. But you know why? Because I have the date of her death, and it was much too early, and I might have met her if she'd lived as long as her mother, or not even as long as that, and then after her death I'd maybe still think of her in a slightly morbid way because I'd know and she wouldn't when and how she died but I didn't meet her and she's always beautiful and grey-eyed and sad even when she's happy because to me she's a phantom and I want you to feel that, too.

Zelda says I talk too much about myself. Nobody's interested in you and your crazy feelings, she says. Her tongue is worse than her *keisaku* stick. I am not an interesting person. Oi, wotcha mate, get my drift? We're talking about complicated things. Agatha's just told Uncle Kenneth about William. We missed it. It wasn't important. It was actually really banal. It was sort of breathless and banal. The dust-cart's gone. If we'd been looking out of the window we'd have seen a chinless guy in round spectacles watching the iron grille of the stinky drains being put back. This guy is going to father a girl who's going to bring forth a guy who keeps the chinlessness thing going and who at the age of nineteen will be sitting on this beautiful palm-waving surfy island with two hundred other guys and they'll all have their hands over their eyes and there'll be this light so bright it makes it through the hands into their eyes and when they open their eyes there'll be this great thunder and incredibly beautiful rising cloud rising in slow motion up and up and up right in front of them and about two days later their skin'll start peeling off and they'll start suffering and dying over years and years and they'll say that the day the Shadow fell was August whatever 1958 – and tough luck 'cos even after my documentary (*Death on Christmas Island*, 1978) Her Majesty's Wankers refuse to take the rap for GBH and murder. I mean, it's not even in the *Encyclopedia Britannica*, it just goes on about phosphate mining and stuff, it's like they're all ashamed or something. Zelda's impressed. Hey, it was in my furrowed brow phase. The budget was so small we didn't make it out there, it was all archive and interviews, it was screened at midnight or something, it wasn't even a fully-grown turkey. Zelda's impressed above all by my modesty. Shucks, thanks. My history of failures impresses someone. There's something Zen about my successes: they empty the mind just like that.

The chinless guy's gone. I didn't mention this but I think I ought to: his Christmas Island thing grandson will father a girl who'll bring forth a guy who'll father a guy who'll father twin girls who'll bring forth, about halfway through this spanking new millennium, nothing but mutants. I'm projecting ahead. Zelda says stop inventing. I'm not inventing, it's statistically certain, hurts and poisons are laid down in the genes, they wait there and then when you think you're in the clear they shamble up and say hi, stranger. Remember Christmas Island, '58? Remember Hiroshima? Remember that stuff they put on the wheat for the aphids and on the backs of cows for the warble fly? Remember that tricky sector on the No. 3 redoubt at Le Transloy that got soaked with mustard? You don't? You think the twentieth century was buried with the twentieth century? You think Shadows fall once only and only once for about ten minutes or something? You think you got away with it? You think massacres and violations and stupid oafs don't have a half-life about the same as Caesium 3 or something? You think Tarkovsky's *Stalker* wasn't projecting ahead? You think you can go visit the Ukraine without hitting the Zone? You think the Zone isn't going to be there in 25,000 years time? You don't think Tarkovsky was a genius? You don't think I'm a fraud? You don't believe in phantoms with silk gloves up to their elbows? You think it's pleasant being thrashed with a *keisaku* stick by the woman you love in a library with the best air-conditioning system *in Texas*?

You think we ought to change the reel? You think we ought to put ice on the top of the projector? You think we ought to have some action?

You crazy or supp'n?

There's a steam train coming right for you.

So you're not screaming and running hell for leather out?

Say, how sophisticated.

I hope you're keeping awake. I hope the twenty-first century hasn't started off with a power-cut. I hope the Rickmansworth Liberation Army hasn't had a go at the building because they're way out of date. I'm projecting. I'm burying the action in a whole load of junk. Zelda says it's like peering through cigarrette smoke. Cigarete has only one r, she says. One r, two ts. It's my weak spot, I reply. I can't kick the habit. I've had hypnosis for it. I wiped out my spellcheck because I ran out of room. I'm over-confident. I ask her to spell iridescent, exaggeration, and millenary. She passes. Shucks.

Anyway, it's not cigarette smoke. It's – begins with ph, ends in ms. I've overplayed that one. There's no longer a chill.

Uncle Kenneth is trembling all over. Minutely, but not quite imperceptibly. He is sitting in the over-padded sofa by the Chinese lamp and is knocking the tassels on the shade with his finger. This is unfortunate, because it really gets to memsahib if these tassels are not completely straight. But Uncle Kenneth is stressed and when he's stressed he has to fiddle with something in the world, something out there, generally the nearest fiddleable thing. The tassels are way out of line now. Some of them are kind of stuck up on the curvy silk of the shade and one of them is actually loose, it's dangling, he's broken an object. It is one of the most unoriginal and literal phrases of Mrs Trevelyan but I have to repeat it at this juncture: Uncle Kenneth is a bull in a china shop. He has large elbows and knees. The house has more china in it than a china shop. He has broken three pretty good plates and a fancy piece of delft in the last few years. That's worse than any of the domestics, who aren't doing too badly either. Lily is second at one Meissen Bruhlsches Allerei-Dessin porcelain saucer dated 1758, one squat terracotta jug of purely sentimental value and a salt-glaze stoneware flower vase with blood-red blisters said to have been plucked from the Great Fire of London but it wasn't, it was a crappy firing. George (he's the manservant/butler, he'll be shambling into view in a minute – appreciate this minute because he is Not Very Nice and looks nothing like Anthony Hopkins let alone Anthony Perkins) is third with one deliberately smashed Sèvres flambé-glaze coffee pot and a Schwarzlot faience dish with hunting dogs sniffing at tousled lovers in foreground which Mr Trevelyan particularly liked to point out to guests. Gcorge is way out first if you take value into consideration. Dorothy has broken one crappy milk-jug in thirty-four years. There was one mentally defective maidservant (I mean, literally challenged, OK?) who tipped over a tray with nine long-stemmed peachblow champagne glasses with milk-white linings and violet rims and eight shattered and she screamed and screamed until she was hit by George, twice.

I wonder what happened to her. I don't suppose anything nice.

Agatha is standing directly in front of her uncle. She wants him to say something. She wants him to take over. She wants him to guard William and herself from the cold winds, from scandal, from the end of the old world. But he's trembling, she can see it, he's buckling, there's a shadow across him, she'll have to cope on her own. We must take matters in hand, says Uncle Kenneth. Should we tell anyone? says Agatha. She's already said this three times. We must indeed take matters in hand, Uncle Kenneth repeats. They're on a kind of loop which is going nowhere. We must get to the station, oh dear, it's all so beastly, says Agatha. Most beastly of all for the poor boy, says Uncle Kenneth. Very beastly, says Agatha. I cannot imagine what he might have done. Should we tell anyone? We must therefore take matters in hand, says Uncle Kenneth. The tassels are a mess. He stares at them. Then he grips the stem of the table lamp and shakes it. The little silken tassels jig about and come to rest, miraculously, in order. Such things please me, murmurs Uncle Kenneth. Dorothy, says Agatha. We could tell Dorothy. Dorothy would know what to do. I know what to do, says

Uncle Kenneth. He feels he is not matching the situation. He feels the situation coming at him from various angles and perforating him in various places and he feels this Shadow across him. Boys have been expelled before, he says. Ssssh, hisses Agatha. It's true that Uncle Kenneth's voice booms. The house has ears all over. It has a dumb waiter in the dining-room and frequently a less dumb waiter at the bottom, catching the booms, leering, saving it up. A glimpse of George, a weeny preview. Uncle Kenneth rubs his hands. A wretched business, he says, a wretched business. He thinks he's sounding like a novel. He wonders what the term depravity might include. He sees red plush curtains and painted ladies but knows it must be to do with boys, with boys' bottoms, which for some reason are in a row bent over while someone is saying depravity in a horrible manner so that the cruel lips dribble and fart. He wishes he hadn't brought over the zoetrope with its nude fellow. It was to cheer Agatha up. Damned difficult to put the lid on, he says. He's quite tubercular, says Agatha in a jaunty way. Uncle Kenneth knows William is quite tubercular, that his lungs are quite scarred, that his wheeze is quite pronounced at times and that his sputum has been quite yellow on occasions. But he still says, ah, yes, he is indeed. Because he quite sees what Agatha is getting at, oh yes. He always does. They comprehend each other, each other's drift, they practically don't need to talk, I wish I had someone I felt like this with, I wish I didn't need to verbalise so much, I wish I was more like me mum, Moira. Ah yes, he repeats, nodding, he is indeed quite tubercular, and has been sent home on several occasions in the past, I think. Once, says Agatha. But once is enough, says Uncle Kenneth. They are sending a letter, we'll have to intercept it, says Agatha. It'll be our secret, whispers Uncle Kenneth. Supposing, whispers Agatha, leaning towards her uncle slightly, he really has done something quite frightful? Uncle Kenneth feels the gelatinous presence of unimaginable frightfulness briefly bubble over the rug at his feet. He has not done, he replies. He has merely shown himself to be too much Willo and too little Randle. Have faith in your brother. Uncle Kenneth is not quite sure that Willo has not indeed committed bestial acts of some unimaginably depraved kind because anyone is capable of anything, however unlikely, it's a rule of life, it's the Shadow. He stands up. He places his hands on his niece's thin shoulders. Let us not sit in judgement, he murmurs, but in honourable love. I have to say that this is not typical Uncle Kenneth. He's speaking like this partly because the play he saw last night is still running round in his head and partly because he is rising to the occasion despite being Uncle Kenneth the unkempt windbag. He clears his throat because the line didn't come out quite clearly enough, he's nervous, he's vaguely frightened of his brother and his sister-in-law and beyond them the dark lump of Randle College scowling as only fear can make dark lumps scowl.

He drops his hands and lets them writhe around together. I suppose we ought to meet the train, my dear. He suddenly feels that the whole enterprise is ridiculous. It is a mountain of immense proportions, he thinks. It is a vessel full of holes and they will be sunk before the harbour exit. But he cannot deliver his nephew to the hands of the mob, the judges, the stony-hearted dreadfulness of society's judgement. (OK, that play again. It was a mediocre play.) Agatha is going on about Dorothy again. She's probably sensing his faint-heartedness. There must be a key, a clever ruse, a devilishly clever wheeze which will let them all off the hook and William to catch his butterflies in peace and plenty. William won't tell us, I don't suppose, Agatha murmurs, we'll have to get in touch with Giles; Giles will telephone us I'm sure, he'll tell us exactly what has happened. Is that important, my dear? I don't know, actually. Agatha's striding up and down the room, it's really lucky she didn't put her hobble skirt on today, lucky for the skirt I mean, she's sort of muttering to herself so that Uncle Kenneth has to raise his voice a little when she comes near. Supposing we told your mother and father— Oh, we can't! Why not, my dear? Agatha fingers her collar, paces up and down, up and down. Because it would be too awful, Uncle. They would do something awful like cut him off, or send him to Aunt Constance in Calcutta, or to some even worse school. Mightn't they forgive him? They will make such a ballyhoo, Uncle, they're like that. I would defend him and get cut too, probably. We would all disintegrate.

Zelda says, hey, you know that's the longest run they've had without you poking your nose in? I say, hey, that's the longest run they've had because they are making the action so fast the sound guy almost knocked over the standard lamp with his mike boom. It's a directional mike he's using. It was hell for him. They were only just touching the levels. Every time my great-aunt went through a cable he got fuzz. He says can't I do something about the fat guy's whistle? I say Uncle

Kenneth's not made to suit your equipment, Bosey – if you don't like it you can mix it out but keep the master for me, OK? I like my relatives untampered with. He says it's the worst space he's ever had to work in. I say watch that fucking creamware ewer, Bosey, its cerulean tint is unique. He's a dark lump, he's scowling, when a Hupmobile 12/14 changed to top second the other side of the street his needles hit red. And I've got to work with these guys, because they're legends, legends in their own time.

George. I have to bring in George. I have to let him be picked up by this craaazy process. I have to pick him up off the scenery and turn him into wafers of celluloid and shoot him back out again so he's a giant making gel of our eyeballs as we angle for the last itzy-bitzy crumb of honey-coated popcorn in a bag that is pure white noise. As a matter of fact, the idea of George being bigger than he is is not a nice one. The idea that some shots are going to show him filling the screen is not a nice one. George is playing George. Those boils and pimples and scurfy bits on his cheeks and that complicated relation of nose to nose-hair is natural. We have no face-paint in this picture, geddit? I'm about to show you the kitchen. The kitchen may not come up to your standards of cleanliness. OK, it's cleaned. It's scrubbed and swilled and mopped and waxed and buffed and generally disinfected because that's Mr Trevelyan's line, it's the family business, disinfectant, disinfectant and antiseptic Ideal for Use in the Home and home starts here but somehow the kitchen in 1913 is not the kind of micro-surgery unit my friends call their kitchen. Neither is it glossy. I said this to Mike at the outset: I said, gloss is out, Mike, just pick up the sheen on the waxed stuff, the sheen of waxed stuff is not the same as gloss. I said to Mike and I said to Sylvia: do you know what it takes to get that sheen on that banister knob? It takes six coats of wax and in between each coat enough buffing to power the Great Eastern. And I mean buffing, not polishing. Buffing is buffing. This sheen has *depth*. Look at it. It is the depth of a thousand hours of buffing. It is the depth of a thousand hours of muscular activity in the region of the upper forearm, mainly. Lily's right breast is slightly larger than the left, it is firmer, she knows this, it is the buffing bubby phenomenon and every maidservant who is not a cripple has it. In Houston we do not know this depth. Our interior wood, and there is quite a lot of interior wood, is gleam'n gloss and has no depth. Sounds like Merchant-Ivory, says Mike. Sounds like Ricky

Thornby, says Sylvia. I have this great relationship with Sylvia: I like my continuity girl to cut me. Sylvia is not continuity on this picture any more: she fired herself. She wasn't being used, she said, you cannot be continuity when no one cares a fuck about continuity. I said continuity is vital in this picture: there are twenty-three crates etc. and Lily's always shifting stuff and it gets right up Mrs T's nose. This house needs its own private continuity person. It needs someone to pad around after Lily and now Milly and straighten everything up. Mr T does this, every night. The painted bits on the ceramic bowls and plates and stuff are always half hidden. It's like they're bashful or something. The candlesticks are the worst. The candlesticks on the mantels (hey, there are a lot of mantels in this house) look like they're not quite sure why they're up there and they're discussing it. There's some military gene in Mr Trevelyan which comes out over this candlestick business. Every night he gets them looking like the guards outside Buckingham Palace and pretty well every morning they go back to discussing why they're up there and looking hesitant. Sometimes after Lily's been through they look like they've decided there isn't in fact any point in being up there, especially in a time of electrical illumination, and seem set to jump it, right out on the edge.

Zelda thinks I should wrap this cleaning thing up. I say I'm not talking about cleaning I'm talking about gloss, I just got diverted a little. Basically what I need to establish before we move into the kitchen is that hey, there's a hell of a lot of dirt and germs and matt surfaces around. This kitchen is not the latest thing, it has not changed since Mr Trevelyan was knee-high, it's kind of settled into itself and looks grumpy and worn and dark. Because it is dark. It has one flex that made it down here somehow and that lights up an electric bulb next to the old gas fitting and the ceiling has a complexion problem. It's got blisters all over it and it sweats. The flex is really thick, it looks like a hempen rope, it comes already-frayed, it loops across the ceiling and if Health and Safety could step down here they'd have to be carried out in shock because the flex is crazy, it's touching damp places and metal places and looks like it couldn't care less, which it couldn't, it's a psychopath, it's waiting to kill. The kitchen is damp and in the summer the damp factor turns into steaminess, it's really unpleasant. This is because the kitchen is buried half-underground. There is actually a window but it's pavement high, long and mean, like it's peering up silk skirts which it is in fact, it lets in about as much light as would slightly ghost a photographic plate. Dorothy practically lives down here. I don't think you people know how much grease and filth this kitchen produces before it's even cooked a thing. I'm talking about the range. The range is a monster. It's Grendel's Grandmother. It has a leak where smoke comes out but even if it didn't have a leak it would manufacture more grease and filth than it does heat. It really doesn't *like* to heat. It only heats if Dorothy talks to it nicely. You have to plan way ahead. If you want to boil an egg for breakfast it has to have about twenty-four hours' notice. Actually, Dorothy doesn't plan ahead. She inherited pots and pans that were kind of permanently bubbling and she just throws stuff in. Mrs Rundell's *New System of Domestic Cookery* she also inherited. Pages fall out each time she humps it down. She humps it down because it's symbolic. She doesn't use the word symbolic or totemic but that's what it is and it's also in memory of Mrs T Senior who told her she must use It and Nothing Else. She opens It and lays her hand on It like It's got great energies or something and then just chucks stuff into the pans that Grendel's Grandmother has a real grudge against but can't do anything about because they were put on there about forty years ago and are actually really hot by now. Right at this moment, if we peep through the steam and lift the lid, there's something bumping around in there that makes you think there might be an actual psychopath in this house but sorry, old fruit, there ain't, this ain't *Homhitch* or *Murder by Weak Electrical Light* – it doesn't give your buffed nails a hard time, it's a family tentativehook, it's dull as real life is dull but wow, real life dullness is extremely interesting, it's a boiled knuckle of veal being re-boiled, in there.

Whack! That was the mutton. Glistening, Mike. Those fatty raw hands are not the mutton or some giblets but Dorothy's fingers, kneading salt in. The mutton is cooked, incidentally. And when I say cooked I mean *cooked*. It was in the back pan from about the Diamond Jubilee (look it up – do I have to tell you everything?) and now it's cold. Its ambient temperature is the same as the scullery where the incredible amount of implements it takes for a Georgian (second time round Georgian without the powdered wig or twelve-foot high hairdo) person to receive food in his mouth gets washed up and dried on the racks that line the scullery like the washed-up timbers of old ships. (Zelda says Ricky, that's the first original simile in a hundred pages,

212

too bad it took you an hour and five ruined paper-clips to get. Shucks an' fanks, darlin'. Did anyone ever tell you you resemble Jenny Agutter from your bad side?) The mutton is gonna be served up cut into hunks but otherwise unchanged. Dorothy's fingers have not been washed all day but hey, they're so raw and chapped and steamed that it's a helluva hostel place for a salmonella or any other kind of germ to hang out in. Those guys are scrambling to get aboard George. He's the ocean liner with luxury fittings and ten-course meals, he's where every self-respecting bacterium wants a part of the action, or at least to retire to and put their feet up after a life of anxiety snucked up between the tiles where tidal waves of Trevelyan Disinfectant never quite got to but it was close. George is coming, he's coming, just be patient if I'm talking to a bacterium now, a crowd of bacteria, my bacterial friends and relations who've made me queasy all my life and are now drinking my whisky – he's gonna dock in in about two minutes, if you're really sensitive you'll have felt the bow wave of his indigestion, it always precedes him by about two minutes if he's heading your way, if you're ultra-sensitive you'll be detecting something else, a swell, a slight swell of something nasty and tense but that might just be the air getting itself set, doing its buttons up, straightening its wing collar, screwing on its armour.

The mutton's for dinner, actually. It's going to get even chillier, waiting. The soup for luncheon is in the most gigantic pan you'll ever see in your life right at the back of the range, it's pea soup, it's sort of green and it's like the planet in *Solaris* – it's beginning to think, it's definitely alive and thinking, and there's probably something down there . . . whatever *is* down there is beginning to erupt, it's a soup the pseud creep would call disrupting, he'd probably like it because he'd be too busy talking crap about Dizzy Derrida or Krazy Kristeva and what they have to say about Milos Forman to even notice how disgustingly out of date the taste is. I mean, this is 1913. How do we know things tasted the same in 1913? How do we know things were tasted in the same way in 1913? These are two quite different questions. While I'm asking these questions I have to point out that there is a minor crisis going on in Mrs Trevelyan's dressing room. You've guessed it. Way above this kitchen Milly the maid is having a spot of bother with the hats and Mrs Trevelyan is rising – actually, she's risen, but she is using the toilet which is off the dressing-room.

From the sound of it (I don't want to be too personal here) Milly is OK for about another three minutes. I'm going to slice this house in half for a second. I'm sorry, this is the only way I can show what an amazing organism this house is. The Steves have the most incredibly powerful state-of-the-art slicers with diamond teeth and they're positioned as only I can position them. This is epic. It'll be a hot knife through cold butter.

Go.

The tiles are a problem. They're slate tiles or something. They don't stay put under the slicers but kind of shoot off. Never mind. We're through, down through the attic, a piece of guttering has come loose, this is the Blitz all over again – there has to be a bath-tub hanging from its pipe and someone in it, screaming. No no, only joking. They're down through the servant's quarters, they're into the upper rooms for guests, a carpet's got snagged in the bit, Mrs T is on the toilet, she's screaming, I forgot about her, her toilet's right in the middle of the house, there's this diamond-tipped slicer roaring through the brick inches from her nose, down it goes, dig that antique cistern, that chain with PULL on a little china knob, the mahogany perch buffed by a hundred bottoms and Lily and still warm – down through the hallway and at the back down through the conservatory, watch the glass, slice through the pavement to get at the kitchen, hit the foundation rubble, keep going because there's some nice medieval death-pits underneath and underneath dem bones there's a Roman hypercaust system pretty well unusable and beneath that there's a thin streak of Bronze Age sludge and some ash from when the whole city was razed and under that shit they've hit rats and I said stop when you hit the rats because that means you've hit the ceiling of the London Underground system but when Steves get going they're petrol tankers, it takes glaciers to stop them, there's this incredible fizz and bang and the whole system's fucked.

Stop showing off, says Zelda.

Zelda's my conscience.

Hey, just take a look at the house for a minute. I'm opening it up like a

214

book and the other houses are getting bad wrinkle, sorry, it's not for long. There. You see how complicated it is? You see those little figures dotted about? You see George coming down the kitchen stairs, Lily making the candlesticks look suicidal in the smoking-room, Dorothy wondering why there are waves on the soup, Mrs Trevelyan hanging on to the PULL chain and getting vertigo, Milly smoothing out the gull's feather which is impossible to do successfully even without the wind, Agatha and Uncle Kenneth putting their outside gear on in the hall, not bothering to get the servants to do this for them? You see how much junk there is in the attic? You see how I've done all this without breaking so much as a milk-jug? You see why the Royal National Theatre in London needs me to handle its revolving stage?

Zelda has tears in her eyes. She says it reminds her of her doll's house. She lost her doll's house in a great depression. She chucked it out. Now she wishes she hadn't. If Mrs Trevelyan falls off her lavatory seat we'll lose the Martita Hunt of this picture and I can't afford that. She's very high up with her eyes shut. I'm closing it, boys. They're still reconnecting the Underground cables. Leave it, leave it. Londoners are used to suffering. Or they're gonna have to get used to suffering, soon. They're gonna be bombed and they're gonna get asbestosis from their gas-masks and they're gonna have Stafford Cripps and they're gonna have Margaret Thatcher and they're gonna be stuck on the Underground for hours in the dark but they're gonna be plucky and valiant and Cockney and Typhoo and their upper lips are gonna grow so stiff they'll look like those Africans who put soup-plates in their mouths and they'll love it.

The Steves are pushing the house back. Gently, gently. We don't want that kind of bump that makes the actors look like they've just been moved on a revolving stage instead of being caught in the middle of a conversation in the grand house of a Russian country estate or something.

Bump. Mrs Trevelyan thinks she might have overdone it with the tonic wine this morning. She drinks tonic wine like my first wife drank vodka. George is in the kitchen. Let's descend, let's – at least let's get out of Mrs Trevelyan's toilet. Even if it does contain one of the earliest

215

toilet paper dispensers known to man, of brass and imitation majolica, now gone the way of all toilet paper dispensers.

Do you have to be so funny all the time?

That was Zelda. It's kinda relentless, she adds. Let up. Listen. You don't have to prove yourself all the time. Sweep the leaves into circles, into perfect circles. Sweeping leaves into perfect circles for five hours, I reply, strikes me as really anal. The fact is, I am not being funny. I had to say this thing about the toilet paper dispenser because toilet paper dispensers are something we handle at least once a day, if you're reg'lar. Women handle them many times a day, Zelda corrects me. Too right, I murmur, blushing. Zelda is my conscience. She makes me blush. But she's got the point. She's ruffling my hair. Not now, Zelda. I'm out to dinner tonight, she says. A date? A date. My heart sinks. I'll bet it's pseud creep, I say. I'll bet it's Todd Lazenby. Right, she says. Don't believe a word of it, I stammer. Just don't! What are you writing down what we're saying for? says Zelda. Why not? I say, tapping out why not? I say, tapping out why not? I say, tapping out – you get the picture, huh? This is unedited action, this is CNN reporting from HCDVA Library, this is instant mush. She laughs. I love you, she says. Hey, Zelda, mnx | pqu |; | kjkfmiqduwyfquwaqkmwqkm

That was Zelda's buttocks laid gently on the keys. It wasn't my command of Serbo-Croat being wielded or something. It was her joke. Then the Granville-Barker weirdo appeared at the borrowing desk with an incredibly complicated request to do with the On Tapp System here – he wanted to call up H. G. Wells' Christmas gift list of 1901 or something, and Zelda's sexual needs were sublimated. This'll be up off the screen and into the wherever it goes when it goes up by the time she's back over here. For once, I thank the weirdo. I've got to be fighting fit to handle this manservant guy.

OK. Geronimo.

He's cracking his knuckles in front of the copper. The copper is made of iron. The knuckles are made of bone. The copper is like the funnel of the Great Eastern and it's supposed to pour out piping jets of water from its tap but it's Grendel's Great-Aunt, it's related to the range, it

216

never has done, it manages something just a bit more than tepid, about the temperature, George has noted, of a man's glue. (You know what he means. He uses expressions that are now historical. I'm not gonna translate. He has as many words for seminal emission as Inuits have for snow. One of them *is* snow, actually, but even he regards that one as pretty pathetic. He calls the luncheon soup glue, too. It's his private joke. Dorothy doesn't like George, not surprisingly. Even in her generous bosom there is no little corner for George. There might be a very narrow window-ledge, way up, really way up, and definitely outside.)

This is George's usual place. He's cracking his knuckles and holding them out to the copper. There's always this wee burn of a chill running through him. If George'd been born a hundred years later he could've been a famous novelist right now, buzzed round to readings where he vomits or whatever and delights the literary ladies with his filthy mouth – because George has poetry in him, like my old dad. It comes out in coarse chunks like cheap coal but it warms, it warms, and none of the middle-class wankers can do it quite in the same way, don't you know. George had a very interesting childhood, he could have mined it as a novelist or as a film-maker for the whole of his career, like I should've done and didn't because I was ashamed and it doesn't work south of the South Mimms Junction. (Doesn't *South Mimms Junction* sound like an Ealing heyday comedy, wrapped up in steam and stuff? But I'm talking, for the benefit of the Yanks and other foreign flotsam among you, blaspheming my Laphroaig with London ice and, Christ alive, *soda* – I'm talking of the M25/A1 coitus interruptus where once my Uncle Norbert's allotment cabbaged its cabbages and sprouted its sprouts. If George says how's your cabbage? and chortles it's because cabbage is one of his fifty-eight ways of saying female pudend, by the by. I have a list of the other fifty-seven. I'm not revealing it. You can make your own and tick 'em off. That list took me agonies of being in this guy's company. I'm still using Dettol in my bath. I have a bath in Houston. I had it installed. I'm British to my tub-wrinkled gonads, okeydokey?)

Still Six: the house. Number 25, Albermarle Terrace, Westminster borders (about three houses down you plummet into Pimlico, OK?). Not sliced in half. I forgot it before. Go see. Sorry about the water stain across the living-room bay. It was there already. But the living-room bay is

identical to the dining-room bay. Accidents of time. Great phrase. Zelda's.

Check the projector, Ossy. Put the ice-bag on top. It has a burning headache by now.

Nice pad, 25 Albermarle Terrace, huh? Up-date, 1994: it looks like a wedding-cake, they've painted everything in sight Dulux Icing White Gloss or something, they've chucked out the art students and they're working hard to chuck out the Polish guy because apparently some Iranian geezer wants to make it his fifteenth home. The Polish guy has actually written to me to aid him in his Fight, he thinks I have some rights in this because it was once In The Family. I say it's now In The Iranian Family and if they want to make a mosque out of the living-room – Allah be with them or whoever. They might be nice people. They are breaking my Life, Mr Thorby, he writes. What is Life, I reply, but the nonchalantly withheld threat of permanent eviction? Ralph Waldo Thornby, Selected Apothegems Of. Poor old Ladislaw. From Auschwitz to Belgravia in one swap. I'll invite him.

Hi, Ladislaw! Help yourself to the wodka, and I mean it. You're In The Wamily.

Dorothy is stirring the soup. George is stirring his body inside its stock, jacket, breeches and boots. Actually, Dorothy is letting the furry wooden spoon with a fissure in it – the only spoon she uses to stir soup, which is why the fissure has this weird deposit in it like uranium or something – idle on the erupting surface of Thought like a Received

219

Idea. Thank you, Zelda. I thought it was original, too. George is letting his furry non-wooden spoon with a fissure in it (one of his thirty-nine ways of saying dick) idle on the erupting surface of Sexual Fantasy like it usually does. I have to say here that George MacPhearson has been doing these usual things for an extremely long time. Basically, no one has been longer in this house than George. He arrived before his voice broke as something so junior he was under the washstand. He's risen above everyone and everything now, *in principio*: risen ineluctably and ineliminably up to being equivalent to a butler on good days and general manservant on most days and where's that bloody footman on really terrible days when Mr Trevelyan is drunk and highly stressed. But George is only paid as a general, which is why he moans a lot. Moans is the wrong word. Carps is better. Carps and cavils and crows. Zelda gave me a pocket thesaurus for my birthday because she said I was ruining my back with the library copy. Really, it was because I was ruining the library copy. She's still dealing with weirdo, it's OK, she won't see that. She loves her books. Her Zen master says she shouldn't have any books. She doesn't, personally. But they're hers, they're hers, they're all hers in here.

Like it's all Dorothy's in the kitchen, except for the clothes brush with *Come to Inverurie* on it, which is George's, for belabouring his lapels and shoulders and thighs. It hangs on the scullery door. Whenever Dorothy goes in and out of the scullery it jigs and taps. *Come to Inverurie, O Come to Inverurie* jigs and taps through her head, she can't help it. She has no idea where Inverurie is, except that she never wants to go there, because it's under a snow of George's scurf. Everything else in the kitchen is hers, down to the last badly corroded oyster-opener in the enormous mouth of the gigantic dresser which was here when the house was built – she reckons the house was built around it because they couldn't have got it down, and the same with Grendel's Grandmother. When she thinks of history she thinks of the big range and the big dresser in the open air, enjoying the sun, before these guys in armour came along and started piling bricks up and yelling at each other in Ancient Greek. Otherwise she is fairly sensible.

Now hold on tight, we've a lot of curves coming.

There's this really weird thing going on in George's face. It's like he's

220

about to give birth to an Alien through one of his cheeks. He opens his mouth wide and you can see right in, you can see this wedge of cooking chocolate his jaws are negotiating with. This is what he usually does, after cracking his knuckles. Dorothy's going to tut in a minute. Wait for it. There, what did I tell ya? She looks at George for about a half-second and tuts again, because if she didn't tut at least twice he'd think he could just cabbage a piece of her cooking chocolate any time. After these two (sometimes three on bad days) tuts, George makes a sound like my doctor telling me I have hypercholesterolaemia very quickly and sinks his teeth into the wedge as hard as their precariousness can take. (Great pun. Thank you, Zelda. She's back. What's hyperwotsit? she asks. Did you find H. G.'s gifts list? I ask back. Don't change the subject, Ricky. It means, my sweet lullaby, every time I get heartburn I say my prayers. Seriously? Seriously – I'm way overdue. When I get to Heaven they're gonna fine me. Doc Zwingli says it's under control, I should take some gentle exercise – yoga and sex and stuff. Lots of gentle sex and a bit of yoga and both at the same time to save time. But – Subject closed, OK?) George doesn't really like cooking chocolate. He might have done about twenty-five years ago but he's too old to change. He likes the tuts. It makes him feel wanted. His mam used to tut at him, before she got into hitting him and the bottle, roughly at the same time, up in Aberdeen or somewhere. Certainly not Inverurie. He stole the hairbrush about a century ago. It is not a family icon. Let's not be sentimental about this guy, just understanding within tight parameters. There are worst things in life than not having a butler/ manservant/footman, and that's having one like George. I stress this now because *Remains of the Day* has been served up in Houston recently and everyone wants a butler who hasn't actually got one already. I'm just putting the record straight. They don't all come looking like Anthony Hopkins. As a matter of fact, most of them over here come looking like Anthony Perkins as Bates and are called Antonio and wear galoshes to serve rum and coke in the jacuzzi and call everyone by their first name. Hi, Ricky, said an Antonio last month. It was at this guy's who owns this gallery I'm trying to ingratiate myself into for Greg's sake although Greg isn't interested, he says it's junk. Of course it's junk. The private view was so private you couldn't see it, there were too many people. I caught a glimpse of baby dolls covered in slime and stuck through with nails. I got talking to this fire extinguisher who turned out to be the artist and I'd already said I thought it was all fake. She was really small, she had a private view of my zip and that was about it, I think she eventually got trampled but not before she'd said she was going to report me for expressing my opinions forcefully, or forcibly. Anyway, this Antonio was somehow gliding around on roller-skates with about three trays of piña coladas and I grabbed a glass as he did an *entrechat* or whatever between me trying to approach the owner and the owner and I said thanks and he said, Rick, any day – which really got to me. No butler should talk to you like that. Anyway, no one wants these guys any more. They've all been fired and everyone's been asking me to take their place because I'm the only person in Houston that doesn't sound like he's playing scales on a slide guitar – I sound about forty-nine per cent English, would you believe it. This is because of this stupid film. I say, hey, it wasn't like that, then I say, how much? I say how much? to the elegantly ageing and incredibly wealthy widowed ex-beauty queens who ask me. There are a few. They still have teeth like pianos without the black notes and their skin is not yet hung out to dry. But it's never enough. I know how George feels. It's never enough when you have to do what you have to do. I mean, they expect me to sound like Anthony Hopkins all the time when I'm just doing it for a party turn, for a giggle, hm, very well, m'lord. And I don't want to do their chiropody. I draw the line at that. The problem is, they don't know where to draw the line. They're not good enough for an English butler. It's what the movie's all about, I tell them. Next thing, they'll be asking me to satisfy their enormous sexual needs or something. Zelda says that's enough lies for now. I say it's important to express oneself. It's not easy being English over here. I'm a minority. I have the right to be oppressed but no one recognises it. They just oppress me. Even this library oppresses me. It has more CD-ROMs than books: I called up Dickens the other day and he was waving to me the other side of this gate called *non-American English*. I had to show my passport and get checked for lice, practically. At least I didn't get punched up. We're a negative quantity, we're a subset, the flagpole's squeaking as the flag is lowered, it's sunset time, the Union Jack's a tea-towel. Actually, I myself am a subset of a subset. I'm *not-quite-non-American English*. I'm not quite anything. This is what the butler saw when he looked in the mirror. I'm not quite anything. This is George's big problem. Maybe we have something in common. I hope not. He's just gobbed against the copper. It actually sizzles. Relatively, against George's spittle, the copper's hot. The gob's chocolate brown. I feel sick. He sticks his finger in his mouth and clears out the last bit of chocolate and licks it. Then – do I have to go through with this? – he smells his finger. Anyone'd think he was married to Dorothy, he's so unabashed about his intimate rituals. Soup be maunderin' at me, she be that ready, says Dorothy. Dorothy isn't reciting poetry, she's just Wiltshire born and bred, she speaks like this all the time, it really gets on George's nerves. Actually, I have to say, it's great the first time you hear this thing about the soup maunderin' at her but it kind of palls when you've heard it about twelve thousand times, which is roughly how many times George has heard it, at a quick calculation (she started using the phrase thirty-one years ago, so it's thirty-one times three hundred and sixty-four because she doesn't say it on Christmas Day because there's no soup of any kind on Christmas Day) – and he sucks his teeth, drowning out the last bit of Dorothy with an amazing squeal. He's wiping his wet finger on his jacket, it's always the same spot, it's just under the last green button and if you had an electron microscope you wouldn't sleep for days for what's patrolling the thick ropes of fibres, guv. Ready, George? says Dorothy. Och, woman, George says. Dorothy has licked the spoon and places the lid back on the pan. Clang. Sorry, Bosey. The steam's making great effects against the electric bulb, it actually looks fake the way it's pummelling against the ceiling. George does this weird sort of growl as he always does and stands up. It sounds like his trousers have ripped because someone's put glue on the chair but he always makes this sound and this isn't silent comedy, is it? He's tugging his cuffs down and wriggling his wrists one after the other. Where's that drat Milly, then? says Dorothy. She's tugging the enormous mouth of the dresser and taking out a ladle. They're both tugging, note. Two gobs descend apparently in slow motion – hey, why not, slomo it is, down they go like brown amoebas tracking through hyper-space – until they blurt and do a kind of mini-mushroom cloud on George's toecaps, one after the other, spilling little bits of themselves out and away and on to somewhere where things will be grateful for it, things which will survive us and our spittle by several billion years and'll still get along fine as they always have done.

George rubs his toecaps against his shins. He gets a kind of smear with sheen in between. The alert ones among you, the ones who love the small hours and haven't gone to sleep or slunk off to coit in the walk-in cupboard, will reckon that George's method of polishing could be improved on. What he needs, you reckon, is a consultant. He needs to be taken aside and given a thorough consultancy. The consultant would tell him that to eat chocolate is OK, but not before you use your spittle as a free leathershine. There would be other things the consultant would advise, things which'd make George cleaner, leaner, more streamlined and viable. For instance, the way George uses the *Come to Inverurie* brush needs viabilising. George unhooks the majolica brush and slicks his hair with it: it works. But now he's belabouring his lapels and shoulders with the same bristles. He's peering into the tiny mirror on the scullery door. The tiny glass somehow manages to contain Dorothy ladling out the soup as well as the consultant. The consultant has a Panasonic notepad and portable phone and tiny TRY ME tie-pin between his wide lapels. OK, the consultant thinks, the scurf's flying but big deal. As much scurf is re-applied and the greasy look of the lapels and shoulders is not just wear, it's hair-oil. He gets tapping. He's here not to advise but to evangelise. Buy another brush. Clarify roles. He's netted three figures in three minutes. Impact's the name of the game. TRY ME. George is viable, he's been impacted, he's clean. The bacterial hordes are running, they know when the game's up, they're instant refugees – billions of them pouring off George to be massacred by the new regime's hostile sweeps and swabs, whole generations lost in nameless zones, a few surviving in inaccessible terrain behind the range. You're getting carried away, Ricky. I am, I am. Piss off, consultant. Your time has not yet come.

The scurf is now alighting, as usual, on George's thighs. He belabours them and grunts. He grunts because he's bending over slightly into the flurry of scurf. Dorothy is ladling out the soup. You've guessed it. If you ever come to luncheon here, skip the soup. Or if you've got any manners have the soup but try to think of the little white bits in it as parmesan or something. Just try.

OK?

The soup's settling nicely in the bowls, already cooling. It's meant to be cooling. The veal's not meant to be cool and it won't be, it'll be tepid. It'll be tepid because it has to make this epic journey from the

224

kitchen to the conservatory. Mrs Trevelyan likes to take luncheon in the conservatory until days when the frost doesn't go from the windows, then she retreats to the dining-room which is about one degree warmer except around the fireplace which is fifty degrees warmer and is up her end and gets the ribbon-ties at the back of her corset curling through four layers. The temperatures in this house'd give the thermometer in your back pocket a real workout, a hundred press-ups a minute, Mercury meets Sparta, it'd probably throw up. I mean, you only have to move an inch and your butt shifts from Saudi Arabia to Siberia in the time it takes to say ouch. These fireplaces are the most inefficient heat source known to man. They heat the air above the rooftops mainly but above the rooftops is about as hostile as Venus or someplace: it's permanent twilight, you wouldn't believe the smoke, the pigeons have emphysema, they just sit there wheezing and blinking like they've just been rescued from a pit disaster or something. And it goes on and on and on. For miles and miles and miles, out to where Uncle Norbert's father's allotment is cabbaging its cabbages and sprouting its sprouts because a fifty-foot prestressed reinforced concrete pillar has not yet burst out the earth like Jack's beanstalk and sprouted a motorway intersection. Down the other end of this brick tube, this chimbley shaft lined with soot and microscopic clusters of small boys' skin-cells, last night's fire is a heap of ash and this heap of ash is due to be swept out at four o'clock p.m. by Milly but right now it's stirring in the down-draught, the down-draught is working really hard at lowering the temperature of the dining-room to a point where the fire arriving at four-thirty will spend all evening trying to get back up to what it would have been if the fireplace had not been there at all. Day after day this is repeated and meanwhile there are these hundreds of thousands of grimy guys underground having the worst time it is possible to have bar being baby-sat by Hisbollah or whoever just so this process can be repeated. Ninety per cent of their suffering goes up the chimney in smoke and hangs over the city like the dark phantoms of the dead – the early dead and the all-of-a-sudden dead who cluster round the pit-mouths on certain nights like their own widows and swivel their eyes and show their bright red tongues as they whisper till the dawn shift evaporates them possibly forever. And for every chimney with its black muscly phantoms crawling out of it there is a pedigree of skinned knee-caps and cancerous elbows and welted soles, Des, it's like a graveyard up here, it's like every chimney-stack sticking up out of the rolling grey vista of roofs is a gravestone, it's like this rooftop view is a big cemetery for small boys and there's not a single name or date on any of them, they've been folded over and forgotten, they handweave rugs in Hindustan for Harrods or serve businessmen's butts in Bangkok these days – these days being nowadays and not this day in the 1913 down-draught of the Trevelyans' fireplace where the ash is actually moving around like I'm playing the action backwards.

You are, practically, says Zelda. You sound like Miss Barnett with the brace. Who's Miss Barnett with or without the brace? I ask, wiping my forehead because that last break got me sweating. Miss Barnett was our lousy history teacher in fourth grade, says Zelda. She was spying for the Russians, we reckoned. We called her Sputnik. She was really left-wing. I wish you'd cut the history and just get on with the action, Ricky. Zelda, I say, I'm a talking Jackdaw Folder, didn't you know? Greg used to have the whole set. They educated me, along with his *Look & Learns*. This was in the days when kids read *Look & Learn* and built the Clifton suspension bridge out of Meccano instead of what they do now, which is learn how to remove eyes and lift fingernails and have sex in three different ways at once and keep a few guys in the movie industry very nicely off, thank you. I don't know what you're squawking about, Ricky. Am I squawking? You are. This is a library. There are people trying to concentrate. I'm sorry, honey-bunch. This is a thing of mine. We've taken kids out of the chimney-shafts to put the chimney-shafts into the kids. We're filthying the insides of their minds. We're callousing their brains. If they rub up their sores enough they'll harden and no longer hurt. Then they'll go out and run the world like it's always been run, only more efficiently. I said to stop squawking, says Zelda. I'll have to bar you else. You've talked about this before. You repeat yourself. I like repeats, I reply. Praise be to the video recorder. I've watched *La Silence de la Mer* forty-one times. I identify with it. It's the lowest budget masterpiece ever. Until now.

Ssssh.

Zelda's hand on my forehead is leaves in a perfect circle. Maple leaves, probably. Maple leaves on raked white sand at dawn in Kyoto with a temple bell somewhere not too close tolling. In other words, it's c-c-cool and consoling. It's nice.

Come to Inverurie's back up on the scullery door. Hey, Lily's down here. Lily is shorter than Milly and has this chin you could balance a candlestick on. She's got the soiled tea things on the tray and George is chortling because I think Lily must have said it's ready for laying as she usually does. George is dabbing his mouth with a tea-towel and chortling. The forks and spoons are waiting in the drawer that sticks, waiting in the darkness, like they're used to this waiting, they're veterans, they've been pensioned off, their silver's been buffed by so many lips and towels it's gone through to something that flavours the food and hits the teeth like ice, like shot in game, like the metal of blood (I've never understood this taste of blood thing, it's like we're androids, it's like we've got a foundry instead of a heart, mine's actually tin rather than steel but there you go) and the orders are that if Uncle Kenneth is visiting and likely to stay for luncheon it's these old guys that are to be lined up. These are Mrs Trevelyan's orders. Otherwise it's the crack troops kept in the dining-room. There's a sudden whisper of a gust that shifts the steam some more and it's cold and smells like coats do when they've just come in. That's the wake of Agatha and Uncle Kenneth's departure out the front door, they closed it behind them ten minutes ago but it takes that long for the draught to work its way down. They've gawn aht, says Lily. Im and Miss Agfa. She only talks like this down here. Somewhere on the kitchen stairs there's a force field that does things to her mouth, when she's up there Agatha no longer sounds like a marketing rival to Miss Kodak, bom bom. But I'm finkin' eel be back, adds Lily. No one tells you nuffink 'ere. Where's that Milly milt, eh? says George. Veal is it? says Lily. Veal and spuds, Dorofy? Dorofy nods, because she's sipping oyster sauce from a big spoon. I forgot to mention the boiled potatoes in oyster sauce. The range is so wide I couldn't include it all in one shot, I'd have to pan slowly, ha ha. The only reason she covers the boiled potatoes in oyster sauce is because a page fell out in Mrs Rundell's. It's a chance combination – and it works, it works. The pages falling out thing doesn't always work: the beef hotpot with *Sauce Mousseuse* did not work. But she read it so long back and repeated it so many times it's established itself and no one notices any more. *Poularde Strasbourgeoise* with hot chocolate on it did not have a hope in hell of working – actually, maybe in hell it would. The menus in hell would be like that, along with those long red-hot tongs. There is a dangerous area in the book where the savouries end and the sweets begin, and the page looseness there is severe. Duck and stewed prunes was a lucky break. It was the only lucky break, in that area.

Tear a page out, get the scissors clipping, we're going outside.

OK. Agatha and Uncle Kenneth are taking a growler cab (a horse-drawn one with brass lamps and stuff, you've seen it in a hundred cossy dramas, it seats two dry and one wet who drives) to Paddington station and they plan to be back in time but it's tight. As the oyster sauce hits Dorothy's intestines the cab is negotiating Piccadilly Circus. There's horse-dung scattering over the tarmacadam and lots of flying advertisements for stuff like Hudson's Soap and, wait for it, Nestlé's Milk and this is big budget, there are at least thirty omnibuses in action and two and a half times that in cabs and the omnibuses and cabs are split fifty-fifty between cylinder and horse-heart which are both thumping really hard to keep up and the number of private motor cars is actually into double figures and there are twelve drays and an old wagon looking like it's wandered off a country lane into the wrong scene and just *thousands* of people who'll mainly be dead by 1990 and in all this remarkable comment on the serio-comedy of London life in which wealth and poverty, happiness and misery, mingle in a kaleidoscopic picture that, once seen, can never be forgotten (can you imagine that on a postcard *these* days?) there's a spattered growler negotiating and the driver flicking his whip and it's amazing, there's filth everywhere, there's dung and soot and mud and litter and the tyres and wheels are just spinning it up and out and even Mike can't stand it, his trainers are black and his jeans are wet and yet all over the place there are these long skirts and somehow they float along and now and again they seem to hitch up like magic. Sylvia's shouting it's not magic it's dress clips, they have these tiny sprung clips dangling from their waists and when they come to dung or something they get into action, it's just practice – and anyway, I yell back, the pavements are clean, they're scrubbed and swept and washed. Zelda says I have a hygiene complex. Maybe I do, but I want to say how amazed I am at the dirt, you could power a turbine on the dung being dropped here and as a matter of fact I'm feeling sick from the smell, it's like a silo with a coal-burning power station next door and a few leaking tins of Castrol at my feet and I'm not sure they've got their perfume consumption

228

worked out – every time a lady floats past it's like she's pickled herself in rosewater or violets or something, it's really thick and cloying and when this stuff isn't around it's straight body odour. Maybe they've all got adapted, maybe their noses have filters in them. Hey, I've got a sore throat just standing in the middle of all this with that jerk Eros prancing about on one leg way up there when he ought to be flying, his wings are big enough, and Mike moaning on at me about the terrible light. It's smoke, I tell him. We are in the Big Smoke. He's coughing into his handkerchief and saying that I told him to read *Mrs Dalloway* and in *Mrs Dalloway* everything glitters and glints fresh as a rainbow and he's got all the wrong filters and why aren't we still in the kitchen? I yell, Mike, shut your trap, we've got wild sound here and Bosey doesn't want you making it tame and Virginia Woolf had the right filters and she happened to be feeling good when she wrote *Mrs Dalloway* and anyway, once or twice a year the sun comes out and it all looks like a rainbow instead of like this, that's London, if you tire of her you tire of life because life's like London, it's a shit-hole – she was never anything else since the first jumped-up centurion with a squeaky voice and bad catullus threw a ford across this swamp pretending to be a river with scuffy foliage all around and a damp problem. Now we've lost the growler. It disappeared between Pears Soap and that terrible thing on at the London Palladium. Mike says it was nice in the fourteenth century, it had apple orchards or something right in the middle and about three thatched cottages with an uninterrupted view of the Tower and the appel orchards sweeten'd ye aere most delitefulie. I holler stop spelling like a corner shop and catch some general atmosphere, we can always cut it in later, no one'll know, a year or two here and there – there'll only be that bastard from Stockton-on-Tees with his world-beating collection of horse-drawn cab whips or motor omnibus leather-faced cone clutches or whatever his wife'll leave him for in about three years writing in as usual with an offer of his Xeroxed specifications at double the price. As if I need these people.

Zelda?

She's gone.

I think she got tired. She's left early. Weirdo's snoring. She doesn't keep official hours always. That's Zen, guv. I think maybe she's psyching herself up for Todd Lazenby Tonight, the pseud creep. He has girls dropping off his every vowel. Even though he's incredibly ugly and quite small and has a lazy eye. Lazy-eyed Lazenby the laser brain. No one understands him, that's why they hang off his every drawl. He makes movies sound like particle physics and particle physics is sexy. These girls bump up and down on his wooden spoon then they go home to Mom and Pop like they've been beamed down from the Starship Enterprise and Mom and Pop chew their hayseed and shake their heads as Miss Spock decodes *Rocky 3* or some other crap and she feels brainy when she isn't, she's actually less brainy than her mom who can at least write. If she wasn't jacked up with Lazenbyspeak and patent Lazenbyseed the girl would have a hard time thinking at all. I try to teach them to think but it's very tough with a class of holograms. The real kids are somewhere else, thinking simple and original thoughts under sweet appel orchards in delitefule aere. I think Lazenby is quite evil, really. I've told Zelda this. And I said he must have AIDS by now. She said are you implying people with AIDS are evil? I said Zelda, you have just committed the sin of syllogism. I'm surprised at you. I donate my boost to AIDS welfare. I—

How the hell did I get onto this? Don't I trust her or something? Aren't we in love with each other? Aren't I sure that This Is It and maybe for always? Zelda Zelda Zelda. Thank you for coming into my life. Back into my life because we had a long interval with no ice-cream some time back. Try not to leave it for lousy Lazenby and a bunch of five-syllable words that sound like diseases.

Zelda has grey eyes. A still of Zelda. Still Number Seven: Zelda laughing at my cake. I baked her a cake for her thirtieth. It didn't rise to the occasion. We had a great time laughing. Hang on a minute, don't rush out to scan Ricky's sweetheart until I say so. Still Number Eight: my great-aunt Agatha not laughing because you didn't when someone was taking your photograph in a studio in 1913 and it was costing your papa an arm up to the elbow. See the grey eyes? See the way she's lifting her head to the light and looking as Burne-Jonesy as possible? See how if she was photographed laughing at a cake instead of looking like the Lady of Shalott in good times she might just pass for Zelda? See how crazy it was to hike up and pin down a tumble of hair like that? See how she has the same tumble of hair as Zelda only in all the other

230

photos I have of my great-aunt Agatha it's not allowed to tumble? See how grave phantoms are and how laughing the living? See how terrible the difference and how terrible the sameness?

Mike and Bosey and even Sylvia are getting really sore at me. They've had a very hard time from the itinerant street traders of Lunnen. They've had cough pastilles and marigolds and oranges and a bit o' rump-work thrust at them and Bosey's needles were on purple. It was like *My Fair Lady* shot by Pasolini or someone and their sleeves smell of juniper berries. I have to say that there is indeed a serious drink problem around here, like there's a serious sound problem. The growler's driver negotiates a city with no zebra crossings and a million horses with iron hooves and cars with brakes as dicky as their steering driven by people with no driving certificates and big electrical trams and bigger double-decker buses without roofs on from which brats in boaters chuck half-sucked barley sugars at his rubbers on a bottle of some unidentifiable liquor a day. I don't know where he is right now, with Uncle Kenneth and Agatha bouncing about inside the tatty coachwork, but what I do know is that he is glowing under his cape despite the drizzle and a couple of half-sucked barley sugars stuck to his head. The horse is not drunk. It is the horse that leads. The horse has The Knowledge between its blinkers. Despite this, it has haphazardly flayed flanks because the driver thinks the horse has only a blasted farthin' inside 'is noddle, you can 'ear it rattlin', it'll pay for the knackers when they split 'im open.

Ah, the misery of the animals, the misery, the misery.

There's no one in the library. Either that or weirdo's stopped breathing. I just dozed off myself. I dreamt I was a leaf being swept by Zelda. I was a very heavy leaf but she swept me into a perfect circle with the other leaves, who were discussing something about Canadian fishing rights, I think. It's really quiet down here. I have banks of books either side of me. Zelda's subjects. I am gripped by a sense of my total unreality. I may not exist. According to Laserbrain I don't. I am just a text, he tells me. I am about as important as a paper on Canadian fishing rights. I am a leaf out of a book on myself. I must not panic. I know why I'm thinking this. It's to do with some biological process in the brain. I've dropped off and I haven't quite climbed back up again. I'm a failure. I'm going to be sixty in a few years' time. My boost would make a great golf handicap. I repeat myself. I tell the same jokes all the time. I don't listen enough. I don't listen because everyone else tells the same jokes or says the same things about the same things or even different things all the time. Why should I listen? Even Zelda – even ZELDA tends to say the same things all the time. I don't care a fuck about sweeping leaves into circles. What a waste of days. Even symbolically. I'm making a film that doesn't exist. Maybe no one'll come to the party. Maybe this film that doesn't exist will play to an empty room. Empty except for myself, which is really empty. What a great metaphor for the brain. I am gripped by a sense of my total isolation. Maybe I'm dreaming. Maybe I'll wake up and I'll be in hospital with minor injuries and a big headache and this doctor with sideburns and a voice like David Niven'll boom well well, we took that corner in the Bond Equipe G.T. 4S Saloon a teeky bit hastily day before yesterday, didn't we now, Mr Thornby? It'll be 2 January 1965 and I'll have dreamt the last thirty years. I'll know all the moves. I won't make lousy films to pay for the great personal statement that never gets made due to the fact that the lousy films are so lousy only my uncle in Melbourne wants to see them. I won't compromise. I'll make great tragic films on a budget so low the unknown actors' astonishing portrayal of hunger and distress comes from hunger and distress. Waste, waste. I hate this air conditioning. It dries my mouth out. The last thirty years can't have been real. This place can't be real. Todd Lazenby can't be real.

Stop.

Don't wipe it. Keep it. Save it and continue. You never know what we might need. No one'll know the difference, anyway. The moon landing shots were filmed right here, in Houston. The caretaker says so. He'll be coming round rattling his keys in a minute. He worked up at NASA. He peeped through a keyhole in '69 and saw Neil Armstrong playing golf in slow motion in a very large grey bunker. It's his big thing. He grabs your neck and looks around like he's expecting to be jumped and hisses in your ear one small step for man, one giant leap for mankind, said Tricky Dicky, and his whole face goes into a wink. You have to run or you get the conspiracy theory in full, and it's long. He wants me to

232

make a film about it. To make a film about these guys making a film of these guys making a film that wasn't. I say to him, you're on the moon, kiddo.

But it's a great idea. I should have had it in '69. It could have been low budget. Just steel walls and grey sand and this caretaker and a few Michelin men bouncing around in slow-motion. An intense study of illusion, astonishingly wrought. Derek Malcolm. With this work, Richard Thornby proves himself to be the Robert Bresson of British cinema. Philip French. I wish I'd taken a corner too hastily, just once.

Here's Loony Tune with the keys. Shucks. It's all for real. It's all too late. It's all my fault. Maybe I should take up golf again.

I could've called it *The Keyhole*. Poster with a big eye in a keyhole. Or a full moon.

Hey, Ricky, stick to what you've got. And not got.

Anyway, hey, ping, lightning-bolt time – there's a flaw, a very big one: You Cannot Have a Keyhole in an Air-Lock. I mean, haven't I seen *2001* twenty-one times? Don't all doors slide or something in NASA? I want to ask him. Here he is. I want to see his face crumple. It's already crumpled. I want to see it crumple some more. Hiya, Mr Thornby. Workin' laayet, Mr Thornby? No, I'm just thinking about keyholes and writing down what we're saying as we say it. This is CNN, live from — I'm lockin' uyup, Mr Thornby, but if you're talkin' about keyholes . . . (Hand-on-my-neck-eyes-all-about routine.) One smaall steyep for — Leonard, you cannot have a keyhole in an air-lock. Not a see-through keyhole. It's physically impossible. It would probably suck out your eyeball. Mr Thornby? Yes, Leonard? I swear to you, sir, I am not a liar. They did not land on the moon. The moon is a virjeyen. Man has not landed on the moon, Mr Thornby. I sayed theyem not landing on the moon with my own eyes. They want to eliminate me, sir. Before I speak ayet. Maybe you want to eliminate me too, sir. I don't, Leona — Maybe that's why you have loored me down heyer, Mr Thornby. It's a trap, ain't it, Mr Thornby? Thank the Lord I've gotten my geyern. The eliminators ain't never succeeded and they is not going to naye no way. Leonard, I was only jo

Shucks. We'd have made a great team. But he blew me away with his forefinger. Leonard is part of our equal opportunities policy for the mentally challenged. Everyone calls him Leonard the Loon. We can't all be fired, not simultaneously. Actually, he's only pretending to be mentally challenged so he can keep the job. Which must drive him crazy. It would me, if I wasn't already.

Lily is saying something important. (I'm sorry about that drivel about keyholes and moons and Leonard and the stuff about my non-reality last week. I've played some golf. I'm up and running again. I ought to wipe it, but I'm superstitious about dumping rushes. Always have been. You never know. We might need an ice-cream break. There was always an ice-cream break at the Enfield Ritz. The Lady with the Limp'd come out a bit too early and you got distracted just when it was really important. She'd stand down at the bottom just in front of the screen and her hairdo would be all lit up and flickered over and she'd be rattling coins or maybe it was her teeth with this big tray strapped on to her like she had the weirdest breasts in the world and you missed the vital bit at the end of the first half, it was like it was really unimportant, the whole thing up there was unreal, she had no respect, she was a breaker of spells and she had a limp which for some reason made everything taste a little unpleasant. Maybe everything was off, or maybe it was contaminated by the cigarette hanging off her top lip because there was ash on my Wall's Choc Special once. Ash or chocolate powder, I wasn't quite sure. There's nothing wrong with limps. They can be very attractive, like moles. It was just that particular limp. And she had very long painted fingernails which you could imagine tearing the screen to shreds. You had to avoid them when you took your Wall's and the red torch made things worse, it sort of lit her nostrils and not much else. I was frightened of her but I liked ice-cream.)

Actually, Lily has just said something REALLY important but we've missed it, I'm sorry, the refreshments vendor came out too early, as usual.

(I just really have to add that one time she didn't come out. It was

234

during *Lassie*, of all things. The first half ended and she didn't come out. The local adverts came up and she still hadn't come out. She'd died. Honest. It was terrible, actually. I cried in *Lassie* but I thought maybe it was because she hadn't come out and I knew life could not be relied upon. Maybe. Her name was Lil. Not to be confused with Lily. I'm glad she's part of all this, now. Phantoms can sell ice-creams and popcorn and Liquorice Allsorts, too, you know. We have a policy of equal opportunities in this art house. The refreshments are real and they'll be on sale in a minute. Watch her fingernails. She won't change a two bob piece for nuffink.)

Wot's vat fing in the sittin' room, ven?

(Hey, I'm gonna drop these phoney phonetics. I can't do it all for you. This is not *Pygmalion*. I am not George Bernard Shaw.)

What thing? says George. Just get on, says Dorothy. Mr Kenneth likes his pea soup piping. What bloody thing then, mite? says George. The thing on the little table, says Lily, with a black cloth over it.

She sniggers into her hand. A lock pops out of its pin. She tucks it back.

I peeped under, she says. She sniggers again. George's face is like a little boy's for a teeky moment, mouth open, forgetting itself. If it wasn't for his bleached-out stubble and flab and skin fissures you could breathe on the lens and have him back in Aberdeen for a second, watching his mother knit. Then it collects itself and tucks into a scowl. He grabs the lock between his fingers and tugs it. Lil says ow but her head goes with the lock. This golf did me good. I'm beating down the fairway fast. My swing is great. I'm not slicing, I'm not scooting off into the rough. Stick with it, Rick. Ow, says Lily again. What the fuck are you snigglin' aboot, mite? says George. Dorothy's stirring the oyster sauce. She's on hold. She only ever intervenes when George starts swinging a fist. He never contacts with it, just swings it, but one day he might. Gerroff of me, says Lily. It were a bloke. She sniggers again and I'm sorry about this detail but a bit of nasal stuff shoots out onto her apron. I forgot to say that she's in her black and white outfit with

235

a little cap because she's just served tea. Don't ask me when she got changed out of her cleaning and buffing cotton but it's like she did it so quick she still smells of beeswax and petrol. She smells of petrol because this morning she was dealing with the washing. Petrol for stubborn stains. I was on a Persil ad once, years ago, and the blood was ketchup. Early days of colour. Dollop of ketchup on a nice white shirt. It looked like a Hammer horror and I got fired. I said it wasn't my fault. We tried blood and it was more than stubborn, it was bloody-minded. I showed them a pile of underpants with perfect skid-marks and said how's about using something more normal, not everyone's hubby's just got blown away by the Krays. That's when they fired me. Dick the Talking Prick. Maybe petrol works better, but it sounds pretty drastic. The wash-room's more like a garage. Sometimes Lily comes in smelling like she's pissed in her knickers, but that's the ammonia and benzine cocktail she uses on Mr Trevelyan's suits, because Mr Trevelyan's suits accumulate stains like he's been strapped to the bonnet of a Crossley Open Tourer going at sixty down a country lane on a summer evening or something. This bit of nasal stuff sticks to the frilly starched bit over her chest and it's really bad luck because otherwise she's immaculate. OK, she has breadcrumbs under her nails but that's because – you won't believe this – she's been cleaning one of Agatha's dresses and it's beautiful, it's pure white silk and you can't wash pure white silk so you use breadcrumbs. Breadcrumbs. I have a great storyboard for a Persil ad: cleaning through the ages. Petrol and ammonia and breadcrumbs, really complicated and foul-smelling and terrible for the skin, then it's all shoved aside by my first wife holding a Persil packet. I could've made my name. Then I could've made my Great Personal Statement. I'm in the rough. I'm hacking out of it now. Keep in the clean, Rick. A bloke, eh? says George. Lily sniggers and says, a bloke without nuffink on. George lets the lock go and Lily tucks it back up under her little cap. They're nae jabberin' in there now, are they? says George. Lily shakes her head. She tugs open the dresser drawer and counts out the cutlery. She bursts into sniggers again, then sniffs it back. A hand-barrow trundles past the window and George watches the blurry boots pass and then the wheels. The window'd give a peep of frillies if you aye twisted your neck like a chicken. He's thought this many times but the window can't open more than an inch and the wrong way. Dorothy's wiping her mouth. He does like it piping hot, does our Mr Kenneth, she repeats. She always says this if Uncle Kenneth is around for luncheon, but Uncle Kenneth never gets it piping. It's weird. She says it way too soon and then forgets about it. The soup is ladled out anyway about half an hour before it's served up because that's the way Mrs Trevelyan likes it, she has sensitive lips, they chap easily, and Uncle Kenneth has to lump it. It's in the bowls and it's accumulating a scum and when the spoons sink in it'll dent really low and then fissure and the liquid part will seep through disgustingly, but no one really notices. We're in England. It's 1913. They liked scum on their food, maybe, like we like gravy. They liked gravy then, too. The gravy boat sails at every meal. Dorothy's gravy is really salty, it's like she has lead poisoning or something and maybe everyone else does because no one says anything, they just pour on this thick brown salty stuff all over their meat and potatoes and whatever and tuck in elegantly, not opening their mouths too much, getting gravy drops on their huge napkins which'll keep Lily really busy the next morning. I'm feeling hungry. Writing about food before lunch is a mistake. Our canteen here makes McDonald's look inconvenient. The people behind the counter use surgical gloves. It's like you're queuing up for an operation. I think they're wearing surgical gloves because they might have AIDS and a cut finger but it might also be because the food's so irradiated they have to protect themselves. I don't know. Everything is huge and varnished. The apples are like balloons and you can see yourself in them. They taste like balloons. Everything tastes like balloons. The inside of a balloon, I mean. The french fries, even. Nowhere else in the world do they make french fries so regular. I sit down with my tub of french fries and try to find one that isn't regular. It's like being in China or something. When I find one that isn't regular I say yippee and hold it up. The regular students chewing next to me look up and they're all as blonde as french fries. Back home we say chips, I shout. We eat them out of the *Daily Herald*, preferably the sports pages, so we can walk into a lampost reading about Stanley Matthews through the vinegar scrim. Not one of them looks the same, and they're soggy. That's the British for you. Not one of them looks the same, and they're soggy. Then I eat the french fry. No one even sniggers. They nudge away from me. They think I'm related to Leonard. They think I'm part of the equal opportunities policy.

Hey, how did ya get off the fairway again, Ricky?

Hooked it with a number three, Glenda.

(Glenda's my golfing partner. His real name is Glendallen. Jack Glendallen. He's really fat. He teaches carpentry someplace and is my neighbour. Love thy neighbour. His wife screams at him and has teeth the size of – shucks, she has very large teeth, even for America.)

Clack. That's the loose tile in the kitchen. That's Lily. She's counting out the cutlery on the tray, aloud, again. George has whipped a white cloth off a wooden rail and slung it over his shoulder. It's for the hot dishes that never are, but it looks good, it's his serving uniform, he rubs a fold of it between his thumb and forefinger like it's his security blanket or something. His stubble is rippling around his mouth because his tongue is pushing against the wall of his cheeks, he's excited. He opens his mouth and looks at Lily's back which is already rounded too much for her age.

Let's go take a peep then, mite, he says. Dorothy looks up but Lily carries on counting with funny little breaths in between each number. Dorothy's settled some salt out of the salt tub on her palm and her palm is upsides over the boiled knuckle of veal knocking in its big pan and her hand must be tough because anyone else's would have been parboiled by now. She doesn't say anything but George answers her anyway.

So we can see what the thing is. We can see what the fucker is.

Dorothy's hand makes tiny sideways movements like it's a shuttle on a loom and the salt's left in mid-air bit by bit from where it falls bit by bit like all those damned souls some of my students go on about, countless white souls falling through the steam into the pot of eternal damnation because they didn't have the right teeth or whatever.

You do be a trial, sometimes, she says. She's blinking because of the steam. She's enormous. She scratches the side of her head where the ear grows out of and some hair's drawn up from into a tight bun. There's a nice little recess of bone she likes to snuck her finger into. It looks like she's almost picking her ear, but she's not. She's done this since she was three, and you can tell.

George clears his throat. He has a hand on Lily's shoulder. Let's aye take a peep, he says, at this birthday suit gentleman. Lily's biting her lower lip and not looking at Dorothy. Her sniggers have died, which surprises her. She wipes her hands on her apron, forgetting she's changed, but her hands are clean. Dorothy slaps her palms together to rid them of salt. She's just ruined the boiled knuckle of veal, but who cares. We're not eating it. Lily scoops up the cutlery like it's a handful of thunderbolts and places it on a smaller tray, a round one, a silver salver, hold this for a moment, this silver salver is THE SAME ONE, it must be, I want to cry, I can't explain this at the moment, we'll miss something, there's a queue back there at the tee-off, it'll take about as long as this film's gonna take, actually. Ho. My hand's trembling. Ho. Ha.

I have to pretend I have never seen this silver salver before, for the moment.

OK. Hit it.

There are glasses on this – this thing. I think she must have put them there at some pre-arranged time, or maybe Milly did, I don't know. Anyway, she picks the insignificant salver up and goes out of the kitchen. She has short strong arms and big shoulders and this is what you think of just after Lily's left a room. Strong arms and big shoulders. Compact, a compact bundle of muscle and hair and chin. Very fine auburn hair but you don't notice it, it's all so compact. Clack. A louder clack because it's George's boot as he follows her out. Grunt. You think of grunts and rippling stubble after George has left. Nothing else much. Maybe a white napkin over a black shoulder, if he has it on. And the smell. Certainly nothing about salvers.

Dorothy looks up at the flex. She thinks of it growing out of the ceiling like a tree root. The old gas fitting looks very old, next to it. The bulb hurts her eyes. She misses the soft gassy light. I'm on the putting green in three. Ten yards. She folds her arms and sighs. The steam has returned to water. It shimmers on the ceiling, it always does, it sticks like sweat. She feels wrong, today. Her antennae are picking up trouble. She doesn't think this exactly. She thinks how her throat is hurting and of melted snow. Melted snow for sore throats. And burns.

239

Her bare forearms are notched with old burns. They seem to be remembering themselves today. Any road, there's hardly ever enough snow, and if there is she forgets to bottle it.

Plop. Down in four. Great run, Ricky, great run.

OK. Number Two. Big bunkers but straight, rolling only a little, a high green on which Mrs Trevelyan's waving at me. George wanted to hump my golf-bag but I gave him a trolley. Glenda uses electric, I use George. It's OK, I wear gloves. My swing's great. Agatha's watching from the woods. She's found a ball. She looks great, white dress against the woods, the dark woods. Texan woods are dark. The leaves begin too low. They're forever green. They have jogging and bike tracks through them in case you forget civilisation and kids and overweight people. Lily is caring for my tees. She has a habit of standing directly behind me. I tell her, think of me as a horse. I nearly took her head off three strokes back. Milly is nowhere to be seen. Ah, there she is. She's standing in the bunker. If I slice I'll hit her. It's the most dangerous place to be on the course, a bunker. Balls like them, they like the sand, the softness. They like to snuck up under the lip and watch you flailing with your niblick, thinking the world is coming to an end and your life is a waste of time.

Tee up. I'm feeling on form.

George and Lily come up the stairs and stand in the hallway. The door into the living-room is shut. George can tell that there is no one in there. He just can. There's silence and there's quiet. Silence is uninhabited and quiet is not. Behind the door there's silence. Once he's established this he moves forward over the lozenge tiles (Bishop to Knight 3) and opens the door. He looks. There's silence and then the clocks ticking and also the chairs hunkered down and relaxing or little and uptight but no one in them snoring or turning their face or not turning their face because he's only the butler. He feels Lily's breath behind him. I'll put this down, she hisses, where I oughta. She's talking about the TOTALLY INSIGNIFICANT salver. She goes off with it into the conservatory. The conservatory is at the end and on the left of the passage that sneaks off into the twilight of the back of the

240

house, beyond the staircase. George feels abandoned. He curses softly (OK, he says fuck) and steps into the room. He knows there's no one in here but he thinks they might all be disguised as furniture, they're going to jump him, Mrs Trevelyan's going to whip off her antimacassar and shriek at him. He grunts and sits on her. He likes to do this. He likes to sit and soil the furniture, it gives him a feeling of reckless abandon just descending from the vertical more than a small bow. He really goes for it today: he spreads his legs wide and rucks up a rug from Hindustan with his heels and allows his hands to loll either side of the low arms. It's one of those antique padded chairs with low arms and a seat that just clears the floor and legs with rickets. When Mr Trevelyan does this he's drunk. When George does this he's being a revolutionary, he's smashing the class barriers, he's subverting the imperial order but only in his skull. If he so much as heard a pin drop behind the curtain he'd be vertical in about an eighth of a second. It's one of the escape valves, it takes off the pressure – if he had a whistle attached to his head you'd hear it peep right now. There's sunlight falling across the floor. It's nice. The polish picks it up where the rugs aren't and throws it onto George's face, so he can't see very clearly. But in the general glare there's something black on a table. The ball's on a terrific lie, bang in the middle. It didn't hit Milly, yet. It hasn't got that far, but I'd have to slice it at right angles practically to hit her now. I'm taking a number one wood, for the hell of it. Here goes.

The something black on the table is like a tiny coffin. This is what George thinks. A child's coffin covered with a black drape. He's thinking of Evelyn's, actually. He liked the bairn. Well, he didn't know he liked that bairn until the bairn was dead, but that's good enough. He mainly liked the bairn underneath because it was the first bairn, and when he was born George was still young enough not to ache all over. Twenty years ago. He doesn't like thinking about the coffin. He doesn't like thinking about the maid coming down into the kitchen steady steady with a bowl and a white cloth over it and him fritting her with a growl so she tipped the bowl a mite and half of the white cloth went red and so did they jes looking at it bloom like a red red rose that's newly sprung in June O. He doesn't like thinking about the way he acted the loon all the way through the illness, down in the kitchen, making fangs out of potato flesh and fritting the maid every time she came down with a bowl full of arterial blood and scummy bits of sputum. He doesn't like thinking about the cough cough cough that was like a clock it was so regular, it filled the whole house, when the coughs stopped you noticed, it was dead queer, it was so quiet. Maybe it was a miracle. Maybe Big Bastard up there had got it into his head to be nice for once and sucked everything rotten out of the bairn's lungs. But no, the coughs'd get going again and one'd get a mite angry with Big Bastard and a wee bit peevish at Evelyn himself for carrying on so. And the missus was terrible, shouting and that. Aye aye. Everyone padding about like bogies. George'd have to bring up cocoa or hot lemon and knock and Nurse Gulliver'd take it with a glare, as if he was Mister Death or something. Then one time when the toffs were out Mister Death took up the hot lemon instead and George was just too late, he knocked and Nurse had a hand over her mouth and wide eyes, she couldn't believe it, he'd choked or something when she was on the toilet, she went into shock and the hot lemon went down again and stayed all day calmly and quietly on the kitchen table while the whole house exploded upstairs but quietly, quietly. The hot lemon was cold lemon by the evening and with a scum. George drank it without thinking and afterwards felt queer. The bairn'd looked like he'd pulled a jolly wheeze, the way he lay there, stark white over a waistcoat of blood and stuff beyond the nurse's shoulder. George grimaces because he's remembering that and the way he was trembling the next morning, serving toast, while the family sat there as usual as if nowt had happened. Only the eyes, all the eyes were bloated, like fish, and it was a bit quieter. He'd had a need to cough. Aye. He'd tried to swallow it out but it crawled up his throat and out it came, and Mrs T had whipped about and fixed him with an awful stare as he wiped his mouth. This is what the something black on the table has tweaked out of his brain, it's like that thing at the music hall, that magic blokey pulling a hundred knotted scarves out of that wee box as the monkey claps. He grunts. He hears a step in the hallway and he's vertical but the rug slips away from under him and he's horizontal again.

Lily puts her hand to her mouth.

Blimey, you all right? She nearly chuckles but it's a sigh instead. You all right, Mr MacPhearson?

He's not dead. He thought he might be. What does it fuckin' look like,

242

he growls. I came over all queer and decided to die. He drags himself upright. He shakes his head. I've sliced. I did something very weird. I clipped the ball and it's heading towards Milly. She's got her back to it. Christ. There's another footfall in the hallway. George and Lily stare at the door like it's about to explode. It opens. It's Milly. I hope she ducks. Golf balls have been known to kill. They can hit the temple and kill. They have terrific velocity. Even my balls have terrific velocity. She doesn't. We're all running over to her because it's like she was karate chopped in the neck and she dropped out of sight behind the lip of the bunker. As I run I'm thinking it wasn't my fault, she shouldn't have been standing there, will I get done for homicide, am I insured, will she sue me if it's not fatal, will she have brain damage, they say there's a ghost of this guy who had a coronary after missing a two-inch putt on the eighteenth, there will definitely be a ghost in this bunker, there are ghosts everywhere, some people walk into these things, they invite it, Milly didn't have to be standing where most golf balls like to go, she didn't have to come into the living-room right at the moment I'm talking about, which is now. And always now.

And now now? TODD LAZENBY IS DATING ZELDA. For definites. He actually comes into the library. We have just purchased the twelve-volume *World History of the Movies* on CD-ROM and he keeps on calling it up. He and Zelda giggle together. It's disgusting. They had a great night out last week. If I show up all possessive she'll run straight into his waistcoat, I know it. He has a waistcoat, a kind of multicoloured Paisley thing, with a fob-watch on a chain in it. Seriously. A fob-watch. Lazenby the laser brain has a fob-watch. I reckon it's this and his lazy eye that clinches it with women. Anybody who tries to compete gets accused of rape. He doesn't. Seriously. It's terrifying. There was this guy called John Blean who was such a sop you could've picked his ear for him and he'd have thanked you. He was the world expert on John Huston. Perhaps he was John Huston underneath. Call me John. Anyway, he winked at a girl in the front row when he was giving a mass seminar on *Cultural Identity in the Western* and he was up in front of the college tribunal. They did him for ocular harassment or something. He claimed he had a sty and it was weeping which was probably true but they'd gone too far, they'd pulled all his nails out by that stage or something and he had to leave. It was a major victory for the forces of progress, I guess. A major victory for the forces of progress would be to crucify Todd Lazenby. You know what he did yesterday? (I won't be long on this, I'm waiting for the ambulance to arrive and I've got sand in my shoes and it looks bad for Milly, but we've time, this is important, I have to get it off my chest and on to the screen where it can snivel and snort to its heart's content forever.) He called up the twelve-volume $1200 plus tax *World History of the Movies* and looked for me in it. Hey, let's find Rick, he said. Zelda stopped massaging his shoulders or whatever she was doing and clapped her hands with delight. He was on this swivel stool in front of the VDU and he swivelled and looked over to me and said, hey, Rick, do you know if it's nice about you? I pretended I was coming out of a trance state of profound concentration and looked over his way (I have changed my place to be in sight of the issue desk, by the way) and said, I'm sorry? I like to be quite English when talking to this creep. I feel an advantage over him, being English, British English. I feel the oaken-hearted ancientness of being British English coursing through my veins and this turns him into a squeaky kind of American hologram, it really does. That fucking waistcoat and fob. I don't need appurtenances like that, old fellow. My blood goes back to Hengest. Or maybe Horsa. Anyway, the ones that cut some softy Romano-British hands off and left the rest on the beach. I've picked up a bit of Viking on the way, the nasty bit that plundered and raped and slew monks. I retroactively acquired some Beaker brain cells and a portion of my DNA is definitely Arthurian Celtic. No Norman. It may seem amazing, but I have no Norman. I know, I know, Normans were really Vikings but you know what I mean. I am pure. I am not continental filth. My seed is so British and ancient it'd grow an oak clump if I jacked off in a meadow. Todd Lazenby is so recent he'd leave a UFO burn if he jacked off in a meadow. Now I have to say that under my British *sang-froid* I was curling up, guv. Because I knew. I knew that nowhere in the million corridors and rooms of those twelve little discs was there anybody resembling Ricky Thornby, or who answered to his name (because Danny Kaye resembles me, but he doesn't answer to my name). I am not even the son of a footnote. I had spent two whole days hacking into those discs just in case the microscopically reliable index had slipped up. Mike was there, as an assistant lighting guy on *Waterloo*. Bosey was there, as a footnote to *Blow-Up*. Fuck it – even my first wife Deirdre was there, under *The Significance of Names to Screen Failure* or something. I wasn't. My presence in the Grand Canyon of World Cinema was less than the echo of that dropped rose petal some very successful poet went on about. It wasn't even the torn-off wing of a tsetse fly hitting the gulch. There was nothing. It was as if I hadn't even stood on the edge and dropped anything down into the Colorado at all. And I get vertigo. OK, I didn't get vertigo when I looked into the Grand Canyon a few years ago, it was too high, it was too big, but I got vertigo looking down into that CD-ROM and not finding myself. I nearly threw myself over the edge in recompense. I nearly smashed it up. That is, I nearly took out the CD and did whatever you do to the thing to ruin it. But I thought of Zelda and how proud she was of this thing, how amazing it was to have got them to swell the budget to buy it. Anyway, I'm a coward, I didn't want to lose my job, and I thought how in the 2001 edition I'd be there, the only guy to have screened a masterpiece with no pictures, no sound, and ONCE ONLY, unique screening, like a great meal, like your one great night with your pin-up. I'd be a crazy ghost trace, a rumour, a cult. So I got up and went home and drank eighteen straight Dylans. Small ones, so I didn't die. I lied when I said I was playing golf. I'm sorry. I was actually drinking and sleeping and telling them I was having a recurrence of my cerebral malaria from the VSO days. I feel better now. At least, I did until yesterday. Until Todd Lazenby tried to call me up, tried to listen out for an echo, with Zelda next to him. It's incredible that Zelda hadn't tried already, but she doesn't really know how to handle machines. This doesn't matter, because no one uses the CD-ROM except weirdo and he can make it talk, literally. The other students are too busy learning to read. I wanted to leave the room, actually. It was like Todd Lazenby and I were struggling on the edge of the Grand Canyon, we had our hands under each other's chin, but I was on the bad side, I had zilch but air the other side of my heels, little rocks were skittering down and he had a definitely evil gleam in his eyes, he was pushing my head right back and my body was following. It wasn't that he was stronger than me or anything, it was just that he was taking unfair advantage of my position, and Zelda was watching, not realising what the hell was going on, just thinking we were having a harmless little tussle on the edge, it's what boys do, it's fun. The only echo was of my long scream. I was screaming inside. Lazenby shakes his head in disbelief, staring into the screen, some junk playing in his eyeballs.

There's something wrong, he says. You're not in here.

He tries the other disc, the *1980 to Present* disc. Zilch. I'm sweating, I'm falling, I'm falling a long way, it takes ages to die. Zelda's frowning. At least there were no giggles. My cerebral malaria week had left its skid marks in my head. I got up to leave. Both of them were looking at me. You're nowhere, Rick, said Lazenby. There's some mistake, said Zelda. I raised my head. I tried to look like Gary Cooper in *High Noon* but ended up looking like Charlie Laughton in *I, Claudius*. I even stammered. I g-g-guess it's not c-c-comprehensive, I replied. The room swam. It started off as a doggy-paddle and ended up Olympic butterfly. I had to sit down. I did, but there was no chair. Men don't faint. I guess I'm gender-challenged. Anyway, I didn't really faint I just wanted to be blown to Bermuda or someplace or have a trap-door open under me dropping to anywhere but the HCDVA library and Lazenby's lazy laser eye. He picked me up. Git y'hands off of me, I growled. It's the malaria, I heard Zelda say. I lie even to Zelda. Yeah, it's the cerebral, I said, I apologise, I shouldn't have white-water rafted up the Congo that time, but I was into Conrad before Stanley, Stanley Kubrick I mean, not Stanley Stanley I presume, old fellow. He's delirious, I heard whisper Zelda. Yeah, I am, I heard whisper myself, don't tell him. Todd Lazenby turned into my bedside lamp. It was all a nightmare, I thought. I was so relieved. Then Zelda strokes my forehead. Boy, you're heavy when limp, she said. It wasn't a nightmare, it was worse, it was real. She and Lazenby had got me to my bed. I was apparently unhelpful. I don't remember. The doctor came round. He gave me Aspirin and suggested a heart-check. There's nothing wrong with my heart that Zelda running into my arms won't cure. Zelda aikido-ing Todd Lazenby in the balls and running into my arms won't cure, I'd better say. If I'm strictly honest with myself, old fellow.

This is ridiculous.

Milly has stood up, she's OK. We don't need the ambulance. Agatha says she might have concussion, her brain might be bleeding, if she gets sleepy we'd better take action. I'm looking at Milly's eyes now. She's standing in the doorway of the London living-room. Her eyes are dilated, but it's the dazzle, we have a specular in here that's getting Mike jumping up and down, it's the polished floorboards where the rugs aren't, it's the specular that's closing down her retinas, it's aperture correction, that's all. Hoi, she's no more doomed than you or me. The whole world's brain is bleeding. Watch out for sleepiness. If your wrist droops, or is it your thumb, it's the apocalypse. It's 999. Milly is thirteen. Look in her eyes. They are definitely dilating. They have coal smuts in the corners and on the eyelashes. Are you telling me she was always doomed or something? Are you telling me that the bleeding can't be staunched, snipped out, my golf slice spliced away into a nothing as nothing as my absence in the *World History of the Movies*, vols 11 and 12?

Too right you are, guv.

George looks at her.

Milly milt, eh? Our Milly milt.

Milly's lower lip darts about but fails to make contact with its partner. She swallows. She's not quite sure what made her come in. Perhaps it was the tea things, but they've been took. Perhaps it was the noises. Sometimes she thinks she's sleepwalking. Her brain is poisoned by Worksop's soap works, by the whole industrial revolution, by her crappy diet, by the way her corset bunches her up.

Lily tells her to shut the door. Lily's not nervous, just corset cautious. Milly shuts the door. It bangs. She can hear the echo go great guns in the hall and up the stairs. George murmurs, aye, we're fuckin' deaf too, and his tongue appears, searching in the corner of his mouth for something, perhaps a crumb, perhaps a sweetness. Milly blinks but watches him go over to the draped object on the table like she can't watch anything else. He purses his lips and sniffs and takes the cloth between his thumb and forefinger and his little finger goes up and he tweaks the cloth off. Lily sniggers. The zoetrope's drum shifts minutely because of the cloth being tweaked off. It's well-oiled. It's a fine piece of nineteenth-century engineering. George's eyes widen. Och, will ye look at him, he says. His tongue explores his lower lip as he looks at the ballock-naked men who are all the same man. You can see his privates and his tuft. Naked as Adam. There's a hedge behind him. Maybe Eve's behind it, waiting. Something stirs inside his breeches,

247

something in his loch stirs, something a saint'd like to chase away. He bends down. What the aye fuck do we do now, mite, he says. You turn the handle says Lily, looking at Milly and sniggering. George looks up and sees the handle resting next to the zoetrope. D'you ken where it goes, mite? he breathes, fingering it. I'm just under the green. Great shot. A number seven'll toss it up. Just let the club do it. Don't overplay. Don't think too hard. Just leave it to the club.

George is stood there holding this little handle like it's a motor car starter with a fancy knob. Where, mite, he hisses, where do I put it? There's no fuckin' hole. Milly is backing off, which for once means she's going in the right direction, towards the door, staring at George the whole time like he's about to shoot her if she makes a wrong move. Lily claps her hand to her mouth and goes ooh, because she's suddenly overcome by the mischief of what they're doing. They haven't a load of time. George's face somehow gets itself into a grin. You can see his awful teeth now. Here, milt, he snaps, sticking the handle out and jabbing it towards her, stay right where ye are. I know where it goes, says a voice. Milly is amazed to find it is hers. George scowls. He showed me, says Milly. She doesn't know why she's blabbing like this. It's nerves. I know the feeling. It's like she's running to catch up a part of herself that's blabbing and dancing just in front of her but out of reach. This blabbing part of her is next to the zoetrope now, lifting the little latch in the side of the base and sticking the handle in the hole secreted under it. She's blinking in fright. She hates this machine. She was alone with it and the uncle and the uncle put his hand on her shoulder and told her how she must run naked through a field of long grass and she'd feel better. She wouldn't, she'd thought. She'd mostly catch her death and expire gracefully. That's what th'manager's wife over at Soap Works did, like. Expired gracefully. After forgetting her umbrella. Clean soaked to knickers, she were, Mam'd said. She's turning the handle. It's heavy but it moves the drum, the drum clunks and moves slowly round. They are all three looking at this thing going round and round like it is the most gripping sight in the whole world, like they are Europeans seeing their first wheel bumping under a barrow in about 3,300 BC and not knowing what to do about it. (I've just checked this fact up. It really shocks me that Europeans saw the wheel so late. I was about 2,000 years out before. Zelda claims she was a neolithic shepherd in one of her past lives, like this guy they found

248

stuck in the ice a few years ago. She likes meadows. She says they were in tune in those days, their god was the Great Goddess, Mother Nature, all that stuff. I'm not surprised she was hanging around then. I'd like to be regressed. Maybe I was her wife. Maybe we grappled in the thick grass of the high summer meadows above the tree-line, above the tree-line of the thick forests of the New Stone Age where there were no Todd Lazenbys not finding you in CD-ROMs and talking gunk. Where there were no golf bunkers. Where there were no movie critics. Hey, it sounds like the Golden Age. Pan was not dead. Eros was hanging around behind every bole. There were lots of rare flowers and my great-aunt Agatha would've gone out with my great-uncle William and had a great time catching butterflies and chasing dryads. I like the sound of the New Stone Age. Maybe we should model ourselves on the New Stone Age. Maybe we should give it a second chance. Maybe I should carve myself a crook. Zelda and I see eye to eye. I'm into Zen and I'm into the New Stone Age. Todd Lazenby is into hydraulics when he's not into words like diseases. He's incredibly unsuitable for Zelda. She's not here today. She's at a conference. Lazenby is one of the speakers. It's something to do with the MLA. I wasn't invited. Well, I was, but I was invited to pay $75, $75 for the privilege of listening to Lazenby and ten other jerks explain why movies are incommensurable figural disruptions of temporal significations. I guess mine were, if only I'd known. They had to hire a coach, there were so many groupies. I said I get coach-sick and I don't like Dallas ever since. Ever since what? said Zelda. Hey, is memory that juvenile?)

I got into the tough grass there, I'm sorry. I hurt the Great Goddess a little hacking out of it. I was like a mowing machine. I overshot the green into the tough stuff at the back. I didn't let the club alone. I didn't hold back. I'm up there now. I'm as far from the hole as you can get without dribbling off the velvet. I'll do my best. This one's for Zelda. I'm trying to stop myself saying that if it doesn't go in she'll leave me. I'm not superstitious, just insecure.

Milly feels the flat of a hand on her back and this means she has to bend down. Life sometimes repeats itself. It's George's hand. He's making her look. The thing's going round on its own now and she lets go of the handle. The walking naked man flickers past her eye. Maybe this is what life as a maidservant is all about. She watches and her

249

throat doesn't even go dry. She's deeply into a never ever and she doesn't care. She's fucked up the hats and she's let a poshy open the door for her and she couldn't hang the coat properly and now she's definitely into a never ever in a big way and all in one morning. Her head's bleeding inside. She's getting sleepy. She's tired. Her mouth is furry and the naked man walks past it, swinging his hands and lifting his feet forever and ever flash forever and ever flash forever and ever and George's face is next to hers, one huge eyeball under a forest of eyebrow, one horrible nostril yanked wide open so she can see everything inside it, like when the dentist came round to the factory to pull the workers' teeth out. The carious ones! Hey, things aren't that bad in Europe, yet. She thinks there's a cat in the room but it's George's throat, it's mewling and whimpering. She feels she's aged about twenty years. She's looking forward to writing a letter. To her mam. She's grown up in one day, and it'll show. The hand on her buttocks is definite. There's a hand on her buttocks. She looks at the eyeball and the hand is a tentacle of it. Incy-wincy, says George. The spider is crawling down the slope of her rump, down into the cave. Her whole body is frozen. She hates spiders. The naked man is slowing down. She hears a voice from the other side of the naked man. Turn it faster, Mill, says the voice. It's Lily. Lily doesn't know about the spider because she's the wrong side. The spider has stopped, as if it senses a big fist about to squash it. Milly opens her mouth to tell Lily about the spider but only a squeak comes out. Dunna fret. Never ever. Christian souls. Expired gracefully. Machines in the factory. A moment's silence. All lined up. Hiss.

The spider bites her.

She's poisoned. It's a poisonous spider. She tries to stand but the spider's on her back again, pulling her towards the eyeball. The eyeball and nostril whisper out of their forest.

Would nae ye both like it, eh? Would nae ye both like a lick o' that cock, eh?

Whassat? says Lily.

Milly has a very open mouth. She knows this language. But here she

250

can't hang it up on the right hook, to coin a phrase. It won't go in the box, to coin another. She doesn't like this eyeball and nostril and bad smell. The thing as it goes round flicks her cap, flick flick flick. Her brother had a thing. It was made of cardboard. You turned it on a pencil, like. A man went cross-eyed 'cos a fly flew right onto his nose. Her brother'd play wi'it for hours. He swapped th'pictures. It got stamped on, if she remembered straight. Mill, says Lily, he's stoppin'. The open mouth which is hers, I mean Milly's, fills with saliva. The back of her head is clamped. It's like a photograph in the studio. That time. She has an uncle on a reasonable income, a shipping clerk, he paid for it, it's Still Nine. Go see it in a minute. She looks terrified. The clamp is the spider. Teeth. Awful teeth appear beneath the nostril. This is kissing. Not quite. About to be kissing. The thing is squeaking as it slows. She presses into the clamp, away from the teeth, but not before the cheek next to it scrapes her lips. She has full lips, she has at least a full upper lip, the lower lip's kind of a pedestal, a cushion for the upper lip, you know what I mean, it's pretty attractive in a kid and in a grown-up it'll be sexy and right now it's indecisive. Oi, move it, Mill, says Lily. Mill can't. She's stuck about a half inch away from this eyeball, lifting her face away with the spider trying to press her back down again. The clamp loosens. In fact, it goes right away and she finds herself almost falling backwards. Her hat is awry. There are hair-pins on the floor. She's panting but she hasn't run anywhere. Never ever. Her face goes blank. Lily's watching her the other side of the drum. The room is echoing with a cry, a kind of dragon's bellow if you can imagine that. George is holding a handkerchief to his face. The fuckin' bitch comes out muffled. The room is frowning, unsure what's going on exactly. The antimacassars are prepared to be embarrassed. The pictures are waiting for her to speak before they carry on. It appears that she actually gobbed at his eyeball. Whassup then? says Lily. She's frowning, but you get the feeling she knows whassup. Milly takes a step back. The clock's carrying on. The pictures are sighing and carrying on because they're that busy. A dray full of churns goes past. Clippety clang clang clop. Dunna lay a finger on me, says Milly. That's what her sister told her to say if anyone except a gentleman with means tried it on. There was more but she's forgot it. Or else, she says, instead. Or else.

Clip then clang.

That was a great putt, only it hit the pole. We forgot to remove the flag. We are idiots. I never expected to get that far. Lily was standing there. She should've hoiked out the flag when she saw what an incredible putt was coming over. Now there's this little extra bit I have to do, but it's a whole stroke. It's unfair, waaaah.

George removes the handkerchief from his face. The whole of his adult life is scowling at him. OK, OK, he happens to be facing Napoleon's full-length mirror. It's not really Napoleon's, it's a nice Napoleon III plaster-mould and gilt mirror out of some Paris dealer's back room but somebody got it wrong somewhere and the servants call it Napoleon's mirror and only George can clean it. He looks away from it. I didnae touch ye, he says. Lily is already walking towards the door. Oh that's it, thinks Milly. He didnae touch me. It was a spider. And if ye do that agin, skrunt, adds the butler, if ye gob at me agin ye'll be on the street afore ye can squeak.

Milly's plump upper lip retracts under its little cushion. She wants to keep blank but her mouth won't let her. This thing about being on the street is really terrible. The house would be the wrong side of her and she'd be the wrong side of it, and the street would be wet, and she wouldn't have a commendation. A commendation, Sis said, is the passport, the lifeline, the Most Important Thing along wi' a clean pair o' knickers. Wi'out a commendation tha'll drop through bottom and into gutter and sell tha rump to them as want to eat thee and send thee to Hell. She knows, does Milly, how easy it is to slide down to Hell because the minister was always saying how easy it was, he was a proper clever minister, he gave her bits to read out of the Bible especially written out in big capital letters and they were always about HELL and CANKERWORM and A GREAT NUMBER OF CARCASES and THE LABOUR OF THE OLIVE failing and bad INDIGNATION and young children DASHED IN PIECES AT THE TOP OF ALL THE STREETS and a load of ARISE AND THRESH, O DAUGHTER OF ZION which came back at you off the bare walls much higher than it was sent out. She liked the bit about the maids leading wotsit AS WITH THE VOICE OF DOVES and saying BUT NINEVEH IS OF OLD LIKE A POOL OF WATER slowly and all that about Zerubbabal's hands and the Lord's eyes running about through the earth which made her feel all tingly in her feet but she'd only had that to read aloud once when it was very bitter out. Actually, this minister was incredibly screwed up and spittly and eventually strangled some street vendor or other and died in prison but in 1913 he was still operative and had really wheedled himself into Milly's personal make-up. She can almost feel the wet street on her bottom and at the end of it HELL MOUTH waiting to swallow her up. The house is the only thing between her and the widest mouth in the world. It was that easy, the minister was right, she'd been here a day and the mouth was a'ready grinning. She nods.

Sorry, she says, I'm sorry.

Lily's at the door. Milly looks at her. Lily's mouth rumples up, it might have been a smile, it might have been sympathy, but Lily has to be careful. Despite the domestics crisis, she has to be careful. George is in with Mrs T, hand in glove and dick also once long ago as goes the legend. You have to look to your own. Milly's too new to have crossed into Lily's sympathy room. Blimey, they've hardly spoke. Lily's one side of the ropes and Milly's the other. There's even a teeky bit of Lily that likes seeing Milly screwed down by Georgie Porgie, though Lily hates the guy. Humanity is like that. It can't bear too much unfamiliarity.

Plop.

Agatha's clapping, at least. She knows what all this means. White against the dark woods. There are no dryads in those woods. Only the phantoms of Injuns long ago slaughtered.

Go see Still Nine. I'm taking a break. Go see Milly Looking Terrified Next To An Aspidistra With Background Of The Heaviest Curtain Ever To Have Not Broken A Curtain Rod, by E. S. Cummins, Photographer to the Anonymous, Worksop. I think she's looking terrified because Mr Cummins has just told her that if she moves her head the clamp will snap it off. This guy still uses a clamp? Uh-huh. For kids, for kids. Also, the mad spittly minister does not like photography and he's told her so. He's Primeval Methodist or something and thinks it's frippery and takes away your soul. He'd have made a great ayatollah. But you see what I mean about her lips, in the

253

still. She's keeping them firmly shut because she has this idea that your soul can escape out of your mouth. At least, it can do if you take the name of Our Lord in vain or laugh too much and too loud.

Go look at those eyes. I'm taking a break. I hate looking at the issue desk with this student in a Hawaiian shirt instead of Zelda in anything.

Happy New Year.

I just remembered that. I don't think I've said it yet. Happy New Century. Happy New Millennium. The dancing should've started. I debated with myself about the dancing. It'll mean some of you people won't watch every minute of the film. It'll inevitably be a distraction, like the hammer drill that always starts up as soon as my class on the Silent Film begins. But this film doesn't have a sound-track. The sound-track is life, it's ambient, it's wild. It's Ossy next to you sucking the wodka out of his lemon slice and it's my granddaughter snucking her ballet feet under her thighs and sighing and it's the dance music swilling over from the next room and it's the bells of London saying turn again Dick you're gonna be a hit this time and it's the pooping and snorting of pleasure boats and the unemployed silence I hope of dredgers and the whittering of bats and the murmuring of a thousand million mouths and hey, I could go on but I won't, it's too complicated unthreading the woof or unwoofing the thread and right now I'm a long way away from this party, I'm in the hum of a place where only books talk and it's so quiet I feel like bringing in a personal stereo and some of that chill-out New Age stuff Zelda's lent me to create an atmosphere conducive to gentle thought because there's something incredibly violent about this quiet, it's like it's waiting for me to get up and start screaming at her over there because of what she's just done.

She's told Lazenby about my project.

Lazenby said two things in reply. He said Jarman's got there first. He said this to Zelda. Then he said it to me. He said it to me yesterday, in the corridor, looking concerned. The other thing he said was that he didn't know I had it in me. He didn't say that to me, he only said it to Zelda. I can't believe that Zelda has told him. I feel raped. I hadn't heard of this Jarman thing. I only know the guy has recently died. It's really bad luck – he's made a film with no pictures. It's called *Blue*. Lazenby says it's a masterpiece. It's a blue screen and that's it. With a sound-track. It's DIY cinema. He was telling me all this in the corridor but I knew it already because Zelda had told me what he'd told her on their date together at Seebug's Fish Restaurant. It had to be Jarman, because I don't like Jarman. I mean, I don't like his work. He laughed at me once, in '69, off the Old Kent Road. It was a matey sort of laugh but it made me angry. He was on my set. He thought the set was naff. Plywood Studios, he joked. I said this is a Victorian drama, it has to be accurate, we have to hide Mr Wu's Fish Bar and Ali's Kebabs. No you don't, he said, and laughed. Now he's gone and kicked me in the groin and I have to be nice about him because he's dead. That's really bad luck, Ricky, said Lazenby. That's kinda taken the punch out of a great revolutionary concept. He had his concerned look all over him, his fob watch was dangling in sympathy, I could've nutted the guy. I hope you didn't have too many fish bones last night, I replied. I find Seebug's is heavy on the fish bones. His hands. I was looking at his hands curled around some jerk's thesis on some other jerk fattening a clip folder. They were pale and unpleasant, like, I dunno – like he bleaches them every evening or something because the rest of him is fairly carefully tanned. They have small black hairs between the knuckles, but not many, you can count them on one finger. I was thinking about maybe what the fingers had done with Zelda the previous night. Paddled with her. Paddled. What a great word. Shakespeare. Hengest and Horsa. Oak trees. I happen to believe Zelda when she says there is nothing physical between them. They just copulate mentally. Staring into each other's eyes. She didn't put it like that, of course. She said it's swell, he is really illuminating on certain theoretical aspects of life and art. But he must have touched her, if only fleetingly, fleetingly. You know, paddling with the palm of her hand, borrowing her Kleenex, helping her fillet her monkfish. Shakespeare. I'm sounding like Shakespeare. She probably tingled. They have only candles in Seebug's. That's why it's dangerous. You can't fillet properly. A guy died there, a rich Indian guy, a lawyer in real estate, they thought it was poison but it was a monkfish's sternum or something. You can't fillet efficiently, I added. Because Lazenby was looking puzzled. My voice was a semitone above the usual. I cleared my throat. Anyway, he said, it still sounds very interesting, this project of yours, Rick. Yeah? Yeah, uh-huh, very interesting. Todd, my son? Yeah, Rick? Go fuck yourself.

Wasn't that unfair? Hey, look, I barely said it. I was already turning away and blushing when I barely said it. He probably thought I said, *go for a car sale*, or *gofer cures elf*, or *go far go slow*, or something that would keep him puzzled in between jacking off over his students and belching monkfish and fennel until lunch. I wish I'd said it loud and clear but I didn't, I dipped it down to about one and a half, it was really ambient, it was more like surf and breezes and Tibetan wind-chimes, it probably really relaxed him. Anyway, it'd only encourage the guy. I mean, if I'd stood there and screamed go fuck yourself so close to his ear I'd have got wax on my nose instead of off-mike and so close to my shoes I practically dubbined my forehead it would've encouraged him to go further with Zelda. He likes competition. What he doesn't understand is how profound my feelings are for someone he just wants to play around with for a while like he plays around with the desirable T-shirts. I feel sick talking about it. I wish I could plant a monkfish's sternum in his morning cereal. Zelda is right now reaching up and planting a book in the shelf where it will smell slightly of her scent for a while. I go round sniffing books every evening, I go round getting high on the day's returns. I'm like a dog, it excites me, we haven't made love for weeks because she has a headache. She has a headache and I had my cerebral malaria. I don't want to go on and on and on and on and on about Zelda but it's killing me. I'm wracked by jealous pains. I am jealous. I want to be very upfront about this, guv. I AM EXTREMELY JEALOUS. Jarman and Lazenby are ganging up on me artistically and emotionally, they make a great team, they completely complement each other. They have already winded me. I never get anywhere before anybody else. I'm Scott of the Antarctic. I eat my huskies. I practically kill myself but it's OK because no one in the history of the world has ever reached this place before and then there's this fucking flag there. Hey, I want to establish a stable relationship. I want Zelda to fill my future forever. She makes my fingertips tingle. We could even marry.

Christ, guvnor, Daisy Daisy an' all that? Get me to the church on time? Eh? Third time lucky or somefink, Cyril?

Mike, kill the lights. I want to listen to my head.

Mike?

Shit, the guy's cans are around his neck. I'm rapping on the glass, the gallery glass. I'm mouthing obscenities silently, I'm a goldfish, all the plugs are out, everyone's cans are around their necks, the actors are farting about with coffee down there, laughing. I hate TV work, I did *Play for Today* once in the really early days and it was a catastrophe. It was such a catastrophe they only pretended to wipe it, they wiped everything in those days, even priceless stuff like Laurence Olivier tap-dancing with Dudley Moore they wiped, it was amazing, it was great, it gave everything an edge, it was like you couldn't care a fuck because you knew it was going to be wiped except I cared a fuck because I was very insecure about my career and Deirdre was in it and she was drunk. My first wife was drunk and it was live. And it wasn't wiped. I mean, it was but there was a bootleg the tech guys showed newcomers to terrify them, it was an initiation rite, it was cruel. It was so live in dem days it went out before it had happened, almost. Before *we* knew what had happened, anyway. It was like life but worse. It was supposed to be exciting. Everyone's sideburns sparkled because it was so exciting. My sideburns were like the crown jewels I was so excited by the idea that I could make the biggest asshole of myself ever in the history of the world because at the other end of the line there were about a hundred and two screens like submarine portholes and all these pipe-smokers and cardigan-knitters and dwarves in ties and shorts who turn out to be kids watching and waiting for me to fuck my career up. Edward Woodward was in it. He was Harald Hardraade. My first wife was Mrs Hardraade, daughter of Yaroslav the Wise, grand prince of Kiev, which suited her down to the toe-nails she used to stab me with in her sleep. I had to do eleventh-century Europe with a couple of box sets and three cameras and a lot of north light fill on a huge blank float which kept running over my wife's toes. She said oh goodness fuck twice, not quite off mike. None of the pipe-smokers and cardigan-makers and dwarves in ties knew what oh goodness fuck meant in 1961 but the crew did and they started to giggle. It was like there was a serious unrecorded earthquake in Old Norway because the grips were giggling so much. My wife kept fluffing and her torque fell off and this boom-arm swung over right behind Tostig's big speech and

259

there were so many noises off it was like it was experimental, it was like it was Lindsay Anderson or something, but it wasn't, it was by Eldegard Peach in his dog-days and we even had coconut shells and the Battle of Stamford Bridge was on hand-held with lots of smoke several centuries before the cannon was invented and afterwards there was me goldfishing through the gallery glass because they were sick of my voice.

I hope you're not sick of my voice.

Fucking goldfish!

That was Deirdre. She hated me by then. We went to Cromer for our honeymoon. I could go into that but I won't. Off-season Cromer. It's not interesting. When I'm tanked up I do a party piece on it but not now. Look at me. I'm shouting but no sound's coming out. I'm yelling at Zelda but she's stamping something, head down, hair beginning to slip out of its complications. I like her with her hair complicated and I like her with her hair all slipped out, it reaches the undercurve of her breasts where the sun doesn't, she looks like Mary Magdalen in the wilderness, I can snuggle up under her hair while she's standing there naked and it's like walking behind a waterfall only warmer. She's caught my eye. Her mouth goes up at one side which I reckon is a smile but it's kind of sardonic, mate. She has this side of her. She's stamping again. At least they still stamp in libraries. At least there's something to hold on to in this chaotic and fast-changing world. I wish I could stand between Zelda's hair and her body right now because there's no nicer place in the whole world and it's so close but my nose is pressed up against the glass and no one can hear me and, shit, they've locked the door. I hadn't seen Dustin Hoffman in *The Graduate* then, this was primordial days, so I didn't think how I looked like Dustin Hoffman in the last reel of *The Graduate* yelling silently through the glass door of the church but I am now. The bastards had locked me in. Then they all turned and looked up at the gallery and laughed. I couldn't hear them laugh but their mouths were opening and closing and they were spilling their coffee and I was a schmuck and there was Deirdre in her cloak, pissed out of her head, smiling up at me in a really triumphant way, twirling her fucking torque.

Horrible, horrible.

A Shepherd's Bush legend. Maybe it's still doing the rounds, creeping about with a trail of slime and rotting fins. Maybe not. Maybe when sideburns come back it'll pop out of the cupboard and get folk chortlin' again, like in the old gold days. Last known sighting, Maida Vale, Sound Studio 3, 1971. I hope some of you lot bloody chortled, at least. Fucking goldfish. Great days, great days. Nostalgia gives you neuralgia, *ouch*, 'n raking up the past gives you back ache. Bom. *Hotchpotch*, Scene Eight, Song Two. Swell, huh?

Back ache.

Bom.

Rake. C'mon, rake it all up. Rake, rake, rake. Don't let pseud creep spoil things, Dickhead. Don't let him in. He's dust. He's debris. He's Hair In the Gate. He's HIG. Hi, HIG. Three chest-hairs and they're in my gate. Blow 'em away, Ossy, blow 'em away. We want a clean picture, clean print, clean as dawn dew.

Right, guv?

Sweep of a brush, as it happens. Silver-backed hearthbrush held by a small hand with a boniness about it. It's Milly's. Milly is raking the hearth in the dining-room and she has an ache. It's deeper than her spinal column. It's kind of fear and loathing combined. She chokes on the ash. The room clears its throat. A wagon goes past, etc. Last night's dinner is about three centuries back, but there's a scent, a staleness, a trace. I hope you all notice the fancy plaster on the ceiling. Grapes or something, leaves, leaves, leaves. Chandelier. Tints of blue. Mediocre pictures. Mr Trevelyan's grandfather at the end, needs a scrub, cream highlights on nose and buttons and that's about it, the rest is murk. She wants to write to her mam. Or Sis. She feels she is slipping towards the mouth. The fireplace is dark and draughty and maybe it is in fact the mouth. Maybe the mouth isn't like a toad's or a dragon's but like a very large fireplace wi'out a fire because the fire is going to come in a bit, and forever. Maybe it's like a very large fireplace turned upside down, so you fall down th'shaft and into th'Devil's arms. If only Milly could scrape out the ash of this minister's ravings she might have a chance, but she can't. The down-draught plays on her neck and she shivers. Then she looks up. There's a darkness because there's a kink in the chimney. There's no sky. She knew a sweep in Worksop who died. He had horrible growths on his elbows. He was about seventy, mind. He remembered going up as a boy. The growths were where he'd levered himself up as a boy. He'd try to get her to touch them but she screamed. They were like baby cabbages. Then they went bad and he passed over. He probably went to Hell because he drank spirits and never washed, he was black, he was black as night and his eyes rolled and he cursed. She shivers again and sweeps and coughs. The naked man in the Wheel of Life walks through her head. She canna stop it. It's like there are thousands of him, o' them, naked, walking through her head. Her dustpan scrapes the tiles of the fireplace

Holy shit. Hey, I'm sorry to chop like this. But Zelda has just come over and said, how's the eternal autocue? Then she laughed. What're you talking about, honey? I replied. She just walked away, sniggering. It's not like Zelda to snigger. It's also not like Zelda to make a technical joke like that. Sure, this thing is like an autocue, it's a rolling script, a portaprompt, one or two of you will have made the same observation, but the way Zelda said it was like it was a running joke. She's never not taken this thing seriously before. It's a Lazenby joke. He's infecting her. Hair In the Gate's trying to break me. HIG's trying to break us. I'm sorry. I'm shaky. It's working. He's screwing me up. I have to talk to her about this. Right now I have to keep going, I have to believe in myself, I have to get my immune system on red alert, I have to prove to Zelda that I am stronger than this virus. She hasn't seen him for a week, he's busy or something, maybe his wife is acting up at last. THERE ISN'T ANYTHING BETWEEN THEM. I'm not jealous. I love Zelda. She loves me. She's said so at least twice. I must stop cracking jokes about maple leaves and perfect circles. Our love is stronger than – shit, I'm not a poet. Steel cables will do. Our love is stronger than steel cables. I could cut the guy's dick off.

I'm not very nice. Hey, I realise this. No one's perfect. This air-conditioning system gives me a sore throat. I would work at home if I could stand being away from Zelda and if you didn't have to sign in and sign out because the Mussolinis that run this place think your brain dissolves as soon as you step out of this dump. Hey, I'm getting nowhere again. It's HIG, he's fiddled with my clubs, he's sent me swinging away into the juniper and gorse stuff that shreds a Reebok in about five seconds. Big deal. See if I care, mate. I'm putting on my rhinoceros hide. I'm hosing myself down in iced water, I'm standing under Niagara, I'm aloof, I'm British, I'm going over in a barrel, I'm going right in, I'm going to stick at it, I'm going to do the longest single take since *The Sacrifice*, OK?

What time are we? There's a clock on the mantelshelf. We're in the dining-room, remember? If you've just gatecrashed on my party because Sting's little raver got too earnest then fuck off out, this is 1913, you're not wanted yet, Ossy has just shot the last Famous Grouse, there are only pork scratchings, there's vomit in the handbasin, I'll invite you next time. Milly is standing up. She's thirteen and her shoulders are rounded already. That's ridiculous. Maybe her birth was awkward. Mine was. I came out crab-wise, according to my father, like I was looking for the john – it was in the blackout, it was in the Blitz, you can't blame me for being cautious. That's why I have a kinked spine, a very slightly kinked spine. Shut up. Milly is standing, just standing. She's staring at the highlights that are supposed to be Mr Trevelyan's grandad, he's somewhere in there, he's lurking, it terrifies her, the door opens.

Mill?

It's Lily. She has one hand on the door, she keeps it there, she leans in and whispers.

Mill? Don't take no notice, girl. Don't take no notice.

Mill blinks and looks away. The whisper is tossed about a bit by the room then slips away into the shadows of the portrait like its lips didn't move, not really. Don't take no notissss.

Lily winks and then the door is where she was. Milly feels really lonely at this point, in this room, really small and lonely and crumpled

263

because the room's full of stuff that is gleamy and unrelaxed and waiting to service mouths that open and close cleverly, without showing anything, and say clever things, and then are gone till the next day. Her cap itches her. Her collar itches her. Actually, it chafes her. She's allergic to starch. She doesn't know this. She just accepts that a starchy collar chafes like a horse-collar chafes a horse. Don't take no notissss. She has this dustpan full of ash in one hand and the brush in the other. The ash-bucket is at her feet. She bends down and slips the ash out of the dustpan into the bucket and there's a small cloud, it rises up, a small cloud of grey ash she steps back to avoid because she doesn't want to grey her pinny. Don't take no notissss is like a key to all problems because Lily doesn't have any problems – it's better than never ever, even. The time, by the way, is seven minutes to four o'clock. Luncheon has been served. Afternoon rests have been observed. Lily's gearing herself up for tea. Dinner is a cloud on the horizon, a dust cloud, it's getting bigger and bigger, it's coming this way, if you put your ear to the ground you can hear the hooves. The ash is cleared. Milly lays the fire. She lights it. She's good at laying fires. The flames are happy, they like the way she's done it, they're settling in for the evening, they relax, they swap gossip and tut and hiss and the log on top of the coal hunkers down to its immolation, dribbling a little at each end. Milly watches all this for a moment, her face quite close, the flames in her eyes, Mike loves it, it's modelling her beautifully because flame does this, it brings out the best in people, it's the best kicker in the business according to Mike, her tongue's showing, it glints, she's thinking, we're very close, she's big, her lower face is enormous, the flames gleam on her tongue, on its tip, because there's only the tip of it sticking out, like a kid concentrating, because she is a kid, concentrating, concentrating on how to save herself from th'mouth.

All the clocks chime. Bells bong outside. Somewhere quite close Virginia Woolf closes her eyes and nods appreciatively at the four circles dissolving in the air. For someone who never had to wash her own underpants or handle a broom, she has a copious imagination.

Whassat? Four o'clock? *Hey*, I can hear you really razor-sharp people yelling, *you've jump-cut four and a half hours, Dicky. Where's William got to? What happened at luncheon? How did they sneak him in? What are they gonna say to—?*

264

OK, OK, don't claw the screen to shreds, don't lose your toupées, go back to your seats, pour yourselves some orange juice, I'm gonna tell ya in ma own good time. My time is your time is their time. Real time is unreal time, and vice-versa. I'm getting to talk like Todd Lazenby. Zelda says I should read this guy Baudrillard because—

Chop, chop.

William is in the attic. He's trying to piece together his life. He was hustled up there by Agatha while Uncle Ken boomed in the dining-room to cover up the creaks on the stairs. William's life was torn up into tiny pieces by Boulter, you remember. You'd better remember. That outside shoot cost a fortune. It's a modern classic. It's in the same league as the last frame of Buñuel's *El*, almost. You don't know it? You don't know the last frame of Buñuel's *El*? When you think this guy driven nuts by jealousy is cured, become a nice quiet monk instead of a murderous paranoiac, and then this last shot of him taking a walk in the monastery garden, up the path towards this hole, this tunnel, this mouth in the hedge, and he's *zigzagging*? He's gently *zigzagging*? And you know what – I caught myself *zigzagging* today, up the HCDVA driveway? You know that?

William is in the attic, in amongst the big iron bed-ends clutching each other at last and the ridiculous prams with torn hoods sliced by baby-snatching gypsies and the bust of Venus with the big tits Mr Trevelyan's great-aunt objected to because it made her come over very queer (it turned her on but she didn't know she had a switch) and the army tent which is not an army tent but a crinoline belonging to his grandmother when she was a healthy young woman which turned nobody on except those with an incredibly fevered imagination and which had to be lowered over her head by two maids with poles as she was always telling William wistfully and a wash-stand with a china dog waiting for the water which will never come though its thirst be great and bustles bustling out of baskets because the Last Day has been sounded and the bustles are trying to find their owners' butts and medical illustrations of lungs and brains and malignantly tumorous tissue on thick board suitable for hanging as demonstration used in all leading hospitals faded by years of nobody looking at them in a leading hospital and Grandpapa's butterfly table with no glass and five

265

butterflies huddled in one corner wondering when someone'll take the pins out and a contraption. None of the kids has ever worked out what this contraption really is. It's huge. It has cogs and springs and wheels. It is black and won't move. But every time they come up here and look it has moved, very slightly. It is not a traction bed from the old St Bartholomew's Orthopaedic Hospital. It is an instrument of torture. It has the mind of a tarantula. It schemes its freedom. It clanks into their dreams and used to make them jerk bolt upright with wild eyes in Big Close-Up, panting, stifling a scream and mostly managing to so that Nurse Ginger-Nob Hallam wasn't disturbed and they weren't cuffed into sense, silly-billy fools.

William is by the water tank. There's a stool with arthritic bamboo legs there and he's sitting on it. There's an old baize card table with cigar burns all over probably because the contraption has been trying to get it to confess but William's elbows are not rested on this table. His head is not in his hands. If this was one of my lousy early films he'd have his head in his hands and his elbows on the table and I'd circle him in medium close-up with a 300-watt yellow-gellied kicker just catching his knuckles and the highlights in his hair. But this is not one of my early lousy films it's my final masterwork and he's just sitting there with his hands in his lap and slumped a little and he's definitely staring out. There's a tiny oil-lamp on the table and that's it as far as luminaries are concerned. The tiny oil-lamp with its little wavering tulip glass is having a hard time making inroads into the shadows, because the shadows up here are well established, they're not often disturbed, they're fat with not having to flee and curl up in corners, they're thick and wheezy and the only thing that'd get them moving is Pierre with his cobweb gun but he's not needed here and the little oil-lamp is nervous about its situation, you can tell that, it's turned up too high and it's emitting a thin vertical of black smoke. But you can just see enough of William to get the general picture. He's very still and he's staring out, out of himself and into a particularly unexercised shadow in the corner that's hunkered down around a really antique web William has examined over the years because it has an amazing number of skeletons in it, it's a family plot, it's still used by the great-great-etc.-grandson who comes out and crawls all over his ancestors like he doesn't care. The light is picking up his white collar, his eyes, his jaw-line, a lock of his hair. (I'm talking about William, not the damn

266

spider.) That's it. If I were to go into his head I would have to pick my way through an awful lot of debris, an awful lot of torn-up things, before I reached whatever is holding him so still. I'm staying out here because apart from anything else there's a fleet of what look like used chamber-pots and some unidentifiable stuff with poles between me and him and I don't want to break this stillness by clattering and banging around, OK?

Ssssh.

The mad brother in the attic.

That's what Agatha is thinking right now, on the edge of her bed in her room two floors below William. She knows her Charlotte Brontë. Except her brother is not mad. William came off the train and promptly went queer, he almost fell, she had to support him in the middle of suitcases and huge white clouds of steam and a lot of highly-paid extras in wide straws or small bowlers jostling and barging all around her while Uncle Kenneth stood there like a lemon saying poor boy, poor boy. She had no idea what she was going to do with him now. Uncle Kenneth had no idea what they were going to do with him, either, but he felt excited.

Right, let's replay. They're standing there. Railway stations always make Uncle Kenneth excited. The whistles and hisses and clanks and shouts bear him up up on a wave and he doesn't have to think, he's hurly-burly, he's hustle'n bustle, he's off somewhere even when he isn't. The trains are ridiculously large. The pistons are gigantic. William looks like an elf. The train belches and wheezes and Uncle Kenneth's mouth is full of its taste. Ah, what we're missing. The Age of Steam. Civilisation now and again finds itself, now and again but never for long – some jerk comes up with something that doesn't grease your face and fill your eyes and nose with smuts and choke you every time you enter a tunnel. Big deal, smart-ass. This scene with Agatha and William and Uncle Kenneth is God's gift to a camera, there's light slanting down like rods through the muck, there's a heap of trunks and the light's catching their brass corners and the gilt on the huge station clock up there which has either lost its small hand or it's exactly midday but either way it's a pleasure checking your fob-watch against it – it wouldn't be the same these days, it wouldn't be the same. Nostalgia gives you neuralgia. Sometimes it's worth it. Agatha is shouting something but so is the train, so are the porters, so is the world because it is midday and everything's bonging. Pigeons aloft in the girders. It looks quiet up there. That is where God resides, no doubt, Uncle Kenneth would've thought if he hadn't been on this hurly-burly high – He's vacated the cathedrals for the railway stations, He knows where the action is. Uncle Ken's thoughts are like that. They're pretty modern but not ahead of their time. His wing collar is askew. His lunettes are steamed up. The noise and steam bear him up. He lands with a bump in the growler cab. Agatha is next to him. William is outside, in front, next to the driver. This seems all wrong but it happened, the driver assumed the young gentleman would 'op up next to him and there was no room for a third inside, of course. I say of course but maybe you don't know a lot about old-time transport. I'm sorry. It's the same cab, they're suicidal, the guy's emptied half a flask of brandy down his throat while they were waiting in the station, he's kicked the horse, he's pissed down an alley where three whores were pissing down the other end and the cab-driver and the whores laughed at each other or at the general situation and the alley fair echoed, it did, it did indeed, it fair echoed with the laughter of the London poor in them bygone days, ho yes, as the trickles met and warmly seethed between the cobbles! – and shrieks too, of delight, of pain, this alley could do you shrieks, mainly towards the night, or in the night, three murders in total and about five thousand four hundred and twenty-two ahem tuppenny uprights, cheap at the price, 2d a rump, luverly out in the air where the fog blows cold and the gaslight's crook and if you'll just come this way please it is probably here by the greasy window that something really horrible happened but all record of it is lost under the Red Star Delivery forecourt the alley's ghost does not frequent any more and neither do we, this way please, hold on tight to your handbags and toupées and arseholes.

So the ridiculous situation occurs: William is outside on his own conversing with the driver instead of his sister. Clip-clop. She slides the window down and sticks her head out to check he hasn't fallen off or been snatched or something. This is when Uncle Kenneth, wiping his lunettes, says, my dear, he hasn't passed away, he has merely been inconvenienced. Uncle Kenneth has this very downbeat approach to life alternating with sudden bursts of hysteria. Right now he is downbeat, he's come down with a bump and he's attempting to clear his lenses of the Glorious Age of Steam. Agatha sticks her head back in and straightens her hat and blinks away some coal-smoke particles and brushes her cheek where a minute piece of crushed tomato and dung has been flung up by the cab-horse's hooves and says, what are we to do, Uncle? It seems so jolly queer not to be able to talk with him. All he has said to us so far is good morning and sorry.

Uncle Kenneth smiles and in front of thinking how lovely his niece looks in plum, wheels the following: Let the boy say as much as he wishes to say. It may be he does not wish to say anything at all. As to what we are to do (here he sighs and replaces his lunettes and looks out of the window at the filth and toil that is and was and always will be London, seeing a donkey sunk under a hod of bricks and a policeman next to it bending his back and guffawing, which is fairly amazing in itself) – my dear, that is altogether in the lap of the gods and they are notoriously unhelpful unless one trusts 'em. This being one of the most unhelpful remarks Agatha could imagine, she peers out of her window again without opening the glass, seeing just enough of William's cape to know that he has not dissolved and thinking how at least he is not dead, that there are many things worse in life, and oh God that's it. She turns round to Uncle Ken who has his mouth wide ready to deliver a second homily even more unhelpful than the first to do with degrees of misfortune and a saying of Mr Newton's for crying out loud when Agatha's gloved hand seizes his forearm so tightly it actually aches and he finds himself looking into a pair of extremely excited eyes. He has often conjectured how two lumps of glistening gristle can take on such vivid and varying states of emotion and has reckoned it is as much to do with the surrounding variations of puckering and expanding muscle as the actual organs themselves – and I myself have ventured to peruse aloud this very question when pissed, considering carefully the eyes of Jason, whose said organs are generally twin vessels of bile and hatred, but getting nowhere, getting nowhere.

What, my dear?

That's Uncle Ken. Cueing in his niece because it seems that otherwise she'll just go on staring at him like one of those mad Bohemian types on opium. The growler jolts and sways through Regent Street. The word Liberty&Co passes just above Agatha's straw four times before she answers. She does so in something like a rasp, or maybe a hiss.

Liberty&Co Liberty&Co Liberty&Co Liberty&Co *I think I know what we must do, Uncle.*

Why does putting it into italics make it hissy? God alone knows, so I'll ask Him. I'll ask God when I get Up There in the clouds and the station girders. The angels have pigeon-shit on their bottoms, they perch so much. The laundry bills in Heaven are outrageous. All that white. Sacred breadcrumbs, holy mangles. Agatha'll get there – she won't even stop to hover and bite her nails while they temporarily lose her papers and murmur in the back room, she'll go straight up, she'll leave St Michael whirling in her jet stream, there'll be feathers flying, she's half there already because the intensity of her goodness is incredible. It's this intensity that's gripping Uncle Kenneth's arm right now as the growler leans over to take the kink past Air Street without clipping a delivery wagon stuffed to the canvas top with tea-chests actually full of tea for once. Isn't that amazing? If I'm not careful the intensity of Agatha's goodness will get us burn on the lens and every shot'll have this phantom on it. Of Agatha. Of Agatha's goodness.

That might be nice, thinking about it. Hey, she's opening her mouth.

Suffering is partly degree, is it not, Uncle Ken?

Uncle Kenneth frowns a little and nods. He's sure he's just said something to that effect but maybe he didn't actually get it out. Something about the swaying of a carriage gives him mild amnesia quite apart from the slight but perceptible sexual excitement the swaying motion and the bumpy padded leather of the seats imparts to one. He blinks to clear this thought and inserts a rose in the magic lantern of his head. Agatha is a rose. The rose is blooming. She's blooming instantaneously, thinks Uncle Kenneth. It's true. Something incredible is happening inside this shit-splattered horse-drawn cab nearly into Piccadilly Circus but not quite because there's a jam. Virginia Woolf is on the pavement passing the cab right at this moment

270

but Uncle Ken doesn't see more than a hat with a feather beyond Agatha's left ear – he certainly doesn't see Virginia Woolf Virginia Woolf Virginia Woolf and Virginia Woolf doesn't even notice the cab because first there is still a lot of horse-drawn traffic in 1913 and second she's very uptight about her shopping because Virginia Woolf was the world's most uptight shopper, it was hell shopping with her, I know this because I once had tea with Quentin Bell her nephew but he didn't like the idea. My biopic idea didn't grab him. It didn't grab *anyone*. Virginia's gone. It was a happy coincidence. If I was still keen on my biopic idea I'd hop out of this cab and follow her with a camcorder at the very least but I've grown up, I'm beyond fame and fortune, I'm serious, I'm really serious, I'm practising my swings at first light and at the setting of the sun and in my sleep.

(It was great tea, actually. The teapot stood on a stand. Elms swayed. Roses bloomed. I fell in love with England for about, hey, an hour. Flying wit and a teapot gurgling and elms, elms, elms. A film-maker chatting idly with a painter, sculptor, potter, author, art critic, you name it, he probably built suspension bridges in his time. There were just the two of us, by the way. Chatting idly under the swaying elms, in '68, in Sussex, deepest most profound and forgotten Sussex, the teapot on a stand and mauve cups Thomas Hardy handed on so the legend goes – and me in my leather jacket, the one with the biggest lapels in Christendom, still smelling of diesel and nicotine and BR lavatories, thinking how I might actually belong if I purchased a teapot with a stand and mauve cups Thomas Hardy handed on and a stand of elms and a sun-hat that once sheltered Saxon Sydney-Turner from the Dorset sun in 1910, my dear boy. What did you do in '68, Dad? Fuck all, son, 'scuse the lingo. Hey, one of the pleasantest hours of my life, as a matter of fact. I relive it when Houston gets to me. Minute by minute I relive it. Sorry, Tariq! Sorry, Daniel! That's the way I am, guv. Unreconstructed. A teapot on a stand. An English rose. An elm. Pre-disease, of course. Of course! Jason doesn't understand. Quintessences elude him. Quintessences elude you, Jason, I say. He knows what I'm getting at. He knows, for Christ's sake.)

It's OK, I'm on the green. Springy little turf, clipped like nose hairs, perfect lie. It was close. I was a centimetre from the Black Hole, a bunker in the shape of England, quicksand you can see these fists sticking up out of and still gripping their wedges, their number eights, their niblicks, their Excaliburs – their score-cards sometimes, if it was a good one and they managed to get it out of their pockets in time. Fine, Zelda, fine, honey. I'm just fine. See ya.

She's busy tonight. She just came over because apparently I was snorting or grunting or something and weirdo complained. I invited her over for a meal. Candlelit, Eno for ambience, lots of laughs over the charcoal-stained chicken, like the old days, like last month, not even that, not even a month. When did the first elm leaf in England start to feel it?

The cab, for Christ's sake!

It's way up Whitehall, it's way up, it's a rear window with two wheels and a hat. I must have fallen off. OK, OK, I'm fifty-something but I'm running, guv. It's got stuck behind the number 11 to Shepherds Bush. The number 11 to Shepherds Bush'll get stuck in the mud outside La Briqueterie in three years time and lean over crazily, crazily, with blokes losing their caps and jumping. Nestlé's Milk. Old Gold Cigarettes. Hudson's Soap. Trevelyan Disinfectants. See that? That last one? Now you know. Sharp-eyes! I'm jumping up hup and holding on by the luggage rail around the roof. William's suitcase is up there. It was in Jefferies' carriage while the gauntlet thing was being performed. It's scuffed at the edges. Pig leather, pinkish, very nice. Trunk to follow. Another hassle for Ags. I'm panting. This smell of dung is really incredible. I never knew horse dung smelt so much. It's not wholly unpleasant. It's better than HCDVA's lilac air-freshener but try telling them that, mate. I think I'd better take a peep in at the window. It's closed. Agatha is talking and Uncle Ken is nodding and his eyebrows are really getting exercised but the racket out here is incredible so you'll just have to wait see, OK?

Hey, I've nearly had my buttocks cleaved off by a beer-wagon. Look at it. Parliament Square. I could've used a film library archive for this clip but no, this is real time, this is the thick of it, this is me having my front teeth loosened by the luggage-rail because this guy must be pissed, it's terrifying, these horses shouldn't go so fast, it's fucking dangerous, why do horses have to go so fast? Why does everyone have to go so fast?

272

Why don't all these horses and antique motor cars just pause for a moment and ask themselves that? Why does the world have to be so jerky all the time? Why is my throat sore?

I'd like to show you William but I can't. My foot's on the back axle and there's not enough space between the body and the wheel and the wheel's spinning round and it's dirty, it's spraying up dung and stuff, I daren't foul my trousers because we're about to attend luncheon and I haven't spare.

Anyway, I'm a coward. There might be another beer-wagon. I can just see the edge of William's cape. Don't worry. He's still on there. The driver is chatting amiably with him – I can see that because the driver keeps swaying out my side and laughing. He's a merry old soul. He's pissed. It must be really annoying for William. I guess if you just imagine him looking stony you'll be about right. Maybe not. Maybe he's nodding and smiling like he's about to start vacation. Life's like that. It never clings to your expectations. He's probably looking really jolly. Life's weird. It wouldn't surprise me. The more I think about it, the more I'm thinking that jolly probably *is* how he's looking, out there on the front seat, next to this drunk who'll kill me if he takes a gap between two omnibuses like that again, Christ in Heaven, blow me down, what a way and a time to go but we're nearly there, nearly there.

Print that! Strike the lot! Munchy-wunchies, yer lazy bastards!

Where's me megaphone, Julie ducks? Me froat's frogged. No one takes any notice of me, these days. Aw, shucks. Ta.

TAKE A BLEEDIN' BREAK, OK?

Christ.

Hi.

I hope there's life out there. I hope I'm not addressing a room ringing
with echoes. I hope I'm not just talking to myself. I hope the projector's
not fucked up. If the projector has fucked up then you won't be reading
this. Maybe I'll have a spare. But never in my life, in a lifetime of going
to the cinema, has any projector ever fucked up. That time the cinema
got flattened in an earthquake doesn't count. It was in Peru. The
cinema was a tin shack. It was a very local cinema. I felt like Tintin or
someone, but actually I was on holiday. I was trekking, getting over the
Deirdre disaster. It wasn't a big earthquake, it was just a very weak
cinema. It didn't even kill anyone. Macchu Picchu was great. I'm
pretty certain I was an Inca in a past life. I felt at home in the Andes. I
was alone for once. I wasn't jabbering. I was way up where the air is so
thin you can hear it rattling around in your lungs and you're scratching
your freak's beard and thinking that there's an incy-wincy bit more to
life than spray-on deodorant and automatic flush and that humanity
might do the planet a favour by shutting Human Progress Inc. down
for a while. Then you turn the corner and there it is, isn't it just great,
isn't it a marvel, really? Five lavatories, a bar, air-conditioning,
Cinerama, luxury berths on the third deck, the works. And they can't
even give you a lift.

Makes you sick, dunnit?

William is up there. He's still very still. Agatha's on her bed. The king
is in his counting house. The queen is in her parlour. The maid is in
the garden. William is up there on his mountain. He's very remote.
He's actually still swaying from the thing that carried him up onto this
mountain, but only inside, only in his head. He doesn't know how he's
going to get off this mountain. Night will be falling soon. Supplies are
erratic. At least his bum's stopped hurting. The oil-lamp makes things

275

think about moving and there are a lot of things in this attic. He's pretty certain the contraption has moved. He keeps it in view, in the corner of his eye, because he doesn't want the beastly thing to jump him. There are a lot of ghosts on this mountain. They pretend to be mice. They scamper behind the wreckage of past expeditions. That disagreeable smell is probably the rotting corpse of that famous mountaineer who never returned. Up he went, into the mist, calm and steady, and the mist cleared and he was gone, the ropes were gone, his footsteps were gone, it was like he had never gone up there but they had seen him, definitely seen him, and he had cast a long shadow over the snow. What a fine fellow, what a mysterious end. Perhaps the Beast of the Peaks had got him. Perhaps he had deliberately vanished. Perhaps there was some disreputable thing in his life that he could no longer cope with. The contraption shifts. It's smelling blood. William my great-uncle gives a little sigh and it comes out as a tiny moan. The noise really shocks him. The whole mountain stops and stares. It's so dashed quiet, up here. It's so dashed quiet. And he hadn't even noticed that nowhere in the house or garden is there the teekiest squeak out of Sparkler. That'll come, that'll come. The noticing, I mean, not the squeak. Not the faithful nuzzle. Not the weight of shaggy head in his lap.

Will?

I'm holding my breath. That was Agatha. She's opened the little door a crack. Great light, Mike – a pencil, a slit, a Chinese right across the boards until it hits the wreckage, but not brilliant, not glossy, not more than ash grey. Then it fans out because she's stepping up and in until everything is covered in ash and she's a silhouette and William feels cold, suddenly. Then it's shut right down again, right down, to nothing but the oil-lamp up this end. Click. Print that.

Willo?

William wants to say something but he can't, his jaw is frozen, he's in this glacier, it's got him by the boot. Help approaches. It's tiny, it's the other side of the range, it's got miles of crevasse and ice-flows and boulders and stuff before it can reach him.

276

Will, it's all right. Uncle Ken phoned and pretended to be Papa. He's been awfully decent. Uncle Ken, I mean. He calls it surprising the enemy by attacking first.

Amazing, how this mountain does not echo. A whisper sort of goes blunt.

Will?

Agatha's standing in view of her brother. She's holding her dress up slightly for obvious reasons. An attic piled with junk is bad enough in jeans but when you're kitted out in a long silk dress with extra-fine lace borders and fancy ribbons and a pair of soft shoes it's like the world's a porcupine. Actually, she could probably walk right through everything because she looks like a phantom in this outfit with nothing but a little oil-lamp to pick her up. Her face is in shadow because there's a thing sticking out between her and the lamp, a small thing with a huge cast, maybe an umbrella, maybe a dead bat. My great-uncle blinks and frowns and then sighs like he did before.

Did you speak to Giles, Will?

She steps forward and puts her hand on the card-table. This is really the most terrific wheeze goes through her head like a clown. Cartwheeling through like a clown. She blinks it off, knocks it on the head with a parasol, kicks it in the butt – shoo, shoo! Will, did you manage to speak to him before . . .

She waves her hand about. It makes great Fritz Lang shadows against the joists. Her face is now underlit. It looks scary. William opens his mouth to yell across the crevasse that he's really quite all right apart from the broken back.

No, not really, he says in such a tiny voice that Agatha has to lean right forward. Sorry, Ags.

Listen, says my great-aunt, putting her hand on my great-uncle's shoulder, you mustn't be sorry all the time. You didn't hurt anyone. You didn't do anything wicked. It was horrible and beastly of them to do what they did. Uncle Ken says Papa was desperately unhappy at Randle, he remembers, it's a horrible and beastly place and if it wasn't for Uncle Ken's illness he would have gone there too, but he was jolly glad not to. Have done. For more than a week.

William nods feebly. He knows all this. I can't go into why Mr Trevelyan sent his sons to the school he was incredibly miserable at. If you're British you'll understand. If you're not you'll go on shaking your head until they come for you in their white coats and scalpels.

It *was* just pictures, wasn't it, Will?

That's the most direct line Agatha has made yet. What she would do if William said no, Ags, it was the one-to-one deflowering of nine new boys and the gang rape of a tenth I have no idea, because she has actually no notion of what it is that boys do to each other that gets them expelled sometimes, mainly when the school needs a moral Hoover. I'm just using an example here – hey, it *was* just pictures, just watercolours in fact, if you don't count the odd fumble and various filthy conversations and the common-or-garden jacking off behind the laurel shrubbery in the Wilderness. Agatha is very inexperienced in these things. She has only the fuzziest notions of these things, like she has only the fuzziest notions how a motor car actually moves along or an electric lamp lights up. So her heart speeds up a bit at this point while she waits for William's reply. His smile catches the shadows on his face and makes big hollows of his eyes. He looks so like Evelyn. Did.

What if it wasn't? says William.

Oh-oh, he's trying to be clever, theoretical, he's doing a Todd Lazenby on Agatha. Agatha blinks a little. William's looking at her. He seems a bit cross, in my view, or maybe anxious. The help that was coming for him has slid back down the mountain. He's all alone again. Why did he try to be clever-clogs? I'll tell you why. What he has gone through today – today! – has left him feeling extremely insecure. He's only fifteen, for God's sake. He's holed up in this attic in his own house because if he were just to say hi, or rather, hallo, hallo, I'm home, how're things, I've just been kicked out of my fee-paying school for painting nude boys, what's for tea? – do you know what'd happen? I'll tell you. There's an even chance that he would never darken the door of this house again. Agatha knows this, Uncle Kenneth knows this, William knows this. It has happened before. Generally what happens is the outcast goes off and serves his country behind the mast until he's either drowned or the black slug in him has been shrivelled to just about nothing by salt spray and salt winds and blistering sun in some profitable but hellishly unshaded part of the Empire. William really doesn't want this. When he was still in the nursery sucking the lead off Giles's soldiers this happened to some distant relation, so distant that by the time the fact got back to them it was three years later and the poor guy had been skewered by Zulus. His crime wasn't even sexual, it was petty theft, it was stealing a shilling or something because his parents never gave him any pocket-money and he'd been desperate for a cherry cake in some lousy tuck-shop. Out he went, bang went the door, the maid pressed herself to the window to see what he would do, he didn't have a bean, his parents sat facing each other in the sitting-room so upright and rigorous you could have waved your dick at them and they would not have budged an eyebrow. He didn't really even go out because he didn't really even come in. He just stood under the portal for as long as it took the maid to see who it was and then a bit longer to be ahem told and then for about a minute after the door slammed to collect his wits and not sob. To be honest, he'd been at boarding school so long they'd practically forgotten what he looked like. When he was at home he stayed upstairs in his room most of the time. At six o'clock he was ushered down and stood in front of them just so they could check he was still alive. Five minutes was all they could stand. They weren't into kids. Meeting them at a dinner you'd have reckoned they were quite entertaining people if you like dry humour and a lot of stuff about horses. I mean, they didn't *look* evil. They were present at Mr and Mrs Trevelyan's wedding. Agatha and Giles and William worked out long ago that only twelve potential guardians not including their parents would have to die for them to end up with these people. After that it'd be the orphanage. Now it's only eight, because there are so many fatal diseases at this period, not including childbirth and cars with dicky brakes. You can see why Agatha and William and even Uncle Kenneth are really uptight about the situation right at this moment.

279

The point is, guv, Mr and Mrs Trevelyan APPROVED of what Mr Trevelyan's second cousin once removed did to his boy, who was called Ashley. Agatha remembers them approving. When the subject pops up now and again, as it does, not even a hairline crack has appeared in the huge windowless wall of their APPROVAL. Actually, this wall is a dam. It's keeping out what'd sweep everything away in a tide of moral filth and squalor. This APPROVAL appals Agatha. She's eighteen, just. There's a big gap between her and her parents. She's not Victorian but Edwardian OK *Georgian*. Her cognisant life has been spent out of the shadow of that miserable old tent. It's made a difference. Her heroine is Sylvia Pankhurst. She's hung around at the back of two demonstrations for Women's Suffrage in Hyde Park. She's seen a woman dig her elbow in a policeman's stomach. Her friend Amy tells her that there are secret classes in hand-to-hand combat and How To Disable A Policeman. Zelda wouldn't believe me when I told her this. I said these suffrage women make Germaine Greer look like a kitchen sink. Zelda has this idea that everyone before 1968 were parents, they just spent all their time yelling up the stairs about the noise and collecting Tupperware and getting their hair done. I said 1968 was a wash-out, it was a fake, it was a student vacation in the woods where the camp-fire and the brown acid does weird things for an evening or two. She thinks I'm hung up about '68 because I was too old for it. You were too young for it, I tell her, you were too young for it. Anyway, 1968 is completely outrun by what's happening around Agatha. These people are inventing things like Cubism and Old Age Pensions and Militant Feminism and National Insurance and the Modernist Novel. It's really incredible what's going on behind these gigs and omnibuses and Model T Fords and mahogany doors with brass knockers and ridiculous clothes that swish and hats that fall off in a wind, they're so tall, so broad. It's really incredible. Blimey, think where it could have got to. But the contraption is on the move. Sir Philistine Fascist is shaking his *Spectator* in the Criterion. He's plotting how to quell the natives. Break their spirit. Give them baubles. Kill 'em in large numbers. Ho yes, Sir Philistine won't be that easily taken. Wha'dya think of it, Trevelyan? Ha? Arthur Trevelyan peeps out briefly from behind his *Times*. His knee is being attacked by the *Spectator*. Trevelyan is having a hard time just at this moment. I won't go into details but it's to do with Izal cornering the market in anti-typhoid measures in India. Trevelyan Disinfectants has sat back on its buckets and is paying the price. Izal have made huge inroads in London hospitals. Izal Disinfectants & Antiseptics are cheaper. Trevelyan had pinned his recovery on the enormous requirements of the sub-continent, the teeming filth and flies, the mass swab that the Empire demanded and which he was absolutely primed to provide. But Izal is 2d cheaper per bucket. He doesn't like Sir Philistine Fascist banging his knee with the *Spectator*. It's vulgar, apart from anything else. But Sir Philistine is a knight, he has connections, he has the ear of Bonar Law. Quite so, quite so, says Mr Trevelyan. My wife is a nervous case, for instance. They are all nervous cases. Society is rapidly becoming a nervous case. I suggest the medieval instrument whereby the scold was silenced. It fitted around the mouth and was locked with a key. I shall take out a patent and go into immediate production if you provide the investment, Sir Philistine. Sir Philistine roars his approval, turning heads. It's good for these heads, they need the exercise, most of them have been asleep under their newspapers and illustrated periodicals for about forty years. I'll tell ya what, Trevelyan, growls Sir Philistine, I'll back ya to the hilt as long as it's not the other damn opening you're plugging up, what? He roars again. Trevelyan nods politely and disappears back into the obituaries. Terrible to say, but Sir Philistine's vulgar quip has stirred Mr Trevelyan into a mild sexual need. An antique orgy is briefly squeaked down in front of the day's dead, hiding the bishops and judges and generals and stuff. He closes his eyes and lets it play itself out. One of the participants is Ruthie. Ruthie does not fit in with the general picture, which is kind of eighteenth-century classical-pastoral. She giggles too much and says gerrofwivyer and her unlaced flopping corset is out of place amongst the gossamery Psyches with their fat thighs and tumbling hair under the ilex. He must see Ruthie. He must fit her in before dinner. He stirs and studies his fob with a frown. Apart from the fact that the guy has a wing collar and mutton-chop whiskers and an antique suit it might be now, it might be one of those City pin-stripes with veined cheeks checking his Rolex in between meetings that keep the free market free and the world in jail. Sir Philistine Fascist is snoring. He always does this, it's embarrassing, he dribbles some sort of coppery stuff. Trevelyan's mouth goes up at one corner, shoving his whiskers around. He's anticipating, he's anticipating. Saliva gathers in his throat. He swallows it down along with some sweet smoke and a taste of antique sherry. He hasn't been smoking, he hasn't been drinking, it's just the air, the air is expensive in here, it's exclusive to the club and it's been built up over about a century to this very collectable miasma. He settles back and closes his eyes. He has pouches under his eyes. He's only forty-five but he has pouches. He likes to close his eyes sometimes and listen to the baize doors thumping away off and the brash and vulgar world tiptoeing past on its muffled hooves like a memory but Sir Philistine's snore is really bad today and Trevelyan clears his throat loudly which always helps. Sir Philistine grunts and twitches his nose like a fly's landed on it and then he lets off. It's foul, it really is, there's something very rotten inside Sir Philistine's guts, my great-great-grandfather closes down the hatches of his nose and breathes through his mouth. The fellow knows Bonar Law. Bonar Law might form the next government. Members are always pooping. You can't bar a fellow for letting orf. You can only bar a fellow for not wearing a tie. That's the worst thing, that's criminal. The second worst thing is to expire under a newspaper so no one notices. Sometimes no one notices until decomposition sets in. When it is eventually noticed there's a lot of whispering and flunkeys bobbing about and then suddenly the chair is empty. Then this guy comes in and swabs it discreetly because there's often some sort of evacuation and even if there isn't it's a symbolic gesture, it's a reassurance, it means you can sit in it as soon as the smell of disinfectant has evaporated and the leather's dry but no one does for about a week, just in case. Mr Trevelyan likes members to expire on site because he can smell his product. It's always Trevelyan's. The reason it's always Trevelyan's is because he's done a cut-price deal with the club. The day they use Izal he'll resign and probably go shoot himself. So he keeps this deal up, even though it hurts. Especially when times are lean. And they are increasingly lean. His eyelid tic is due to this leanness. It tics away uncontrollably in meetings and just before he goes to sleep. I'm leaving him in the chair because Agatha and William are having an interesting conversation in the attic about ten streets away and I don't want to miss it. Notice how I'm really concentrating and not thinking about Zelda and HIG too much. This is because I've had a break. I've been off set for about a month. The Mussolinis, anyway, were wondering why I was spending so much time in the library. They don't like the idea of their employees spending too much time in the library. It means they might be spending HCDVA time on research, instead of their own personal time, like after midnight or just before dawn. So they gave me three extra classes and five hundred essays to mark. It was really about fifty essays but the students can rewrite, it's a divine right, it's liberal and progressive and so they take all your comments and the notes they took down when they wasted an hour of your life asking you why you gave their work of incisive genius a lousy grade and they hang 'em together and come back and you give them a slightly less lousy grade and encourage the use of the comma and the full stop and even the semicolon from time to time and the whole process repeats itself. Meanwhile Zelda was seeing Hair In the Gate. I got very depressed. I took my phone off the hook because these dumbo students kept shouting down it. Now they've all got straight As because I'm a great essay-writer, I know my stuff, there's nothing I do not know about stuff like the impact of the moving image on social discourses and the impact of social discourses on the moving image – it's all in here, tap tap, and I can't blow the Hair Out of the Gate. So I'm concentrating. Zelda says hey, it's platonic. I say I never believed that stuff about Plato. So I'm concentrating and not in the HCDVA library. I'm in my study, I'm busking a bit part in *The Life and Times of St Jerome*. We go out once in a while, my sweetheart and I. To the zoo, last week. It has great colobus, they like doughnuts, they keep looking around like neurotics who've just realised why they've lost. I could watch them for hours. Zelda prefers the cheetah. I can't stand the cheetah. I can't stand watching the fastest animal in the world searching for somewhere to get the acceleration up and not finding it, not ever finding it. I'm patient. One day I will tell him to lay his hands off. Not yet, not yet.

Chopper over the roofs of London, why not, we're in a hurry, it's only my salary a minute. Smoke, smoke. 1913 roofs of London with amazing telephone poles like combs with handles and someone's severe hair loss, 1913 pigeons swaying in clouds around that crazy Column with the amputee on top, as my dad'd put it, who had no bloody respect for nuffink, still hasn't, by Gad, traffic, terrible traffic, I mean really terrible, all complicated bits and pieces with horses on the end and buses holding on to their hundreds of hats, squiggly lanes, the flash of the river, no blocks on the docks but of bales and tea-chests, bless my socks no aeroplanes, not today anyway, they've only been going about ten years, vitamins less, seven according to my *Cyclopaedia*, bet you don't know Who Discovered the Vitamin and, hey, you're into

283

your health, you're into your rattly supplements and you don't know the name of the guy who discovered the vitamin in 1906 because the really useful people in this world, the quiet and good ones, are never recalled except in dusty lessons on afternoons too long and hot to be real. Right, we're nearly there, Biggles old boy. We'll land in the square at the top of the street. Clip the branches, raise the leaves, flatten the grass, meet our shadow, a shadow unknown on this earth in 1913, a shadow out of H.G. Wells, we're scaring the daylights out of that nanny with the perambulator, we're blowing her dress right up and out, her straw hat's flying, she's shielding her face, she thinks it's the end of the world or a very large fly, we're floating over a 1913 lawn, I'm jumping out, I'm running at a crouch like they do in the cop films, I love it really, I'm James Bond in 1913, the very large fly swoops away to a dot, I swat it, the nanny has passed right out, I wave my smelling salts under her nose, she swears which really surprises me, but she's OK, she knows who invented the mass motor car, she says Henry Ford, but she can't put a name to the Man Who Discovered the Vitamin, to the quiet and good one, to the chap who brought nothing but the wealth of health to millions, so I tell her anyway, she has a nice smile.

Go look it up, potato-brains. Make it the first information byte of the new millennium. Get off on the right foot. Maybe he was a relation to the other one. I should've asked Louisa.

Here's the house. Aw, hell. Just get straight in through the roof. We're phantoms, aren't we? I've got a quarter of a century to go before my very first crap pleased my mother no end because it meant I worked, I could join the human race, I wasn't a rough guess.

Darkness. Blink it thinner. Mike, this is barely stirring the emulsion. The oil-lamp's shielded by the joist. We've come in by the wrong side. Hey ho. Float straight over, cutaway joists and junk, not too close, aaaand stop. Pull focus. Rack down. William's profile floatir g. Agatha submerged because she's stepped away. They feel a chill. That's us. We carry a draught around with us. Is it surprising? Given everything?

She hasn't replied to his clever-socks question. That's evasion. It's like when Zelda asked me how's the dramadoc going? and sniggered, like the autocue time. I evaded. I asked her that thing about vitamins, which she's really into. She didn't know. Dramadoc. That's HIG. Blow him away, blow him away. Agatha's wringing her hands. She has smooth soft hands because she never wrings anything else. She applies cream every evening as part of her toilet on her face and her hands and, I feel embarrassed saying this, her breasts. They tend to chafe against the starchy corset, they need it, especially the nipples. I feel shy about this because she's my great-aunt and I'm in love with her in a totally phantasmal way and it's nothing to do with the shapeliness of her bosom. She sighs. There's a lot of sighing in this film.

Oh, Willo, I do so want to do the right thing. I do so want us all to be happy.

What a word, huh? Happy. The way Agatha says it, it's like it's got to be picked up with tongs. Sugar-tongs, coal-tongs, whatever. Don't touch it with your fingers. Don't dirty your dress. Happy flits through William's mind like a dryad. I don't personally think in terms of dryads and stuff but Willo does. He kind of believes in them, like Zelda believes in auras and I believe in Zelda. He's not even chasing this dryad, he just watches her pass, because he's accursed. It's a great word, accursed. In the school carriage, bouncing around because Jefferies is the kind of driver who'd pass you on two wheels in a souped-up crap convertible if he was around now, my great-uncle decided this. He watched the trees and hedges flash past in the railway train and decided this even more decidedly. Things are so frightful and beastly even Nature and all her attendants will surely shrink from him. He might wander forever, forever accursed. Yes, he has always felt sorry for Marsyas. (*Marsyas*. Marsyas the satyr, dumbos. Don't you know yer Ovid? Flayed by Apollo for cheek, for playing the pipes way way better than him, Charlie Parker versus the tin-whistle. Ye gods, what DO people learn these days? Sorry, Willo. Carry on.) Yes, he feels the same, he feels flayed – he feels as if Apollo's minions have taken his skin off and pegged it to the tree just because he played the pipes a touch better than number one. Now he wants to tell Ags this but can't summon up the energy. The main thing is not to keep thinking he's about to wake up any minute in the dorm at Randle. It's all real, dashed real. From the shake of his shoulder before early call to the sneaking up the stairs while Uncle Ken boomed at the new maid who'd emerged unexpectedly from the dining-room, it

285

was most definitely and decidedly *in veritas*. Yet he's numb. It's exactly like the time he fell off his bicycle and got the bump on his head, the concussion, the queer noises when people spoke. I hope you noticed that thing about Milly. She's flitted in and out but it's important. The queerest thing is that although he can't summon up the energy to move or to say much or even to feel frightened by what Ma and Padre might do when they find out despite Ags's best efforts there's a little excited elf in him running round and round and round. It's like going really awfully fast on one's bicycle down Parson's Bottom even though one knows it's terribly dangerous and could jolly well finish in a broken neck the other side of the bramble hedge. We know what he means. He'll be blown away too soon to fall in love but if he had done, if my great-uncle had made it through just one more day or the war had finished just one day sooner he'd have gone on to fall in love and lived frightfully dangerously for as long as the madness was on him. You know what I mean – it's love, it's *amour propre*, it's *Michelle ma belle*, it's *amor vincit omnia*, it's crazy, it's thinking you're the only one on the planet smitten like this. Zelda tells me there was this guy who loved her so much he put a paper bag over his head each time he came into college in case he saw her because she'd said definitely no way, Otis. How did he not bump into things? I enquired, circling her navel. She reckoned he had pin-holes or something. He taught TV studio lighting. He lost his job. That's living dangerously, guv. Ho yes. I bin my paper bags the second I empty them. I'm a coward. I'm into safety. I don't want my head where the soft fruit was. Hey, William's head's shifted. Look at it. In about three years' time it'll be wearing a stupid tin hat and it'll have barely stopped growing, it'll be tender, it'll be soft and the air'll be full of stuff trying to pulp it. Right now it's full of thoughts that are pretty bruised. The fact that he doesn't reply to Agatha's sugar-tongs makes her unhappy. She looks away, down to where there's just the sneakiest slit of light making it through the door but not much further. There's a smell of oil from the oil-lamp. London is rumbling outside. It's a different rumble to the rumble you can hear right now in the early hours because I'm presuming, guv, that even though everyone's partying and stuff the rumble will be carrying on, it never stops, the day it stops something really terrible will have happened, like mass extinction of the human species, or maybe something good, like totally silent motor vehicles – but even with totally silent motor vehicles there'll be the movement of people over pavements and people jabbering at each other or ringing each other up or whistling while they're building things and generally shoving stuff around because the rumble is not just traffic it's the mulch of every sound that's made, it's brown noise, it's compost, it breaks down even a baby's scream or the monkeys in the zoo or Zelda grinding her coffee or me grinding with Zelda or HIG practising his heckelphone, for God's sake. He plays the heckelphone. He plays it really well, apparently. I don't even know what a fucking heckelphone is.

I was going on about this 1913 rumble. Bosey is saying something to me: he's sticking his mike out through the roof and saying the audio signals are different because this rumble is mainly hooves, there's something bumpier about this rumble. I say, yeah, Bosey, like it's not quite mulched down, like the hooves are a whole load of brambles that don't quite mulch down properly. He's wearing his cans, I'm goldfishing. But, yup, I can believe it. It was shattering down there, my ears practically bled, it was cast iron striking stone to the power of ten. Roll on Mr Whoever Discovered the Pneumatic Tyre. I'm so ignorant.

The rumble is a sea lapping at the house, thinks Agatha. Great thought. The flood lapping at the ark. The ark is full of beasts saved from the waves. Nice beasts, dangerous beasts. Stupendously dangerous beasts. Oh, gosh. Devouring types of beasts. The sea is full of fish. Sea-serpents, monsters, aquatic dragons. They've found skeletons, fossils, terrible lizards with teeth the size of perambulators. Dinosaurs. Giles draws them. Tyrranosaurus Rex. Brontosaurus something. Uncle Kenneth has pictures of dinosaurs for his kinetoscope. They wobble and loom above the aspidistra, snake up onto the ceiling, shiver and gnash and wail. Maybe not wail, but she used to imagine them wail. She used to gnaw her ribbons and sit tight. Scaredy-waredy. There are so many things to be scared of: injury, disease, mental affliction. Incredible. I'm saying incredible, not her. It's because I'm reflecting, I'm reflecting how in a year's time she'll be handling broken bodies and won't think anything of it. She'll be suturing and bathing and unpeeling pussed lint and won't think anything of it. She'll be feeling the knobbles of split bones and the warmth of vomit over her fingers and won't think anything of it. She'll see shit in a man's trousers and a penis go up when she swabs around it and won't think anything of it. War will get her onto a set that suits her, suits the kind of person she is, because right now she doesn't ken who or what she is. She just flaps her hands helplessly and reads and sews and waits. That's why she's kind of excited now. She's made for better things, tumtitty-tum. The thunder sheet's in action, there are villains to be squashed, she's got her stage paint on, she's screwing up her courage, her hand is at her forehead but it's her doing the saving, not being saved. Actually, she's got it all worked out.

I'll bring you something to eat, she whispers. Whatever you do, don't move around too much. We're right above the servants' quarters, remember, Willo. She gives a little nervous laugh. Oh, Will, it'll be all right. I've got it all worked out. Oh dear, it's all so frightful, but it'll be over by this evening, I promise. Right will prevail. I'll be back within the hour. Trust me, Will.

She's so GOOD. Maybe they don't make 'em like that any more. She flits out. Not quite smoothly out because her hem snags, as I knew it would. It snags on something really prosaic: a nail. The big HIG could write a twelve-volume treatise on the significance of this clip because he's full of crap, he can spin it out of nothing and everyone applauds because he's the Emperor, inne? There's a bit of embroidery left on the nail. Let me tell you something. When I visited this house in '90 I went up to the attic. It was full of purple paint cans and plywood sheets and zinc sinks and heaps of unused polystyrene ceiling tiles left behind by the moving tides of interior fashion, it was really sad, and I found the nail. It was a big nail, sticking out at the bottom of a mainbeam. There was a tiny yellow thing on this big nail. It was a scrap of embroidery. I took it. I bought a locket in a junk shop on the Portobello Road, just a tinny thing, nothing special, it cost me a fortune but it was tiny and it clicked tight shut and that's where I keep the scrap of my great-aunt. Round my neck. It's better than ashes. Some people go through life without anything snagging 'em. They die forgotten, leaving nothing but dandruff on the terrible suit. Being snagged's great. The door clicks shut. William closes his eyes and thinks about the woods behind Hamilton Lodge. A dryad flits, or maybe the sun shifts over a blackberry sucker. Maybe there's no difference. Agatha's a trooper. She's terrific. He always considered that she didn't really think much of him, that she preferred Giles. Thinking that she does really care about him makes him smile. Catch that. That smile is secret. He feels

288

warm all of a sudden. She's really terrific. They could run away together and live in a cottage somewhere like Aunt Rose and Uncle Jack, who never found anyone better but don't sleep together, of course. They could read and talk and garden and he could create the most important butterfly collection in the British Isles. There are lots of butterflies at this time. There are lots of hedgerows and wild banks and thick woods and unpoisoned meadows. There are also some cheap cottages – David Herbert Lawrence can even afford them. It's not all that crazy an idea, just näive. He's fifteen. Let him keep that smile. It might have seen him through if the world wasn't full of maniacs who run our lives for us and don't smile like that, not ever, not like that.

I'm really drained.

Life is shit.

You know the trouble with all my films? They were deliberately B. B as in Bad. B as in Bloody. B as in Bollocks. B as in Boring. In other words, they were lifelike, they were exactly like life. Not like life out there, I mean life as filtered by your Brain. Life out there is by Fellini, OK? But life in here is by me. You wouldn't believe what my Brain gets up to. It believes in love stories turning out happily, it believes in things in general turning out happily once the rough patch is over and I get a new door lock because the fuckers smashed it to get themselves in – once I get a new door lock and sell the house and throw in the job for a part-time lectureship in Danish Cinema at Tahiti University where Zelda has just been appointed Chief Librarian. I'm serious. I'm serious not about this appointment but about the fact that I go round believing in this crap. I go round watching these really terrible B movies in my head and believing in them. I lie awake at night and when I'm not watching my Brain screening an intimate account of all the possible things that can go wrong with the human body as if I *need* these fucking medical lectures, this asshole lump of grey broccoli is screening stuff that makes *On Golden Pond* look like *The Bicycle Thieves*. What do I do about it? Zilch. I give classes on stuff like Neo-Realism and the New Wave and Redemption and Illusion in the Works of

Robert Bresson and Illusion and Redemption in the works of Carl Theodor Dreyer to about three students and a hearing-aid and meanwhile I am engaging my attention with the kind of crap that used to go on at the Enfield Ritz when the main print had got held up or mislaid by some poncy pea-brain at Ponders End Plaza or nicked or left out in the drizzle or eaten by giant sewer rats or something. I hope you don't mind me saying this. It's like a public health warning before the main feature. This one's coming in the middle of the main feature. WARNING: HUMAN KIND CANNOT BEAR VERY MUCH REALITY. Keep those B films rolling. At least you're the star, you might get an Oscar if you act bad enough. Zelda says she thinks she's in love with the creep. Maybe it's his heckelphone. There goes Tahiti or wherever. I came back kind of disappointed and found my house burgled. Done over. Smashed up. They say it's drugs wot do it. I made to make myself a cuppa cha 'cos that's the Blitz spirit, innit, but they'd taken out my fuse-box. I mean taken out as in killed. Shotgun, maybe. For the sparks. I'm glad I wasn't in. Hey, it was probably some of the students, they know my timetable, maybe the creep wants to keep me on my toes. I made to telephone Mummy I mean Zelda I mean my friend Carol happily married with twins who likes me and we swap British comedy classics because she's British but the telephones had been taken. My studio went dark. The reel clattered out. I was off the air. No B films, no reruns of old soaps, no nothing but Des Pear in his terrible suit and an imperial litre of Famous Grouse, Duty Free, with a stupid Union Jack round its neck.

I wish my grouse was fucking famous. Like Baudelaire's or someone.

Bom bom. Or maybe oof. Great stuff, Des, great stuff.

Then this phantom enters. She stands there in her silk robe and stares at me. I've got the nadgers. I'm practically dribbling. I raise my glass. To Agatha, I say. To goodness. To beauty. To love. To you. She doesn't say anything she just looks. Ricky? Christ, it's Zelda. It's the moonlight. Moonlight does wonderful things. She steps over the wreckage and sits down next to me. I thought you were my great-aunt, I say – you know, Great-Aunt Agatha. I think I've mentioned her. What's that, Ricky? says Zelda. Apparently I am inarticulate. Funny, I thought I'd said it clear as daylight. Every time I open my mouth my sync point is out by about a quarter of a second. It's like the blahdy Ritz all over again. She strokes my hair or what's left of it after fifty-five years and Des Pear's little number. The crickets are zizzing like crazy. I drink rarely, I try to say. Ssssh, that's OK, she says. I'm giving up my project, I go on. It's too draining. Masterworks are too draining. I'm pulling it. I have accepted that I am a complete failure. I turn. Christ, it's not Zelda. The grey eyes have worms in them. The hand is like ice on my scalp. The silken robe is stiff and yellowed and there is a cobweb across the underarm. I'm so scared I cannot move. I swallow. I'm even scared to swallow. This is death, obviously. I've probably had eighteen straight whiskies, big ones. The mouth with its awful teeth opens. My great-aunt's voice comes out, clear as daylight. Remember, she says. Then she flits out without snagging on anything but there's a small greenish evacuation on the rug. (There was this morning, anyway.) I cry. I sob. I'm not sobbing for myself. I'm sobbing for her and what she said. Because the way she said it – it was pleading, it was very pleading. I have such a responsibility. I like responsibility. I've never really had any responsibility before. Greg and Maura just grew up, it was mostly Deirdre who did it all, things were like that in those days. I just read poetry to them and took them round the Science Museum and to *Custer's Last Stand* in Sensurround which was a mistake and fished a bit on vacation and got them Edward Woodward's signature and stuff and then suddenly their shoes were bigger than mine. At least Greg's were. Maura's were just higher. Now I have responsibility. I sat there in the wreckage of my house and sobbed because I knew it was all going to be OK and life is shit. It was all going to be OK *because* life is shit. Basically this is a promo for my new attitude. I'm going to try to stay out of it now. I'm not even bringing my clubs. I'm just gonna sit at my desk in the wreckage of my house. I have a new fuse-box. At least they didn't touch my computer. I don't have to use my plume and inkpot and get chapped lips from my tongue helping out. You know why they didn't touch my best friend? Because the phantoms stood round it and rippled their ectoplasm and pointed at them and went ooooh. We're in this together, it was a great performance, it beats Securicor any day. Zelda, honey, go screw yourself. Go screw yourself. Todd Lazenby, go stick your dick in Spielberg's clapper-board and keep it there. You're a fake. You have no clothes on. I'm a little kid, I am humiliated, but I have a great responsibility and you wouldn't even begin to have the teeniest-weeniest inkling of what this means, creep.

That's sour, but understandable.

Now shuddup, son. Your muvver's 'ad enough of your yap yap yap. So 'ave we all. Yap yap yap all blahdy day. Even the wallpaper's 'ad enough, look, you're peelin' the blahdy wallpaper wiv yer jaw-mag. Puddesoginnit. All roigh'?

All roigh', Dad, all roigh'. Can I 'ave a bob for the flicks? Cor, fanks. Fanks, Dad!

Phoney, so phoney. Even my ur-accent, my real one, sounds phoney. The rain in Spain falls mainly on the plain. By Jove he's got it. The heinous in Venus falls mainly on the penus. How true, by Jove, how true! Now button y'lip, mate, or I'll zip it for yer.

Ahem.

The new maid, Milly Stephenson, hesitates before opening her door. It is a habit. She opens her door and enters her small room crouched beneath the attic. She doesn't have to crouch because she's small. But the room is indeed extremely low. A small pan of the furniture: water jug, small pan, cane chair with rickets, iron bedstead, hook, chest of drawers with missing knob and spotty three-sided mirror, small table with frayed edging of pink chintz nailed to it, nail-heads rusted, Polanski patches of damp and general rot on wall, tiny rug on bare boards, tiny rug has tinier hole in it for catching the big toe, bed has bedspread of white muslin that has seen better days in the guest suite of Mr Trevelyan's great-aunt before a guest spewed up on it after a great Victorian Christmas in 1853. Tallow candle because there's only electrics in the corridor. Oil-lamp someone forgot to refill and Milly's too new to mention it. Window with view of roof-tiles and pigeons, mid-opaque due to collected grime, north-facing. In the time it's taken to pan all that Milly has donned her black tea-serving uniform with frilly apron and frilly hat and frilly detachable cuffs and frilly detachable collar. It's OK to look now. She's doing something with her hair. A pin drops. She picks it up. She pokes it back in. She studies herself in the mirror, smoothing down her general frills. Creak. She looks up. Creak creak. Her chest flutters. She holds her hands tightly

together in front of her apron. Ghosts. Mr MacPhearson said watch
the ghosts ha haaar. Eyes widen. Creak creak creak. Tongue in her
mouth. MacPhearson's tongue. Gob. Dismissal. No commendation.
The gentleman's hand on her shoulder. Naked through the grass.
Naked gent through the Wheel of Life. What the Butler Saw in the
Pantry. Nay, the Master Bedroom. Creak. Ghosts. Boy in hall. Uncle
in hall. White face and Miss Agatha in hall turning like Milly were
th'ghost, queer uncle pushing her back into dining-room and booming
at her till her ears split about some Irish situation and locomotives. He
took a breath. She nodded. The young master will need his room
turning out, she said. What young master? said he. The young
m-m-m-master as I have just seed, sir, she said, bobbing. Stammer
come back. Creak creak. Queer gentleman with eyebrows puts
eyebrows very close to hers. Bad breath. Needs Dr Swillshake's Extra
Strong Menthol Fluid Beats Bad Breath Every Time Says Leading
Dental Surgeon. There is no young master in this house, my dear.
Both young masters are at school. You must be referring to the
tradesboy delivering Miss Agatha's new, ah, new, ah, new skirt, yes,
yes skirt, a very charming one too, a yes skirt. I see, she said. Yes skirt.
Well then. That settles that. Now, my dear, don't let me interrupt you.
Or I will be in a great deal of trouble! Queer uncle leaves her alone in
dining-room. Creak. Tradesboys deliver skirts. Well I neveranee.
Creak creak. Slow hexaminationary of ceiling like it's a big cake o'
soap, for blemishes, bubbles, foreign matter. A variety of maps on it.
Faces. Oh. Faces looking at her. She shivers. Under the bedspread
with the yellowy stain is her rag doll. It has no mouth. When she prays
to God she sits on the edge of the bed and holds her doll. This is what
she does right now. Small clock on table with nailed pink chintz chimes
tinnily because it's on the hour, it's time, she'll be late down Amen.
Doll goes back under bedspread. Agnes. The name of the doll is
Agnes. Smooth down frills. Creak. Don't look up at it. Look sharp. Yes
skirt. Tradesboy wi' white face. Yes skirt. Black hat. Posh black suit,
posh shoes. Leave room backwards because the Devil likes to leap on
weak spines. Door closes. Room empty. Shoot pigeons fussing blurrily
through window-pane with grimy glass and blue curtain which is too
short. Creak. Scuffle. Creak. Print that, like.

Down below, downstairs upstairs upstairs downstairs in her lady's
chamber and out again, tea served, two different lots of tea 'cos

memsahib's imbibing it alone in darkened room, drawn curtains, headache, Aspirin Does Wonders For Your Overstrained Brain Says Leading Nurse, other tea in conservatory, Miss Agatha and queer uncle almost whispering, so do likewise wi' *will that be all sir, fresh pot sir, very good sir miss* bob bob out again traps for the unwary everywhere ay and the olive trees blighted and blasted yea what a lark what a plunge who said that smooth frills down again dear Lord protect me from all hurt and bogies and the stuffed rat on the landing and Mr MacPhearson specially him cut.

I'm sorry about this. I just want to get to supper. Stream of consciousness makes me sick. Nobody thinks like this. But I'm doped up and I'm keeping it. The cutting-room floor's looking like my barber's after the Grateful Dead freaks who'd decided to join the Hare Krishnas came in that time. Fuck off, Thornby. Just quit yacking and get to supper. WE DON'T WANT TO KNOW, SON. WE DON'T WANT TO KNOW WHO BUILT THE WORLD'S FIRST BLEEDIN' SWING BLEEDIN' BRIDGE. Do watch your language, dear. He's only trying to inform us.

George is belabouring his lapels and thigh, etc. Dorothy is stirring whatever I said they were having for supper ages ago, last year, when Zelda loved me. That's Sylvia's department. She's got the Polaroid. She re-hired herself after I broke down by the wrong stuffed lemur and wept. Don't expect me to remember. I'm falling apart. It is something meaty and tough and grandparenty. It is early evening. I can't be more specific. Try saying specific on a lot of Texan ten-gallon gut-rot and hashish. Yeah yeah, hashish, hashish. I'm crumbling. I'm Samuel Taylor Coleridge, I'm Thomas de Quincey Jnr, I'm Jack Kerouac, I'd be so lucky. Zelda's left me, pretty well, jogging and pole-vaulting with Pubes In the fucking Gate. PIG. Hey, that's genius. PIG. I was never happy with HIG. It sounded affectionate. *Pubes In the Gate, PIG.* Well I never. Harry Hashish hath done it again. I feel nauseous, however. My father is turning my ears into broccoli. He's only trying to inform us, dear. I need a vacation. I need a weekend off. I need to join my other neighbour Jake G. Firth Jnr and go drag some illegal immigrant around from the back of a Jeep on the Mexican border. I need to take a pot-shot at some tires on the freeway. I need to freak out in the way they do here. I need to go to NASA and ask if I can be on the next shuttle to inner space man, I need to leave skid marks on the interstate highway instead of in my underpants. I need to kill someone.

I burnt an essay today. Like burning a thousand dollar note. The fifteenth rewrite. It cracked me up. I just burnt it. Fuck off, student. Go cheat off someone else. On the end of a match I burnt it. Oh, it was SO SATISFYING. Smear marks on the silver. Someone's whingeing on about smear marks on the silver. It's the butler. It's the chief domestic. It's Anthony Hopkins disguised as George MacPhearson. I hire only stars, Welsh stars, Welsh stars so costly you can't make out what they're saying and what's more George MacPhearson is not Welsh. There are pimples on George MacPhearson's neck a blind person'd want to pop, they read I KEN HAIRY BITS in braille. Let him whinge on. Let him overact. The smear marks mar the silvery shine, the mar smarks sear the shivery saliva by the light of the silvery moon, my dear, my love, by the light of the silvery moon, my pussy, my love, by oh fuck. Aye, George, aye. I'll inform Lily of the matter. Dorothy is patting something. It may be blancmange. It goes up her arms as she pats and turns her into THE THING.

Ricky, you're being irresponsible. Seriously. He's pissed, he's completely shashed again, guys. Let's cap up and tail out the takes.

No, no. I'm sorry, I'm sorry. I'm a genius. I'm Baudelaire. I work best horizontal. I want a cam remote on the nike and a scrim on everything and no zooms. I'm a genius. I want a rifle mike but watch it hey there are gonna be a ton of reversals, reaction shots, catchlights of candles in aghast stares, quietly aghast stares over the dinner-table, just candles actually, no luminaires Mike, real dark, shut right down, not even a day for night, barn doors tight, nothing, no scrims, no nothing, not half a lux that isn't candle-light and a merrily blazing fire and one electric standard lamp, circa 1911, in the corner, OK? No buts, Mike. No buts. I'm a genius. I know what I'm doing. These are gonna be voices out of the murk, catchlights of eyeballs, taffeta rustles on the buzz track under silver and crystal pings, and that's it. Murk.

Bridging shot. WHERE'S MILLY? WHERE'S MY STAR? CHRIST, HOW CAN I WORK WITH THESE PEOPLE? Rick, you got the megaphone the wrong way round. We can't hear you. You're very faint. Mike's been dead ten years. Bosey's married with three kids. Sylvia's in Spain on the plain someplace. Pierre's unemployed. Joe Gel's HIV but is doing just fine. Julie's I don't know where she is. Ossy you know about. I'm sorry he was like that with you. Maybe he's insecure. It's been rough lately. Can you hear us? We can't hear you. You got the megaphone the wrong way round. It needs polishing. The Brasso is all dried up in the tin. Ah, here's Milly. We had problems with the detachable cuffs. She has very thick wrists. Here's George. He has a very thick neck. We have electric light in the dining-room. We have dusk through the long windows. We have a buzz track of *Residential Street, Westminster, 3 November 1913*. Do you need any bells?

Action.

The Devil finally leaps in the dining-room. Pssst, milt, d'ye ken where *he* is? She finds her mouth is too dry to reply to the Chief Tempter. She shakes her head. The frilly detachable collar buffs her chin. The silver forks in her hand have smears. She's only just noticed them. Brillo For A Brighter Finish. Turn out the young master's room anyway, just in case queer uncle was having her on as is his wont. A finger in front of her face. It has a queer nail. It's grown funny. It would, belonging to the Horned One. She can't pray because she's holding silver. Oh ay, he is a clever-clogs, that one. The finger is old and hairy. As old as sin. It points at a picture on the wall opposite, th'other side of table. The table is a very very very very long one. She put that in her letter to Ma and it weren't a bull. It is a very very very very long one. It's very very very very dark, too, and takes an age to bring up right. George the Devil-In-Pathetic-Disguise has a spatula in his hand, not a toasting-fork. The spatula is for measuring, it has notches in it, it's laid between glass rims and edge of table, glass and napkin, plate and side-plate, candelabras and salt-cellars, pepper-pot and wee bronze figurine of Victory with the bubbies, and top and tip of the Devil's dick when it's saluting the Queen, as George jests inaccurately – I mean, everyone knows the Queen is dead and the Devil is nae able to get it up high enough, ho ho ho.

That was lousy. Take it again. From the top. I'm a genius. Dicky

Attenborough would be satisfied but Dicky Thornby ain't Dicky Attenborough, OK?

The Devil leaps on her weak spine in the dining-room. A finger obtrudes in colossal close-up. Beyond it in deep focus a picture of Mr Trevelyan a few years back in morning-suit and tie, albeit the same gold as the studs in the leather chair, Mr Trevelyan the Big Wallah in his office, pigskin-gloved hand on a bronze figurine of Victory with pert breasts, no grey hairs as yet. D'you ken where *he* is? Again. D'you ken *where* he is? Nope, again. D'you ken where he *is*? Pssst milt. You forgot the pssst milt. Keep the pssst milt. Spray her detachable collar and the exposed nape above it where the hair's drawn tightly up. Rock and roll. Take twenty-eight or whatever it takes. Action. We're losing the light outside. Get a move on. Pssst milt, d'you ken where he is? That's great. Think about breakfast. Don't act. Robert Bresson's primary rule: actors get in the way. Pssst milt d'you ken where he is shake of head he grins oh the Devil's smile he takes her chin in his hands and brings her ear up to his mouth her eyes are blank her mouth pouts under the pressure of the fingers on her chin snibbin' in the front parlour he whispers so her ear floats away on a foaming wave snibbin' an' snortin' in the front parlour aye gettin' his wee pinkie to plug the gap o' some downy doll-mop aye we ken it all we ken it all we keep our eyes skinned ha haaar.

I'll buy it up to doll-mop. The rest sounded like Long John Silver practising in the mirror.

To plug the gap o' some downy doll-mop. She swallows. Smears. Mr Trevelyan stares across and down at her over the table. He looks surprised. Chin released. Skin springs jauntily back to its usual position because she's only thirteen. But spots. Bound to be spots. Soap and water. Pear's For a Better Complexion. Don't say nowt, by 'eck. Just nod. She nods. She lays the silver with him watching. Think about breakfast. He begins to measure. We ken it all, aye we ken it all. We keep our eyes skinned, aye. There's a tremor in his voice. He sounds uncertain about something. I'll tell you why. It's because he doesn't know this squit of a wench, maybe she'll shop him, maybe she'll keep it all to herself till one day she'll write a letter to someone high and heavy and the ceiling will come down on his head. He moves a glass a quarter of an inch till it meets the notch. He glances at her from under his eyebrows. A squeeze and a squirt. That's what he'd like aye out of her but these squits niver come on easy. Side-plate to candelabra. He stiffens underneath his breeches. He leans across for *ha* silver salver (totally insignificant, oh Christ) to Victory figurine and the edge of the table presses against his Jack Robinson. Aye aye, we ken it all, he sighs. He sounds sad, she thinks. At least he didn't. He's not the Devil any more. He was never the Devil. The Devil smells of soap and hair-oil and sulphur because you can't hide that. Stink of sulphur. Can't be hid. Gets under the nails. His nails smelt of cabbage and he didn't. The Devil would've. He's just a poor lost soul. When the Last Day comes and th'Trumpet blares he won't even be cinders, won't even be ash, nay, he won't even be enough to prick wi' a pin-'ead. She hears the echo the Prehistoric Methodist-or-whatever-it-is Chapel makes after Mr Dougal has blared. A fine echo. Never ever hold it by tangs. Smeared any road. There's this part of her I don't like, even through a scrim of dope. It's all bunched up and knotted and even if you dropped acid on it it wouldn't uncurl. It's like a tumour, it's a tumour of primordial bigotry that sits cruelly in a fair young lady, hey ho the wind and the rain and the rain it raineth every day in Worksop, that's the trouble. Mr Dougal rubbed up against her brain until the tumour took seed and grew. It bleeds, it's a bruise, it's tough, it keeps her going because the fallen won't even be cinders. She places the last fork and thinks about Mr Trevelyan doing something in the front parlour, sniffing and snorting or whatever it was, and playing with dolls. Or a mop. A doll out of a mop-head, like Sis's. Funny folk, down here, Ma. Probably picking his nose. A gentleman never picks his nose. Dear Ma, Mr Trevelyan picks his nose (snibs, they call it) in the front parlour. She isn't sure where the front parlour is in this queer house. Maybe it has summat to do wi' them creaks. His nibbs snibs. A bubble of laughter escapes her mouth. She puts her hand to it. Oh 'eck. Mr MacPhearson pats his hand with the spatula like he's about to welt her.

Pat pat, pat pat.

Moral worth is in the consequence. The true is the name of whatever proves itself to be finally good. That is Mr James, not myself. I subscribe to it totally. The important word is proves. One has in one's thoughts the ideal as well as the purposive. Good is an active sort of realising. It is not a marble statue. It is not an idol. It is more, let us say, an electrical current that lights a lamp, or rings the bell, or—

Yah, yah. This is Uncle Kenneth sounding forth, or off, in the drawing-room. No one talks like this any more. Not many talked like this then. *It's because he lives alone*, whispers Mrs Trevelyan. This is what stops Uncle Kenneth in mid-flow. Mrs Trevelyan is whispering to the cat. Mr Arthur Trevelyan, amazingly, is picking his nose. Hey, he's doing it as a gentleman should, discreetly, pretending to examine one of a pair of spatterware vases on the dresser. Actually, Uncle Kenneth is incredibly nervous. This is why he's talking so much. He's talking about Pragmatism. He could have talked about freshwater fish or the history of Bolivian tin-mining for all anyone in this room cares. Anyone being his brother and his sister-in-law. Mr Arthur Trevelyan has cleared his left nostril and is turning, nodding his head as if he's understood which he hasn't because he's still pooped after Ruthie's little giddyup. The three of them are pretty smartly dressed but they're not going out. This is how people dress for dinner EVERY DAY in 1913. Uncle Kenneth is as smart as he ever will be. Rumpled, spattered with ash, odd spats, crooked collar, but SMART, basically. He's blinking through his spectacles at his sister-in-law. His brother goes hmmm. Then he says, and what about God? He has found that what about God can be interjected at almost any point in a conversation provided the content is of sufficient substance to take it as a cover for not having the faintest idea of the thread, hey ho. Hashish does amazing things to one's intelligence, huh? Uncle Kenneth is on opium. Now and again. For his gout. Ah, he says. He points a finger in the air. Mr Trevelyan looks up as if he's admiring Orville and Wright conducting a loop-the-loop. Very droll, very droll, 1913 humour. Quite quite alone, whispers Mrs Trevelyan to the cat, who purrs because she is pragmatic and no great judge of human character. Mr Kenneth Trevelyan takes a pretransmission sip of his sherry. He smacks his lips. He withdraws his finger from assertive service. What is this dope doing to me? He opens his mouth. God, he says. A very pertinent point, Arty. Mrs T flinches. She can't stand their nursery relationship. She closes her eyes as if she is enduring with enormous fortitude someone ramming a needle up her asshole. What a saint. The point being, says the Bore For Tonight, that as my friend Mr

Ferdinand Schiller pointed out in his most recent lecture, Pragmatism cares for we humans more than it cares for an abstract, you see. Of course, I am not by any means stating that God is a mere abstract, but that our belief in Him most certainly is, if it is not rigorously examined AS AN IDEA. An idea with decent, or shall we say otherwise, consequences. He pauses. Mr Arthur Trevelyan is inserting his jiggamy into Ruthie's thingummy all over again and jerks. Hm, I see, yes, yes indeed, indeed, Kenny old chap. Mrs Trevelyan is looking tragically at the carpet. For instance, continues Kenny old chap, if you were to call this little glass of mine an idea, then whatever use I make of it, or do not make of it, you see, will change the, ah, the meaning of it, of the idea, of the glass of sherry, d'you see? Beat. Two beats. But it's still a bally glass, for all that! cries Mr Arthur Trevelyan, waving his own glass about and letting loose a few drops over the rim. Mrs Trevelyan shudders because she can't stand and never has been able to stand the sound of her husband's voice raised higher than a murmur. Mr Kenneth Trevelyan blinks benignly at his brother. In the Idealist sense, yes, says he. But our world is a frightfully mucky place, don't you know, and full of stuff. And stuff says bunkum and fiddlesticks to Idealism. Bunkum and fiddlesticks! Where is Agatha? asks Mrs T. It is not like her to be late. Bunkum and fiddlesticks adds Uncle Kenneth very weakly, nervous again and really failing to disguise it. I'm sorry? Mrs T eyes him sharply. I still think the drift is dashed off course, says Mr Trevelyan. Dashed off course. He blinks determinedly. Or deterministically, because that's how he likes to think of himself. A determined Christian determinist. Anything that'll show up the flippy-flappy nature of his wife's brain, or of women in general, as a net does a species of butterfly, or better a pin.

Catch that one, PIG. Match that.

OK buy it, I'm gonna hug my pillow.

Tomorrow same time don't be other than too early. Bring the Asprol, Julie. And the Brasso. I've never been more on form. Don't forget the Brasso. The Brasso, OK? I can't work without I can shave in my megaphone.

Great days, great days ha haaar.

A match flares.

Big deal. It's George lighting the candles. It's nobody's birthday.
Actually, today *is* my birthday, remember? Hope you liked the steam
train cake. Yeah, it was supposed to be a steam train. Exact repro of the
Flying Scotsman attempt by my father on my eighth birthday, the one
and only time he made an effort, green icing all over the kitchen walls,
the fact that it looked like the Blob from Venus was neither here nor
there, I was warm and tingly all over because he'd made an effort,
when I think of that day I think of my father as my father with green
icing on his nose grinning at me and not some guy who'd shuffled on in
place of my real one while my real one was circumnavigating the globe
on a raft armed with nothing but a bow and arrow and a fishing rod and
nineteen packs of Bisto gravy and the Meccano set I never had in case
he got bored mid-Pacific. I hope you've sung Happy Birthday to Me.
The day this particular match flares it was nobody's birthday.
Nobody's birthday in Number 25 Albermarle Terrace, that is. Milly
thinks of Lucifer when the match catches on the side of George's shoe.
Seriously she does. Those of you whose brains are irredeemably
damaged by drink and drugs and automobile exhausts and nuclear
leaks and pesticides and stuff will need to be told how matches used to
be called lucifers or lucifer matches just as I used to be called Spotted
or Spotted Dick. And also how matches are no longer called lucifers
generally speaking in 1913 except by stone-deaf hags in remote little
villages like Bracknell or Milton Keynes or certainly Zennor because
Zennor is the last place on the list of the guy going around with his
megaphone telling everybody to drop the lucifer and he's slow and old
because he's been doing this since about 1871. He struck out from
Abbas Combe in Somerset for Abberley way up near Droitwich and
then down to Essex for Abberton and then back up near Droitwich
again for another Abberton for crying out loud and then he looks at his
list and groans because Abberwick's Northumberland and huddled up

in Abberwick with the wind moaning off the North Sea about men not being men any more as in the days of St Cuthbert as if anyone called Cuthbert could be anything but a wimp he orders another malt because Abbess Roding is south of Bishop's Stortford and anyway he's not sure anyone's taking any notice and these are the days before tarmacadam and it was a bad winter but he has faith, he has a mission, he is systematic, he isn't fooling around, he tosses back his malt and clutches his little lamp and wraps his cloak tight around him and out he goes into the freezing Northumberland air with his tinderbox dry and so stumps on through mud and storm and snow drawing a line through his names with a great quill, dreaming of the warm hearth and warmer ale in *The Tinner's Arms* in Zennor, of the ancient sea-pickled Cornishmen striking their lucifers against hob-nails and hearth-stone and hearkening to his tales as they make bubbling noises in their clay pipes and laugh ha haaar.

You might meet his ghost one day, on the road to Manderley or wherever he snuffed it from old age and exhaustion in 1915, with the Ws still to go. You know how many places beginning with W there are in the British Isles? Over 2,250. The last place he visited was Vulcan Bridge, Cheshire. Vulcan. God of fire. Fitting, huh? Hot pants of the Industrial Revolution, I presume, where England first gave the world the Judas kiss of Vulcan's devotion. Sounds pretty unlikely, doesn't it, even without the poetic flourish? Like it sounds pretty unlikely how this septic isle, this dearth of majesty, this bleat of Mars, this Antony-Eden-semis' paradise, this abortion forced on Nature by some sod to breed insurance salesmen and the perfect lawn, this crappy bunch of inebriates in their little world, this old turd bobbing in the grisly sea, could once have stained so much of the planet in imperial red, as every classroom in 1913 was witness to on at least one wall, oilcloth maps bumping their rollers in a breeze, waking Henry Peterson from his poetic slumber and giving him another idea for a scathing pastiche (*England & Other Versions*, Gooseberry Press, 1958).

George's lit the candles. I'm sorry I'm just trying to impress I know, I know. I've got 2,250 takes to go and most of the story is not yet rolled and I'm running out of raw stock. You know why? Because Zelda fair lady of Zennor I don't think (Duluth, her folks are from Duluth for crying out loud) is not around me to cajole and curmudgeon and cosh.

303

Or cuff. Or click her fingers. Or kiss me on the nape and say, honey, it's story time. We want the story. Then it was: honey, it's narrative that should be foregrounded if you want to hold our attention and remember the use of the colons and the kiss was gone, it was a light touch of the fingers. Then it was the expectation of a touch which was unbearable because it prickled my neck and how's it going in a really flat Duluth kind of voice as she passed with three volumes of Howard Hawks's memoirs between her thumb and forefinger. It's going fine, I'd say, it's going fine. I'm foreplaying the narrative but not grinding yet. Then she'd cuff me and chuckle. Her chuckle was enough to get me leaping out my chair and pressing myself to her but I never did because there are video cameras in the HCDVA library just in case there's any groping or profound intellectual enquiring going on in college time. Aw, shucks. Cor fuckaduck. Cockalorum I'll be dandy. Wot, me be 'arf a crahn abaht it? Nail me in me cawfin on me old cock-sparrer I'll be singin' diddledee doi dow. I'm a chickaleary cove, when it cometh to it, cor blimey blow me dahn guv luverly toms at twice the price mate.

Grope for Jesus, grope for Jesus. This is going through Milly's head like one of those naff crawler captions on bigots' TV. It's what Mr John Dougal yells when he lights a lucifer. Then he blows it out. Like George blows his out. And grins. Dim the lights, Mike. More. OK. Merry blaze of fire George stoops to poke unnecessarily but it's habit. Aye, we ken it all, squit. He sounds sad again, thinks Milly. He leans against the mantel stiffly in all senses of the word and pokes. Firelight picks out the sweat and grease on his face, the shadows of his boils move around like they want to get away. His eyes blaze. The sulphur is matches, thinks Milly. Ay, it is matches, it's only the matches. She's too nervous about dinner and the soup and not spilling the soup to think any deeper on George and Hell-mouth for the moment. She pats a napkin into a more erect shape. It flops. It's like a rabbit's ear in a picture she once saw in a toy shop. This makes her feel homesick for Worksop. Not really for Worksop, more for her lean childhood and the smell of her mother's frayed apron-hem which was a mixture of brats' saliva and boiled apples and raw herring. Roughly. The slap of her little bare feet on the damp cobbles of Worksop is interrupted by a growl from George. It's not a growl, he's hawking into the flames. They hiss and recover. He's staring into them like he'd watch TV if it

304

were around now. Hey, he's a flames addict. In millions of homes around the country people are settling into an evening of flames gazing. Sure, they're knitting and sewing and playing cards and chess and reading the newspaper and books and periodicals and getting plenty of exercise bobbing up and down to Beethoven's Fifth Symphony because each disc lasts about three minutes and there are twenty-two but mostly people will just be staring into the fire watching the coal flutter or the logs flap and thinking about things for themselves, rewinding the day for the edited highlights, musing on the future and the past and why beef always repeats on them and how his false teeth always click into place when he's finished doing that acrobatic thing with them'n his tongue and whether there'll be mutton on the menu tonight because the wife's looking like the Lady of Shalott's come round again for cocoa and whether *Ta-Ta Ragtime* at the Hippodrome is as saucy as *Hullo Ragtime* last year and why God allows children to fade away and debts to accumulate and earthquakes to happen in faraway places and the privy to foul each time Aunt Violet Maud stays the week and on the meaning of life. Now we have it all done for us. Now the soft flickering chattering glow's just converged primaries signalled to a four by three aspect ratio out of C-format head drums turning and ticking slowly someplace faraway and writing onto our broccoli the gabber and gash and gunk that no one really wants in their own living-rooms but it's better than musing deeply on the meaning of life, the fickleness of love, the random access of misery, the WYSIWYG of fortune, the accumulating zits of time on the epidermis of memory, or maybe it's vice-versa, I can't quote my own verse perfectly because I giggle too much, I blush and I giggle and I tear it up, I trash it, I watch TV instead because there are some great late-night movies on PBS.

Grope for Jesus, Milly murmurs to herself. George picks up the Indian gong and whacks it just once but it's enough. It makes her nigh jump out of her skin. He chortles, showing his gums which are wolverine to say the least. She blinks so quickly it turns him into the picture Uncle Stan took her to with the mummy in it which'd made her scream but instead of screaming she stays blank and turns away and fiddles with the candlesticks. Oh. The mummy's coming towards her. Its hot breath is on her neck. It's only an actor dressed up in about twenty yards of lint, said her Uncle Stan. Don't be frit. The hot breath turns

305

into a cold hand. It somehow gets between her detachable collar and the nape. Aye, the cold hand says, we ken it all, squit. Here they are. Don't slip up or Georgie-Peorgie'll make ye cry, aye. Then the cold hand leaves. The candlestick by now is on the very edge of the mantel. It's good to know some traditions continue. Here they are indeed. She somehow gets to where she's supposed to go, halfway up at the back, next to the picture of Mr Trevelyan, waiting to wait on. She's so far from any light source it's hard to make her out, but she's there, she's there. She'll always be there. Her afterburn has never decayed, even when the place was empty in the mid-fifties and she looked out of taped-up windows or when the ground floor became a dental surgery in '59 with plywood partitions blurring the bedrock. Patients as they were sinking into their own nonsense of gas saw her with a huge soup-ladle leaning over them and tried to bob up again and did to well dones and a free tissue but couldn't remember. She'd tune in for a second between the Cripps-approved easy chair and *The Five Stages Of Dental Rot* wall poster and those of a nervous disposition in the days of low-speed drills squealed and everyone looked at them. A dentist with all five stages on the cobbler's-children principle blistered his lips on his Player's Special when she walked towards him down the corridor with a steam iron as he was closing up very much alone. O chaser of shadows, fleeter after dreams! You think I'm joking? Hey, the landlady went white when I enquired after the resident domestic on my last trip over. Tenants had left because of less, what with the lethal electrics, the impossibility of escape in a fire, the diseased carpets, the deaf Pole's TV at night, don't mention the blasted ghost if you please my dear it might dent my nice little earner, it might upset the boys from the Friends of Rachman Society, they might want to have a little word, if you get my drift.

OK, OK, you don't believe me. Christ, Uncle Ken's still going for the Bore of the Year, Belgravia Section. Fast forward the soup course until he's stopped. In out, in out, in out, napkin whipped up to mouth and back, in out, in out, heads jerking and the soup gone down in five seconds flat, not a drop spilled, the conversational drone a witter like bats or Japs. Stop. Play. I've played this scene a thousand times. I transferred it onto video for edited highlights, my own personal use, but you're gonna see it once. I know it by heart, I know every word before it comes, it must have been really irritating for Zelda watching it with me, like it must be really irritating watching *The Graduate* with Dr Lazenby who knows the songs by heart and has a voice like a weasel on heat. I could score every chink of silver spoon on bone china and the slippings of silk against silk and the discreet burps and the pad pad squeak pad pad of George with his bottle into something that'd have Cage turning in his grave like an organ-grinder's organ. But you're gonna see it once, once only. Unique print. Nothing happens in this world MORE THAN ONCE. It's called entropy. It's called there goes the echo. It's called decay and rot and fade. It's called wiping and shredding. It's called pulling down the studio to build a parking lot. The fickleness of life and love. So listen and look. You won't get another chance like they didn't get another chance. Meat course. Where to goodness is the draught coming from? says Mrs Trevelyan. That's Bosey passing her with the rifle mike but we can't tell her that because even if I shouted in her ear I'd be goldfishing – it's like there's an inch of gallery glass between us and them and it's enough, we're silent but we raise a chill. Where indeed do draughts arise? ponders Mr Trevelyan. He fingers the long stem of his crystal goblet. George fills it so discreetly it's like being served by bad breath. Where indeed do they arise? he asks again. That's the kind of useless question that he can wheel in front of his own thoughts because his own thoughts are about as viewable as a multiple pile-up on a freeway right at this moment. They concern Ruthie. Ruthie *sniggered* when he unbuttoned his combinations facing her instead of slipping behind the hanging plush as per usual. Confounded cheek. Their firkytoodle was dashed dismal. He stroked her diddly-pout with the flat of his foot as he always did and she sniggered again. It put him off. The walking on moss to the rivulet's edge went quite awry and he withdrew his foot and rose and dressed and chucked a shilling on the rumpled coverlet and left her with a slam of the door. Beastly confounded cheek. Harlot. Painted harpy. Mistress Much Too Quickly. I am asking a straightforward question, repeats Mrs Trevelyan. There's no need, Arthur, to dress it up. Is the girl ill? Uncle Kenneth lifts his head from his fork. He reads jerkily from the crib card Julie's holding up, or seems to. She maintained, that she had little appetite, but would, join us eventually. Ah, says Mrs T, thank you for telling me. I would have done, says Uncle Kenneth, but I have only just remembered. Mrs Trevelyan eyes him, superciliously of course. The leaks of fluid at the corners of her eyes glint in the candlelight. She is allergic to dust and smoke and stuff and the fireplace now and again puffs its fumes into the room and outside London's rapping its foggy knuckles on the window-pane to coin a phrase and her eyes are leaking. Uncle Kenneth feels very nervous and she picks this up. He's run out of drone. He's thrashed Pragmatism and hasn't the energy to think anything new about the Irish situation. I won't argue with you, says Mr Trevelyan. He says this like he's decided it long ago and is skipping a few lines to save time – you know what I mean. Uncle Kenneth swallows his meat and it's noisy. It's because his oesophagus is restricted by nerves. *Where is that confounded girl* he's thinking behind his jolly but really hammy grin. He knows where she is. She's walking up and down in her bedroom rehearsing her lines. He can't bear it. Mrs Trevelyan sighs and fiddles with a potato. Underdone, she says, inform Dorothy the potatoes are underdone. This is because the potato does not fall apart the instant it's touched. They are quite agreeable, her disagreeable husband announces. Mr and Mrs Trevelyan turn their heads towards Uncle Kenneth as George stirs discreetly in the background. I like them any old way, shouts Uncle Kenneth. He didn't mean to shout. Mrs Trevelyan's eyelids twitch as the sound waves smash into them. Now here's a subject, thinks Uncle Ken. His knife lifts in Rhetorical Gesture 3. Perhaps we shall be like the Emerson-Palmers, says Mrs Trevelyan as Uncle Ken's mouth opens, who partake of their meals quite separately, they say. Jack Sprat could eat no fat, his wife could eat no lean, contributes Mr Trevelyan in a knowing sort of tone which could quite easily be susceptible to a sexual interpretation. Holy shit, this goes on EVERY EVENING. Can you imagine? Mrs Trevelyan smiles sardonically. OK, maybe not sardonically, maybe it's just the candlelight on her allergy reaction, but to Milly the maid in the shadows it doesn't look terribly friendly. Mr Trevelyan looks up and catches this look and blinks and frowns because this look of his wife's seems to turn his forehead into a fish-tank full of his brightly-coloured thoughts in murky water. Amazing how he can see this the length of a table you can measure in yards in this sort of dimness but they are used to it, their eyes haven't been ruined by neon and floodlights, they can open their pupils right up and read by one candle without getting a migraine. Those were the days. Day for night, night for day. We don't know what night is. Night never comes to Houston. It is one eternal blaze and wink wink wink of cop cars. It gives me a headache just popping out for a Kentucky at three a.m. That's what you do when

308

you're single. You eat Kentuckies and there's no one to lick your fingers for you. Aw, shucks. Shuddup, will ya?

Agatha is not pacing up and down in her room. She's sitting very still by the window and listening to the wind in the wych-elms or whatever those very large trees are outside her window – hey, I reckon they're wych-elms because the first time I visited in '88 they were very ill and white and now they're dead and down. She's trying to work up some Sylvia Pankhurst spunk in herself, but her tummy is liquid. This is only about the third time in her life she hasn't descended the moment the gong sounded. The first two were owing to illness. She's staring out the window and wondering why life tends to be either intolerably dull and miserable or intolerably blissful. In the sigh of the wind through the wych-elms she hears the sea and it's taking her away from this place. She doesn't know where to exactly but vaguely through the sea-mist she sees an island and this island has a handsome ship-wrecked sailor on it who turns out to be a relative of Captain Cook and so widely read he can read to her every night under the stupendous stars without a book in his hand. They have a heap of children and together they work out the Perfect Society. And the time comes for them to return but Agatha won't project that far ahead, she has an intimation that the vessel that finds them carries their destruction in some way. Maybe all the sailors have the plague or something. Maybe on board there's a pretty daughter of the captain seeking a handsome gentleman to elope with. She'd better be going down. Golly, they must almost be through the main course. O Lord, give me strength and spirit to do right this evening. To do the right thing by Thee.

It seems a long way down, ho yes it does. Her shot-silk dress is viridian. You and I say blueish green but I'm trying to be pretentious, I'm trying to inject some quality into this movie. Zelda used viridian for about a month. It was one of the first things I noticed about her. Isn't the lawn viridian today? she'd say. Snot green I think, was my rejoinder. No it wasn't. I never had the pluck. I just nodded and went hmmm and tried to look like Marlon Brando about twenty years ago. It was because she was reading this fat English novel by by by by Byatt, A. S., Mrs, and I said ah, yeah, my pal Jeremy Freeman just missed the rights to that because I phoned him, he was really possessive about *Possession* chuckle chuckle. I was still trying to make her notice me in those days.

Zelda went through this stage of calling everything stuff like faded periwinkle and saturated moss because she was reading this woman and I couldn't stand it, it was like living with Mrs Windsor & Newton, she was a walking Dulux sampler or something, she'd stroke my hair and say it's definitely going frosty flint. I think you mean slug grey, I'd reply in a kind of frosty, flinty way. And at least, honey, it's not guano white, I'd add colourlessly. OK OK, joke over. Dr Turd Lavatory was reading the same book. I realise this now. I realise that shared reading habits lead straight to the shared bedlamp. She has only one bedlamp. Like me. It makes for very short bouts of reading. This shimmering pigeon's throat of a sea-green dress laps after Agatha kind of reluctantly down the stairs. I don't mean the whole shimmering etc. dress, I mean the bit at the back that's busy cleaning the runner. She crosses her fingers as usual, as she has done for about thirteen years, on the thirteenth step. The pictures go on being pictures, kind of smug and into their own thing to do with cows and churches and never hanging straight, but she's too nervous to correct them this evening. She turns at the head of the stairs and oh God brushes the loop on the sash window and there it is. The stuffed lemur with the crooked grin. Wrong shot – Gordon you ape, git the lens round. There. Down there. Pull focus. *The dining-room door.* Wow, big deal, so what's new, it's been there for half a century or something. What's new is the fact that it's scary, it's about as enticing as the lid on a coffin. So she leaves her dress alone and holds the banister. She's very still. There are clinks and clunks coming up from the kitchen and a water-pipe gurgles. She's not into water-pipes so she doesn't know it's a water-pipe exactly but take it from me it is, it's about an inch under the plaster to her right and why it's gurgling is to do with air pressure, it's not someone upstairs it's someone in the kitchen, one of the servants, it's a noise Agatha has always known so she's never thought about it, it just happens, it's the house musing or clearing its throat like it moans and cackles in the night. Needless to say her heart is beating wildly and if we now have a big close up of her hand Gordon we can see it's trembling. At the same time she's thinking how she mustn't touch her dress before wiping her hand because the banisters are waxy, they haven't been buffed enough, that's the new domestic and it'll spoil the shimmer. Then at the same time as some clerk in her brain is typing this out there's another one painting in four-foot high letters IT MIGHT GO WRONG, IT MIGHT ALL GO FRIGHTFULLY, DREADFULLY WRONG. Zelda would like this. This is narrative.

310

Agatha's foregrounding the narrative for me but she doesn't like it at all. You know the feeling. It's the difference between a shaggy pony you go to sleep on and a lean stallion with a very bony spine. Up to about five minutes ago Agatha was enjoying the gallop in a sort of elated way but now she'd rather like to get off. She's not used to it. She usually spends a lot of her time gently bored on the shaggy pony. But I'm sorry, Ags. Sometimes plot gets hot. Right now it's very hot. It's like when Dorothy tests the iron by holding it near her cheek. Agatha touches her cheek. It's flushed. We're ready.

But. What would life be without buts? Top-heavy, I guess. OK.

But the dining-room door looks like it's closed for the duration of the human species. On the other side of it are her parents and her uncle, we know that. But she can't imagine this quiet family scene in candlelight without a whole load of stage smoke billowing around knees and sharp white fangs in the dark mouths that turn to greet her. She can hear a rumble of voices the other side of this door under some traffic clip-clopping past the other side of the front door. It's going echoey. She could hesitate here until hesitation turned into lassitude and lassitude turned into total inertia. The attractiveness of that prospect is awe-inspiring. But the dogs of fate have got her cornered. They're slavering and chomping at her shot silk. For William's sake she must outface them. She must throw them meat to deflect their hunger, their frightful rage, their wanton cruelty. She takes the last few stairs with an uncertain tread but at least she makes it to the lozenge chess-tiles and the peculiar cool echoey vault of the hallway. She sighs slightly, poised on the brink. The white enamel finish of the door is the blank sheet of her future, upon which no message is discernible. (Thank you, thank you. But don't clap between movements.)

Cutaway into the dining-room, please. Right through the wall, through the cutaway wall and up and along and round until we've an over-shoulder shot past Mrs Trevelyan's puffed taffeta of Mr Trevelyan which includes the door behind him. A complicated manœuvre, but one I used to be famed for in my Russell rip-off period. I do think it the most frightful bore, says Mrs Trevelyan. Uncle Kenneth clears his throat, not to speak but basically just to clear his throat. Maybe also to avoid having to say something. I don't know what

311

the thing that's a bore is but since it's one of Mrs Trevelyan's catch-phrases we needn't fret too much. It might be breeding Pekinese for a living, it might be the unfortunate exhibition at the Marlborough Gallery which made her giddy, it might be Lily's problem with the candlesticks – I don't know and I don't care and neither should you. We mustn't get distracted. This is a BIG SCENE. It'd be better if Zelda were here but writing into a void is better than not writing at all and descending into alcoholic dereliction. Did I say writing? Don't I mean filming? Oi oi – is the purity of my calling sullied already? Can't I just zip my big mouth for more than two minutes? If not why not? Is it a nervous problem? Am I suffering from logorrhoea as Zelda said Mr Lazenby pig-brain suggested good-humouredly once quite recently before she fell into his outsize trap, before she was pinned struggling on the end of his outsize dick?

Yuk. At least I can spell logorrhoea. Someone who can spell his own condition can't be too sick. I mean, most of us won't even have bleedin' *heard* of the condition that'll finally shut us up for good – the one some runtish little clerk'll copy carefully down in some unbelievably depressing room with an adjustable metal shelving system, as if black Quink and a Parker and an adjustable metal shelving system stuffed with the Files of the Dead make up for everything, for Christ's sake. I thought it was cancer, I remarked. I thought me mum died of cancer. It went on forever, the way he wrote it. Two words, one ending in us and the other in itis. There's a name for everything, mark. There's a name for the tightening of Uncle Ken's red lane and for the running sores under Mrs T's chin and for Mr Trevelyan's foot-happy way with Ruthie's moss and for what's happening right now to my great-aunt's guts as she poises on the brink with her hand on the knob. Diarrhoea would be too simple.

She'll be learning all this soon, y'know. All these sises and ismuses and itises and rrhoeas. And what with it being war there'll be so many on one body they're bound to miss a few, it'll be ever so messy and slapdash, there'll be conditions overlapping with other conditions and conditions so grave there'll be nothing left of the original owner and conditions for which medical science must have given a name to but nobody can find it slipping about in the blood as they are so they just invent one and add itis or ismus or rrrhoea on the end and bury them quick, hey ho. But I'm skipping. Agatha has no conception as she stands feeling the slightly slippy brass knob in her hand of WHAT HORRORS ARE TO ENGULF THE WORLD IN LESS THAN TEN MONTHS. Isn't that crazy? Don't we all just love that wickit little sense of Dramatic Irony when we see those old old films flickering merrily away, all those innocents bustling nattily along in their bustles and bodices and breeches or playing accordions in the picturesque ghettoes if we're talking of later, doesn't it just *so* excite us, stoodents of mine, think about it, discuss next week, more particly its use in any one o' Mr Hitchcock's works, the video library is open till five o'clock, now scram, you've got I see here Mr sorry *Dr* Todd H. Lazenby Jnr on Strategies of Demystification and Disruption in Brian de Palma's *The Untouchables* (1987), containing the doc's *pièce de résistance*, his Eisenstein cross-reference, the perambulator bouncing down the steps while everyone gets blown out of their huge lapels, isn't he amazing, so intelligent and elegant and original, the most obvious movie quote in movie history and Dr Lazenby's spotted it. Don't miss this class if you're a complete jerk.

Tosh, all tosh.

He wouldn't know what a barn door was if it trapped his dick, Jason. No, Mr Thornby? No, Jason. Fill 'er up, lad. Don't repeat me for Christ's sake. Don't repeat me. There's a good Englishman, there's a fine builder of bridges between nations, there's a worthy forger of links between the British National Party and the Ku-Klux-Klan, southern Texas branch.

Jason of the Largolouts. She used to chuckle at my jokes.

When we kissed, the hesitant flicker of her tongue in my mouth bespoke her youth. God I love her still. God? Hoi, I'm speakin' to yer, switch yer deaf-aid on and swivel yer Zimmer this way for once.

That's blown it. I'd better grope for Jesus if I don't want to end up less than cinders. Sometimes I feel like I know exactly what George feels. It's creepy.

Doomed. Aye, doomed.

She's coming in.

I mean Agatha my great-auntie, not Zennor or whatever her name still is. IjuswannasayveryquicklyihopeyouraspissedasIam, folks. Otherwise this might have gotten irrititus of the spleen or something.

She's comen in like the dewe on the flue.

Not quite, to be honest. She closed the door behind her with a degree of force unnecessary in the technical circumstances, everything being well-oiled and pretty well hand-constructed in this house. Bosey's needles jumped. It was a mistake. It was nerves. Right now she's just standing a little in front of the door, nor-nor-west of her father my great-grandfather's right shoulder and overlapping slightly with Mike's elbow so clear it, Avens yer bum.

Thank you.

I find these family occasions very difficult. I had a family once and now I just have a kind of testical familiarity with various photos pinned up in my kitchen so it's a shock to see the real thing, to see Greg with eye-bags or Maura with sagging breasts or Hilda *with* breasts. They never smile like they do in the photos. Here's a still of my kitchen pin-board. Still Ten or maybe Eleven, I can't keep count, I never watch my rushes. Go see it. Anyone'd think my family were beach bums but that's the way it is, everyone in family snaps is having a whale of a time on the beach or in front of castles or round a table with pink eyes but that's the flash, not the Australian turps. I look at this still and I think, hey, I created all this. All these good times, all these weird people with shifting hair and lousy cameras, they're to do with me and my sex drive. If it weren't for my sex drive my kitchen pin-board would be empty, or at least it'd have only the Rothkos and the Blackfoot calling an echo out of the canyon and the Houston Big One ticket and the garage bill and Dr Lazenby's face out of the HCDVA staff journal which I use for dart practice 'cos one day I'm gonna thrash Jason in the Green Man championships and the quote from Tarkovsky on the back of the Dunkin' Donut napkin and stuff. No, it wouldn't have the Lazenby picture. If it weren't for my sex drive I wouldn't have noticed the guy existed, probably, because he's indistinguishable from all the other

314

androids out here who jog and play tennis and work out and cheat their wives and think Robert Redford's their shaving mirror.

Go see my pin-board. If you think it has no place in a historical drama then you're wrong: these people are intimately related to the people who are sitting in this dining-room frowning and they're frowning not because me and the crew have suddenly become visible or audible, no – there ain't a cable or a lens in view, not a click or a shuffle in earshot, they're sealed tight in 1913 and we're behind the glass watching the bellies of the sharks swoop over us so close it makes us scream but don't worry, the glass'll never ever break, the water'll never ever gush out along with its sharks and sea-snakes and polyps and trilobites in long shot-silk skirts and top hats and detachable wing collars because the glass is not glass it's perspex, it's spun out of where you're at, we can even stick our tongues out and go nyaaaa.

OK? Right. Action. Take however many it takes. As was my famous hallmark phrase. I was a cocky bugger in them days, great days.

My dear, what is the matter? That's Mr Trevelyan, twisting round in his chair. Agatha attempts to swallow but her throat's pistons have grit in them. There is a jug of water on the table. She picks it up. Ah, Kenneth appears to be in on it, whatever it is, says Mrs Trevelyan. Mrs Trevelyan's uncoiling her venomous side. Actually, you'd have to be an invertebrate not to notice Uncle Ken's gaze fixed on his plate instead of on Agatha as it would have been if he had not been in on it or had been a less lousy actor and now his head jerks, a dead give-away, he doesn't know where to put his face because snake-woman is glinting in every shot – he grins ridiculously at the Victory figurine like he's admiring her breasts and snake-woman's this formless shadow on the edge, it's like the way he makes his ectoplasmic presences, controlled light spill, oh good grief the breasts are moving, it's blebs of candlelight sliding over them because Agatha is replacing the crystal jug, maybe he should be looking at her, he drops the grin like a curtain and looks at the base of this glass flaring the candlelight and her eyes closed above it.

Right, she's drinking. He has time to check up on his brother. The whites of his eyeballs show as he does so because he doesn't want to move his head, he doesn't want things to get more blurry than they are already. Arthur is blinking nervously. OK, he's blinking nervously because a goblin in his brain has its hand up, its suggesting that Ags is about to pull back the plush and show Ruthie Dunnet in a loose corset smoking. The goblin wears spectacles and has a book under its arm and looks as if he knows about these things. Mr Trevelyan stares hard at the winks and snatches of candlelight in the cut crystal of the base of the glass. Surely not, he thinks. He glances at his brother glancing at him. Oh good God. He thinks oh good God because the whites of his

317

brother's eyeballs get instantly closed down by a reflex action of contact-avoidance to use Zelda's phrase after this course she went on called, I dunno, *How To Open Up* or something, like you're a tin of cat-food, and it looks very suspicious. Ken is currently auditioning for the part of The Man Who Has No Idea What It Is He Might Be In On Even If He Were, but he hasn't got a hope of getting it. Surely to hell not, thinks Mr Trevelyan, surely to bloody hell-fire not. His wife is a black rock at the far end. He refuses to smash himself upon it, he steers his head back to Agatha. She is clasping her hands tightly in front of her and looking at the corner of the table ditto. At some point she must have put down the glass, we missed it, I can't do everything. It's William, she says, in a shaky voice. The little bespectacled goblin is taken outside to be tossed twenty-five times on the end of a hay-fork while Mr Trevelyan provides drinks all round and dancing long into the night gratis.

Oh? he says, frowning slightly, inclining his head forward, like he's releasing a mildly difficult turd. For those who don't know English people we're talking Pavlov here, it's a classic response to a very dramatic situation. Mrs Trevelyan is not classic, she'd have sent Pavlov screaming out the laboratory.

William? she cries.

Her sickly boy. Her favourite son. She can see the coffin draped in sable already, she'll have to order it and no flowers, the whole procession's disappearing down a vast chasm that used to be William, her lovely little boy and such hair, such eyes, such teeth!

William?

Her little cunning snaky construction has been demolished as decisively as Milly's slum will be in 1963, it's been replaced by an enormous tower-block of dread with broken lifts and Evelyn's piss-smell. I received a telephone call from the school, says her daughter, my great-aunt, William's sister, Hilda's great-great-great aunt. Hilda was the one waving a spade in the middle, next to the Rothko. Hiya, Hil. I hope you're still with us out there. You got her brains, baby.

318

A telephone call? quavers Mrs Trevelyan. She's blinking very rapidly. Her breath has gone into short supply. She was asleep, knocked out on tonic wine, for most of the afternoon. The telephone would not have woken her up. When? she demands. Mrs Trevelyan is a very demanding person, especially when she's nervous. When? comes out like the yap of an unpleasant little dog, something like my neighbour's which has a personal dislike of me and pisses against my garage door so I get wet when I swing it up. Agatha lets out a short sigh. This is going extremely well. It's going like clockwork, thinks Uncle Kenneth, smiling encouragingly at Agatha. He really is hopeless. He's smiling at her like she's doing a party turn or something, like she's reciting the whole of *Dream-Pedlary* by Thomas Love Beddoes – If there were dreams to sell, What would you buy? and so on. She stands in just the same way and recites it in the same sort of sing-song. OK, she's not a wonderful actress either, but Uncle Ken's not helping her. He should be screwing up his napkin with one hand and his face with the other, if you see what I mean. Or something less melodramatic, perhaps, less like the penny awfuls where they keep throwing their arms around and swooning just because Frankenstein's come out of the cupboard and more Stanislavskian, thinking about what he had for breakfast if he were playing this guy who hadn't spent the whole of luncheon discussing exactly what Agatha's now saying, and how to say it, and in what order. But he's lucky, because the small glinty part of Mrs Trevelyan that notices Uncle Kenneth practically mouthing Agatha's next line like some hopeless kid in a school play just thinks he's had too much sherry and wine and probably opium because the block of dread is overshadowing every damp mean slum of suspicion and she probably didn't unscrew her face-powder lid right. She's just flicking the day back to see if she can recall unscrewing the lid with three revolutions because if she did it with four or five that would explain it. That's why he's dead. That's why in the middle of a trigonometry class he just keeled over and went pale and passed away. But she can't recall anything revolutionary or devil-may-care in the way she took off the lid of her face powder.

Ye-es? comes from Mr Trevelyan. His goblin party is over and he's getting the hangover now, he's thinking maybe it's even worse, the goblin with the specs is to be replaced by a goblin in a black hood with skeletal fingers. He swallows reasonably successfully and wipes his top lip with a forefinger which smells of pea soup and eau-de-Cologne. Oh God comes from somewhere in his belly. Uncle Ken however is leaning forward and almost gesturing go on, you're doing jolly well, and I took the call, and – wow, he's so totally hopeless, but Agatha turns her face towards him and gives him a look of such incredible anguish that Uncle Ken momentarily believes it and sinks back into his chair. Agatha is good on looks but not so good on the lines. The reason she's looking at Uncle Ken with incredible anguish is that she's completely forgotten what comes next. She knew she should never have learnt it all by heart but Uncle Ken absolutely insisted at luncheon, he dipped his spoon into the raspberry jelly and insisted so absolutely he let go of the spoon which slowly disappeared from sight never to be seen again this side of the kitchen. Talking of downstairs, I ought to mention what the servants are doing upstairs. George has got his bottom teeth in front of his top teeth and his eyes are popping out because he's remembering Evelyn and William is his next favourite bairn and something's up wi' the wee one. Hey, does nobody like Giles, my grandfather Giles? Milly is looking mentally subnormal or challenged or whatever it's called in the corner, trying to work out what to do with the gravy boat she's holding because it's quite heavy but you never ever plonk a dish down when someone is making a speech. William is the young master she didn't spot going up the stairs but she'll turn out his room any road. The stuff is welling at the spout and she rights it. From where she is the young lady looks like a ghost. Now that's ironic.

Agatha is looking ghostlike for obvious reasons, one of them being the fact that she has dried up. If I'd thought about it I'd have brought a crib card and got Julie to hold it up by Camera Two ho ho. Now I think I've mentioned already – hey, cut the old ham bit, I *know* I've mentioned already – the fact that Agatha's favourite party-turn apart from playing Schumann's *Rêverie* on the piano-forte and singing one or two French folk songs is reciting Beddoes's *Dream-Pedlary*. I promise you this isn't a set-up. That's what she recited until recently, until Christmas 1912 to be precise. It's a great poem. Dr Lazenby had never heard of it or even of Thomas Lovell Beddoes because culturally-speaking he's a prime-time yob. Anyway, there's this great stanza in it all about raising the dead because that's the most expensive most desirable dream of all if the dead you wish to raise were desirable and how that really is just a

320

dream. Agatha looks at Uncle Kenneth but he isn't any help and then she looks at the room in general without pulling focus on anyone in particular and she just knows that everybody is hanging on her every word and if she screws it up now it'll be for ever but her brain is working overtime in the back recesses full of adjustable metal shelving and filing cabinets and the indefatigable little clerks with their little typewriters and rubber bands who can locate you anything if you can locate them and these are the guys who are yelling at each other with the red light flashing on off on off and the electric bell ringing and the telephones going which means a real emergency and there's this one little fella with a skin problem and a stutter who has just found the Beddoes file underneath a pile of Gamage's catalogues and he's waving this verse around and the guy on the trolley snatches it from him and hurls it into the suction tube and phhhooooit out it comes, clear as daylight, exactly as she always recites it, too high and too earnestly but still clear as daylight and with a heavily pregnant pause after *joy* and this kind of siren that turns out to be the vowels on *vain*—

> If there are ghosts to raise,
> What shall I call,
> Out of hell's murky haze,
> Heaven's blue hall?
> Raise my loved long-lost boy
> To lead me to his joy.
> There are no ghosts to raise;
> Out of death lead no ways;
> Vain is the call.

Uncle Kenneth brings his hands together but a single soft clap is not clapping and he gapes with his hands stuck together wondering if the whole caboodle has just skidded off the road or shot right ahead. Agatha doesn't say the last verse. She just wonders how to fill the next hole for about ten seconds until she hears the sobbing, the snorts from the other end of the table and realises that it has gone better than she could have dreamed of and it's all she can do to stop herself skipping on the spot. Uncle Kenneth turns round and watches Mrs Trevelyan looking remarkably unattractive as she quietly weeps and almost unsticks his hands and shakes them in the air as one does at a football match when a goal is scored. Mr Trevelyan is gazing at his napkin on his lap. His boy is dead. It is quite the most devastating news ever inflicted on his personage. Because Evelyn's was expected. It is worse even than if Agatha had told him Trevelyan Disinfectants & Antiseptics shares had completely collapsed and Izal and Sanitas had joined forces and conquered the subcontinent with their damn travelling packs and easy-to-carry pails. Just worse, because that would be confoundedly ghastly. But this is definitely ghastlier. He's trying to remember exactly what William looked like, because it's three months now since the trot down to Wiltshire and really since then he's been so confoundedly busy and of course school. His pictures of William are not up to date. In fact, some of them are as up to date as my pin-board pictures and one or two of them show Evelyn's face instead. The main one shows William on the lawn in the arms of the governess. Ah, the governess. Stroking the blond top of his boy lapped in her fragrance. When he lapped her she fled back to Switzerland and his wife started that queer thing. His wife is Mrs Beatrice Trevelyan. He has to remind himself sometimes. He raises his head a sufficient number of spinal notches to bring *noli me tangere* into view. She's a pale ovoid with glittery bits that are not all jewellery. There are glittery bits on her cheeks and on the tip of her nose and just underneath it and he thinks Beatrice. I'm sorry about the stuff glittering on her nose, I really hate that in the cinema because the screen is SO BIG but she's not going to wipe it, her hands are numb, out of it, neurasthenically traumatised, sleeping it off in her lap. Good God comes out of Mr Trevelyan like he's been punched in the belly. Then a groan because he's just remembered what Willo looked like, serving on the sloping court, not a bad swing, decent sportsman underneath it all, tolling of the bell, sunk too fast to call 'em down, no holding of his little hand in the Sanny, short quick gasps, not so little hand, quite big really, lifeless now, my son is dead with the golden top. There's a hole in the pale ovoid over there which is a mouth. His own is also open, he discovers. Grief is so damned ugly. His neck gives way and he has to catch his head before it rolls off onto the plate. His napkin takes a drop of nasal mucus in its stride just as the parquet takes the gravy-boat. This is the worst never ever shattered but no one reacts except Milly's feet. They have never been mutton before and the gravy is mucus warm. She dropped it through an involuntary action of her hands. Involuntary is my word, not hers. You can tell a lot about me from my use of the word involuntary. She wants to stoop to pick it up but the whole situation says don't stoop, don't stoop. Her feet remove themselves before they're eaten and she watches the gravy advance as if the world is on a slope but stays blank. George growls somewhere deep inside his throat, I don't know exactly where but it's deep, it's practically in his stomach, maybe it is his stomach. He's confused, awful confused, which is not surprising. The serving-maid has dropped the gravy-boat and the main course has been interrupted by a party turn and there's snortin' and snivellin' all over the shop and Uncle Queer-Arse is beaming from ear to ear. Basically, he's not at all certain what the fuck is happening. If someone could tell him what the fuck was happening he'd get the drap to mop up then take her down to the kitchen and welt some sense into her but he's not quite sure what the fuck is happening. He would like to switch on the electrics. If he switched on the electrics this carry-on wouldn't carry on. He doesnae ken it, he doesnae ken it at all. Not quite true. There's a little ken that kens it but it's been walled up by the rest of him, which is quick-dry cement. This wee ken is beating its fists against the wall but the wall is set rigid, glaring at the drap's ankles with the sauce all over them and aye he could eat 'em he could to the shapely bone. Amazingly but please take this on trust 'cos there are kids out there and the screen's SO BIG there's a wee mouse moving aneath his britches, fattening itself up on these ankles. If you find that gross or unlikely then I'm sorry, go watch the dead rockets bob on the water.

Talking of water, that's exactly what Agatha wants but if she takes another sip it'll be embarrassingly like her party turn so she works up some saliva instead. Because the snorting and snivelling is actually authentic she doesn't feel like skipping on the spot and saying oh yippee any more. What should happen now is questions. She glances at Uncle Kenneth, who is beaming from ear to ear. The telephone rings. The beam drops and on to Uncle Kenneth's toe apparently. Ouch, says Uncle Kenneth. The manservant racks his back as straight as it can go, which isn't very. Shall I take it, Miss Agatha? he says. Oh no, says Agatha. Oh no, don't. I shall take it. Mr Trevelyan seems to be nodding. It'll be the school, he says. Good God, it'll be the school. It'll be the school, good God. Why didn't you tell me earlier? comes out of the black hole in the pale ovoid. I have to take it, says Agatha. Uncle Kenneth has both hands on the table as if he's trying to stop it levitating and he's playing Uncle Kenneth Trying Not To Panic At The Unforeseen Intrusion very well. He'll get the part, no sweat. Why, why didn't you tell me earlier? Good God. I'll definitely take it. Oh dear from Uncle Kenneth. The rifle mike's a blur and Bosey's training for the London Marathon or something. The telephone's terrible, it's like an old alarm clock, even through the door it's loud. The crew're crashing into each other and binding each other up in cables and Mrs Trevelyan's getting terrible draughts. She shudders. Why, oh why didn't you? she wails. Suddenly the volume is awful, the whole situation is crazy, she's wailing and Mr Trevelyan's standing up and knocking his goblet over and saying good God it'll be the school and Agatha's trying to open the door the wrong way and Uncle Ken's slapping the table to keep order and Milly's just blank and George is doing his growling thing again and hey, let me out, all we need is Buñuel in here for the ceiling to pay a call.

But I'm not Buñuel.

I'm not Buñuel I'm Ricardo Thornbia, notorious once, married twice, forgotten thrice, celebrated part-owner of an Alfa Romeo 1750 Spider Veloce, low, streamlined and sporting, whose every move the paparazzi click their tongues at if only I could get it off the blocks. Why, oh why didn't God freeze-frame 1968 just before Jim Clark skidded and *Spangles & Starburst* crashed in jeers at Cannes? Ah, Ossy me old chum – remember them hairpins above the azure Med's glitter, Louisa's headscarf turned into a wind-sock, her sunglasses audition-ing me in Technicolor as she turned and stuck her tongue out and I said hadn't you better watch the road because she was crazy, I was a coward, I never had the guts to just enjoy going over the edge practically give or take a sprig of thyme here and there like you had, Ossy, like Louisa, like the rest of our gang who didn't want to grow old anyway, who thought I was already practically behind a Zimmer frame because I didn't know the words to *Penny Lane* or was it *Arnold Lane* and would quite like to be sending postcards when I'm sixty-four instead of cheering every time one or two of the perforated disc wheels around carefully buffed hub-caps mirrored nothing but the far blue horizon with distant yacht and the rubber trying to get a grip on a hundred feet of air? Hey, was it surprising I never jived the night away when all you sods did was tease me about the way I gripped the windscreen frame and said oh God oh God oh God? I realise this now

324

– you always put me on the worst side, the side facing the sea, I don't think you realised about my vertigo but if you did realise you're all even bigger bastards than I thought you were then and anyway I got the girl, I stroked the pussy-cat, I freaked out on the taste of her Lauren Bacalls, OK?

Sometimes I think it would have been better actually to have gone over.

How about that?

Well, guv, when I'm back in London I open up the arm and a leg of a rented ten square foot of garidge in Hendon and give the hubcaps a wipe until I see my face and each time I'm older but the Alfa isn't, Greg wants her, but I'm hoping Hilda'll take it because she wears these great headscarves and has the right Polaroids and anyway Greg'll just throw her into a quarry or cover her in plaster of Paris and call it *Occurrence #3* or something. I'm talking about the Alfa, not Hilda. I have these dreams where the Alfa's being winched up out of the sea and Louisa's in it but she's all bone, she's all picked clean and there are thousands of people watching from the cliff, jeering in French. Or maybe they're cheering and can't pronounce it properly. The Alfa'll survive us all, accruing, accruing in value even if I don't so much as touch it wiv an adjustable. Isn't that a crazy thought? I wish I were accruing in value. I sign the paper tablecovers in Dunkin' Donads and they make me pay extra. I tell them I don't like your doughnuts anyway they have holes in, they remind me of lavatories. Then I tell them in England they don't have holes in. Neither do the doughnuts. We invent the complicated bits first, that's our way, we're geniuses, we're above holes, we've put the ugh in doughnuts. We get a lot of splash-back but then we're not fussy. By now I'm saying this outside the door, I'm yelling it actually, the security guy is calming everyone down with his Magnum, get back to ya donuts, folks, get back to ya dunkin', it's OK, he's not armed. Shit, what a life. To be taken for a psychopath when all I'm really telling them is I am slain by a fair cruel maid and he only lives that deadly is in love. Sometimes I just tell them that but they still scream. No one here speaks the RSC's English, there's the rub. Cor blimey blow me down what a load o' cobbler's awls. Nah where was I, guv?

The telephone. Sorry about that interlude. I hope it gave you some time to visit the toilet or some fresh twenty-first-century air. I mean, it's not been fouled up yet, has it? It's not been fouled up. Unless you've been working real quick. Cordite, I guess, from the fireworks. Booze belches. Smoke out of people's insides. A lot of radiation from all those power stations swilling around in vodka right at this moment. (Your moment, I mean. And probably my moment back now if we only savvied it, mate. I'll 'ave an 'arf, ta. Yeah, if we only savvied what went on we'd all call it a day, mate. All call it a day. Ta, mate. Cheers. Seen me Black Spot anywhere? Ha haaar.) Hey, I hope you've found your seat. Hi again. If you've missed anything, don't worry. It was vital. But don't worry. Worry gets you nowhere. You've probably just missed meeting the person who will make you happy for the rest of your long life together. You looked the wrong way at the right second. Blame your neck-muscles. Blame the bore who called out to you to come tell them all about Switzerland. Who is the same, which at my window peepes? Or whose is that faire face, that shines so bright, Is it not Cinthia, she that never sleepes?

Almost certainly. Raped by a wolf in sheep's clothing. Hey, one small step for mankind. I know my mythology, I know my poetry, I'm extremely cultured, I call my jeans Frank Levis and my goldfish Stendhal 'cos it's red and black. I used to be into anthroposophy. Greg and Maura went to an anthropoposopical Rudolf the Brown-Nose Steiner school and look what it did to them. I've spent the last half an hour trying to say anthropoposoc whatever the fuck it is, I used to say anthrax, I've had to change to a dry shirt. It's a great test of inebriation. You can only say it if you're inebriated. Anthrax. So I can have another one, or two. Cheers.

The telephone.

THE TELEPHONE.

Look, I'm really fucked. Basically what happened is Agatha got to the phone and it was fucking Boulter. At first she couldn't get her tongue back into her mouth from wherever it was hiding but by the time she did Boulter had finished telling her about the articles belonging to your son being placed on the 8.15 London & South Western from Basingstoke non-stop to Waterloo tomorrow and was sending white

326

noise down the mouthpiece which was him belching from nerves. Because, let's face it, after having

Mr Trevelyan is standing right there. I mean right behind Agatha. He's grabbing at the phone. It's because Agatha's tongue said good evening Mr Boulter before she could stop it. Mr Trevelyan regards Mr Boulter as a fine sort of chap because he uses Trevelyan Disinfectant to swab the corridors and Trevelyan Antiseptic to swab the sick and welted. There's a brief tussle between father and daughter which is totally silent apart from the echoey scuffles and squeak of shoe-leather on highly-polished ceramic. If we can turn ourselves into sound waves for a moment and pound along the wire we'll get out the other end without having to hire a jalopy but remember to duck because there's this giant pile-driver which is Mr Boulter's finger tapping the earpiece. Hey, it's quiet in here, you can relax. The boys are in Study Hour. Mr Boulter likes this hour. He drinks in it. Actually, if we could go over to Upper School Library for a second and just peep in through the door to see them at Study the silence would be kind of broken because the prefects have not yet arrived and we'd probably either be lynched on the ends of some ties or at the very least get Volume Three of Gibbon's great work in the mouth and a buttered bun on the lens so let's not, let's just enjoy the quiet in Boulter's room.

Aaah. We're no longer sound waves, by the way, Ossy. You can take your carton off now, it's losing its milk-bottle tops, it reminds me of your amazing designs for *Dig It*. Well tried. Aaah.

He's tapping away at the earpiece again, scowling. Maybe we should be back in Albermarle Terrace. There's not a lot going on in here. Maybe he'll offer us some of that veteran port. It's all over his whiskers. I hope he sucks it off. I hope he develops cirrhosis of the liver pretty soon, sucking all that port off of his whiskers.

Ah. There's a voice, at the other end. It sounds like a duck speaking Japanese but Bosey's getting a directional mike on it, don't worry. Relax. These are really comfy old sunken armchairs. They're made like this by Public School Supplies Inc. It's in their Period Headmaster's Study range. They come complete with bloodstains and dog hairs and pipe-ember burns and butterflies-in-the-stomach. But I am

327

not at this school. I AM NOT AT THIS SCHOOL. I try telling myself that in my dreams but I don't believe myself. I go to night school every night. I wake up exhausted. I've taken more exams than all the Japs put together. I'm disappearing into this fucking armchair. It smells of one hundred volumes of Queen Victoria's memoirs. Bosey, get that mike fixed quick. Ah, we have it. I'd have nipped back to London by steam train but this film's shoestring, it's crazy, even *Clive's Seasons* had proper laces. Shaddap.

ing.

Indeed, Mr Trevelyan. I understand your sorrow. The affair is most unfortunate.

Unfortunate, Headmaster? Is that all it is?

Unfortunate, yes. But remember, if I may be so bold, the action of Diogenes. Who struck the father, sir, when the son swore. Burton's *Anatomy*.

The allusion escapes me, Headmaster. I have lost a son. It is not surprising.

Never lost, never lost. Say not good night but in some brighter clime bid me good morning and all that, what?

Your – your tone, sir, dash it, strikes me as somewhat airy for the leaden hour. You will soon be firing off at me how the darkest one is just before dawn or when bale is highest—

Then I will be more to the point, risking bluntness. I urge you, sir, not to spare the rod. One must never forget the *facilis descensus Averni*.

Confound it, sir—

Uncuff and pull back and birch the rottenness out of him. For he is too soft, Mr Trevelyan, he is too soft and that is, if neglected, fatal. A disease known is half cured, as we say. We do know the disease. Alas, we do. My advice only, of course. Take it or not. Now his effects, as I mentioned to Mrs—

328

What the Devil are you blithering on about, sir?

Blithering, sir?

Blithering, sir. Your tone does not fit the circumstances. Indeed, I do not catch your drift at all. If you're speaking of the late condition of his lungs—

Lungs?

The softness of his chest, as it were—

Facts are stubborn things, Mr Trevelyan. I speak of the softness of his heart.

Ah, his heart!

High shriek from Mrs Trevelyan just detectable as backing track. Great stuff, Bosey.

Yes indeed, Mr Trevelyan. Dig deep, dig deep. To root out such a weakness, the blow must be very hard.

It is, it is.

Good.

Good, sir?

I say it is good. The harder the better.

I take that exceeding ill, sir.

I am sorry you take so ill, sir, such amount of disinterested advice as your son's nurse – for that is what I was, in a manner of speaking – can, indeed must, peculiarly proffer. A good, hard, rugged nurse, Mr Trevelyan. Rods of iron have no slack. Christ, something in Ancient Greek. Or, as Herodotus put it of the fleet at—

329

Once again your drift, sir, quite escapes me—

I speak of the unfortunate battle of Lade, between the Persians and the combined fleets of the Ionians, the Samians and the Lesbians. Sounds great, huh? Bosey's giggling. Shaddap. You know, of course, why the Greeks were routed, sir? They were routed because they refused to submit to a few days of rigid discipline. Something too quick in Latin, shit. They made their choice freely. They freely chose a lifetime of slavery over a week of slavery, sir. They preferred to live soft and good gracious how they paid for it. I am, as you may know, sir, an Old Sedberghian. And Sedbergh's motto is *dura virum nutrix*. Homer's description of Ithaca, Mr Trevelyan, rendered into the Latin for those ignorant of the Greek. It has held me steady, sir, throughout my life. The thick and the thin. Ha yes. *Dura virum nutrix*.

Sorry about these fossilised bits. I hope Hilda's relaying what *dura virum nutrix* means. OK, something like a cold bath and a ten-mile run in driving hail and a spot of self-flagellation is better for you than a six-pack of Guinness, twenty Rothmans, a great long-play video and a couch. Mr Trevelyan's totally gobsmacked. I just want to say in the pause how really wonderful Mr Sparta 1913 looks while he's saying *dura virum nutrix*. Really wonderful. I mean, take those ginger whiskers. When he gets excited there are these little blebs of spittle all over them. He's also got very round shoulders and he's blubbery. If you took a rod of iron to him he'd just splash. I don't want to kind of prejudice you because this movie's liberal and tolerant and wishy-washy but I thought I ought to fill you in. Just in case his speech about the Greeks and stuff was making you sit straighter or something. I'm sitting very unstraight. In fact, I'm getting bad curvature of the spine down here. I'm a real A1 Ionian. If I'd been born in Sparta I definitely wouldn't have been the amazing success that I am. I'd have been

Sir?

I do not get your drift one iota.

Then my words have been cast upon the wind, alas. As for your other son, sir, he has given neither cause nor opportunity for reprobation. A quiet, but steady sort of feller.

330

While my great-grandfather's getting his broccoli around that one it's just worth explaining that Big Cunt is mentioning my grandfather in case Mr Trevelyan feels moved to remove him which would be a nasty little dent in the school's finances what with the recent losses from killer stuff like 'flu and cut thumbs and the latest outbreak of Randle Cholera courtesy of the antique sewerage system and of course Trevelyan Minimus's exit. As the Bursar has put it many a time: fees *alere flammam*, General. It'd have been neater as fees to feed the flame but the Bursar has no ear and wants to make people think he's educated. He isn't. Actually, he's pretty innumerate. He counts on his fingers but the little one was taken off by Gordon of Khartoum's pet chihuahua or something in 1884 so the accounts are all way out. Heck, you don't believe me. I tell you, this place is a nut-house. Even the mashed turnips smell reminds me. Of where Louisa ended up, I mean. Just in case you were thinking I'd had a spell within as well or something. Give over, mate, give over!

bation? What the deuce do you mean, reprobation? What the devil do you intend by it, sir?

Boulter's got a frown on and he's picking his nose really thoughtfully. He always does this when he concentrates. It can get embarrassing in class. His whole finger just disappears sometimes when there's a knotty bit of Theocritus to deal with. But no one, absolutely no one, sniggers. Weird, huh? His finger's coming out. OK, guys, duck.

Phlegmy clearing of throat. I use the term, sir, in its censuring sense. Ah, of course, you have not examined the offending evidence.

Sir?

The pictures, sir.

The pictures?

The pictures, sir.

What pictures, sir?

331

The, ah, *the* pictures.

Christ, this conversation's not exactly the M4, guv. Merry Old Oldsmobile, son. Average speed eighteen to twenty-four m.p.h. The Post Office must be laughing all the way to the banco. I hope they improve things with the profit, I hope they get rid of the guys frying their sausages on the cables or whatever. Hey, Boulter's hand is trembling. It's good to see him suffer a little. He was hoping he wouldn't have to cover this ground. It's rocky. No, it's swampy. Bosey's doing a great job in the circumstances, getting cramp and stuff. Mike's got a 500w kicker on Big Cunt which is getting a nice sheen off the phone's nickel-plated metalwork. Wish I could nickel it, nudge nudge. It'd go a bomb down in Houston. The repro

pictures I assumed by now, clearly erroneously, the content of which would have been imagined by you sufficiently clearly to have needed no illuminating additional discourse therewith. Sir.

You – you speak of certain articles of a pictorial nature belonging to my late son, I take it?

By him, sir. Engendered, as one may put it, by him. Art of a sort, sir. Your son was an artist in his time here, of the stripling Bohemian type. Did you – did you – did you by any chance just now use the term late, sir?

I did. Any objection?

Only that I am of the opinion that it is a word causing a deal of confusion. I tell my pupils to keep off late unless in the sense of tardy or – or – and ah, what is more, your son held no position. *Quondam* is a very useful—

Good God, sir! We're having a lesson in grammaticals now, are we? *Quondam? Quondam?* Will *quondam* do? Would God I had died for thee, O Absalom, my *quondam* son! Piffle! All piffle!

Boulter clicks. The penny's dropped. A whole new area of his brain starts whirring. It makes him dribble on to his whiskers. He sees a break in the crackles and makes for it.

332

Good gracious. How very – how very unfortunate.

There's unfortunate again! Confound it, sir, your attitude is most disagreeable. I can only think you are quite inebriated.

Inebriated, sir?

Inebriated, sir. That, or of a most cruel disposition, that takes its pleasure in twisting the knife. Twisting the knife, sir.

Dead right, me old chap, on both counts. Inebriated *and* a right bastard. Well done. Boulter's tongue appears like a nervous water-rat's snout in the foam-flecked tangle of his beard. Thank you.

When, ah, exactly how and when did your son, ah, ah, pass, ah – away, Mr Trevelyan?

He's wiping his brow clear of some really impressive sweat-drops. He's shaking. He's thinking that perhaps it'll be said that he went rather too far. Delicate boy. Shame, remorse. A hammer to a pin. There might be a scandal. Good God, there might be a fall in numbers. The Bursar will wave his Mahdi scimitar around again and one'll have to take cover. My back's going straight. I'm half out of the chair. This is enjoyable.

Am I to understand, sir, that you are unaware of the exact circumstances of his – my dear son's – passing away into a better life?

Oh. Oh no. I am. Indeed I am quite wholly ignorant of the fact. Quite, quite ignorant, sir.

Mr Boulter wants to swoon. He's taking a swig of 1908 Old Ruby straight from the neck. Mr Trevelyan gets an earful of Big Cunt's oesophagus flushing. Bosey's eyebrows go up. He's not had such a great time since he recorded the Niagara Falls for Brian Eno. Or someone.

I – I find – I find that most confoundedly odd, sir. Nay, I find it shocking.

Good gracious, how should I have known? I have received no call from you since my own this morning! This morning! Only this morning!

Careful, Boulter, you're into your whine mode. You're also tipping your transmitter and it ain't gonna work properly if you do that. That's better. Keep a hold on yourself. Durex virus neuters or whatever it is.

own this morning, sir?

My own this morning!

Dash it, we received no call from you this morning—

Ha, beg to differ. I talked to your – to Mrs Trevelyan. Deuce, to the boy's mother, sir.

You talked to my wife?

No, I talked – yes, yes, the same. I assume the same.

Ah.

You know what he's thinking. He's thinking that Beatrice was pissed again and too *hors de combat* to remember receiving the call or maybe she blanked out from the shock.

Are you – are you absolutely certain you talked to my wife, sir? To Mrs Beatrice Flora Barkiss Trevelyan, sir?

OK, I was wrong. He's Mr Smartie-Pants 1913. Sorry.

As certain as one can ever be, sir, at the other end of a telephone apparatus and with an ignorance of the full appellative of she who certainly and without a shadow of a doubt claimed to be your wife, sir. The wind, the wind.

Coincidentally Boulter lifts his bottom and releases a pocket of it. Bosey gags practically but sticks to his post.

Then, sir, I think you are mistaken. She who is most certainly my dear wife has made no mention whatsoever of having received a call from you, Headmaster. I doubt in the circumstances she would have forgotten it.

Ah. Then either I was mistaken or – or fooled by an imposter!

There are no imposters in this household, sir. It was undoubtedly my daughter you spoke to and who took the message from you. She was too upset to tell us immediately. She has just done so. She has done so in a befitting manner, sir. In stark contrast to the manner in which you have conducted yourself in this wholly tragic business, Headmaster.

Tragic indeed, sir, if he has as you say passed to a considerably greater weigher of souls than I.

Hey, don't get too modest, Boulter babe. It doesn't suit you, it really doesn't.

I think we can assume that he has gone thitherward.

Of course, of course. Good gracious oh dear me. A most unfortunate business.

Unfortunate again?

Unfortunate, yes.

Oh no, oh no. This conversation is on a LOOP. Hey, let me out, they're getting nowhere quickly, it's like listening to a spaghetti junction or something. But you get the idea. Boulter thinks Trevelyan Minimus has topped himself and the bastard feels bad about it in various ways while Trevelyan Extra Maximus thinks Willo succumbed to some lung thing overnight and Boulter's abreacting or just lush. I think a résumé is necessary because traffic is very boring to listen to, especially when it's looped. Now let's out. I'm feeling my claustrophobia coming on. I need a drink. Bosey mate, leave the guy his port, it'll give you a headache, it's been there nearly a century. Like the

335

conversation. Like the phone. Like the *Titanic*. Like the 1 in 5 deck of the *Titanic* and the guys all singing on the prow.

Last one to slide off please kill the lights.

Hope the period puddings are something to write home about. Leave me a couple of éclairs and a chunk of sago because down our way the sago's cold. Dorothy had made this great sago pudding and for once she'd chopped the beef suet finely enough and not completely smothered it in powdered loaf-sugar and even the custard was not too lumpy. But no one apart from Uncle Kenneth's touched it. Lily's come back down saying there's still some to-do on the telephone and memsahib's having one of her squalls and George's tic is back after a long time in hibernation. The sago has to be eaten straight off or it goes kind of quick-dry cementish but only Uncle Kenneth's touching it. Dorothy is more than a mite upset. She was already a mite upset because of the potatoes complaint George was really careful to pass on to Lily when Lily came up to clear the decks of the mutton course trying not to notice Miss Trevelyan and Mr Trevelyan grappling in the hall because if they murder each other it'll be in the papers and it never does to open yer mouf more'n you can get a farving in let the ticking clock guide the boiling crock see no evil hear no evil speak no evil busybodies never have anything to do stewed cheese and onions good for sound sleep and bunions.

Hey, don't snigger, we all have our little tags, our chapbooks, our

Good Things Said For Every Home And Household. I mean, I do. Like: *How hide from oneself the fact that it all winds up on a rectangle of white fabric hung on a wall?* (*See your film as a surface to cover.*) (Thank you, M. Bresson). Or: *Not artful, but agile* (thank you again, Robert). Or: *Shooting. Agony of making sure not to let slip any part of what I merely glimpse, of what I perhaps do not yet see and shall only later be able to see.* (Same guy. I'm flicking through my red leather notebook and it's in alphabetical order. It's Cocteau next. There are two hundred and twenty pages. It's all really serious, OK? No Hollywood gags, no immortal bitching, no Howard Hughes on the very simple engineering problem of Jane Russell's brassière or Groucho Marx on being around so long he knew Doris Day before she was a virgin or Mae West on a hard man being good to find and that kind of wisecrack bumper-sticker stuff Dr Lazenby learns carefully by heart to make young girls' breasts wiggle up and down behind their wet T-shirts which reminds him of Joe Pasternak on Esther Williams [*Wet, she was a star*, dumbos. Where have y'all bin this century?]. I never lend my chapbook, old chap. It's been buckled by the sun or maybe the rain. Zelda once said that it shows a basic insecurity in me. I replied Zelda, *No psychology – of the kind which discovers only what it can explain.* She said there you go, you can only reply in italics. Try to believe in yourself a bit more, find the inner voice, the core thing, the silence. I replied Zelda honey, *Debussy himself used to play with the piano's lid down.* I have eleven more pages of Bresson. No wonder people think I'm a genius.)

Mr Trevelyan's just come off the phone. You could take a mould for a new Western Electric Company earpiece off of his ear. He's white. Agatha is also white. Whiter than usual, I mean, which is very white indeed because getting a tan is something only the agricultural labourer does at this time and anyway it's November. They're back in the dining-room staring at this glass bowl full of sago and custard. No one's said anything for a few minutes. Agatha's finding the sago and custard incredibly de-inspiring. It seems to be weighing on her brain as it usually weighs on her stomach. As a matter of fact, this is a projection on her part. Life in England in 1913 is fairly sagoey. I suppose life in England has been and always will be fairly sagoey. Sagoey the way Dorothy makes sago, anyway. So it's not the sago that's lumping around Agatha's brain so much as the brain lumping around the sago. Although I reckon that if you had to keep going off a diet of stuff like jugged hare and broiled rumpsteaks and cold beef with Yorkshire Relish and suet pudding when the sago's off and hashed mutton from yesterday's boiled leg of mutton in a quart of brown gravy and beef-and-potato pie as a nice change from fish cakes followed up by a touch of tapioca or maybe macaroni with black treacle on it – hey, you wouldn't exactly be feeling light on your toes, would you?

Mr Trevelyan's had to sit down. Agatha has sat down because, hey, she just did – it's uncomfortable being the only one vertical except the servants who are always either vertical or stooped or on their knees. Mrs Trevelyan's about to blow her nose in a small square of embroidered chiffon which is the 1913 equivalent of those pink paper tissues that disappear like candy floss the minute they touch any nasal mucus. Uncle Kenneth is eating some sago. His stomach always comes first, as he jokes, because actually physically speaking it does. He's like General Sam Houston who had to wear a girdle to stop it spilling over his dick. And I live somewhere named after this gross slaughterer of the indigenous peoples. Otherwise Uncle Kenneth bears no resemblance to General Houston. For a start off, he'd be a catastrophic general. I know, I know, in ten months' time that'd be just fine but you know what I mean. He never does the appropriate thing. That's why I like him. The point is, we should've stuck with the phone conversation because it became transparently obvious towards the end, just after we quit and hailed a Basingstoke-bound dung-cart that there had been some serious miscommunication. That's the story of my life, actually. I never stick it out quite long enough. I mean, I nearly got almost blown up once but I left the hotel about a day too soon. I was on vacation in Sri Lanka and it would've made a great dining-out story and, OK, no one was killed, but I could've got shaken and stirred and maybe taken a few cuts here and there and it would've improved my self-image. But saying you missed it by a day doesn't exactly get the forks clattering on the plates. It's like National Service. I just missed National Service by the time Awxford had bin and gawn and my carefully-rehearsed mental problems had cleared up but I wish now I hadn't. Zelda was amazed that I'd never been a soldier with my musket fife and drum. She reckoned I must have been at least a Desert Rat or stumbled up a few French beaches under withering fire or whatever. Yeah yeah, guv, you've guessed it. Dr Turdsville was in Vietnam. He was a fifteen-year-old conscript or something and went

340

through Hell and unfortunately out again the other side. He's seen things, said Zelda. Ricky, he's really seen things you and I will never understand. Uh-huh? Uh-huh. Well, he probably killed people, Zelda. Mi Lai and stuff. You never know. Women and children, babies, pet kittens. They were all stoned. I've seen the film. Yeah, she said, looking like a kid who's just seen Arnold Schwarzenegger for the first time and has got him confused with Arthur Schopenhauer. Yeah, we'll just never understand what the guy's had to suffer, Rick. Holy shit, it's that mothering thing, you know? She thinks she's Jane Fonda or somebody. I tried to get this damaged look in my eyes and pulled down my mouth and started murmuring meaningfully about the Blitz except that I have no personal memory of the Blitz, it stopped about a day before I was old enough and anyway I was knee-high in cow-dung near Llansantffraed Cwmdeuddwr never getting beyond the new address in my letters home while John Boorman was running around in shorts and sepia tones in what was left of Poplar or wherever and something about the poor old Jacksons next door and their dog – I can't go into it now – got Zelda into hysterics. Every time I opened my mouth I felt like an Osbert Lancaster cartoon. That was the last time we lay with each other. Now the damaged look's real. Maybe it's the hashish. Mrs Trevelyan's blown her nose. All Clear. Shaaaddaaap.

think I wish to ruin your digestion, Kenneth.

I do not, I certainly do not. I've always been something of a sago chap. It goes down very easy—

Preposterous. The whole thing is spiteful and preposterous. That is all, at present, I can manage. One would have thought shame would have impelled a certain loss of appetite, if nothing else.

Hunger makes the best sauce, my dear.

Of two evils the lesser has been chosen, Beatrice. It goes without saying that I for one feel considerable relief.

Then why say it, Arthur?

Because it might be forgot, otherwise, in the rush towards the new situation.

I am rushing absolutely nowhere. I am too debilitated, my nerves are shattered, I have made a great fool of myself in front of the servants—

Mother, William lives! Does that not outweigh all other considerations?

I think you did it quite deliberately.

Did what, Mother?

Chhum chhum, my dhear sish—

To try to conceal faults is but to add to them, brother-in-law. A pity that does not extend to speaking with your mouth full of pudding.

I did not do it deliberately, Mother.

Agatha is crossing her fingers under the table, just in case you were worried there. Uncle Kenneth has swallowed his last dollop and is wiping his mouth on his napkin for once. George and Milly are clearing up the gravy and the wreck of its boat in dead silence, like they're doing it underwater. At least, Milly is, down on her knees, bottom in the air. George just watches, bent over a bit, with his gargoyle look shifted around by the fire, looking like he's in the opening minute of *The Maid's Seduction* by Charles Pathé or whoever. He'll be placing his hand-tinted hand on her apron ties in a second, then'll bunch her skirt and petticoats right up and on to her back and tickle the hand-tinted globes poking out of her open knickers like he's testing a very large apricot and maybe she'll turn her head round and smile at the camera and FIN will flicker up and the screen go white and this cute little classic'll end up being flapped at hopelessly by a projectionist who was careless with his roll-up and charcoaling a secret cinema around 1921. I lie, I lie – George is way too ugly for a cellulose nitrate skin-flick. He's Charlie Laughton. He's way-over-budget unfinished epic. We're lucky to have him.

Mr Trevelyan's hands are flat on the table, as if he's about to get up. But he isn't. If all these people were aeroplanes their altimeters'd be going like windscreen wipers. What I mean is, they're kind of up and down simultaneously and desperate to land someplace if only the alpine crags'd stop looming. Wheeeeeeeeaaaaahhh.

Please, don't be cross, Mother.

Now if I was Mother my heart'd go from stone to maple syrup as quickly as it takes Dorothy to turn blancmange powder into blancmange, which is pretty quick. But I am not Mother I am great-nephew, and never heard Agatha say please don't be cross great-nephew, because I missed her by about twenty years, which is a big miss but not a lot when you take into consideration the six million of them we've been loping around for. Mother is Mother. And it doesn't matter what the hell you hit her heart with it just stays stony. Sure, it fizzes and sparks and gives off belching clouds of green smoke like something I remember doing once upon a time in a chemistry class but when you've opened the windows and gagged and waved all that stuff out until the lab clears you've got the same basic stuff intact. It's very depressing. So Mrs Trevelyan just fixes Imploring by Burne-Jones with to put it basically a look from the Extremely Nasty range and says:

Do try, my dear, to act the adult now and again.

Phew! What a scorcher!

Imploring by Burne-Jones turns into St Sebastian by I dunno Goya and needs its blisters repairing. OK, quit the gallery, Ricardo. Agatha's face is hot, she only just manages to prevent an excess of salt water by widening her eyelids so it gets soaked up by her eyeballs or something and emits a short sigh. This is not going at all well. In fact, it's going frightfully awfully badly as Custer did not say during his Last Stand. When I think of Custer I smell vomit, it's complicated, my daughter couldn't take the whoopings on the wide screen, I bought an ice cream afterwards, or maybe two, with chocolate flakes sticking out of them, I totally spoiled her and now she hates me. The decent forces are always getting routed by the forces of spite and bitterness led by General Ill-Will. Custer's Cock-Up was an exception. And they don't even know that William is up in the attic waiting for his grand entrance. It'll be a grand exit at this rate, like the second cousin once removed who was very much removed. Papa is a better bet. She turns to Papa.

I only did what I thought right, Papa. It was to – to soften the blow. I never imagined—

To frighten a fowl is not the way to catch it, my dear.

But Papa, I didn't mean to frighten!

This is actually going catastrophically, thanks to Boulter's call. Uncle Kenneth lets a sagoey belch out the secret way, through his nostrils. Mrs Trevelyan turns round and flicks her hand at the servants. This means piss off, basically. George ratches himself upright and growls at the wee milt. The wee milt nods and picks up the tin bowl into which the gravy and wreckage have been interred and stands up and blinks. There's nothing hand-tinted about her. The smell of Dorothy's gravy is the most unerotic odour ever devised. For about a century all you can hear is two pairs of shoes making for the door at a respectable pace. George willnae scarper for no one. Butlers niver scarper. They hold their heads high and sedate and stuff. The door closes. Everyone breathes out audibly in the life-saving realisation that they haven't performed this function for about a century. Inadvertently Uncle Kenneth breaks wind. He does something fussy with his napkin to cover it. It looks like he's waving the pocket of gas away, but he didn't mean it to look like that. A lot of things he does are inadvertent. I wish I was more like Uncle Kenneth. I'm a very advertent person, but I still end up screwing things. Screwing things inadvertently is better. I won't go into this now.

Mrs Trevelyan's face is causing Gordon on Camera Two some big hassles. Have I mentioned Gordon, Gordon the Great Grip? My oversight if I haven't. Also, we were never close. I was never close to my grips. They didn't have to do much except grip the camera and move it where I told them to, or not move it at all in my Antonioni phase. They all wanted to pan and travel every other shot, because they were bored, they barely had to grip. I said *This is to separate the eye from the body. One should not use the camera as if it were a broom.* Oh yeah, guv, oh yeah? If only I had believed in myself more. If only I had thrown myself at Robert Bresson's feet and cried, *Je serais votre garçon du thé si vous teach me everything you know*, then about ten years later come out forged in a new likeness but not just Robert Bresson Jnr, *non* – by then I'd have outgrown my master and got my own megaphone. Instead I just went and let the grips do their travels and pans and zooms snickering up the tracking rails and thought, hey, Orson Welles hose-piped like crazy, Tarkovsky pans like he's looking for his car keys, it can't be that bad. I had no belief in myself. I kept borrowing drums and banging them, telling myself they were my own. Did I hear some yob cheers out there? Is out there still inhabited in these early late hours? Sorry, I was on about Mrs T's face. The hash does terrible things to the way you say terrible. My great-grandmother's visage vaguely resembles the other Mrs T's visage about a second before the other Mrs T sank the *Belgrano*. I repeat. The other Mrs T sank the *Belgrano*.

You ready out there for a relevatory revelation?

It's a crime-reality clip, man. Here goes. We're in Buckinghamshire, England. We're peeping through some beeches at this cosy little mansion with nice red roses in front of it. This is Chequers. Chequers is what the Trevelyans shout when they check in chequer but there's no connection. The Attorney General's just whipped open the door of the PM's study having dissolved the speed limit down the M40 and up the A4010 and got most of the gravel drive into the red rose beds and She turns round and fires this question at him about whether it's legally illegal to sink a hostile ship heading hostilely towards the Exclusion Zone'n Our Brave Boys and the AG looks like he's swallowed the door-knob which is actually still in his hand and after a few seconds of non-thought in the full glare of Her glare he says um no in a kind of extra-dry sherry sort of way and is about to add several ring binders worth of caveats when she picks up the telephone receiver and shouts Sink It so loudly the AG practically salutes and it's his joke *Sieg Heil* type for whenever She's the other end of the line.

Wars start in all kinds of weird ways, but that's one of the weirdest, folks.

You know who told me that? A judge. A judge on a plane. I travelled

345

First Class in those days and they had those posh lounges, remember remember? You probably don't remember because you were jemmied into Economy Class getting to know your knees intimately if only you could focus that close or fumbling for your crusts but I promise you they did, it was in the swollen lump on the top, I used to worry about what would happen to us if the pilot decided to fly under a bridge or something. I used to worry a lot in those days. Anyway, Judge Bollocks and I were spread out all through the polar night in these huge armchairs up in the lounge pod of a 747 working our way quickly through several gift-packs of Courvoisier on the Old Bailey and boy, did I learn a lot. I had enough scenarios to keep me in jail for the rest of my life, I was a swaying D Notice, I felt incredibly vital and dangerous, I got convinced the stewardess had poison on the tips of her eyelashes so I stopped tickling my cheeks with them but by the time I was carried out on a Heathrow stretcher my tapes had been ninety-nine per cent wiped, I could only remember two of the incredible relevations but no one was interested, they just told me to stop upsetting the Non-EEC queue with my bad language. I tried to get my pal Jerry Freeman hooked into this *Belgrano* thing and also into how the Ayatollah had been put there as a thick stooge by the CIA and how he'd just gone AWOL to their amazed amazement but Jerry said, Ricky, you look terrible. Go find yourself some Alka-Seltzer and I might give you one of our teaser promos to play around with.

Cunt.

Hey, it's all true, I tell ya! I wanna be taken seriously! I want Special Branch to break down the door and seize my canisters! I wanna be gagged by the British Establishment! I want Zelda to come and visit me in my bare cell! Yeah. I want her to weep her heart out and beg my forgiveness and my shaven head to nod all but imperceptibly eventually and my bruised and battered lips to touch hers about three hours before a brute hand-tinted hand drags her off and says here's your cup of tea, miss, sorry about the milk, it's that nasty pasteurised stuff but you know how it is, it's so much easier to keep in the station with all this toing and froing and funny hours'n that and you get used to it, I suppose. Funny how you get used to things. Hang on, I've just got to give him a little kick and then I'll get you some sugar. Oof. Lumps or powder? They say there's no difference but there is, there is.

346

Great days, grand days.

My great-grandmother's face. OK, so who's the *Belgrano*? Hey, let's be
a bit more period, period. So who's the *Titanic*? 'Cos, OK, maybe it did
take about 3,000 years to make that iceberg and about three and a half
seconds for that iceberg to blow its nose on some steel and turn Mr
Trevelyan's second cousin into a dinner-jacketed rest home for
molluscs but my great-grandmother's face is not exactly soft and
warm, baby. TITANICEBERG! That's not my joke. It's what some
wag of a teenage Lloyds Insurance clerk scribbled on his jotter on 16
April last year before his boss saw it and dropped him out the window,
according to Mr Trevelyan. The problem for Gordon the Grip is that
however hard he tries he can't get the focus right. There's something
really hairy going on and it's to do with Mrs Trevelyan's face having
this quiver all over it. That's the main difference between it and an
iceberg. Icebergs don't have nervous problems, they take it easy for a
long long time and then when they're ready just drift around for a few
years giving everyone else nervous problems. We know the type, huh?
But Mrs Trevelyan's not like that, she gives everyone else nervous
problems because she has too many and to spare. So Gordon can't get
a grip on this thing and he's saying Ricky, we got gnats – and I'm saying
don't worry, if she ends up looking like something by Francis Bacon
that's fine by me. The quiver is actually the muscles in the face getting
beat up by the nerve guys. These guys are high on tonic wine and
dandelion coffee and Crappy's Miracle Elixir and are having a great
time. Mrs T lifts her chin up and lets everyone see her neuralgia, just
in case someone out there is still in doubt of the extremity of the ordeal
she is undergoing. To the prickle of the face is added the twinge of her
running sores as they unstick from the embroidery around her throat.
Hey, don't feel sorry for her. That's the whole point. Polish your salver
and look at her through that. Anything else and you'll be turned to
stone she'll suck and spit out. Don't be a prune, OK?

Then there's this sound of tissue-paper tearing and it's her voice. She's
asking a leading question so wake up, the fireworks are pre-war issue,
the Thames flows on softly, there's not gonna be a revolution.

Where is he, Agatha?

The dance band stops mid-rag. Glasses tinkle. A 300-foot gash appears in Agatha's chest. Don't panic: up to four watertight compartments can be flooded. Now all the fifth watertight compartment needs is some diving boards. Her heart jumps anyway, holding its nose.

Who – who do you mean, Mother?

Out of the neuralgic mist looms a small smile. At least, one half of the mouth kind of pushes up and stays there twitching. Try it. It makes you feel just what Mrs Trevelyan's feeling right at this moment.

Don't overdo it, my dear. You've never been an awfully good fibber, right from when you swore blind you had not wetted your drawers one long-ago morning.

Uncle Kenneth bows his head to hide his flush. Ninety per cent of it is shame at finding the idea of his niece in wet drawers dashed erotic. The other ten per cent is fairly selfless embarrassment on her behalf. Agatha looks away. She doesn't have a lot to look away to, but some dwarf chrysanthemums on the little round table under the standard lamp in the corner are really honoured to have her attention for a minute, especially as this is their last day on earth because Mrs Trevelyan has a thing about wilt, and these are either suffering from hyphomycetous fungi, or are just old. Being a dwarf chrysanthemum in 1913 is not exactly prestigious, you don't get poems written about you and stuff, like the tea roses and the lilacs and the white flags of iris or whatever. Being an old dwarf chrysanthemum is sad because there isn't a lot of poignancy in being an old dwarf chrysanthemum – not even Henry Peterson wrote an elegy to an old dwarf chrysanthemum. The nearest he got was a mention of frost blight on his asters in *De Profundis* (*Willesden Wedlock*, The Aphid Press, 1967).

The fifth watertight compartment is now an aquarium. I know what these flowers feel like. Agatha doesn't because she's like Zelda, she's full of sap, she's got juice and it's tingling at the tips of her fingers and on the edges of her lips and sometimes at the base of her spine when she just sits on her dressing-table stool with nothing but a chemise between her buttocks and the cushion so she can feel the velvet making an impression. I have to say, without any kind of snigger, that this chemise is silk. I've tried to get Zelda to hire a complete neo-Georgian outfit because I told her I said you know what some guy once said? He said that if you haven't taken an early-twentieth-century lady's clothes off you haven't known real love or real joy. It's like an archaeological excavation, getting through to the body. You have to take along a Thermos and have tea-breaks and stop for sandwiches. By the time you get to the breasts you've taken a degree in costume making and you've still got to unbutton your spats and your waistcoat and your combinations and make sure your fob-watch doesn't get stepped on and stuff and don't forget your bowler hat, you've still got your bowler hat on, sir, and you realise the maid is in here and expecting to have a romp too and she's got all those detachable frilly collars and cuffs and stuff let alone the hairpins. By the time you've undone the apron ties and separated that little starched scarab with your blunt fingers you can't hold her hand and get to the first one yawning in the bed without falling over about three day's worth of washing and ironing. As Jean Cocteau put it, and he'd done it in his youf, in PARIS for crying out loud, *It's as eef a murder has taken place, non?* Oui, oui. Zelda didn't buy it. She was into No Loitering. She'd sit on the bed in what she usually wore at the weekend and quite frankly there wasn't a lot of difference. I mean, if it was shorts and T-shirt disrobing took about two seconds per item equals four seconds and one for the panties if she'd bothered equals five and if it was her Zen robe thing she'd just lift it up and over her head like she was changing channels and there she was, nude under her hair while I was still lining my shoes up. The fact that what I really liked was the challenge of the hunt kind of escaped her. I said I liked to glimpse to start with, just to glimpse her honey-coloured skin flickering through the trees, you know, the Diana or is it Daphne chased by Apollo thing – that maybe she could keep her Zen robe on and just lifted up while we did it but she said honey, only listen to the voice of pines and cedars when no wind stirs and anyway you might stain it. She made me feel really fetishistic. Maybe Dr Lousebrain likes instant nakedness like he likes instant philosophy.

Beatrice.

Yes, Arthur?

Arthur is discomfited by the fact that she says yes Arthur without looking at him, without so much as a tilt of her head. It often happens. He doesn't feel like the Big Chief of Trevelyan Antiseptics & Disinfectants when she does this, or the Head of the Trevelyan Household By Law, or even the Sole Source of Cash. It's like being a mainbeam with bad woodworm. But when you're up against someone with a face like an iceberg and nervous problems, you've got to navigate very carefully. Twenty-four-hour look-out, full radio contact with the International Ice Patrol, keep to the right shipping lane. Right not as in right or left, but right as in correct, in case there's some fatal confusion, because the left might be the right one, in this case. He sighs and folds his hands together. It's queer how they do it without getting in a tangle. All those fingers.

Beatrice, I think we must take this whole thing coolly. Keep your head cool and your feet warm, as Father used to say. It's all damned awkward, but nothing worse.

Nothing worse, Arthur?

As we thought it to be, only half an hour ago, my dear.

Thank you for reminding me, Arthur. I do believe I had quite forgot. Silly me.

Arthur tuts and purses his lips and lets the air out slowly, which is what he usually does when Beatrice fires her sarcannons. Tuts and blows and pats his cavalry horse and turns to Wellington and says, I do believe, sir, my leg has been took clean orf. It's hopeless. He withdraws his hands and knits his brows and slumps a little. The table stretches out before him like, you've guessed it, the Valley of Death. Half a league, half a league, half a league onward. Half an hour ago he was blown off a cliff. A ledge caught him, bruised but still kicking, by Jove. The ledge is frightfully small and very high up. Be thankful for small ledges. My son is not dead. Hurrah! Hurrah!

You remind me, Arthur, of the man who struck a brick wall with his head repeatedly because it was so very pleasant when he stopped.

For God's sake, Beatrice, be thankful for small ledges! I mean mercies! Nay, not small ledges at all, but great ones, a great mercy I mean in this case! Our son is not—

He never was, Arthur! Anyone would think that he was Lazarus raised miraculously from the dead! You are falling for their little wicked game!

Whose game? What game?

To visit on us a greater evil that wasn't true in order that the lesser but still considerable evil that is true be heartily welcomed. I will not play this game, Agatha, Kenneth! I will not! Where is your brother?

He is upstairs, Mother.

I thought so!

She leans back in her chair, triumphant. This is a touch horrendous. Forget the *Titanic*, it's gone, the iceberg's a lousy metaphor, I used it because everyone else uses it here – it's only sixteen months, their attention span is longer than ours by about three seconds under sixteen months, they're still shuddering, the 1,513 drowned are still scattered on the sea-bed of the nation, to quote Henry Peterson's one famous line (*On the Bridge*, privately printed pamphlet, 1956). I wanna go Tennysonian, Miss. You may, Thornby. OK, long slow pan, wide screen, a tad slomo. The victory pennants are fluttering, the crows are cawing, the riderless horses snort in the mist, one with an arrow in its flank tries to rise and the arrow whoops bends just like rubber and it's one of my great unanswered questions: Did Bresson mean it to bend? I'm talking about the closing frames of the finest film in the world ever: *Lancelot du Lac*. You know how many times I've seen it? Twenty-two. No piece of white fabric has ever been covered by anything so great before or since. Dr Turdsville has never seen it. Godard is God, he says. Sure, I remarked, Godard is good, but not God. Bresson is possibly God. I think I've seen *The Pickpocket*, he said. So that's where you learnt the trade, I replied. You picked mine right under my heart. Hey, Rick, let's call it quits. It's been a year now, huh? The thing is, you think the guy's making no effort. You'd think he'd pretend he knew

351

every last shot of Robert Bresson. You'd be wrong. He *is* making a great effort. He's making a great effort to show how the tinsel town commercial crap is great art. He'd turn a dog turd on his shoe into great art, because he can talk. He can talk students into thinking a commercial for Pepsi-Cola is as good as *8½*. I'd like to shut him up, actually. I think he's dangerous. I'd like to ride into town and clean it up. Make it safe for great art. Make it safe from Mordreds and Morgan le Fays and all those men and women with urinals instead of percipience in their upstairs. Upstairs? echoes Mr Trevelyan making me jump. Yes, I suppose he must be. I suppose he must have gone somewhere.

In the attic, adds Agatha.

Agatha is Guinevere, only no Lancelot has ever actually touched her. She's been stuck in the nursery reading Tennyson and Scott and the Earl of Beaconsfield and hasn't yet gone neo-realist and certainly doesn't know what a man's lips feel like. She's the same age as Hilda. Hilda's her great-great-great-niece. Hilda (hi, honey) is very lucky to have been brought up in the late twentieth century instead of in the early bit. She can wear shredded Levis and shoot heroin and shave her head to the scalp and get laid every day if she wants to without being a member of the destitute classes. Hilda is bright, she reads Dostoevsky and stuff, she's awf to Awxford soon. Agatha is also bright but won't be awf to Awxford soon because her mind also has to be kept virginal for whoever comes clopping up on his fat charger before she's on the shelf at twenty-three. This is beginning to make her cross, mainly because it's perfectly tedious. She's hanging around at the back of these meetings in Hyde Park where women with large heads and small hats or maybe small heads with large hats shake their fists and shout but she also likes Tennyson and Scott and the idea of this tall dark handsome fellow coming up to her at the next tea dance and murmuring how she reminds him of Guinevere. It's tricky. I don't know what got me on to this. It doesn't matter because no one's said anything for a couple of minutes. I think they're musing. Mrs Morgan le Velyan's surveying the rout. Maybe they're not musing – maybe they're thinking *what the fuck do we do now*? genteel version *circa* 1913. I mean, in the attic is such a ridiculous place to be. It's only just striking Agatha how actually frightfully ridiculous it is. It's going to take him ages to come down, clomp clomp clomp clomp on the three flights of stairs, past the Boy Picking His Verruca, past Albert the One-Eyed Lemur, past the cows and churches and the tiny frightening anatomical one of a whale and everyone'll have to wait and it'll be frightfully awkward and beastly. She should have had him all prepared, hair brushed, shoes polished, waiting in the drawing-room or wherever. Mother sees through everything. She ruins everything. Papa is so awfully weak. Uncle Kenneth is useless. Now one supposes that Willo will be banished. She can almost hear the tumbrels rattling and the knitting needles prattling partly because she's just re-read *A Tale of Two Cities* and has fallen in love with Carton this time instead of Darnay, know what I mean.

Then he must be fetched, mustn't he?

That was Mrs le Fay, now Queen. Uncle Kenneth closes his eyes and tries to dematerialise himself, but the sago won't let him.

Yes, indeed, murmurs Mr Trevelyan. Yes indeed.

What are you going to do? murmurs Agatha.

That depends, does it not? shouts Mrs Trevelyan. She isn't really shouting, but it sounds like shouting after all the murmuring. Uncle Kenneth's eyes open and so does his mouth.

Quiet, snaps his sister-in-law. Uncle Ken's mouth snaps too but shut. He lets out a little nasal sigh which reminds Mrs Trevelyan deep down of the way Willo sighed in his cot as a golden-haired sleeping infant but it's so deep down it needs a bathysphere and doesn't even bubble.

We have not yet comprehended, she says, why he has been – ah – um—

Expelled, proffers Uncle Kenneth.

The term is quite familiar to me, thank you. A horrible, ugly term, like expectoration.

Spit is worse, says Uncle Kenneth quite unintentionally.

You are the Devil's own of a bore, sometimes! shrieks Mrs Trevelyan.

Beatrice, please be calm—

It has come, it has come!

Beatrice?

My attack! The – the strangulation! Help me, help me!

Good God!

Mr Trevelyan is entering the Valley of Death with his gallant six hundred, he's standing up and leaning forward and saying are you all right, Beatrice dear? and it's half a league, half a league, half a league onward and someone had blundered and volleyed and thundered into the jaws of death, into the mouth of Hell, Beatrice dear, are you all right, shall I fetch the doctor? Are you all right, my dear?

She's got her fingers underneath her collar and the embroidery is straining but she's not blue, she's breathing in deeply and shuddering, she's definitely all right. It's a great performance. Mr Trevelyan is really worked up. The Light Brigade is no more. He'd kept it in reserve but now it's in tatters. He's puce. He's lost control. His nerve lies somewhere between the candelabra and the silver butter-dish. Keep it light, keep it light is his motto. But sometimes, to Carry On Quoting, his not to reason why, his but to do and die. He yanks his napkin from his throat and hurls it onto the table. Hurling a napkin onto the table is not a big thing, though. It just kind of flops and doesn't even knock over his goblet. He's definitely not reasoning why any more. He's exerting his authority. It helps that he's on his feet. He puts his knuckles on the table and leans on them with a really authoritative demeanour, trying to push the chair back with his calves to give himself space. Unfortunately the chair is caught on a ruck in the rug and so it's riding up on his calves and practically tipping over. He has to bend his knees and the chair descends to a less precarious position but Mr Trevelyan does not look impressive on bent knees. Gordon wants to crawl out of shot to help him out but I wave a no-no, this is how it is, *no part of the unexpected which is not secretly expected by you.* Tighten on a

354

foreground candle flame, pull back focus to get his face medium close up, Gordon, it's all on the dope sheet, everything's predetermined, get to it. Hey, stop moaning, I don't know why my great-grandfather doesn't lift the chair away himself, maybe his knuckles are nailed by now and anyway the fact that the chair is bobbing up and down really wildly as he tries to get it to slip off his calves and he's looking like he's jacking off through a knot-hole in the side of the table or something is not our business, just crank and catch him, catch his roar, it's an important moment for this guy, it's an important moment for the whole darn enterprise.

All right! Let's stop fidgeting and fardling and have done with it! I'll tell you why they've given him a one-way ticket! The boy has drawn obscene pictures!

Mrs Trevelyan's hand comes up to her chin no mouth maybe nose nope, sorry, it's carried on all the way up to about a foot above her top hairpin and kind of stays there so we're pulling back a little to include it, it has a nice sheen on the thumb, it's not a gesture you see very much these days and I'm talking about 1913 now.

Arthur! Not in front of our daughter!

Not theft, not punching somebody in the head until his ears bleed, not poaching or truancy or tying a skeleton to the chapel bell, but obscene pictures!

Oh!

His chair nearly tips over and Agatha's half out of her own to take a catch but it doesn't, it jiggles, it rocks back safely. It's weird, but it's keeping everybody on their toes, this high-backed fairly heavy chair with what are either chocolate whirls or stylised dog-turds on either corner, it's making them quite anxious underneath all the other emotions. I'm sorry about all this shouting. When these people erupt they really erupt. I have to stress that this is not a normal dinner here. A normal dinner here is about as exciting as bread sauce. I mean, it's not every day you think your son's dead and then find him resurrected in the attic. It's raining, by the way. In case you like to be kept up with the

355

weather. You can hear it in the hooves and the wheels of the gigs and the rubber tyres of the automobiles. You can't see it because George closed the thick curtains about an hour ago so I thought I'd tell you in case you'd forgotten your umbrella because there are about twenty-three in the hall but I don't think now is the time to leave, frankly. Have some sensitivity, for Christ's sake. Let alone some *politesse*. This isn't the 1990s. OK, it's safe to open your eyes again now.

Do you mean that he *purchased* them, Arthur?

Purchased produces a minor spray of spittle which falls mainly on the condiments her end. Arthur blushes because actually he's the one that purchases obscene pictures. When I say obscene I mean 1913 obscene, like a couple of plump Parisiennes with corsets round their ankles and authentic black suspenders looking like they're delousing each other, or a butler tickling the bare globes of a maid's behind as she cleans up some gravy. OK, maybe not gravy. Maybe some spilled madeleines, one of which she's licking with a long tongue and not thinking about Proust. Hey, we've come a long way in eighty-odd years. Maybe there was hardcore stuff then too but it hasn't yet come the way of Arthur Bertrand Edgar Trevelyan, and I'm not sure he'd like it if it did. Ruthie's got a fairly hardcore side but so far he's not bitten into it, not like the Cabinet Minister whose transexual double-barrelled name she can never remember and who's into defecation and Georgian water sports. I have to say, while on this subject, I did a very sneaky thing last month. I thought that Dr Todd In The Hole might like to take advantage of this great Introductory Offer to *Labia*, a high-quality monthly catering for all male heterosexual tastes in full frontal colour. It cost me a fortune but I know Zelda really hates pornography. I think I forgot to say that over the last year (hey, you think I've shot this dinner scene in under a year or something?) Mrs Todd has left Mr Todd and gone with Weeny Todds to live with her parents in the Vermont hills while Mr Unfaithful 1996 gets his arse sorted out from the bed-springs. You know what he did? He got Zelda to come and sort it out for him, on a fairly permanent basis. Is it surprising I'm doped up a lot of the time and risking Death Row or whatever they do to you here in sunny Texas for puffing on a joint and pretending to be a freak? Not that I look like a freak. I wear my hair balding and my tie knotted and

356

my Levis creased in all the right places. The only weird thing is this paper bag on my head. But they can't drag you around behind a pick-up for wearing a paper bag on your head. Hey, it's accepted round here - one of the highlights of Texan culture is wearing big white pointy bags on your head with large eye-holes and a flaming torch in the right hand. Anyway, I only wear it when I go into the HCDVA library and there's never anyone else there except—

Oh Christ, why do I have to be so funny all the time? Why can't I be Ingmar Bergman or someone? Or maybe Woody Allen pretending to be Ingmar Bergman? You know how many wives Bergman had? Five. How many mistresses? Twenty-something. And the guy was still fucking miserable.

Where was I?

Crank back.

yyyyou mean that he *purchased* them, Arthur?

Of course not! Good God! He painted them with his own hand!

With his own hand? You mean, he did it all by himself?

Look, I really think—

I know what he did, Papa. It's quite ridiculous. He painted a few nudes, that's all. Like they do at the Art School. Don't you remember how he kept painting the nymph on the stairs and that one of Hermes in the conservatory and Laocoön wrestling with the serpents at Hamilton Lodge—

And a very fine watercolour of the fellow taking a thorn out of his tootsie, adds Uncle Kenneth.

Do I? Vaguely, says Papa.

If you wouldn't mind sitting down, Arthur. You're giving me a headache with your bobbing.

357

I'm not bobbing! Good God! I've had a very stiff day—

The chair tips over and they all bob. They sigh and everyone except Big Chief Mainbeam of course resumes their seats. He tweaks his trousers just above the knees and stoops and rights the chair and sits in it with a huff and then puts his head in his hands trying not to think about the penny papers tomorrow or his tucked-away album of French cards or Ruthie's scented underwear on the chair behind his left eyebrow.

Do you mean to say that he asked boys to sit for him, without a stitch?

Yes, Mother. He tells me their subjects were mythological. I do believe they were in the best taste, and those silly fools—

Who are you speaking of?

Those, Mother, who twist everything to mirror the sickness in their own minds.

Specifically?

Mr Boulter. And the others, the other beaks.

That is confounded disrespect, Agatha! cries Mr Trevelyan, who was thinking far worse thoughts on the Randle fellows a few minutes back, which is why he's over-reacting now.

Your elders and betters, dear, adds Mrs Trevelyan. Do stop shouting, Arthur.

Dash it, is it damn surprising? shouts Mr Trevelyan. Mrs Trevelyan closes her eyes as if the sound waves are breaking against her face – which actually they are, of course. Gordon is happy because the neuralgia's gone. She's in focus. She's so precisely in focus you can count the hairs on her chin wart and the pimples on the side of her nose revealed under the talcum powder by the recent deluge. I mean the pimples were exposed under the talcum powder, not the nose, because the talc's thickly applied but not that thick. Her fingers are no longer

358

tucked into her collar. You have to remember with my great-grandmother that she's a flash-flooder, she's tectonic, she's very much on a fault-line. She'd be a dangerous country to live in. She'd be the kind of country where tens of thousands perish in mud-slides and collapsed cinemas and stuff so often that it'd only just make the fourth news item everywhere else for a couple of days. Mind you, it'd have to be a place where the prevailing climate was English. I mean, Mrs Trevelyan is not exactly California.

Mr Trevelyan huffs again, in floral italics. Seriously, he does. He actually huffs. He takes a good swig of his wine. Ruthie and his combinations. The whole damn day's gone skew-whiff. Good God, it has. And it ain't over, not by a long chalk, old chap.

The shame of it, murmurs Mrs Trevelyan. She gets up. She goes over to the window. Gordon is so surprised he loses his grip and gets some camera-shake but it doesn't matter, it looks avant-garde. She's at the window holding the curtain back a little. There's a yellow light coming through from the fog and the street lamps but not enough to more than give her a touch of jaundice, which is fairly suitable. Great effect, Mike. He uses real gas, you know. Nothing but real gas gives that sort of blurred glow out of a lamp. Oh, the frightful shame, she adds, in case anyone was in doubt.

Please try to understand, says Agatha.

That was a bold, even crazy, move. Uncle Kenneth's closed his eyes again. The sago's causing him problems. He'd like to loosen his girdle but feels in the circumstances to unbutton his waistcoat and loosen his girdle would be disrespectful and might well bugger everything up, if one could bugger it up any more than it was already buggered up. The idea of William stuck up in the attic waiting to be summoned or is it summonsed is either droll or pitiable, he can't decide which. A small hysterical pocket of mirth is making plans to expand in his belly but it turns into a cough which makes his dear brother jerk a bit. His brother either swims around benignly or jerks. It is most trying, and got from Mater. Mater jerked when she died, come to think of it, in that very chair during that frightful luncheon with Mr Quill, or Spill, or whoever it was was trying to lay hands on her cash. Jerked and burbled and fell head-first into the rougemange. The rougemange was garnished very tastefully with sprays of white jasmine, one of which had affixed itself to Mater's cap when they lifted her up. If it wasn't for the rougemange mud-pack, it would have been rather touching, with the jasmine spray. Rather touching.

I understand perfectly, says my great-grandmother, allowing the curtain to fall back into its usual evening station. She'd like to be a curtain. Just hang and be drawn and maybe cleaned at long intervals. There's being drawn and being drawn, she reflects. This is one of her rare jokes, but she doesn't share it. She only shares her nervous problems, remember.

Yes, she sighs, I understand perfectly, quite quite perfectly.

This is crap, actually. Her mind is in total confusion. She has absolutely no idea of what to do with this situation. But she says it anyway because it sounds nicely sinister, and people who sound nicely sinister give the impression that they are also totally in control. Not very deep down she's really terrified of confronting Willo. Really terrified. She's floating back to her chair. She sits down. Gordon was ready this time. His knuckles are white. That's the sign of a great grip.

I suppose we'll have to bring him down, says Papa.

Giles telephoned, says Agatha.

Mrs Trevelyan is brushing some imaginary insect off her puffed shoulders. She pauses in mid-brush. She's a film still. We can make that Still Eleven or is it Twelve but you don't have to leave your seats. If you hadn't seen the film you might think she's inspecting her nails discreetly to one side. You might. You'd be wrong. Never trust a still.

Giles? she murmurs.

He very kindly telephoned and said they were utterly and completely beastly to Willo. They made him walk the cestus, if you know what that means. They did it to that other fellow—

You forget, my dear, that your father was at Randle.

So was I, sniggers Uncle Kenneth.

He stops sniggering pretty quick, and looks serious, but really, you'd think he'd make *some* sort of bloody effort. The guy's about as switched on as a shorted patch-panel ho ho. He frowns and lowers his head as if he's about to say grace again. His brother tuts and sighs.

Good God, did they really make him do that? The devil of it.

Dashed hard, says Uncle Kenneth.

The devil of it, repeats his brother.

Mrs Trevelyan gives up being a still and does actually inspect her finger-nails. For an upper-middle class woman of the Georgian period, they're not perfect. She also gets crumbs on her tea-gown that lodge themselves for days. Get this: she doesn't change her tea-gown every day. A faint air of neglect, as some ex-Harvard ponce at HCDVA put it to me last week, just because I'd forgotten to do my fly up and my socks were fallen or something. OK Mr Clean, I said, lend me your bicycle-clips and I might lend you my nose-hair clipper. He flushed, he really flushed. No one messes wid de Ricky Thornby, OK?

What else did Giles say? murmurs my great-grandmother.

That it was frightfully blown up, and that it was all for art – and nothing, you know, outrageous, and that he was just a scapegoat.

For what? asks Head of Household by Law. A scapegoat for what, dash it?

I'm not sure, says Agatha in a rather uncertain manner, which is a big mistake. But I suppose—

Suppose what? snaps the Mother of Mothers.

I suppose that it was all – for all the usual reasons, Agatha says finally.

Limp, huh? Really limp. An undefended rear. Roland in the Pyrenean pass not blowing his trumpet. Pearl Harbour in the sun, shirtless guys in dark glasses lounging on the decks, gazing up into the clear blue welkin of Hawaii, that Sunday morning feel-good feel as the face warms up. Me just nodding like an idiot as Todd Lazenby starts borrowing books out the library for the first time in years. Agatha has not examined this thing about the scapegoat. It's confused in her mind with the idea that actually it was better being the scapegoat than the other goat, the one upon which the LORD's lot fell and who was killed and had his blood sprinkled with a finger of the priest whose hands were full of incense beaten small until he threw it on the mercy seats and clouds covered everything and in went the blood. It was one of the Swiss governess's favourite passages. Lo, she came for a year between Nanny Dreadnought and Ginger-Bits Hallam from some Alpine slope where the church was Zwinglian or something and had a penchant for the gory bits or the bits that if you did the same thing now you'd end up in a great deal of trouble. She'd always say the bit about the goat getting patted on the head and sent off into the wilderness by Aaron like it was the worst thing that could happen to you, yah? But Agatha reckoned that the goat didn't really know it was stuffed full of the iniquities of the children of Israel, it just trotted out into the wilderness with the run of all the juicy little thistles, or whatever goats like to munch on. She ventured to say this once as Miss Schimff was tucking her up in the nursery but Miss Schimff really abreacted, her nostrils went all huge over the candle and her eyeballs rolled up to Heaven where they were given a polish and bowled back down again to crush Agatha against her pillow and her doll, the woman was actually sick in the head and became a branch of the Eighth Day Adventists or something. The situation is further complicated by the fact that Willo actually murmured something about it being jolly to be back home when they were up in the attic because anywhere's better than Randle. A further possibility is that Willo will only become the real scapegoat if he's sent out into the wilderness now, because getting sent back home is like getting sent back into the byre, not into the wilderness. This implies that if Madre and Papa do what was done to the second cousin once removed they will be visiting their iniquities on Willo's head which opens up a whole new vista for Agatha, because up to now she's never thought of her parents in terms of bearing iniquities, just that they could be a bit more like Amy's parents who are frightfully decent and jolly and spend most of their time having musical soirées and talking about the latest books, instead of bickering or looking depressed or spending the whole afternoon lying down with a headache in Mother's case. I'm sorry about having to have dredged all this up out of Agatha's mind but, hey, this isn't a soap opera, this is an extremely complex masterwork and extremely complex masterworks don't treat people like most of us treat people normally, they treat them like their minds are more than a lump of sago, they turn them round and round in their hands saying O what a wondrous thing is man and then drop them on the floor usually, because life is not about dropping sago on the floor it's about dropping glass, priceless glass, glass from Mesopotamia or sixteenth-century Venice or someplace, the only known example of, because each of us are only known examples of, and we need to remember that.

OK?

Don't complain. You haven't had a lot of Today's Thought in this film. It's just that Zelda and I passed in the corridor this morning and she had a different perfume. That's really serious. She always had this kind of musk and patchouli fragrance before and now she's into something they spray around shopping malls, the kind of stuff that gives artificial flowers black spot and if you're under a paper bag it can be dangerous, I practically suffocated, but it's OK, I have to know what it's like because in a few reels' time we're gonna get a lot of gassing and guys in gas masks thinking the sound of their breath is the seaside. And I reckon that under this air freshener she's the same person but unhappy. I think she's unhappy. I'm freeze-framing the dining-room scene because what I have to say is really important, so Mrs Trevelyan'll just have to lump being stuck with her hand in the air and her mouth open and wait a minute before she attacks out of the clear blue welkin of Hawaii or whatever.

She's definitely unhappy. Zelda, I mean. Her eyes had red rims, she didn't look like she'd just blown in from the Garden of Eden as she usually does, she had a coffee or some such stain on her jacket. She wears a jacket these days with fairly powerful shoulders. Believe it or not she wore a black leather skirt last month with a zip down the side and it finished above her knees. It's getting crazy. I left her an outaprint

Pelican book on Zen Buddhism which I picked up in London last fall and it came back into my tray with *In one blink of your eyes/You have missed seeing p.!!!* written in red biro on the cover, which is not easy because the cover is the glossy kind biros slip over and it looked very ugly. It hurt me. Actually, I couldn't understand it. I mean, I couldn't work out what *p.* stood for. I thought about it all through my class on Bergman's symbolism and it was a lousy class, I'll admit. I kept saying *The Seventh Peel* and *Piled Strawberries* and *Persona* which was OK. Persona was OK I mean. I also said *Alexandra's Fanny* instead of *Fanny and Alexander* which is a very in-joke between me and Ossy, remember m'old fruit? It was embarrassing. Dirty jokes are banned on pain of castration in this college, it's like working in a Victorian convent or something except that Victorian convent girls didn't wear desirable T-shirts without any engineering and shorts so short you wonder where the thighs are going to end. But these girls are really sensitive. I take a cold shower every morning in case their libido detectors start bleeping. Then when I got back home for me cuppa char I looked at it again under my Pinewood pup and realised. I'm talking about the book here. It was Zelda all over. Zelda the hyper-efficient librarian. *In one blink of your eyes/You have missed seeing p.111.* I certainly had, honey. So, hey, I looked up page 111. *Dried Dung.* The verse appears under the heading *Dried Dung.* Hold the book open and keep the camera still, OK? (Ignore my thumb, I'm sorry, I tried to get Sean's – Sean Connery's – but he never takes bit-parts these days.)

DRIED DUNG

A monk asked Ummon: 'What is Buddha?' Ummon answered him: 'Dried dung'. *Mumon's comment:* It seems to me Ummon is so poor he cannot distinguish the taste of one food from another, or else he is too busy to write readable letters. Well, he tried to hold his school with dried dung. And his teaching was just as useless.

> *Lightning flashes,*
> *Sparks shower.*
> *In one blink of your eyes*
> *You have missed seeing.*

His teaching was just as useless. Yeah, but whose? I've put the haiku down in my chapbook, after *Zeffirelli.* Zen or Zelda, it doesn't matter. It's all about movie-making, really. *Zen and the Art of Making Better Movies.* I was talking about Zelda in distress. Basically, as I see it, she's losing her grip. Her core silence is getting filled up with dried dung. I think that's what she is trying to tell me. She needs rescuing. But she'd never admit that she needs rescuing. I don't think for more than about three hours that she's saying I, Richard Thornby, am dried dung. The point about the storm and missing the lightning flash is interesting. I think it means that she was really in love with me but I missed it somehow, I didn't do the right thing, we should have gotten married or whatever. Either that or this paper-bag-over-my-head business is the wrong attitude and Sir Lancelot would never have done that, he'd have kept his eyes wide open and seen how Arthur was away the whole time and Guinevere was sighing a whole lot and gazing at him over the drinking-horns – which Sir Lancelot did realise, and pretty soon got his hands under her mantle and plugged the holy in her grail. Cor blimey. People are so blahdy complicated, son. Like your muvver. Your muvver is so blahdy complicated. Thank Gawd I'm not. I'm simple. Oh you are, Dad, you are. You gettin' cheeky again, Dick me boy? Probably, Dad. But I'm so complicated I'm not quite sure. Thwack. Complicated enuff for yer, son?

Good old Pop. Down in Havant, now, in a Home for the Unbelievably Old. Havant and Houston. How can Havant and Houston exist on the same planet, for God's sake? How can Dad and son be so blahdy different? Zelda. Stick to Zelda. That'd be nice. What do I do? Maybe the pornographic magazine thing was a mistake. Maybe I should just act diffident. It was a whole load easier when you could go out and kill dragons and green giants and stuff for ten years and then come back a bit dusty and browned with bow-legs and maybe a dented bascinet and some hauberk sores but basically intact and heroic and with a lot of Personal Development. Sir Lancelot acting diffident under his bascinet would make for a dull movie. Maybe I should challenge Dr Trash Loosebowels to a joust. Or a duel. The thing is, he'd probably take me up and come along with some serious armaments, this being Texas. I probably wouldn't even be able to hold the pump-action wotsit up and I'd just get spattered all over the cacti. It wouldn't be worth it. Hey, I'd rather act really diffident.

Holy shit.

I've just realised something. You haven't met my grandfather yet. I mean, you have but only in a non-speaking part and he was lowering his head. You've been watching this thing for about five hours into the next millennium and you still haven't met my grandfather. I've screwed this whole movie up. I should have been in the trenches by now making sure the special effects guys had got their act together for, wait for it, you've guessed, don't go OTT about it ho ho, THE FIRST DAY OF THE SOMME but instead we're still stuck in fucking 1913, we haven't even finished dinner, I don't know what I've been up to for the last five years. It was thinking about what my grandfather would've done in this situation *vis-à-vis* Zelda and Toerag Liceface that made me jerk. I literally jerked. It was like I'd got a golf ball in my mouth – which actually has practically happened several times here because of the crazy lie of the fifteenth green which I can piss on from out my study window and do so pretty often in the early hours which is why it's been returfed so much not taking into account the fat-arses who can't swing a club to save their lives. It's incredible how I never realised before that we hadn't got further than one day and how my grandfather's still on hold, getting really bored in the caravan. It's a nice well-stocked caravan of course, but he's been waiting in there five years for crying out loud except for one stint standing under a lime tree for nine hours plus. There's lots to read but I mean back numbers of *Screen International* and *Alfa Romeo News* and some toilet paperbacks with cinched pages along with Sylvia's *Continuity Monthly* and Ossy's *Just Seventeen* and Mike's *Practical Fishkeeping* and Bosey's *International Broadcast Engineer* and my *Making Better Movies* which I'll have you know I contribute to under a pen name and have done so for many years can't keep you going forever and a doi, can it? I think I owe it to him and to you to get his call sheet ticking. This means keeping my great-grandmother on freeze for quite a while but that's OK, you won't mind, there's so much to get through and so much to explain.

If she starts to thaw out, alert the army.

Shaddap.

I hope the toilets are not blocked, by the way. I think the millennium will start with blocked toilets from all the throwing up that's bound to occur. I really hope you're not suffering from that. Don't start snoozing or snoodling too much, though. Maybe you should snort some ground coffee beans or something, because this is going to need some concentration. There's so much to get through I'm going to have to step up the leisurely pace somewhat. Before we Sikorsky over to Randle, though, I have to tell you something I learned today because if you were in any doubt about what a complete jerk Dr Lazenby is please don't be. I sat down right opposite him at lunch in the HCDVA canteen and we got talking. I didn't even spill my coffee accidentally over his french fries or tell him all about the various hiccups with me old man's artificial sphincter because this is my new policy. I'm being nice to him so he'll eventually tell me how Zelda's doing. My other policy is to sneak up on his – Christ, their – house at night and hook my fingers on the sill and listen in, but that gives me the creeps because look what happened to wotsername or was it the rabbit in *Fatal Attraction* (another of Tosh Lipflap's fave clips, I haven't actually *seen* the fucker) and I don't want crickets in my pants. Anyway, we got onto books because I know he likes to flaunt his ignorance and I asked him what his favourite twentieth century novel was and he said *In Ballast to the White Sea* by Malcolm Lowry. Oh yeah, I said, I really like Lowry too, *Under the Volcano* of course, great portrait of a personal disintegration, yup, *In Ballast to the White Sea*, pretty good, but by no means one of his best. This was supposed to be my diffident put-down, really subtle, but he just laughed, the cunt. I could see his french fries mushed up in his mouth because he's got no manners, he's American remember, his grandfather stretched the severed vulvas of Apache women over his pommel probably. Anyway, when he'd quit spraying me with french fries out of his mouth I asked him what on earth was the matter in my David Niven voice, which made these coke-sniffers from my *Cahiers* seminar snigger at the next table. It's not easy being diffident in Texas. Then about five desirable T-shirts came up and asked him something inane about their assignments and when they'd levered themselves off him and the air had stopped wobbling up and down and pretending to be a multiplex-brassière he leaned forward and said, Ricky, the thing is, you couldn't have read it. My suit of diffidence was getting metal fatigue but I was still David Niven and when I'd got my oesophagus back into action I said, oh, really? No, he said, it was never published and the one and only manuscript was lost in a fire back in 1944. The way he said back in 1944 like it was the Golden Jubilee of Queen Adelaide or something was almost as irritating as the fact that I'd just made a prime-time berk of myself. So how come you say it's your favourite book, smart-arse? I didn't actually say smart-arse I said Todd but he'd have got the message, you wouldn't believe how much emotional colouring you can give the name Todd, you can really cram the sub-text into that cute little holdall. Then I got this lecture for about three hours on Absences. I thought until halfway through that he was talking about abscesses because I don't know if I told you my tinnitus is getting worse, I keep thinking I'm about to take off down a runway or sitting in a dentist's waiting-room or something, but by the end I'd very much got the point, he wasn't talking dental at all. I couldn't really see him clearly because of the desirable T-shirts hanging off of his every word but I didn't need to. The guy is a complete fraudster. He likes *In Ballast to the White Sea* because it is a complete not said, it is all intertext, it is a margin of margins, it is an event in metalanguage as the Big Bang is an event on radiowave receivers, it is a whisper of white noise, it eavesdrops on us but not us on it, it remembers nothing, it is what will have been done and does not allow the return of the same, it is ultimate rupture and total non-closure, he really talks like this when he gets going, Zelda used to echo it, I'm Granny in the back of the Morris, I think it's a load of frightful twaddle, the guy's a jerk, I wish I could figurally disrupt him with a loaded Magnum. OK. Nuff said. Giles Trevelyan's call sheet. Tick tick tick.

But I just have to add, which is the whole bleedin' point, that as he was spraying me with this gunk I really did feel seriously homicidal towards him. It's worrying. I'm actually a very unaggressive person to the point of being a nancy yeller-belly knicker-skidder, in the local parlance. Zelda once gave me *Feel the Fear and Do It Anyway* as a birthday present but I can't handle reading it. You've no idea how my wrist trembled when I was filling in the form for that pornographic magazine. A lot of you won't find this easy to believe out there who knew me once. I left *How to Deal with Difficult People* in Zelda's tray last month and actually ran out of the building like I'd left a bomb or something. Flippin 'eck, son. Your dad crawled up French beaches under withering fire an' that. Yeah, yeah. That's probably the whole problem. Never mind yer grandads, son. Never mind yer grandads.

Mind yer grandad, OK?

While we're choppering over a lot of 1913 gorsey scrub where Heathrow now is and highwaymen once were or so they tell ha haaar you can take a stretch on the veranda and check out how the sun's doing beyond the horizon curve. Because I reckon it must be the First Day fairly soon. As in First Light. As in It's the Dawning of. That's exciting. It's not? Hey, you shouldn't have drunk so much. Just because it's Ricky Thornby Enterprises Inc. wot picks up the tab. There goes Greg and Maura's inheritance. Dig in, dig in. Neither of them need it. Maura doesn't speak to me anyway so she and the bloke wot stole her from me can fuck off. Hilda'll manage. She'll manage whatever, come rain or shine or whoever doesn't deserve her. Good old Hil. My genes, my genes!

Naah. Her great-great-great-aunt Agatha's. Obviously.

Poetry break. I hear poetry's very popular again in England, ever since that film a couple of years back, the one about funerals and marriages that grossed the mostest bucks in the history of British film-making hey wow. You think I'm out of touch? Actually, I was lucky. I picked it up on the flight over just a couple of months ago when I had to stay a night with my brother Des, it's complicated, there was this funeral of the only nice aunt in the whole phalanx so I said over a pre-transmission Scotch, hey, maybe I can read some Auden in thick Scots and Muriel replied in her frostiest mode, the chapel is always well-heated, Dick, which would have been a great joke if she didn't need her ears syringed. Des knew what I was on about. He's my bruvver. We have things in common, unfortunately. He didn't say anything, he just did something hypertechnical with the CD and there it was, the Scottish gay guy sobbing over Auden. We listened to the poetry in dead silence except for Des and Muriel's dog, it's a Mexican Hairless, it has complex stomach problems since it swallowed a barbecue stick at the Theydon Bois Summer Whoopee and that is NOT a joke, it's called Cheryl, I call it The Thing from Stanmore Kennels in Smell-O-Vision which upsets Muriel so I keep saying it. The poetry continued. I blushed, I felt like a surf-bum in Switzerland, I wanted to bury my head in the carpet which is the easiest thing in the world at Des and Muriel's because apart from anything else they were staring at me triumphantly, they'd made it onto my closed set of dropped quotes in leotards swanning around with long cigarette-

370

holders swooning over daffodils and stuff and were saying *howzat, prick?* So after the first track I waved my hand around and it was very lucky, the film was dire rear but I'd waited for the credits as usual to see if any of the old gang were focus pullers or dandruff creators or whatever and a couple of the stars' names had stuck so I poked my neck right out and said yeah, yeah, Andy told me he'd done a bit of Wystan. Actually, I don't know Andy McDowell from Robert Burns but I got away with it because the doorbell rang and it was the phalanx led by Cousin Frank with the loud voice and colour-matching problem so Des and Muriel swallowed it like a peanut going down the wrong way, I hope it's still mouldering in there.

Here's the poem. As never read by me old mate John Gielgud bless his soul, but you can imagine it, you can imagine it, complete with bad scratch:

> Dishonourable omens where a cry
> suspends itself from marriage
> and the curlews weep over the silver mere. . .
> the mudflat's mute calligraphies
> where the froth flourishes its fetid trace
>
> and nothing's in its place
> bar the ice-ground glens, apostrophes
> on market vendors' boards, the queer
> austerity of horse and carriage
> as they flee the television's lemur eye
>
> once more and again and once more, O Pitys!

Hey, not bad, huh? I remembered it by O so lonesome heart. I think 'tis roughly right including the Pitys. I said thank you, Henrik, pity about the spelling mistake at the end and he said codswallop, O colossus of modern ignorance or words to that effect she was a soughing fir tree changed thus from the loveliest of nymphs by the desire to escape the lustful Pan get me another I'm skint thoroughly he snapped a branch and wove it round his head and some pork scratchings for old times' sake, my boy. It's his greatest poem but everything's relative. The reason I know it by heart is that it's dedicated to me. *For Richard Thornby*. About a year before this I took him out for a drink and I said, Henry, you're the greatest living Randleian poet under the age of

371

fifty-eight and I want you to know that. How about writing me an adaptation? OK, I was desperate, I'd been let down, my budget was a trickle, the project was up against the wire with its hands up, I bought the second round because Henry Peterson was incredibly mean, I knew I'd be waiting all night if I didn't. This was in 1973. There's something really depressing about that date. I think there were paraffin lamps giving the plastic flowers droop because the oil sheikhs or the miners or maybe both were bringing down Western Civilisation as we knew it and Heathrow was full of highwaymen again but I liked the paraffin lamps, the light was soft, it smelt of old times, you could look at Henry without feeling nauseous. His eyes lit up. He hadn't been praised for decades. At least since his mother died. What to adapt, he growled. Henry had this weird grammar, you got used to it. My grandfather's diary, I said. His face loosened and I feared for his eyeballs. Hah, he commented. I removed my dark glasses and found my beer and sipped while he cogitated or whatever. It was disgusting beer. This was 1973. You had to drive out to somewhere turfy like Wiltshire in those days to get anything that wasn't What You Want. Your grandfather's, he grunted. Your grandfather's diary. Yes, Henry. My grandfather's diary. His eyeballs were really teetering. He leaned forward, I leaned back, I didn't want gristle in my lap, the paraffin glow was slanting dramatically across his skin problem. I felt like Apollo 11 on the approach. Not *Nostromo*, not *Middlemarch*, not *The Forsyte Saga*, but your grandmother's diary, he growled. *The Forsyte Saga*'s been done, Henry. And it's my grandfather's. He went to Randle. I know he went to fucking Randle, Henry spat, for so did I. I know for how you went to Randle, Henry. I know for how you fucking know that, director fellow of films, for haven't you so said in too many letters, my boy? It's Thornby, call me Rick. The point is, Henry, watch that ash, the diaries are an intimate account of my grandfather's life at Randle. Unpublished. Unabridged. Hey, it'll start with the linden tree avenue in deep perspective, a carriage raising dust, a gravelly voice-over—

Shit, what's the point in telling you the whole history? Peterson was hopeless, an old hopeless vitriolic soak but just as I was realising this well into the fifth round on my bloody slate he took to the idea with a vengeance, he opened his eyes so wide I could see they were well attached actually, he became really excited, he started *taking notes* on a Watney's mat with his one good finger-nail. Look, the guy was a bit of a

372

legend in certain circles, I thought it would be one of those mismatches that strike a spark that lights a cult classic on a par with, I dunno, *Penda's Fen* or *Culloden* or something. 'Cos it was going to be for Beeb 2. The bloke was dying an inch a day, I saw it as his swan-song with me on the bank taping it and then shrugging off the glory. Yeah yeah, I'd always considered him one of the great post-war poets, man, pity you were all so deaf. I had fairly long hair and shades and said man in those days, I was very embarrassing because I was too old but I so wanted to be hip, I wore Indian beads for about a week and then my hair-line decided to give up the struggle and started journeying to meet the back of my neck. I really know what the Aral Sea is feeling like. I still dream I have hair other than the rampant stuff up my nose and in my ears and concealing my dick. OK OK, I'm not Yul Brynner, but it'd be better if I was. Zelda used to tousle my head and I'd panic. Peterson had lots of hair but it looked as if it was trying to leave on the next tramp steamer out. No poet ever smelt as much except probably Chaucer. By the seventh round he was singing. He was singing songs he and his old drinking boyo guess who in the Fitzrovia days made up on the spot to upset the barmaid only Peterson remembered them and Thomas never did and then died before it got embarrassing. The What You Want Is Warthog Piss was really getting to me. My head was in my hands. He wanted to see the diaries straight away, he was demanding a contract, he said he wouldn't start without whatever Dylan got for *Under Milk Wood* slapped on the table right now. Llareggub backwards, I said, but he didn't get it. Hey, I was always sticking my neck out in those days only it was usually into a noose with drinks on Albert Pierrepoint ho ho. All this particular little follow spot in my head illuminated was Henry fucking Peterson clutching me trouser-belt (Indian pig-skin, man) until the day he expired, which was not a day too soon in my book. '76, if you missed the whitewash job in the *Randleian* and the crawly mention in *Wolseley Words* (he had a bootiful green livericd 1931 Wolseley Hornet and a luverly little 1939 Wolseley Ten Saloon wot once belonged to Lord Nuffield and is now appearing in many an adaptation, I'll have you know – the nearest the dear old soul got to one, tee hee). And all I got aht of it was a poem I don't get. It's called *Lights Out*, 'cos that was going to be the title of the cult classic. The line about the carriage on the TV screen is how I saw the cult classic kicking off. Once more and again and once more 'cos it was going to be, wait for it, a trilogy. I showed him the diaries in the end because I had some burning questions. He kept ringing me up and reversing the charges and saying he was putting the call on expenses. Who's that, darling? (Crazy Louisa's bathtime query. Luverly more than crazy she was at that juncture. Hey, the bathroom door's open. She's soaping her breasts with a coppery oval of Pears and letting the delicate curve of her Susan Hampshire neck get nibbled by the Apple Blossom Oil, to quote myself. I could write great scenarios in those days. I was an *auteur*, fuck it. We tried asses' milk but our fridge wasn't big enough.) Henry Pestersson, sweetheart. Henry who? Henrik Pestersson. A Swedish poet, huge, blond, worked with Bergman. He wants me to adapt his opus but it's way too gloomy. I need to *swing*, man! Darling, swinging finished years ago, I've told you so so *so* many times how hanging around Carnaby Street in those dark glasses does your reputation for incisive contemporaneous statement no good at all. Pass me my loof—

Ah, Louisa my love, my crazy woman, I think I want to meet you again after death, on that great set in the sky where the doors open to clouds you can't fall through and no one ever swings themselves on the gaffer tape. Or herself. Or herselves.

Shaaddap, son.

These diaries.

The fact is, I could just fix a lens on 'em. I could do a Sean Connery thumb but he wasn't available and anyway that isn't what the cinema's abaht, is it? *The cinema is truth twenty-four times a second. Merci*, Jean-Luc Godard. I mean, you wanna some action, huh? My grandfather's Randle diaries are not full of action. They go on and on about soul and porter and bladderdash and God and nymphs and queer rippling sensations which he discusses with Barstow who sniggers, dash it. But they'd have made a great frame, a great hook, something for the Henry Peterson I thought existed to get his caries into and wow it would have been swinging and wild and beaten poor old Lindsay Anderson by a bit, if only. And there's a great little nugget of a drama in there. It stars Hubert Lightfoot. Uncast as yet, Henry, but I'm putting feelers out, don't sweat, stay cool. It starts on the playing fields of Randle and ends on the killing fields of Flanders. Henry, the genius, noted immediately the anagrammatical potential of Randle and Flanders. There's no F in Randle, Henrik, I'd say. But he was too excited to notice. At least he spent his last years excited. I just tagged him along. I'm still pitching the back-up, Henrik, I'd say. These broadcasting bastards are all lip. I mean, it's a ginormous budget. Just hang in there, man.

Christ, I have so much to tell St Peter about. Let's hope there are no massacres or mud-slides or civil wars at the same time. I'll hold everybody up and the Pearly Gates'll buckle or something. It'll be worse than Eisenstein. I've been such a bastard, in my time.

This thing happened I need to tell you about. A week ago. A week before Willo's boot, I mean, not a week before the end of the millennium or a week before me sitting here looking out at the fifteenth green and watching some fat-arse in pink flannels from Sunset Homes get a birdie. Hey, he's good. You wouldn't believe it. And in this heat. OK, sorry, I know you're pressed, I know you want to join the Welcoming of the Millennial Dawn in Hyde Park and bang your drums and triangles because you won't be around for the next one, nor will Hyde Park probably. But I really need to tell you about this thing wot happened to Giles my grandfather at Randle about a week ago, it's in the diaries, I read it, it's relevant, it'll all tie up in the end, or get tangled up, tangled up because there's no one here tying anything up, OK? This is the truth twenty-four times a second. THIS IS THE TRUTH.

The afternoon of this day a week back opens with bladderdash. Bladderdash is written in the diaries like this: *Bldsh*, or sometimes *Bosh*, ironically. It didn't take a lot of research to decode it, just a few costly rounds with Henrik. Actually, the day begins with *Brrr. Cold. Light frost on Pod! Kpprs. Trigmy & beastly P. T. Gardiner snitched my waistcoat for a jape. I welted the beast with tie. Ouch! Rst beef & sago (verdict: guilty).* P. T. isn't Gardiner's initials, it means Physical Training. You see why Henry was useful. I could've got reet muddled, lad, by all this pubelic skewel tosh. Then it's *OTC* like it is every day with a little remark like *dropt rifle* or *OOS again* or *oh wot a lot of frightful SWANK*. I said Henry, I presume OTC is not Over The Cop or Overdid The Cannabis but Officers' Training Corps. I presume OOS is not Out Of Sync as in lousy cinemas but Out Of Step. And SWANK is not what you think it is you fin de sick bastards but the first indication of my grandfather's pacifist credentials I'll have yer know. All right, all right, just an incy-bit tarnished by *Field Day Exercise on Pod. Present: Fairly Big Wigs from Aldershot – no Generals tho. I was not, thank the Lord, a DARKIE this time. Barsity was. Played the corker – refused to drop when I shot him, just carried on whooping like nigger minstrel gone compl. dotty. Frightfully good fun, but Major Wormsley ticked Barstow off no end & H. P. thunderous. Ho ho. Some use in these japes, I spose. Civilisation kept intacto. Felt quite excited in nice RED uniform, firing away. Red so much grander. Green safer of cse, but give me red any day & I'll risk the pot-shots. Wd go back to helm & halberk in a jiff, if came with crimson plume attached.*

Get the idea? He'd survive about a minute at HCDVA, wd my grandad. Wd all our grandads. Dads. Wd most of you out there – pink or black or brown or yellow or even purple 'cos Ossy's present if you were given an HCDVA thought-scan, you intolerant bastards.

Bldsh. We're all out here on the pitch and it's raining. Or maybe it's just very heavy mist. Anyway, it's England. It's not Flanders. If I was a low-budget genius like I am I could use this pitch for The Greatest Battle Scenes In Ve History of Ve Cinema and I probably will, if ve mist keeps up. Frandles. Frangincourdles. Out of the mist comes Mike, in his best duffel. It has beads of moisture all over it like a duffel has beads of moisture all over it. When it's damp. Don't expect me to be a poet when I've got wet tussocks and mud instead of feet. Mike looms up and then is gone. It was a vision. Mike is dead. There's only me and mist. The whole crew is not here and they never were. I'm alone. I'm cold. I'm my grandfather. Somewhere near the other end of the mist which has no end is the rest of the mob. The game swayed up this end and my grandfather alias me gave the ball a dashed good boot and the mist swallowed up all those eggy chaps who take life far too seriously and think the bladder should be dashed for when really the whole thing is frightful poppycock. Actually, I'm kind of only half right about the egginess of the other chaps. No one, repeat no one, takes bladderdash seriously. Not even the bloods get cut up about it. Not even the bloods. Indifference is all. If one gets into a real scrap it's not the game but the natural inclin. of the fellows. So little care is ta'en of the score that even when the damn thing flops into the enemy's ditch for the 5th time & chalks up a point, it is Bad Form to cheer. This is all in the diary, OK? And the *Sunday Times* refused to serialise it. Maybe they thought it was fake. Maybe they thought it wouldn't sell their lousy paper. Maybe the fact that bladderdash is totally extinct now the Old Randlers don't have their ceremonial Prize Day bout since one of them choked to death on their dentures in the scrimmage means that no one's interested any more, it's about as gripping as dodo shit or the History of Fleet Street or watching indoor fireworks. Some jerk's bound to have brought some indoor fireworks. Sorry about that. Wave your sparklers around and pretend you really appreciate the gesture. Imagine being this jerk and continuing to be this jerk in the new millennium because it'll take more than a new millennium to change him. Sad, huh? Like it's sad being my grandfather in the middle of a bladderdash game a week before his brother's due to be given the boot in the way he was given it and it's raining and, hey, he had to play this fucking thing on the Very Day Itself can you imagine. Life can only get better. Unfortunately, this is 1913. This is pretty well the peak. This is certainly, if not the actual peak, one of the approach slopes. The actual peak was where we all know it was. I'll get there, I'm looking forward to it, I'm looking forward to strawberries and cream under the sighing elms and Rupert passing his latest scribble and the tinkle of bicycle bells or maybe flocks of sheep or maybe it's those vicars under floppy hats as they lean over the gate and scratch their mutton chops and wave halloo through a cloud of gnats. It'll be a nice break. I deserve it. We all deserve it. No one scratches mutton chops these days unless it's from adhesive irritation. Whoa hey the bladder's coming our way. The fellows are floundering after it. Someone's given it a jolly decent tonk and here it comes. As Last Domino it's my grandfather's unavoidable duty to collar it. Kendal is pulling Sandicot round by the sleeve over there wheeee which is rather beyond the pale because Sandicot has not touched the ball yet but as all bladder-dash *aficionados* know even if they don't know how to spell *aficionado* there are no pales in bladderdash, you can bloody well Whirl a fellow until his brain separates into its constituent parts if you want, you can actually pin a chap to the ground and get the whole team to trampoline upon him until he's disappeared into the mud if you so desire but that would be bad form because it's a touch keen, what? The fact that only one person has ever died playing this thing (not counting the stupid Old

Randler with the lousy dentist and the eleven or maybe twenty-five wheezy chaps whose pulmonary fluid may have been topped up by a little stint of it in fairly uncomfortable weather) is only remarkable if you apply normal everyday rules of conduct whatever they are. My grandfather slides over and collars the ball fairly deftly but because he's thinking about cigarettes and how he'd really like to suck on one right now his mind's not with it and he just stands there holding out this inflated mud-pack ready to kick it but someone else does it for him and not very accurately so quite a few levels of knuckle-skin go flying too and he has to suck his fist after shaking it some. The fist tastes of blood and mud and stuff and it stings. The fellows slip around yelping after the ball and not even Barstow comes up to see if I'm all right. Bldy rotter. Youch. This is the taste of Agincourt. Out of the forest on the edge of the Pitch comes the damsel with her lint. The mist is clearing. The forest is deep, its craggy oaks and flowery brakes and mossed stones go on for as long as the ocean goes down and down. About five miles, actually, but I don't think my grandfather is a very literal guy. Let him be poetic, for God's sake. No one's allowed to be poetic these days meaning the other end of the sickle. No one's allowed to believe in forests being so deep and oceanic they might contain nymphs and knights and stuff. Hey, Giles my grandfather believes in Pan. He's standing there in that fucking awful sub-marshland about a board-rubber's throw from an incredibly unpleasant boarding school to which he has welded half of his youth sucking on a torn fist and gazing at this scrappy little oak wood under drizzle and thinking how he might just spot Pan cavorting in there on his hairy goat-legs. I mean, isn't it ridiculous? Amazing but true. My grandfather's view of the world is basically a lot of England divided between the shallow bits and the deep bits. The shallow bits can be anywhere and so can the deep bits, but generally the deep bits need to have trees or at least some kind of shady greenery except that there's a view of the downs near Hamilton Lodge with nothing but a few juniper bushes on it and a lot of sheep plus shepherd of which (Christ, this shepherd's really important, he was hell to cast because no one has a face like that these days unless they've been pegged out on the beach in Antigua for about three months – I've ended up with this hippy traveller guy with no front teeth and a slight limp and extremely distressed skin. The limp and no front teeth look great, he was set upon by a consortium of major English landowners for picking a blackberry or something and he'll get dubbed over by Ben Kingsley pretending he's got no front teeth because this hippy traveller guy cannot do accents, OK? I mean, he's from Hemel Hempstead for crying out loud. He and my grandfather have had some great conversations in the caravan over the last five years. But no one hangs around off set forever, with or without free cups of tea brought by Julie Patchouli and the latest *Grip Weekly* personally cinched by me. I'm running way over schedule. It'll be *I, C-C-C-Claudius* all over again, which won't be too bad, actually)

I'm sorry, I lost the thread of my spool, the screen's a white-out and the audience are putting on their Polaroids, a cheery groan goes up with the smoke, the projectionist takes his hand out of his trousers and doesn't even smell it, he's so keen to rectify the situation. With a razor.

OK. Splice. Sorry about the hop, the razor was blunt, he's only a projectionist.

that there's a view of the downs groany cheer near Hamilton Lodge with nothing but a few juniper bushes on it and a lot of sheep plus shepherd of which the bottom has definitely not yet been sounded and it's hard to say why. Or why not. It certainly has nothing to do with grammar. It might have something to do with it being incredibly spacious and having a lot of sky thrown in, but that's just too visual for my grandfather and me. I'm not a very visual person, it may surprise you to hear. This I think is the reason why I've never made complex masterworks before and why I feel basically lonely. I mean, the world is really into visuals. Cor blimey innit 'arf. When I said this to Zelda recently through my paper bag she couldn't hear me so OK OK I took the bag off and repeated myself with my eyes closed. She said I'd been taking drugs and I said not the mind-bending ones just a lot of Aspirin for my broken heart cross my fingers hope to die which was a calculated risk and she sighed and said anyway Baudrillard got there before you concerning this visuals thing. I said Baudrillard could be a Swedish dental surgeon for all I've read the guy and the way you pronounce him. What's interesting is that Zelda did not say anything about Zen Buddhism. Dr Tosh has entered her in more ways than three. How did I get onto this. I was doing really well. The game is doing really well too. Willoughby-Vern is being Whirled. This is pretty well a tradition. Willoughby-Vern has a monocle and no chin and can gallop in a straight line on his own land until the priceless chestnut drops dead under him from exhaustion, theoretically. I'm sorry if this guy sounds too clichéd but there we go, THIS IS THE TRUTH. Withery-Vermin gets whirled really spectacularly at about this stage of every game because it's at about this stage of every game that he's discovered trying to look like a thorn bush instead of playing up and playing the game and wheeeeeeee round and round and round goes W-V until his brain is separated into its constituent parts which makes very little difference to his thought-patterns because his thought-patterns are basically a series of parallel lines to do with horses and money and monocles and stuff and now he's shrieking that he'd only stepped out because he was feeling dashed seedy. What his parallel lines have never picked up on is the possibility that his shrieks are what make whirling him so incredibly satisfying for the chaps and also that you can't step out of bladderdash because theoretically the bladder-dash pitch has no limits and you can run with the bladder to Land's End if you're so inclined and the only reason Hastypudding (the original and authentic tinted-by-hand name of the field, dumbos) is churned to treacle is owing to the position of the ditches at either end. NOTICE I DID NOT SAY TRENCHES. I AM NOT ONE FOR OBVIOUS PARALLELS. MY MIDDLE NAME IS SUBTLE.

I'm afraid to say that my grandfather really enjoys watching the Willoughby Whirl, it gives him a quite delicious thrill, it says so in his diary. HOWEVER, a week from now there'll be an exception. Didn't enjoy the WW today, too cruel to my mind even tho' the rotter was grinning all the way through the cestus this morning. If this whole beastly episode makes me a better person then some good will come of it. I pray it does. Wheeeeee. While Willoughby-Vern's bowels are turning to custard the bladder lands in the enemy ditch for the fifth time and it's a dunk hooray dammit. Not that Giles my grandad could care a toss. The virgin damsel in the silk mantle is binding his wound while the nymphs and various assorted elfine spirits watch from the skirts of the greenery his shy fortitude. Willoughby-Vermin travels through the air as usual and vanishes. The victors return to the middle over where he was last seen. He's there, actually, but he's very well camouflaged. Maybe if he'd rolled around in the mud just before the First Day of the Somme instead of striding out in clean togs with his stupid swagger-stick and the Willoughby-Vern coat-of-arms stitched

380

brightly on his tunic by his dear mama Lady Ursula Augusta Branswick Throckmordant Willoughby-Vern *née* Huck and known affectionately as Poppy for some really insider reason ironically he wouldn't have had his head blown off. But there we are. The sole scion of the family, too. Hard cheese, Willers. Hard fucking cheese.

OK, I'm not a better person. I'm not my grandfather. I didn't watch my brother go through Hell and out the other side. Actually, if I'd watched Des go through Hell up the linden tree avenue I'd have probably been pretty happy. And vice-versa, speaking for him. Des is my brother, in case you've forgotten or just come in disgustingly late or don't know me too well. Frankly, we would not have chosen to come into the world out of the same womb only three years apart and to share the same bedroom for most of our youth so that each night I went to sleep with the smell of Des's socks up my discerning nostrils but there we go. Fate *accompli*. At least we only shared the same bed for seven years. Kids tended to in them days. Nuffink improper. Des did have this thing about his bottom, though. He'd show it to me every night and laugh. Eugh. He was always fundamentally thick, was Des. Something interesting's happening on the pitch. Some of the guys are edging towards the school side. Nyah nyah I know why and you don't. It's a historical secret. It's extinct. It's gone down with stuff like fossing and pluved and a perspers to the Five-Mile Hump.

Aw shucks, OK, I'll let you in on the biggest secret of the century. The reason these guys are edging towards the school side instead of floundering after the ball on the wood side like the sporties and the thickies is because the ten-past-three bell is about to clang and bladderdash changes into hotbathdash because first come first in and the boiler has a limited capacity despite its titanic proportions. And we're talking jugs and basins, remember, not high-pressure taps and showers and jacuzzis and stuff. Now you know. Giles starts to edge over which is risky because edging over like this can get you a Guinea Whirl and that's the whirliest and the whirler can grab anything, not just your right sleeve as in the Penny and either or both sleeves as in the Shilling, he can swing you round by your hair or your ankle or even by your testicles if they could stay on long enough. It's called the Schoolside Forfeit and you have to weigh up having hot steamy water being nice to your limbs against the possibility of the worst Whirl in the world and actually that's how the one bladderdash death occurred, his name was Julian Tremlett and he was really cold and so new he didn't understand that hovering around North-West Thorn at five-past-three when the ball was flopping around South-East Thistle was running an incredible risk but he did have a dicky heart, it wasn't really the fact that they spun him by his right foot so many times and he couldn't keep his face up that long. I don't know why I'm going into this thing so deeply, maybe it's because I am probably the world expert on the game of bladderdash, I could start a Bladderdash Club in Houston and charge the earth and clinch the TV rights and it'd be like Eton fives and its crazy court, we'd have to recreate Hastypudding down to the thistle patches and the slippy ditches and the big dead rotten log across the middle and the kind of boggy miasma which has a lot to do with the school's sewage outflow or so the legend went. Something tells me it could really take off, only the stadium would have to be ginormous because it'd have to have the oak wood for Outers and the school buildings for Schoolers or at the very least the school bathrooms because this edging towards schoolside thing is an intrinsic and very exciting part of bladderdash, don't get me wrong, without this life risk involved the game'd be a whole lot less complex and it comes right at the end, it'd keep the stadium on its tippy-toes to the final ten-past-three clang which is right now ringing out and no one's got a Guinea Whirl or as it's called affectionately a Dead Tremlett, I'm sorry, I was really hoping you'd get to see one, it's disappointing, they're all floundering and sliding and loping out of it and off and my grandfather's pathetic bit of edging over has got him nowhere because he's slipped, he's going to be the last off apart from Willoughby-Vern who's that walking silo over there looking for his monocle.

I mean, to be really authentic you'd have to recreate the whole planet because bladderdash had no boundaries. Think about it. Bladderdash has no boundaries.

What a concept.

I cornered Todd the Backward Dot about this last week. He was stuck in this corner with a fire-extinguisher nozzle up his arse because I admit I was over-excited, I got too close, I didn't give him enough space and the rubber plants grow really big here, I guess the corner couldn't really handle him too. Hey easy, Rick, he kept saying. Easy, easy. I know it's easy, Todd, you just gotta have nerve and an extremely large stadium. A stadium as big as our planet. Because the bladder can go anywhere. You can theoretically be whirled on the Graham Land peninsula or in the suburbs of Bujumbura. Though edging schoolside would be fairly tricky, what with the time-zones and the compass points to be got right. But it's all feasible. Everything is feasible. Aim high, I say, aim high. Grab what you can. Make a buck out of a doe, Todd. He actually pushed me off in the end, he tore my paper bag which I'd forgotten to doff because we were only just outside the library, it was my favourite paper bag, I could sue him for assault and invading my personal development. Rat-arse.

Giles Trevelyan is standing. I mean, he's not moving. Even Lord Walking-Silo is half across the meadow and the meadow is between the treacle and Back Wall and not slippy. But Giles Trevelyan is standing in the treacle. I think I said before that because of the cesspool outflow or whatever the treacle stinks. You can't show a stink in a movie except through reaction shots and Smell-O-Vision never took off – but since Giles is really adapted to stinks by now, Randle stinks I mean, and since this is 1913 and most places stink of horse dung and urine through the coal smoke anyway my grandfather is not too bothered by the whiffs so there's no reaction shot available. I could cut one in like a noddy in an interview but there's no one else on the pitch and anyway this is a complex masterwork, not a fake pile of glossed-up junk. You're very lucky that I'm telling you about the smells as we go along because most movies don't and that cuts out a great deal of the orfentic trouf, dunnit? I mean, eyes are just spectators, it's the other four or maybe five but let's not get too furry that go right in there and ravish, OK? Like for me the Blitz is basically brick powder on the tongue and the stink of burst gas pipes, the stink of burst gas pipes being extremely relevant to this heyar location shoot and you'll see how in a minute, *tight-rein the horses of impatience* (shuddup, Henrik). OK, OK, I exaggerate: the pert finesse of Zelda's profile particularly from the right side does something to my bowels even through the safety glass of the HCDVA library but I'm talking about calling up, not reading the moment. I'm talking Proust here, I'm talking dunked madeleines, I'm talking Pears soap lathering to my

infancy and stuff and the fact that Giles Trevelyan is stood stock still in
the middle of the bladderdash pitch is important because it's not just
the churned-up treacle he'll be recalling pretty soon it's the stink, the
stink peculiar to the bladderdash pitch and ten times ten to the power
of ten THE FRONT LINE TRENCHES. Holy Moses, I've just
blown the Brian de Palma Prize for Discreet Allusion '96. We're
circling Giles right now, he's quite small and distant in the middle,
Pierre has built an amphibious tracking rail like a Hornby-Dublo Set
No. 2008 right round the pitch and we're travelling on it wheeeee. It's
not a Whirl, but it kind of recalls one. It's slow. There's mist blowing
up. The colour's bleached right out to variations on the colours blue
and brown. Giles in his cutaway breeches is stock still and small out
there or *in* there I suppose and definitely sad and he must be fairly cold
too. I'm cold. I can't get used to this lousy climate, it's like living at the
bottom of the Atlantic in a cold current without a wet suit, it's amazing
anybody can sum up the zip to keep going, guv.

I'm hanging on for the summer. I happen to know that the summer of
1914 will be twenty-four carat, you won't see the hayricks for boaters
and blazers and their impossibly lovely cousins in embroidered lawn
squealing oh so prettily when they flit barefoot over some expired
gramophone needles. Bet *you* didn't, nyah nyah. You did? Oh. OK, but
I'll bet you half the cost of the total this party of mine you're leeching
off's putting me back that you didn't know that the spring of 1914 is
going to be really wet and nasty and'll nip most of the fruit-tree
blossom dead just to give a very large clue but no one spots it.

Around we go. It looks like the pitch with Giles shivering in the middle
is turning but that's an illusion. There's so much mud it's kicking up
from the tracking wheels and spotting the lens, so what, it's looking
good. My brass megaphone's saying so. It's also telling my grandfather
to hunch his shoulders a bit more. The rest of the guys have been
sucked into the Back Wall. The mist's creeping and it smells evil.
Maybe it's coming out of the ditches. If I was really naff I'd have a kind
of echoey shells-exploding-and-bullets-whistling effect suggested
quadrophonically and maybe music but I'm not, I hate quadrophonics
and background music and I spent twelve years at the feet of M.
Bresson and M. Bresson said to me once in about 1953 when my
blackheads made smiling dangerous *It is only recently that I have*

suppressed the music and have used silence as an element of composition and means to emotion. So this circling scene is in silence. If you have a crisp packet in your hands freeze. If there's anyone insensitive enough to be yakking in the other room or on the veranda or even in this room for crying out loud throttle them somehow but silently. Thank you. We've nearly done a complete revolution. Giles is turning on the turntable of the world and his face is turned away and down and I haven't the foggiest idea what he's thinking, it doesn't matter, what's important is the image and holy shit he's moved, he can't hear me yelling, he can't hear me even through the brass megaphone and Christ if he keeps to this trajectory we'll go straight into him and he's kind of walking and turning at the same time which makes me feel very giddy and I'm saying hold on to his face, we're all phantoms, we'll pass through each other and out the other side and maybe there'll be this little ripple of a chill through the broader chill but basically that's it, his face is coming really close, I think we're going to meet, Gordon's getting shake because he can't believe he can be a phantom and I say there's Mike over there with his funny little cardboard thing and he's definitely a phantom just hold on to his face, you mean Mike's face, no dope I mean the face that's filling the screen right at this moment and is nicely streaked with black miasmic mud we're in his head now, it's really echoey, we're inside the great whale of my grandfather's head and it'll be fine once we've found the eye sockets to look out of but right now it's pretty jolty in here, it's like that London trip in the growler we took two years back, I feel seasick, we're heading over the meadow and because the tussocks are big he's taking big steps, it's dark, it's booming, it's trickling with something, things are really active in here, I know exactly what Pinocchio felt like when he found his poppa in the belly of the Great Shark, I know what he felt like in more ways than one, it must be the hashish but I'm kind of melting into my grandfather, it's a wild and frightening trip this, I reckon I AM my grandfather, I'm walking towards Randle College for Gentlemen's back wall over a damp meadow and I've had a person transplant, I've overdosed on the diaries, I've not slept enough, I'll hang in here until I find his tongue.

On the other hand, mebbe I won't.

I've had a break. I just got back. I'm still glowing and leaving sand around the place because I have some impenetrable crevices on my custom-built body. Hi. I hope you got to the loo and had a great jive or whatever in the meantime, m'dears. I sold my Michelangelo sketch of a foot and flew to, wait for it, *St Lucia*. Zelda knew this. I made sure she knew it. I sent her postcards c/o Dr T. F. Lazenby Jnr with *Wish You Weren't Here* and *Not Thinking Of You* and stuff. Hey, it was a great break. I'm cured. I've thrown away my paper bag, I'm not jerking so much. He didn't. Sorry, that was a bad cut, we jumped some, I've razored out some garbage about not meeting Derek Walcott, forgive me, every movie must have its flaw, it's hop, it's hair in the gate, it's clock on the mantelpiece that wasn't there a second ago, it's bendy arrow, it's wrong stuffed fucking lemur. Actually, I told Zelda in some of my cards how we were getting on fine, Derek and I. She's a fan, she thinks he's the Greatest Living Poet. I also told her that Paradise is overrated, here is better, you don't have to lose your soul to reach it. Youch. When I wasn't hunched over my picture postcards trying to juggle space for the amazing stamp without wiping out half my message I spent most of each day trying to leave my body to enjoy itself in the sea, on the sand, on the wicker bar-stool. Not a lot on the wicker bar-stool. Mostly flat out on the sand with my eyes closed. It was hard work but by the second week I'd got my eyelids to stop blinking too much when they were shut. That was the secret. I thought about things like surf and Zelda and surf and surf and my complex masterwork and Zelda's chin and nose and eyes and breasts sometimes when no one was looking or I was rolled over on my tum-tum and surf and surf and surf and why the hell surf sounded like it was just about to stop. And then I'd wake up again and the surf'd be going on just the same and it was quite a relief. You see how difficult I found it to relax. But it got easier. I snorkelled and snorted and used the pool and stuff and didn't drink too much. I relaxed totally on the last day or would have done if I hadn't had a background atmospheric of nerves about the flight back and packing and unpacking and term starting up again and my program or pogrom as Rick the Wag heads it for the totally humourless stoodents who wouldn't know what a pogrom was if it hit them in the face and hey, I'm getting worked up again, *total relaxation is only available the day you're on the flight back from it.* Sayings of Thornby, Volume 28, Personal Development section.

But I've quit my paper bag and the dope. I'm hanging on to the Scotch. Cor blimey progress is relative, innit? It's not any old whisky and it's certainly not the napalm they drink out here with Coke for crying out loud it's old and peaty and oaken, like me.

So I have to pick up on my grandfather in a fresher state of mind. I mean me in a fresher state of mind, not him.

Youch. My toes are burnt. I was just wriggling them. I always forget my toes. I did meet a girl. We got to the stage where she was camomiling my toes on the penultimate day and giggling because I was Ambre-Solairing hers and yelping but this was on the beach and when we came off the beach we had dinner and then we had a walk along the beach in moonlight and then it was warm haired arm in warm smooth arm and then I had this idea that life was like a Hemingway novel and was just a series of thens but nevertheless and however and needless to say got their act together and despite the beauty of the phosphorescent foam and the perfume of the sea breeze if you can call an aerial massage a breeze and my inimitable attractions she scarpered from under my very lips, guv. I think she was a neurotic, actually. She was a German painter or maybe potter or maybe cocaine runner about Zelda's age and I think she thought I was very wealthy and famous yeah yeah. I stood for about two hours staring at the ocean under a full moon but no one circled me with a tracking camera or even without one. Apart from the thump of the surf or maybe a distant disco I was alone with my thoughts. Actually, I had incredibly significant revelations while staring at that ocean, like how incredibly insignificant I was staring at that ocean.

And old.

Yup, old. Old in a really superficial way, because if you're staring at an ocean like I was staring at an ocean you feel actually you haven't really got used to being around at all yet, you could do with a few more years, like a hundred thousand or maybe a couple of million, just to get used to things like surf under moonlight and the soft inside bit of a girl's arm. But I felt old and was worrying about my eye-bags for crying out loud when in the whole movie of the planet the history of civilisation isn't even a single frame, it's not long enough, so what am I, I'm a jerk who needs a hairpiece, I'm not even significant enough to make my insignificance significant.

But me muvver loved me. She thought I was significant, I guess. Wrapped up in me black-out curtain, bald as an egg, not yet realising how lucky I was. I mean, I could've been a mollusc, or Himmler's daughter, or Des. Imagine that. I could've been Des. So close.

See what lying on the beach for two weeks does to you? And there's a white rectangle where my Michelangelo sketch (OK, OK, maybe School Of) used to be because my walls are grey with Houston atmospherics. Anyway, I like white rectangles. *Build your film on white, on silence and on stillness.* Too right, *mon cher* Robert. I do most definitely feel fresher. My grandfather is in the bathroom. That was scary, being inside his head. That was scary. Now he's in the bathroom contemplating a cold bath. I don't mean my bathroom. That would be even scarier. I got a chill just then, thinking that. Maybe he is in my bathroom. I believe that click just now was a cat. Or maybe my dicky swivel-joint, right hip. I've had a dicky swivel-joint ever since Peter Brook leapt on me in a drama game in 1966 when I was briefly considered as the guy to film *Marat/Sade* but I shrieked too loud or maybe I swore at him because wow did it hurt. It's Peter Brook in my set-the-table-in-a-roar number but actually it wasn't it was Glenda Jackson. OK OK it was some guy who now plays mainly period bank tellers or runs a pub in Weymouth called *The Boring Rep* or something but he was in Brook's gang and he did leap on me to Brook's precise instructions softly spoke. I'm not a liar. But it lost me the contract. Big deal. My call is higher. I am not an archivist. Repeat. I am not an archivist. My grandfather is in the bathroom of Cavendish House. It is a very large bathroom. It has a high ceiling no paint has ever succeeded in sticking around on. It is like a Roman bath without the comfort. The steam is causing our lenses some problems. Basically all you can see is a blur. The pinkish shiny bits are limbs. There's a queue. The water under the wooden slats is black. I'm sorry about the temperature: some jerk smashed a window last week with a calker ball. I can't go into what calker is right now. The northerly gusts are punching up the steam and making it very desirable to be immersed in a tin basin, but as the tin basins are shared you can't wallow without your dick ending up under the guy's chin, which however attractive that might sound to some of you this is a public place and you'll just have to be happy with splashing the four inches over your upper torso's goose pimples and remember that hot baths soften your spirit and declined the Roman Empire and draw your legs up pronto or the other fellow'll think you're making advances with your big toes.

Sorry about the silence. We've got problems with the sound. Bosey's tapes don't like the steam. There are some great sounds here with the echoes and tin basins and water pouring out of jugs and so forth, it's a pity. It looks kind of interesting, though, all this blurry nude stuff in silence so maybe we won't dub it after like – ah, there we go. Bet that got you jumping out of your bean-bags. OK, it's noisy, but there are twenty-odd naked adolescents in here and a lot of water and metal and bare surfaces and the wooden slats are wobbly, they smack and creak and things. That whoosh was Girtland tipping a jug over his head. He'd saved the last fill-up. Now he's sponging himself. There's a break in the steam, you can see him and so can my grandfather. There's a hot pipe in the middle with towels on. Barstow's whipping one off and rubbing himself vigorously. Beastly luck, Trevelyan! he cries. We only caught this because Bosey got a lip mike to him, there are so many cries and echoes it's like a naff nightmare sequence, all we need is a church organ.

Barstow is my grandfather's best friend, the fact that they call each other by their surnames most of the time has nothing to do with their feelings for each other. I call Dr Lazenby Todd and I hate the guy. People I have never met before like stewardesses and bank tellers and stuff say hi Richard. My name is open on all sides, it's flowing away, it's everybody's to do what they like with, they might as well take my trousers too while they're about it, like they're generally taking my money. I feel really dispersed sometimes. Mr Thornby has walls around it. When I want to I'll invite you into Ricky, and maybe even

390

Rick and the other ones. But no one except the mad floor-cleaner at HCDVA calls me Mr Thornby any more. Master Trevelyan has a towel over his shoulder to keep him warm. He flicks it at Barsity but misses. The queue shortens because two basins have their three minutes' sponge-down time up simultaneously, if you get what I mean. Barstow vigorously rubs himself some more and laughs. Still, I expect there'll be a drop or two of hot, Trevels, if you search for them hard enough, old fellow! He disappears for a minute behind some magnificent samples of early twentieth-century English youth as they go grab their towels. Actually, one of them has a bow back from a drunken midwife or something but generally these four are pretty marmoreal. Marmoreal is a big word for you people I know, it means *like marble* – Zelda gave it me as a present after reading it in some poem or other and I use it frequently because people out here are always saying hi how are you but really what they're doing is showing you what excellent and very expensive dental care they are having so my reply is frequently marmoreal, thank you. Now generally I am just nodded to, which is great. I gave Zelda *syzygy* because I'm a whizzy guy and I think it's what angels do. Ho hum. I don't think she uses it much. These moving Discus Throwers are currently trying to sneetle each other's towels. These towels are small squares of linen, by the way, that only just meet around the waist, because Athenian Warriors do not disappear into half a ton of deluxe furry cotton like we *fin de* softies do without instantly losing their manhood, so sneetling another chap's towel is not that easy. Sneetling is something else I haven't time to go into, but it does mean that Barstow is jostled around a bit. Barstow is definitely not marmoreal. Actually, he has a stomach. He's got out from between the classical nudes and is right next to my grandfather. You wouldn't believe my grandfather's goose-pimples. The warm steam is teasing them a little but they're not reacting. Barstow is wrapping his towel around his waist but as usual it's a quarter-inch from meeting so he just holds it there.

I've got some porter, he says. He says this to the slats which if Tarkovsky was doing this movie would have a few hundred frames to their own because there's some great bath-spill swilling past under them, some great flow full of grass blades and mud and the occasional piece of lint and various clouds of blood although these are pretty small. But I'm not Tarkovsky. That fact has given me some pain in the past, before his TED (tragic early death, stoopids) at least, because at the moment I reckon on balance and after much consideration it's better to be alive. My grandfather is examining a bruise on his thigh. Porter, repeats Barsity. He hisses this at the slats. He's pretty certain he can see an ear down there, or maybe an eyeball. Top notch porter, Trevels. Molten gold. You can help me with my elegiacs. Bring a toasting fork. Stroke of four. Some devil's snitched mine. A surge tickles his feet, because Kidlinton has just tipped some guy who's nameless on the credits and shall remain so because my budget is limited and you won't believe how much you have to notch up the payment just because they're called something out of his basin and it's the baby with the bathwater syndrome. Trevels also watches the steamy water swill past and away and shakes his head. Dash it, enough to make one feel seriously indisposed, he says. The waste, the shocking waste. There's a smell of antiseptic, by the way, from the soap around the place. You'll be glad to hear it's stopped raining. I hope Mrs T hasn't begun to thaw out yet in a week from now. I hope the candles on the dinner table have not started to quiver. I hope it's not a strain on the sprocket holes in your head, keeping the frame frozen in the gate like that. The more I think about it, the more I think it might be a long time before we get that scene up and running again. A long time. So file it away in the still store for now, OK?

Barstow is shorter than my grandfather and he has to go up on his toes to get anywhere near the ear so he does. He's about to risk saying porter again when Trevels nods and says I'll bring my toasting fork, Barsity. Barsity grins and goes back onto his heels. Someone's turned round in the queue and is talking to my grandfather. It's Kidlinton. Just in front of Kidlinton is Lord Walking Silo. I don't know how Walking Silo got in front of Kidlinton but does it matter? Actually, it does. It's relevant to what's about to happen. The diary was fairly inexplicit about this bit of the action-packed day but I've not had twelve years of analysis for nothing, I can read between the lines like my analyst could read between the lines of my cheque-book oof. Walking Silo is going to bag a basin for Kidlinton. There's cash involved. This is not what Kidders is chatting to Trevels about. What he's chatting about doesn't matter, and there's an infernal racket coming from the locker-room which is making hearing anything intelligible difficult anyway. I think the four magnificent marmoreals

392

are throwing their boots at someone, something like that, I dunno, guv, I'm not of or in their class, am I? One of them has just been sent a telegram from the Palace for making one hundred not out but since he's deaf, blind, and suffering badly from Alzheimer's I don't suppose it made his day. Still, I thought I'd let you know. The other three did NOT perish in THE GREAT WAR but made it through with various minor disabilities and decorations and became fat sagging purple-nosed braying chairmen of various minor corporations and konked out at various moments between 1960 and 1978, so there. I'm sorry about that. It would have been poignant nay more appropriate to have had their beautiful forms draped brokenly across the corners of some foreign field but sorry mate, nuffink doing, LIFE'S LIKE THAT, it puts the apostrophes in all the wrong places, it nips up on you and doesn't nip up on you, I'm not one to change VE TROOF.

My grandfather is feeling the boiler. He's out of the queue because he's realised with a soggy kind of flash that the very last person in a queue doesn't have to queue because no one else is going to snitch his place. As he's realising how tepid if not actually lifeless the boiler feels he's simultaneously but only briefly wondering why therefore queues don't just sort of dissolve as each last person drops out but then of course the other dropper-outers would snitch—

A large cake of carbolic smacks against his ankles. Ouch, he cries, I say, look here! I know only the Royal Family now say I say look here in a similar situation but not in 1913, please try to understand that my grandfather is not an an an an anachronistic joke. If Hilda and her privately-educated pals were his age in 1913 they would also be likely to shout I say, look here! if Smedmark smashed a cake of carbolic against their ankles with a cricket bat, although given that this is a place of steaming male nudes it would be extremely unlikely Hilda and her female pals would be in here, stripped or unstripped. Smedmark is the Norwegian Ambassador's son and he's now whooping as once Vikings whooped when they split monks in half from tonsure to scrotum. He's now loping over. He's tall. He's very tall. Past silly mid-off to ze boundary, what? he says to Giles. Rotter, Giles mutters. The bathroom is practically empty now so you can mutter and be heard. Giles is not feeling inspired right at this moment, otherwise he'd quip. Smedmark slaps Giles on the shoulder. A four, I think, don't you know! He takes being Captain of the House Fourths really seriously, but actually no one else wanted to be Captain of the House Fourths. I'm full of useful little nuggets of bitchy information like that, if you're interested. My grandfather can be quite acerbic in his diary. You're not interested? You mean bitchy nuggets lose their crunchiness with the passing of time? Hey, you don't say. Maybe you should quit the idea of that autobiography, Ossy. Maybe no one'll be interested in what we all got up to in the swinging sixties and the strangled seventies. Maybe the fact that I once called Joe Losey an accident is not a burning issue any longer. And so forth. Lord Walking Silo is blinking white-eyed through his filth right next to Giles. He has a jug in his hands. He smells miasmically. Over his shoulder is a towel with the bright coat-of-arms stitched on by Lady – by Poppy, I haven't got all day. Otherwise the towel is regulation. Giles steps back and lets him drain the very last of what might be called reasonably-heated water out of the boiler tap. I say, Willers, would you like some porter? (Smedmark's pissed off out of it by the way. You can go home, Niall. You're no longer needed. Thank you. I'll call you. Actually, it was hell to get a real Norwegian. There aren't many of them. Icelanders are even worse. Tell me, how many Icelanders have you ever met in your life? You mean you've been to Iceland? Shucks. Shaaaddap. This is a reasonably important dialogue between Silo and Trevels. All ears, OK? Lip mikes, Bosey m'boy.)

What's that?

Porter. Would you like some porter?

Rather!

Then let me in first, there's a decent chap.

In first?

Your bath.

Oh.

I'll just be a jiff. And you are rather soiled, old fellow.

Thought there was something in it, Trevelyan.

In what?

In the porter.

Burnt malt. And a toast to his majesty. Huzzah huzzah.

All right. Since we're toasting. When?

Four of the clock. You'll have to skip Hall.

I say, what a tragedy.

Barstow's study, half an hour. Now mind out, you lucky chap. I'll be breaking the blasted ice soon!

He takes the filled-up jug from Silo and humps it over to the basin and finds Kidlinton already in there with his eyes closed. He adds the clean water to the soiled and tests it and smiles and neatly flips his towel on to the rail and steps in and touches bottom and leans against the back of the basin and it's reasonably pleasant. He doesn't wonder how Kidders got in before Willers given their queue positions. He's not the CIA, for God's sake. The other basins are empty both of water and personnel. A couple of chaps are rubbing vigorously beyond the rail which is now cool. It's nice, the quiet. My ears are ringing more than usual. There's just the slop of water as Giles tries to snuck in an extra inch of his torso and bathes his knees basically to keep them from going Alpine. He closes his eyes and smiles in the kind of reddish darkness because he's thinking how thick Willers is and how he'll most definitely end up at Sandhurst, the silly prawn. This is not the most generous side of my grandfather but life at Randle is not a ball, it does not make you into Jesus or someone. His hips are being stroked by something fairly coarse. He opens his eyes. Kidlinton's knees are very low in the water. When the ice-caps melt they'll be the first to go.

I say, Willers, don't get this opportunity every day, do we?

That was a murmur. Well done, Bosey. It was so private and murmury it didn't even echo. We caught it clean. There's something coarse now stroking my grandfather's scrotum. I'm sorry about this. There's no certificate on this movie but I know there might be children out there so all I can say is that the water is very opaque. Actually, it's grey. The coarse thing is Kidlinton's foot. Anatomically speaking it's the big toe's ball-joint. Fortunately Kidlinton opens one eye and so retracts everything into his half of the basin and his half of the basin's water empties itself over his end, which is a frightful bore because, I don't know how to say this, but the lowered water level exposes the top of my grandfather's member. So there.

Gawdelpus.

Actually, I've had enough of this bathroom. It's the echoes, partly. They're really over-assertive. I reckon the echoes talk to each other at night, snigger and snort and stuff while the boys are sleeping away their youf. I can't stop thinking of Kidlinton's stumps. He's really embarrassed and blushing and doesn't know where to put himself and there's only about two inches of grey water between himself and my equally embarrassed grandfather and all I can think of is these stumps. It's probably because of the underwater scene with Kidlinton's toe-joint. I mean, it's really weird to think of it not being around in about a year's time because Kidlinton joined up very fast. He joined up very fast because he writes poetry and is very sensitive and went to France on holiday in 1911 where he fell in love with a farmboy, surprise surprise. He was in France the second time about three weeks when his legs converted fairly instantly into stumps from the knee down, or up, or whatever. Go see the still. The guy in the trendy jacket with a fag and limp trouser-legs stuck in the Bath chair next to the toothy nurse is Kidlinton. The fact that he's smiling is not because he's happy. He ended up being trundled around the shrubbery every day by his mother and went alcoholic, which is not surprising. I'm sorry about this. I like to think he went alcoholic after Willoughby-Vern got his head blown off but I don't think there was that much between the two, actually. The diaries reckon there was cash involved. I dunno, guv. This is really depressing. Go see the still anyway, people. Go get your dose of *pro patria mori* as a little teaser promo for the Big One Coming Up. I mean, it's going to be the most orfentic recreation of ve Great War ever screened, innit? No holds barred, mate. No holds barred.

I've just got to get through some narrative thrust first and we'll be there behind the old barbed-wire tralala. Don't go. I mean, just go look at Legless (not my nickname, the world's cruel, his cronies harshly laughed their way through the brittle twenties etc. etc. while he dribbled and belched) and come back. Forget the Hyde Park thing. There are no fountains spewing out Bollinger anywhere, that is an evil rumour, this is Great Britain, the fountains are probably not spewing anything out, the basins are full of fag-ends and lynched revellers and empty – I repeat empty – lager cans. This is the dawn of a new millennium. Legless we stumble into fresh fire and feel the something something about each something heel. You know what Henrik should have done? Started a Rent-a-Quote service. It'd have cost me a fortune. I hope his executors aren't watching. Greg and Maura's inheritance is not infinite. Nothing is infinite, these days. See ya in a mo, people. See ya the other side of my golf-game, at least, with Glenda my only friendly neighbour who's got a great handicap. He's visually challenged in one eye. Seriously. Oof again. Youch. Hey, my elbow's out of practice, I hit my funny-bone on your breastplate, I need this little break, I do.

I hope you don't think I'm making anything up. That would upset me. Kidlinton pays Willoughby-Vern to play around with him and clearly it was very exciting to bag a bath together. Hey, it's all down in the diary. Trust me. Willoughby-Vern is hanging around the boiler, by the way. I don't know if he was actually paid to get in the bath with Kidlinton or whether it was synchronicity. It's amazing that anyone'd even think about getting in the bath with someone as soiled as Silo but maybe Kidders was into bad smells and fouled water too. Actually, I'm not bovvered. What does bovver me is that my grandfather found himself in a very awkward situation and that maybe the way he reacted, which was to think of his great-aunt in her adjustable spinal carriage in order to get his member at least below the water surface and then write all this up in his diary, means that at the time he was totally sane. What I mean is, he didn't bottle anything up like my analyst claimed I always have done. Actually she didn't say that, she didn't say anything at all except hi and thank you when I signed her over my week's wages so she could keep her couch in Leathero, she just nodded, but I could tell absolutely and without a shadow of a doubt that that's what she was thinking all the way through my gabble, my really intimate gabble, and it made me really paranoiac to think she was thinking that. I had to stop after twelve years or I'd have gone crazy, I'd have started to think that she was doing this just for the money and that basically there was a world-wide professional conspiracy going. Whatever, when my grand-father got out the Beastly Thing Was Down and W-V got in and said ouch because the water was frigid but he had it to himself 'cos Kidders was already rubbing himself awfully vigorously & for a v. long time by the window as if *Roma te tenet et amor.*

Hey, I've only just realised. That little Latin bit's a palindrome – it says the same on rewind, Ossy. *roma te tenet et amoR.* See? Now that's smart. Like *Madam, I'm Adam* or *Able was I ere I saw Elba* or *Todd, evil-lived dot.* My grandfather's writing's really neat, by the way, but I have problems reading it because he uses a bin taf I mean a fat nib in Welsh bom bom. I reckon the Latin's ten out of ten, however. I'm not bothering with the Greek. This is the Dark Ages, OK? Actually, the real Dark Ages was quite a nice time. Houston was a prairie with little animals and some quiet Indians who knew them and the oil industry was just something you did in olive orchards around the Mediterranean and if you kept your head down you could spend your life growing oranges or illuminating books or selling unguents door to door between the forests. I could have snucked down nicely into the Dark Ages and maybe learnt Ancient Greek for a start-off. These are the Darker Ages by about fifty lumens. I mean, no one reads Ancient Greek any more and about *thirty-five million people have died in wars since me mum danced in the street for the one and only time with Mr Glover the nice Air Raid Warden or with anyone else for that matter* and that's being on the safe side, I may have missed a million or two here and there but generally not here. *Snug & raw was I ere I saw war & guns.* Hey, we'd best be gittin' on thar, Toto. Yip haieee. Crank that scenery roll till it smokes.

I hope Mrs T is not getting cramp with her hand up like that. I hope there aren't too many draughts in the attic with William's condition and so forth. It's hell keeping everyone happy. They're setting up in Barstow's study but there's very little room. They're always moaning. They want me to build a set. They say I should've built the whole school like Fellini built a hydraulically-tipping ocean liner and Joffre built the teeming wretched unbelievably poverty-stricken slums of

Calcutta but what do they think my budget is? Twenty million? I lost my golf-game, by the way. I always do with my neighbour. He's not trying to direct a movie and teach pea-heads and study the art of homicide all at the same time while suffering the agonies of unrequited love. Or requited, I can never remember which. I have not made love to a single girl since Zelda picked Toadflax. Bastard Toadflax, to be botanically precise. BASTARD TOADFLAX, *Thesium humifusum*, prostrate to spreading, inflorescence terminal, flowers five-merous, calcareous grassland, local. Sounds bad, huh? I ringed it in my wild flower book and Xeroxed it and faxed it over to them a couple of days ago. He's developed this tic. I don't know whether he's developed this tic because of my one-way correspondence or whether it's just age or his wife getting at him from Vermont in every which way but it's ugly. It involves one nostril, it's difficult to explain, no two tics are the same, I should know, I've studied my mirror for years. He's cracking. Actually, the reason I lose my golf-game with my neighbour is because whenever I start to win I feel bad about his eye and his breakdown five years ago and his wife's inoperative cancer and the fact that he's fat and his underpants show and his daughter hasn't kept in touch. As soon as I start thinking this he streaks ahead and I feel really sore but I guess I'm just too nice for this world, huh, guys? Weren't you always saying I'd make a lousy Joseph Losey? Aeiough and other naughty noises. One step nearer and I fire. Fool – you can't shoot a banana! It's— BANG! BANG! Swine – it was loaded! Of course – you don't think I'd threaten you with an unloaded banana? Now come on, tell me – where is Fred Nurk? I used to know them all off by heart like Greg knew Monty Python off by heart and drove me round the bend but you know what? Apart from the rent-a-quote stuff like *Dear mother she was like one of the family* or *You're acting suspiciously suspicious* that's all that's left from all those times crouched at the wireless negotiating a cease-fire with my blackheads and then at the gramophone spraying my gin and wondering why Peter as in Sellers refused to work with me when I could do Bluebottle and Bloodnok like no one else could and word perfect too and even to his face at those great Chelsea parties, remember? Aeiough. Ha ha he he. The egg stains were holding my suit together. I'm not the Laramie man, I'm the Harry Lime-type man. Silly zither music. Holy shit, it's all gone, the whole works, even *The Dreaded Batter-Pudding Hurler of Bexhill-on-Sea* has evaporated. Louisa broke my albums, no one in Texas laughed, Zelda laughed but only

400

when I was trying to be serious. Nothing happened, but it happened suddenly. He's fallen in the water. You filthy rotten swine, you. That was *The Goon Show*. Hey, the worst thing about being alone is laughing, because you start to worry.

OK, they're ready. Action.

Giles Trevelyan goes up the back stairs and along the passage to Barstow's study. Barstow is struggling with his fire and looks rather black. There's no poker so Barstow takes Trevelyan's toasting fork and deals for rummy. Sorry. Aeiough. This is school days but not the 1950s and me muvver bringing the Bovril and pretending to chuckle. I'm looking at me muvver's father in 1913 watching his best friend poke the grate with a toasting fork at school but otherwise there's no connection. Barstow exits to lavatory and scrubs his hands while my grandfather skewers a slice of bread on the fork and props it on the fender. Barstow comes back in and wedges a chair against the door. The film crew are down to the minimum but it's tight. Mike is half out the window watching the sky, because it's very changeable. Giles opens the tin of tongue. The porter bottle is hidden in the coal basket under a layer of coals and it's taken out and wiped down with Giles's handkerchief 'cos Barstow lost his up on the eleven yesterday. Detail, detail. Giles gets rather black and so the chair is removed from the door while he goes out and cleans himself up in lavatory. The film crew are muttering mutinous and fairly rude things which I ignore. They want everything easy and clean but I can't oblige. My grandfather hears someone coming up the passage and thinks it might be Willoughby-Vern so he hides himself behind lavatory door. (It's always called just lavatory in the diaries. *Lave* as in wash. Stick with me.) It isn't. It's Pantile's fag. Pantile's fag is pretty astonished to see Trevelyan behind the door and thinks he is about to be jumped. He's also pretty. He grabs a plate and flees. Giles goes back to the study and this time Barsity produces a pair of laces and ties the handle to the fairly sturdy gas-pipe that runs along the ceiling from study to study for reasons of illumination. Slow pan of gas-pipe for those who're not concentrating, tighten on string tied round it, tilt down string to handle it's also tied round. GEDDIT? The porter goes down splendidly. Bosey's getting cramp against the desk. There's a knock on the door.

I say, chaps, are you in?

You know who it is. For latecomers – too bad. Ask the attractive person
sitting next to you but whisper and don't keep your hand on their knee
for longer than is essential. Good luck. Invite me to the wedding but
I'm allergic to duck. Seriously. I like ducks. My first word was quack
because me muvver wheeled me through Enfield Town Park every
day. We couldn't throw them bread because this was the war and we
ate right up what only a duck would eat in peacetime so they just
quacked and quacked and I didn't understand why we couldn't satisfy
them like the black marketeer's kids were doing and basically I think all
of my problems go back to that. I blame Hitler. My analyst opened her
mouth at last and said that's projection. She's Jewish, by the way.
Hitler wiped out her parents and grandparents and just about
everybody else in her family and there was I going on about ducks in
Enfield Town Park. It's not surprising she broke her professional
silence. Actually, she made me jump. Barstow chews his toast and
winks at Trevels. Trevels has raised his hand to warn Barstow and kept
it there, because the chair he's on has a Devilish Creak. He has a mind
to reply no, we're not in, because the inbred halfwit would probably go
away but he doesn't reply at all. The door-handle moves timidly but
makes no impression on their patent lock save a squeak from the gas
pipe which is sagged anyway. I like this, it's moving, my middle name's
Carol Reed, we've got tilt on the camera. Footsteps die down the
corridor, even. The rest of the school is quiet because it's hunched
over its desk preparing for class and this makes my grandfather and his
best pal both uneasy and stimulated so Barstow waves the elegiacs
around in front of Trevels's face but they make no impression. It
seems Trevels has broken the deal and Barstow is getting aggrieved so
my grandfather gives him the last slice of tongue.

What was Willers wanting with us, Trevels? Giles's mouth is full of
tongue so he can't speak. I say, you didn't tell him, did you? I'll bet you
made a wager. The guilty party swallows his tongue and washes it
down with a swig of porter. Porter is not port, by the way. It's beer. It's
really dark. It tastes like someone's left their burnt toast in it for about a
term. Trevels holds his mug out but Barstow puts his hand over the
bottle. Buggering hell, says my grandfather. Elegiacs, says Barstow. I
know something you don't, Barsity, murmurs my grandfather. He

belches. Barstow waves the miasma away but it doesn't have many places to go to. Actually, with five members of the film crew crammed in here and Ossy's underarms even with the window pulled up it's pretty objectionable. Barstow has just asked what it is that Trevels knows that he doesn't. Ah-ha, says Trevels. Ah-ha! echoes his pal. And this is before A. A. Milne got his act together. You're a qualified scug, says Barstow. I think we can safely say that that was an affectionate piece of abuse, by the way. Trevels nods his head. Definitely mashed, he murmurs. Mashed, who's mashed? Ah-ha, says my grandfather, waving his empty mug about and passing right through Mike's waist which freaks him out because it's like an omen. Who's mashed on who, you dirty prawn? demands Barstow. My grandfather's elbow or maybe it's his thigh hurts and he discovers the two are connected. He removes one from the other and gets it right. He holds out his mug. The elbow was on his bladderdash bruise. That's great continuity, Sylvia. Sylvia is currently negotiating some personal space with a gas-lamp bracket and a camera crane. Who the hell thought of bringing a camera crane in here for crying out loud? I did. OK. I wanted the crazy overhead angles apparently. Just watch yer heads and cor blimey stop moaning. Barstow's pouring the rest of the porter into my grandpop's mug. It's swallowed. The mug won't go past my grandpop's teeth so he removes it from his mouth and places it on the floor. The floor's on hydraulics and tips up and down, up and down, and you thought this was a dime movie, huh? But he gets it there, he gets it there.

Kidders, he says. Barsity is clearly fairly piqued that the mug took the last of the porter for granted and he's looking pale, too. Barstow, not the mug. As a matter of fact, the porter smells more like port than beer so maybe it's kind of old and strong and wired-up like me. Somebody is playing squash. Hey, you can flick matches into one of the squash courts from Barstow's study. The chicken-wire is pretty active so the play is not exactly top-hole, don't you know. Mike's still out of the window and I reckon he's watching the game but he's not blocking the light so I'll leave him, he's not on camera for this one, he's given precise instructions, he's only got a few years to live, give him a break. Three shillings, says Barstow, it cost me three shillings. He's staring at the fat but empty bottle on his desk. The name Kidders eventually makes it to his cerebellum and his face swivels back to his pal. It's plump and sweaty, this face. It looks younger than it is. It could be about ten. On the other hand, it could be forty-two if the lens was fogged up, which it isn't. It's one of those faces which never go ripe. It kind of hangs around the ten-years-old phase while its hair goes grey and its eyebags baggy until suddenly it withers up completely around seventy-one and looks ninety. There are worse fates.

Kidders? ventures Barstow. *Mirabile dictu*, yes! cries my grandfather. Oh Christ more Latin. *Mirabile dictu* what, exactly? presses Barstow. My grandfather holds the chair together and blinks at Barsity. Kidders and Willoughby-Vermin, says my grandfather. A door slams way down the corridor but Barstow jumps anyway. And vice versa, adds my grandfather. Now he's flicking at his tie for some reason. It's blue with orange spots which are meant to be there and it's silk. Barstow's tie is regulation black and cotton. Giles Trevelyan is something of a daredevil, I'll have you know. If you cross the Pod wearing a non-reg tie without being snaffled and hung up by your thumbs and lashed forty times or whatever the forfeit is you get a cad point, don't you know. Giles Trevelyan has run up three points and only eighty lashes or whatever it is. That's fairly good going. He's flicking his hair back. There may be some kind of oil in it. He spreads his arms carefully in case the hands go flying and one passes through my waist this time. My kidneys chill.

Willers is mashed on Kidders, and vice versa, he says. Long live good King George until his due demise. I say, hisses Barstow. So do we all, says my grandfather. The bell starts donging. I don't know what this bell's for, I'm consulting my timetable, it's very difficult to keep track. It appears to be the four thirty-five for tea and sausages in Hall. I'll give it a miss. Both pals are looking at the door but neither make a break for it. There's either a lot of boys running down the passage or Bosey's set the speakers up very cleverly. Now there's silence and no hiss. It must have been boys. The squash has stopped. We can pretty well assume that the whole of Randle College is in Hall hunched over their tea and sausages with the exception of these two. Trevels has his eyes closed and Barstow has his mouth open. The eyes open and the mouth closes. Barstow's chair creaks. It's a great creak. Creaks are some of the most difficult things to get right. I say, Trevels, how the hell do you know? I hope you're not too shocked by a vicar's son saying hell and stuff, but there we go. He gets it from his father. His father is not a hallooing-over-the-gate type of vicar but a cantankerous old bastard with a sherry problem and a rectory so big and dark Mrs Barstow gives him a ball of wool if he has to go off up to the lavatory or someplace but if you go into Little Haddlesdon and so much as hint that maybe a fresh young face in the parish would get God's purpose going a tad more rapidly the little old maenads in crêpe hats there'd tear you into pieces and eat you.

How do you know, Trevels? re-enquires the vicar's only son of his errant pal. Dum-dum steep our brows in slumber's something balm, nor harken what the spirit brings, something joy and calm, why should we only toil, the roof and crown of things! Sorry about the Tennyson bit but this is what is currently rolling through Trevels's cerebellum and he's got his eyes re-closed. Dash it I must learn it by heart because it really has got life to a T's now rolling through, hand-cranked by Enorches the betesticled who's giggling under his grappa-leaves. His knee is being unscrewed. My grandfather's, I mean, not Enorches the betesticled's. And from the craggy ledge the poppy hangs in sleep, he hears himself murmur about two seconds after he does. My grandfather again, not Enorches the well-hung. I say there, off my knee! also emerges but frightfully loudly and it wakes him up. Barstow's hand is on his knee. He claps his own upon it. The devil you know, says Barstow, which translated into *fin de* sickle lingo means you bloody well don't. 'Cos that's what poppies do, says my grandad the adolescent prig. You're allowed to be a prig when you're adolescent, OK? If you're not really irritating at the age of sixteen you'll be really irritating later, when it matters. Des was really sensible at sixteen. So was Maura my daughter who's not kept in touch and married a very unpleasant person called John-In-Insurance who thinks I'm an Unacceptable Risk. So there. They go to sleep, continues Maura's great-grandfather who would definitely have been an unacceptable risk. Come to think of it, John-In-Insurance would have had a lean time if he'd been active at this period because a year from now there are going to be a lot of healthy young very low-risk men converted overnight into very unacceptable ones. John-In-Insurance would have been sweating bricks and Maura would've had to sell the Toyota Land Cruiser with the buffalo guard because there are a lot of buffaloes in Stoke Poges. What a nice thought.

They slumber on craggy ledges without falling off, continues shortly-
to-be-unacceptable risk. That's deuced clever of them, I say! He starts
falling off. He's not a poppy, obviously. He's certainly not a poppy as
you or I understand it because poppies blowing in a field of corn do not
mean the same thing to my grandfather at this juncture as they do to
you or me unless you've been sealed off all your life in a loop tape of, I
dunno, *Dallas* re-runs. Or happen to be one of my new students which
comes to the same muchness. I mean, most of my noo stoodents only
think a lot of Jews were gassed in the follow-up because Spielberg told
them so. I ask you. My grandfather hangs on to his straw hat because
Barstow is pulling at his roots which is unfair. He hits the floor and the
chair hits him and his straw hat goes rolling off through Bosey's legs.
Barstow is now taking the poppy's shoes off. Giles Trevelyan studies
the chair's canework microscopically. His uprooted feet are being
tickled but the giggles are Barstow's very nearby. It has to be very
nearby because the mean dimensions of this room cannot be
exaggerated and one's feet are quite near the rest of one's body, when
you think about it. Sylvia is stretching a little now the chair is down.
Mike has fallen out of the window or maybe he's come in and is
trapped behind Gordon the big Grip. The camera cane swings across
an inch off from the top of my head and I suspect intimidation. I'm
used to it. I intimidate myself. I won't go into this now. There's no
time. I'd need at least two-score years and sixteen to go into it.

Barstow looks as if he's about to say I feel fucking awful. Actually he
says I feel hugely seedy but it comes to the same thing. Trevels
suggests a cocoa. Wow, an amazing moment of sobriety which can
happen when one is completely pissed, but since there's no response
from Barsity he reckons he just might have imagined he said it, or not
really said it properly – which is true, because no way can a hum be how
about a cocoa, old chap? This reminds my grandfather of relieving
oneself in a dream only to wake and find one's member stiff as a
cucumber and heaving oneself out of bed and stumbling through the
cold and the dark and releasing oneself into the *pissoir* with
tremendous relief only to find oneself marshalled halfway through into
the ranks of the Emperor Napoleon's guard of honour still bursting
and cursing one's ill fortune because one hasn't been anywhere but the
other side of one's pillow and Boney is on his way sporting a
rhinoceros's horn and it's really Ionescoesque. Not that my

grandfather thinks it's Ionescoesque, I'm not that careless, he probably thinks it's burlesqueesque or whatever if he could manage to say it without his head falling off. Burlesqueesque or not, he's pretty much that way now bladder-wise. If someone could attach a rubber pipe he'd do it out of the window. A Patent Piss-Pipe for Gentlemen in Need (accompanying ink sketch – seriously). Made out of the Finest India Rubber, new design This Season, Guaranteed to withstand the heaviest Usage, light, fast, cleanly, compact, elegant, comfortable, Adjustable to any Size, durable, easy to Learn, no slippage, no Stooping. Sound familiar? Ddot takes the smallest size, by the way. Don't ask me how I know. Hey, I'm saying nothing. I'm just commenting. I was told by a school pal in about 1953 that we were all the same dimension when fully up. I harboured this illusion through thick and thin, despite some fairly nasty observations from women I fancied were hung up or trying to be Bette Davis at the time. Now I know we aren't. There are legends around. So be it. At least Ddot and I share something, except that I'm not screwed up about it. I think he is. When Zelda comes back to me chastened I won't mention it at first. When I do we'll laugh. Laugh and laugh. That'll be nice. On the beach in Antigua or someplace. Cor blimey. Gawdelpus. Vat'll be ve day.

I say, Barstow.

Do you?

You haven't got a piss-pot, have you?

'Course not.

Would you mind awfully, old fellow, if I used the empty bottle?

Yes, actually.

Thanks, Barsity.

He lifts the chair off his face. The chair falls onto its side and Gordon says fuck, but it doesn't record because we're phantasmal presences and phantasmal presences don't record. My grandfather sits up. Would you mind closing your eyes out there because this is a fairly

407

undignified action that's about to take place. My grandfather begins to undo his fly and after about half an hour or maybe five minutes of giant buttons he's done it. He kneels. He the full bottle back on the floor. Sorry about the jump-cut. It's just that watching my grandfather piss into a bottle for several minutes is not very interesting so I got the razor out. I could have left it and just put my hand in front of the projector like Mr Malim used to do in the Southgate ABC whenever two mouths approached each other it was said but I may not be amongst you, who knows, who knows what tomorrow will bring let alone the dawn of the new millennium.

I say, you beastly scug, you've hit Demosthenes!

That was Barstow. He's been practising that line in the caravan for days. He'd tend to over-emote it, make it intentional and personal. I kept saying to him, I don't want you to act, Fatty. I wasn't being offensive, I've got the young Fatty Arbuckle on this one. Charlie Laughton couldn't make it. I don't want you to act, *the thing that matters is not what you show me but what you hide from me and, above all, what you do not suspect is in you.* Anyway, the line's fine now. Demosthenes is his little tin soldier in Frenchie uniform which gets thrown across the room fairly often, particularly during a Greek prep. You really are a filthy scug, Trevelyan. Barstow's looking very pasty, actually. He picks up Demosthenes by his hat and waves it around. Trevelyan's buttoning up his flies while still prostrate. Demosthenes is wiped on his trousers. Bosey was hit, too, but it went right through him. Mike is definitely stuck behind Gordon, telling him to get more tilt on the camera because Mike has watched *The Third Man* seventy-one times, for crying out loud. Gordon and Mike have a complex relationship. It ought to be symbiotic but it's not, it's tricky, it's like trying to sweep maple leaves into a perfect circle with someone else holding the broom. Grandpa Trevelyan stands up, kind of. In half an hour he will be exploring the functions of angles in Geometry so maybe he's started early. They might even do some rotating. Either way it'd be pretty nasty in his condition. I'm also worried about Barstow. He looks like someone's thrown a bag of non-wholemeal flour in his face. He's putting Demosthenes back on his desk but slowly. Trevelyan is trying to work out how to rotate or maybe transform the chair so one can sit on it, but it's tough. There are a lot of mathematics involved, a lot of squiggles and arrows and indices. I say, Barsity, he says, did I mention cocoa a minute ago? No, says Barsity. Ah, I could have shworn I did. The chair is upright with some asterisks and arrows around it. Trevels shakes his head and after holding his ears on he transforms his body into a sitting position on the chair. He doesn't need to attend Geometry. He knows it all. He's beginning to think maybe the porter wasn't such a frightfully good idea after all. Mind you, he's not eaten much today, it was salt beef and tapioca again for lunch, he's thinking how he'd better break into his herrings over in his study and then cadge a ciggie off Lyons or some fellow. The door-handle is moving up and down all by itself. Or he could purchase some fags off Jack the Lats, who cleans the school conveniences and does a roaring trade in Woodbines if you don't mind the marks of his calling on them. Remarkable, how door-handles can do that. I have to point out, by the way, that it's not one of us trying to get out. Or trying to get in. I know who it is. If you're thinking it's Willoughby-Vern, forget it. It's much much worse/but it's not Holloway-Purse. The gas-pipe is having a tough time up there, because the string is 1913-tough and well tied. People knew about knots in those days. The pipe's kind of bouncing up and down and making a weird noise all along its length but the boys in the other studies are used to it making weird noises, like they're used to the little farts of gas you get when lights are turned out at night and the psychotics are getting ready under their blankets for whatever but it might just involve you, old chap.

Three guesses what Barstow's doing. No. No. No. Bad luck. You might have got a free copy of my Maurice Barrymore poster. I could've bleached out the coffee stain on his tuxedo and ironed the paper because his legs have got sag, it's been in my toilet for ten years, it smells of something pretending to be lavender. He's playing Captain Swift as usual. Zelda hated the centre parting and the arrogance. I said it's not arrogance it's swagger, there's a difference – he was born in a dungeon on the Jumna River, the dungeon had a great view of the Taj Mahal, women fell over their crinolines trying to touch him, he toured Texas where surprise surprise a sheriff practically shot him dead in 1878 – he was a soak and extremely famous and completely forgotten except that his son was John Barrymore. You mean you've never seen John Barrymore? Corluvaduck. Me eyes are saucers. You mean you've never seen John Barrymore in *Beloved Rogue* catapulting into the

409

medieval boudoir wiv a fevver in his cap or even in *Grand Hotel* with that Greta wotsit y'know GARBO for crying out loud? You mean you don't know how this idol of idols and star of stars became a bit-parter of bit-parters and a tosspot of tosspots, hollering in the hollow rooms of his mansion for the next Jack Daniels and maybe a chair? They don't make them sink like that any more. Barstow's snoring. Maurice stays in my toilet. My grandfather's got hiccups. The door-handle's causing the gas-pipe a simple engineering problem, as Howard Hughes said of Jane Russell's brassière. (Hey, I quoted this in my class on Great Screen Idols last week. I'm up in front of the tribunal tomorrow. I think I might just get away with my car, my home, and my job, but I'll probably have to wear this little yellow *S* sewn on my lapel for about three weeks. I'm smiling a lot at Vyshinsky, alias the Vice-Principal, alias Dr Smith. He chairs the tribunal. It doesn't help. I say hi Vyshinsky and smile but he doesn't get the joke. He's never heard of Vyshinsky. He probably thinks the Great Purge is some kind of laxative. No one likes to laugh here. Not at my jokes, anyway. People disappear after laughing at my jokes. I have to use the stairs and with my heart-condition because it's dangerous to go in the elevator with a lone woman and there are lots of lone women. They think if you get in the elevator with them it's just to snuck up close but hey, the elevator is small, you can't help invading their personal body space even if you're pressed up flat against the mirror on the far side and if you actually try to say how nice the weather is or something between floors they scream. I'm serious. The worst thing that can happen is that the elevator gets stuck. It happened to a new guy on the staff with one of my students and although she wears a desirable T-shirt she's really nervous and it got stuck for an hour. He was up in front of Vyshinsky and the others and really went through it. Apparently all he said into the blackness was hey, I'm a claustrophobe, how about you? with a kind of nervous snigger. Can you imagine? The stoopid idiot. I'll let you know how I get on.)

My grandfather looks at the gas-pipe and holds his breath. Because of the hiccups, not the gas-pipe — hey, my grandfather is not that anticipatory right at the moment. The section of the gas-pipe with the biggest problems pops down for a visit as the door opens and John Barrymore practically falls in. I finally got John to play Hubert, Hubert Lightfoot. I thought it would be kind of interesting to have the young

410

John Barrymore play a villain. Anyway, he looks the part. Oh my God, he says, oh my God. What an amazing actor, really. Probably the best Hamlet ever. I'm honoured, guv. Hubert Lightfoot stumbles across to the window and grabs the sash-cord and practically guillotines himself. He yanks the upper section of window back up and takes a breath of ungassed air. Because he's stepped on Barstow's toe, Barstow jerks awake. Silly fools, cries Hubert. Barstow says Oh my God and thinks he's having a nightmare because Hubert Lightfoot is in his study and he meaning himself has just burped. Trevelyan's thinking how beastly fuggish the air is. Too right. I didn't think Lightfoot would take so long to arrive. Papers rustle on the desk by the wide open window as if someone's doing a prep. I thought you'd like that detail. The room feels really crowded again. Bloody fools, cries Lightfoot once more, what the deuce are you up to? Since Barstow is the one being addressed, Barstow makes a small high sound at the back of his throat. He very much wants to go to the toilet suddenly. Lightfoot is Captain of House and has a togy with five knots in it under his waistcoat and Barstow's bottom is getting really scared. He doesn't want his bottom to let him down, but there's nothing much he can do about it. The porter bottle is on the floor by his feet. We're all being really careful not to knock it over because none of us want piss on our shoes but Barstow doesn't try to secrete it. He's given up. His only hope is that he gets the togy from Lightfoot instead of Holloway-Purse because Lightfoot doesn't break the skin too much. Trevels is pointing to his mouth to indicate that he can't speak because he's holding his breath. His face is pretty purple. Hubert Lightfoot is looking up at the bit of the gas-pipe where a gas-pipe should have been. It's what Ddot the Smallest Size would call a disrupted figuration, but Hubert doesn't call it that. Instead, being John Barrymore the silver-screen matinée idol and man of action, he stuffs his handkerchief into the open end of the pipe until the hiss dies down. Then he looks at the other open end and turns and whips off Barstow's tie a trifle brusquely and plugs that one too. My grandfather bursts into the land of the living and raises a finger.

I don't think that's strictly necessary, old chap.

Barstow picks himself up off the floor and checks his throat's still roughly where his collar was until a few seconds ago. Lightfoot glowers at my grandfather. It's a fantastic glower, a classic Barrymore glower, hardly a facial muscle working except for the eyebrows but it gets Giles's hiccups going again. That thing about the tie not being necessary was fairly impressive given the state of his brain but also fairly unimpressive given the state of the situation. It gets worse. A lot worse, actually. Stick with me. Lightfoot will have a pencil moustache in a year's time but right now you'll just have to imagine one because remember he's still at school. His upper lip curls up and then stretches out into a fairly unpleasant sneer, as sneers go.

Don't think you'll make a bloody fool of me, Trevelyan.

He whips out the tie from the end of the gas-pipe, or strictly speaking the beginning of the next section of the gas-pipe with no gas in it, and tosses it on to Barstow's head. Barstow's been sick, by the way. I wasn't going to mention it because you try cutting between the great John Barrymore in the performance of a lifetime and Barstow being sick on the floor but I guess I have to or you might think we're beginning to feel comfortable in this cute little snuggy-hole. OK, there are gusts through the window, but these gusts are English and Bosey's started to sneeze from the lousy little grate and its cheap coal. See how we're suffering for our art and you. Thank you, old chap, whispers Barstow. I've just stopped you topping yourselves and probably taking the whole house with you, come to that. That was Lightfoot, by the way. I say, I thought it was only distressed lovers who formed suicide pacts. That was also Lightfoot, plus sneer. I have to slip in here how Lightfoot is known to Agatha via Amy. You don't know Amy but Amy is Lightfoot's second cousin and Agatha's best friend. Amy is very nice. In fact, she's extremely attractive in the broadest sense of the word and laughs a lot at my jokes, which my great-aunt doesn't. That's unfair. I'm guessing my great-aunt would not have done whereas at least Amy has the advantage of hearing them even though she's fairly deaf and you have to shout a lot, but at ninety-something I don't suppose I'll even have ears to hear with. Lightfoot doesn't know his second cousin awfully well but on each occasion he's enjoyed her company, the cad. He's met Agatha twice, once actually at Hamilton Lodge where he addressed Giles as Giles and was quite nice to him even on the croquet lawn but that only makes the whole thing worse. He more than enjoyed Agatha's company, he was actually stricken by it, which makes the whole thing even worser. You'd think that he'd try to suck up to her brother, would you not, but he doesn't. He's not schizoid he's just complicated. Or maybe he's simple. He never liked Giles Trevelyan and it really subliminally irritates him, I think, to see a dim echo of Agatha Trevelyan's features and amazing grey eyes in the silly little prawn. Anyway, he and Giles do not get on. Lightfoot beat Trevelyan fairly badly with a togy a couple of months before the first meeting with Agatha last year, I think I'm right in saying. This is quite apart from the previous unofficial infringements of my grandfather's personal space which started from the very first day four years back when little Giles was suspended by various slightly less junior chaps including Lightfoot over the central well of the house where at some date in the previous century a new boy's green suspenders had failed to hold out and had consigned their contents to the fairly unappealing career of a spook in the dim-lit basement three floors below. And Giles suffers from vertigo, like his grandson. I can safely say that so far, in a pretty uneventful life, those were the worst five minutes of it. Too bad they didn't stay that way.

Sorry, I thought I'd better fill you in. Don't fall for Hubert, for God's sake.

Giles's hiccups are really taking off his dignity. He is about to raise his finger and rout soundly this charge of sexual misconduct and attempted suicide when he finds his finger already in place. That's a great start. I have to hicform you, Lighthic—

Hubert. Call me Hubert.

What?

Family friend, old chap.

This takes my grandfather completely off guard. His finger is lowered. Barstow's searching for his collar-stud in a kind of discreet manner, still on his knees. I hope for his sake it's not in the puddle of vomit. You wouldn't believe the smell in here, actually. I wish they'd just get on with it so we can get the hell out of here, guv. My grandfather's momentarily stricken with the thought that Hubert Lightfoot might end up as his brother-in-law. I know the feeling. C'mon, just get a

413

bloody move on. I need to expectorate. The gas has really affected my sinuses for some reason. Sylvia actually looks green. Apart from anything else, guys of this age smell pretty disagreeable anyway, like my neighbour's tom-cat or whatever. It brings it all back.

Porter, eh?

Hey, Lightfoot's picking up the bottle. He holds it to the light. There's some liquid in there, if you remember. If you don't, *tant pis*, or *Aunt's in the smallest room* if you want to add to your Amusing Subtitles collection (*Les Beaux Draps*, 1935, 15 mins, director unknown, only print thought to be in Japan along with Frank Tuttle's *Puritan Passions*, 1923, alongside some great lost Goyas probably).

I say, what damned consideration, you've left me some. Barstow's got his mouth open to tell him that it's not porter actually but something else, only his knuckles are being rolled against the floorboards by his pal's foot and he squeaks instead. Actually, adds Hubert, that bratchet Vermin told me you were up to something. He seemed stupendously sore about it. Why's it warm, heh? Been trying to mull porter, have you?

Giles nods his head. Um, one does in the right circles, Hubert.

He also smiles and makes a steeple of his fingers. Barstow groans. If he was in a war film he'd be the podgy little sergeant with round spectacles and permanently open sweat-glands who gets mown down at the climax despite having done all he could to avoid action. He *is* in a war film, actually. I mean, these are just the preliminaries, hey, your eyeballs are getting themselves burnished on THE GREATEST MOVIE EVER MADE ABOUT THE GREAT WAR and Barstow's down for the battle scenes. Or one of them. He's down for the most disastrous and bloodiest day in the history of the British Army, actually, which is fairly bad luck on him, given the fact that he's not exactly Gregory Peck or Rod Steiger or Steve McQueen or whoever. If you told him that fact right now he'd blink at you and probably laugh or throw his lead soldier at your head if you were a pal of his because I think the very last image of himself as a grown man that he'd ever slip into the magic lantern show would be of Gerald Barstow in a real battle because he is probably the worst OTC cadet in Randle history and he is morally opposed to all forms of bloodshed. But life springs crazy surprises, dunnit? I mean, whoever around our family Bisto table ever considered I would be a movie-making genius, for God's sake? No one except me. And I was incredibly wrong. Until recently.

You're black-rotten drunk, Trevelyan. I could have you gated for the rest of term.

Wow, big deal. The Randle grounds are quite big enough for two chaps to be imprisoned in for a few months, you may be thinking over your Alka Seltzer if there's any left. What you haven't considered is THE SHAME. Gated chaps have a big yellow *G* sewn on to their foreheads or somewhere equally visible. They also get about fifty of the best as a kind of soupçon. Their parents are informed by letter. It's suggested that all pocket money be suspended. It's also suggested that all contact, written or otherwise, be suspended. With the corollary that of course if the fellow falls mortally ill the parents will be immediately informed and vice versa. These people have hearts, for God's sake. And it has to be pointed out that there is nothing honourable about being gated, even among the chaps, because it's generally for middling misdemeanours like drinking porter in the study or attempting to gas yourself or maybe both at the same time. I guess it's like having herpes with I HAVE HERPES hung round your neck or positioned next to your begging cap. You wouldn't get much money that way, at any rate.

That's why Barstow groans again. Hey, he can't wait to leave this hell-hole. As soon as he leaves he's going to become a writer of amazing theological treatises musing behind a fragrant screen of flowering wisteria and stay that way until his state funeral. He can even see the plump maid come out onto the loggia and replenish his tea-cup. Loggia, because he reckons it might be in Italy – he reads a lot of Browning and Ruskin and there's a framed Fra Angelico next to my elbow here. I know it's a Fra Angelico because it says so at the bottom where the scissors have cut it out from some magazine. The colours aren't too bad for 1913. I think I might have known it was a Fra Angelico but I could have got him muddled with Fra Lippo Lippi, to be honest. I'd really like to say to Barstow that things might not work out quite like that but now wouldn't be the time. He looks extremely pasty

415

again. Cor blimey luvaduck. Hubert Lightfoot's leaning towards the chaps still with this giant urine sample in his right hand. He smells of games pitches and some mentholy stuff you put on enormous but weary muscles and has a stupid little blue ribbon thing on his lapel which means he's a Captain of House. If he couldn't spell Thucydides one wouldn't mind, but he can. Tighten on his face, Gordon. It's got to fill the whole screen. Great stuff, great performance.

On the other hand, my dear fellows.

Giles brightens immediately. Profile shot of Fra Trevelyan's brightening face against the Fra Angelico. The Fra Angelico is of the Magi bringing myrrh and stuff which is a nicely subtle link because Lightfoot's other hand is famous. It's the left one, it's held out while its partner twitches the togy and it gets heaped up with ices and shillings and French postcards and whatever other sucks happen to be available until the togy in the right hand stops twitching. My grandfather once tried to tell my great-aunt about this little incy-wincy flaw in Hubert's character but she ran off over the lawn and lost her straw hat to a trailing honeysuckle tendril under the gazebo. Ho hum. Love blinds, as little Josef's devoted mother never said. Don't I know it.

Hubert's still leaning over with one eyebrow slightly raised. It has to be said that he's in a long and glorious tradition of Randle extortionists, it's not an idiosyncracy, Stalin was Ivan the Terrible and all that. The camera crane's just gone right through his face but it wasn't meant to be an augury. Hell, not everything can be an augury, even in 1913. I mean, I've seen amateur cine films of Pearl Harbour, guys on the decks sunning themselves and stuff in fuzzy colour, and you think every time they look up at the sky it's a portent. Everybody got up as normal in Hiroshima that August morning, to quote the first line of my very first movie, shot in the streets and parks of Enfield with a Super-8. I've lost the print. It was kinda like *The Bicycle Thieves* without the bicycle. As my grandfather isn't saying anything but is still trying to deal with his hiccups Lightfoot comes in with an offer.

The rest of the porter and ten Woodies, he says.

416

He rolls the urine sample around a bit. Seriously, he doesn't realise. Basically the porter went so fast through my grandfather it's still pretty well porter, if a bit tangier. Barstow closes his eyes and slumps against the wall under the window. He takes off his spectacles. He would like to say don't drink that, Lightfoot, it's Trevelyan's piss, but he can't. Neither can my grandfather. He wishes he had in fact left some porter instead of drinking it all and replacing it with an inferior version because he doesn't fancy being gated and flogged and stuff and ten Woodies is pathetically small, so maybe this is why he's not saying anything. Instead he lets the air out of his cheeks and nods with very wide eyes. The liquor is just beginning to clear from his head which is unfortunate, because the iceberg is about ten feet away.

I'll deal with the porter now, says the bottle. The smokes by tomorrow. Plus a shilling for my trouble.

The reason the bottle says it, is because Hubert's mouth is so close to the opening. It's how the BBC used to do aliens from outer space before they got technical. That shilling sting-in-the-butt is classic Lightfoot. Giles nods again and leans out to touch the iceberg. Lightfoot has the bottle to his lips and is tipping it back. Sylvia actually has her face in her hands, looking out through her fingers. Gordon's got shake. Bosey's got a lip mike very close to Lightfoot's starchy little sticking-up collar to pick up on the gurgle and swallow, but we can always dub my bath going out later if the collar makes contact. The urine sample certainly makes contact with the inside of Hubert's mouth because after a very small pause it comes straight out again and all over Barstow the other side of the room, which shows how fucking small the room is. Can we wrap up now? That's what Sylvia's expression is saying to me. Yeah, yeah. I don't want to hang around for the reaction shot. If you're thinking it's just disgust you're wrong. It's disgust and humiliation, because a gentleman knows when he's made a right dickhead of himself. That's why my grandfather got away with the whole porter episode and Hubert didn't get his myrrh and stuff. It's all down there in the diary. Exit Hubert until the world-renowned trench scene with it all bottled up, if you don't mind the expression. Let's go get some fresh air, let's leave my grandfather laughing and Barstow sniggering. A great victory over the forces of evil. But they'll come back, they'll come back. They always do, like migraine dots. I hope yours aren't obscuring the dawn.

Reel change. We're getting there. Hey, cross me 'art guv, there really are some classic scenes coming up, stick with it, unfold your legs, you'll get varicose veins, relax. The People's Committee found me guilty, by the way. Vice-Principled Vyshinsky said I was generally upsetting a lot of people, it wasn't just this thing about Jane Russell's brassière. He mentioned the paper bag over my head and that comment (in my movie history class two *years* back for God's sake) about Norma Talmadge being the most beautiful woman ever to have appeared on the silver screen. Norma Talmadge *was* the most beautiful woman ever to have appeared on the silver screen or even the golden screen for that matter, I replied. Our Dean's crew-cut kind of quivered all over like it had been electrocuted or was maybe recalling how once it had had something to toss and shake in a summer breeze or in the back of a Chevrolet Bel-Air Convertible doing one hundred and five up the ocean freeway and she fixed me with one of her dirty looks. You also said, she growled, that the beauty of the silent movie stars has never been surpassed. Too right I did, I replied, you can't have a goddess with a drawl or, just in case you think I'm being anti-American or something crazy like that, clipped vowels like this. There was a general sigh, like I'd confessed to chain-sawing twenty-five nuns over a period of several hours. My imitation of Celia Johnson was a wash-out. Vyshinsky stirred behind his purple waistcoat, the one that gives me migraine and I've told him so on several occasions but it's made no difference, he goes on wearing it day in day out, it smells and has Persian cat hair on its lapels which is maybe why I sneeze whenever he comes too close. Your job is on the wire and the wire is kinda shaky, Rick. I object to the use of my Christian name, I retorted. Uh, don't you mean your *first* name, some prick from the literature faculty of the University (HCDVA is affiliated or infibulated or whatever – hey, didn't you know?) pointed out helpfully. No, I replied, my first name is Archibald (lies, lies). My second name is Richard but I am not about to say hey, I object to the use of my second name. The prick droned on

420

about imperialist discourses and other but he never said what other it was just other and I frowned imperially but Vyshinsky waved his hand and said we'll leave it for now, Hal. I said hey, I haven't finished, I object to the use of the name by which my dear mother used to refer to me, I mean can you imagine Vyshinsky yelling Comrade, you have been found guilty by hot flat-iron of dismembering the Soviet state, wrecking the economy, subverting the military-industrial complex, reintroducing the capitalist system, murdering Comrade Secretary Kirov and plotting the murder of Comrade Lenin so I reckon your wire is kinda shaky, Nik.

He didn't like that. He and the others really didn't like that. Apparently Sue G. Yass (I am not fabricating, she teaches *Getting In Touch with Your Vocal Chords* or something over in the drama section) had a grandfather who laughed at a joke about Stalin's dick in a bread queue in 1936 and knew all about it and didn't take kindly to, etc. She got really emotional. I said Hey, you haven't told me what happened to him. What the hell do you think happened to him? she said, in her best Cincinnati Latvian. I presume he ended up in front of a tribunal, Miss Yass, I replied, in my best Trevor Howardian. Vice-Principal Vyshitski's fist makes mincemeat of the crap pile of papers he's shoved in front of him to make it look like he can read. Do I need to go on? Basically I have been severely reprimanded, Rick. Rick has lost whatever microscopic chance he had of a boost to his boost or being put in charge of the Canteen Check Committee when Buster G. de Carrion retires (I am not joking, that name is for serious, he's a nice guy actually when he's not picking his nose). Hey, it might have gone to my head. As my daughter used to tell me I don't need to grow up, I'm better off in the pre-operational stage, I don't need to ask why it is that I fail when I do, I just do. What hurts is that they'll touch my pension. My pension is decided by the College Pension Committee if I live that long because I'm not using the elevator whatever and my shared cupboard is three floors up. Hey, I found myself in front of Sue G. Yass in the canteen queue today. She was fairly hostel. I nearly got a plate for her and could have been up in front of the tribunal again for gentlemanly behaviour, it was really close – I so wanted to ask her if the joke about Stalin's dick was a good one but said anything with no mashed yeast in it please instead as a kind of in-joke because I know she thinks Woody Allen should be strung up but I got zero reaction

421

from her and the counter-lady just carried on talking over her shoulder in Spanish while working the vegetarian's macaroni with a whaling-spade or something. Then I saw Zelda sitting on her own and dropped my plate on Sue G. Yass's ankle-bone I think it was, which is probably more painful. She screamed. It was a horrible moment, I thought maybe in some time-slip I had stuck my head inside her body-stocking or something (she wears this lycra skin-cling dance outfit all the time and keeps running her hands up and down her body like she's lost her wallet which is impossible, you'd see it bulge right out, maybe she's looking for her vocal chords) and apologised a lot. Everyone was looking at us, there was this terrible silence. I know what Mr Yass Snr Snr felt like now in Stalin-on-Don or wherever it was. Your vocal chords are definitely down there in the right place, I said, I saw them. She said actually she felt very very sorry for me and my immediate family and walked off with her pile of french fries and three really heavy cream puffs. I don't know how she does it, she must work out like crazy. I kind of nodded ruefully and tried not to look like an unsuspected serial killer so that everyone could get talking again and glanced over to where Zelda had been and she still was. In the kind of lousy films I used to make there'd have been an empty chair instead and I'd have chased after her shadow down endless corridors and into the sewers of Vienna or someplace. But she was still there in this complex masterwork called life. I swallowed and walked over to her with an empty tray and put it down opposite her and she looked up and I felt about sixteen because for about a century our eyes hadn't met and she has these very grey eyes. I hit Sue G. Yass's ankle-bone, I said. I dropped my plate by accident, may I sit down? Zelda started sniggling. Her mouth puckered and I thought she was going to cry but instead she sniggled. I guess other people's misfortunes, etc. I felt this sniggle too but I could sense the security cameras swinging onto me and had to clear my throat and think about operations. This wasn't difficult because the canteen team all wear surgical gloves which is why I don't eat much at the canteen quite apart from the macaroni problem and the sesame seeds that get stuck in my bridge. Then I sat down. This is more like Hemingway, I thought. This is going thennishly. Maybe there'll be a few moreovers. I looked at my tray and realised I had not gotten (sorry, sometimes I like to show off, I like to pretend I'm a chip off the *Mayflower* instead of a chip on my shoulder) any victuals. I waved my hands around. I guess I forgot to get anything, I said.

Where's the paper bag? said Zelda. I couldn't believe it. Her grey eyes were looking straight at me and she was being so, well, straight. The canteen started going really echoey. As a matter of fact, it always is echoey, it's like an aircraft hangar with rubber plants but it got even echoeyer because I realised that Zelda had *moved out*. Her eyes had red rims around them which meant I guessed she had emoted about it but basically she seemed in very good shape. I smiled ruefully and tried to pick my coffee up because I was looking at her and normally there's at least a coffee on my tray but I ended up pretending I was doing hand flexions, I did not want Zelda to think I wasn't mentally A1 grade – it's OK because this is the kind of place people do hand flexions in, there's a mime and dance module, students are always working out and doing back-flips over my head and stuff, it makes them feel sexy and vigorous and different from their parents who only jog twenty miles a day. I allowed my hand to take a break on my knee while I cleared my throat which I don't need to do manually, the body's a great invention. Then I flushed for a few seconds because I'd forgotten the question. It may sound incredible, this, but you have to remember what Zelda does to me even when she's not about two feet away with her eyes locked onto mine. I swallowed. Then I remembered the question. As long as I kept thenning I was OK. Oh, the bag, the paper bag, I tossed off casually. I wanted to get to the point. The years telescoped. It was as if she had never departed from my personal shores. My dogged loyalty and incredible patience had paid off. I could have hung Todd Lazenby by his green suspenders (have I mentioned his green suspenders already?) and kicked the chair away and watched him piss in his pants to no purpose. I could have chloroformed him and laid him down gently in quick-dry cement on my new patio so only his face was showing and practised my golf swing using the nostril that doesn't tic to anchor my tee nice and firmly absolutely needlessly. I started to think of him as quite a decent guy and probably wrecked now more than I was because he had nothing left – his wife and kids had gone, his dog had recently been put down owing to some kidney malfunction apparently, he didn't even play golf, his Vietnam experiences would be falling over themselves to come back and haunt him under the skilled direction of Oliver Stone, he was going to have a very tough few years and his hair loss was definitely getting worse. I didn't say any of this of course, I just sighed and smiled ruefully and watched Zelda sniggle so much her hair came loose and fell across her cheek. I nearly tucked it back but cleared my throat again instead. I was about to say so you've moved out only she clapped her hands kind of lightly. I'm sorry, Ricky, she said. That's OK, I replied. It's just that I feel happier than I've ever felt in my life, she went on. So do I, I smiled. Do you? she said. Her grey eyes were shining, like pebbles just after the tide's gone out. I nearly said that, but her hand was holding mine, the one I'd left out on the tray doing flexions. I was about to say will you marry me but she said I'm so glad you *un-der-stand* instead. The instead is mine, by the way. I nodded because I didn't quite understand what she meant by that but I didn't care because emotions lie too deep for words and stuff. She squeezed my hand and said how she always knew what gentle candle was burning in my heart. Thank you, I whispered, or maybe gasped. A person may appear a fool and yet not be one, she pointed out. He may only be guarding his wisdom carefully as Zengetsu put it. You could put it like that, I murmured. Congratulations, someone yelled in my ear. Maybe he didn't really yell it, but after all this murmuring it sounded like a yell. I nearly said thank you but he was taking Zelda's hand and shaking it. It was Vyshitsky. Thank you, said Zelda. When is it to be? shouted Vyshitsky. He always wears this purple waistcoat instead of a jacket, by the way. He was nearly clubbed to death by the National Guard in Berkeley or someplace about thirty years ago and reckons that gives him the right to wear purple waistcoats and no jacket for the rest of his life. I think I might have mentioned the purple waistcoat already. Too bad. This weekend, yelled Zelda. She was looking at Vyshitface pretty much as she'd been looking at me, with shining grey eyes etc. Vyshitface shouted some more and then squeezed my shoulder as if I was some Alzheimer's victim on a day's outing and pissed off with his pepperoni. If I hadn't sneezed I'd have thrown up. I wiped my nose on my tie and felt really hungry all of a sudden. I guess I'd better get my lunch, I said. Then I added, hey, what's up this weekend, honey? You're not thirty are you? I thought you hit that three years ago. Zelda frowned. Oh Jesus, she said. Oh Jesus? I enquired. Oh Jesus, oh Jesus, she repeated. It was like my born-again student's paper on *Soviet Cinema, 1918–1945*. I gave it a pretty good grade, some things are not worth the damn risk, at least she didn't go on about Eisenstein directing *The Battleship Potemkin* in between breaking the atom like the others did. No one's told you then, she said. I thought the way you came over someone had told you and the wisdom come out at last. No one tells me anything, I chuckled. I was hanging on to my knees because they were jerking around a bit. Oh Jeezus, she said again, I'm so sorry, Rick. You mean you haven't sent me an invitation? I chortled. No, said Zelda. You're getting married to Todd Lazenby and you haven't sent me an invitation? I chuckled. Cool it, Rick, said Zelda. OK, maybe it wasn't a chuckle, maybe I shrieked. But he's already married, I ventured to point out while my universe was falling past me like that great scene at the end of *Quo Vadis?* probably. The divorce came through last week, said Zelda. She's completely cleaned him out and kept the kids, the car and half of the house but he doesn't care. We'll manage. We've got my room downtown. We'll manage there until we find something maybe outside in the woodlands, one of those woodlands schemes that are going cheap right now. I want to hear birdsong in the morning. Real birdsong, she added. Oh, is it canned at his house? I chaffed.

Oh, fuck it. I'm so embarrassed telling you all this.

I thought you'd be pleased, she said. I know it's crazy but I thought it might make things more definite, bring some closure into the thing. It certainly does that, I said, trying to look like Paul Muni in *Scarface.* Oh, Ricky, she said, is your indigestion back? No, I said, I'm working out how to end my life as messily as possible. Ricky, oh Rick, you couldn't have seriously thought. . . ?

Great, huh? Hold ellipsis while the whole of the Holy Rickety Empire tumbles into the panicking togas, polystyrene pillars bouncing around and stuff, flames shooting out the sinking triremes, the Colossus's head rocking and rolling, D.W. Griffiths swearing into his megaphone, Nero on the balcony with his fake lyre looking fat, Burt Lancaster in the wrong film again, basically fucking catastrophe with no sound but the jet-engines of my tinnitus taking off and the ticking of my eyelids which I thought I'd got under control but it's been a very bad week.

Yeah, I said, I guess I did. I'm just an ordinary Enfield boy, really. You're a what? An ornery Enfield boy, Mrs Lazenby. Rick, you're the only person who's miserable about this but I think that's because you've gotten too much attachment generally speaking, you're trying to hold the running stream between your hands, you have to try to let the water go and enjoy the sparkle and the gurgle. The *gurgle?* Or whatever, she said, fairly impatiently I noted. Christ, what a load of crap. What a load of codswallop as me dad used to say. I've got to get on, I can't waste any more time with people like this. I thought Zelda had a brain. The Dot has rewired it. Or maybe she always talked like that and I didn't notice. Yeah, yeah, love blinds, throws acid in your face, wears dark glasses in the cinema when you're trying to find a vacant seat and the movie's started with a night-scene, all that. People in love ought to have white sticks. They go on cliff-top walks when they shouldn't. I give it a year, before she finds out about his problem.

Because Dr Lazenby has a problem.

Hooked now, huh?

His problem. Everyone has problems but I mean this is a Problem. I have not been pretending to be his shrubbery or his shower-attachment or a louvre on his louvres but my neighbour with the inoperable wife knows someone who knows The Dot's cleaning lady and this cleaning lady blabs. I can't bring it to the attention of Vyshitface or someone because they'd just say I was oppressing a minority of one or whatever. I say a minority of one because I cannot believe anyone else in the world would share this Problem. But then I'm just an ornery Enfield bloke, guv, as me dad was wont to say when I started shouting at him about D. H. Lawrence and stuff. What a son I must have been. I ought to fly over right now and nip down to Havant and apologise. Anyway, for all I know everyone except me is doing it and it's me who has the Problem because I'm not doing it. Zelda wouldn't believe me if I told her, she might get her fiancé to sue me for slander, it's incredibly easy to find yourself in a sued situation these days. I think I'll just hang fire and wait, mate.

Zelda couldn't have been serious about not being serious.

I may edit all this crap out but not now. I want you to understand the terrible conditions of this movie's production. My golf-game's collapsed. My favourite goldfish is listing. The weather's the kind that'd wipe out an army in the old days and there are big problems in the Crimea. Maybe we're running the general feature backwards.

426

Zelda, Zelda. Zelda. My great-aunt is talking on the lawn. When one looks at something, does it change? How do you mean? says Giles. Well, how can that tree be there and here at the same time? It's not here, says Giles my grandfather aged seventeen on a warm lawn in 1914, just outside Fawholt, Wiltshire. Yes it is, says Agatha, it's in me, it's making me feel jolly and pleasant, looking at it. Therefore it's sort of inside me, it's sort of changed. Giles sighs and lies on his back and looks up at the sky. I know this guy in Houston who has a huge TV screen and all he plays on it is ambient stuff, clouds and sky mostly, occasionally tossing tops of trees, sometimes just the ocean breaking against sand for three hours. He likes Mark Rothko, too, he sits for hours in the Rothko Chapel, that's how we met. The sky Giles is staring up into is fairly ambient, there are just these tiny puffs of white cloud which look like they are meteorologically impossible because the rest of it is so blue. I'm talking English blue, not Texas blue or Mediterranean blue or St Lucian blue. I'm talking 1914 blue, too. The right side of 1914. I just had to get onto this lawn or I'd have cut my wrists or something. I'm running out of time, actually. Between *Zelda, Zelda. Zelda.* and *My great-aunt is talking on the lawn* there were about a hundred yards of rushes, two years' work, but I got my razor out and practically waded through them to answer the phone. It was Greg, my son. He's got an exhibition at the University to which the College is fellatioed. Well done, Greg, I said. There are some people over there who'd really appreciate your work. How are things, Dad? Things are swell, Greg. You sound more Yanky every time I phone, Dad. That's because you don't phone very much, next time you phone you won't be able to understand me, unless you're into Mickey Mouse on slomo. You sound upset about something, Dad. That's because Zelda got married and is still in there. Zelda? You remember Zelda, Greg. You met her when you came out in '93. You mean that nice brunette with grey eyes? I do mean that startlingly attractive brunette with grey eyes, Greg. She got married? She got married. When? Two years ago. Hey, bad luck, Dad, you should've told me. Naw, it wasn't worth it. I'm coming round.

It was a great exhibition. He's into carpet squares now. Just carpet squares laid out like a carpet and called things like *Carpet Squares #3, Pink Series*. He doesn't even lay them himself, he got Easifit Floorings Inc. of Houston to lay them. The prick from the literature department thought it was the most exciting thing he'd seen since, aw, since Sherrie Levine's photographs of Ed Weston's photographs three years ago, aw, how do you find her work, Greg? I expected my son to say who? but instead he said really quite interesting, actually, if a little latent.

Latent?

I'm just a ornery Enfield bloke, guv.

I burned the rushes, by the way. My friendly neighbour complained. He's got really tetchy since his inoperable wife finally went the way of all inoperables. I said to him just after the funeral how we're all inoperables when you think about it and he didn't like that. I meant it to be comforting but the thing about round here is that old people do not really believe they are going to die. They've all watched *Cocoon* and even *Cocoon The Return*, for God's sake. They reckon if they work out enough and have enough sexual activity and dress in shellac shorts and tennis shoes they'll just keep on treading water forever. Anyway, my golfing partner is my golfing partner no longer. He complained about the smell. Sure, celluloid is fairly evil-smelling when burned but I couldn't find a refuse bin big enough to handle it. You'll want to know what classic shots went up in smoke, I guess. Hey, some great ones. But all art is mortal. You wouldn't believe how much art and books and stuff has sunk to the bottom of the ocean or been blown up or burned down or flooded out or whatever. It's amazing there's any art left, actually. *Time had made the highest bid/and fire was the fastest reader*, to quote dear old Henrik (*The Vandals*, Maggot Publications, 1974). When the talkies came they put the silents into the furnace. You wouldn't believe how many were put into the furnace or anyway used as ashtrays by peg-head projectionists. About EIGHTY PER CENT, actually. All those silents and no one said a word. They just curled up and glowed and turned into dribble. All those beautiful golden women up in smoke. Now they're being screened night and day in the great Cultural Centre in the sky where God and the angels get free admission to everything that's gone from this world worth crying over. They had to build a very large extension after Dresden went up but it's OK, it's not made of concrete with hand-painted rain smears but of gossamer with the dew still on it, for crying out loud. It's hell to hang

428

pictures on, actually. I'm back on the Laphroaig, by the way. It's so pricey out here, guv, I thought it might curb my consumption but it hasn't, I'm just going without me HP Sauce. Shaaaddaaap.

> Time had made the highest bid
> and fire was the fastest reader.
> Art was a scratch on a dustbin lid
> and Orpheus, the little bleeder,

It goes on, it goes on. Twelve hundred lines of it or something, most of it lost when he exploded. Did I tell you he exploded? Pretty well exploded, anyway, in the way flambées explode. He was drinking brandy and he kept missing his mouth. Then he decided to light his briar pipe. He had the full text and only copy of *The Vandals* on his lap. It was his life's work. Bits of it survived. A team from the British Library or somewhere spent about five minutes piecing it back together until they realised it was crap. I have a few more verses. I will one day publish them in an extremely limited edition. Somewhere in the manuscripts department of the great Cultural Centre in the sky they're using it as lavatory paper. OK OK, maybe angels don't crap. But maybe they do! According to Henrik this was a vexed question in the Middle Ages, the best minds tussled for months over stuff like this. Hey, I miss Henrik. He knew things. I didn't appreciate him, I was too busy swinging my arse off, man. At least he could read Latin and Ancient Greek fluently. He really could read it like he was reading the newspaper or something. He was born in 1914 for crying out loud. Maybe as Agatha's brushing her hand over the cropped lawn and making the cut grass blades jump up Henry Peterson is pushing his head out between Mrs Gertrude Peterson's thighs perish the thought.

I've just realised over the last few days that I haven't got very far.

I mean, I cut two hours' or something worth because it wasn't strictly relevant it was just atmosphere building thinking that might speed things up somehow but hey, we're still nowhere. Mrs Trevelyan and the others are still frozen I hope in the dining-room because I wanted to Put Things Into Context. I've wasted two years of my life. Zelda is happily married. I'm nearly fifty-nine. I have a heart murmur. My jowls need a pulley system. It was never serious between Zelda and me.

429

My complex masterwork by which I shall become immortal is about an eighteenth into the storyboard and way way way over budget. Time is the highest bidder. William is up in the attic. The whole crew are sunning themselves in Wiltshire, it's very nice actually, we've been hallooed to by a vicar in a floppy hat with kind of mutton-chop whiskers because he thought we were someone passing but we weren't, we were a shadow scrimming a sunny patch of greenery and afterwards he prayed, you could tell. The sunny patch of greenery is now an Ideal Home Exhibition gone wrong, there are real people with problems in there, they have strimmer problems and marital problems and Edwardian-style conservatory leak problems and next door's TV problems. It wasn't there in 1985. I've been away a long time. I reckoned that if I didn't go back I wouldn't ever go back. It's very nice being in Wiltshire with the sun on your face but we have work to do, for Christ's sake. Norma Talmadge is on the lawn stroking the cropped grass. I was very lucky to get hold of her. She's been playing Zelda as well as Agatha, by the way, if you haven't noticed the likeness. She's very glad to be speaking. Her greatest work went into the furnace and now she's getting to speak. I take back everything I said that upset Crew-Cut and Vyshitface and Hal the Computer and Soggy Ass two years back. She has a golden voice, too. She's very adaptable. She can play an American screwball badly into Zen, birdsong and these green suspenders holding in some kind of lower form of life as well as my great-aunt aged eighteen going around in white muslin that mustn't get stained on the lawn or else. That takes some doing. I don't mean that my great-aunt is in the suspenders along with Toadlice, Ossy. Give me a break. What have you ever created except fuzz, huh?

I'm badly in love with Norma, of course. It's complicated. But I know she is completely unattainable. I'm a year and a half off of *sixty*, for crying out loud. She has a chin that'd make a yob weep. That alone. But the chin is attached to everything else, everything else kind of flows out from the chin and round those grey grey eyes and oh the mouth and ends up being perfect all the way down to her toes. My kind of perfect, anyway. She has a normal voice. It's not deep or sexy or anything. It killed her career but it's perfect too, because it doesn't act. She was very worried, but I said, hey Norma, *the Talkie opened its doors to theatre, which occupied the place and surrounded it with barbed wire*. How true, she said, and her mouth did something thoughtful that made me have to lean back and stare at the oak beams for a minute. That was Robert Bresson, I murmured, you'd have liked him. Did he do silents? she enquired. I tried to ignore her eyelashes. I flicked a beer-mat casually (we were in the pub in Fawholt, it has a very nice little snug where you don't get guys who try to tell you about foreigners and stuff, you don't get anyone normally except this wheezy labrador who lies across your feet for some reason, he's surprisingly heavy, please don't ruin it by driving out after the movie and celebrating the first day in honour of me, you won't all fit in and the garden backs on to a battery pig farm unit) and said, no, but his films are kind of silents with sound, if you see what I mean. The sound is very important. The noises become music. He doesn't call it cinema he calls it cinematography. He reckons cinema is just filmed theatre. But CINEMATOGRAPHY IS A WRITING WITH IMAGES IN MOVEMENT AND WITH SOUNDS. I tore a used-up page out of my diary and wrote it down for her in block caps in case she forgot it. Norma was stroking the labrador's head. Its belly was on my feet. Thank you, she breathed. There was something remarkable about her pale hand on the golden kind of velvety stuff on the skull of the labrador. The labrador smelt, actually, but Norma's scent neutralised it somehow. Her curls swept the beer-mat right off the table, they were that long. I was concerned for her hair getting beer in it from the puddles on the table but then I remembered that you can wash your hair in beer so I didn't say anything, I just breathed in Norma Talmadge's scent of rosewater and musk and sunned skin and something they must have put into the clothes in those days because they all smell of it, all those old clothes, all those folds of silk and muslin and lace and stuff. Maybe it's the lavender they put in the drawers. Maybe. Oh, Norma. The old labrador does not know what it is getting. It does not know what hand is caressing its velvet. I just watch. It farts for God's sake but we ignore it. Laughter bursts out from the other bar we're affiliated to by a small hatch but we ignore it. I am alone in England in a country snug with a pint of real ale and Norma Talmadge and it's summer and the windows are open and the shoot is going fine and I'm not even thinking about the Great War scenes coming up. I must not drink too much. If I drink too much I will get maudlin and gabble and stare at Norma Talmadge's bare forearms until they flicker out. The secret is

431

not to stare at her for too long. One must only glance. If one stares
too

Christ, I've passed out.

Of course I'm OK. I couldn't be telling you I've passed out if I was
still passed out. It's just that I wanted to let you know how finding
oneself lying on the bathroom floor is not funny, particularly if you
think your mother is about to come in and stroke your forehead and
then it hits you in the belly that she's been dead thirty-two years and
you're on the other side of an ocean to boot, mate, with a Texan
mosquito on your nose. The doctor asked me what my regular drink
was. I said Laphroaig. He couldn't even spell it. What is that exactly,
Ricky? I said Islands Scotch, strong-flavoured with a u, peaty. He
said my name isn't Peter it's Bob, Ricky. He looked at me real
concerned. Can you believe it? He's given me pills. My murmur's
building into a rumour. I've always ignored rumours, as a rule.

My main incy-wincy problem with Norma is her accent. She can
handle Zelda but Agatha's giving her problems. I refuse to dub over, I
dunno, Celia Johnson or somebody. Hey, we'll work on it. I'll take her
out on picnics and we'll stare at the sheep-sprinkled downs and I'll
put on my Polaroids to cut the glare off her white muslin and lead her
gently through the exercises. The rain in Spain falls mainly on the
plain. You should see the way her lips cope with that. I don't want
you to think she's a drawler, by the way. She's not. She's US posh,
for God's sake. She can handle it. One day she'll come in and it'll be
there. Don't act, Norma. Free yourself. Free Agatha. Free the real
Agatha from the fictitious Agatha you had imagined. Richard, is that
that French genius who liked silents again? Yes, Norma. If I say
anything profound it's normally on permanent loan. Have another
cucumber and watercress sandwich. This is the summer of 1914.
Relax. The rain in Spain falls mainly on the plain. The bombs on the
Somme aren't falling on the Tom. Not yet, not yet, anyhow. The
Irish situation is what we're supposed to be worrying about right now.

I like it. She calls me Richard. Only my mother ever called me Richard.

One day she cried. Almost on my shoulder. I have a squeaky voice, she said. It's a lovely voice, I replied. Your eye-liner's running. We were facing a wheatfield, by the way, to put you in the picture. The wheatfield is in wide screen format. Don't watch this scene on TV, it'll make a nonsense of it, you won't even be able to see us, we'll just be a brown dot and a white dot close together, a cinema screen is one hundred times larger than a TV screen, watching a movie movie on TV's like admiring the Mona Lisa on a postage stamp, it's a travesty – hey, why do you think I only show stills in my classes for God's sake? OK, there've been complaints, I've had letters from Crew-Cut and others over the years saying the students are complaining, didn't I know HCDVA has the biggest and bestest video collection in Texas, I should use all the facilities available and stuff and I reply yeah yeah, but we don't have a facility called a cinema with a standard or even wide format screen and popcorn and a till lady with carmine lips and some framed stills, do we? I don't want to go into this now, I have some very important scenes coming up, this movie's way behind schedule, Bosey's drinking too much extremely real ale, I'm getting sunburn can you believe it. So this wheatfield is like a copper ocean breaking in front of us in wide screen and Norma Talmadge is in tears. Silver tears are running down her cheeks. I'm sorry I couldn't fit a full-size wide screen in the suite, by the way. You can imagine the problems. I did the best I could. Drinks are still on the house. I hope no one's snoring. Maybe some tea or coffee would be nice, it must be about that time of the morning, unless tea and coffee are being given up for the millennium. It's a really lovely natural voice, I said. I was a star, a great star, she cried. Now I'm not even in the *Encyclopaedia Britannica*. Now the only thing people remember me for is what I said to the autograph hunters after my retirement so-called. What did you say to the autograph hunters, Norma? You mean you don't even know that? I may have done, but it's slipped my mind, honey.

She stood up. She was magnificent. Her hair was tossed by the breeze, you couldn't really tell the difference between her hair and the ocean of corn because just at that moment this great cloud shadow was moving over it. She spread her arms out. The breeze was exploring the billowing possibilities of her muslin and lace. I shaded my eyes because I'd forgotten my Polaroids. Sheep-bells sounded across the valley completely naturally, we're not talking Boseysound here we're talking untampered wild track – and I jerked because there was a shepherd with a crook in the combe shading his eyes in the same way I was shading mine and it was him. *The* shepherd, for crying out loud. He's got some scenes coming up, he's fairly vital, stick with me. Her voice rang out. OK, OK, maybe not without a certain nasal quality but basically lovely.

Go away, go away! I don't need you any more! That's what I said. Go away, go away! I don't need you any more!

Her arms came down and she looked at the ground. I almost clapped but I didn't think it appropriate. She had freed the real Norma from the fictitious Norma. Now she can play Agatha, I thought, once we've found the accent. I took a bite out of my tongue sandwich and nipped my thumb. She came and sat beside me again. She had no shoes on, she'd taken them off because the grassy bank was soft and warm. Perfect feet. I guess the talkies took away what I had to say, she said. I grunted. My mouth was full of tongue. I think you've had that one before, sorry. The wheatfield hissed and rolled. Maybe it was barley. Maybe I got the clean effects wrong, but no one'll notice. No one knows what fings like that sound like any more.

Hold wheatfield.

I'm thinking. While I'm thinking just enjoy the wheatfield or barley or whatever it is. We're too late for poppies, this is July, maybe there are one or two but they're lost in all the copper. I had some Technicolor poppy shots against green corn that practically bust the lab printer but they went up in smoke and got in my neighbour's eyes instead. Too bad. I'm thinking how tricky this shoot's going to be. Norma's ready, the crew's ready, the scenery's ready, the house is ready. Everybody's ready except me. You're ready, even.

I am nervous, actually.

I have some great actors, don't get me wrong. I have a great crew. I have a great audience. I have a great landscape. We have great weather. OK, there's been some thunder, but it's been way off, over Gloucestershire or Oxfordshire or wherever. We have the largest collection of period agricultural machinery and real live shire horses since they weren't period. My extras are well-behaved and have crooked backs and bad teeth if they need them and all the right tools and they're ready to go and they don't overact, either. I'm nervous because I don't know whether I am mentally in the right condition to cope with it all. I am also in love with my leading lady. The last time I was in love with my leading lady it wrecked everything and we got married and then she killed herself. Moreover I have some very difficult scenes ahead of me. They are actually very personal. The phantoms won't like it. They won't like it at all. And there's something about the atmosphere. The atmosphere is not healthy. We sit on the lawn and discuss the shoot timetable or how Milly carries the bucket up the stairs realistically so it doesn't look like she at no point in her life has ever carried a bucket of water up some back stairs because the girl playing Milly was born and brought up in High Wycombe in a four-bedroom Wimpey for crying out loud – and I don't like the atmosphere. Actually, it frightens me. It's ridiculous sitting here on the lawn in the summer of 1914 and not feeling self-conscious about it and hey, maybe that's what's frightening me about the atmosphere. Everyone's waiting without knowing they are waiting. I'm watching my great-aunt sweeping her hand over the grass and I'm wondering how I get Norma to act like that, like it doesn't look as if she's waiting for something just because this is July 1914. I mean, Henry Hopeless-Poet Peterson couldn't help being born in July 1914 and I can't help it that my great-uncle and my grandfather did what they did in July 1914. The fact that the world is just about to fuck itself up in the biggest way yet in the history of the world has nothing to do with this very personal and frankly embarrassing incident to do with my great-uncle and my grandfather and Millicent known as Milly Stephenson while they were in the country house in the summer of 1914 with vicars hallooing and gnats clouding and brooks burbling and picnic cloths getting settled down all over onto stiff tussocks that kind of refuse to flatten out until the crockery gets weighty enough or some smart-arse with a monocle that never drops out finds the clover patch.

Still time, go see. Number oh heck Thirteen.

I'm glad you made it back. Because you never know.

It's from Uncle Kenneth's home-made movie called *The Family Outing*. The white streak is not a bird's-dropping on its descent but a scratch, it's a very old film, it hops and flares and sparkles and then bleaches out for a moment right in the middle of a crazy croquet game in this meadow like there's been a nuclear strike thirty-odd years too soon. Mrs Trevelyan is hidden behind Giles doing a tango with Mr Trevelyan's shooting-stick because Mr Trevelyan doesn't like sitting on the ground but right now he's gone off to look at the perch in the river. I guess Agatha blurred herself looking round at William putting the teacup on his head. Dig that hamper, huh? It tied on to the back of the motor car. The last shot in the film is of dust, a very large cloud of white dust. I guess they didn't really leave Uncle Ken behind cranking away so he had to walk back with the tripod and camera and stuff, it was a kind of set up, they stopped and reversed after a few minutes and Uncle Kenneth loaded the motor car and then off they went probably covered in white dust because they would have had to have reversed into their own cloud before it had settled and Mrs T moaned about it all the way back while Mr T shouted underneath his goggles. I have no idea what he was shouting, they passed me on the road and even though it was an Adler Open Tourer with a maximum speed of around forty-five m.p.h. it was too fast and fairly noisy and anyway I was choking, my eyelashes went white, I got flint-chips in my mouth and stippling my kneecaps, it was awful. Adler is German, by the way. They kept her hidden away down here until it was safe to show her in about 1925 and between 1914 and about 1919 they went round in a big and extremely comfortable Napier Torpedo instead. Hey, Mr Trevelyan could afford it, the disinfectant and antiseptic line was booming all of a sudden, business had never been so busy, even his patent portable packs plus bandage and tweezers went down a treat, they built an extension on the factory, he could've bought twelve Napier Torpedoes if he'd so desired, that clever-socks at the Club didn't open his mouth again about Trevelyan losing out to Izal – even if clever-socks hadn't been dead by the time things got really going he wouldn't have opened his mouth again.

See what I mean? I can't help it. I just can't help mentioning the war.

Actually, I'm in a fairly bad way. My nails are too long. I have stubble. I smell. I've really declined. So what's new? you cry. Thank you. Well, my nails are longer, my stubble is thicker, my smell is worse. OK? Hey, my ex-analyst would've said that I have placed myself completely beyond sexual reach where it's safe, Rick. Thank you, Moira. I would say it's because I am fairly depressed but I know you have to pay for this incredibly luxurious fortieth-floor apartment somehow. Yup, Zelda is very happy in her woodlands home listening to birdsong and her husband going to the toilet every morning. They come to work together in the car, it makes me puke. Then he lectures some desirable T-shirts on disruption and deconstruction and fragmentation and instabilities and decentering and conflicting layers of information and why e.g. Ricky Thornby is a prehistoric jerk for thinking *Citizen Kane* is an incy-wincy bit better than this Pepsi Cola commercial we're going to discuss right now for two and a half hours with a whole lotta words that sound as if they kill you in the end after a lot of suffering or like an in-house NASA journal for propulsion engineers and then he goes back in the car with Zelda to his nice little newly-constructed woodlands home and watches *Citizen Kane* on cable before centering himself between her legs and resolving all conflicting layers of information therein oh yuk, oh gross. Meanwhile the guy who's billed as The Most Unreconstructed Conservative In The Western Hemisphere lives an incredibly progressive life. I mean, he can't even find the cap to go on his hooch if he doesn't finish it in one night, he's so fucking decentered or whatever. The Laphroaig got too expensive. Blow me down. I think there's every chance I might just wrap up eternally before my complex masterwork is finished. Or maybe the noo millennium will come along sooner than I thought and you'll all be watching a white screen.

Laserdick'd really like that. He'd say it was as original as that book of Malcolm Lowry's he caught me out over. The one that got burnt in the

440

fire. He really liked my son's carpet squares, did I tell you that? Or maybe that was Hal the Computer. I get confused. Except that Hal the Computer looks like a dry-run for the Bearded Lady in *Freaks*. Todd is clean-shaven. Maybe he can't. Maybe he has some pellicular defect.

It's pointless. My anger is pointless. This born-again guy suggested I pray for him every night. Todd Lazenby, not the born-again. Nice positive prayers, he said. Prayers you can warm your hands at. Sure, I said, but we know who's tied to the faggots and screaming. The born-again said I was lost and would probably go straight to the Devil without passing Go. Hey, you play Monopoly? I cried. Yeah, he replied, I picked it up while I was trying to convert students in England. So now we play Monopoly once a month at my place. He cheats, I think, but it's company. He gets all the hotels in Mayfair and stuff. The most I get is a side-alley in Whitechapel where Jack the Ripper operated probably. It's something. He'd like to play for real cash, he says, but I said that would kinda spoil it, Clifford. He has this terrible aftershave. I've told him. He just says he'd like to meet Jesus smelling sweet. I scowl at him from under my matted hair-line but he's concentrating too hard to notice. I think he nicks me spondulicks when I go out to the whisky crate or to the toilet but I can't prove it. Sometimes I call him Des. Ho hum.

Norma says if I don't start shooting she'll quit.

I say to her when you quit acting I'll start shooting.

I'm rehearsing all of them over and over. Cor blimey. It ain't like the old days, guv. We had idiot boards in the old days and one walk-through and then cranked. Now it's day in day out till it's on auto and the soul starts to show. Norma says she's had it up to her eyes with my Frenchy genius and I say honey, that means you're nearly there. We're all nearly there. The phantoms don't like it. I can feel the chill rising up from my toes. Or maybe it's – nah, rumours are for weak ears, as me muvver used to say.

OK, action. Let's rock 'n roll. Let's make this lean, clean and hungry for more.

441

I mean, Norma's made it, she's there, she's got it by Jove so here's a still. See what I mean? Uncle Ken's favourite star but afterwards, after my great-aunt his niece died too early he'd cry if Norma loomed up on the big screen because hey, what's the difference? He had to be carried out one time, *The Secret Rose*, 1925. Norma Talmadge as Guinevere. Went up in the furnace. Go see the still but come back toot sweet, OK? This shoot is gonna be so lean, clean and hungry for more you won't have time to think how fucking awful you feel now the light's on full outside but keep the curtains closed, for God's sake. This is an art house. Light spill kills. Don't bleach me out checking to see if the grey has something different to it. It hasn't. The Thames and the sky are relations. There's a smell of burnt cordite and lavatories. People are walking to work over the bridges for crying out loud looking even more hunched up than usual for obvious reasons and with *briefcases and rolled-up umbrellas* and you get a voice-over from that old scratchy disc you never gave back to the library of Robert Speaight (great guy, great guy) reading the whole of *The Wasteland* – something London bridge, flowing over something something, probably endlessly, O so many, I had not thought death had undone so many, I must learn the fucking thing off by heart *this week* so I can impress people round the dinner-table and generally feel culchured and anyway everyone used to learn everything off by heart *and* wrote amazing letters every day, I feel really inadequate now, really modern and grey and inadequate. Hey, you suddenly have this terrible idea that NOTHING IS GONNA CHANGE except you'll have more cheques refused, 19'll be hard to let go of, some of your cheques'll be dated a hundred years ago. But I can't help you on that one. Relax. Watch the movie. There are some great battle scenes coming up, cast of millions, no newsreel library footage of fake attacks or army-surplus boots splashing past in mud endlessly until the actor gets too dizzy, no pathetic shots of barbed wire and this lifeless hand lying really gingerly across it, no smoke pellets or flash-bangers or, for Christ's sake, poppies – fucking *Poppies Waving About In Corn* (11.5 secs) filched off of some nature programme in 1971 with all the colour drained out of it and bad sparkles. This is not *One Day's Night Too Early* (dir. Thornby, 1976, 70 mins, unscreened) for crying out loud.

This is my great statement. If I can find the cap. Because attached to the cap is the bottle. And kind of attached to the bottle but only extremely loosely is the liquor. And I need a slug right now just to get me feeling lean, clean and whatever.

Go see the still while I check out my plumbing.

Oh, Norma. O Norzeldatha goddess of the golden upper world who never wears carmine and smiles softly at me. Forgive that belch. Hurry up please it's time. Find your fucking seat without manhandling everybody's crotch and keep your headache down. Another interesting movie fact. *The Birth of a Nation* tailed out with the whites shipping all the blacks back to Africa only the frames went into the furnace along with the take of the Ku-Klux-Klan guys castrating that wicked fellow in black boot-polish who gets murdered and you're supposed to applaud. D. W. Griffiths makes Jake over the way look like Robert Kennedy. I'm full of interesting facts like that. Hurry up please it's time. That reminds me. I know the whole of *The Wasteland* off by heart. My heart's fairly unreliable so the rumour goes but here it is. April is the cruellest month, breeding lilacs out of the dead land, mixing memory and desire, stirring dull—

Maybe she didn't like me sounding like Robert Speaight. I even got the scratches and the dust static in the right places. I think Norzeldatha is one of those deities who vanish easily. If you look at them too hard or quote poetry or whatever. Shucks. Cor blimey luvaduck. Here's to me muvver.

Anyway, it's a Bank Holiday. No one'll be flowing over the bridge looking like death. I forgot that. Instead there might be one or two flowing under the bridge looking like death. Stay alert.

Take Five. Jazz in the interval. And you're still complaining?

Action.

For God's sake, before I disintegrate.

Shaaaddap, son. Or you git a clip round yer neck and strung up by it.

Twilight. Crane down slowly through leaves and tighten on lit window

444

with a frame of some fragrant climber grown too thick Sylvia's shaking
to simulate breeze and in homage to all the great classics that start like
this, the only difference here being that we're not inside Pinewood
we're outside, we're in the perfumed twilit garden of Hamilton Lodge
Fawholt Wiltshire, des res *par excellence* and certainly not Des my
brother's sort of res but yer actual double extra clotted cream desirable
toff stuff, once affiliated to enormous country mansion but enormous
country mansion got burnt down in 1823 when old Lord Tutt last of
the line dropped his bedside candle on pre-safety regulation blanket
and whoomph. Bumpy sort of graveyard feel to the nettle and briar
patch at the end of the lawn if you're masochistic or phantasmal
enough to want to feel it being only indication of enormous country
mansion, even in 1914, right side of. Is this lean enough? Probably not.
Less history. OK. Squeeze through window without breaking it and
here we are in the company of a post-prandial Trevelyan family *sans*
Mr T who is busy up in London obviously because the business is
really shaky, not enough people are disinfecting or antisepting
themselves, maybe Hamilton Lodge will have to be let or even sold,
horror of horrors. William (ah! he has not been Removed, that's a
relief, innit?) and Agatha and Giles are playing a card game. Mrs
Trevelyan is in an easy chair resting her eyelids. Dorothy is taking up
some curtains and giving a rocking-chair a hard time. It's a nice room,
if a little musty for some reason. The gaslight is soft and patchy and not
very good for reading or for Mike, but Mrs Trevelyan's Tennyson is
face down on her stomach, so no one's reading. Dorothy is humming
and the rocking-chair's complaining and the antlered clock from
Baden-Baden's tutting at how time flies as it always does and there's a
nightingale, it must be, outside and now and again the slap of the cards
and Mrs Trevelyan's stomach which she can't do anything about,
maybe it's the weight of the book so she lifts the book and adjusts her
spectacles and her long face notches downwards so her chin triples up
– she's put on weight since we last saw her, or maybe it's just sag, we all
have it, it's called decomposition – and tries to read some. The
splendour falls on castle walls And snowy summits old in story: The
long light shakes across the lakes, And the wild cataract leaps in HA!
That was William. It made her jerk. Do you have to, dear? she says.
Her nape hits the antimacassar. Sorry, Ma, says William. Mother,
please, sighs Ma. Mother or Madre even. But not Ma, Ma is—

She wants to say common but glances over her spectacles at Dorothy first and the coast is clear, Dorothy is deep in her curtains.

Common, Mrs T breathes.

She turns a page. She knows these poems pretty well off by heart. She kind of flickers over them and actually it reassures her, seeing that no one's come along and sneaked around changing the words here and there. Bosey's in the village with a pair of huge speakers for the far-off dog bark in case the wheezy labrador doesn't. It doesn't. Far-off dog bark courtesy of Bosey and a couple of whopping woofers *oof*. Hit that funny-bone. Mrs T raises her head and I'm sorry but her face fills all the available space, you're lucky this isn't wide screen or you'd have her ear lobes and the grease on the antimacassar as well. The dog bark makes her think of death. Don't ask me why, I'm not Mr Nosey. Old yew, which graspest at the stones That name the under-lying dead, Thy fibres net the dreamless head, Thy roots are wrapt about the bones. She finds 'In Memoriam' so she can check up the rest of the section which starts off with Old yew etc. To touch thy thousand years of gloom. She sees that line before the others, it's her favourite, gloom is actually her favourite word, she can snuck right up into it and hide. O not for thee the glow, the bloom, Who changest not in any gale, Nor branding summer suns avail To touch thy thousand someone going up the back stairs. The maid, it's all right, it's not the mummy from the newspaper serial or Mr Hyde or Frankenstein from *Frankenstein*. To touch thy thousand clink. There is definitely a clink. There's the thumping of someone going up the back stairs and a kind of clink like they're dragging after them a ball and chain. Mrs T's nerve count goes way up. She fingers her skin problem above her tea-gown's fairly low neckline. She didn't change for dinner tonight, she's still in her tea-gown with cake crumbs down the front and no corset, she's getting to be a slob but it's family and her flesh has only just found its non-corsetted position, it takes hours, it's like a sponge getting back to normal in very slow motion after being squeezed or whatever. Who is that? she says, querulously. Martita Hunt who's playing Mrs T wanted to know how to say that line so I said querulously and wondered where the word had popped up from. Sometimes things happen like that. Martita had to have querulously explained to her so my God-given moment was a waste of time. My great-grandmother waits for an

446

answer and discreetly smells the finger that's been fingering her sore problem and it's the usual smell, no change, it stinks.

Did you hear something, Mother? says Giles. He's a little bit older, his skin is tighter over the muscle and stuff, he's kind of a man now, nine months can make a lot of difference at this age or even at fifty-eight. He's holding up a card like a semaphore flag or something. The other two are out of focus in the gloom. I don't want people to see Norma Talmadge too abruptly in this scene and swoon.

Going up the stairs, says Mrs T. But it doesn't matter.

Milly, I'd a-thought, says Dorothy. She twists round in her chair and the wicker's really having a hard time now. Mrs T sighs and blinks so fast it reminds her of the monster scene in *Conquest of the Pole* so she stops. I'd a-*thought* Milly, Dorothy goes on. Yes, yes, says Mrs Trevelyan. She finds Dorothy's fat helpfulness trying at times. Binker out! comes from the card table. It's Giles. Giles has binkered out. Don't ask me the rules of Hamilton Snap, for God's sake, not now. Sorry, it's not Giles, it's William. They pretty much have the same voice sometimes. My mistake. I don't make many. William's raising his hand and showing three fingers. Oh come on, Willo, says Giles, you can't give up that easily. I can and I have, says William. Giles tuts and looks across at Agatha. She shrugs in profile edged out golden by the gas-lamp on the side table. Not a great start to the scene for Norma but I'm not dealing in tinsel here. Anyway, says Willo, I want to check up on my catch. What did you find today, dear? says his mother. Willo stands and tugs his jacket straight. An uncommon variety of a common butterfly, he says. You and I might think poncy smart-ass sorry arse but remember, people talked posher in those days if they were posh, like they looked posher if they were posh. It was the same at the other end, they kept their clothes going for decades with a darning needle and they talked pretty well in dialect, things were more different when they were different, no one wore jeans for a start off – I mean not one of my stoodents wears a skirt these days, the only difference from the back is that the girls' bottoms tend to push out and wiggle and make me look at them, it's a great shame, I'm an unreconstructed romantic – even Zelda's wearing jeans for crying out loud and they all talk like they're chewing the same gum. Shaddap. Is that exciting? queries my great-

447

grandmother. William makes a face – I can't be more specific, the light's bad. It all depends, he murmurs. I never understood the pleasure where your father was concerned, says Mrs T. What *is* the pleasure in it? William frowns and scratches the wrist under his left cuff. I am referring to your interest, my dear. She catches a small eructation of stomach gas in her fist. A fairly sizeable if dismantled hunk of beef is currently battling its way down and things are not incredibly tip-top in there, take it from me.

William is trying to deblush himself. It involves digging his nail into his palm and wiggling his ears a bit and thinking white. It never works. He's blushed because of his mother's selection of words and the vow he made this afternoon on Wot Hill and the recent mention of Milly the maid all kind of going into the same hot soup of his brain and spilling over his face. I'm not saying Mrs T selected words like *pleasure* and *your interest* deliberately but some of the deliberate wires in her brain are crossed with some of the undeliberate and the result is electrocution if you get too close. Hey, it's only nine months since the classic sequence up the linden tree avenue and the oft-excerpted clip of Mrs T realising that her younger son wasn't deceased but instead had brought scandal and ruin down on the family head so things are bound to be a bit tender still. I had a lot of incredibly subtle development but it all got up my neighbour's nose and in his eyes because I went crazy and panicked and – hey, don't cry over spilt milk as me muvver'd say, dabbing her eyes. If I'd kept it all in you'd have left way before the end, or gone to sleep on the floor, or maybe the hotel cleaners would've started to hoover around your feet for crying out loud. There's nothing more depressing than outstaying your welcome and having people hoovering around your feet. Maybe that's how Death'll come – maybe Death'll come not with a scythe but a hoover, in a hotel cleaner's outfit, before you've checked behind the bedside-table for anything embarrassing like screwed-up tissues and skid-marked underpants and the middle spread of *Labia* and stuff. Oh shit. I feel depressed now. I've booked the suite until midday, for Christ's sake. If they start to hoover and pick up the Twiglets and broken glass and underpants and barbed wire and stuff before midday then tell them scram, OK? SCRAM, like that. Unless they're non-white, in which case the palefaces amongst you be politer because we of the unhealthy hue have a lot of colonial shit to expiate, you're not on a cocoa plantation or something, we might as well start the fresh dawn as we mean to go on. On second thoughts, don't say SCRAM like that even if they're white, UNLESS they're stoodents from New Zealand or Texas or someplace hired for the day, in which case the class oppression thing doesn't apply and you can just kick their butts right out. See how sensitive I am, guv?

This vow. Basically it was to stop tossing off for the rest of the hols. OK. I said this scene was going to be personal. He was up on Wot Hill which is just off Mirsdyke earthwork and it's a fairly amazing place, I've been there five times other than for the shoot of William standing up there with his arms crossed making this vow so that the Ancient British god asleep in Wot Hill'd take notice and make sure it was kept, and the first time I could see way out to the Black Mountains of Wales for God's sake and decided to settle for good in the English countryside because the day was beautiful, there was this goldeny haze, the only sign of a pylon was this little flashy thing and the corn was high and the trees were full and there was even a steeple sticking up and two villages over to the left with real church towers for crying out loud. The next day it was heavy cloud cover, I was on another planet, we had to postpone the shoot, I felt terrible. I kept bumping into pylons and bungalows and refrigerator trucks unloading and stuff and when I got into my hired car with the sticky clutch (Ford Escort, what else, we have to keep the budget down somehow) and drove out on to the high downland again I got a flat tyre from an incy-wincy coil of barbed wire some agricultural jerk had left on the side and there was this incredibly depressing report on the car radio about something, I think it was on drunk Eskimos or maybe disappearing gypsies, I can't remember now, this is two years back, it stayed grey for a week would you believe which is why I'm still in Houston, Texas, despite its complete lack of aesthetic or spiritual qualities apart from the Rothko Chapel where the flies know me really well by now. The point to ram home with delicacy and candour is that William is fairly screwed up at the moment but only fairly, he'll make it through, he'll be mentally strong and healthy enough and basically totally ready to play an extremely important, progressive and influential part in the History of Twentieth-Century European Painting by the time that fucking howitzer's on its recoil and flipping the leaves on its camouflage net, it's all right, I musn't exaggerate for the sake of dramatic interest or whatever. Fuck it.

Sorry.

He's been at home now for nine months. He has a periodic tutor by the name of Frank Franklin who's very intense and trying to write a novel about this tutor who's very intense and they get along fine. Maybe twenty years back it would have been different, naughty William would have gone to sea and served behind the mast or whatever. He's been developing his drawing skills and getting deeper and deeper into lepidopterology. Basically he's coming through. He's lucky he's got a mother like my great-grandmother and a father whose business is going through a bad patch so he can't take anything else on board and who is actually a soft-hearted guy like me. If he had a mother who cared it might have been stickier, because once Mrs T had accepted the situation she forgot about it, she has a short attention span, he's lucky. OK. This was all in the burnt rushes. It's complex and contradictory but it took about a quarter-second for the howitzer shell to undo it all. You see why I burnt it all. Why am I making this movie? Shaddap.

William is sweet on Milly, to use his own lingo. I have to get this across. She's fourteen. He's sixteen. It's sweet and innocent whatever that means. Romeo and Juliet. She's on the balcony of the class divide. Dig a bit deeper and it goes sour. She's his servant. She polishes his shoes. She dresses Agatha, tightens her corset and laces her up and stuff. She leans over William at dinner and he gets excited by her sweat and starch and hint of cheap scent and the petrol which is from her trying to get a stain of tomato sauce off not doubling as the house mechanic and hearing her breathe as she doles out the meat or whatever. Her bust is pretty well fully developed and she has a nice smile and raven-black hair and a full upper lip and a kind of calm to her, a something else behind the bustling around that he'd quite like to get to know. I can't stand telling you about all this when the Hoovers are going to be around my great-uncle's feet in about four years. He wasn't even twenty-one, for crying out loud. Mrs T burnt every drawing or painting he ever did in protest at something, maybe war. All I have left of him is the citation and some photographs and Uncle Ken's decomposing movies for God's sake. Not that I have them personally. I have to go begging for them when I'm in England, I have to sneak up to the big front door and press the bell and practise my Trevor Howard routine and yell good morning, Mrs Halliday, it's Richard Thornby here into what I think is the intercom grille and if I'm lucky she'll open the door or rather the buzzer will go off in my left ear as I'm crouched to it and practically kill me with a coronary but if I'm not really quick I won't give it a push in time and the buzzer'll stop and the door'll dislocate my shoulder practically and she never does it a second time, not in the same day, because she's a paranoid.

My half-aunt, for crying out loud.

She regards me as a nuisance. She tolerates me. She's cut-glass, she has a voice like Celia Johnson's with a few chips off the rim but it's the real thing. I kind of shamble in like Lon Chaney Jnr in *The Wolf Man* and ingratiate myself as best I can but basically I'm the virus, I'm the half-blood, I'm the Phantom of the Opera she can't exorcise, I'm the nuisance on the carpet, I'm the unpleasantness. You don't know what it's cost me to get these images for you people. I just hope you've stuck it out because you won't get a second chance: King Kong fell one hundred and something floors but it doesn't take me one hundred and something floors, it just takes a river. Mysterious, I am being mysterious. Stay alert. Oof. I was born within nasal shot of the Thames, guv, it's my river, it's me farver's river, it's me grandfarver's and his grandfaver's river, they slipped about in its guts and put the shat in Shadwell and the rat in Ratcliff and the fiddle in a ha'porth of liveliness – they could trace their lineage back into the shadder of a tun of porter on a Ratcliff wharf wivart a moon to cut the bilical by, if yer gits me drift.

I've got spittle all down my shirt front, I'm getting over-involved in my voice-over. The VO's OTT RT, as Ossy'd put it. Ossy only ever talked in initials. Hey, Ossy? Y'still aht there, son? IOU a clip or two on the Rs, A, Oss m'boy?

Shaddap.

William is about deblushed by now because he knows it's all top-hole secret really and while I was emptying out about my grandfather's only surviving daughter or child come to that Giles has said killing, it's the killing. Oh no, says William, oh no that's rot. Giles is looking up at his

451

brother and striking the edge of the pack on the table ready for shuffling – maybe there's a technical term for that but I don't want to get anxious about it now, you know what he's doing and he says what's rot? It's rot to say it's the killing, says William. Agatha's watching them spar and she has a tweak of a smile in there because she knows that one day one of them'll win hands down and they'll both be grumpy and sort of lost. Giles spreads his arms out wide so his jacket lapels stick out. Well if it's not about slaughtering the poor little things – What *is* that girl doing then? interrupts Dorothy, looking up. She came in early on her cue but it sounds great, I'll let it roll, my grandfather's looking peeved but forget it. The thump and the sort of harder sound have been continuing underneath, it's pretty creepy, it's like an ambient slow motion disco or something. Would you go and see, please? says Mrs T.

She's said this with her eyes closed, so it's an undirected instruction. William is still fairly worked up about Giles and the killing thing so he doesn't respond straight away, he just does the buttons on his jacket up like he's about to go outside, he has to be careful at nightfall with his pulmonary condition. Mrs T opens her eyes and stares at the ceiling. Would someone go and see what is the matter, please? She's getting anxiety tics on her face, someone had better move. Dorothy begins to fold the curtain. Righty-ho, m'm. This is not really right, Dorothy is into off-duty blue on the dial of her day, everyone knows that – at least until the last little red stripe which is cocoa and locking up and kicking out the cat, hey, it's always been like that down in Wiltshire. Why do you think the wicker takes her shape so nicely?

Shooing out the cat, this summer. Not kicking. No one kicks a heavily pregnant cat unless they're my brother Des aged ten. Seriously! I was there. And I didn't throw myself between them. I didn't do anything. I am weak. I have no spine. He was into wiping out the local fauna and now he keeps carp and a rare thank God breed of I think dog but he's still brilliant with chemicals, he takes *Pesticide Monthly* and they really value him at Bayer, the warble fly doesn't stand a chance and neither do the cows, probably. If you bring up this thing about warble fly treatment and mad cows and why everyone seems to go senile or at least tremble earlier these days he comes at you with a knife. But he loves his carp, he worries about them, he leans over and talks to them and it's all I can do not to tiptoe towards him on a hand-held and guess the rest.

I'll go, says William. I feel a real shiver through my solar plexus right at this moment and not just because of the unpleasant memory trace. I'm thinking that maybe if William hadn't said that – I wouldn't be around to shoot this scene, I wouldn't be haunting Mrs Halliday, I wouldn't be victimising her in this way. Agatha's stood up now. I don't mind going, she says. We'll all be storming the door at this rate, says my grandfather. He's shuffling the pack semi-professionally. Dorothy's twisting around to face Mrs Trevelyan, the wickerwork's popping out all over the place and it's sharp. I don't believe as she's up to mischief, m'm, she points out helpfully.

I'll go, honestly, says my great-uncle.

He makes for the door a trifle hastily, he reckons, so he contrives to look stupendously indifferent as he opens it. He turns round and surveys the room definitely stupendously indifferent to anyone not attached to his chest via a stethoscope and clears his throat of a little tumbleweed of sputum.

I've got to look up my burnet, anyway.

APPENDIX

Those of us present at the party given by my father on the last day of the twentieth century (the generally accepted last day, not the official one) and the first day of the twenty-first century at the time the film projector was knocked over have all given their own versions of events. Hilda Brand (my niece), Ossy Cohen, the person on the sofa who turned out to be a homeless vagrant called Jock, the projectionist Joe 'Gel' Parker, Mrs Victoria 'Indisposed' Halliday (my half-great-aunt), and myself. The fact that none of our versions coincided is owing to the fact that we were all in various stages of inebriation or recovering from various stages of inebriation, and that we were in different positions in the room. Or rather, rooms. I believe only Ms Brand was watching the film at the time, as she had done throughout. That's why I've decided to take pen to paper (not my usual line) and give as clear a picture of events as I can, taking into account the various now yellowing press cuttings and unofficial correspondence between those present and myself, as well as the report finally drawn up by the Thames River Police. I am grateful to Ms Hilda Brand for overseeing the typescript.

Perhaps the first point to clear up is the number of reels remaining unshown – apart from the half-finished one damaged when my father attempted to remove it from the projector. There were fifteen. If one discounts the suggestion that many of these were blank, that makes another ten hours at least of film. I cannot believe that my father seriously meant *Haunting Mrs Halliday* to continue for another day. He was well aware of the time problem. The room was booked by others for that night: the hotel staff were adamant that we had to be out by midday on 1 January 2000. In the closing minutes of the film as shown and apparently 'interrupted' there were several mentions of Hoovers in connection with death and certainly with the end of the film. We

454

could hear the Hoovers on the floor below – which had been particularly riotous through the night, one person having been ejected summarily through a closed window – at about the time (according to my niece Ms Brand) the Hoovers were mentioned in the film. This leads me to believe that, contrary to press reports, my father was fully aware of the length of his film almost to the minute and had timed it to perfection. Therefore this calls into question the idea that he was a fruitcake and had no notion that his film overran by ten hours or that it would be forcibly halted in mid-showing.

It was, it must be emphasised, my father himself who pulled the film out of the projector at the point just shown. The tear comes a few inches after 'burnet, anyway'. It was again my niece who pointed out the rather curious coincidence of the word 'burnet' (meaning a type of butterfly) and 'burn it'. Apart from that, it does seem a very odd place to end a ten-hour movie if that ending was, indeed, deliberate.

It might be appropriate here to give the relevant dictionary definition of 'burnet' (*Shorter Oxford*): 'A day-flying moth of the genus *Zygaena*, typically dark green with crimson-spotted wings'. Ms Brand (who is, I might point out, at present studying English at Oxford) has drawn my attention to the fact that William Trevelyan (my great-great-uncle) had told his mother he had caught an uncommon burnet. This would probably mean one with four instead of six spots on each wing. There is, as it happens, a very tatty specimen in the glass case thought to have belonged to William Trevelyan and now in the firm possession of Mrs Victoria (*née Trevelyan*) Halliday, and it does appear to have only four red spots on each wing – however, its colours are so faded it's pretty hard to tell. Ms Brand has also drawn my attention to the idea of these red spots being somehow a hidden reference to the breaking of Millicent (Milly) Stephenson's virginity – an event which, everyone agrees, was just about to happen in the movie. From the three reels dredged up with my father's body from the Thames, and painstakingly repaired with some limited success by Mr S. T. Longley, a retired Pinewood laboratory technician who recalled my father with some affection and who was also responsible for the last-minute processing of the first reel, it appears that it is Giles Trevelyan, and not his brother, who 'has his way' with the young maidservant. *Zygaena* also recalls perhaps Dr Todd Lazenby's widow, Zelda, with whom my father was besotted – but that's something else and certainly not my idea.

It certainly wasn't mine, either.

Phantom of the Opera talking. You'll never get rid of me that easy. Screams, chairs turned over, Ricky Thornby more Thames slime than flesh making a puddle on the carpet and wondering why no one's saying *hi, good to see you back, come on over, that was a great movie*. Greg, I apologise. You sound nothing like that. I'm not great with voices and I'm in England and your new Chinesey girl has nicked my resident umbrella or some sod has and no one's invited me for dinner. I phoned Mrs Halliday and she said to give over pestering her – if I went on pestering her she'd alert Scotland Yard or whoever. That really screws things up. It really screws me up, too. It's kind of raining. I'm nervous.

Why am I so nervous?

Maybe I'm not up to it, guv.

Maybe when the crunch comes my teeth'll just fall out.

Cor blimey luvaduck. I'm feeling slimey. Maybe I should torture myself and take an English shower. Maybe that phone call has screwed me up tighter than I thought. Maybe it's because I was sitting next to this aircraft mechanic on the flight over with my stubble growing into my knee-caps and my stomach negotiating a cease-fire with some intractable turbulence. And this aircraft mechanic from Vancouver kept telling me how he was gonna give up and open a store because it wasn't worth his while handling all these crap components these days, all made in Taiwan or someplace, not worth the polystyrene they were badly shipped over in. I had to watch this incomprehensible crap with dicky earphones that picked up the hard rock channel while this small but totally vital component badly lathed by some child slave in Jakarta or wherever was working itself loose and we'd only hit Newfoundland. I wish I could just be beamed up Scottie or something or fly astrally like Clifford says he can, but then he also cheats at Monopoly.

My flat feels creepy actually, it feels like it's been slowpanned while the phone rings and rings with no one answering and there are these crimson stains on the walls. My son's got this new girlfriend called Me who eats all my dry goods and leaves bloodstains or maybe paprika splashes on the walls – I was already sore. Now that little sore has been completely out-sored by something that's gotten right into me and it hurts.

I mean, I've kind of been keeping mum about Mrs Halliday, I know, but that doesn't mean she wasn't very important to me. Like Jason of the Lagerlouts is very important to me. Like the Chairman of the College Pension Committee, Dr T. Lazenby, is very important to me. Like Jeremy Freeman of Viper's Bugloss Productions Limited (extremely limited) is very important to me. Like Houston and its dot-to-dot college is very important to me. Like Vyshitface and Crew-Cut and Hal the Computer and about nine and a half of my students are very important to me. You know why they're very important to me. They make me feel nervous. They make my mask go all lopsided. They scrim my life vision and stand in front of my projected image and blow smoke into my self-worth and trample on my head to get to their seats. Maybe I shouldn't wear sandals. I have very good sandals, actually. Small-country-trampling heavy-duty sandals made in Germany. Listen, if you lived in Houston, Texas, you would wear sandals so as not to get yourself confused with everyone else plus my big toes like being wet-nosed by stray pooches, it's one of the only times they get appreciated. My problem – hey, my problem is that I'm confused with myself. I was hoping that this complex masterwork of a twelve-hour motion picture would kind of deconfuse me. I was getting there. Lon Chaney Jnr was getting there. But this phone call from my half-aunt has screwed things up. Basically I have no access any more. You know why? Because some prick went and told her I was not writing a history of the Trevelyan family from 1721 to 1918 for the Texan Trevelyans who might think they share three corpuscles with the founder of Trevelyan Disinfectants & Antiseptics big deal but that I was making a movie and in this movie were some dark secrets in Big Close-Up.

True, true. Dark secrets in BCU. *The Return Of Spotted Dick*. Knock knock, knock knock, knock knocketty knock. Tighten on her eyes,

Mike, tighten on the wet whites of Mrs Halliday's eyes above the tulip-glass of the flickery oil-lamp as she fumbles with the big key and breathes through her mouth because in under the door creeps this puddle and it really stinks, it's evil, it's unadulterated Thames sludge, it's all the drowned of London town including dogs, cats and babies and about two thousand years of tipped shite and industrial effluent and costermongers' peelings and it encircles her slippers with the pink pom-poms and she screams.

Hey, I can't examine my great-uncle's butterfly collection or my great-aunt's correspondence or my grandfather's intimate diaries or the fat photo albums or Uncle Ken's home movies or what remains of the Trevelyan library any more while Giles's daughter watches TV in the next room with the sound turned up so high I have to stick wax plugs in my ears or go crazy, the canned laughter starts to sound deliberate, I start thinking it's applying to me, I start to feel as if all this stuff lying around is some kind of joke and that there's something really hysterical about the old butterflies for instance or Uncle Kenneth's home movies the time I hauled up my antique projector and threw my relatives onto the wall with various backdrops including Hamilton Lodge plus different shrubs and trees and kind of quick shadows and a wheelbarrow and Agatha jerking from round the corner and shading her eyes in that beautiful long dress and so forth while the elm trees swayed around like they were showing off and me thinking this is probably all that's left of them even though they look so huge and animated and then this wave of canned laughter coming through like it was all ridiculous anyway and why don't you give up, you jerk.

Hey, it was very depressing but I felt at home, I felt I was sharing something I had every blahdy right to share, I felt in touch with myself, the Wolf Man began to look vaguely human, I was getting there. She was even making me tea the last two times, she began to lose this thing about being indisposed today and she'd press the buzzer longer than a quarter of a second. Never at no time did she ever use the word pester. It's a really awful word. Zelda used it last year. She said my husband and I would appreciate it if you stopped pestering us, Rick. Cor blimey, guv, I come over all unnecessary with scabby warts and some disease with a German name which makes you smell and hunch over and dribble and say hey, Zelda, please don't call it that. Bother or bug or even harass yes but not pester. I'll stick with pester, Rick. OK, so be it. The Pester Man slouched off up the HCDVA corridor leaving a trail of scabs and green stuff and never approached his true love again. The movie bombed. No one could care less, actually.

That's it, innit? No one could care less.

Bleedin 'eck.

Make visible what, without you, might perhaps never have been seen.

Oh, Norma. Everything you admire about me is out on loan and way overdue like my Enfield Town Library copy of Wittgenstein's *Tractatus Logico-Philosophicus* due back on 3 April 1949. You know one of the three things that wakes me up screaming at the peak coronary hour and if you don't know which the peak coronary hour is don't ever find out because if you're awake at that time you just get really stressed thinking you're in the peak coronary hour which is probably why it is? It's Miss L. G. 'Loofah Face' Hope waving my fine in front of my spectacles. Not that I go to sleep in my spectacles, but I'm always wearing really thick spectacles in this nightmare and just beginning a productive conversation with the Warner Brothers I've waited fifty years for. OK OK, it was *Arthur Askey's Annual 1939* not Wittgenstein but Miss L. G. Hope didn't split hairs and if you're wondering why I got the '39 and not the '49 *Arthur Askey's Annual* it was something to do with the war, blame Hitler, I got the most up-to-date one in the building.

Hey, London always makes me feel gloomy. It's the shit on your own doorstep thing apart from the weather and the food and the badly adjusted diesel engines and people who look like they could do with eating more fruit or something. London is the shit on my personal doorstep and I always step in it because you don't look, do you? My first memory of my home city, I say to interested parties back in Texas, was a hanging bathket. A hanging basket? No, a hanging bathket. There was this bath hanging in the air where a bathroom had been and maybe someone scrubbing their back with Miss Hope's face. It was hanging by its plumbing and it had weeds growing out of it and kind of drooping prettily over the side, it was a hanging bathket, I found it amusing, I

459

pointed and laughed but my mother jerked me because she said that's where Mrs Vernon had joined her Maker. What a place to join your Maker, a bomb-site, the dust'd get into the seals and the wings'd fall off I reflected but not out loud. The interested parties in Texas show their dental work understandingly and go back to talking about commodities or polyphylesis or the origins of the medieval guild system or whatever, I don't know, it depends who's present and unable to quit their career mode for even a couple of hours. I tend to drift off in these things and find my face in the *ice*-cream as opposed to the ice-*cream* but it's just as unpleasant and never very popular.

You wanna know what happened, huh?

Still Fifteen, from my short VD, *Home with Mrs Halliday*. Take a break. The white and yellow stuff in the chair is the white cat lying on what's left of my great-uncle's summer flannels. The black stuff on the wall is my shadow.

You were ages.

It's not that those things in Mrs Halliday's place tell me a great deal, guv. They're not exactly teeming with information or *clues* if you wanna make me out to be some kind of shifty sleuth, streuth. It's just that they reassure me. They tell me that it was all *reeal*, that these people actually did exist for God's sake, that they moved around knocking their legs against *reeal* furniture and went up *reeal* stairs holding on to *reeal* banisters that didn't shake and wobble along with the walls and opened *reeal* doors that went somewhere other than a ten-foot drop with Joe Gel winding some cables at the bottom. If they were real then so were my grandmother and my mother and me. Because basically there is so little left of them, so little that they might all have been a rumour, even my grandmother at the top of the stairs oh Christ suddenly and my dear old mother for crying out loud when she was young. And I don't believe in rumours. Maybe I should make the rest of the film silent with me doing a voice-over like the voice-over in Mrs Z. Lazenby's favourite film after *Bambi* (*Jules et Jim*, by the Truffle), really dry and matter-of-fact while these amazing very passionate and profound things are going on. Maybe I should do that. If I don't do that I'll crack up and furnace what I've had printed up so far and annoy my neighbour because I've processed about five hundred yards of celluloid and it cost me what Greg got for one of his carpet squares out of some unhinged private collector with gold-handled lavatory brushes which is half of my savings, for crying out loud.

Or maybe I should just crack up. Maybe I'll just sit here in this lousy little empty kitchen and decompose like one of those early Warhol films. Letting it roll for hours and hours while I just sit here and decompose. *The Decomposition of Ricky Thornby, 30 hrs, dir. Richard Thornby, 1998.*

But the hoovers'd arrive just at the most exciting moment, when my eyeballs fall out or my kidneys flop onto my toes. Or something.

What would *Robert*-to-rhyme-with-despair do? *Robert* would not despair. *When you do not know what you are doing and what you are doing is the best – that is inspiration.*

Why am I outside everything and everybody, *Robert?* Why am I always sneaking up to their windows through the shrubbery and pestering them, *Robert?* Why have you made so many great complex masterworks that strike the inner soul and me not one, *Robert?* Why do I seem to see through everything and everybody and comprehendeth them not, *Robert?*

Quoi?

He likes the *Jules et Jim* idea. He thinks it's my only hope. *Shooting is going out to meet something*, Richard-to-rhyme-with-bizarre. *Nothing in the unexpected that is not secretly expected by you, OK?*

OK.

Hi again, crew. You've been so patient. We're going kind of silent. Sorry, Bosey. You can pack up your woofers in the old kitbag and jack me a lip mike. Sorry, Norma, for all those wasted times on the sheep-sprinkled downs and stuff. I'm doing all the voices. This is the eleventh hour. The Hoovers Are Coming. Here's what we do. William has the line about the burnet then we cut into me wrapping the rest of the story up while you move around enormous on the silver screen. Thus.

William has the line about the burnet. Action.

He goes out of the room. He moves through the kitchen and up the back stairs. The steps are of brick but dip in the middle. Basically a lot of damp and gloom. One gaslight at each turn and a tiny window halfway up. He looks through it at the front drive where the carriages and motor cars used to deposit luggage and attached guests and the gravel's moving because the moon's a day away from full, Mike's got a gobo over the blue luminaires and Clifford's waving the flicker-stick, he needed the job, sorry, I don't want you saturated with detail.

Breathe.

William's now noticing nicks on the steps, bright new nicks like someone's just begun carving a waterfall and had to go answer the door or something. He's nervous. The top floor's floor creaks and he thinks about ghosts and goblins and stuff – he thinks particularly about the phantom new boy in the basement of Cavendish House and he has to kind of sigh and blow a few red admirals out of his stomach. Then a great whine which is the door opening at the top of the stairs though he can't yet see it, it's round the turn. There are these little clicks and clinks and a thump which his feet pick up at some very subliminal level. Also a hissed *bust me* that makes William's mouth fall open.

Shadow. The shadow first, on the wall at the turn. Me in my expressionist mode. A shadow like my clothes always made on the chair in the bedroom, probably a psychotic monk. Hooded. Vile smell courtesy of Des's socks.

Then her. Unhooded. Or hooded by her hair which her hair-pins have mostly let out on parole. Quit the jokes, Rick. Hit the bone.

The maid. Millicent (Milly) Stephenson. Bent over a big metal bucket, both hands on the handle, taking it a step at a time. Blouse, long cotton skirt, big boots. He coughs. She looks up, there's an intake of breath, the bucket thumps back onto the step and water splashes up golden in the gaslight. Big saucepan lid bobbing on top. Bust me, she exclaims again but under her breath. William swallows.

Do you want a hand? he proffers. She blinks, her tongue explores the corner of her mouth. She's three steps higher than William. William feels a bratchet. Screech outside. Barn owl, says William. Glances through window: Clifford's doing great things with his flicker-stick, Bosey's got hiss on the Scotch pines, the black tops of the elms against the night sky are approaching ogres.

It's got a nest in the barn, he says, but where you can't see it.

The light's too poor to see my grandmother's spots.

Can I keep this up?

Yup. And now you know.

My grandmother's looking down at the bucket, biting her lip. Blouse unbuttoned at the neck, hair really astray. William mounts two steps. Let me help, he says. She looks at him and gives this little nod. Their hands sit side by side on the handle like a couple of kids on a gate. Mrs Lazenby'd be really impressed by this.

Hold that, Mike. Hold their hands tight.

They lift the bucket and the saucepan lid rocks and some water splashes out. She grunts, he wheezes I'm afraid. They get it down with a few more nicks and spills and they giggle. Lower it thump onto original earthenware tiles outside scullery. Phew, I say! He wheezes and coughs and takes out his handkerchief and wipes his mouth on it but there's no blood and the sputum's passable.

I had to do it up there, sir, she says, she's took a fancy to me.

William flushes of course. OK, she's lifting the saucepan lid. He bends over and takes a squinny. He makes a face. Rats but with these big snowy feet and they're bobbing about. Tighten on one. They have very swollen eyes but tight shut. Oh, he says. He feels nauseous. He looks at her.

My great-uncle and my grandmother stand together in the dark little back entrance outside the scullery and don't know what to say. The summery night air's sneaking in under the original outside door that doesn't meet the original tiles, there's a hint of honeysuckle and evening primrose and stuff. I think that is a nightjar. A moth hits the door but softly because it is only a moth.

Silence.

465

More silence.

I wish you'd shut up in the back there. There's such a thing as soft-pedal lovemaking for God's sake, it doesn't have to sound like a pack of wolves. Ay. She said as to deal with it straight away. That's my grandmother breaking the silence, which is fine. Mrs Abbot said. She's either massaging her thighs or wiping the flat of her hands on her skirt. Mrs Abbot.

My great-uncle nods and he closes his mouth.

On ma bed, snorts my grandmother.

On ma bed, she repeats. The little Devil.

William's blush would power a jet turbine. Thank God it's gloomy in here. Des didn't flush ever, he just stayed pasty. I did. Of course I did. I flushed very easily just thinking about flushing. It was a no-win situation. But then Des doesn't have a very flushable face. It's like school brawn. That silent few moments a few moments back will appear a lot of times in my great-uncle's sketchbook, and once as a completed painting about the size of a person. It went the way of all inflammables with his other more personal effects gratis my great-grandmother. I was going to study the painting with a magnifying glass this trip because it appears in one of Uncle Kenneth's snapshots only slightly out of focus but I can't because The Police Will Be Alerted if I try to axe Mrs Halliday's door or jemmy a window or winch myself down through the roof out of a stolen Harrier powered by William's blush. Shame. Take it from me it's a remarkable painting.

THE WASTE.

So much fuckin' waste, mate.

> How many and how more were the violins unsung
> By the fingers something over Dachau's stack?
> Smoke cannot play the Einsteinian rag
> Nor blear its own eyes to feel the lack, the lack!

Thank you, Henrik old friend, fellow pesterer and toss-pot but not now, not now. Later, maybe, in the bar after the screening. For old times.

Christ, I'm older than he was when he was old.

Plip. That's the hairpin dropping into the pail. My grandmother dabbles about in the water for it. My great-uncle wants to tuck her curl back but misses the opportunity and anyway he feels frightfully seedy watching her bared arm being nibbled by the dead OK you've twigged kittens. She lifts her arm out, on the end of it is her hand rising up in slow motion trailing a ribbon of water and the hairpin's there and she sticks it into her bun and her wet skin gleams, obviously. Note that, Mike. The water in the pail rocks gradually. Because she has her arms up William's lungs are taking in a fair amount of her body odour, which is sweetish. She's gone and made a downright mess, says my grandmother. Hey, she has my ears, small and neat. Pardon? squeaks William. He clears his throat. Maybe his broken voice is getting itself fixed again. On ma bed, she says. Blood'n stuff on ma bed. Oh, how frightful, says William from about two hundred miles the other side of the class divide, how quite frightfully awful. The maid has never spoken to him like this before. He's never given her the chance, actually. I'm thinking we should have had an establishing clip of Calypso the pregnant cat but I'm sorry it was furnaced. You're not that dumbo, anyway.

Little horror, she says, it's 'cos I makes such a fuss of her.

My great-uncle nods. He feels he's confronting life and death in its profoundest vestments. This is Frank Franklin's influence. Frank Franklin is D. H. Lawrence without the background or the red beard or the genius or the poor health, which is a tough thing to be. But Frank Franklin maintains that the country life of blood and soil and sex is vital and profound and that we are all attenuated beings, so he's making progress. He's not yet touched William's knee. He'll do everything he can to join up instantly despite his club-foot and'll fail and turn deep pacifist and practically vegan and weep uncontrollably at William's funeral and throw himself into the grave at Agatha's funeral which we'll come to, he's a rival, I tracked him down to a low-slung cottage with a lot of cats in Shropshire and stepped on his hearing-aid BY MISTAKE in 1989 when I was on my general recce but he was totally ga-ga, it was OK, he posed no threat, he'd burnt the letters from her in about 1928 because he'd learnt them by heart I think his mistress or maybe just helper said, she was a mine of information, he died about a month later aged something totally ridiculous but not quite a century.

Have you killed all of them?

Oh ay, she says. She looks down at the kittens as if she has just decided to suckle them or something. They're revolving slowly with outsize paws because they've landed on the other side of the water from a great height or maybe depth and are just recovering. They're blind, thinks William. They came out and the first thing they knew was horrible. The only thing they knew. They were refused.

They were refused flaps around in his head like it's broken in from somewhere else and can't get out. It is from somewhere else, actually – it's from something his father said last week when he'd motored down for the weekend, he was on about the Club and a couple of chaps who tried to enter without ties or spats or longjohns or something. My grandmother looks down at them like she's thinking how cute they are. She's about at her peak right now. This'll be the happiest she'll ever be. I'd have preferred a backdrop of spring flowers and Austrian mountains because it's hell shooting all this in a few square feet of black hole on an extremely uneven floor even with a bazooka mounting on the Number One but no one chooses where their happiest moments come, mine was in a bus shelter in Uxbridge, I'll explain it sometime but not now because we have a little technical wizardry to perform at this point. OK. Sometimes my great-uncle has nightmares involving linden trees falling on top of him and right now the linden trees are racing past him like he's in a motor car. He swallows and leans against the wall because the last thing he wishes to happen is to faint in front of the girl. The linden trees are superimposing themselves in front of his face. They race past him and go on forever and in flickery black and white. The whole Frank Franklin feeling has vanished, frankly. It's this thing about being refused. I want a few seconds of the supered flashing avenue over my great-uncle's cold

468

sweat and staring eyes so tell the sod who's standing up in front of the screen to duck down or fuck off, we can't cope with more than one super at a time and anyway, his face isn't flat enough.

Thank you.

Little 'orror, murmurs my grandmother.

Little 'orror would've been an expression my mother would've recalled my grandmother using a lot if I'd asked her, like *my, my* or *not on me onions* or *joining the Maker* are expressions I would've recalled my mother using a lot, if you'd asked me.

The flashing-avenue super has gone. There's just the face now. Look at this face. Those of you not draped over the bean-bags under someone or maybe under the bean-bags will have begun to note t

Sorry about the jitters. Kitchen-knife edit and the Romanies haven't been around lately with their whetstone. I decided the time wasn't ripe. Stick with it. We've lost about a second, twenty-four frames, not a lot happened.

Did you not mind awfully, doing it?

She shakes her head with a little puzzled frown and about the penultimate swatch of black hair comes loose from the bun at the back. Her lips are kind of hovering away from each other. She has my mother's lips. I mean, my mother had her lips. I see it now. I never saw that before. Who needs a magnifying glass? Who needs Mrs Halliday? Who needs a mirror? We need a spade, says the maid. Pardon? says the young gentleman. We need a spade, sir, she repeats. You'd think this'd be a never ever but it isn't for some reason. Maybe deep down she's very embarrassed at being in the tiny entrance bit between the scullery and the ancient outside door that doesn't meet the tiles with the young gentleman – or maybe she's just lonely for God's sake and this loneliness has overridden all the rules. I don't know. All I know is that my grandmother is getting Master William in on this whole operation. Don't call me sir, William squeaks. Hey, this voice thing is really unfortunate. There's a stupendously awful silence, stupendously awful, broken only by a moth. YOU CAN CALL ME WILLO, IF YOU WANT. Then he says it, but quieter. He clears his throat again. I'll call you, um, Milly. That'll be terrific, actually.

If you were never incredibly embarrassing at sixteen, you're either lying or you were in a coma for a year, OK? Stick with it. How do you think I feel, huh?

I don't mind butterflies, he adds. He thinks it's adding but it's not of course. He's fairly confused by her look, which is appproaching the pop-eyed. I don't mind butterflies, he repeats, but they're different. You just put them in a chloroform jar or whatever. He isn't sure when exactly a chap puts an arm round – Pantile told him when and he's forgotten but the when can't be much more whennish than right now. Her eyes relax some. She bites her lip and studies his collar button. The mess on the bed, thinks my great-uncle kind of echoily. Hey, something about the mess on the bed disturbs him. Maybe it's because it makes him think of the mess he sometimes does into handkerchiefs or his sputum jar out of his throat. We need a spade, he says, like it's his idea. His arms are nailed in about five places to his hips and his thighs. She's breathing through her nose and her nose is flaring. William wonders why this should be so dashed miraculous. She dips and picks up the bucket again. It makes him jump, this big movement. Her dress brushes past his flannels, it actually touches his white flannels. I think Gordon caught that, I hope he caught that. She lifts the latch on the outside door and opens it. Her fingers on the black latch have the same effect on my great-uncle as the flaring nose. Perfumed night air enters, it's really a relief. Then she's gone. Never ever call a master by his Christian name. That's what did it. Stephenson the Rocket. The outside door starts to swing back because the world's on a tilt or whatever and he catches it with his foot. It bumps against his foot and stops there like it's a bit put out because it's a very old door and not used to being interrupted these days – it's taking it easy, it hasn't got long to go, it's in its senescence, it's fraying at the bottom under the impact of about a million boot-strikes because the boot-owners' hands have been around a tub or a cheese vat or a couple of muck-knockers or something, it'll be ripped out after two hundred years of un-complaining service in 1958 and replaced by a glazed door you can't see more than a blur through like the world outside's a lavatory and

470

which'll be ripped out obviously by the new people after thirty-one years and replaced by a thick varnished oaken slab with wrought iron hinges and six Chubb locks like the world outside's New York and William blinks out into the blackness with his hand on the very special frayed and scarred original door not appreciating it or consciously anyway. The various rustles might be her or they might be Sylvia setting up the next shoot or even bats. Damn, he whispers. Blasted rotten damn. I mean, the blackness is really black like I've got a lens cap over the whole thing but it's OK, we're out to the widest aperture now and there's a practically full moon coming up any moment and some stars and wow we're going infra-red.

We're not really, it's just that William's got his night vision sorted out and he's crossing across the yard. The cobbles are fairly plump under his pumps and for some reason *Daddy Has a Sweetheart and Mother is Her Name* is running through his head, maybe because Giles has played it fifty-one times on the wind-up this hols already with Lillian Lorraine's voice kind of floating over the lawn like the garden should shut up and listen – especially the innumerable murmuring bees and Ags's croquet mallet. The historic door bumps shut behind him and makes his needle jump a bit. He's really edgy. He tacks up to the stable wall the other side and listens. She's dematerialised.

How black-rotten hugely damn tedious.

Ich habe gelebt und geliebet.

I *refuse* to have Uncle Kenneth's amazing baritone singing Thekla's song from *The Piccolomini* dubbed over the night breeze through the elms just because the moon's riding up and William's murmuring this line from Schiller which Uncle Ken has rendered over his brother's and then Agatha's so-so keyboard accompaniment ever since Willo can remember, I *refuse* to cosset your romantic sensibilities, so be happy with a little helpful sub-title jittering around under his youthful moonlit profile, OK?

I have lived and loved.

Look, at sixteen all your past lives were close enough to touch,

471

bunched up right behind you, you had this great world-weariness, the older you get the thinner they get until at about twenty-five they leave you to it and go phut out of your present life, by the time you're sixty all you're left with is yourself and the mirror. Let's have it, hopelessly scratchy plus hiss, me in the mirror looking out at you expertly spliced in for the half-minute it takes:

> Das Herz ist gestorben, die Welt ist leer,
> Und weiter giebt sie dem Wünsche nichts mehr.
> Du Heilige, rufe dein Kind zurück,
> Ich habe genossen das irdische glück,
> Ich habe gelebt und geliebet.

Softly from the German trenches over no-man's-land it'll waft, of course, but Willo won't be anywhere near the right sector so some totally philistine twerp'll yell fuck off and the beautiful tired voice'll stop and the Brit trench'll chuckle and jeer quite a way along its length. Some of the cobbles are glistening. There's wet on the yard. Go softly with that flicker-stick, Clifford, there are no leaves between the moon and this yard and we have to see this glisten clearly, it's a kind of flaring wake my great-uncle takes about five seconds to follow. He's practically decapitated by the washing line. OK, I exaggerate, but it's a shock, his head is young enough to be full of ogres and elves and squeaky night gibberers as well as Schiller songs, Arthur Rackham has patted it and muffed up his hair and sniggered. He smooths it down again and follows the gleam and glisten past the new garage to where the cobbles shrug and give up and hand over to earth and stones and then weeds to you and me but probably some really interesting wild flowers to people like William who bother. He doesn't bother right at this moment, he just walks right over the ramping fumitory and the scented mayweed and the yellow vetchling and I could go on but it'll take all day because it's so rich. Bats flit and stuff. He's pretty certain she's gone up to the old vegetable garden. It's where potato peelings and cabbage-leaves and all that rot end their days, anyway, if Cheery Matt the pig-man doesn't come by with Carrot the one-eared donkey. It's got a brick wall around it that looks as if it could be about ninth century and someone maybe Uncle Kenneth said something about a monastery and the brothers hiding their jewel-encrusted valuables from the Vikings. Actually the wall was built in a fortnight in 1803 but don't disappoint the kids.

The old vegetable garden is now rank, to use my great-grandmother's term. It was rank in 1914, I mean. It's currently a lawn clipped to about a molecule thick with a brick-and-glass receptacle at one end where this creep lives who shouted at me in 1992 just because I was trying to locate exactly where the kittens were interred and my great-uncle had his First Kiss. OK, this fancy metallic-finish puce Vauxhall cavalierly turned up groan and there was a pause and then this guy got out and came across the lawn and asked if he could help me and I said yes you can lend me a spade, I'm trying to locate where my grandmother buried the kittens and my great-uncle kissed her and my biro has made very little impression but he disagreed, he called me a Vandal and shouted at me to clear off immediately. I mean, I'd poked a hole about the diameter of a niblick's divot off a bad lie but everything's relative, he was very upset. There was a sweat stain beginning under his armpit and ending under his tie knot. You couldn't see the other armpit because he had this pale jacket slung over his shoulder hooked on to his finger by the tab and he smelt of hot interior extras and lousy aftershave and something that told me his pink shirt was 89% polyester. The only sign of the wall was a low thing at the back with cement pots at very regular intervals. There was a fairly hefty pause after he'd shouted at me to clear off, I could hear the Vauxhall-something tapping a toothpick against its teeth, all we needed was a swirl of dust and a few tumbleweeds and maybe a barber-shop sign swinging. I cleared my throat of my summer asthma and said I'm sorry about your turf but I reckoned the bones might still be in this world or under it to be precise. Actually I said I'm sorry about your smell but corrected myself, I was a little edgy, I don't believe he heard however. He took two steps back but left me the personal odour in question to deal with so I wheezed through my mouth. He started snapping at me. I mean snapping like dogs snap. I nearly fell into his pond. It's hard backing away holding a video camera but it turned out to be a great shot, jerky for a jerk. I slipped out between the Arizona cypresses before he could turn the sprinklers on me and spot the lens. The woman in the big-house-which-once-belonged-to-my-grandfather was watching from an open window. I'd already encountered this woman on my production recce a couple of years earlier, she had a voice like a car-alarm. She yodelled Well Done John and that if I came again she was going to alert the police pretty well as Mrs Halliday said it last week although Mrs Halliday sounds like sloping English lawns with big copper beeches and this crappily-paid gardener raking on it somewhere. Maybe the police are snoozling all the time in their leather chairs with bluebottles circling their truncheons and need alerting, I don't know. I shot her yelling at me and she shielded her face and backed off out of sight into Agatha my great-aunt's bedroom. I wish I could have taken a shot of Hamilton Lodge and her backing off into the interior shadows through the spokes of this really great bicycle that was kind of stuck upright on the front lawn and overgrown but it had been removed about two years before, there were just about five hundred turf-squares and some pastel-hued all-weather paving and these fancy shrubs with the price tags fluttering in the very pleasant breeze bringing the perfume of cut hay from another planet. I waved goodbye though from where my great-uncle's having breathing problems because he's in amongst the weeds and it's thistles and old man's beard and stuff and it makes him even wheezier. There is a sort of trampled path but he can't locate it. Jeremiah was supposed to have scythed it all two weeks ago but Jeremiah's slow, he's eighty or something and the boy he works with is mentally challenged so Mrs T gets very sweaty under her lace collar about it all but reckons he'll grind to a halt this winter and she can get someone of incredible drive with huge muscles and flowers woven in his pubic hair or whatever but she's in for a surprise because anyone of incredible drive and huge muscles and flowers woven in their pubic air is about to be seriously indisposed for four years and Jeremiah is all she can get so this rank section stays rank for quite a few more seasons but it's OK because Willo's the only one who gets wheezy off the rankness and before Jeremiah grinds to a halt in 1919 he meaning Willo'll be dead along with all Jeremiah's replacements with incredible drive and huge muscles etc. except for one called Enoch who's fairly close to Mrs T's fantasy model except that he now wheezes more than William and Jeremiah put together and only makes it through a couple more seasons before the war finally taps him on the shoulder in the main rose-bed where he breaks a few rose-buds tight shot of scratch across pale cheek under half-lidded eye just too late for the memorial mason so he gets a little brass plaque all to himself after a helluva lot of pushing and shoving on the part of his widowed mother kind of set into the base in 1929 for God's sake by which time she's passed on but only just and the main rose-bed's a tennis court, tic tac, tic tac, tic tac oh shot, jolly well done, deuce. And you think I'm gonna get the girl in the end. Well I never.

474

William meanwhile is battling on through the weeds because he's driven by something that's making him salivate, frankly – along with the night conditions, the summer night conditions. Hey, you don't need a Bel-Air Convertible and a West Coast road to feel excited, you can feel excited in the weedy bit of an English country garden in July 1914 if the set-up's right. There's the old vegetable garden wall. He can tell it's the wall because the moonlight's catching the ivy that's all over the brick. Mike's saying is this what you meant all those years ago about great night effects? and I'm saying Mike, take it one luminaire at a time. Where the ivy's not gleaming fairly eerily is a black arch-shape because that's the arch with the door wide open on one hinge and several ivy-tendrils and William makes for it and steps through and stops to let his wheezes ease a bit, which they don't really, they'll probably keep him up all blasted night. Maimed animal floats through his head now. He spits softly onto the old vegetable garden which is basically lumpy earth covered in places with loops of stuff like wild clematis and bramble along with the odd prehistoric-looking cabbage and plants that smell like fennel but aren't really and some black nightshade in flower right now which Jeremiah and Uncle Ken had told them was deadly after Giles had swallowed a berry by error when conducting a theosophical ceremony in 1911 but Giles didn't even have gripe, the rotters. William swallows and calls her name as loudly as he can without bringing everybody to the glimmering windows of the house about fifty yards back, which means he sort of hisses it into the darkness.

Milly?

Aye?

He jumps. He didn't expect a reply, leave alone a reply from the region of his right knee and so dashed quick. He wants to run because it must be an ectoplasmic entity or the Queen of Elfland or something but sees the water silvery in the pail and the little lacy bits on her blouse moving around like those really embarrassing parties where they had ultraviolet lights and you'd come out of the toilet with glowing flies if you were careless and had white underpants and you'd keep wondering what it was about you that people found so funny and if you were a teenager (I wasn't, I was always about forty-nine with dazzling dandruff) it could really screw you up for life, a thing like that. Actually, she's about five yards away and ultraviolet light has not yet been invented or maybe discovered or perhaps *harnessed* is the best term. I'll just superimpose a really embarrassing fact on this shot of my grandmother dealing with the kittens in the old vegetable garden while my great-uncle is getting his head back on – Dr Dott put on a wild show with the stoodents called *Sigfreud's Follies* last year and, wait for it, he used *ultraviolet light* and a *stroboscope*. Whacky, huh? I told him afterwards I'd worked for correction *with* Peter as in Brook and Peter hated UV and strobes and that was in the early seventies when they weren't embarrassing for second-rate discos only. Actually, I started to say this but some jerk interrupted me saying how wonderful the show was and hugging him so I tipped my Californian dental mouthwash over the Doc's pansy dance-pumps instead and retired early. I should have been a missionary in the Congo after all but it was me dad's suggestion so I never took it up, guv.

It's so quiet in the old vegetable garden you can hear the moths or maybe it's my grandmother's fingers in amongst the weeds. We've got sound back, by the way. I could do all the voices but the effects were beyond me and Bosey told me he was going to play some Deep Purple at full volume out of his Bose two thousand-or-whatever-watters at the crucial moment if I didn't go back to doing a talkie and I know when Bosey says something he means it and hey, playing Deep Purple in a little country village in July 1914 might upset one or two people, especially the hallooing vicar and the alcoholic squire and certainly my great-uncle although it would've prepared him some for the kind of aural levels he's going to encounter in a couple of years, I suppose. Bosey's really looking forward to those trench scenes, it's the greatest challenge of his career, the sound's going to make The Who look like they're playing through a wind-up and it's going to go on and on and on – I really hope we make it before the Hoovers come and I jump from the veranda into the greasy waters of oblivion with all those reels because it's going to be the summit of my artistic career, those battle scenes.

Did you bring th'spade, sir?

She's looking up at him. The oval of her face is slanted across by the moonlight, it makes her nose look kind of hooked and catches her right eye and neatly sculpted ear.

Oh, crikey, says my great-uncle. There's another silence filled with an incredible multi-track collage of extremely soft rustlings and whoopings and I think clickings and probably the black nightshade curling up for the night. I forgot, confesses my great-uncle. Dashed silly.

She appears to be scrabbling in the earth with her bare hands. I'll do that, he says. He could go and fetch the spade but his wheezes and the fact that she might disappear into patches of moonlight in the mean time stop him. Honestly, he adds. I'm not quite sure why he added that because he has no intention of getting down on his knees and making a hole with his bare hands because of a slight technical problem, which is to do with his white flannels and the fact that Madre would have his guts for green garters if he so much as flecked them with the tiniest crumb of Wiltshire sod. So he kind of hovers uselessly listening to his own breath and trying to stop it whistling so much. He can see the kittens in the pail, they interrupt the moonlight, it makes him feel nauseous again. Milly the maid goes on scrabbling away and a weed flies over her shoulder. He looks up at the stars. Faint gulfs of white light and the wink of eternity. He's not sure where that line comes from but it's dead I mean jolly accurate. The elm-tops look very high and sway but they can't be swaying really because saying there's a breeze would be overdoing it. By the way, the light that reaches his retina from one of these stars started out at exactly the moment a young female iguanodon was crossing the point on the planet taken up by the old vegetable garden and masticating some bracken at the same time, which is more than some people over Houston way can do. He looks back at my grandmother. The iguanodon light wastes itself on the weeds and the ivy and the back of a shimmery beetle snootling around by my great-uncle's left foot. This beetle couldn't care less whether this is 1914 AD or 50,000,000 BC it'll look and act pretty much the same either way and will continue to do so although life'll get tough around the 1980s when this lot's grubbed up and some Bayer killer chemical's put down for the creep's lawn by Walters Homes Ltd.

My grandmother's looking up again. The moonlight catches the bottom lip and now the top lip. Her eyes too.

This is where Bosey would've played *Storm on the Water*, OK?

Instead there's the multi-track collage of night sounds and my great-uncle's wheeze. Very very very very faintly there's the sound of talking through the open windows of the house about fifty yards away but you'd only register that if you had supersonic ears. I'm travelling away from my great-uncle and my grandmother at this juncture, I'm afraid. There's something called privacy. I'm feeling a snoop. The arch is over us for about a second and there's a naff movement of the ivy at the top because Gordon's wearing his stupid hat and it caught and you can see the leaves flapping back like a camera's just tracked through but I'm not retaking this, we haven't time, you dumbos won't notice. There's an interesting conversation going on in the sitting-room, we're almost there, we've got a bit of lawn to go now, get that honeysuckle scent, maybe we'll stop for a few seconds just to admire this garden. That dark humpy mass at the bottom is the woods. Otherwise it's rhododendrons and azaleas and fancy roses and stuff with a sloping lawn and that big creepy tree is a yew and over there is a hornbeam and that one's a tulip tree and you can see them all again on Uncle Kenneth's home movies looking really agitated beyond the sparkles and the tramlines and Mrs Halliday's or whoever's thumb-prints as if they're afraid we're not going to notice them or something just like lousy extras are. I mean, even a game of croquet between the kids looks neurotic unless you're on slomo but then they kind of get overwhelmed by the celluloidal deterioration, it's difficult, and, hey, now I don't need to think about it because I have no access to my family's archives, for Christ's sake.

It's peaceful here, huh? Maybe the conversation isn't that interesting. It's only politics, actually. That tubercular bearded student-guy Princip shot the Archduke about a week back and Giles and Agatha are telling their mother who Princip is. It's coming kind of muffled through the open windows behind us. I don't think I'll shoot it because Ossy'll say it's too predictable, next thing you know Ricky'll be inserting that clip of the Archduke and his consort coming down the stairs to their motor car with about five minutes of life to go except the quality's so terrible you can hardly see them, there's this weird burst of light like an omen, maybe a burn-out or a specular, and then that's it: nobody was cranking away next to this Princip guy or on that particular street as the vintage car with the ostrich plumes sticking up out of it and blowing around approached – it wasn't like Jack Kennedy in Dallas and the guy whose name began with Z, Zap-something, Zapludel – anyway the guy with the home cine whose little spools took the dime-store Kodak past the shutter without a hitch into the most famous clip in the history of humanity. Imagine taking that little number out of the camera without widdling in your underpants. Someone's laughing. I know why it is, it's Giles's joke about Princip having no princips. They're laughing because actually they're not really aware of the situation. They're not really aware that this conversation about the Balkans and where exactly Sarajevo is and what's the difference between Servia and Bosnia makes me want to cry because they're quite enjoying it, it makes them feel intellectually excited, they can show off in front of their mother and Dorothy, they're that kind of age, they've both of them read the papers down here because the days get kind of baggy and playing Chopin in front of billowing curtains all day is OK if James Ivory is the director but not OK if Ricky Thornby is on the megaphone and they don't realise that this conversation has about seven million phantoms listening in including a pair of spectral teeth in a jawbone which is all anyone ever found of Willo although they didn't know it was Willo's jawbone, they just put it in a sack with the other bits and pieces and carried on hoeing. I'm talking about 1953. These seven million phantoms are having problems fitting in, they're jammed onto the lawn and beyond and maybe we'll have to relay the conversation on loudspeakers Bosey wherever you are but it's OK, it's very calm and peaceful out here in the summer moonlight and English nocturnal wildlife is relatively low-key, there aren't even cicada and a billion crickets to drive you round the bend or some fucker playing his parents' Doors album so the whole block can appreciate how wild he is or maybe to drown out my neighbour's TV. These seven million phantoms are just listening very very quietly, they aren't even nodding their heads and grimacing wryly like I'm doing, they're just holding themselves very still and very evenly spaced even through the rose-beds and stuff just listening to the conversation as it sort of pads out over the air about as softly as a moth trying to get through a closed window or whatever until it peters out about a wood and a field away where the last few latecomers are joining up but they'll have it explained to them, don't worry. I'd like to be able to say that Willo the jawbone is right in the room behind Agatha's head or wherever but he's not, he's somewhere out there with the others, I can't even see

479

him and I don't really fancy moving, if I turned my head round they'd probably just kind of all vanish and we'd be back to the lawn with just blue moonlight and long shadows over the grass and very pleasant smells because the last of the hay's been cut today which is why you can just hear some group-singing from the village direction thataway and I think a fiddle, I'd like to think it was a fiddle, I'm a sucker for

> The older England of byways and slow apple turnovers
> And the steep-stacked haywain,
> The brand-new England of highways and spaghetti flyovers
> And the jam-packed airplane

leaves me chilled. Hey, Henry, sorry for taking liberties but there were some things we saw eye to eye on and no one else reads you anyway, not these days, you're not so much neglected as abandoned. OK, that brand-new stuff's not so brand-new now but it seemed that way when Henry wrote it in 1961, like the millennium seems brand-new to you people out there but hey it's not, it's only new in name and number, it's actually got all the same sparkles and tramlines and thumb-prints and vibrating hairs because you handled it too quickly, it was still green and wet and you were clumsy, you should have laid it out on the table and let it dry really slowly and given it a chance, you've fucked the print, there's only one, you've already gone into it all wrong, all the same pinheads are running the screening and all they want is money and power and fuck the cost – hey, you're caught right between Princip's gun and the big guy's ostrich plumes as they flounce and bob after his head that's turning round in slomo to catch a specular off the muzzle, I'm sorry about that, if I was very naff I could superimpose my great-uncle's lips approaching my grandmother's mouth but this is an art-house movie of the highest quality and I won't and anyway I've got so excited the seven million phantoms have sighed and turned to blue moonlight which Mike's done just a fabulous job on, the moths love it, Agatha's leaning out of the creepered window we swooped down through if you remember and breathing in the night air and saying how sweet it smells so Gavrilo Princip must have bitten the dust as the evening topic and by tomorrow Mrs Trevelyan will have forgotten the difference between Bosnia and Servia and where exactly on the map Giles's finger tapped Sarajevo because there'll be other more urgent stuff to chew on like domestic rape.

The cat. We forgot the cat. It's here, it's by my legs. It's called Calypso. My grandmother made a fatal mistake: she should have left Calypso one kitty, she shouldn't have wiped out the whole lot. That's why the cat's kind of upset, y'see, son. She's mewing and looking around for what's supposed to fasten on her teats like I once fastened on my mother's would you believe. Agatha's looking out the window and saying what's the matter with Calypso and Dorothy's replying with some nugget of wordly wisdom but I can't catch it. I think Bosey's still up in the old vegetable garden with his goose-neck or I'd have stuck it through the window above Agatha's head and picked up the nugget but sorry, let's just assume it was something like Calypso hev goed an hed her little-uns most like, chit. She shouldn't really be calling Agatha aged eighteen chit but old habits die hard, like overcooking the sago or sucking her teeth and her dialect always thickens when she comes back to Wiltshire anyway, by the end of August she's practically indecipher able. Agatha's disappeared from the window. In about fifteen seconds she'll be out on the lawn in the blue moonlight looking stunned because the cat's not got a big belly any more and there's blood on its tail and no sign of the kit-kits. She wasn't party to the plan. It was Mrs T's plan, actually. She just about stomachs Calypso who is a kind of summer visitor from Littlejohn Farm up the lane knowing which side of her paw is buttered but the idea of a heap of squirming mini-Calypsos makes my great-grandmother vapourish, as a matter of fact. It's not really my grandmother's fault, she was carrying out instruc-tions, it's what she's paid peanuts to do by these people, like I'm paid peanuts to carry out instructions by HCDVA and most people are paid peanuts to carry out instructions by the jerks in charge under their fucking ostrich plumes. If I drove around Houston in a vintage De Dion Bouton wearing ostrich plumes on my head and carrying a sabre they'd probably shoot me too or maybe drag me around behind a pick-up next to Gomez or Felipe or whoever but it wouldn't fuck up the century and kill my great-uncle and seven million others too just for a start-off because I am incredibly insignificant, I'd just be another tiny addition to the long list of Houston homicides and in fifty years my grandson would not be making a film about me, I'd be about as obscure as the sexual behaviour of *Tyrranosaurus rex* and that's very obscure, it's one hundred per cent guesswork as a matter of fact. Hey, a *Tyrranosaurus rex* coupling with another *Tyrranosaurus rex* must have been one of the grandest most awesome most thought-provoking sights in Nature but phooey hard cheese it's as lost as Calypso's kitties' little skulls because NO ONE GOT IT DOWN ON CELLULOID. It thought-provokes because watching from behind some scrubby little shrub and chewing the dust-clouds an extremely unintelligent two-storey eight-ton killing machine reproducing itself might get you wondering what the purpose of life on earth might be, like seeing the Western Front even on a good day got my grandfather and great-uncle wondering what the purpose of life on earth might be but I don't want to jump the gun. Here's my great-aunt. Her dress looks great in the moonlight. It rubs against the lawn and makes a sound like the sea just before you clear the dunes and see it and shade your eyes if the weather's jolly. They're all going down to the sea in about three weeks' time and it's that particular little trip William and Giles will keep reconstructing in their heads moment by moment when they're stuck up to their pips in slime and listening to the gas-gong and various metal things pretending to be yachts' masts tinkling and clinking as the wind blows down the trench and how the sea's backing down the shingle and sucking at the pebbles'n their hot toes but it's only the machine-guns having a crack way up the line even though they can catch a whiff, they can catch that really special whiff of the sea and it's not gas blowing from way down the line and making the back bit just where the palate goes soft you can't reach with your tongue even though you curl it right back all tingly. Hey, I'm terrified of injections for God's sake. The idea of some person I don't know very well puncturing my fairly immaculate and completely bio-degradable wet suit with an inch of sharpened steel deliberately is only outdone by the actuality, like thinking about Mr and Mrs Lazenby kissing one another on the lips is only outdone by the actuality. I mean, I only have to smell the antiseptic interior of a clinic to feel the terror of all mortal creatures in the face of personal extinction, it's a real problem, I think if I'd have been in my great-uncle's or my grandfather's puttees I'd have been very unhappy and extremely anxious while serving my country. My great-aunt has followed Calypso and Calypso is heading where the iodine smell of her kitties tells her to go, which is fairly unfortunate because a cat's nose is never mistaken. Agatha's rustled past me but I'm staying put. I like this lawn, it's the kind of soft lawn Texans only know when they're handling a putter and even then there is no comparison because a putting-green in Texas has about as much charisma as the Vice-Principal whereas my great-grandparents' lawn makes me want to take my sandals off and quote poetry and think about the mystery of existence until dawn streakes the empyrean and the birds wake up. What's amazing is that my great-uncle and grandfather did think about the mystery of existence while waiting for the dawn to streak the empyrean standing up to their pips in slime which is probably more than you've done while dry and warm and having a very nice time at my fucking expense, thank you. Judging from the letters I have perused and am no longer allowed to for crying out loud they certainly considered the mystery of personal existence out there. I mean, if you were stuck on night-watch next to some block capitals in red paint on a plank saying FOR FUCK'S SAKE DON'T FUCK ABOUT HERE! in a sap-head on the Somme in exactly two years from the lawn as it is at this moment you'd be fairly philosophically inclined, too. FOR FUCK'S SAKE DON'T FUCK ABOUT HERE is about as straightforward as you can get and comes after the day Willo's had his typhoid inoculation back in the medical tent with the ginger nurse who likes to cut round bullet damage with her nail scissors and pour in boiling Jay's Fluid or something so he isn't feeling tiptop anyway. Coupled with that is the nuisance of probably the most frightfully unpleasant stench he has ever encountered, because to make a stench like that takes an awful lot of long-dead people lying around and pretty non-existent lavatorial facilities for the ones who are still living along with details like two-week old unfinished tins of beef lumps and mud fairly well rinsed by chlorine gas and deep green pools with some kind of froth on top you try not to dip your toes into and think about what might be swaying at the bottom. Willo spits like his mother does after George has passed through but it makes no great impact, like air-freshener makes no great impact on the HCDVA lecture hall after Doc Lazenby has wowed the T-shirts with his Pepsi commercial and I'm trying to get both my audience members to come a bit closer so I don't have to shout. The night is fair and there are stars and Very lights and flares and flashes while against the firmament the nearest iron posts grow coils of black barbed wire and that's all I can see of *terra firma* unless I take a peep through the periscope where everything looks like my train set has just been trampled on in the dark, it's all so d— shrunk and smashed, Ags. I'm so sorry to hear your holiday weather was variable.

For Christ's sake, I've taken notes. I'm not inventing any of this. This

483

is just a teaser promo for what's coming. There are great epic sweeps of wide-screen format downland and touching details and the noise is Sensurround and will give you temporary tinnitus, I'm sorry. We're talking yer actual Western Front, mate. I have laid twelve miles of tracking rails and fifteen hot-drink dispensers and as for machinery we have three moonshots and four cherry-pickers and five cranes with twenty-one-foot pythons hired by some pinhead who thought that soldiers had telescopic necks and the seven million phantoms are my extras, actually. There is a liquid mud section of about fifteen square miles and a cornfield-blowing-with-poppies section of one square mile and a meadow-dotted-with-cows section of a half square mile and an uncut grassy section of no established dimensions they have a very interesting way of mowing using machine-gun bullets. We have corpses in varying states of decomposition down to the semi-liquid with hatching eggs of flies and a great drone effect from their parents I'm thinking of playing some sitar over if Robert will allow that. There'll be cracked mugs meeting dented lips or maybe vice versa and circles of Highlanders playing concertinas and singing softly in bare knees and slomo spews of brilliant white chalk-dust twirling up into the summer blue and sudden rain streaming over this head wound while the owner's cheeks and lips suck in and puff out like he's a mental deficient trying to blow out a candle and very gradual pans of prayer parades with now and again a chap keeling over until the dumbo of a chaplain realises they're being snipered and a long interior take of a stoup by a church door rocking its water back and forth as some bombardment proceeds way off and the water is oily with a fly struggling on its back who's nevertheless been places.

I'd like to have *Tyrranosaurus rex* coupling but Spielberg has the rights. Yeah, yeah, I know, he's got everything covered.

The lawn's so quiet. I'm walking out to the middle. Maybe I should just carry on walking out until this picture's behind me. Maybe I should just let everyone do it without me or just pull the plugs. Maybe I shouldn't put my grandmother through more than she is about to go through. English grass is always cool at night. It's very cool on the soles of my feet. I'll probably get a cold and then a fever and wonder where Zelda's got to because she's a great nurse. Thinking about Zelda these days leaves me numb and hysterical simultaneously like I've just had dental treatment and somebody's cracked me a great joke about the US cocaine trade. Bosey must be waiting for us back at the old vegetable garden because this conversation in the sitting-room wasn't ever slated up. I almost love Bosey. He has a mug with IT'S ALWAYS FRIDAY on it and permanent kind of brown lip-marks because it's fifteen years old, he hangs on to things, he kind of stoops over it and sips, he's six foot four with a frame like a boom-arm, it's useful for a sound person, dwarves would be very bad sound people. He'll go on recording without me and you dumbos will have to work out what's going on from the sound track only. It'll be good for you, it'll do your hangover a great service working out what these rustles and clicks and gasps mean until Agatha says in about three minutes oh Willo, what have you done? with her voice flopping back off the old walls of the old vegetable garden like Echo is now on crutches or something. It could be the National Knitting Colloquium 1914 or it could be man-slaughter or it could be David Attenborough getting very close to that little shimmery beetle if you remember it and looking like he's got no problems wondering what the point of life on earth is, it's to give him a great career.

I think I'm highly strung tonight. I need this lawn. The world's falling apart around me. We don't need to dunk our biscuits but we do, we take the risk, my mother always took it and she spent half her life getting her fingers scalded hooking out the bit that had stayed dunked too long and fallen in, she was like that, she was heroic in her own way, she came from a great line.

Behind me there's a flash and a glimmer and another flash. That's my grandmother running out of the old vegetable garden, the moonlight's picking up her white bits and her face, she's got her skirt up to clear the weeds but I'm imagining that, I can't see clearly enough from out here in the middle of the lawn and the soft kind of coppery light out the windows is enough to get in the way because she's run between the old vegetable garden and the stables and past Agatha and this is over beyond the lit windows of the sitting room where Mrs T's actually playing some Rachmaninov incredibly proficiently on the piano, it's really amazing, it's floating over the lawn and it's like Rachmaninov himself is playing it and we've got to see this, it's not dubbed over or anything, I'm padding back to the house on this soft cool grass and the music's getting louder, she's a concert pianist, my great-grandmother was undervalued, I'm looking in and there's the cards on the card-table and there's the rocking-chair emptied of Dorothy and still in shock and there's the piano and oh fuck there's nobody playing it, the keys are moving up and down like a virtuoso ghost has sat down and I'm so scared I have a saliva problem, I need to spit, I'm getting swish on the picture because I'm turning to spit, I'm sorry, I shouldn't be using a video camera in situations like this but I was afraid I'd miss something, it's just a backup, I have to keep all my options covered, there are so many holes in the world, there's a real live phantom in there for crying out loud and maybe it'll come up on the playback like a kind of burn in a top-hat – we don't know about phantoms and we don't know the sexual maturity of the Great White and we don't know what Zelda sees in Dr Dot Laserprinter or why people like to kill each other as much as they like to procreate or whether beyond the two foot of peaty gloom in front of our Loch Ness bathysphere there might be the most important scientific presence of the millennium passing by.

I've got myself extremely scared now. There's the night at my back. There are voices from the old vegetable garden. A man hanged himself in the woods so they do say – on certain windy nights you can hear his boots creak and a face sway or something. 1914's creepier than 1998, I can tell yer, guv. There are no comfortin' jet-lights winking at you in the night sky, no street lamps to night for day at the corner by the new estate and no new estate at all just a massive rick you think is a house until you tap on the hay and sneeze, no comfortin' murmur of the motorway like a way-off bombardment but just very dark hills and clumps of copses and stuff, no TVs winking through Cinemascope front windows but flickery candles illuminating gargoyles peering out to see who it ben't, no security lamps going incandescent just because you've strayed an inch too fucking far for crying out loud but a kind of shuffle of something maybe the mad aunt behind chicken-wire probably, and fairies and stuff. I mean, the place is crawling with fairies and goblins and elves and sprites and various species of ectoplasm and nymphs without corsets or even dresses or even underthings and most of the bit-part gods and goddesses let alone witches. Seriously. It's all this lack of artificial light, son. The countryside's like a well when the moon goes in and when it's out there are faces pretending to be shadows of leaves and branches everywhere, it's like right now they

486

know they're in their terminal time, they're holding the short end, the big scissors are about to trim, they've heard the rumours and are coming out in force to get the wind up the chaps. Like the rats. The rats are simply everywhere. We prong them with fixed bayonets or trample them underfoot. It's bloody awful. Funky Partridge made Bewland pop off a few rounds tho' Bewland said it attracted return fire from Jerry and ping sure enough it did. Bewland went on firing half-mad with Partridge who said righty-ho, Bewland, you can stop now, but he wouldn't. Ping ping. All right, Bewland, that's enough for God's sake man! Ping ping ping. Rest censored. This piano is crazy, I can't look, it's stopping. I'm looking. Mrs Trevelyan's popping up from the far side of it with a box. I'm tromboning in on the label. *Rachmaninov Playing Rachmaninov, Genuine Recording.* Hey, that's a kind of phantom. I saw his fingers hit the keys only his fingers weren't there. I'm not too embarrassed, just disappointed. She's taking out this big roll, it's a pianola, she's putting another one in and closing the little door, the handle must be the other side because she's dipping out of sight again – it has a concealed hand-crank option as well as the pedals, obviously, I think she does this every night, it stills her nerves. It sounds like Debussy now for crying out loud. I nearly am crying out loud because Debussy makes me do that. Here's Bosey. He's annoyed with RT, I can tell, and Mike behind him with Gordon looking gripey, and Sylvia shaking her head by the rain barrel, and Joe Gel and Pierre and all the great gang hopping from foot to foot on the lawn in the moonlight as if they're really mad at me and making such long shadows.

Such long long shadows.

With Debussy by Debussy kind of padding over the lawn and into the woods. And they still look blahdy cross but, hey, they're not, they're not mad at me. They just want the green light for the big scene. We've all somehow got to cram into my grandmother's little attic room up there, under the eaves. They know why I'm looking up. They're all looking up too, with Debussy over us as if I've forgotten Robert for a minute. Everyone, even Ossy for God's sake, even the Steves – everyone is looking shy and tender. No film crew ever before in the history of film-making has looked so shy and tender as they look up in the blue moonlight at a tiny window in the eaves and wonder how the fuck they're going to get the equipment up there and in time. As a matter of fact, no film unit has ever looked shy and tender The End. Mine were always different.

Reel change. I got back to find a note on my door. It said TO RICK. It was the wrong side of the door, I saw it as I was closing off the world and welcoming myself to my little hallway with its one raffia mat and its two golf cups and its three Oscars and its five Dinky Foden flat-beds in a bullet-proof glass case and its *Twenty-Four Views of London Conveniences* postcard set no one out here appreciates – they think cast iron went out with the Stone Age, like gaslight went out with Shakespeare, they have a great sense of chronology in Texas. I tell them not to get anxious, they'll feel at home in London these days, the cast-iron conveniences were not convenient, people could actually see you being convenienced, it was terrifying the number of women who screamed and fainted in the Stone Age when they passed one of these things and saw your elbows jerking either side of your gaberdine – now you get airlocked into your own personal space and it takes American Express and power-jets it so clean you could probably eat your Big Mac off the bowl if you got stuck or the Third World War broke out outside just as you were hiking your pants up or jerking your elbows or whatever and you reckoned it was better to keep your head down until it blew over. They think I'm present-challenged when I go on like this, they think I'd like to spend my life next to the cast-iron urinal with the real live gaslight at the river end of Cheyne Walk watching the sweet Thames run slowly or softly or whatever it is and all my friends bobbing about in their whacky boats, yacking the night through over candles with the sixties ahead of them to go on yacking and being way-out and arty in and watching the dawn come up above the last lamplighter in London Town cadging a Senior Service off of me guv so as we can watch the river togever, ta, watch it take its time to flow and not be existentialist about it, just happy for God's sake, happy under our natural chin-stubble, the city stretching and beginning to roar, the last lamplighter and the most exciting very young film director since Orson Welles contemplating the first cuppa char comin' up in the

Lyons Corner Arse where Harold Pinter's takin' notes and the costermongers are stretching their woolly mitts abaht a bun.

They think I'd really like to go back to that time or something crazy like that, they actually think I'd prefer that to contemporary Houston. I mean, really, let's be serious for a moment.

This note. It's very weird finding a note taped to the inside of your front door, actually. It's like finding a double-glazing call card in your Y-fronts at the end of the day or something, it makes you feel somebody's been in where they shouldn't. I handed my suitcases over to the floor and peeled the note off and it took about half the paint with it which was distressing oof yer gettin' there son. I unfolded the paper and got Sean Connery to do the thumbs at last. Tighten and hold. Oh Rick, I came to TALK but you're away. I need to talk to someone who'll UNDERSTAND what I'm going through. I figure you've forgiven me enough by now to UNDERSTAND. Everything is entanglement. We must cut ourselves off from objective things. We must stop muddying the past and clouding up the future. We must live pure clear water lives and let the sun touch our pebbles. Basically there is kind of a big Problem I cannot come to terms with so I'm cutting loose. I feel crazy. I have nowhere to go. You're crazy enough to UNDERSTAND, Rick. You're so DIRECT. I'll call sometime. Z.

Z.? You mean, Z for *Zelda*? You mean it's not Zoot the window-cleaner saying *Hi there I Visited but You Were Out* a little over-zealously?

Ah, nope.

Zelda has a key to my house. She never bothered to return it to its original owner and I didn't encourage her to either. Only a librarian could locate an ex-lover's key after five years. It probably had its own shelf-mark for crying out loud. Hey, why aren't I hitting my head on the ceiling with joy, huh? I did. I swung from the chandelier and stuff and ruined this big guy's five foot putt for a one under par on the fifteenth by opening the window and yelling hi world but it almost dislocated my jaw all over again so I shrieked, I can't go into that now, a small tactical error, guv, it's old history, I swallowed some Aspro in whisky and read the note again about one hundred and thirty-one times and held it up to the light and squirted lemon juice on it and generally tried to find some living cast-iron proof that she was about to run up the drive and into my arms forever and I'd better move the car so she didn't have to squeeze past and into my arms forever which wouldn't be quite as attractive. I poured myself another couple of gills to breathe with and felt the sun touch my pebbles through the translucent water of my jet lag all of a sudden, my pebbles were really sparkling and there were these golden fish now and again and I was cool and sublime and probably full of Suchness or *li* or whatever Zelda used to call stuff's innermost reality and my jaw's stopped aching. Maybe if I changed my name to Ri-Kiu Tonbai which is the way the Japanese exchange students say it I'd fly straight into the bull of her heart with a glass of water on my elbow if you know what I mean. I forgot to say that there is a flower on the dining-room table where there wasn't before I left for England. I think it's a Spanish iris. It's a little jaded but basically it's the colour of summer skies with a golden heart and the perfume is all that plus Zelda's right cheek and it's in the Hopi vase we bought together in '91 when we checked out Arizona and paid the mesas a call. If it's Zoot the window-cleaner on a heavy sales pitch after all I'll be very disappointed and maybe strangle him with his telescopic ladder the next time he visits.

I knew she'd find out sooner or later about the Doc's Problem, by the way. I thought she'd already found out about his Problem and just been unbelievably Zen about it, actually. You'd probably have to be incredibly enlightened and be able to balance on one elbow on the edge of the Grand Canyon for ten days having your feet tickled with a goose feather or something before you could live alongside the Doc's kind of Problem. I want to give you all this personal angle before I get onto the big scene in case you think I'm a little hyper or something. The crew are on the lawn looking up and I'm just standing there so happy I am actually crying. I am waiting for her to call me because I tried calling her at her woodlands habitat and I got the guy with the Problem so I just called off without vocalising anything more than a shriek of delight. I keep sighing really profound sighs because if I don't keep sighing really profound sighs my tummy-button'll pop or my ears fall off or something. It's very difficult to make a big movie when your leading lady has fallen back into your arms and is as heavy as a labrador after all and her cheek is actually warm and doesn't flicker and silver over to nothing or whatever. What's interesting and I hope it's interesting for you is that my ardour has not altered or diminished, it's like my ardour for Zelda is my *li* which is bleedin' reassurin' at this stage of my life, guv. The library opens tomorrow but I don't want to meet her in the HCDVA library for God's sake – I've left a note saying I'm back, you have brushed me into a perfect circle and the winds of five years have not blown me awry, please call, I'm waiting, your ever-friend R. I didn't mention love as such. I think we have to tread carefully on this one, I have to be as cool as I dunno my local chemist's or something or maybe not that cool, that'd be icy. I have to be her calm harbour with little yachts plying around and I probably shouldn't have said I was waiting even. I also have a movie to wrap up. Hey, the sunlight is touching me pebble bed and the waters are clear all the way to the sea. I must not take conscious aim.

Thwack.

There's this biscuit in a hand because my grandfather is having a biscuit right at this moment. We're in the big country kitchen and my grandmother has just flickered across the side lawn but my grand-father had his hand in the Squire's Chemical Food For Delicate Children jar at that moment so all he registered was the outer door opening and shutting and someone going up the back stairs and the kitchen door sort of bumping on the latch in sympathy. He's eating the fairly stale Marie at the kitchen window which is open. It's open because the kitchen is incredibly hot, Dorothy keeps the stove going all summer, you could leave a loaf to bake on the kitchen table and now the cool calm and collected night air is taking over a little and Giles is contemplating. He's contemplating whether to join Willo in the study and have a titter at some of Padre's saucier books or slip out to the shed and have a smoke, basically. His favourite saucy book is the one by Mr Muybridge full of butt-naked women doing jolly queer things like cartwheels and leapfrogs and bashing each other with pillows in photographic sequence. It was a present from Uncle Kenneth, naturally. One can see their very fairly pleasant top ballocks and their twat-rugs clear as day and the same with the men, their John Percies are frightfully exposed, if you blink right it all seems to move for real. Golly. Right now he's happy finishing his biscuit while the garden sort of slides around under moonlight.

Hm.

The flowers are at their strongest in the evening, it's amazing how really sweet they can smell, you can sup them like you sup blushful Hippocrene cooled a long age in the deep-delved earth etcetera. The clematis over the old well is probably the sweetest. Maybe a pretty lass's skin smells sweet. My grandfather's thinking that the sweetest part of a pretty lass's skin is at the neck, probably. He can really imagine nuzzling into the neck and smelling a kind of night garden scent that isn't cologne or rosewater or essence of vanilla or whatever but just the natural excretion of a pretty dark-haired lass whose teeth shine when she smiles. He's leaning on the chapped window-sill and wondering when exactly he'll clock up something like this on his girlometer. Pretty lasses with berry lips and grassy-scented necks and blouses frilling over what my grandfather cannot actually imagine exposing to the air this side of Paradise are really pretty far and few between. He'd held Amy's hand about a fortnight ago and that had practically made his head melt and he wasn't even sweet on Amy but a girl's hand is a girl's hand, it couldn't be more different from a chap's hand. I mean, a chap's hand in bladderdash or whatever is thick and blunt and no nonsense whereas a girl's hand is always about to be the petals of a lily but hasn't quite decided yet, especially if it's attached to a slender and animated being descending a rather difficult slope through long grass that catches on skirts frightfully and is dependent on the chap's hand for balance. The fact that this was the first time since the onset of puberty my grandfather had touched the skin of a girl for more than a few seconds may amaze you but there we are, his hand has still not got over it, it's still registering the micro-pressures of her palm and the thin undersides of her fingers as they negotiated the slope to the bottom where for a few awesome and rather blushable seconds in which anything could have happened except that the rest of the party were waiting by the car and Randolph gave a blast on the horn, the stinking rotter, which rather queered things, they stood together hand in hand. Randolph is Amy's cousin, by the way. I'm really sorry about this but he's leaning there on the hot bonnet of the clapped-out Jowett he's picked up for a song laughing under his boater in the jolliest possible way because he is basically jolly and decent and has a great tenor voice with a black circle looping his head and I can't do anything about it. OK, here goes: he'll disappear into some mud on

494

the Ypres salient carrying a duck-board and the duck-board'll float up about three minutes later but he won't. He wasn't even carrying the duck-board in the right direction, some thoughtfulness-challenged moron had given him the wrong order, his men had to bring all the duck-boards back again and start off in the other direction wondering where their leadyloo with the nice voice had got to. When Zelda used to go on to me from the other side of the beeswax candle about the lotus flower being the symbol of enlightenment because, Rick, its roots are right down there in the deep mud of human passions while its flower is up and turned to the purity of the sun I'd say maybe that's what happened to Randolph, maybe the fact that he went down without a sound means he's singing somewhere nice and sunlit now in his spotless flannels and summer jacket with that curl tucked down behind his ear like it always was.

Here's Randolph. Still Sixteen I think. Get up off your collective butts and pay your respects. The cropped elbow belongs to William. The girl sticking her tongue out between the elbow and Randolph is Amy. The amazing motorbike is Randolph's, he's keen on motorized movement and he's fairly wealthy. The shadow over the lawn from the bottom edge of the frame is yours, you're a lousy photographer, while you're there just check out the Hoover situation in the corridor. If it looks like they're shooting *Worms from Outer Space* on a very low budget tell them it's a Bank Holiday. Tell them if they try to come in Mr Thornby will throw himself into the river then adjust your wrap-arounds and try to look like Paul Muni. Then say how we're still on the razzle baby and that they should beat it. If that doesn't work invite them in for a cocktail. Just throw all the stuff left at the bottom of the glasses into a jug. Call it Rikki-Tikki Snakebite or Pharyngal Flush or Helloover Surprise or something. Play for time. Imagine missing the last reel or even the last five seconds of *Citizen Kane*. Huh? In case you ever have missed it it was the name of the sledge, by the way. Like the policeman did it. This movie is just as tantalising and me dad in't around to spoil the finale. He's hanging on in Havant. At least that's very likely given how fighting fit he was on this last trip. He calls me Cyril but that's usual. Cor blimey. The cat's late. Never work with animals. The kitchen door leading into the tight interior space where my grandmother and my great-uncle played one of the tensest scenes of unrequited love since Francis X. Bushman and Beverley Bayne in *A*

Romance of the Dells opens. Giles turns his head in slomo while the creak increases his heart rate because it always has done, ever since he was teeny in a frilly dress perched on Dorothy's knee while she podded peas or whatever and sang lost Wiltshire songs of phantom lovers it has done, because the creak sounds like a creature in torment, a phantom lover come to claim his own from o'er the brine O massy me those bogglin' eyes, those scarlit lips – all it needs is oil but Giles is dressed in white. No one enters which also increases his heart rate. He pooh-poohs the idea of phantoms but the pooh-pooh wouldn't blow out a match. He swallows and thinks about leaping out through the window but only thinks it, he doesn't actually move a muscle, the only muscles moving are around his heart and they're working overtime but he's young, he's not approaching sixty with a history, the door bumps to a rest against the kitchen sink which it's been bumping so long now there's a little niche for it in the stonework which was there until 1989 when Hob & Home Fitted Kitchen Specialists got invited in with some fairly powerful tools and a big budget and a lot of really-what-you-need-heres so if you want to see this nick go to the back and round until you spot this tasteful plant container against the brick and separate the lobelia a little, it's there on the left corner, it's proof that everything I'm pointing at is direct reality, OK? Just don't get collared by the cunt or the cunt's wife who think they own the place, he's a real live professional crook, she's his moll Best By About 1973, they know all the right people, you'll be in deep waters with a slow puncture, don't mention my name, just pretend you have a frontal lobelia problem or summat.

It's the cat. Actually, it really is a creature in torment. It clears the table from Giles's sight-line and brushes his leg. Giles goes hmph because he's embarrassed at getting into such a funk and shoves the thing away with his shin I have to say gently in case you think there's any violence being done to animals in this movie except for the kittens, OK, the kittens were a problem, I'll tell you later, I STILL FEEL TERRIBLE ABOUT IT then checks his turn-up for smears. The cat is looking for its brood, obviously. Giles has no idea where they are and as a matter of fact couldn't care a jot. Willo's the one who likes animals and birds and butterflies and all that. Giles likes sheep, though. The landscape down here is covered in them and they're pretty much like shrubs that move when you get close and he also likes shepherds mainly because of their leading role in classical love poetry although the shepherds round here with their prematurely-aged skin and hand-me-down bowler hats and completely out-of-date capes don't quite fit the bill when you get up close, like the local milkmaids when you get up close. His turn-up seems to have a smear although the light's not good, it might be a shadow. The cat's really mewing now, it's painful, it even gets through to Giles's miniscule St Francis area and he starts to frown a little in sympathy. This is where everything went wrong. Or right. Depending on whether you think Ricky Thornby is a Good Thing or a Bad Thing. It was one of the staging posts, anyway, with a fork off to the left saying This Way Just As Interesting but he didn't take it. My grandfather looks at this cat which is now by the open door and remembers all those stories Nurse Ginger-Moustache Hallam used to read to him about animals leading people to someone in distress and takes out a Jeremiah Woodbine from his inner pocket and places it between his lips and touches the tobacco with his tongue for the dashed gorgeous tangy savour then tucks the treasure back again and says righty-ho, beastie, show me the damsel! which is incredible when you think about it because he was joking, what he really expected was the beastie to lead him to her kittens in distress from a local badger or fox or whatever – not the damsel my grandmother, not my mother, not me for God's sake whose little face he knew by touch which is better than nothing but I cannot eat hard-boiled eggs. I cannot even shell them without wanting to throw up.

I don't want to get onto this now. The crew are following the cat and my grandfather up the back stairs and if I turned round now and said hey, hold it, I want to show this thing about my grandfather and Hubert Lightfoot and the gas mask's eyepieces they'd probably trample me underfoot because they're really committed now, I've never had a unit so committed, it's like they want to get this domestic scene over with and onto the epic war stuff as soon as permissible and not be screwed around by me anymore. Hey, I don't blame them. I'm hyper at the moment because Zelda still hasn't called but here we go up the back stairs and I'm very nervous, if the cat suddenly decided to jump out the window or Giles Trevelyan decided to take the left fork and go back down and out the back door and suck on a Woodie behind the rhododendrons I'd be less than a nice thought, I wouldn't even be a phantom no one remembers the original owner of, I'd be not-I and non-attainment and Zelda'd say lucky you, you've achieved the totality of void or some crap like that. Cor luvaduck.

But, hey, it's all on the pianola of life. It's all on the big roll that plays the same tune using thirty-five notes simultaneously at moments. I'm using this profound metaphor only because as we're mounting the stairs after the cat and the teenager in the natty white flannels the pianola is playing again, it's coming over from the sitting-room like fairy music with some bass vibrations and it's quite creepy, actually. I keep seeing those ivories moving up and down by themselves and it reminds me of a very terrifying moment in the Enfield Ritz, it was a *Phantom of the Opera* rip-off and this grand piano started rippling its keys and the guy who'd murdered the virtuoso out of jealousy screamed and I screamed and it was very embarrassing, Des and his girlfriend sniggered and moved places, I think it was called *The Revenge of the Concert Pianist* or something but I can find no trace of it, it must have been a very rare print, maybe it was so bad the studio furnaced it, maybe its phantom print lives on, maybe if you got yourself locked into an ABC somewhere and the caretaker's footsteps have died away there'd be this click and whirr and up there on the curtains'd ripple the same grand piano clip over and over, totally silent, while you try to scream but no sound comes out, I've got myself sweating again, it's the concept of all those furnaced silents playing sight unseen somewhere with this blind guy at the back suddenly leaning forward to touch my face, maybe I've drunk too much this week, I need my leading lady to climb up to me on her telescopic ladder, I've got my first sophomore class tomorrow, we're doing the treatment of water in *Psycho* for crying out loud.

We're on the top floor now. We were going to do a shot of Giles looking out the same little stair-window William had looked out of about half an hour ago but Calypso just kept on going up and so did my grandfather. Never mind. The top floor is very dim, there's just one inky-dinky lamp hissing away under its broken tulip, this is really the roof, I think my great-great-grandfather converted it when he bought the place so as not to waste a floor on the servants because in those days there were hundreds of guests all the time and it was crazy trying to negotiate the crinolines. There's this little spill of light from under one of the doors up here, Mike's telling Gordon to zoom in on it because

498

the cat's already there, it's kind of sniffing the light like the light might be butter, Gordon's saying he doesn't like to zoom at this point, not when he's walking with a camera anyway, what does Mike think he is, the trombone-line in a military band or something – and Mike gets huffy, he's tense, we're all tense, the corridor's narrow and there are too many of us, it's always like that for the big scenes, everyone and their lover comes along to watch, the whole village, the whole goddam universe suddenly including Hilda my granddaughter who's operating the clapper-board, I like that, it makes me feel like Jean Renoir, but there are too many of the others and I'm saying I want Camera Two in the old vegetable garden where Norma's waiting with my great-uncle and Norma Talmadge does not like waiting but no one's listening to me any more, the pianola's rolling, they've pulled the celluloid from under my feet, maybe I should let it roll and see what happens, Robert as in flair would've let it roll, my grandfather's stopped now and everyone's bunched up behind him jabbing their elbows into each other's faces and Bosey's making rude hand-signals at this best boy's boyfriend who's stepping on the cable and it's bleedin' chaos, guv. I cover my eyes. I want to shout cut but I can't, this has got to be a running take, I keep thinking of the last running take in *The Sacrifice* which lasts as long as a reel for crying out loud and how Andrei must have been so nervous and maybe he knew he was dying, maybe he knew that if the house didn't burn up like it should or one of the tracking-rails screwed up he'd die for nothing, and maybe he was smoking and coughing while the whole thing went right and the house burned up and the ambulance came and went and the little boy watered the dead tree and I stood up in the National Film Theatre London and applauded which was very embarrassing because none of the other really anal pale people there joined me but I couldn't stop, my eyes were streaming, even when somebody said ssssshhhhh I couldn't stop. Ssssshhhhh as if the most important thing in a movie's working out the date by the fucking roman numerals, ass-hole. I clapped and clapped and clapped some more. Even when the theatre was empty I was clapping. So what's wrong? I expect you all to show your appreciation at the end of my complex and extremely moving masterwork by doing more than raising your eyebrows at your partner and looking for your coat, as if you've just watched a bus-stop for God knows how many hours. I expect you to clap and cry like it's, I dunno, Verdi – Verdi's *Requiem* and you're a Neapolitan, OK?

I'm alone in the corridor. I'm leaning against the wall and it's still damp from the winter and so is my shirt from exertion and I'm completely alone. They're all in there, they all went in while I was jabbering about Andrei Tarkovsky. I'll watch the rushes tonight, I'll have the dailies printed up and run them through tonight. I trust these people. I can hear murmurings through the slightly open door. I can hear my grandfather and my grandmother about to become my grandfather and my grandmother. I don't feel like going in. I feel a snoop going in. The door clicks shut now. What you can see of this corridor is very unpleasant, its roof is leaning and low, there's brown wallpaper up to my hips and then it's distemper of the kind of yellow you don't want your teeth to turn into. It was amazing the way Calypso the cat pawed the door. She actually hung on the handle and opened it. I've never seen a cat do that before. The light went up a few notches and my grandfather's face in the corridor had this sort of golden glow on it like he was looking in at the stable in one of those Old Master Christmas cards because the light in that room is candlelight. Even if the cat hadn't done that I think my grandfather would have found his way in because he'd had his ear to the door and was looking concerned. Bosey's cans were picking up sobs. My grandmother was sobbing in there. I know why she was sobbing, actually. It's because up in the old vegetable garden my great-uncle had decided her moonlit mouth was definitely wanting nothing more in the world than to have him approach and stick his lips out and rest them on it and then to see what happens, maybe a bit more pressure or something or even this thing about tongues Pantile was always going on about. It's a mistake many have made. At HCDVA many have made this mistake. If a boy student wants to do a bit of courting he has to take his lawyer along with him or forget it and have three ice-cold showers a day. Maybe I'm Granny in the back of the Morris but I think it's a shame the girls are so uptight about the boys, most of these boys are not sexual psychotics, they're just as scared as the girls, everyone should be going into it together. I wish my grandmother had not reacted so dramatically but maybe in her case there were complicating factors, like the religious maniac back home and her never evers and the whole socio-economic set-up in 1914. I mean, my great-uncle and my grandmother were not equal in this, it's worse than me trying to move my mouth towards a desirable T-shirt during a tutorial, there's this whole thing of taking advantage, Dr Lecherby takes it all the time but he's OK because he does it kind

500

of sneakily and the girls hang all over him. It's the spotty hunchbacks with polystyrene teeth who get it in the neck, they just need to say Hi, Candy, I was just wondering if you'd like to come back after Ricky Thyroid's drone and see my unique collection of Japanese nose flutes or something and thunk, they're strung up for rape. Right now what is going on in that room is probably rape. I'm not looking forward to watching the rushes but I have to. I said to Mike the minute they actually start doing it you leave the room and take the unit with you, OK? He said I was a prude or words to that effect and I said I am not a prude or words to that effect I am just aware that most people know what happens when a boy gets into bed with a girl, this is not a movie for people who need to be reminded, it's like Candice Bergen said, you just rock your head from side to side for about ten seconds and have a mild asthma attack and roll your eyes up until you see the whites and die a little, it's easy as butter. Anyway, my grandmother is under age. We could get arrested.

Hey, look, *why am I here?* Why am I standing in this corridor like a sneak or like that time Mr Rowlock asked me where King Harold met his end and I said in the eye sir because he didn't keep it skinned sir and he really exploded over the snorts? Do they know this gas-lamp leaks a bit? Do they care? Or maybe it's the diesel fumes off the cherry-picker's hydraulics. I'm wondering if Mike really needed the cherry-picker's hydraulics for the approach shot through the window because apart from the fumes it'll have screwed up that lovely lawn, we're vandals, we don't need to drop onto that little window under the eaves like we're Special Branch or filming a Grand Prix race or something, this is possibly the most private moment of my grand-parents' life and I'm tearing it open, I don't know how everyone could've fitted in there, the pianola's stopped, I feel sick from this gaslight and the diesel fumes or maybe I'm claustrophobic, I need a big space to breathe as a matter of fact – I occupy whatever volume I'm placed in, I thin right out over the hills, I really feel I could hike right now actually, I could go out onto the high chalk hills and roam free or maybe tramp the Ridgeway track in the footsteps of the ancient nomads following the wild deer and wild oxen or something and probably drown in a moto-cross rut. Christ, the door's opening. It's the cat, the cat's out. The door's closing again. The cat's coming towards me. I really think the crew should be leaving now. They

501

should've followed the cat out and wrapped it up on that. I think I hear voices through this kind of skylight next to my head, I think it's my great-aunt and my great-uncle, their voices are floating up from the garden and the cat's stopped, it's turning back before it gets to me, maybe it has a sixth sense, it's tail's vertical in case I want a close-up of its butt which I don't thank you, it still needs cleaning up, it's kind of dried out now which is worse. Hey, I really hope William and Agatha don't get messed up with what's happening in that room, the diary doesn't mention them at this stage but you never know, there might have been some tactful scissoring, the cat's scratching on the door again, the door's staying shut, the crew aren't showing, I'm very angry at them, it must have started by now, this is breaking all my rules, I think I'm going to go in there and pull them out physically, all twenty-four of them, it's crazy, I'm striding up the corridor, I've got my hand on the door handle and actually I'm scared, I'm pushing the door handle down, I'm pushing the door, I'm opening the door, I'm chilled but it's February so the sunlight's just blinding and when I shield my eyes there's bare floorboards with mice droppings and a smell of wet paper and a broken chair and a cast-iron bed but it's folded up against the wall and the main body of it has a bungee-tie woven between the springs for some reason and a plastic I think Cindy doll with rocking eyelashes and no legs and a roll of lilo and a dead ESSO can and a fairly successful fly paper and an upside-down beetle in the sink which has no tap and a pile of very damp 1983 *Swindon Evening Mails* under a roof-leak which make for great reading if you're in here for eternity and have time to turn the pages without rending them but I'm not, not really, not this side of life anyway. I just stand here and wonder where everybody has got to.

Nobody has a monopoly on the truth.

Actually, that's Zelda. It's one of the many things she said to me last night. My Dr Dot identification alarm bleeped instantly and I silenced it with a slug of whisky. I was hoping Zelda'd be rolling her head from side to side and having a mild asthma attack and stuff by now but instead she was perched on the end of my sofa and I was in my cane chair only Mr Agility knows how to sit in without buckling. She just

502

turned up, by the way. It was really pouring and there she was in the porch with rain streaming off her leather skirt like she'd been to my class on the treatment of water in *Psycho* and she even has blonde hair, Norma won't like this, Zelda's gone platinum in some kind of protest, she has a sixties wave and bob, if I screw my eyes I get Louisa looking at me all over again, I must not mention my mother or my grandmother I must not mention my mother or my grandmother I kept murmuring to myself the whole time she was patting her hair with my *Secret Life of the Owl* dishcloth and talking. Yeah, yeah. Zelda knew about the Problem right from the start and doesn't mind it as long as he clears up afterwards, it's her who has the Problem, she reckons the Todd with the luminous brain is not quite synched in with her soul situation as it stands at the moment and wants out but there's this teeny little hitch and it's Weeny Todd Jnr sucking his thumb and peeling his eyes or just about inside her belly and waiting for lift-off. Hey, the way she talks about him he is definitely the kid at the end of *2001* come to save the planet or whatever in Cinerama. Cor blimey luvaduck. I kept saying Zelda, I have to watch my rushes and she said just put them in soak Rick, this is so important, she wasn't even blahdy listening to me, guv, after five years of intermittent communication here she was and I was just a noddy, I might as well have put a screen around her and bought some popcorn, it was about as uninteractive as Interactive TV or whatever. She kept fidgeting with her nails and I loved her so much but she was way up there, on the screen, it was hopeless, I realised with the force of a gong-strike that frankly it was all over, the lights were coming up, I'd dropped popcorn all over the floor, there was one sticking to my sock, I couldn't squeeze the bag into the ashtray, it kept expanding and dropping onto my knees like *The Non-Biodegradable Thing From Mars* or somewhere, but I felt a great calm. I felt reborn. I said this to Zelda, I said I'm experiencing a great Zen satori here because I realise you are completely unattainable in this life but I don't hold it against you, I want things to work out very well for you and weeny whatsit, I think you should leave the father by ten o'clock tomorrow because he has a lecture to give at 10.05 on the latest Coca-Cola commercial Pepsi, she interrupted, it's always Pepsi, I've typed it out six times for him now, he likes clean copy but it's practically the same lecture every year and ditto for the Levi's and even the Volkswagen number, it makes me sick. She said all that, not me. My satori was deepening. She has little worry-lines at the corners of her mouth now and I wanted to smooth them away but no, I had accepted the truth and this truth I most definitely had the monopoly on, son. I wanted her to go far away with her weeny whatsit and live by a lake with a nice gentle guy into trout fishing and composing kind of Philip Glass stuff with polished pine timbers everywhere. Houston doesn't suit her. It doesn't suit me but hey, I'm leaving too. She was talking and talking and this is what I was thinking the whole time and that I had to go view my rushes but remember Fellini, don't get stressed about it, it's all in the can, Mike told me it was all in the can and I trust Mike Avens, the Cindy doll is on my mantelpiece, I must not mention my mother or my grandmother or owls.

I think you should take a long shot hower, honey, I said. Correction, great slip. I think you should ease out under my jet-powered shower unit, honey.

She didn't even chickle.

Hey, c'mon, cor blimey, who do you think I am? I don't even have a blade big or certainly sharp enough. It was just to get her out of the way while I watched my rushes. I love Zelda. But if I look too hard she vanishes. This whole thing has nothing to do with the kid waiting for lift-off inside her. Even if the kid looked exactly like its father down to the green suspenders I'd rear it with my own hands around its neck. No, seriously, I'd bring it up like me own, guv, like one of me own, 'cos it's kind of in the family, innit? It's kind of a family tradition, innit?

She took a shower while I watched my rushes. It was soothing, thinking of her soaping herself under the shower without me watching. It was also comforting because it meant she couldn't hear the rushes, all showers completely deafen, someone could walk right up to the plastic shower-curtain with an upraised cleaver and you wouldn't know, not even if they yelled out just before the blur established itself as an old lady holding something above her head. I don't want Zelda to hear my grandfather and my grandmother on the soundtrack ever, I want her to go and live by a lake with this very gentle guy and watch the herons glide low with her kid next to her, laughing and so forth. I don't know if she will do this. She's talking about going back home to her mother in Duluth, which is not on the lake I had in mind, not at all mate, cor luvaduck no.

The rushes were remarkable. Here's the unedited version. We're all proud of what we did. We were so happy afterwards we had a big barbecue on the lawn. Uncle Kenneth turned up. He's a vegetarian, he got on pretty well with Mike. Then this helicopter landed and blew the barbecue over and we leaned into the air and our dresses and flannels went kind of ecstatic. Hey, it was CNN. They'd heard that things were going on following the seeding of my mother, they wanted in on it, I said listen, preserve your energy for the War To End All Wars that's about to fuck up the century, have a sausage, there are no fake ingredients at this time, relax, your helicopter has completely wrecked the azaleas and the lawn doesn't need combing, leave off the media attention, these people are going through a bad time, the vicar hallooing over the gate has lost his floppy hat and his side-whiskers have turned into rabbit's ears, Zelda has walked out of my life, seven million people are packing their suitcases and feeling nervous about dying before they grow old, Hubert Lightfoot is on a motoring jaunt in the highlands of Scotland and my grandfather's eyes are very well thank you but the old guys with ostrich plumes and very bad posture and terrible breath are getting generally disgruntled, forgive me if my speech is a little slurred, let me introduce you to Gavin Simpson originally from Hemel Hempstead England, he plays a Wiltshire shepherd, he's been incredibly patient, his big moment's soon to be here, do those rotor-blades have to keep turning, it feels a little windy, it feels like an Altman wedding or the end of Vietnam, why are you bristling with cameras, you've fucked up the private party, isn't anything sacred any more, I think they're in the sitting-room, I hope this isn't going out live, it is, OK, I'll shaddap, I'm shaken by events and up to my main neural highway in Laphraoig or however you spell it.

Click and whirr and kill the lights. You know what it's like watching rushes? It's like the end of your dream when you're turning over and not finding anyone next to you and then touching flesh and you know the dream's spooled out and you're not where you were just now but here, in a hotel in Sweden with Ingmar Bergman's latest after all, and there's a lot of work to be done and Zelda's gone. Basically, it's a mixture of the good, the bad and the ugly. The good parts are chance, the bad parts are not, the ugly is in between. It helps to be situated near a litre of some great Scotch. There's Hilda with the clapper-board. Great days, great days. I'm never going to finish this movie. It'll rank as the most unfinished great unfinished movie ever made. I can't believe she forgot to hug me. I've expended so much of my energy on this woman and she forgot to hug me. Actually, she came in and had this shower and some lasagne and some sleep and some burnt toast and some honey-nuggets and some coffee and walked out without ONCE TOUCHING. Not even my hand on her shoulder or her hand on my shoulder. Not even elbow on elbow by mistake. I'd never ever do a scene like that in a movie. It's too ridiculous. She just said thanks for the breakfast, Rick, I think I'd better be going, you're a good person basically, if our lifeways don't meet again then may reality bless you and went. It was still raining a little. Instead of saying hey, Zelda, our lifeways have been meeting ever since we bumped into each other and paired up in the Upper Cretaceous, all that bloody giant bracken and bog-asphodel to negotiate if you remember and they're going to go on meeting until the sun turns the Eiger into the kind of ice-cream I used to serve up in the glow of those honey-candles if you also remember I nodded and then called out do you want an umbrella? She didn't hear me and I didn't grab my umbrella and lope after her in my slippers and we didn't embrace on the sidewalk in the streaming rain with Mike's crazy little cardboard thing waving at the rain-machine operator to open it right up, I just frowned a bit and then closed the door and sat down to watch the rushes and then remembered the breakfast stuff because I can't stand working until the breakfast stuff's cleared. So maybe the very final word passed between me and Zelda is umbrella.

I wish she hadn't dyed her hair, that's all.

I just wish she hadn't.

I just wish my neighbour's daughter hadn't chosen that day to visit. I just wish she'd stayed on very bad terms with her father.

Because the rain wouldn't have sneaked in between her tyre treads and the tarmac and made her slide towards the sidewalk and Zelda.

And the way Zelda screamed at her made me go to the window. OK, it's fairly irritating having someone almost clip your ankle with their hub-cap and then lift a curtain of dirt-brown water which has to drop somewhere but, hey, it wasn't my neighbour's daughter's fault, and

506

you don't need to scream at them like that. And watching Zelda looking like Louisa screaming at people was incredibly unpleasant. It's kind of screened out all the other Zeldas I knew. It was a shock to see Zelda screaming at someone, actually. It was like she couldn't care less about anybody, not me or Doctor Pepsibrain or her mother in Duluth or anyone. The way she screamed under her platinum and then walked away around the corner and out of sight, she could have been anyone. Anyone.

I'm sorry. We've missed some.

He's looking down, he's watching the cat sniff my grandmother's hands right now. She's on the bed and so is the cat. There's this stain on the bed. There are only two candles in here but he can see it's a fairly unpleasant stain because the bedcover is cream. We keep jerking between the stain and the cat sniffing my grandmother's hands. The damp patch behind is out of focus but it still looks like India with Ceylon too big. This is a shot of the dressing-room table now. It has a bottle of facial lotion and a circle of crochet and a yellow – hey, give me time, we're onto my grandfather's face now, these guys are jumping around like hell, anybody'd think there was a fire-fight going on in here or something, my grandfather's mouth is opening and closing because someone's fucked the sound, it's probably to do with the cat, we need Hilda because she's working with deaf people at the moment, maybe the best boy's boyfriend walked on Bosey's cable and snucked the jack out, Bosey'll go and throw himself off the Telecom Tower or wherever when he sees this but it's coming back in about three seconds, don't get stressed up, the talkies are about to surround us with barbed wire, I could have shot this on an antique camera with a hand-crank like they're about to shoot the War To End All Wars on a couple of hand-cranks but you bastards would only have yelled and stood up and got my grandfather and grandmother on the back of your heads and fists and stuff and here's the sound, it's like coming up out of water, it makes my grandmother's shudders look reasonable because we can hear them, the shot is of my grandmother down to her boots on the edge of the bed looking over at something and we're checking up on it, OK – it's that crappy little picture of St Francis in a bamboo frame Sylvia upturned about fifty junk boutiques to find and we're coming up very tight, it's enormous, it's bigger than the screen, you can see

507

there's a dead mite trapped between the glass and the right eye, it's a great shot, that's what you call divine or maybe benign chance, it recalls the icons of Andrei Roublev at the end of *Andrei Roublev* except it's nineteenth-century Sunday School junk and has a ripple in it from damp or something and his face is the colour of rhubarb pie and the birds on his arms are unidentifiable they're so botanically indecisive and now we're cruising down his torso onto his naff sandals where a red squirrel's looking for protection and there's this crop of yellow primroses and another squashed gnat, I'm glad they obeyed my directions, sometimes the crew go AWOL and do all the obvious things like not pan over in microscopic close-up a crappy picture of St Francis circa 1880, they think stuff like that's pretentious, they think the kind of jump-cuts I do are schizophrenic, they fear for my mental health, they think I'm going to go the way of all Rothkos or at the least end up making video shorts three hours long of red circles floating slowly down or white light extremely gradually slanting across a blank sheaf of heavy art paper to a Bali gong or whatever when all I want to do is touch bottom.

Seriously.

You can hear my grandmother's breathing, she's miked up so close. The bed doesn't have a creak it has a kind of mild asthma attack every time she shudders. No wonder they put in the bungee-cord about seventy years later, it clearly needs some firming up – it's a very bad bed for young growing backs and reminds Giles my grandfather of the cast-iron Randle beds and glancing off that particular neural pathway is a left turn sign-posted Self-Abuse he tries not to look down, instead he takes the right fork where Poole's waiting like he waits pretty well every night with this amazing shaggy-dog story that kind of unrolls and unravels through the darkness or maybe some faint moonlight falling across bright red blankets the colour of bright red blankets and finally everyone still vaguely awake groans because the Mystic Hindoo Candle the height of the Great Pyramid or twenty thousand and one school brekkers kippers balanced nose to tail is reached and climbed up perilously by Ug-Kaar-Spat the *ne plus ultra* of the ancient seekers of the meaning of life and THERE IS THE TINY SHIVERING FLAME and he sneezes.

Dark, all dark.

Oof. Youch. You rotter, Poole.

What happened actually was that the summer storm that's brewing up sent a gust through the crack in the window and the candles momentarily horizontalled, they were really hanging on by their finger-tips to the lip of the wax for several seconds and my grandmother went eh. So did I. I thought maybe someone had walked in front of the camera or stepped on my shadow or something. The light's back upright and there's Calypso, she's slipping out the door, she's nosing it open and slipping right out – she must be very confused

509

by all the pheromones of her birth fluid, it must be tough. The candles are smoking quite a bit from their bad experience. There's a strong smell of candles in here. I think I've got time to give you a sneak teaser of this great scene in Amiens Cathedral of all places because they're not saying anything at the moment and I might as well make some effort to stop you leaving to stand in the cold grey drizzle of the new dawn or whatever and link arms and sing with total fucking strangers just to have something to tell your grandchildren about instead of telling them what a great movie you saw, THE movie for Christ's sake, the one that only had one screening so if you missed the end you missed the secret, the clue, the syzygy to rhyme with whizzy guy, the burning sledge, the *here's looking at you kid* with the propellers strobing on the tarmac, the girl walking right on past down the long probably lime avenue so he lights up, he just lights up, the puff, the payoff, the oof, the pummelling of Poole sometimes if it wasn't good enough, the darkness, the *real* darkness, OK, I haven't.

so kind, sir, as to shut it tight?

There are these shadows all over the walls. It's fairly expressionist but that's Mike's thing. In fact it's nothing to do with Mike it's to do with the position of the candles.

Would you be so kind as to shut th'door, sir?

My grandfather closes his mouth which is not what she meant. Up through the floor comes this vibration which is the grandfather clock in the study sounding nine o'clock and because this is Sensurround it gets my priceless collection of fake Roman tear-vases from Pergamum tinkling and the Oscars in the hallway nudging each other. Now he's closing it. That's an incredibly sexual moment, obviously. Unless you're very extrovert or get turned on by risk even very slightly ajar doors cause problems – with a slightly ajar door you don't know whose eyeball might be catchlighting in the crack or whose ear for that matter but as soon as an inch of hollow plywood's set between you and the rest of the planet you have the impression you're secure, you're private, things can start heating up, they get done to a turn, it's crazy.

And things are definitely starting to heat up up there now. The

510

swallowing's me, by the way, I have a loud swallow, especially when it's a gill at a time. Now it's my grandfather's swallow. He's just swallowing his nerves while keeping his back to the room. I think he's studying the flies preserved in the varnish or maybe the grain of the woodwork for the moment because he can't face this little sloping room with its small feminine articles and major feminine article he's just shut in. With him on the right side or maybe the wrong side depending on which self-adhesive moral sticker you want to apply. Owing to the fact that he's closed the door or blame the Phantom of the Corridor the cat's returned and is nailing the varnish on the other side.

Good grief, that cat, says my grandfather. I'm about to have the maid.

He doesn't say that last bit, he thinks it, but it's like he's said it. He can't bear the fact that he's thinking this and the maid in question's about two feet away with her feminine articles. He can't believe that two people can be so close together without knowing everything about each other instantly, but I could tell him right now that I know about one per cent of anybody else including Zelda Lazenby *née* Wick and about five per cent of myself. And given that the only contact between him and her has been over silver salvers and wobbling rougemanges or now and again a brief encounter of sleeves on the stairs followed by a whiff of wax polish and maybe the armpits again if it has been buffing day, he knows about 0.01 per cent of her. But knowing 0.01 per cent about somebody does not stop a person from having extremely intimate physical contact with that somebody, it's very very strange. And the fact is that my grandfather has about twenty-four stage and screen melodramas to fall back on if he dries up, along with all that rot the chaps go on about in the dorm. All that sexual rot. With an all-star cast of house laundrywomen and dining-hall servants and milkmaids on the local farms let alone the pubescent domestics back home generally unclad and giggling and the shape of keyholes so it's like he's walked into the penny pictures with the projector whirring and found himself up there on the screen which is quite a coincidence actually, if only my grandmother was Mary Pickford it'd be perfect because my grandfather aches for Mary Pickford's curls and neat chin and so forth like about seven million other chaps. I need to put this whole thing into context or I'll feel I'm the result of a crime without attenuating circumstances which ain't a cosy feeling, guv. And these guys in ostrich plumes are getting ready to screw the century and hand Randolph his duck-board and William his howitzer shell and Giles his fucked-up gas mask and nervous problems which I feel for one outdoes my grandfather's crime by about seven million to one. His buttocks are tingling right now. Mine are, anyway. He's turning round finally, it's like the biggest effort of his life to turn round finally, it's like he's in liquid mud up to his breast-pocket or something, but he makes it. The most obvious thing would be to mention the cat but he'd rather not, the stain's still glistening on the bed-cover. My grandmother blows her nose on her handkerchief which uses up a bit of time. Those shadows are amazing, every time they move an inch it looks like an earthquake or the Ice Monster's in town.

Charming picture, says my grandfather.

She looks up and because he's waving his hand around like a traffic policeman she hasn't the foggiest what he's on about. And then he doesn't help the situation by saying *C'est un banquet charmant au sein de la nature, Où chacun a sa place et trouve sa pâture*. Her mouth is now right open. That wasn't Henrik in his Rimbaud phase by the way it's off a postcard Nurse Ginger-Whiskers Hallam purchased in 1903 of a bird charmer in the Tuileries Gardens at Giles's insistence when the Trevelyans were travelling continentally for a month and it did not matter one jot that this guy in a big walrus moustache and greasy cape and soiled trousers too small for him had a pocketful of crumbs, Giles reckoned he was the tops – especially with the bird muck all over his shoulders like a hard frost as Uncle Ken pointed out and this pigeon on his hat like Sir Lancelot as William pointed out, a little forward for his sailor suit as always. It's French, my grandfather's saying. Then he blushes, because he was about to say it's a French postcard of a bird-charmer. But if you dumbos didn't know this already that sentence in 1914 or at any date from around 1880 is lethally loaded because a French postcard in 1914 means one with a girl in a corset up to but not incl. her nipples licking a baguette or lowering her buttocks onto the Eiffel Tower or unlacing her otherwise completely unclothed mistress's leather boot while this jerk in an oiled walrus holds out some lilies with the edge of the backcloth showing behind the tin tub with the discarded frilly knickers arranged tastefully upon it. So my grandfather brakes in a cloud of flint-chips and manages to say St Francis and the birds instead. He steps over and picks up the picture and the bamboo frame comes apart. He holds the bottom piece of the frame to stop the glass falling out and pretends that it's not an incredibly cheap and shoddy frame coming apart in his hands but looks at it with his heart beating very hard as if it's Piero della Francesca and sees his own face in the glass and what a stupendously silly fool he looks.

Frightfully charming, he says.

This is about the crappiest dialogue I have ever seen in any film but stick with it, this is how it was, I'd have preferred the line leading pretty soon to me to have been instigated during something you could have spliced unedited into *The Rainbow* or whatever but hey, sorry, this is the truth, truth mumbles and sends the fly on the wall off to sleep unless the fly on the wall realises that *every movement reveals us*. My grandfather's wondering how he's going to get this collapsing icon back onto the little bedside ex-milking stool intact, it's like he's come in here and smashed up her toys or something, her presence next to him is a very complicated thing, she's a blur next to him but it's a very complicated blur involving downy golden hairs on forearms and precious cheapjack articles and the sound of breathing and the hint of armpits under a cotton print dress with tiny red roses all over it and these dark locks coming out of their pins and surprisingly dirty fingernails and as he's trying to pretend not to be pressing the bottom piece of bamboo back into the glass and the backing and the little tacks in each corner he gets this very clear image of her whole life from birth to now, she's drowning inside his head, he's slotted his coin into the peep-show, flap flap flap. There's a baby and a little girl and a bigger little girl and then a little big girl and then right now where there's kind of a girl and a woman at the same time with her little bedside treasures and her feminine articles and a rag doll not really wanting to look over the cream bed-cover and finally this fellow in white flannels next to the bed and it's him and the penny drops and it's dark again, it's that gust, Clifford's going great guns with the thunder-sheet the other end of the lawn, tell him to cool it, it's not the Second Coming yet, just because he lost a Pall Mall hotel last night. Giles looks up and the light wavers on again and he wonders how anyone could survive these draughts. He feels quietly moved by his viewing of *The Maidservant's Life* but of course he doesn't wipe away a tear, it's like a very submerged sob that never makes it past Jules Verne level. As a matter of fact he's getting irritated by this picture, it's like he wants to hold her life in his hands but his hands are full, he gives up and rests it on its back on the stool because if he tried to place it upright it would probably collapse.

Dennis Price plays this guy called Jack Yates of the City Imperial Volunteers with a damaged dick and a brandy problem in that Amiens Cathedral scene, by the way. Just in case you're thinking of pissing off out of here. And the drizzle's getting worse, it's kind of sleety now. Stick in the warm for a few more hours, pour yourself a Buck's Fizz or an Essex Fuzz or whatever. Go for it.

My grandmother's wiping some glitter off her nose, she probably couldn't care less about this picture or not now at any rate, now it's just part of her general sadness and she feels the bed bounce and it's him, *he's sat beside her*, tweaking his flannels up like no one under sixty does these days. I'm leaning right forward in my seat now. Like I used to lean forward in the Enfield Ritz and sometimes slip off and crack my tooth on the ashtray especially if it was that bit in *Great Expectations* Des used to remind me about after Mither had flicked the light out and the clothes on my chair were doing their Son of Werewolf routine and the hairs on my back were proving they existed. I hope I don't crack my tooth on my knees because there's no ashtray in front of me, only a sheep-fleece rug with attached thistles from my uncle in Melbourne who's trying to find *Will There's A Way* on video and keeps writing to me about this. I'm not going to disappoint him, he's nearly ninety, it might finish him off, it gives him a purpose in life outside of his scuba-diving and bungee-jumping and stuff.

Hey, they're not very close in fact. I would say there's easily two feet between them. He's gone as near the end of the bed as he can get without having a drypoint of the cast-iron rods on his thighs and she's nearly on the bolster.

Basically they're staying very still for a moment.

It's like you wouldn't know the camera was working except that the light's unstable, the candles are jittery, this draught through the crack in the window is making the celluloid work for its living.

514

Dennis Price. And, hey, *Alec Guinness*. Yup. Alec Guinness as Parkes. Actually I have the whole Ealing stock company scattered through the rest of this movie. Parkes is Giles's batman. Wot a character, cor lumme, patter like there's no tomorrer which there probably ain't, drives Giles up the bleedin' wall. He gets blown up fairly swiftly but it's the *young* Alec Guinness, he's not that fantastic at nineteen. He has this great running gag wiping his little spectacles on his sleeve every two minutes but his Cockney accent's hopeless. After the shell lands on his head or wherever Giles finds these spectacles unscathed in the general pulp and sends them back to Mrs Parkes the dear old mum (Margaret Rutherford) but, wait for it, *he wipes them carefully first*.

It's still just the light moving, and probably their internal organs.

The first movie was a cave-painting, by the way. It said so in this article in *Time* magazine I picked up at my heart specialist's last week. How the bisons and wild antelopes and mammoths and so forth were painted onto irregular rock so when the tallow-lamp arrived out of the pitch-black they all shifted around, the shadows jittered and swayed, it was a very early use of the Starlight enhancement to Quantel's Mirage Digital Video Effect, it was basically a shade modifier, this is the kind of junk Dr Laysemendtoend comes up with and no one giggles. But if I were to add that excuse me you're talking steaming shite, there is no correlation between DVEs and the kind of magic my but I'm not sure your ancestors were into, these people were continually profound, they drew animals like no person could draw animals now because we're full of steaming shite and watch DVEs instead of how a bison's hip-joint ripples, they allowed the animals to come into them and let them out through their finger-tips onto the rock like I've let my grandparents come into me and out through my fingers onto the rock and now they're both just sitting there moving but not moving in the candlelight, the whole fucking class'd be on a hysterics loop-tape.

I guess you're moving but not moving in the dawn light or maybe ten o'clock light by now of the new millennium. I wish sometimes I could move but not move in the dawn light of about twenty thousand years ago minimum. I have this very strong urge sometimes to be prehistoric because being post-historic you don't have the wind and animals and leaves of grass blowing through your mind, you just have an incredible

515

amount of gunk and junk, it's like being a waste tip where the only beautiful thing is the wheel of gulls and they're laughing.

I feel very Walt Whitman sometimes, as a matter of fact. I really feel like cleaning meself art, guv. Fade the gulls to faint, for God's sake.

I don't want to know the void though, I was never into this void thing of Zelda's, I'm a really unZen person actually. Basically I think I'm a Great Prairie person. If I could get my head emptied of everything except rolling silvery grassland to the open sky I'd be right there, I do believe. I know you'll be tittering to hear Ricky Thornby of all people talk like this but hey, everyone has their secret, their quirk, their personal planet. OK, they're moving again.

I feel awfully like a smoke, says my grandfather.

He's turned his head a few degrees towards my grandmother at least and somehow the Woodbine's got into his hand. My grandmother nods. It's kind of a dutiful nod, like he's just asked for some more cocoa. There's a lot of rustling of clothing, I think the mike must be badly positioned or maybe clothing in those days was noisier.

Do you? asks my grandfather.

She turns her face and looks at him square on with her mouth open so he can see the little glistening cave of it and then at the fag then back at him and shakes her head. It's amazing that her eyes meet his for more than it takes for me to sip my duty-free Laphroaig once and replace it on my Shad tea-chest if you think about it, because up to now she's never actually more than kind of glanced off of his eyeballs when stair-passing or wielding her majolica crumb-brush on the tea-table in front of his knees. I hope you like this shot of my grandfather's eyes which are blue-green not kind of mud-green like mine and of course Willo's. That's the last time you'll see them in extreme close up until 1917 when they'll be encircled by a gas mask and blinking with some very heavy scuba-diving breathing going on but I'm not trailing that now, there's no time. My grandmother's raven eyes drop to his breast-pocket and she says I didn't mean to hit him sir in such a quiet voice it makes my grandfather lean towards her and the bed has to be rushed to hospital.

516

Sorry?

I didn't mean to hit him, Master Giles.

Who?

Master William, sir.

Hey, if you have a fruppenny bit for five frows and don't lean over the string and get free of the balls through my grandfaver's mouf you could win a lead duck, they were collectors' items down the Portobello Road in my heyday, roll up'n 'ave a go guv, he's not going to be like that for long, he's going to taste the Cologne water and the candle wax and the armpit-sweat etc. on the inside of his cheeks and snap it shut like right now. See? Too late. He thinks he might have sat on the stain. He stands up and sure enough he did. He didn't look, it happens sometimes, the seat of his white flannels has picked up the cat's afterbirth, he's twisting round to look and Milly has stood also and is doing things with her hands in the air and she says I'll wash them straight off, I'll bleach them straight off, sir. He looks at her now and starts to snort, no, laugh. This is crazy – he starts to laugh. He's got this big slime patch on his white seat and his fingers are crooked in front of his mouth like he's trying to catch his laugh or something and my grandmother's holding her hands out like she's going to take his trousers right now for God's sake and I don't know where to look, I'm blushing, I'm embarrassed at these people like I used to be embarrassed at my parents when they came to School Open Day and my mother's high heels kept catching in the holes in the lino and my father'd wear his sharp suit and try to comb his hair in the staff-room bottle-glass and say cor lummy every time Miss Bellerby rippled past. I survived though, my scars are barely picked at now, the school was authentic Jacobean with huge oak trees and beams with real wood-worm so they demolished it and put up a whizzo H Block in pre-stained concrete with extremely large rectangles of glass that gives a great view of pre-stained concrete with extremely large rectangles of glass that gives a great view of your tiny face trying to find your tiny face which leaks in 1953 and the saplings didn't make it, they got some disease – but there's lots of ground cover at the foot of the security fences so the Miss Bellerby Memorial Fund for the Advancement of

517

Natural History Studies has something to go on, she'd have been quietly proud if she'd not got giddy while examining a buck's-horn plantain somewhere about an inch too close to the edge of Wales and seventy-five feet too far from the shingle six weeks before her retirement, I was surprisingly sad, when I told my dad in the Home he said cor lummy and I practically fainted, it's the one and only sane response he's made to date since the stroke.

It's OK. My grandfather's stopped laughing. Just like that, like I've yelled CAT and we're to do it again, like a passionate kiss can end just like that when you yell CAT and the guy turns his face and you'd think he'd just been biting a sour apple or something.

But I wasn't in the room, no one yelled CAT. Hey, all twenty-four people crammed into that room could have yelled CAT and my grandfather wouldn't have heard them, he's really in his own world now, his eyes are burning because the laughter made them leak a bit and now you've got this great candle-flame specular in each one just over the retina which my grandmother even notices but it's hard for us, they're not in extreme close-up now, the crew missed that one. Instead they're tightening in on the hands. My grandfather's hands are closing around my grandmother's hands and my grandmother's hands are sitting inside my grandfather's hands like a baby rabbit. Like that time the late Fawholt gravedigger came out from behind some geranium pots and gave him something soft to hold that rippled and then just trembled while his heart leapt around and Nurse Ginger-Sideburns Hallam brushed hairs from his sailor suit lapels and got tense in 1905 or something.

Don't hurt me, says my grandmother.

Ladas Cream Baking-Powder thinks my grandfather because there's a Ladas Cream Baking-Powder tin full of hairpins or maybe insects just beyond the maid's head, on the window-sill there, and right now his eyes are kind of skirting her face because her face is looking surprisingly distressed.

Why should I want to hurt you, Milly?

You're hurting me hands, she says.

He realises he is but it's nerves, her hands haven't got the pliability of a baby rabbit, they're quite bony. Sorry, he says. He relaxes his grip a jot but the baby rabbit doesn't try to escape. This is very complex. She may not be trying to remove her hands because she's too frightened to resist or because no one's held them for about nine months since Sis and then her Ma held them at Worksop station and it's quite nice having your hands cupped. Or maybe there's something sexual here, just maybe, but I have to tread on tiptoe through this area because there are a lot of people in white coats and round spectacles just waiting for me to slip up and say hey, come on over and see my Japanese nose flutes or whatever.

Or maybe it's all those things at once. Maybe if you were to take a deep emotion sample the tube'd be full of different soils and industrial poisons and some bits of bone and pottery and you'd be in the lab a long time sifting it. He lets her hands go. He steps back. Her hands weren't the same as Amy's were on that slope, the maid's hands are bonier. He feels incredibly nervous now, he doesn't feel he's achieved anything, the fag's between his lips, it must have got there when the lens was sampling the light on my grandmother's neck. I've spilt my fucking Laphroaig, leave it, let the fleece get happy. Now there's a low angle on his shoes, they're involved with this apron on the floor, this big white apron either Sylvia remembered too late or we just didn't pick up before – it's the one my grandmother untied and tugged off her shoulders and hurled away before bursting into sobs about ten minutes ago when she was on her own. He lifts his feet up and out like he's in liquid mud again. He actually picks the apron off the floor and holds it in front of him.

I say, ah, what do you mean you hit my bro? he says.

He's looking at the apron as he's saying this, it's as if he's asking the apron why it hit William, this must be what Robert means by automatism and the cause following the effect and making the objects look as if they want to be there, it's completely illogical. Ladas Cream Baking-Powder also runs through his brain, there's a pink stain on the apron, his cigarette's moving up and down because he wants to chew his bottom lip but it's tricky with a fag in the way. My grandmother's also looking at the white apron. She has her mouth open like she's about to whistle and make it lift its head and prick its ears or something, she's seen this three times at the local lousy music-hall, it was grand the first time, not so grand the second, totally pathetic the third. This reminds me of a great exercise I did with Peter as in Brook the day before I got blinded for several seconds by tear-gas outside the US Embassy, that was quite a week, life's been downhill ever since, we got this grey cloth and pretended it was a very sick person who had to be carried off this mountain in Tibet, we carried it down across the lino of this big low room for the whole morning, the worst bit was crossing the stream in full spate from the melting snows by the fire extinguisher, it was a very rocky mountain with extremely thin air, Peter was sitting like a Buddha on his rug, he didn't help at all – this very sick person was heavy and delicate and definitely groaned when I lost my footing on some terminal moraine, I think he survived though, we all had some strong tea and Peter thanked us and hugged me. I forgot to switch the camera on. It'd have looked very naff, I told myself, weeping afterwards. It'd have looked so incredibly naff. Maybe I didn't say naff in those days. Maybe I said something else like it just wouldn't have swung or its soul would've been out for lunch and then about twelve hours later I had gas in my eyes, maybe it's a family tradition, I was weeping some more by this upside-down coach with everybody screaming and I'd lost my bandanna, it was crazy, a crazy way-out week, man.

All these things, I forgot them for years, now they're coming back clearer and clearer.

OK. I'm watching. My grandmother's mouth is filling the screen. There's a specular on the upper lip where it's wet. Clifford's going great guns again with the thunder-sheet but this ain't Texas, Clifford. Out of the mouth peeps this red tongue. It wipes away the specular which returns instantly and that much clearer. It's definitely a flame.

He tried to have his way with me, sir.

Human lips are a miracle, the way they flex and touch. Hey, the flame's still there. For once my crew obeyed my dope sheet precisely so here's to they. No more lips. No more whisky. I'm sucking it off the fleece, I'm getting a thistle up my nose. *Tant pis.*

My grandfather keeps staring at this apron in his hand. The apron is her. It's developing very slowly into a fetish but he doesn't know this, he just finds holding it fairly strange in terms of its effect on his sexual chemistry. It kind of overflows all creamy out of his hand and its tie is dangling onto his shoe and he might as well bury his face in it like those weirdo *fin-de-*previous-*siècle* poets did with their mistress's lavender-sprinkled soiled underpants but he doesn't, thank God, he just tries to say instead *I say, you can't be serious, old girl* but he knows he's in a complex masterwork not a big-budget British feature in drip-dry gloss for the hard-hat housewives in Ohio so instead he mumbles, he mumbles *God, how appallingly silly.* My grandmother's brought her hands up to her face and her face is emerging from her fingers like, say, a mayweed from its calyx (I learnt so much from your ripples, Miss Bellerby) and there's this gust that hits the window-pane. It must be Pan, thinks Giles, it must be Pan trotting over the lawn with his pipes and without really thinking about it he brings the apron to his chest and holds it there like a teddy bear or an article of clothing belonging to someone he feels very strong sexual and maybe emotional feelings for. This is taking years, I'm sorry, I had no idea it was all so delicately-wrought, I really hope the critics use the term delicately-wrought about this scene because I'm generally associated with fairly broad-stroke stuff but I've changed, I don't have dowel-head producers breathing down my neck who think delicate films die.

How appallingly silly of him, he adds in a murmur. He definitely murmurs it this time. Actually, I thought he meant the first time how appallingly silly the whole idea was and that we were going to have at least a few minutes of my grandmother persuading him it was true and that sweet Wiliam did try to have his way with her and then my grandfather stomping about the room denying it and waving his hands around but no, this is not photographed theatre, this is irresistible reality, and in irresistible reality people believe things really un-expectedly, like I believed Zelda was going to leave me for ever the minute I saw her out there in the streaming rain waiting to come in and I was right. Anyway, my grandfather looks really terrified all of a sudden because his younger brother might have kissed a girl before he

521

has. He knows for definite now that his younger squit of a mildly tubercular brother has tried to have his way with a girl before he has, but trying to have your way might not include much of your way, it might not have included any way at all beyond the first step, the beginner's lunge, the grip at the wrist or the elbow or the waist or wherever – I mean, the mouths might not have come into contact, my grandfather's reputation might be intact, tomorrow or even tonight he could sally forth and seek some incredibly loose woman on one of the farms or something and damn well do it until her eyes pop out and the hayloft collapses. Then he remembers that the last of the hay has just been gathered and that probably all the haylofts are booked for the night. He feels quite angry now in amongst his terror, it's like Willo getting a Rudge-Whitworth bicycle before him three years ago – Willo didn't get a Rudge-Whitworth bicycle before him three years ago, Giles got it three years ago and Willo got his last year, but it's *like* Willo had got a Rudge-Whitworth bicycle before him three years ago for Christ's sake, do I have to explain everything in five stages like an air-stewardess conducting a slow movement with an orange inflatable nobody watches because the in-flight magazine has some nice turquoise beach pictures and they reckon that if the plane has to land in the sea knowing which toggle to tweak between finger and thumb in a gradual forward motion while blowing into the red one marked D or whatever isn't going to be the primary concern, the primary concern's going to be how hard can I pray and scream and hang on to my loose bowels simultaneously?

Oh cor lummy, he's doing it.

He's kissing her.

I missed it. I mean I missed exactly how he got from a state of Edwardian or OK Georgian respectability into this mess. I got too worked up about this anger thing. Christ, now they're being zoomed up on. We don't need it. All you can see is my bare wall covered in snog, and there's a lot of saliva bubbles, it's unattractive. This isn't important, basically. What's important is at what point and how he lunged. Unless he lunged out of nothingness like Zelda says you should lunge or go to the toilet or whatever, but my grandfather is not Zen, he always lunges etc. out of something.

522

I wish they'd dunked the lip-mike off. It sounds like my neighbour's jacuzzis emptying simultaneously.

I've turned my back. I've always hated kissing in the cinema. Actually I missed the crucial crux because I was thinking of Des the whole time and how Des got his Hornby-Dublo before I did. OK he was older, there's no comparison, but the point is – I didn't get it *even when I was eleven*. It was a crappy hand-me-down little circular basic set No. 2008 with rusty points but it was Des's and I didn't get to use it until I was seventeen when I could put my fags in the funnel and stuff and make my first girlfriend not laugh by laying myself down in its path or doing Keystone Cops gags with my Dinky Humber. I think she just thought I was underdeveloped emotionally. Elizabeth Margaret Heel with an e. She became a beautician, she runs some place in Waltham Forest for the removal of unwanted Waltham wattles or whatever – she moved up in the world, she missed the tramp-steamer out, she could have dealt with my eye-pouches, she could be power-sucking my ass right now. Hey, she probably still wears a beehive and a giant striped brooch and snogs like a rubber doormat and hates Aertex short-sleeves because blokes have bony elbows or something. Or maybe she's dead by now. The faces behind me have become two again, they're reflected in Stendhal's bowl, it's a great fish-eye effect in there, it needs cleaning actually.

I mean like that, says my grandfather. He's looking awkward and not just because of the Van Eyck distortion and Stendhal listing in his head. He's wiping his mouth now. Clearly he must have mumbled something we didn't pick up about whether Willo actually kissed her and she didn't give a snappy enough answer so he lunged. I'm feeling uncomfortable, Stendhal. I was born out of original jealousy. Cain and Abel stuff. Very negative vibrations. Maybe it's inheritable.

My grandfather's looking unpleasantly aggressive. I've kind of seen enough I'm thinking and maybe you're thinking after ten hours. Here's some deluxe fish-feed, my finny friend. Actually, one of the fins is looking frayed, his list is back, he's no longer able to explore the bit between the wreck of the *Titanic* and the cliff of flint off Wot Hill because he can't steer very well. My grandfather's either moved completely out of shot or the goldfish bowl's not inclusive enough, he

523

might have slid round the side of it, I'm turning to check. OK, he's not out of shot, he's standing near the window far right in kind of shallow focus and Milly's in the middle with her arms held over her chest although she's not stripped yet. Now he's looking surprised, it's like April, it's being very changeable up there.

I think he's surprised by the way the kiss felt.

You know why he's so surprised and why my grandmother's just standing there looking totally blank, staring at this completely worn-out little rug at her feet which has suddenly appeared, I thought this was a continuous take, I wonder sometimes if Sylvia's got my nerves in her sights – it's because the first sexual kiss of someone else's mouth is fairly surprising. It's like you've never realised before how *biogenetic* everything is. It's like everything is mouth creating more mouths, that's all there is to life, you forget to breathe or swallow because you're concentrating hard on not hitting their nose too much with your nose but it doesn't seem to matter, the world is basically very wet and warm and out of this primordial saliva this fish thing is crawling up and it means business, it's turning into a fat toad that's no longer going to toe the line – fuck it, you've gone through life with this kind of bony elbow feel to everything once your mother's stopped squeezing you and stuff and suddenly the bony elbows are gone and you're somewhere plump. Oh Zelda. Oh grey-eyes. Oh show me a hayloft and let's loosen all the crucks.

I apologise. Sigh bubble. There's a little bit at the bottom, about half a gill. It'll see me through, thank you. Asses up.

OK, my grandmother's nodding. Her hair's right out of its pins again. Some voices come up from the lawn and go away again, the pianola's just registering in the floorboards, the nightingale from Abyssinia's in its usual position on the second branch of the third hazel beyond the potting shed and the fiddle's fiddling afar thank God because the local musicians are terrible and the songs go on for three hours each especially when the hay's brought home and just in time because hey, it's about to bucket, the gusts are full of an impending storm.

I'm not sure why she's nodding, but each nod's getting more hair

524

falling over her face and it's attractive. I did not inherit my grandmother's beauty. It's a very particular kind of beauty. It's not beauty beauty. It's the beauty of something that might have been happy. Right now this beauty is not really formed, she's only fourteen for God's sake, her skin's still recovering from thirteen years next to the Worksop Soap Works and other gunk like a virtually vitamin-free diet – she still keeps her head too low and sniggers nervously at George's jokes and negotiates her never evers but she might have made it, she might have developed into something amazing, maybe Agatha would've helped her to night classes if not day classes and talked to her fairly unpatronisingly about suffrage and stuff like she did in actual fact but it was too late by then, my grandmother was already broken.

Crack. Thunder and lightning. Seriously. Maybe my projector will blow up. We have Texan storms out here in Houston. We have the Rothko Chapel. We have people leaving Earth without having to die first, we have an eye-research unit at the forefront of world sight, we have some fabulous golf-links. I'd like to show y'all round some day. Maybe I had better switch off. Go see the new day for a minute. Go sing your hosannas while I find my axe. These crates are hell to open, guv.

Power on. I'll take the risk. I can't stand the dark any longer, hey, I've kept all the house lights off, you can't bring up the house lights before the end of the movie unless it's the interval and we've had that, I'm a professional, the ghoul in the garden's just Ricky in a flash of lightning the dry side of the patio glass but it's sheer terror each time.

Look, I'm very sorry to have kept you people. If you leave right now you might just catch the £19.99 one-finger buffet in Trafalgar Square with a free Twiglet if you show up by midday and maybe a stack of sherry trifle if you're willing to use your elbows because we know the English like their desserts, they like them more than they like sex or social welfare or the blue whale. We're basically a mixture of bony elbows and puddings, bony elbows and puddings creamed over with this money thing – if you hike up an English person by their loud ankle socks and shake them really hard out drips this unpleasant kind of detritus and it's all the times they've thought about saving money mixed up with all the times they've thought about having more pudding, it's extremely unattractive, all that's left for me now in my mother country is meanness and lemon cheesecake, everything else is non-essential outlay or something, it's bleedin' depressing guv, that'll be thirty-two quid and we don't mind if you rahnd it off to forty not having no smallish and don't forget the little blessin', it's not easy negotiatin' life and keeping you hentertained, all these people and all these bleedin' turns, never a dull moment, lucky I has the Knowledge and you has the wherewivals. Ta mate. You're a toff. Enjoy yer Twiglet in the fahntin and don't get it wet. Cor luvaduck. Reminds me of V. E. Day – V. D. Day as we used to call it. CAT, wrap up, print that, get rid of the guy. Or there's the £2,000 two-fist buffet at the Hilton, if you've not cleaned me out with your mouth sufficiently. They have this great swing band there I do believe, it's playing a hundred years of Your Favourite Classic Melodies, it works out at about £50 a twist with half a glass of wine included but all the nice people'll be there of course, all

527

the nice people who've made me ache for England, they'll all be there with their huge mouths and horizontal bosoms and self-adhesive ostrich plumes twisting and shouting themselves into pole position for the new one just in case you lot out there reckoned the new one was gonna be in good bleedin' taste, roight? So where're you goin' then, guv? Shad Thames? Ratcliff Highway? The end of the bleedin' road?

The projector's spooled out, by the way. There's just this light, this nice white light which cuts out the terrible strobe effect off the lightning because even my walk-in pool's lapping in darkness, it's the way it has to be, I have to frighten myself, I have to wait for the usherette to show her nostrils above the red torch of desire, I have to sit out the spooks and the thunder and the awful daring of a moment's surrender which was Henry Peterson's fave line, he'd fill himself up to the eyeballs with barley wine and his bladder'd definitely surrender, he'd sway to his fave line then yell DAMYATA while the only thing that was getting wet were his slippers, those were the days, all of us with our mackintoshes on and swaying along in Frank's place, *The Jack of Spades*, ha yes, *The Jack of Spades* known affectionately as *The All Trades* or sometimes *The Jack Off* – remember, Ossy, me old mucker? And Christ, whatever happened to Frank? Dear old Frank the Lisp and his splendid aspidistras on the bar we spent ten yearth requethting the name of with our umbrellath at the ready for crying out loud but he never fell for it, dear old Frank, he never fell for it, just went on sucking up his liquid fortune out of our livers – great pubs, great days, great sodding shame they turned them into wine bars for drip-dries with interindividual assignments, sodding great tragedy, nothing stays still unless you switch the bugger orf.

You know what's wild, man?

I'm more and more sounding like my close relative in Havant used to sound before he got jammed on rewind. Help. At least I don't look like him. At least I got away with something.

I cut the rushes because I needed a break, incidentally. I needed to get over this Zelda thing before watching my grandmother Doing It. I've been looking at this blank white wall of mine if you discount the picture-hook in the middle for about five hours now, it's very interesting, it's stayed blank, surprisingly.

Hey, I haven't even asked the unit what happened. They came out from my grandmother's room and looked at me like I was Bluebeard on the prowl then made straight for the bright side of the *Half Moon* where apparently they misbehaved, they made fun of the karaoke evening in aid of the £1 billion Dick Scanner or something, Gordon especially lost his grip, he did his Gene Kelly routine where there wasn't room. So? Listen, they'd worked hard, it was a difficult shoot, plus one of the Steves is not happy about his overtime rate and is trying to turn them all against me, I think he's a plant, he's a very rare member of the Workers' Revolutionary Family or something so I don't like to step on him. At some point I am going to have to wash the rest of my undies, they can't stay dirty for ever, they'll fester, my mother'll shout at me, I'll be locked in my room with Des's football socks which she never notices because of her adenoids – hey, I *liked* not changing my undies, Blisto for Whiter Whites gave me testicular pimples, or maybe it was the scourge of nits my dear family tended to be blamed for because Mr Munro without an o or an e so there's no relation in spite of his hamster eyelashes and total absence of body hair reckoned my father wasn't a stickler for baths which he wasn't oh no but neither was Queen Elizabeth one had to point out sir and one what had just done the pointing-out sir was given the opportunity to help Mr Munro find his psychological wholeness of being and flogged stupid until one what had done the original pointing-out pointed out once more fairly quietly while tipping the blood from his shoes into the nearest aspidistra because it keeps their leaves shiny as does milk sir that one had not meant the newly coronated royal sovereign herself by St Harry and King George good gracious no but the first one, the one wot stuck pancake all over her face and smelt dead, sir, by your living grace.

My trouble was and is that I have made up for two lives of complete subservience with my lip.

Complete subservience. I like that.

There are those who completely subserve, and those who are served. Basicerly, through a fogged lens. I'm going to load the projector again very soon. I may close my eyes but you'll still be able to see for God's sake if you're still out there, if you're still in your seats and not flinging yourself around to the hip rag of groovy Vera's latest or something because, hey, I know I have a lot of competition. I hope you've wiped out the Hoovers from Mars by now politely.

Right.

The first person who can tell me what Amazing Truth is revealed in the last few frames of this complex masterwork by a British director who used to be one of the youngest will receive my deeply cherished *Now Showing* enamel sign in excellent nick two-by-one off of my bedroom wall bought for a favour off Wilton Road and definitely once screwed to the brick of the very first cinema in London, guv.

The Bioscope, dumbos. The Biograph in my day but it was still the Bio. Let's go-o to the Bio-o my perfectly adorable something, maybe just thing. Norma gracing the posters, lots of columns, lots of nice plasterwork, fancy egg-and-wotsit stuff around the top, whirly wallpaper, soft seats, majolica ashtrays. Plush, y'see. Nice'n plush and you didn't have to be flush. Me dad used to slip in when he was doing his pot-plants-off-the-barrer spell arahnd them parts. Slipped in between the plus-fours below the sightline of the ticket lady and down to the fourpennies, twisted his cap abaht and stretched his pegs and plunged into grey-eyed Norma big as a bleedin' mansion between the fluted columns. While somebody was nickin' his barrer wiv firty-two pot-plants hangin' off of her – me old man roamin' the streets after lookin' for a place to throw hisself off 'cos me grandad were terble crooel wiv a belt and practically slept wiv his barrer. So there's me dad on Waterloo Bridge, the old one what was pulled dahn in the last to-do, past midnight, sort o' gazing into the swirl, the 'orrible black greasy swirl as is abaht to swallerimup when tap tap tap

Forget the fake gorblimey act. It doesn't suit you, Ricco me old soak. It makes you dribble and ache in the wrong places. Cor, hark to that thunder.

Tap tap tap. Tap. Tap. Tap tap.

Along the road comes this chap done up to the nines in top hat, tails, cream waistcoat, shiny pumps, white cane, the works. His cane's tip-tapping the balustrade on top of which is me dad contemplating his demise. The toff stops and taps his cane on me dad's butt and practically puts an end to him there and then 'cos me dad has to whirl his arms about to keep from toppling right in.

Oy, wotcher guvnor! comments me dad.

Then he sits on the granite ledge with his legs the safe side and starts to snivel. This is 1921, year of the BIG HEAT when not a drop fell on the parched ground and hot winds raised eddies of choking dust and the rivers were diminished everywhere according to *The Times* weather report I caught on microfilm the day before yesterday such is my zeal and in case you thought *The Wasteland* was straight off the top of his head. Me dad's eight years old. The posh blokey settles back onto the white cane with the ivory grip and says quietly to the lantern pole *what have you lost, dear lad, what have you lost?*

Me dad can smell the drink on the blokey's breath whirling around in the cold night air what got into your bones like this 'tomic radiation does nah happarently and then this cab clops past and then nothing, just this silence, just me dad snivelling and stuff and the greasy water clapping against the granite footing far below and maybe a horn way off towards the sea and basicerly silence, Bosey. How am I doing? Am I doing OK?

Hey, please, we haven't far to go now, stick with it, ignore the blood on my forehead, I'm tailing out what you've already seen, it takes time, I forgot to do this before – my grandfather's running backwards down the stairs now and he's taking the biscuit out of his mouth, the pianola's playing John Cage, William's hurtling out the vegetable garden without looking, the bucket's getting tugged up the stairs, we'll be zeroized any moment.

OK. What have you lost.

The posh chap puts a fag in his mouth and lights it like he's cradling a little rabbit or something but there's no wind, it's still, it's force of habit, he doesn't want his position given away. Then the eyes light up in the flare and they're blank. It's like he's rolled his eyeballs right up but he hasn't, that was Des's trick along with farting in time to *You Are My Lucky Star* and firing bogies from his nostrils at the end of his Stuka dive while I was trying to get through my Schopenhauer. My old man doesn't think of Des though because Des has not yet been summoned out of non-being by the archangels' trumpets to play his part but what me old man does think of is shelled eggs, a couple of shelled eggs all glistening and white so we couldn't have a devilled or coddled or hard-boiled egg in the house, me mum'd have to poach, fry, or scramble, it was his little quirk. And Des'd do his eye-rolling routine behind me dad's back, which frayed me mum that much quicker, the bastard.

Then this posh blokey takes a good pull on the fag and it glows and it's like the mist and the cold go out of him because he sort of smiles and the smoke smells sweet. Me dad wants to ask him why he's not wearing dark glasses. 'Cos while the topper's rim cuts the gaslight off from most of the face except the mouth the eyes sort of glow all pinkish every time the fag's sucked and me dad's still got *The Moan of the Mummy* flickering in his head from the matinée for Christ's sake. And there's mist curling up off the river and between the balusters and around his ankles and he's lost the barrer.

I've lost me barrer, sir, whispers me dad.

How careless of you, says the blind toff but sort of softly, like it's happened to him or something. How distinctly careless of you.

He takes another good pull and holds it in, then blows it all out through a very pursed mouth. There's loads of this sweet smoke and out of this smoke comes a hand holding a thick wad of something. A cart clops past full of fresh fish from the smell of it and me dad snivels all over again and when he looks up the groper's gone.

But the thick wad's between his legs. And it's all notes.

Hey, I like to think that toff groper was me old grandad, young.

But it probably weren't. There were loads o' young gropers tapping about in them days, smoking Turkish and saying *dear lad*. An' that were that. But you're well clear of them toffs, I'd say. Well clear. You keep to your carpit squares, son. There's honest rub in them carpit squares. Oh yes. There's more than a Conan Doyle on a double-barrelled's parsley in them carpit squares, son. You're well bleedin' clear of them toffs, I'd say. Well bleedin' clear an' if you've got a spare smoke for yer old dad I'd be very grateful. Ta. Well bleedin' clear of CAT, print that, get rid of the guy for Christ's sake.

Get rid of the bridge and the fresh fish, too.

Dear lad, says a voice from the darkest corner. It's a kind of recess actually. Maybe it's a house porch. There's a stripe of gaslight and a pair of shiny pumps sticking out. It's a growly kind of voice in my accent. *Dear lad*, it says. Hey, all we need is a cat and some slithery zither music and Harry Lime'll be resurrected in my grandfather's eyeballs because the very last time, oh yes, when I was not yet ten, oh Mum, I HAD TO TAKE HIM – I'll get onto that, I get chilled just thinking about his kind of fidgeting flickering stare right next to me, I was too young, I couldn't tell him who the Third or even the Second man was and I think I failed him, I failed him – he got run over by a No. 77 never saw him guv the next week or maybe the next month and I've been looking at this blank wall for five hours and I'm tasting the ashtray for crying out loud and I can see Louisa taking the wrong door at Plywood or was it Peeling and falling away forever and I can see the last held shot of maybe the lime probably the lime avenue in deep perspective and the girl growing and growing and carrying straight on past whoever played Orson Welles's friend, shit, my memory's rotting, anyway this famous actor bending his face to light the fag cupped in his hands so maybe he'd just been in the to-do that had recently finished or maybe there were gusts funnelling down the avenue with THE END twice in each eyeball next to me and hey, I wet my longjohns.

Great days, great days.

The house'd smell of muffs.

I've rewound. I'm up and ready to head out the rest of the rushes. All I need to do is turn this big switch and my wall will be full of flesh tints probably. Tears are pouring down my face. I didn't mean to pick up on that dining-room scene so early. I was keeping it frozen until the very end. We still have the whole war to work through, they're all waiting for me out there, Mike and Bosey and Sylvia and Pierre and Joe the Gel and Gordon the Grip and Clifford with his fucking thunder-sheet and all the big Steves lined up ready to twirl the flats and floats and dry-ice canisters and eighteen-pounder batteries on the ends of their little fingers, all ready and set up and waiting out there with hundreds of thousands of extras and Hubert Lightfoot and my grandfather and Willo with his lucky flint off Wot Hill tucked in with his butterfly book and forty miles of barbed wire and stuff and wet-hire period artillery and the right type of gas helmets and the perfect kind of light haze to the morning and for once a canteen staff not doped up on the rum rations and the Hawthorn Ridge mine gone up nicely and the sub-Gordons gripping the cranking handles and the *Birdsong* people tied up and gagged somewhere in GHQ's enormous wine cellars with their paper poppies stuffed up their noses and this silence, this amazing silence after the one-hundred-and-fifty-thousandth shell has been lobbed over and the games-whistles and the bagpipe-nozzles waiting to be blown in the lips of the non-speaking parts and all the right and meticulously-researched attachments nicely buffed and oiled and catching the sunrise and hey, I haven't turned up. The brass megaphone isn't going to flash and the clapper isn't going to clap and instead there's Julie tiny and silhouetted against the wide-format perfect morning haze and rolling silvery grass to the horizon where Mike's got his funny little cardboard thing held up and she's coming this way and running and panting right up into a close-up so close you can breathe in the sweet patchouli on her long neck and Sylvia says oh fuck, he's not coming, the bastard.

So they'll all go kind of muttering back to the canteen pantechnicons and have some coffee and croissants because what the hell, a blown budget's a blown budget – and spend about nine days rolling up the barbed wire and filling in the intricate honeycomb of rats' alleys and pumping out the water from the Ypres salient for the Passchendaele sequence because the local farmers are going down with their pesticide booms and all this time I'm watching my wall in Houston with tears streaming down my face because SHE'S THAWED OUT, you didn't alert me, the candle-flames are fattening and her arm's coming down and the curtains have, I think, yes, they've settled into their station and you didn't alert me, we'll have to make do with a hundred yards of stockshot and establishing sweeps and archive clips and apologise to the phantoms while I'm mounting the steps, the heugh of steps, it's too late to turn back, my mother's got my elbow in her glove and her hand's in her glove and she has a great grip, she could have worked for me, she has such a great grip the enormous door is practically ricking my neck before my little polished shoes have so much as touched the stone, I've kind of flown up, I've kind of flown up here.

Heugh.

That was the noise my mother made at the top. She was already disintegrating somewhere internally important, it started early. Cue in Henrik:

> That high heugh I stumbled up
> Into my rich hell,
> Dashed from my lips the honey-pot of home,
> Its sweet innocence dumb to tell
> How the womb hoards like salt all pain to come.

And so forth until you run out screaming. I said hey, Henrik, lift your face off the bar and tell me what this word is right here.

Heugh, he murmured.

Heugh.

HEUGH! he yelled.

OK, OK, Henry, watch the tankards, they're imitation splatterware or something, I just needed to know, I need to know everything, I need to know above all why the stone steps of Randle College are described with a pant instead of a word, it's kind of interesting.

His hand comes down flat on the bar but just misses it and he forward

535

rolls off the stool into my lap. A cliff, he says. A precipice. The steep side of a quarry, an excavation. A mine.

He didn't say that, of course. I'm dubbing over with some dictionary definitions his mouth saying it is a fucking word you half-baked bumpkin, you unlettered prole, at the level of my navel while I'm trying to get rid of my glass on the bar without spilling too much. Then he went to sleep and I almost stroked his hair. Almost. Because I was plunged into reminiscence suddenly, my mother was at the top of these other steps and going heugh and I felt very sad and salt was being applied to my early wounds or whatever, I was climbing the cliff again, I wanted to cry like I'm crying now but Frank was wagging his finger over the aspidistras and saying none of that in here, Mithter Thornby.

Thorry, Frank, I said, without meaning to.

I think I loved Henry, somewhere very deep down where boys compare their conkers and stuff.

Oh Gawd. And I've run out of even used tissues. Heugh. And when the enormous door opened it was like burying your face in an old lady's muff. This again, says Moira. Yup, Moira. This again. They've thawed out too early, it's the dead season, the rerun, the same old B chiller out of Ealing you reckoned I'd seen too young or something, you kept asking me for the title and the main actors.

Aw, *I* was the main actor, honey.

You always are, Ricky. There's the rub. Take a bit-part for a while. You'll find your whole perspective on life kind of shifts.

Moira doll, shuddup and listen. That's what I'm spending my life savings on you to do. I've only just realised that this couch is not real leather. Now that's cheap.

The door opens and I'm burying my face in an old lady's muff but there's no old lady yet. I sneeze as usual. I say as usual but I don't remember the previous time, I was too young, memory begins at five or something, everything before that's wiped like most of my early TV

536

stuff was wiped thank God. I say as usual because I'm projecting forward, I sneezed every time after that and there were four more times, I was nine when all this stopped. I'm in an enormous hall with black tiles and white tiles I'm not sure about, there are stains all over them, they feel slippy. My mother did not ring the bell or operate the claw-knocker I would have liked to have operated under normal circumstances, she just turned the big knob and walked straight in like she knew the place, like she'd lived here or something. Heugh, she says again, quietly. We wait a little. My mother is keeping her hand on my shoulder and I'm keeping my hands in my pockets, I have this new jacket with soft pockets I was incredibly against wearing because no one around our street wears jackets with frilly collars and cuffs and stuff, let alone knickerbockers. I feel like I'm someone else, in this outfit. I feel my head is balancing very precariously on my collar. I feel like these shoes and these knickerbockers and this frilly green jacket are about to realise their mistake and eject me. OK OK, Moira, I'm getting there, it's only your lunch-break, the Kentucky stays open all day and all night down there where the sirens mewl, it's never not finger-lickin' gross.

My face is so scrubbed I don't know it any more, the loofah's revealed a whole new level I'm still rearranging my features on. My mother is staring at this picture on the wall. There are two pictures, actually, kind of tied together with a ribbon that would chip if you tried to undo it and with the same kind of shit-brown frame that might have been gold or something once and there are bits of the moulding that have fallen away and it's white underneath. We need this detail, Moira. That wasn't your tummy rumbling, it's distant thunder, there's another on the way or maybe it's the old one. It might rain this time. My mother's staring at the picture but there's a glare problem, all I can see is the light through the hall window bouncing off and making me slit-eyed. Then she lifts me up and I see it's not a picture, it's a mirror, because behind the dust there's me grinning out of the glare at me grinning to see me grinning with my hair cut like that and then another me behind me that's grey and is not grinning, oh dear, but that's the only difference between us until I stop grinning which I do right now because I'm scared. I'm staring out like the one next door but that's a girl, she has a ribbon in her hair and pale OK grey eyes. My mother is pointing at the two mes not counting the reflection and saying that's

537

him, dear. That's you. Just do as you were told. No crying, this time. Afterwards I'll buy you a packet of Smarties. Two packets of Smarties. And a lolly. And a Dinky lorry.

I nod with my frilly collar up over my nose because she's still holding me up and the jacket's too big for me and heugh, she puts me down and coughs a little but tries to shut it up because there's an echo, it's like a church, maybe the huge stairs lead up to Heaven. I've just noticed the stairs. My mother's looking at her watch and I'm trying to figure out whether the person looking down from the top of the stairs where they go round all flat and start again higher is real or just another picture. I want to point her out to my mother but I don't want to make the picture come alive, I don't want the picture person to see me pointing at her because frankly she's terrifying, she has black hair shooting out of her scalp and these stains on her apron and big jowls and also my mother's nose. In fact it might be my mother turned into a witch or whatever if my mother wasn't standing right next to me looking at her watch and dusting something off my shoulders at the same time. The person picture at the top of the stairs has something in her hand, it's a cloth, it's the kind of cloth my mother uses to buff our very few buffable objects mainly on the mantelpiece above the gas fire. Also our wireless. Moira's grunting something about buff. Moira, it was my favourite word, I was five, it made my lips go funny and my head jolt. Hey, where were you at the age of five, checking up on your libidinal development or something? Your curtains are dirty, by the way. It's no good having a shiny surgery if your curtains are discoloured. You've been over-handling them in your lunch-hour. You're supposed to lick your fingers for Pete's sake.

The buffing-cloth's moved, it's being shaken, I can't help it I go heugh too and grip my mother's coat-pocket lapel. My mother groans. I feel woozy. The buffing cloth's rippling at us on the end of this arm and a lot of dust comes out and makes its way down slowly over the stairs. The witch is definitely narked about something, her face is screwed up into this paper ball and I want to go, I want out, but my mother says oh Mum and yanks me across the tiles towards this other door, it hasn't changed a lot since we last encountered it, it's still like the lid of a coffin, they're all pretty well ready behind it with their fangs and smoke and clawed hands, the witch is starting to come down the stairs and kind of muttering and spittling at the same time and the more I gaze totally terrified at her the more I see my mother, but stop shifting kind of knowledgeably Moira and get this: she was my mother's mother so there was nothing particularly neurotic about my observation, we should be congratulating my little self on being a perceptive little blighter, I noticed a lot of things aged five.

OK, the door's opening, I don't know whether my mother knocked, she was put off that time by the apparition, the times to come she'll wait until the clocks strike quarter past two, they had their sago very late, it was cold, only Uncle Kenneth sampled it and he's not in there, he has actually dematerialised like he wanted, there's not even a place laid for him now, I hope Sylvia's remembered that, the one time she has to fuck up the continuity on purpose she won't, she's so *reliable*. People are so *reliable*. I'm sorry, Moira, I think I've just broken a castor, just put it on the bill with interest along with my id. Go get your chicken. I don't like the way your lips are moving, like you know what I'm going to say next or something.

Hey, at least we have the door between us and the buffing-cloth, be thankful for small mercies, the fact that everything facing me is probably worse'll just get me nicely in trim for the next six decades, I was trained up young. There's a fire at the other end and there are candles fattening on the table and the curtains are drawn and there's a blank where Uncle Kenneth's pudding plate should be. Well done Sylvia. I don't know why the curtains are drawn, Moira. It's been like that since 1918, the whole house has been like that since 1918 – where there are curtains to draw they are drawn, the indoor plants have a very hard time, it's to do with being plunged in morning according to my mother, but it's the afternoon now, I don't twig it, I just want to get back to the bomb-site and dive-bomb the cats and my chum Monty Rowland with the caliper.

Here here, says Moira. Or a dead ringer for, if you know y'grunts, pardner. But I cain't quit. The scene has me in its sights and its finger ain't goosin'. OK. Cacti off. Dark panelled dining-room on, don't tear it. In front of the fire is this kind of basket with a handle at the back and in this basket there's a shadow. The shadow says, the child? I've just noticed a pair of shiny pumps sticking out of this kind of recess by the way, just a little to the left of the dwarf geranium table which Sylvia's left quite rightly but without the dwarf geraniums, I think I'm going to hug her after this, I need to hug someone standing in for my mother and my wives and my lost love. The shiny pumps might be a spare pair or they might have someone in them, I actually don't want to look, it was the only time they were there because we were early, we'd not waited for the big hand to hit three, normally they were under the head of the table joined to Mr Trevelyan playing Mr Trevelyan. My mother's saying yes ma'am, sorry, but. The shadow is now a sack with a head on it, the firelight's playing behind it, the flames are happy but they burn. I have to walk to the sack. I know this because I was told, we've practised it in the yard even though the washing was out and it was sheets week and every time I walked forward I got a damp ghost attacking my face, it was gusty yesterday, but my mother didn't want to practise outside with all the nervous net curtains and stuff. My mother didn't say walk towards the sack, Moira, she didn't use that term, she was a sensitive woman, she said walk towards the nice old lady in the Bath chair. OK, I can't see the taps but it's dark, the firelight and the candlelight are reminding me of unpleasant things, they were called blackouts Moira, London was badly bombed, you may have heard about our minor role in your country's victory at some time or other, we had a lot of deaths including our charming next-door neighbours, the Jacksons. I'm walking towards the nice old sack with the wobbly head with the help of my mother's palm in the small of my back for the first few feet while my heels are finding very little grip on the parquet but then those weeks of practice tell and I go into automatic, kids are very easily drilled, I'm not even considering the bright green Dinky Foden flat-bed that's coming my way, my legs are just slotting in and there are no damp ghosts sailing to America, there's just the length of a very long table and there's someone else, it's amazing I never noticed her before, she's turning her head as I goose-step behind her chair and she's incredibly lovely, she has grey eyes, she's dressed in white, she's probably an angel, she's much much older than me and each year she got older and more like a grown-up and each year I fell more profoundly in love with her, her name was Victoria, we were half-bloods, she was really my older sister and she would take me away but she didn't. She married some jerk called Halliday, a property agent or something and I got into films, Moira, in case you didn't know this. He died. She didn't. Anyway she was and is my half-aunt and not my sister

540

really. Now I'm haunting her, I'm haunting Mrs Halliday and she doesn't like it any more, she's threatened me with lawyers, the police, the works. I don't know where Victoria has got to, but I found the dress. A part of it. On a nail. I'm sorry about all this emoting, I'll wipe the mucus off your couch if you can lend me a tissue, put it on the bill, the rest of it was in the V&A, it was off-cream, Mrs Halliday had donated it, I held it to my cheek and rocked and the expert with the buffed finger-nails said I wasn't to, could I please leave, he turned very sour suddenly.

Each time she gave me a smile. She hadn't touched her sago. The dress was a little small for her, I think people have generally grown.

There. I think I've completely wrinkled my tear-glands, actually. My ears are wet. Your ceiling is beginning to clear, Moira. It has a cobweb.

I'm there, anyway. I've made it up there. It's OK, the sack is in fact the nice old lady but there are no taps, the water would just drain completely out between the wickerwork, leave alone the bit where her legs come out. I was that sort of kid, I was extremely sceptical at a very early age.

Heugh.

Her arm's up. She's staying like that with all these cracks in her face getting worse in the firelight and my collar itches. I'm just staring at her with my mouth open and scratching my groin. So what's changed? thinks Moira. Great joke, pity you didn't make it, you could do with a sense of humour, honey, like you could do with getting rid of that trouser-suit, they're back in fashion. OK. Her arm comes down and the cracks get really wide and she turns her head. What we'd practised was her saying something about a willow not being afraid and I just had to peck her on the cheek and that was it but instead she talks to the other end of the room.

You're not in your seat, Giles.

This isn't what we'd practised. And I really badly want to widdle. My mother kept asking me if I wanted to widdle all the way here but I didn't want to widdle all the way here, I don't have that big a bladder, you're not laughing, Moira, you're asleep, you're sliding off your swivel chair. Now the widdle's desperate, it's one of those widdles that you can't just enjoy not giving into for about an hour, it has to be instantly obeyed or it stabs you. It is stabbing me. On top of this problem the spare pair of shoes has become a man with white eyes. He's stepping out, he's feeling his way to the chair at the other end of the table and it's OK, he's sitting down, he's not going to take me away to Mars or Transylvania or wherever. The candle flames are sort of in his eyes but there's nothing else in them, he's got them rolled right up better than Des and keeps them there so I widdle. It's amazing how you can widdle silently if it's not into a toilet amplification system – at the end of my large widdle I don't think anyone was the wiser, I really don't, perhaps my knickerbockers were thick enough to absorb, I can't remember, all I remember is terror and shame, Moira. I think you're really getting my money's worth, actually. I hope you're all OK out there. If anyone's left in the last few minutes pity them.

I was warned about the man, of course. I was not allowed to say he was my grandfather. I was not allowed to go oooh at his eyes or say cor blimey, ain't they 'orrible, just like a coupla coddled eggs wivart the shells? I was probably not allowed to wet my pants as soon as he appeared either but that wasn't specifically mentioned. Moira, I just want to show you this clip for a minute, mind your head, there's a great patch of blank wall above your thoughts and hey, howzat, my antique projector just happens to be set up and crankable so here goes.

Flickery shot of Captain Hubert Lightfoot on the edge of a shell hole. I mean a very large crater with a bunch of guys and some pools at the bottom. They're lifting up this guy in a mess on a couple of poles with canvas stretched between which is, Moira, a field-stretcher circa 1917. The guy in a mess is not important. I mean, he is important but not to us, particularly. I'm not paying him more than a half-day basic, anyway, despite the two hour make-up job, the budget's crazy. OK. Gas. That's someone shouting gas who's not in a very good way, he's stumbling towards the crater but it's not easy, he kind of fits in with the general landscape which took a lot of time and effort to get this bad, it's like NASA's moonwalk practice room times about one million and wet. Captain Hubert Lightfoot shouts gas very robustly but he doesn't take cover in the shell-hole like you or I would, he's sensible, he's not a dickhead who thinks that gas isn't heavier than air. The guy in a mess I'm afraid slides back down and screams because his protruding shin-bone catches on somebody's belt while the bunch of guys basically panics. Or it looks like they panic. We should have some floral titles soon because their lips are having a tough time from their teeth. Here they are. There's no piano accompaniment, I'm afraid. This is not Charlie Chaplin.

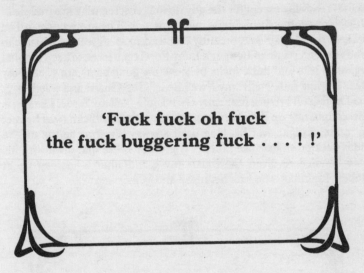

'Fuck fuck oh fuck
the fuck buggering fuck . . . ! !'

Basically they're getting their gas helmets out of their gas packs like they've been trained to do using official stages one to seven except that the stages have got cinched together and there's this guy screaming and no one's shouting out the numbers and it's musical chairs, there are always some quarterblokes who've forgotten both and even more halfblokes who've forgotten their spares – in the few seconds it takes Captain Lightfoot to hide his pencil moustache and assorted features behind some big goggles and rubber tubing, the bunch have become a gaggle of yelling yobs. Amongst them is Second Lieutenant Giles Trevelyan. He's yelling but his yelling is not panic, it's control. He's given his spare helmet to this really thick oick from some other regiment who happened to land up in the same crater, don't ask me why, I don't even know what the fuck's going on here exactly except that they were lifting out this guy in a mess who's still screaming and it was probably this screaming that kind of stirred up the panic when some gas shells were dropped, although I didn't notice these gas shells dropping at the beginning, maybe they were off the spool. Someone's cooking some onions somewhere, imagine. My grandfather's got his helmet in his hand but this other hand grabs it for God's sake, there's not even a tussle, it's just yanked away, the onions have had a whole clove of garlic added, my grandfather is now the only person with his face still showing except for the guy no longer screaming in a puddle of possibly yes definitely his blood and some sick. The former post-office clerk with early hair-loss recently engaged to an expecting typist who sends the creep a tin of Benger's Baby Food each week to keep his vital organs in trim and thick socks because my gum-boots are v. cold my Dear Darling little Nellie my Sweetheart God Guard and watch over you Darling till I return home my Own Little Nell my Sweet Darling is now clambering up the side of the crater with his officer's gas helmet not quite gastight over his face until anyway his arms go up and he slides back down because Hubert Lightfoot's shot him dead with his ivory-handled revolver. Obviously my grandfather is looking up at Hubert Lightfoot who lifts his mask and yells.

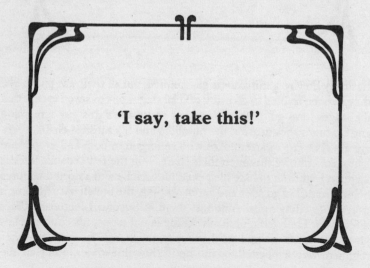

'I say, take this!'

I hope you don't mind these floral titles, we have smells but still no sound except my heavy breathing. There's more dramatic action in this clip than in the whole of my long life, it's like a day out with the Knights of the Round Table or the Houston coke cartel, it's called living dangerously or maybe just all at once.

A gas helmet's flying through the air, heading into the crater. Hubert Lightfoot definitely threw it although the film's got bad hop and some terrible tramlines. We're jogging through this practically frame by frame now, the moving image is for the moment broken right down to its bare essentials so as the thing curves or maybe jerks through the air you can see that there is DEFINITELY NOTHING LEAVING IT THAT SHOULDN'T and anyway it's a nice *hommage* to Godard, it's the killing of Kennedy on Kodak, it's *Blow-Up* with me old mate David Hemmings oh where is he now? Jog, jog, jog. What's that flying out, mate? A speck of dust on the celluloid. A wake of I'm afraid a boat over Loch Ness. The President's important bits of brain.

Jog.

Jog.

And jog.

Whatever's behind's swished right out but it's only mud and the helmet's all over the place, we lose it for a second, shit, you try shifting a hand-crank smoothly in a mustard gas attack, guv. King of Gases, King of Gases, mustard. Right royal persistent little fucker. A fist's coming up and it converts to fingers.

They're Second Lieutenant Trevelyan's. They catch it. He didn't stick at silly mid-off and last domino all his school career for nothing. We're on fairly normal speed now. This onion and garlic fry up is getting ridiculous, I feel like waving it away, maybe you've farted, Moira. Maybe it's thinking too hard about that Kentucky Fried.

How can I be *so gross* at this juncture?

Phew. He's pulled the thing on, he's biting the rubber, his nose-clip's

545

clipped, he's got half a gallon of saliva and nasal mucus with nowhere to go, he feels sick with the flange pressing back his tongue like this, he pushes the thing out from behind his teeth with his tongue and it squashes his nose but he's sitting there calmly with the other chaps looking like a dry-run for something by Wells and the oh fucks have practically given out like the last little shuddery kind of sobs. The guy in a mess is dead. There is absolutely nothing different about the air or the light but there is. Flickery close-up of my grandfather's eyes encircled by metal and rubber. They're blinking. The onion and garlic is kind of mildly irritating them. He places a finger on the glass of his eyepiece but jabs his eyeball. He feels the same lurch that you'd feel if you placed your nose against the unusually clear perspex of a 747 porthole as it was lifting off the runway and you had to pull your head back in fast out of the draught minus your toupée. He lifts his mask away from his mouth.

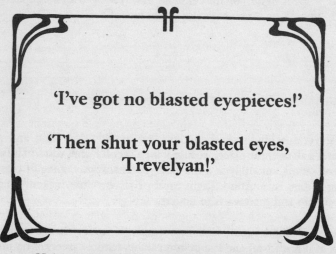

'I've got no blasted eyepieces!'

'Then shut your blasted eyes, Trevelyan!'

That was Hubert. Flickery film spools out to white just before we can tell whether Captain Lightfoot is guffawing evilly up there on the lip of the crater. Nothing is crystal clear but I have to say that for the second time in this movie *j'accuse* because hey, I'm Rick the dick, I've put several things together and they click, I don't think Hubert Lightfoot was making a helpful suggestion or anything although it's just possible because closed lids help. He must have got his lips blistered shouting it

because he lifted his respirator away from his mouth like I had to lift my
respirator away from my mouth each time I kissed my parents goonight in
the Anderson, I had this allergy to warm rubber, it made me look like I
was an early shaver using war-issue laundry soap. Holy shit, I'm
beginning to think that the main handle in this movie might have been
Evostuck and'll come off in the boiling water of your relentless scrutiny.
Maybe Hubert Lightfoot was a hero and not a vengeful bastard after all,
maybe he deserved his posthumous VC for doing something incredibly
useful like trying to shave a pillbox bristling with machine-guns with only
five men and his gumboots a couple of days later, I don't know. Shit.
Anyway, no one leant my grandfather their eyepieces. A hell of a lot of
mustard-gas shells must have been plopped because within half an hour
his eyes were tingling and within an hour his tear-glands were working
overtime and his eyeballs were stinging frightfully and he had a headache
and could only whisper. By the time he'd got himself to the First-Aid post
which was a slightly deeper ditch than the others with FIRST-AI on a
post and some blankets and a doc with blood instead of gloves and
serious stubble his eyelids were bladderdash balls and he was weeping
pus. It gets worse. By the time he crawled into the medical marquee
behind the lines the conjuctiva at the interpalpebral aperture was
projecting between his bladderdash balls and fighting it out with his
palpebral conjunctiva for space, it looked very distressing as my
mother used to say. By the time the doc got a look at his cornea – which
was not easy because Second Lieutenant um um ah Trevelyan was
now severely photophobic and the slightest inky-dinky particle of light
got his eyelids blepharospasming which for you dumbos too young to
have read line by line the *Air Raid Precautions Handbook No. 3 (Medical
Treatment of Gas Casualties) Price 6d Keep It With You At All Times*, son,
means that they shut tight despite their oedematous and septic
situation – it the cornea please follow was grey and hazy and in about
three hours went as orange as the vomit on the edge of his bed because,
hey, he could never find the bowl quick enough and anyway his
laryngitis and headache and gastric pain and septic skin-blisters made
him want to die let alone the nausea, so the little ginger-haired nurse
with the nail scissors told him off for missing each time totally
fruitlessly.

Moira's gone out. I think she might have gone out to get her Kentucky
Fried. I hope she brings back some grapes for my grandfather but
washes them first, you never know what agent they might have applied.

OK, you're all on tragedy-overload, I know, boats tip over and planes crash and schools get sludged and there's famine and slaughter and rape and plague but to put you right into the medical picture I just have to tell you that he got severely ulcerated corneas and was one of the very small minority to suffer total loss of vision from mustard gas, he was unfortunate, he might have stuck around and got his head blown off like Willoughby-Vern or serious brain damage like poor old Barstow had already got in the first minute of the First Day of the Somme, yup, the really serious drooly kind which left Trevels wondering what the point of existence was as he walked out between these cleverly-clipped rose-beds on a fine spring day a few months before without a stick or a zigzag because, God, Barsity was a terrific chum and still is if only he could do more than dribble on the pillow and say heugh now and again.

Heugh.

Where was I, Moira?

Wet, cold, scared. But I'm not up to my knock-knees in a scummy pool of this 1917 shit-hole, my Darling, my Sweetheart, I'm talking 1945, this is nearly six months into peacetime, this is London about to have a ball under Cripps and it's drizzling. My soaked groin is getting pressed against the basket with the nice old morning lady's hand on the back of my head kind of thrusting my face into her neck which smells like the dead mouse I've kept for a month in a matchbox as an experiment. Both are kind of sticky and yellow with this lacy stuff over them and I'm wondering if it's because it's the afternoon that she's decaying, I've always been the speculative type, I want to be a ministry scientist when I grow up and save the world from diseases and Martians and darkies. I'm sorry about the darkies aspect, I am only five, I am still catching things off my dad who is always right. My dad is the same in the afternoon as he is in the morning so I don't have a lot of evidence to go on. My face unpeels from the neck and I can't help it, I wipe my mouth on my sleeve which is a neverever as my mother keeps saying.

Now the photo, Moira. Moira. Please keep your eyes open when you eat. I'm paying you to keep your eyes open at least.

I can see there's this photograph of me. It's on the table but cupped by the hand that isn't circling around looking for impetigo or whatever on the back of my head which is of course shaved to the bone and permanently chapped I suppose from exposure. The terrifying man at the other end clears his throat, he seems to have a problem, he makes funny little raspy noises like our old dog who's dead, son, dead as a nit. I was never coddled, Moira, I was never coddled. Hard-boiled, maybe. Scrambled definitely.

This photo in the other hand is the type that if you dropped it it'd break – we have one at home of my mother looking young and beautiful about three hundred years ago on our mantelpiece, it's jenwin paw shlin and don't you lay a paw shlin on it, son. I'm really hoping the nice old lady with the decaying neck'll be careful with this thing because it's me, it's me in an even toffer outfit leaning on this pillar with a plant on the top and not really smiling and I'm a bit older at this juncture, which is clever. I'm wondering through the crackle of her fingers on my shaved nape if my face in the photo is going to move like hers is moving but it doesn't, it stays exactly as it is and I stay exactly as I am.

As I always have done, Moira. Leave me your thumbs to lick, at least.

And then her fingers find my impetigo just when she looks into my brown eyes so close I'm practically knocked out by the fumes on her breath like I knocked out the mouse and she says it.

So I jerk back instead of looking sweet, this time. Every other time to come when she says it I'll look as sweet as you look right now but without the frown, Moira, without the frown under your eyebrows and the grease all over your cheeks.

Ah Willo, Willo, don't be afraid.

But because I jerk, this time, she jerks too and her cracks kind of bunch up into one and the photo gets gripped so tightly I'm afraid for it and then worse-than-Des-as-Blind-Pew at the other end of the table starts singing softly about willows and a bosom and a knee and the nice cracked lady goes *sssht* so that dribble buzzes the sago and side-slips the nude lady next to the salt and prangs into one of the candle flames

549

which ducks for a second but Blind Pew doesn't sssht, he hisses *what the Devil is there to be afraid of, Mother?*

And, OK, I explode into snivels because I am so afraid. But not the other times. The other times I'll be damaged enough, Moira honey. Time's up? Too bad. You've got grease on your sapphires.

We haven't done the silver salver routine. Aw hell.

We haven't even started watching the rest of the rushes.

I'm almost sixty.

Sixty. That's incredible.

Sorry, folks, I was mumbling at the back, people like that are extremely irritating. IT'S GREAT BEING SIXTY, HIYA, THANKS FOR ALL THE BIRTHDAY GIFTS, I'VE BEEN CRAVING FIFTY-EIGHT CAST-IRON BOOT SCRAPERS SENSITIVELY REPRODUCED FROM THE ORIGINAL VICTORIAN MODEL FOR MANY YEARS NOW AND THE NINETY-THREE DISCREETLY PERSONALISED EDWARDIAN SPIRIT FLASKS WILL COME IN VERY USEFUL ON ALL THOSE SPORTING OCCASIONS, THANK YOU VERY MUCH. YOU'RE ALL SO INCREDIBLY IMAGINATIVE.

It was too long, that room was too long. You've no idea how long it went on for. I'm very glad it was divided for the dental surgery. If I can just finish. Thank you. I did this only six years running according to my mother on her deathbed and the next four times we did it properly all the way down from the attic because the witch was locked away, and because that was practically the first time my mother was really talking about this very important thing I'd thought maybe was a B thriller or even chiller in the Enfield Ritz that I had badly suppressed all this time I got up out of the chair and held her upper arm very delicately and lovingly and would have hugged her, naturally, if I knew it wouldn't have made her scream. Because she was already gripping that wooden bar thing on chains freely supplied on demand by the National Health Service in those days, you're supposed to yank yourself into a sitting position with it so you can tuck into your cauliflower cheese while your loving sons and daughters arrange the pillows behind your back but she was using it to get her body up and out of the pain while I just kind of watched with my mouth open like I was watching a *Rin Tin Tin* rerun or something but this was my mother, this was not a *Rin Tin Tin* rerun or something – this was the dying of the person who gave birth to me and suckled me and gave me meals and held my head when it hurt or stroked my forehead when I was being sick and took me out to the pictures holding my hand because I didn't choose the pound, I chose the ticket, the first movie I ever saw was *Great Expectations* which was crazy with a big iron gate in it and there were sandbags in the lobby and a guy with a black moustache on his mouth and gold moustaches on his shoulders showing me and my mother our seats, it made me stay in my seat with my mouth open for longer than anything else in my five years of life had ever done, especially more than going to speak to God in the place that smelt of rubber boots did. Then she lowered herself back onto the pillow and sighed and I let go her arm and stroked her forehead but she winced so I didn't ask any more questions, I decided to wait a bit, I got Des and me a cup of tea at his helpful suggestion and when I came back upstairs I'd forgotten the sugar because I always forget my brother takes sugar apparently so I went downstairs and tried to get my feelings about Des separated from my feelings about Mother and when I went upstairs with the sugar bowl she'd fallen asleep and before she could wake up to look at me one last time trying not to think really negatively about Des she'd started that weird kind of shunting thing with her breath with a name like a short and probably really crabby headmaster of a lousy public school but it's the guy who invented it and it means the final curtain, it's like the credits going up all the way to the bit about *Sweets & Soft Drinks are Available for Your Refreshment in the* and the doctor came in and pulled off his George Orwell spectacles and told Des while I tried to get into the doctor's sight-line too this thing about the weird breathing like he'd just made a guinea on the two o'clock at Aintree or something, which he probably had as a matter of fact, he cleaned his spectacles on the edge of his jacket really vigorously, there was dandruff stuck to the ear-clasps, I couldn't ever imagine him dying, he hooked them back on and hummed to himself and adjusted the Gough's Stalactite Caves Cheddar ashtray on my mother's dressing-table like it had been a couple of inches too far to the left for thirty-five years and there was this dust and a curly black hair where it had previously been which I don't think he noticed even though he looked up kind of frowning. I think he thought because I was dressed like an existentialist I didn't care about my mother so he didn't make an effort to soothe me at all and Des by that time was phoning whoever you phone, he's a great organiser, he came back in and he and the doctor had this very organisational conversation I didn't understand and then the doctor said he'd be back straightaway but I don't remember anything else very clearly except nodding and having this used hairbrush down my throat I couldn't swallow while Des talked very impressively. I don't know how I can watch the rest of these rushes. Maybe I should get my razor and wrap up on that shot of my grandmother's hairstyle loosening up. We have so much to get through. We have to plot out really carefully this scene with Hubert Lightfoot and the gas helmet, we have to get the right kind of gas helmet or there'll be about fifty letters a day from gas helmet experts who go to gas helmet conferences and swap rubber flanges and nose-clips or whatever, we have to get that take right first time because eyes are eyes are eggs, you can't de-coddle them or put the shells back on bit by bit like you can't ever put my grandmother back again by not watching the rest of the rushes. I have to accept that. I have to accept that she's very cross and hates me and is standing at the top of the stairs in her stained apron between the stuffed lemur and the fern for ever, I really have to accept that, I really do, because she loved my mother. And as I said to Maura I mean Moira the fact that she loved my mother so much is a very impressive thing, it's even noble really, and her hate was kind of noble too, Moira's murmuring standard archetypes, I ignore her even though it's incredible that she should say something, she has flakes just of batter I hope all over her neck, I carry on as usual, I say how there was no going back on this love because once it had turned to hate there was only the standing at the top of the stairs and the looking out of the long landing window by the stuffed lemur there for hours and weeks and years until the morning the neighbour with the Kenneth Williams nose noticed you could see her feet. Maura wouldn't understand this, she said did anyone put their hand on my knee during one of these movies. I said hey, I looked up and I saw her at the top of the stairs looking down very cross and hating me because I had taken away her daughter finally in a manner of speaking, she was clearly mentally unbalanced by everything, she was holding a buffing-cloth but five years running everything I touched left dust on my hands, everything was either sticky or dusty, there were these candles burning but there was still no shine anywhere except off the eye-whites and on the ape's forelip which hasn't featured yet and off my new shoes and at the corners of my great-grandmother's mouth and stuff if you don't count the silver salver of course, that comes with the ape's forelip – hey, it was the kind of light Mike Avens'd come back from the grave for. I would have noticed that, Moira – my mother was very particular with our very few polishable objects. I learnt how to buff off of her in fact, my bronzed Oscars are much shinier than Spielberg's, I know in which compass direction to apply the leather and how to breathe at the end and how to kind of flick away the fog so this face looms up. I also know how to lay a ten-course table for civilised people with incredibly refined taste and inflatable stomachs, I know where to place the thing that tips the plate so you don't waste the melted butter after your asparagus *c.i.f. Londun* steam-tugged off of a big ship that very same dawn and carted straight onto the slippery-lippery cobbles of Covent Garden fresh as a daisy guv has been swallowed silently. I know how to apply eyewash without wasting a drop. I know a lot of things you people don't know for that matter.

I hope you people appreciate that. I'm waving from the back row. Hi there. It was a great party. My mother and my grandmother'll be clearing up, relax, we have a lot of scenes to tail out, my crew are waiting for me as usual, they're amazing, I underestimated them, they're still up to their pips in blood and water and Mike is already out there in the barbed wire walking steadily forward with his funny cardboard thing over the exact point my great-uncle landed a shell on his scalp and Mike carries on walking straight through the barbed wire because once he gets an idea in his head you can't stop him, nothing'll stop him, he'll keep on going now until the mist and smoke swallow him up forever and I'm crying, there's a fly on the wall, the light's superb, it's light through water streaming over my patio glass and the fly just stays there with the light streaming over it like a waterfall and Mike's disappeared, he'd really appreciate the subtlety of the light on the little wings so I won't swipe it, I'll let it roam over the faces and bodies of my grandparents and the really staggering epic sweep of the war scenes if I can find the cans because we've shot the establishing stuff, between *matter* and *I hope you* about a minute ago we actually got to shoot a hundred yards of guys struggling over parapets and lifting up into the air and very gradual pans of blacknesses with these lights rising and falling slowly now and again on a hand-crank. We may not use any of it but who knows, who knows. I'm so tired. I've stopped crying now. I threw Moira out of the window and came straight back but she's used to it, she has a safety net to stop anyone on the sidewalk getting flattened. I'm wiping my swollen eyes so I can see better but it's still crazed because of the rain, the weather's terrible, the helicopter's taking off in a storm and my hand around the whisky is moving slowly underwater. Actually, I don't think anyone including my neighbour's been out on the golf course for a week. The divots are full of frog-spawn or a chemical leak from Mexico or somewhere, maybe it's something they put on the grass, they're kind of sudding over and it's the same with the bunkers, the water in the bunkers has got this weird frothy stuff on it like they're modelling for the Third Battle of Ypres sequence but they're all the wrong shape and the new Niteplay floodlights show them up really clearly, OK, thank you, we'll let you know, I want my shell craters to be round and silvery under the Very lights and shell bursts and stuff like some age-challenged nose-dribbling manservant's tripped up with a big stack of silver salvers buffed to mirror-glass by my grandmother or something, the flood-lights are shielded somewhat by the streaming rain which explains the waterfall on the wall and all over this room and my gutters are playing, I dunno, *Indeterminable Variations for Twelve French Canadian Lead Conduits #XXXII* by John Milton Cage Jnr extremely proficiently given they are solidly American and plastic. The air is miasmic as a matter of fact, there are lots of pretty fatal illnesses hanging around in it, the skeeters don't have enough needles to go round so they re-use them on my ankle-bones. HCDVA's had three power cuts and the brand-new CD-ROM unit with its General Houston paunch roof is a swimming-pool which I think is a much better idea but Dean Lazenby doesn't agree, he's quite upset about it actually, he says it has nothing to do with General Houston's paunch problems, it's a Frank Lloyd Wright reference making play with the concepts of ingressive growth and textual creatressism that was not sealanted good. I'm having to push the sound up really high because it's loud out there, there's a lot of indeterminate music being created but we haven't time to hum along, my grandfather's in molestation mode and my grandmother's remem-bering what her Sis told her which is that if a young gentleman wants to have his way boing boing remember to take your clothes off and fold back the bed-cover and put a handkerchief under your bottom or it's

554

extra work after. I'm sorry about this, Sis was only trying to be of assistance, she knows the score, she was in service herself until the Soap Works needed to replace her grandmother in the boiling-room which was better remunerated if a little less comfortable. A little advice goes a very long way sometimes, some people base their whole conduct on a little advice given at a crucial life-stage like your first day at school or your first day at college or your first day in the office or your first day tucked up in the terminal ward – hey, there's always some lifewise person ready to grab your elbow and yell something at you in your sensitive ear you'll bring up all those decades later in your retirement speech after they've handed over the office Warhol's rollerball-and-ink of The Exterior of the Main Building By Day Signed Andy in a clip-on frame for forty-five years of complete subservience you'll smash the corner off of staggering home on petrol substitute from California wondering if maybe you took that little long-ago advice a little seriously because even the senior executive's representative sniggered but then he's only young with spots. Hey, I'm not expecting a gold watch next month. I'll be very lucky if I get a farewell party because the only other person retiring is the totally bald assistant security officer I'm very frightened of actually, he still challenges me very sharply after all this time, all the other departures are non-essential layouts or layoffs or louts or whatever, they're just going to kind of slink away. Nothing much is happening up there, by the by the by, they're just looking kind of blank with water streaming over their faces and clothes and their hands are wondering what to do with themselves other than cover their owners' faces. At least my grand-mother's stopped nodding but not quick enough to save her hairstyle, which is tumbling over her shoulders and practically down to her waist and certainly down to my Congo poof if you count the waterlight effect – I cannot believe that it could've been so incredibly long when you think how neat it looked on her head, it's like it's grown instantly and her face is very small inside it, it's like she's disappearing behind this black curtain and my grandfather hey ho nonny nonny no is parting it, he's got a hand in there and he's just holding back this raven curtain of hair and waterlight and he doesn't say anything, he just clears his throat and then his Adam's apple kind of squeezes up and pops into view from behind his tie. The face inside the curtain seems anxious now, the blank look has been replaced by this fairly anxious kind of unstable one which isn't just the terrible weather here because let's face it my grandmother has committed probably the biggest never ever

555

outside of stealing a silver fork which is to strike your employer or close relation of. Meanwhile my grandfather's feeling this great bond with this person because of the kiss, he can still taste her mouth, it seemed frightfully easy and straightforward and it's still sending out jolly pleasant warm types of ripples all the way to his toes and his top-knot across which the fly is now walking and out onto the out-of-focus window beyond and on to his huge mouth suddenly because he's smiling gently. Hey, fooled ya. He'd smile gently in a Merchant Livery but he's not in a Merchant Livery he's in a Richard Thornby and going places. This rain is remarkable. Voices float up again from the garden as voices only ever floated up from the garden in those days and Giles the sexually-aroused glances at the window with the fly on his eye. Actually, I'm getting irritated by this fly. But it has this connection with Mike now I can't shake off, it might be Mike come back with compound lenses for eyes and a pair of wings for the aerials. Leave it.

I forgot to say incidentally that instead of smiling gently and getting the hard-hat housewives of Ohio swooning and immediately telebooking their UK trip Oxford-Stratford-London-Solihull food poisoning and coach crash included Giles my grandfather frowned. God knows why he frowned, let him frown, he probably doesn't even know he's frowning although he's finished with his glance towards the window beyond which the floating voices are no longer being relayed by Bosey on the cherry-picker who suffers from vertigo for crying out loud so get him down, get him down, I'm shouting through my cupped hands because we're post-megaphone, it's too late, I'm watching the rushes, I'm in Houston in the monsoon season and there are probably twelve bloated golfers floating past if only I had the courage to shield my eyes and look, it's all wrapped and in the can, it's way too late, my grandfather is already taking my grandmother in his hands and breaking her up in a manner of speaking, he nosedives into her nape under the black curtain and takes a deep breath of the pheromones situated there while Milly my grandmother stares with really wide eyes at some mould in the shape of Borneo on the wall, she's being jogged around a little by this head sucking or whatever at her neck. I wish I knew what she was wondering. Because my grandfather has some minor acne at the end of its cycle on his right forelip and isn't too adept with his cutthroat yet she's probably feeling a bit of roughness and also some warm maybe wettish exhalations on her jugular as he breathes in and out very deeply. A part of her is probably also wishing she could join her Sis in front of the Soap Works' boiling pans in spite of the caustic soda suds and jets of steam and sudden hisses and burbles and occasional unfortunate disfigurements and horrible smell and having to go up the clang-clang ladder and stuff and the fact that the one day she replaced her poorly grandmother it reminded her of what was to come to the sinful herd into which one is at every single instant of one's earthly breath within one and one only plucked hair's breadth of being tugged into save the Lord. The mould of Borneo is becoming her sister's face shouting to take every article off and turn the bed-cover back in front of a huge boiling pan Sis'll fall into at the age of fifty-one in the Year of Suez, it'll get a mention on the front page of the *Worksop Weekly Post* but they'll spell the name wrong a year before the Soap Works' official closure and the dismantling of the boiling pans and five and a half years before the last person to know the one about the little grey curly-wurly right in the middle of the cake of yellow De Luxe tells it during the Worksop Ex-Soap Works Workers' Weekly Social and upsets a distant relation of mine. Now my grandfather has emerged from the curtain and removes a strand of it from his lip. God he tries to comment but the word gets caught up with his Adam's apple and comes out like a cough and he has to swallow again. Now he's smiling a bit because he's embarrassed by this high register cough and his breath is too big for his lungs, he needs lungs like eighteenth-century iron-smelting bellows operated by donkeys or whatever. Every time he breathes in he's getting what can only be described as a succulent helping of Milly the maidservant's personal fumes and there's something very sweet in there which if he wasn't standing under the mental and in my case visual equivalent of the Victoria Falls would recall the lawn newly mown by Jeremiah or maybe the bluebells around the nymph's pool after an April shower, something erotically poetic or poetically erotic anyway which would not explain the eighteenth-century iron-smelting process going on in his groin. I have to be absolutely straightforward about this: he's basically right up and running now, he's bolted, his flannels are under strain, he'd need to be high-pressure hosed by melt-water pumped straight out of the East Siberian Sea or something to slow him down and get his tie looking at least straight. The point is that her neck was not just a divine rose-garden at dawn it was soft and very fairly pleasantly warm and he did actually feel the blood beating beneath his lips but hey, only the flickeriest flicker of that Dracula picture he saw with Uncle Kenneth at the Bioscope entered his head at that moment and was instantly

557

outscreened by the Battle of the Alamo flashing away in his forebrain and which is still flashing away right now while his eyeballs take in Milly the maidservant's blouse's slightly lowered neckline because he is only three buttons away from bliss now, the bud is a rose is a rose and the nymph raises her hands to be pursued through lime grove and thicket to her pool in the woods where Echo calls and calls and Pitys turns into a fir-tree and Syrinx whispers from the reed-bed, the tallest and loveliest reed of them all – hey, he's not really thinking all this while his palms get to find the knobbly bits on her shoulders fairly exciting and his thumbs feel the collar-bones are pretty alarming even through the pleats, it's what he wrote down afterwards in green ink in the bald light of the breaking day in the small shed with the torn tennis nets and the freshly-oiled croquet mallets and Jeremiah's trays of scrunchlings he and Willo'd giggle over for obvious reasons in the far-off innocent days and which I spilt some Tesco's Instant Arabian Gut-Ache over at Mrs Halliday's in '93 my hand was trembling so much. I was upset, I mopped it extremely delicately with my British Airways throw-away personal face-freshener I'd kept for my weird son-of-godson's cabin handouts wall collection but it was OK, the ink was so old it was permanent if it wasn't permanent before, my half-aunt won't know the blemish is not period in the extremely unlikely event of her opening the diary because she is totally disinterested in her father's intimate life, it's like the fact that she does not know about my grandmother. Once he'd met Elspeth Marjorie Clinch at the end of a long corridor in St Thomas's in 1935 he was taken in hand, he was plucked out of the gloom of that dreadful house with its unhinged domestics and all the shutters perpetually shut, Mr Thornlight, for reasons to do with the war and grief, the first one I mean, and he and Mama bought a dear little flat in South Kensington cross-cut to me nodding and fade.

Crap. I was there. You were there. I am not Mr Thornlight but little Dick Thornby, you smiled at me just once a year, I had a big wet leaf once stuck to my shoe, my mother hadn't noticed, it had survived the brutal interrogation of the doormat, it came off on the parquet, you gave a little giggle, your father tilted his head enquiringly and I felt this flush, you looked so lovely and kind in that yellowing dress, in the candlelight, I was deeply attracted to you, you had such lovely grey eyes because in those days you didn't wear thick bifocals, oh his hand on her bosom, his head on her knee, sing willow, willow, willow!

OK, OK: I didn't say it. I didn't take a high-dive into her calm and rock her off her inflatable with my belly-flop yarooooouch. Pink halo time, Mike, breathe on the lens. Thank you. Elspeth read books to my grandfather and he played her Rachmaninov on the pianola and'd pop out for his aromatic Turkish dark twice a week and once a year in grim November this little snot-nosed scamp'd take him out to the pictures or vice versa, it was never quite clear to Victoria probably, dear dear Victoria, who liked Papa's eyeballs the way they were and took him for long walks in her best white kid gloves. She was and is a very proper person with my nose. If she's out there – SORRY, AUNT VICTORIA if you don't mind me calling you that, just this once. Comfort her, give her a hug and a highball or something, take her out for some air, hey, I haven't got all day.

She's out? She's stopped trying to rip up my screen? OK.

He was knocked over by a bus, for God's sake. It slew him before the days of bleeping pelicans, blimey, never saw him guv, just stepped straight out under me nose, came straight outa that posh baccy shop and wallop, won't never get over it. Clip of some archive stuff of big red London buses and those terrible coats. Clip of a vicar with one of those terrible haircuts throwing some soil in and Victoria helpless with grief yelling Daddy, Daddy, oh my daddy. Fade, because the Thornbys weren't invited or anything but it was OK, the Enfield Ritz was a whole lot easier on the nerves.

Now go see the still of Mrs Halliday waving her hand at me. It's right at the bottom under the one of the croquet match I didn't bother you with because we cut that scene, it went on and on, my grandfather came last and William ribbed him and Agatha won as usual despite her dress, you try operating a croquet mallet in a long summer dress of this period, the swing between your knees is severely affected, she was a remarkable person, she nursed soldiers with stuff like I dunno fractured olecranons and cross paralysis and corrosives poisoning and lacerated pretty well everything it's possible to get lacerated and remain alive and how to bandage every part of the body right up to the little fingertip without looking in her *British Red Cross Society First-Aid Manual No. 1* all the time which I'm afraid I took, it has her name in pencil on the front, she's underlined some bits and I like looking at the bits she's underlined, Mrs Halliday won't miss it, it's just a crummy little soiled contusion-blue clothback with the pages falling out and there's nothing about Spanish ladies but I think it was in her pocket when she keeled over in the corridor with a sputum jug in her hand they had to deal with very carefully because the lid came open and the stuff was purulent, the mops were out, the place stank of Trevelyan's Carbolic Acid Solution Invaluable In Our Present Emergency Ideal for the Tropics Be Safe Be Sure Says Leading Nurse In One Of Our Foremost Teaching Hospitals as she was carried away on a blanket because, hey, the stretchers couldn't keep up with the cases, tens of thousands of people were keeling over and dying and William got turned into a lower jaw and maybe the phalange of his little finger before the news got through to him, it was a terrible week for my relations, the bells were ringing and people were whooping and fireworks were banging and Mrs Trevelyan was on her bed staring up at the ceiling with a touch of the influenza herself watching a fly negotiate two of her children waving over Evelyn's golden head just where the hairline crack behind the light-flex started to open dreadfully frightfully wide. Mrs Halliday could be waving hallo too but she's actually telling me not today, not today, we are indisposed or words to that effect. The pavement slabs are the ones right outside her house where I'd crouched behind some uncollected burst bin-bags with a scarf around my nose to filter out the odours unfortunately for the return from her daily outing to Tesco's, it was a little aggressive of me but it didn't work, I stood up and forgot to lower my gas scarf, she started to shout and the street's Neighbourhood Watch scheme dropped from the trees, I spent about three days in hospital with a bald Securicor guard sitting on the end of my bed and telling me about his poetry just in case I released myself, I got absolutely no compensation when my jaw worked enough to explain the situation, England really terrifies me, it's full of big slobbering dogs only just keeping their owners in check and mothers on leads, if I smile at the kids they report me, I have to go round like a bit-part in *Return of the Zombies* or risk an interactive complication. Aw hell, let's haul up for a second and count dead glasses, folks. Go bring to bay some highballs for y'hangovers and eye the dead ringer for Ricky's nose. Go see the still. It's good for your circulation. I hope you've been circulating anyway in the breaks. I have some very interesting friends and I have some relatives too. Aw hellsapoppin. Here come the tumbleweeds a-blowin'.

Welcome back. It's still raining. I've stood outside, I'm cooled down, it's safe for you to come out from behind the chairs now. Click 'n whirr. If you need this detail, I hope you notice that exactly one tear has made it over the top of my grandmother's right lower eyelid, it's broken through the oil barrier and the lash barrier and once the oil barrier has been broken through you're pretty well crying, it's to do with films and suspension, if it wasn't for the oil barrier we'd be going around with tears hanging off of our chins the whole time. There's another one just above that fucking fly and now they've got it in extreme close-up, the tear I mean, it makes the fly look like a miniscule foreign body, I can always rely on Mike and sometimes on Gordon. These physical details speak volumes, son. While I was shuffling for a position at Robert's feet he spoke one day, he spoke about involuntary actions, he said the hands *par exemple* get a cigarette to your lips without you knowing it, you find the cigarette in your lips and light it, hands are mainly their own masters like your bodily secretions are their own masters – hey, my movie will be the first movie to show war as basically a great quickener of bodily secretions, the First World War was the most bodily secretory yet, it was incredible, the classic opening shot'll be of

562

this glittering saliva string as Second Lieutenant G. S. A. Trevelyan
lifts his gas helmet at the end of gas drill and snucks out the rubber
flange and the nose-clip with about a pint of nasal mucus attached and
that's just for starters, he's still in fucking Aldershot, wait till we get to
the Continent, mate, just you bleedin' wait you bleedin' bleeders etc.
Hey, I'm going to slow-pan this Vista Vision cavalry attack over long
autumn grass at dawn and follow it up with a panaglide of these humps
with a brown liquid oozing out of their unlaced breeches the dungflies
really go for. I'm going to have a very long held shot of this guy walking
away to the water-point with a billy can like Bresson had this very long
held shot of this guy walking away with an old lantern in *Lancelot du Lac*
except my guy's muddier and has a limp and is singing over and over
again until it's so distant even Bosey gives the thumbs up and takes the
windshield off the mike

> O Mary Anne
> fill up the can
> for your honour, John Reilly,
> is dry

and then when he's just a kind of khaki nick in this extremely broad
vista of mud he'll stop because that's the water-point and the wind'll be
sounding and there'll be this faint kind of gonging and from right to
left something'll scrim the light a little floating across and he won't
come back, we'll just hold that shot so still you'll realise the nick is no
longer upright and you've already forgotten the song.

OK, the secretory aspect in that last shot is fairly concealed but you get
my drift, guv, you get my drift. Hey, my grandfather is now wiping away
the tears from my grandmother's face. She would really like to be in
front of the boiling pans instead of right here under the rainlight on my
plain wall. My grandfather smells of tobacco and biscuits and linseed
oil, he's been oiling the croquet mallets this afternoon following that
croquet game we cut. There's also some tangy sweat around even
though he's changed since the croquet. Right now Agatha and my
great-uncle are playing croquet verbally with my great-grandmother
who suspects something's up, they're in the drawing-room and Julie
Patchouli's in charge, she's doing just fine, the canteen staff are not
drunk and Willo's struck cheek has just about returned to its normal
tint and he's not angry, he's just pretty dashed ashamed and

humiliated and expecting to be blown sky bloody high any mo, actually
– there's this superimposition of a linden tree avenue over his face
surprise surprise but in fact the old bag gives up just maybe because
Martita's had what the canteen staff would've had but it's great
anyway, she goes over and operates the pianola instead so we quick-
fade the linden tree avenue and the potentially dramatic encounter just
goes kind of puff, the love of his life whose ripe lips just kind of rolled
away in the moonlight like an apple in the dashed impossible bobbing
apples barrel at the Fawholt Summer Fête where Ags always cleans
out the hoopla just looks awfully pasty the next day and incredibly
unmashable all of a sudden and Giles smokes his head off by the pool
in the wood and Ags reads, then they all whirl down to the sea and I
have to waste a whole day hiring the wrong type of period bathing huts
because Sylvia's got sunstroke thank you Sylvia.

Did you really and truly hit him? my grandfather enquires.

My grandmother nods. There's something about this beastly hitting
thing my grandfather doesn't awfully like, frankly. His lips purse which
is an ugly habit, they got very pursy in the trenches and his platoon
went round mimicking him and he blushed the colour of his blisters
when he realised but that's to come, it's all sketched out, the poppies
are looking droopy because we're way over schedule, if I don't look
pretty zippy they'll be baling up the wire and filling in the trenches and
the steam train people'll be organising *Weekend Tours of the Battlefields
Via Zeebrugge* already, we'll have missed the whole thing, it'll get
reduced to a voice off and those establishing shots and some stock clips
out the library for crying out loud. My grandmother's lower lip has
kind of swelled up, it has a tear which refuses to fall off it and instead
rolls into her mouth and naturally the salt sample makes her feel she's
really sobbing her eyes out which she's not, she's keeping herself in
check, her nose is running a little though, it's got a catchlight off the
candles, sorry about that, I did warn you people out there and hey, the
reason my grandfather's developing his mouth pleats while he wipes
away her tears and the iron is being smelted is because some fairly
green and unpleasant corner of his stomach reckons that William has
somehow received a more intimate interindividual communication
than he Giles has and this little reckoning is screwing up the smelting

564

process, there's dirt in the bellows, one of the donkeys has a severe limp.

I say, he says very softly, how absolutely bloody.

My grandmother lowers her head and my grandfather pulls out his handkerchief which is pretty clean if a little linseedy from his hands and she takes it so the nasal mucus and most of the tears never make it to the floorboards. It's quite all right, contributes my grandfather to the general welfare box of human kind, leaving his hand on her head and realising that heads are actually a lot smaller than they look. Because he's taller than her and looking down he gets a bird's-eye view of her blouse and what happens inside it beyond the poverty-exaggerated clavicles which is not much because her chemise breaks its foamy lace or maybe lacy foam against the golden sand of her chest about an inch above where it gets interesting. Nevertheless the well-held position of her arms each side of her ribs and joined at navel height by the finger-bones as if in prayer kind of presses each side of her chest and makes the blouse and the chemise fall away a bit from the neck so there is a kind of an extra plunge into the dark he just stares into with the iron-smelting process doubling its production. Any really naff poetic reference by the way is not screwed out of my Muse but Giles's, I very much doubt whether my grandmother's skin was anything but Worksop white with industrial air-pollution pimples but candlelight does wonders for flesh tint, whenever I'm wooing I always use candles, it softens the blow when I take my Lon Chaney mask off after the HCDVA Fancy Dress Brunch, the Lana Turner cut-out doesn't scream and run out the sliding doors and fall into an unflooded bunker as happened in my first year, she just carries on smiling at me wherever I stand in the room even if I flatten myself against the same wall wot she's leant against, guv – trusting my neighbour doesn't try to knock a nail in behind her head she stays like that all evening without flinching even when the doorbell rings, it's the special delivery postman who always rings twice ho ho with a letter from Zelda ex-Lazenby now back to Wick I feverishly tear open while this guy's still standing there expecting a fifty-dollar tip or something for getting his motorbike wet. This is a terrible admission but I hugged him. It's a terrible admission not because it might suggest I'm keen on young guys dressed up in leather motorcycle gear the colour of newly-applied tarmac which is fine by me even if it were one hundred per cent true but that it meant Zelda saying she was thinking again by Hotpost Services wiped out any profound reassessments I'd recently made of her position *vis-à-vis* me and got the Victoria Falls unblocked again except I was going over in a barrel. The young guy got fairly excited too and said he'd one more Extra Hot to make and then he'd be right back and he didn't mind keeping his motorcycle helmet on but not his leathers, he wasn't into that, and I had to pretend I was and that I was also into flagellation and laceration and suffocation and tying my guys up in barbed wire with the odd tenacious strand of slightly scorched traveller's joy still clinging to it dressed only in the rank badges of a second lieutenant in the Wiltshire Yeomanry which got him incredibly excited so eventually I said I had a bit of a headache as a matter of fact what with my Lassa fever playing up and he backed off so I could Chubb the door and read the letter again. I'm sorry about this kind of extended cross-cut but I have to share my life sometimes, this happened about twelve hours ago, I haven't washed any more undies since, my grandfather has spent twelve hours contemplating the darkness beyond the golden beach and the chemise foam, he's gone deep, he's probably lost all sense of time down there where the world shuts off and only coral blows. Basically Zelda my lovely my honeydew my linden tree avenue with the Elysian fields at the far end instead of Jefferies and his coach wants, yeah, to settle by a lake with her weeny Todd and a very sensitive guy who'll fish and compose and make her laugh but she wants to do it in Canada for crying out loud and I've got to get learning how to fish and compose fast. Yup, I'm Henry Fonda with less cracks. I keep telling myself it'll work, I've got at least ten years of total bliss before my casting-arm starts to get stiff or I forget my one-liners or my *Indeterminate Variations for Five Aspens and a Woman Bathing Naked* shows a certain lack of youthful vigour. Oh, and she's had the baby. It looks exactly like him. I can handle that. It would be worse if it looked like his great-uncle or something. Anyway he has the kind of face that gives Identikit artists a bad name, it's incredibly unseizable, when I think of his face I think of basins, I don't know why, the features just kind of slip my sprockets and get swooshed away – I mean, I really know what Zelda means about the totality of void at the centre of being when I stare at her ex-husband over the french fries he never likes to share with me. His attraction for the desirable T-shirts is that they can decal their fantasy man onto it very easily for Pete's sake – with me they just see five

566

generations of costermongers and two generations of dog shit gatherers overlaid very successfully by two generations of antiseptic and disinfectant manufacturers and the nose of the rich layabouts on my great-grandmother's side. I'm serious about the dog shit gatherers, by the way – my great-great-great-great-grandfather and his son got fruppence a bucket from the tanneries, you're very lucky you don't live next to a period tannery actually. OK, the family business had to start somewhere and it wasn't like you think it was, the pooper they scooped by hand was called Pure and my great-great-great-great-grandfather and son were Pure-finders and they were trusted, they didn't leave a whole load of air between the turds like some of the really enterprising ones did, they pressed it down firmly even though it was never weighed because as long as there was some of it higher than the rim of the bucket it was OK, they'd have got on very badly nowadays, people who don't leave a lot of air between their dog turds have basically had it. Every year I put on my Gregory Peck look and say to my classes that when your ancestors were stretching American Indian private parts over their pommels or strapping General Houston into his stomach girdle my family were finding Pure so folk could go out in decent hand-stained leather without soiling their homes or the homes and shops of others. Clink clink. Cor luvaduck. You're a swell toff, guv. Ta.

Hey, beforehand I was too depressed to watch the rushes. Now I'm too happy. I can't phone her because she's in this Zen nunnery on some lake north of Ottawa. She's there for weeks and she wants me to think about it. She says they have a great crèche set-up. I think weeny Todd might be getting a bottle instead of Zelda's breast. That surprises me. I'm frankly surprised she's on a Zen retreat at this time but I think it probably means Tiny Todd is not everything to her. There is absolutely one hundred per cent zilch doubt about her feelings this time: she said I want you my closest friend to share my life with me, you always said you changed all your kids' diapers each time, I think we can make it work, when I shut my eyes in *zazen* meditation you always float into view on this orange cloud holding an Alfa Romeo magazine like that time I drove us out to Austin for that illustrated lecture on Suzuki by his oldest pupil and you vomited because you were reading the magazine and NOT because of my driving!! It's a great way to start because I can clear you very quickly and still myself before having to nod for the *keisaku* stick. The *keisaku* stick kinda hurts! The head nun doesn't hold herself back, she's called Jean Riley and is from Montreal originally and is very aware and watches TV a *lot*, especially the cop serials and she has them on really loud but nobody likes to say anything and anyway they can't because we all have to take this Vow of Silence, *even me* (!!), we can talk for ten minutes when the sun clears the pylon cable. Although she's so enlightened I think that nothing disturbs the still pool of her mind. There's going to be a lot of snow here. Rain makes these great gurgly noises and touches my cheek with tiny fingers. Please take lots of still time and reflect deeply on everything I've said. With meant love, Zelda. See what I meant? I've reflected deeply for about one second and am ordering up some snow chains by Hotpost Services because no way can you get snow chains in Houston. I like the sort of poetic line about the rain, it means Zelda's going back to her haiku, it's a good sign, she's probably rinsed out the platinum and gone back to natural brown and moccasins with something billowy in between, it reminds me of my late youth and early middle age, it tells me that time can stop. Sod the movie. I'm sorry, guv, a hartist has to live too. My grandfather can carry on looking at the coral in a comfortable vertical position flippers up high for another few days, I've reported sick, my Africa period has come in useful again, nobody calls round to check on my progress, my stoodents will be universally deprived of my classes on Carl Theodor Dreyer but since it takes about five sessions just to get through to these thinking telegraph-poles that he's Dreyer as in live wire and hair-drier and hell-fire not threadbare or hair care or Lord's Prayer or even the brassière of yesteryear which gets a few shocked inbreaths and some forms completed, I don't think they'll be in their deathpods weeping about it on their grandchildren's silver foil all-in-ones around the middle of the twenty-first century somehow.

Ho I'm so excited.

Forget the snow chains. I'm going up anyway. I'm flying up. I've looked at the map and remembered that I am at the bottom of an extremely spacious continent and Zelda is fairly near the reasonably habitable top before it gets to be timber wolves and instant melanomas for several thousand miles till you hit the duty-free igloos and my beat-up 1958 DAF Sedan max speed fifty-seven m.p.h. would take so long to make it I'd be dribbling onto my bunions at the lakeside instead of showing Zelda my swan-dive and it's dangerous going out in it anyway, the low-loaders and the stationwagons and the refrigerated trucks don't notice me, I come up to about their hub-caps if I'm lucky, a '58 DAF Sedan is 142 inches long from chrome to chrome, it's my Monsieur Hulot *hommage* but no one in Texas has ever heard of Monsieur Hulot or even of *hommages*, they think you're imitating the local swamp frog or whichever – hey, most people round here have stuff parked in their driveways with ten-gallon cans on the top like they're ready to scatter some cattle skulls across the Staked Plains or take a splash up to their canvas through Big Bend country and come back with a cougar or two stretched over their hoods when all they're used for is to go grab a drive-thru burger at three a.m. one block up and knock my geranium pot off with their buffalo guards, it's ridiculous, I mean I could just tootle along the interstate and hold people up a little and then wave to them nicely as they eventually pass but waving nicely does not stop the rolled brolly pointing at you from turning into something you think you recognise from that computer-enhanced blow-up of maybe a person on the knoll in that TV documentary about *One Day in Dallas* too late to duck – let's face it, you've irritated them and these are not the right guys to irritate, apparently about ten per cent of the human population outside of your regular homicides would very much like to kill people if given the social opportunity like war or civil anarchy or religious strife or being born in Sicily or Miami or São Paulo or my part of Houston or a jerk holding them up in a DAF Sedan with a hole in the floor and MY OTHER CAR'S AN ALFA ROMEO, SERIOUSLY in the rear window and there are a lot of faces behind the wheels on the interstates, the chances are not good of having Thomas Jefferson behind you all the way to Ottawa back. Hi. That was a bad splice. I'm back. My soul has been trampolined and the stretched fabric couldn't take it, I hit the concrete, I wasted an airline ticket, I'll tell you sometime but I have my art to get on with.

I thought about getting my Congo machete and trimming out all that stuff about Zelda's letter but it's evidence, it's evidence that I am at heart a passionate and irresponsible dickhead.

O O O Yarooo

Christ, Hotpost Services just called with my snow chains and it was the same guy. I hope you were joking about your Lassa fever, he said, because here are your chains. I undid them in front of him and wrapped them round his neck very tightly I'm afraid to say. Thank you, he said, thank you so much. I slammed the door on his nosepeel and pulled down the blinds and tried to think Howard Hughes. I even pissed into one of my jam-making jars and it was quite sexual so I've stopped that. Hey, maybe Howard Hughes is not the right model, he had this private screening room at Columbia Pictures where he'd jack himself off for God's sake. I am not going to jack myself off in front of you while watching my own rushes, this is not a pornographic movie, there are all sorts of people out there who would be very upset. The guy keeps tapping on my window, I can hear his chains rattle, if I didn't possess a clear and rational mind I'd be holding Des's hand by mistake or something. Instead I groan now and again and yell out that I caught it off one of the original missionary nuns but he just says thank you so much and could I sign the Hotpost Safely Received form or something which is a clever one, everyone's so darned clever, they keep pulling me around because I don't get air between my dog turds and he's probably one of the ten per cent, it's lucky for Zelda that I'm not one of the ten per cent as a matter of fact, I just feel sorry for the very old nun with the rake, if she'd waited two more minutes before sweeping her first-ever perfect circle of one hundred maple leaves in fifty-eight years of continual sweeping I'd have been out of there, I wouldn't have rearranged it with my foot into a broken heart, it just looked like a pretty regular O to me but I guess these nuns know when they see the real thing, I can still see her sobbing on Zelda's crew-cut because this old nun was not short, in fact she was taller than me and really thin, I hope I haven't snapped her into pieces. This was last month. Today is the first of the month. Fooled ya. She might be dying of grief by now. Zelda with a crew-cut's just as beautiful surprisingly because she has very reliable features. I shouldn't have gone up. Jean Riley the head nun must be a very impressive woman to overrun my charms but maybe Zelda will be happier with the pure life. I hope she presses it down. I told her this, I told her while the dust was still settling from her dumb show I guessed was the Complete Story of Human Kind from the first slow motion kill to the last slow motion kill but it wasn't, about a minute from the end I realised it was *Why I Am Staying Put & Don't Need You Anymore* and I started to do some semaphore because the vow thing was very strong, I stayed mute, I looked like I was guiding about five jumbo jets into their landing bays simultaneously but basically I was saying hey, I don't believe this, this is terrible, you can't do this to me, why why oh why etc. and then eventually I did a Marcel Marceau thing about how my great-great-great-great-grandfather & Son always pressed it down, they were totally reliable and deeply honest people and I hoped that she would learn from them and not leave lots of air between or use a bucket with a false bottom which was the other trick, guv, there were lots of tricks, there are always lots of tricks, the people with lots of tricks ended up flattening the honest-to-God buckets plus attached fingerless mittens with their BMWs, whoops, never saw it mate, that's how it goes, here's what I think is the state of my inner void, Zelda O Prisoner of Zenda.

That's when I did the maple leaves thing. It was quite difficult, actually, making it look like a heart broken in two, the jagged bits were really unclear and so was the arrow, she probably thought I had a couple of sperm whales on a barbecue stick in my inner void but I wasn't exactly about to put a title on and sign it, now was I? If the ancient nun had actually once opened her mouth and told me to fuck off or had stooped down to my level and whispered that this was the amazing zenith of her long and tortuous spiritual path and could I not grade her life's peak flat for my particular ten-lane superwide I might have stopped, I might even have tried to mend it or at least got it roughly back into a perfect circle, but she kept her vow of silence all the way through except for this incredible *yip* that suddenly came out as I tried to make the last maple leaf look like the tip of an arrow which is not easy and I really jumped, I think I might have had a satori or something if I hadn't been so keyed up and suffering from some awful stress-induced indigestion from the celery salad on Air Canada and it was her, it was the first big sound she'd made for fifty-eight years and it was not happy, I could see that, she was sobbing on Zelda's skull which must have been like sobbing with your cheek on a cactus but I guess that was the point.

Hey ho. Everything I do leaves this tacky stuff at the bottom of the glass which turns out to be guilt. I wish I could come out of things really clear. I wish these experiences could kind of burn me into something pure and clean enough to be poured into a Bugatti Type 35E radiator

571

or whatever. *I'd* be so lucky. I think I'll go clean my teeth instead. I need to take another time-lapse snap in the bathroom mirror for my art house short *The Rise & Decomposition of Richard Thornby* (USA, *c.* 1983–?, 2 mins).

Hey, Dean Lazenby sidled up to me this morning and asked if I had heard anything. Yip, I said, your wife is a Branch-of-Something-Zen nun for life vowed to silence and your son is going to be reared speaking in *Kojak* reruns. You know what he said to me from under his fatigue shadows? He said Thornby, the nicest sight of my life's gonna be seeing your butt walk out that door for the last time. Can you imagine? The first straightforward and understanding *We Try Harder* man-to-alien helpful answer I've ever given him and he chooses that moment to hit back, finally. Thank you for using my surname, I replied. You're the first person in twelve years in this country to do so. I appreciate that. Then I ducked because he swung his Samsonite and hit the fire-alarm instead and emptied the building. I don't think my gold watch has even been ordered from the special hand-sewn place in Geneva Makers of Timepieces to Rich Ass-Holes Since 1234. I think I'll be lucky if I get an unframed biro doodle by the assistant security officer of the front of the HCDVA building by night with various armaments and exaggerated genitalia and wrongly-taken telephone message as a matter of fact. I hope they don't try to dock my pension, guv, that's all. I'll fire-bomb the place if they do. No I won't. I'm all lip. I'll stand outside with a HANDS OFF MY PENSION placard and bob it up and down every day until the pension's no longer required. Meantime the seasons will pass and nice students will put blankets over my knees and wheel me up and down in coffee-breaks and feed me tidbits and I'll tell them stories of cabbages and kings and Robert Bresson and Andrei Tarkovsky and they'll all pronounce Carl Theodor Dreyer like they were born in Esbjerg or somewhere. I'll have a role in life, I'll have so much of a role that when I'm gone the Ingrid Bergman look-alike who liked to hug me lengthily will organise a plaque welded into the pavement with a brief but moving inscription like RICKY STUCK OUT FOR JUSTICE HERE 1999-2038 or RICKY THORNBY: HE SHALL ALWAYS BE RECALLED, THE STOODENTS.

Shucks.

I'm so cut up about the Zelda thing period. I was going to say I'm so cut up about the Zelda thing I can't feel anything but hoovered right out, only that sounds too full and rich for what I'm feeling. I hope I didn't misunderstand Zelda. Mime was never my forte and I didn't have my granddaughter with me to lip-read. I told my love to fetch a pen but she mimed this really complicated thing about ink not being allowed before the third gong, it looked like she was starting a Rank feature by Kurosawa or someone. It was weird because when I was doing my mute yelling thing she started to wave her arms around too and looked kind of imploring and pointed at the temple and tapped her head and crushed her hands together in front of her chest and with this Kohl pencil around her eyes or maybe just fatigue from rising at three every morning I could see why Norma was a star, if it hadn't been for the crew-cut I'd have spread me legs aht and turned me cap rahnd and plunged right in. This went on for about ten minutes while the old tall nun was sweeping the ninety-ninth maple leaf into miraculous position beyond and I had to take a break, I had to sit down on this stool because it's very exhausting emoting silently, it had been a very physical experience. Zelda kept looking at me down on this bench and either doing a repeated take of the shower scream in *Psycho* or saying sorry over and over, I wasn't sure. If it hadn't been for the gentle rasp of the rake and the odd maple leaf hitting the dust and the second or maybe third series of *Kojak* in the distance and now and again a gong I'd have thought I was deaf or maybe underwater, what with me tinnitus 'n that, guv. Then she started all over again but this time she was doing the moon race all the way from V2s to Armstrong's small bounce for mankind and even the buggy it looked like, the grey dust puffed but I didn't believe it, it was a studio set up, they never left Houston Mr Thornby sir, I got off what turned out actually to be a small Buddha and wrote IS IT FINISHED PERIOD with my foot by the Sea of Tranquillity and she didn't pause she just hunkered down in her habit and put a question mark on my question because she's very particular and then YES came out of her fingertip.

I didn't have deep focus on.

I'm sorry, but while I was putting a full stop with my heel after YES because I'm very particular I didn't notice how the tall old nun had just put the broom down and lifted her hands in exquisite joy, she was just a kind of background blur, she could have been a dead tree or the Rape of the Sabine Woman in soapstone or something. I was very upset obviously and vocalised it and it was really shocking, it was like the whole world had waited for this moment, this crackly voice came out and instead of cheering Zelda covered her ears and looked broken so I carried on some more, the whole courtyard was echoing really astoundingly and the tall old nun stood very still, I think I ruined her moment, I think I put barbed wire all around her peak moment, if I'd not talked so loud she might just have had a few more seconds of timeless realisation or whatever but at that point I went for the maple leaves, I used my foot and then got right down on my hands and knees yelling my head off while Zelda kind of leaned without actually falling over and when I'd finished and the tall old nun had yipped and made me jump and wept on Zelda, Zelda looked past the tall old nun's thighs at me and said out loud really steadily GO AWAY, GO AWAY, I DON'T NEED YOU ANYMORE and the courtyard repeated it in case I hadn't picked it up the first time, thank you very much courtyard, how thoughtful of you, I'll be thinking of you in my nightmares.

It was extremely hurtful actually. It was more hurtful than anything she'd said yet and she'd broken her vow but only once.

Maybe once is enough.

My grandfather would probably think so.

The naughty postcard sequence has started, by the way. Flap, flap, flap, it's a great peep-show, it's called *What the Hell's It All For*. The guy with the chains has given up getting me rattled, I heard his motorbike just now or maybe it was the Son-of-Mike-the-Fly in my ear but I think I've just concussed it on my rolled-up *Time*, the one with the big cover feature on my impending retirement. The apron-strings have come undone. My grandfather undid them but my grandmother helped because untying bows when sexually excited is not easy, they turn into Boy Scout specials the second you grab at them. My grandmother is not sexually excited. I'm sorry to say this but she is actually about as sexually riveted as a soap boiling pan. She's kind of repelled and scared but isn't showing it, Robert would be very proud of her, it's amazing, she's a dead ringer for his Jeanne d'Arc, it's like that

574

great trial scene which surpassed Dreyer's as in tyre's last silent masterpiece on the same subject my dear children – she's acting her whole being and her whole being is so profound my grandfather's taking the surface calm on trust because he isn't the scuba-diving type and never has been. There are these hands all over her smelling of linseed oil and then she finds herself topless. I have my eyes shut. Or maybe they've snuffed the candles. Or maybe the film's come off the spool or maybe this is where Mike obeyed my instructions to call it quits as soon as the lens got more than its usual quota of flesh tints.

I think however my grandmother's showing up in the moonlight, or maybe it's the moon outside right here and now.

Hey, let's not quibble, it's the same moon, anyway. It's coming in through my window and past the fern and pretending to be a movie on my wall. That could well be my grandmother peeled like a banana down to her waist very faint on a bad exposure but I'd need to stop the projector and do a blow-up, it might be the moonlight, there's quite a breeze blowing the moon about and there are leaves in the way or maybe they haven't taken the flicker-stick off Clifford, it's dark, if you were out in the woods tonight you'd see nymphs all over the place, elves and stuff, sprites with silken wings and probably a hoof in the wrong place with a goaty smell out the dingly dell. You'd probably be very frightened and bump into the shepherd from Hemel Hempstead getting into his part by the big pool, some boldly practical person like me dammed the stream about a century ago, the village girls go bathing there at this period – yup, that's the very faint laughter you heard from the room, well done, you're on the ball, you'd make a great buff.

But siddown on the leaf mould and keep quiet about it if you please, jerk. Gavin's rehearsing. He's rehearsing his part like he's been rehearsing it in the caravan for the last decade or whatever. He's never acted in his life before. I went for his face and missing teeth because I'm scrupulous, if you remember. Right now he's rehearsing how to watch these girls with big shoulders and generally very firm bodies lifting their arms and walking into the pool, it's a beautiful and touching and lyrical scene and Richard Thornby handles it with acumen and tact, there's moonlight dappling on shoulders and elbows and stuff as these girls turn round and try not to laugh too loud with

575

their upraised arms over the bright ripples and the slime of human passions underfoot and some frogs losing their meditation time and the lily-pads staying curled up while the water surface is measuring bust-sizes absolutely accurately in the deep part at least while trailing these gilded hay bits right back to the ones still dressed in air and itchy down to their thighs or even toes 'cos it takes some time for these nymphs to leave the warm gusts for the cold water so hey nonny nonny no our shepherd has dangerously wide eyes and his hand's doing things that the bracken shadow is concealing except for the glint of his satisfaction, I want you just to grunt, Gavin, when the nymphs are departed you'll stay there for about five weeks until you're needed.

If anyone's sitting nearby on the leaf mould, don't stare. Pretend you're moonlight on a blackberry sucker, OK?

I'm not sure exactly which days you'll be needed. I'm talking to Gavin, not you, for once. You're a background blackberry sucker, you have to start somewhere, just stay that way, the maids'll come picking you in a couple months, be content and patient and get rooted. OK, Gav, just hang around an incy bit longer, I'll order up some more *Bit-Part Monthly* back numbers or whatever, you're an integral part of this story, you'll be way up there on the major credits unlike the ham who's doing the blackberry sucker stick right where you are and DON'T MOVE, whoever heard of a blackberry sucker moving across during a big scene, huh? Do you want to fuck everything up for me?

So, if you go back to Hemel Hempstead or hitch y' canvas to some Traveller's wagon-trail way out Shropshire way I'll be left high and dry, bub. Listen. The day after these flesh tint sequences under moonlight William and Agatha go on this vital walk over the downs and they talk about sex, kind of. William catches a tiny blue butterfly and that'll be in close-up with NO MOZART and then he'll give it in its chloroform jar to Agatha who tries to appreciate the gesture because it's well meant, it's a thank-you for her incredible understanding and kindness and wisdom, Ags, you really are a frightfully wonderful person, you know, it's a rather rare type of common blue and it's yours all in mid-shot but, hey, the closing hold'll be extreme long shot from your point of view, Gavin – Willo and Ags'll turn into two nicks in this wide and lonely Vista Vision downland ocean anticipating the Somme to come and we'll foreground the shoulder and this old oilcloth cape nicely flapping and the hand around the crook and maybe your left ear if the big red curtains are properly drawn back, you'll be watching like you watched the Fawholt milkmaids flickering under the moonlight and rocking the lily-pads as the silver measured their midriffs because Isaac Flower the younger not to be confused with old Isaac Flower see up Ulvers way weren't it 'arry aye I will have another 'n all seein' as you're the 'arfbrain as is payin' in return for a load o' cobblers IS VERY ATTRACTED TO AGATHA, Gavin.

Heck, he's in love with her.

Deeply, deeply.

I want to make this angle clear but subtle. This person is a normal human being but very lonely up there with his flock. And the fact is that Agatha in her blindingly bright summer frock of translucent muslin over white lawn Mrs Halliday donated to the V&A in 1990 for crying out loud and which I have actually handled in their store-room because I got permission but not to take it out and anyway it was in fairly bad shape, it smelt of railway stations for some reason and had a couple of rips in its organdie and was generally off-cream but I have the locket at least, it bounced for a while against her throat, if you scan it electronically I think it might have her voice somewhere inside like the walls of the Tower have screams somewhere inside, so nuts say – the fact is

Fuck, I've lost it. Don't move, don't move, it'll come. Your black-berries'll be huge and black in time, just let yourself sweeten on the woodland floor, you might learn a lot in two months.

Here's to nuts.

Gavin, I want you to show how nuts this shepherd is. Don't worry about the sheep, we have a real live agricultural sheep technician on set to take care of the flock – all I want you to do, Gav, is concentrate on not acting how nuts you are on my great-aunt. Is that really much to ask, huh? I mean, Christ, I'm keeping you in food and water and prime-cut hashish, quit moaning about the open road, there are no open roads, Shropshire was won years ago, your wagon's got tail-lights, you'll only go get your last tooth knocked out by Lord Walters or someone. *It's come back*, I told y'all it would, OK, stick with me – the fact is that Agatha in her blindingly white summer frock is more than a nymph she's a goddess, you watched her gathering fistfulls of bluebells last year and couldn't speak for a week, his eyes went funny, his mother thought he had the ague and did something with sneezewort. The tense but famously tender takes of William and Agatha in the meadow amongst the hogweed and horse-flies and hums when they're discussing the kiss, Gavin, THE kiss, Gavin, you don't have a kiss but you get to die for Christ's sake, I'm talking about a kiss that missed but enough of a kiss to make William think that kissing can make babies because, hey, my grandfather never owned up, it's complicated, Milly kept blank, my great-uncle William never touched anyone else right up to the shell landing on his tin hat with him inside it because he'd watched Milly swell and pop for crying out loud – these meadow scenes will include you, Gavin, as a dark and distant disturbance of the generally green and whiteish landscape beyond all this.

All this, Gavin.

Heck. Why do I have to WORK with these people?

Listen. Put yer bleedin' backpack back down and listen. You've got some great and immortal moments, buster. Following Agatha's untimely loss when the crests no longer sway their grasses around her whitely shimmering form we have the major climax, we have your ginormous exit, we have the bubbles.

We have the bubbles and then we have nothing but the still silvery sway of the pool under moonlight, Gavin.

All you have to do is walk in, slowly.

Not jump. The old blokes in the pub said you most definitely didn't jump. I was relieved, it took two hours on my slate to get to that general agreement, like it took two hours the previous evening to get them to stop playing fucking dominoes in the corner and talk to me over the karaoke crap, we nearly got thrown out for reminiscence-yelling or something. Jumping's naff and really uncinematic if it's not slowed right down but unless you climbed a tree in 1919 your jump would've been off a two-inch tussock and we'd have had to have freeze-framed it which is even naffer, I've got over that phase a long while back, Gav. We could have you taking off your waterproof cape and your waterproof boots and gittin' Scamp to sit, *g'buoy*, then shaking this beech about a bit, just the leaves shaking like in that Dennis Potter thing, then the jump but they most definitely said Isaac the younger walked 'isself in like 'e were takin' a bath only 'e carried right on an' that's the truth, innit?

All for love, see, all for love.

For a bit o' skirt.

For my great-aunt, actually.

Oh yeh? Make it a double o' Johnny Walker Black agin, along wi' the 6X, if you don't mind. Your great-aunt, eh? Let's think now.

Very slowly, Gav, so the pool doesn't actually notice anything's cleaving it. Right up until your big hat floats off by itself. Then just stay under for about two minutes until the last bubble's popped on the barely moving surface over which some damselflies are getting famous for two minutes. Hey, you walking slowly into the silver will most definitely be judged probably the finest thing Thornby has ever done, I have the cape you take off and fold up and place under a tree just before right here on my shoulders because it's wet outside, it took me eighty-one years and half the Half Moon's liquid stock to get my mitts on it, just appreciate how important your role is to me, Gavin.

The blackberry sucker's moving. See to it, Sylvia.

Quit moaning, of course you can stay down there two minutes, you've got a metal leg, if it was wooden you'd have had problems OK but there's a lot of iron forged by the Fawholt blacksmith under your stump, it's the way Isaac wanted it, he was terrified of woodworm or rats or something, like I'm terrified of flying twenty thousand feet over the Arctic ice-sheets, we all have our weak spots, for Pete's sake.

579

Hey, it makes things easier. I wouldn't want you to walk in with a pile of film cans around your neck or something or walk in with nothing and two good legs and faff about on the surface trying to keep your head under so Gordon'd have to wade in disguised as a lily-pad and thrust you down or whatever, that would be hopeless.

Maybe the limp'll cause ripples. I think the limp will definitely screw up the total calm idea. No scene in the history of movie-making has ever been free of this kind of technical hiccup so hold your breath for a while, the main thing is DON'T ACT. You're a mechanism, Gavin. A mechanism.

I don't quite know when we'll insert this scene because I don't want it to rub up against Agatha's funeral which is THE BIG ONE. Hey, there'll be a great deal of your distressed face held staring at the far crest where you watched her shimmer once I suppose, I hope it won't mean you have to hang around too long but we'll use a dummy hand for the really murky underwater shot and you won't be needed for the skeleton a coupla cagoules arm in arm discover in the infamous drought year of '76 when even the pool cracks because decades-old skeletons have a special lustre to them, Gavin – yours won't be seasoned sufficiently, even the special effects guys throw up their sprayguns on that one.

Chuck me some secateurs. This blackberry's sucker's on Last Warning.

So, Gavin me old mucker. When Startlingly Fluorescent Cagoule One screams there'll be just the skeleton with this rusty scale model of the Eiffel Tower attached to its right hip kind of spreadeagled under the Coke cans and used boom-arms and the other half of the Cindy doll. We won't require you then, Gavin, you'll be out on the Big Trail by that juncture.

If we cut the whole drowning thing don't get upset, for God's sake, don't go running out and jump into the Hemel Hempstead Municipal or something, it's all a question of time and motion and being a nut.

Yeah, the old lady with the incredible boil on her eyelid was right, I think she had some romance in her and I love her because she'd only drink lemonade, it was a pity she had to slip in the snow or she'd still be around to clutch my elbow and tell me things between the gravestones – she even kicked Calypso once when she was ten, the cat went feral and nicked her bread 'n dripping or something. Hey, she understood what it takes. She understood what a very strong commitment to the fact that you have loved someone even though that someone has pretty well ignored you and your needs it takes. I told them this after they'd given me an HCDVA Executive Half-Page Diary for the year 2000 with full colour portraits of the management instead of the quadrophonic megawatt hi-fi system plus *A Sentry of Your Favourite Melodies* (great joke, great joke) in a five-volume set they lavished on the assistant security officer for a lifetime of devoted terrorising while pumping his hand and hugging him – January was Crew-Cut in shorts and August was Vyshitface with his five kids at his boots and December was Dean Lazenby holding his Samsonite in front of a rubber-plant before his breakdown obviously, it must have been too late to change it, you can even see a fire-alarm but I don't think it's the same one. Shame, I'd have preferred a doodle by Baldie Head actually, my ten-minute speech of thanks was greeted by the sound of the air-conditioning and someone's electronic wristwatch alarm or maybe it was the secure hospital's secure-van reversing for me, I dunno, I made a crack about the sound of one hand clapping which reminded me of Zelda so I waved my glass around so much my lemon flew out and said hey, the fact that this is probably the crappiest arts college in the universe run by people who would sell our ass-holes in plastic bags if it turned a buck and who wouldn't know a good movie from Baldie-here's dick and you're subserving it does not prevent you from walking through some long grass into a pool in an English bluebell wood for love and grief so slow and steady it stays as still as it was before you entered right up to your neck and beyond though it probably will, it probably will. I was very heated by now, Vyshitsky removed the lemon from his lapel after some new guy who picks the management's noses for them had pointed it out to him and he didn't know what to do with it or me, so he gave it to the nostril-crawler and left. They all left as a matter of fact and without so much as a bleedin' by-your-leave, guv, just a kind of mumble and one of them broke wind I think accidentally and none of them looked at anything except the carpet squares and then the door-knob. All except Baldie Head who wanted to get even

581

about this heyar reference to his total heyar-loss and the other praaavit thing the Lord forgive me in that order so I stopped doing my hand-cranked projector mime and gave him my executive diary I'd tucked under my armpit in the kidneys and tried to walk through the glass door like that shot cop in *Bullit* but just kinked my straight Trevelyan nose. Then Baldie kinked it some more and I've had to sell my Oscars to pay for my bridge replacement, I'm sorry, I was hoping to do a slow pan of my several Academy Awards at this point ending on my bare feet about halfway up the wall turning slowly from side to side. Shucks. Too bad. My nose is better, thank you. I look like my dad now. Or maybe Steve McQueen.

You're ripening. Stay put.

The moonlight is definitely my grandmother's right shoulder and clavicle and not my fern, by the way. Plus dear Christ a bit of her hip. The ghoul hopping around is my unclothed grandfather taking his final sock off, probably. There's a smell of snuffed candles which makes him sneeze and he says sorry and shakes his thumb because he didn't wet it enough. Now my grandfather's where my grandmother is which is on the bed. Rosebud, he whispers. Seriously. The picture-hook kind of travels over his mouth and then his ear and ends up just above his head over the mould stain and her hand. What the hell is her hand doing up there. It's laid flat against the wall and the only giggle is some faint laughter from the wood where she really ought to be situated right now, bathing, bathing happily and nakedly and forever with the others in the silvery pool by the light of the moon laid like a silver salver in the darkness with my head hovering over it not knowing which to take, the pound note, the pound note or the one bob ticket, the one bob ticket or the pound note 'cos SPECIAL CHILDREN'S MATINÉE ONLY meant as much to me as GREAT HEXPECTORATIONS in them days, son – cor blimey, I couldn't even read me own future.

Hey, there's never enough time to choose. The third gong is striking. The door opens and this ancient ape with frost on his shoulders and a glittering forelip enters. My mother steps away smartish. He's holding this woodland pool under moonlight. I'm projecting, I'm not thinking that at the age of five or even nine, it's just that we've done some aerial

582

shots of the woodland pool and it's an obvious Thornby cross-cut, he's coming right over and up to me and the woodland pool is thrust under my badly wrinkling nose, I'm looking into it and I see myself, maybe I've drowned, maybe I know the undersides of lily-pads intimately, Christ, the white-gloved thumbs each side are getting a bit shaky and their owner's breath's whistling like it's about to depart for Paddington toot toot and there's another drop of mucus on the nicely buffed silver with my face in it, my face oh Gahd, my sweet little nippery face down there with a pursed mouth, a fat pound note with the King of England over one eye and a little yellow one bob ticket over the other, I could read that much, I could read *1/-* for Christ's sake and I wanted to take *both* plus a Dinky flat-bed and Smarties after but life's not like that, my face is really huge down there and this voice comes out of the darkness and says *choose, dear lad, choose* – it's really loud despite the hoarse quality because there's an All-Comers Niteplay and they're thousands of 'em, I've had to keep my head down, they're swinging some very wild shots and getting Texan angry about it, I'm crouched very low for my age watching my big face up there looking down at me and this hand's coming out, I can't decide which side this is being shot from, maybe I'm the reflection side for fuck's sake if the face is on high, it's terrifying, there's this growl in Sensurround *willnae ye make up ye mind shrimp* which helps this 3D silvery hand come right out and you should see the actual hand but you don't, it's just coming straight for us like a fucking steam-train, the whole cinema's full of screams, these huge fingers are lunging right out for my throat but it's OK, before I scream it takes the yellow thing floating between us because it likes the fancy curly-wurly way BIOGRAPH is written for crying out loud, it was as stupid as that, I raise my head an inch above the sofa-back and a golf ball practically shaves my left eyebrow but the face with the giant hand has evaporated, the silvery mirror has evaporated, it's been taken away along with the pound note and the lavatory smell, there's just a couple of eyeballs left, a giant pair of white rolled-up eyeballs in a stripe of Niteplay lights or maybe it's Mike come back with his specials or maybe it's bastard Des my bruvver or maybe it's Lightfoot gagging or maybe it's my mother's eyes getting checked for death by Doctor Orwell or maybe it's Jefferies playing the beast through the carriage window suddenly upside-down and hissing who's a dirty rascal and I gasp a sweet little high kind of asthmatic gasp that makes the eyes sink back and down into the darkness because listen, dumbos.

You missed it. Happy New Year. Hey, before you all tip over the chairs and the glasses and my antique projector in the rush out just take it easy, slow down, the rest is in the cans and they're fairly waterproof.